JACKHAMMER

A NOVEL

BOB MACKIN

Jackhammer is a work of fiction. All incidents and dialogue, and all characters with the exception of some well-known historical and public figures, are products of the author's imagination and are not to be construed as real. When real-life historical or public figures appear, the situations, incidents, and dialogues concerning those persons are entirely fictional and are not intended to depict actual events or to change the entirely fictional nature of the work. In all other respects, any resemblance to persons living or dead is entirely coincidental.

ISBN: 1491207566
ISBN-13: 9781491207567
Library of Congress Control Number: 2013914878
CreateSpace Independent Publishing Platform
North Charleston, South Carolina

This book is for Paul Feeney (1963 – 2013),
a Marine and friend who left us too soon.

PART ONE

1. THE ADMIRALTY, LONDON, MAY 10, 1940, 7:34 P.M.

Channing Brown stretched his long stiff legs. The Roman numerals of the old clock on the far wall told him he had been sitting on the hard Windsor bench for fifty-eight minutes. Brown stood and walked to the tall window that looked out on the twilight shadows on the Horse Guards Parade. He rejected the idea of a cigarette and returned to the bench to refocus his mind on what he would say – in very few words – to a man who spoke far more than he listened. But that was ever the case when he confronted Winston Churchill.

Across the large reception area, the stunning brunette from the Women's Royal Naval Service was typing at her usual fast pace, her eyes fixed on her steno pad, pausing only to put fresh paper in the old Underwood. Brown noticed that she showed more gray hair since Prime Minister Chamberlain had named Churchill First Lord of the Admiralty.

Brown yawned, a mix of tension and fatigue. The day had started early and, from the look of it, was far from over. Eden, Atlee, and Beaverbrook had each separately entered and left Churchill's office since Brown's arrival. Daybreak had brought the news that Hitler's paratroopers and Panzers had invaded neutral Holland and Belgium. Now that the so-called "Phoney War" was over, Brown needed the green light for his special project, one made far more important than ever by the day's events.

Brown ran his fingers through his black and gray curls, then straightened his bow tie. Twenty-six years of service in intelligence, espionage, and bureaucracy had taught him to prepare, prepare again, and prepare one final time. Only then could he report with a compelling confidence. He always forced himself to imagine how he would handle interruptions and impatience. Once he had prepared himself for the worst, the worst never happened.

Brown refocused on his message – the thoughts, not the words. Trying to remember words would only trip him up. He tapped his fingers on the tan leather portfolio on his lap. It held the two-page report that would document his oral presentation. He had typewritten it hurriedly right after his bedside telephone rang at just past four that morning and a Wren with a Yorkshire accent told him that the First Lord wanted a "concise" written report of not more than 350 words on "Jackhammer" by 0:900 hours. He had delivered the report an hour before deadline, but Brown was sure from experience that Churchill would have had little opportunity to read it. Brown resisted the temptation to read again what he had written. He might find a typo, a misspelled word, or a way to say something better – too bad, and too late for that now.

A familiar mood returned, as it often did at moments like this. It was like it had been at Oxford when he was a 400-meter runner on the University Track Club. In the hour before a race, his mouth would sour and his bladder would require repeated trips to the comfort station. He would question what he was doing – dressed in short pants and running around an oval course before hundreds, sometimes thousands of people. He wanted to hide and take a nap or a pint. Then, just moments before the start of the race, with no time left to worry, his command of himself returned. He was ready for the test, confident that his months of training would stand him well, if not with a win, well then, with the best that he could do that day.

As Brown stood to stretch again and turned toward the window, he heard a clear unmistakable voice resonating from across the room. "Channy, good lad, come chat with me." Brown turned to see the bright blue eyes of Winston Churchill.

A wave of Churchill's right hand guided Channing Brown to the inner office, to a small chair opposite the large desk. Once seated, Churchill leaned forward, perching himself on both elbows. "As you can see, the office hasn't changed much since the last war." Lighting a fresh cigar using the still-burning tip of the one he had just smoked, Churchill eyed Brown. "I've missed you, Channy," he said, "but there's no time for nostalgia this evening. At this very moment, the Dutch find themselves up to their necks in Germans. They ignored our warnings, some based on your reports. By now every mother's son in Holland has got the message. They have opened the dikes to flood the countryside, but too late. German tanks had already raced over the Ijsselmeer causeway. Queen Wilhelmina may still be in Holland, but it doesn't seem that she can stay there long. Other reports show that King Leopold and the Belgians are no better disposed to confront their uninvited company."

Churchill glanced up at the large wall clock, which told him it was just eight. "But now, lad, let's discuss your memo."

"Sir, I believe . . . "

Churchill raised his right palm. "Channy, would it surprise you to know I've already read your memo? Well, I indeed have. I did so while motoring back from Buckingham Palace, where I had a chat with His Majesty earlier today.

"Now, hand me the copy from that portfolio of yours and let me read it once more. I must be absolutely certain that I understand every word of it. My copy's already secured in a safe here at Admiralty."

Churchill laid the document flat on his desk blotter and fixed his eyes on the first page.

TOP SECRET, EYES ONLY, UNOFFICIAL

DATE: *10 MAY 1940*

TO: *THE FIRST LORD OF THE ADMIRALTY*

FROM: *CHANNING BROWN, CHIEF GROUP D, SPECIAL OPERATIONS, SIS*

RE: *OPERATION JACKHAMMER*

The purpose of this memo is to provide background on a most secret and discrete initiative, and to recommend decisive action with regard to concluding the above-mentioned operation.

BACKGROUND

Since early 1934, this unit has, among its other initiatives, been working to put in place an agent capable of eliminating the present head of the German Reich. I emphasize that the idea was only to have the person in place – in a position where he would be able to strike when, and only when, he received a definitive order to do so. For the most part, private monies have funded the project. It has never been an official enterprise of His Majesty's government.

PROGRESS TO DATE

Following a worldwide search by our best agents, we have recruited a person capable of fulfilling that mission. This person's special talents, plus our investment of substantial human and financial resources from SIS, have enabled him to advance to the point where he needs only the green light to plan and execute the final phases of his mission.

We have secured the documentation and records of the enterprise in a separate safe office in another part of London to minimize security risks believed present at Whitehall. (We believe the First Lord is sufficiently familiar with the aforementioned internal security issues that this communication requires no further elaboration on that point.)

CONTINGENCIES

While his cover appears more than adequate at present, you will understand that nothing of this nature is ever perfect, especially in a state where police are curious in the extreme. In other words, our agent's true identity – and the purpose of his mission – could be discovered at any time.

It is also critical to understand that the agent accepted the mission on the clear proviso that he would plan the timing and execution of its final phase – with his own escape and survival a priority on par with actual fulfillment of the mission. For that reason, he has insisted that all attempts to communicate with him must cease once the mission enters its final days, owing mainly his own healthy realization that any confidant, no matter how strong or loyal, would crack if captured and questioned.

A "Go" order will allow our man to identify the place and time, and allow him to plan the final steps of his mission.

RECOMMENDATION

The undersigned respectfully requests that the First Lord recommend to the Prime Minister that, given the events of this day, he order our man to execute his charge.

PROBABILITY OF SUCCESS
It is not practical to measure the chances of success at this time.

Respectfully submitted,

Channing Brown

Churchill set his burning cigar in a standing ashtray and spoke in a soft tone.

"Well, Channy, what you don't know is that there's been a change of some significance since you wrote your splendid memorandum. You see, when I saw the King this afternoon, His Majesty asked me to form a new government and I have accepted."

Churchill did not wait for Brown to respond. "It will be a coalition. We need all bloody factions in this fight. Everyone is cooperating. Chamberlain is being quite magnanimous. Atlee and Labor have agreed to come aboard. Chamberlain will address the nation on the change at nine, less than an hour from now.

"The reality – given today's events – is that you have already spoken to the Prime Minister, and he accepts your recommendation. By all means, order your man to proceed. But before you leave, allow me to ask two questions."

"Of course, Sir."

"How soon?"

"It must yet take time, Sir. He has trained and applied himself well. And he will not be careless. He must, however, move in measured steps."

Churchill paused to relight his cigar. "Channy, you must report directly to me on our man's progress. Don't go through the Foreign Office or SIS. As you have noted, Whitehall now harbors too many security risks – too many Oxford and Cambridge types, admirers of the Soviet model. We dare not trust those young buggers, especially with Stalin and Hitler allied since their bloody non-aggression pact.

"Now tell me, how will your lad do it? What weapon?"

"That's the beauty of it, Sir. He'll use no gun, no knife, no poison. Instead, the idea is that he'll use his God-given fists to – as our American friends might say – punch the living shit out of Adolf Hitler, and leave him dead as stone.

"If he plans well and is very lucky, he'll live to tell us exactly how he did it."

Churchill nodded and blew a smoke ring.

2. ST. NICHOLAS ARENA, 66TH STREET AND BROADWAY, MANHATTAN, OCTOBER 7, 1932, 8:10 P.M.

No one saw it. It was just too fast. But even the screams of the crowd in the packed arena did not keep the fans at ringside from hearing young Timmy Farrell's jawbone crack. The punch came in the twelfth second of the third round. The game, red-haired lad from Limerick had thrown the first punches of the round, a left hook that missed and then a right to the chest. His opponent, the more experienced and stronger Karl Ludwig, countered with a left jab and a lightning-fast right square on the Irishman's big chin. Farrell fell like a wet towel. Ludwig had scored his twenty-second consecutive knockout. Farrell left on a stretcher as the crowd turned its attention to the next fight on the Friday night card.

Karl Ludwig was fast becoming a minor celebrity in two worlds.

In one world, he had captained the Columbia University boxing team and won the Ivy League middleweight championship in 1924 and 1925. He won every time he fought in the three-round bouts that always preceded the main events at the St. Nicholas and Sunnyside arenas in New York. He used his reputation as a prizefighter to help run a popular and successful instructional boxing program for teenage boys in Manhattan's Upper East Side and Harlem.

In his other world, he was Karl Ludwig, M.D., a resident in orthopedic surgery at New York Hospital on York Avenue. The boxing was an avocation. It helped pay for medical books, rent, and bootleg beer. It also helped to start a small nest egg that would soon help get him to San Francisco, where he and

Dr. Fern Wagner, also a resident physician at the hospital, would begin their respective medical careers and make little Ludwigs.

8:25 P.M.

In the gray light of his dusty dressing room, the kind assigned to those who fought preliminary matches, Karl stepped from the shower and dried himself with the fresh towel he had brought from his apartment. He combed his light brown hair, parting it neatly on the left. He dressed quickly – in a crisp white shirt, navy blue cardigan, and freshly pressed gray wool pants – grabbed the canvas bag that held his boxing gear, and walked down the dim hallway to the office of Irv Levin, promoter of fights. Rail thin and bald, Levin was never without his trademark untied polka-dot tie.

"Sit down, Karl. Take a load off," Levin said. "Wet your whistle. It's on me." He gestured toward the floor and a desk-side washbasin filled with beer bottles and melting ice. "Nice and fresh, just in this afternoon from Montreal."

Levin pointed at Karl's right hand. "That right of yours, Karl. It's so fast and strong. It could kill. With good management and more hard training, you could beat anyone." Karl gave a gentle nod. Levin had made the pitch before. Karl knew Levin was a schmoozer.

"Once again, Irv, no sale. I'm a doctor, remember, with less than a year of hospital residency left before I can start my own practice. Besides, I'm twenty-seven and I've been fighting three-round preliminaries. I'm too old to start training for ten and fifteen rounders."

"Not if you trained full time. I'm telling you, forget this doctor stuff. It's dreck. Who's got money to pay doctors these days?"

Karl spoke with only the faintest hint of a German accent. "Sorry, Irv, that would put my career as an orthopedic surgeon off for years. And I could hurt my hands. It's just too risky. I know what happens to boxers. Too many of them end up broke, blind, or dead. I'd rather save my hands, keep my wits, get rich, and die fat, old, and in one piece."

"Well, think about it," Levin replied. "Hell, Karl, the newspaper story writes itself. 'Surgeon mends bones by day, breaks jaws by night.' You could fight that other German, Schmeling. Hun against Hun. A good fight here in New York and then rematches in London, even Berlin. Think about how people would rush to see a doctor who also happened to be heavyweight champ. You could buy your own hospital."

Karl took a long swallow of beer. "Sorry, Irv, I'm too old for wet dreams. We're not in Hollywood in the Roaring Twenties. We're in New York in the Starving Thirties. Now let me have the hundred bucks you owe me for breaking that kid's jaw. I need some sleep. I go on duty at the hospital at 4:00 a.m. for a twelve-hour shift."

Irv Levin grinned and handed Karl a white letter-size envelope. "You're a good schmuck, so I doubled your money. Spend it on a good time with that lady doctor girlfriend of yours. Tell her to come to your next fight. She dresses up the joint."

Karl nodded. "I'll be sure to bring her next time. And I'll bring her uncle too, next time he comes here from Germany on business. He's seen me box before, and he's the only one I know who can afford your ringside seats."

8:40 P.M.

Back in the hallway, Karl opened the envelope and removed two one hundred dollar bills, then searched in the half-light for Timmy Farrell's dressing room. He found young Farrell on a rubbing table, with a bloody, split upper lip, and a swollen jaw. As Karl eyed Farrell, he felt a hand on his shoulder.

"The lad can't talk. Hurts him too much. I'm sure his jaw got cracked. I heard it snap. And his lip, it's bad too." Karl hadn't seen the other man in the dim light. The man spoke in a soft brogue, the kind that came from deep in the chest. "I'm Timmy's uncle, and I saw your last punch from his corner. He's a fine young fighter, but your right just came too fast and too hard, but it was a clean hit. We've no complaint."

Karl looked at the stricken young Irishman, then back at the older man. "You're probably right about the jawbone, but I know someone who can help." Karl put his hand on the older man's forearm. "Take him to New York Hospital, York Avenue at 68th Street. You'll want to use the emergency entrance. Slip the nurse in charge a buck and ask for Dr. Josh Greenberg. He can reset that jawbone. There's another doctor he should see tonight too – Dr. Fern Wagner. She's a plastic surgeon, a really good one. She'll fix that lip up so there's no scarring."

Karl eyed the prostrate young boxer, then turned to the older man. "Now one final point: When he's able to pay attention, tell him to keep his left up to guard himself. He dropped it midway through the first round and again in the second. That's why I got him in the third."

"But the medical help . . . What will it cost?"

"The cab ride to the hospital will be about a buck," Karl said. "What Dr. Greenberg and Dr. Wagner do will be on the sly – free and off the books. Just don't blab about it, or all three of us could get in trouble. If the duty nurse is in a good mood you might get a free room for the night. I'd slip her a buck too. That should do it."

Karl reached into his jacket for the envelope Levin had given him and handed the man one of the bills. "Here's a C note for medicine and bandages. And for soup and oatmeal, which is about all he'll be able to get down for a time. Then he'll need a dentist. There's a good clinic on East 33rd. Now, let me help you get Timmy up and dressed and we'll get you into a taxi."

9:10 P.M.

As the rattling Third Avenue El carried Karl homeward, his thoughts turned to Fern Wagner. Tomorrow night, after finishing his shift at the hospital, he and Fern would drink Dortmunder, real German beer smuggled in off the Bremen, the German ocean liner that had docked that afternoon at Pier 43 on the West Side. They would drink it at the speakeasy in the basement of the Bavarian Inn in the German-American neighborhood called Yorkville. He jumped off the train at 86th Street, ambled down the iron steps, and headed for his apartment in the crisp autumn night.

3. THE BAVARIAN INN, EAST 86TH STREET, MANHATTAN, OCTOBER 8, 1932, 7:00 P.M.

In the dim barroom light, Karl Ludwig and Fern Wagner climbed onto the familiar wooden bar stools. He felt no fatigue from the previous night's fight, or from the long shift at the hospital. Being with Fern energized him. Fritz, the bartender, a recent émigré from Leipzig, knew that they both wanted Dortmunder.

Fern's chestnut hair fell just to her shoulders, framing her chiseled cheekbones and dark green eyes. She accepted the tall glass of beer and put her free hand on Karl's forearm.

"Thanks for the great job you and Josh did on Timmy Farrell," Karl said, planting a soft kiss on Fern's forehead. "I saw him this afternoon, sitting up in bed reading A Farewell to Arms. Maybe it means he'll quit boxing. Not a bad idea."

"I know. Josh told me your punch pushed the boy's jawbone back so far it just missed hitting his brain – a pretty close call if you ask me. You could have killed that boy." She spoke perfect English. She had learned the language first during her school days in Berlin, then in London and Oxford, and in countless conversations with Karl and other colleagues.

"You know, I don't want to kill anyone. Josh said his jaw was weak. It could have been injured in another fight."

Fern frowned and pointed to his beer glass. He had already consumed half his beer. "Hey, you must be thirsty," she whispered.

"I could drink a tank."

"Let's drink to Governor Roosevelt winning the presidential election. Then we might get legal drinking," Fern said in her unmistakable Berlin accent.

Karl downed what remained of his beer. "Roosevelt has my vote. He's been a good New York governor. He'll get Prohibition repealed. Just imagine, drinking in barrooms with windows."

"Don't have to imagine. I know what it's like," Fern said. "Things may not be perfect back in Germany, but you don't have to hide to drink – there are wonderful open-air beer gardens and street cafés."

"Sounds nice, but I've no intention of ever going back," Karl said, putting his hand on Fern's shoulder. "Especially now that it looks like Hitler and the Nazis will take power. I'm an American, and I want *us* to be Americans. In fact . . ."

Fern put a soft index finger on his lips. "I know, Karl. I have to get going with my U.S. citizenship papers."

"Well, we don't want our plans all screwed up just because you're an alien."

"Karl, I won't let things get screwed up." She leaned forward and kissed him on the nose, clasping both his hands. "Seriously," she whispered, "you need to understand that I'll do it, but I need time. I'll do it before we get married. I promise. But, Karl, please know something else – it's not that easy for me to stop being German, especially now that Hitler and his thugs are growing stronger and more popular every day. Try to understand, Karl. What I'm telling you is that leaving Germany now is like running away, like quitting."

"Running away? Quitting? No *Liebchen*, leaving Germany isn't running away or quitting. It's common sense. Thank God my mother had the sense to send me here."

"You see things another way. You came here as a boy, nearly twelve years ago. I've only been here two years. I still have family in Germany, and I love the place despite Hitler." She took another long sip.

Karl knew she meant what she said, that she always let him know where she stood, and that any attempt to change her mind – or her timetable – would never work. The more he pushed the citizenship issue, the more she would delay.

After a silent moment, she pushed her nose into his chest. They hugged to celebrate not having a fight.

4. NEW YORK HOSPITAL CAFETERIA, AUGUST 21, 1930, NOON

Lunch tray in hand, Karl scanned the noontime crowd in search of a seat. He saw Josh Greenberg, his oldest and best friend, at a corner table with a woman in a doctor's white coat. She was laughing at whatever Josh was saying. Even from thirty feet away, he could see she wore no makeup and didn't need any. Josh waved Karl to the table.

"I see you got the egg salad. So did I. I think they made it last week," Josh quipped.

Josh introduced Karl to Dr. Fern Wagner, noting that she'd arrived from Germany just two weeks before. *"Willkommen in Amerika,"* Karl said, and they immediately began speaking German. Fern wanted to know of Karl's childhood in Germany, especially in Berlin. Josh stayed quiet, even though he spoke fluent German. After three minutes, Josh excused himself. Karl responded happily to Fern's interest in his childhood memories. His life in Germany had never interested his American friends, except for Josh, whose parents came from Frankfurt and taught Josh German before he learned English.

Karl had been talking for thirty minutes straight when Fern interrupted to offer to get them some hot coffee. It gave Karl time to force down his forgotten sandwich and discover that he had lost his appetite.

"I must apologize," he said when she returned with the coffee. "I've subjected you to a monologue," he said in German. "Except for Josh, I haven't talked about Berlin to anyone in years, except to the older German immigrants in my neighborhood. They love to talk about 'the old country' and 'the old days,' but I know very little about Germany now. I've spent close to half my life here, and I plan to stay. I love this place, New York and America – and I want to see more of it. I may even begin my practice in California. I've read a lot about San Francisco. Sure, things aren't so great anywhere in America right now, but I'll bet it's a picnic compared to Berlin when I was a kid there."

She pushed her coffee aside. "Tell me, what do you like to do in New York?"

"One of my favorite things to do is talk with the Americans – fighters at the gym where I train for boxing matches, people on the El, in speakeasies, and at the storefront boxing clinic in Harlem where I teach boxing. I like meeting storekeepers and businessmen, even Wall Street types. I raise money from them for the clinic."

A bell rang in his head – he was talking far too much about himself. "As you can see, I like it here. I became a citizen on my twenty-first birthday. But let's talk about you."

Fern's chin rested on her clasped hands. "You appear to be quite a busy fellow – not much time for a walk in the park, or a girlfriend."

"Not now. You're right. Josh and I used to chase nurses back in college and medical school. Actually we weren't that good at it, and now, we're far too busy."

Fern leaned forward. "Well, after a fortnight in America, it's nice to meet a man who doesn't consider himself a Casanova – quite refreshing, really. Tell me, Dr. Ludwig, are you a man who can have a friendship with a woman without trying to sleep with her?"

Her direct question stopped him. A serious question deserved a serious reply. "Let me say that I've learned that there are three levels to the male-female relationship – friendship, passion, and love. And each is very different, although we all tend to get them mixed up, especially men. Women are much better at making the distinction."

"Right from some textbook, and not really an answer, but an honest try nevertheless," she responded. "Can you offer an example, something concrete, of how things between a man and a woman can grow in time from friendship to love?"

Karl didn't answer for a moment, then sat back. "By having a lot in common. A relationship could grow between an orthopedist who resets jawbones and a plastic surgeon who treats people disfigured in fires, car crashes, and even prizefights." He saw that she was still looking at him, but that her gaze had shifted from his eyes to his forehead.

"Again, I've said enough. Next time, it'll be your turn to do the monologue. Do you have time for lunch here tomorrow?"

"No, but I'm sure we'll run into each again soon." She rose and left quickly, without looking back.

Karl scolded himself for showing that he was so eager to see her again, especially so soon. Bad strategy. He should have known better.

When he did see her in the days that followed, it was in the busy hospital corridors. She seemed always to be going in the opposite direction. Then she was in the OR with him, polite but all business. She would say, "Good morning" or "Good afternoon, Doctor," in her clear Berlin accent, but never said his name. He wanted to hear her say his name. He wondered if he had made so little an impression that she didn't even remember it. As time passed, he found himself on the constant lookout for her, holding conversations with her in his mind. When he did run across her in the hallway or the cafeteria, she was always with other doctors or nurses, seemingly intent on whatever she was doing. Twice he saw her in the library, making notes on a portable typewriter. He let her be.

5. 137TH STREET AND THIRD AVENUE, MANHATTAN, DECEMBER 24, 1930, 9:15 P.M.

The December night had a smoky red look as the snow fell. Karl jumped from the ambulance and saw that the fire had not yet reached the third and fourth floors of the burning tenement.

"Can we get a ladder to the fourth floor?" Chief Fire Inspector Barry Cavanaugh barked to his crew as Karl approached. Cavanaugh knew Karl from other fires. "There are lots of burns here, ugly ones on kids' faces, Dr. Ludwig. Damn, when will they learn not to put live candles near Christmas trees? One girl broke her leg falling down the fire escape. One of your fellow residents, Dr. Wagner, is working on the burns. She came dressed to the nines – straight from some Christmas Eve party, I guess. But she had her medical bag over her shoulder, the one she always carries. We've given her bandages and stuff, Doc, but she really needs your help with that broken leg now."

9:17 P.M.
Karl found Fern in a full-length blue velvet evening dress, a thin sweater barely covering her shoulders. At first, she didn't see him. She was patting a bleeding brown face with gauze. He saw that she'd already dressed the wounds of five children, three with their faces bandaged. Another child, a boy of about five, lay dead on a stretcher, eyes open. Karl shut the boy's eyes and pulled the

damp, snow-covered blanket over his head. Neither Fern nor Karl had time to comfort the boy's grandmother, who knelt on the spot, fervent in her Hail Marys. Other adults milled around nearby, some crying, others kneeling and praying in the whirling snow.

9:22 P.M.

Their eyes met in the dark. "Hell of a Christmas Eve," Karl said.

"Tragic," Fern shouted, loud enough to be heard over the noise.

Karl saw that the long stream of water from the fire trucks had begun to control the fire. A queue of six – shivering in bathrobes, pajamas, and blankets – two of them bleeding from the forehead, stood before Fern.

"Fern, why don't you get them all to the hospital? You can treat them better there. Take the ambulance that brought me. Josh Greenberg's in the ER tonight. He can help you."

"Offer accepted," Fern shouted over the confusion.

As she turned toward the ambulance, she lost her footing on an ice patch hidden in five inches of fresh snow. He helped her to her feet, picking up her sweater, which was wet with snow, and the small bag she had dropped. It didn't seem to go with her party dress.

"The bag holds my surgical instruments," she said, goose pimples covering her well-toned shoulders.

"Here, you need this," he said, removing his blue wool jacket.

"Thanks, but you'll freeze."

"Only for a moment."

"See you back at the hospital."

6. NEW YORK HOSPITAL, DECEMBER 25, 1930, 5:30 A.M.

Their work done, Karl – now wearing a borrowed Fire Department jacket – and Josh Greenberg walked toward the hospital's York Avenue exit when they saw Fern near the revolving doorway. She said hello to Josh, then turned toward

Karl. "Merry Christmas, Doctor. And thanks for the jacket. Saved me from a bad cold, I'm sure."

"Keep it for now, it's still snowing."

"Thanks."

She turned toward the revolving doorway, but only for a second, then spun around. "Karl, if you're interested, there's a 6:00 a.m. Christmas Mass at St. Catherine of Siena on East 68th Street. Would you care to join me? Afterward we can go to my uncle's place for an early Christmas breakfast."

"Sure," he responded, happy at last to hear her say his name. They said their holiday goodbyes to Josh, who remained on duty.

7. EAST 85TH STREET, MANHATTAN, DECEMBER 25, 1930, 6:55 A.M.

The street and sidewalk were under a foot-deep blanket of fresh snow. Fern put her arm in Karl's as they walked. Her free hand held the white purse.

"That white purse?" he asked. "It doesn't seem to match your gown."

"When you don't wear makeup or lipstick you don't need a purse," she said. "As for the bag, an old medical school professor told me to always carry my instruments, because you never know when you might need them."

"Pretty good advice . . ."

"We're almost there," Fern said. "It's the second townhouse from the corner, off Madison. And for heaven's sake, it's all lit up. Uncle Frederick must be up already. Last night he hosted a Christmas Eve dinner party for a few German expatriates and some American and British friends. I was enjoying their company when the call came about the fire."

"You uncle may have gone to bed and forgotten to turn them off," Karl said.

"Not Uncle Frederick. He doesn't waste electricity, and he's a compulsive early riser. He does a great deal of business by trans-Atlantic telephone and cable with the London and Berlin markets before the sun's up on this side of the Atlantic, but probably not on Christmas Day."

"Sounds ambitious."

"Yes, quite so."

"Tell me, what does he do?"

"Uncle Frederick owns things, a tool-and-dye company, an aircraft parts manufacturer, a tractor company, a pharmaceutical company, and an investment firm. He does it through a holding company called Wagner Industries. It's based in Berlin, but the investment firm keeps offices in London and here in New York."

"So he's *that* Frederick Wagner," Karl chuckled. "I've read about him. I'm impressed, really."

As they neared the snow-covered steps to the brownstone, the large front door swung open and a man emerged. Frederick Wagner stood erect atop the stoop in a navy blue turtleneck, a snow shovel in his right hand. He wore no hat, letting his thick black hair protect his head against the cold.

"Fern, Merry Christmas. Now I don't believe I know this gallant lad who has obviously let you use his jacket. You left here in such a rush last night. I almost went after you with an overcoat, but I didn't want to appear to be a doting uncle, and I knew that you would manage somehow."

"Uncle Frederick, allow me to present Dr. Karl Ludwig, an orthopedist and a colleague from the hospital. He's a Berliner by birth. And last night he was my hero."

"Well, get inside, both of you. Fern, please get out of that lovely but damp evening dress and fetch yourself some dry clothing. And while you're at it, get this lad a thick wool sweater from my cedar closet. I've just made fresh coffee. It won't take fifteen minutes for me to shovel this snow away. Then we can have a proper Christmas breakfast. And Karl, you can assist Fern in the kitchen. I won't need any help with the snow. It's fresh and light, easy to shovel."

7:20 A.M.

Bacon sizzled in the large iron skillet as Fern whisked nine eggs for scrambling. She added some grated cheddar to the eggs. Karl began toasting large slices of pumpernickel. At Frederick's request, he set the table with fine bone China that bore the Wagner coat of arms. Once back indoors, Frederick squeezed several fresh oranges for juice.

"You missed a wonderful party, Fern," Frederick said, as he poured ample portions of juice. "Smart people, sparkling conversation, and many laughs. And, yes, your mother called. She's in England, I believe, visiting some old chums from the years when you and she were there with me. All I could hear was that she wished us both a joyous holiday. It was a bad trans-Atlantic connection."

There was little conversation as they ate. Each was too hungry for small talk.

"Karl," Frederick asked, pushing his empty plate aside and pouring more coffee, "do you still have family in Germany?"

"No. My mother died shortly after I arrived in New York. She sent me here in 1919 to live with an uncle. He died several years ago."

"And your father?"

"A surgeon, killed in Belgium very early in the war – in August 1914."

"Most unfortunate. But you have obviously had some good schooling and have gotten all the way through medical school. How did you manage?"

"I've been lucky. My uncle taught at a good private school here in Manhattan, so I went there because there was no tuition for the immediate family of faculty members. I had scholarships to college and med school, and now I do some prizefighting. It pays a bit more than I need to cover expenses."

Frederick nodded.

"I do believe I've read about you. I try to follow boxing. There's a good German boxer on his way to the heavyweight championship, Max Schmeling. Do you know of him?"

"Everyone's heard of Schmeling. But believe me, I'm not in his class. I fight the preliminaries for small change."

"Well, I should like to see you box."

"I fight a week from Friday night at the St. Nicholas Arena, just across town from here. You're welcome to come, but only on one condition."

"And what might that be?"

"That you bring Fern."

"You'll have to ask me first," Fern laughed.

"I'm asking you now. It'll all be very proper – with Uncle Frederick, we'd have a proper chaperon."

"Karl, I hate to disappoint you, but we don't need a chaperon," Fern laughed.

Frederick took the last of his coffee and stood. "You're about to lose whatever chaperon you have. I've arranged for a car to take my skis and me to the Flushing Airport, where a plane will fly me to Vermont for two days of skiing. It should be interesting. They're experimenting there with a mechanical lift to carry people up the mountain. I would have invited you, Fern, but there was just no time. It's sort of an impulse thing. I hope you don't mind. You can be sure I'll invite you next time."

Fern sat back. "Please be warned that if you invite me I shall come. But only on the condition that you invite Karl, and that he accepts."

"I've never skied," Karl said

"So you'll learn. It's something we can do together. Or would you rather that I learn to box?"

"No, I'll ski."

Moments later, Frederick was gone. "More coffee before I send you home?" Fern asked. He nodded yes.

After she resumed her seat across from him, she sat back. "Do you know why you're here?" she asked.

"Because I gave you my coat last night?"

"That's only part of it – a very small part. The real reason is that you had the good sense to leave me alone and not impose your company on me in the weeks since we first met in the hospital cafeteria. Remember, you wanted to see me the very next day. I wanted to see you the next day too. But, Karl, we never could have kept up that every-next-day pace. It would have become an obligation."

He sat back. He knew she had a point. He did not respond directly. "I saw you lots of times, but you were engrossed in what you were doing, it seemed."

"Indeed I was. I always concentrate on what I'm doing. But, Karl, I saw you and could see that you were busy too."

"So where are you going with this, Fern?"

"To an understanding, I hope. And, if I may presume, I'm pretty sure that you're as interested in me as I am in you. But we both have incredible obligations, responsibilities, and yes, opportunities, both as individuals and together."

He could feel her self-confidence.

"What you're saying is that we've got to keep our heads about us. I think I can do that," he said, reaching across the table and placing a hand on hers.

"I think we can too," she said, almost in whisper. "You can't dote on me. It would make me spurn you. What's important now is that we separate our professional and private lives as much as possible."

"Well, there may be places for efficiencies, you know, for coordinating what we do, being in the same place at the same time. I can think of one way we could do that," he said.

"How?" she asked.

He moved around the table toward her. Fern stood and placed a finger on his mouth and grinned at him. After a warm kiss, she rested her head on his chest. "Page one of what could be a great book," she whispered. She looked up at him. "But let's not skip to the next chapter. If we do that, neither of us will want to finish the book."

"So?"

"So now I'll send you home. When we next meet, I'll see you in your shorts – your boxing shorts, that is – at the St. Nicholas Arena. I see a conflict between your being a doctor and a boxer. You're supposed to heal, not hurt."

Karl and Fern began having frequent cafeteria lunches and dinners near the hospital at delicatessens and speakeasies in Yorkville. He helped her draft articles for medical journals in English. She didn't need much help, but it meant they could spend more time with each other. Twice she endured the stench and filth of Stillman's gym on West 57th Street to watch Karl train. And though reluctant at first, she sat through his fights, as many as she could. When Frederick was in New York, he would escort her. Frederick proved to be a boxing aficionado.

Later that winter Karl learned to ski and ski well. He took several bruising falls, but after a time his natural athleticism helped him keep close to Fern, who proved to be an expert on the mountain. In the spring and summer they went to baseball games at the Polo Grounds. The first time there, Fern thought she would see an actual polo match. But she took to baseball right away and soon came to know names like Mel Ott, Bill Terry, and Carl Hubbell.

8. BERLIN, DECEMBER 15, 1919, 4:30 A.M.

Over a dusty tobacco shop on the Dorotheenstrasse, in the flat she shared with her son, Marianna Ludwig wiped her nose with the last of her clean handkerchiefs. She had not slept that night thanks to a persistent cough. Marianna never fully recovered from the influenza that had afflicted her back in October. She could no longer take the crowded streetcar from her apartment to the homes of the few Berlin families still affluent enough to pay for their children to learn to play works of Mozart and Liszt on the piano. These days, Marianna had only enough strength for a half-dozen sessions a week at the upright piano in her small sitting room. She had left a larger and tastefully furnished apartment on Unter Den Linden not long after a Belgian cannon shell killed her husband, a doctor in the Kaiser's army.

Marianna managed to pay the rent, but the apartment was cramped, its sitting room barely large enough for the piano, the daybed where fourteen-year-old Karl slept, and the card table where he did his homework. Marianna saved as much as she was able so that Karl could remain in a good school, one under the demanding academic regime of the Jesuit fathers. For money and food, Karl worked both before and after school as a kitchen helper, dishwasher, and busboy in a restaurant near the Pariser Platz.

When the shrill ring of the wind-up alarm broke the silence, the boy sprang to his feet. Marianna cut a thick slice of black bread, which the boy consumed. He bushed his teeth and dressed for the winter morning. At the door he paused to give his mother a tight hug and was gone.

As a kitchen helper, the boy's job included pilfering foodstuffs from boxcars at the railhead near the Friedrichstrasse Bahnhof and delivering them to the restaurant on his way to school. On a good day, there were bags of flour. On better days, there were potatoes. On the best days, there were fresh greens, grapes, and even oranges from Spain and the south of France. On rare occasions there was meat. All of it was scarce and very expensive on the black market *and* in restaurants and cafés. The idea was to steal whatever was available from the poorly guarded boxcars. There were no rules. Karl would have to fight boys from other restaurants over who would get the most and the best. He often arrived at school with a black eye or a bloody nose.

On this gray dawn, snow had been falling since midnight, accumulating to more than a foot and hiding the rail tracks. Through the swirling snow, Karl could see a tall horse pulling an open cart carrying sacks of potatoes. Karl thought about the potatoes, a decent morning's take, if he could snatch a bag and run with it. He started to move toward the cart just as a whistle from a switching engine startled the horse, which began to run, only to trip on a rail switch and fall to the ground in pain. A policeman, who spent most mornings looking the other way, rushed to the stricken animal and saw immediately that it had two broken legs. Two shots from the policeman's pistol killed the animal and at once attracted the attention of the rail yard vagrants and young looters with whom Karl competed. Several of the boys drew knives and began cutting away the meatier parts of the unlucky animal. Karl moved toward them, wanting his share. Fresh horsemeat would bring a premium price at the restaurant, far more than potatoes.

Another lad, taller and at least fifteen pounds heavier than Karl, jumped in to cut meat from the horse's underbelly. Karl kept his knife in his pocket, but knew that he needed to stop the larger boy from cutting away the choicest parts. He rushed the lad from behind, grabbing him at the waist, and rolling with him in the snow. The surprise forced the other boy to drop his knife. Karl tried to pin the lad down, but the other boy kicked his way free. The two stood upright in the swirling snow, trading punches as the other scavengers gathered to watch.

Karl landed a hard left to the stomach, but took a hard right to nose. Then, as Karl was winding up to throw a wheelhouse right, he slipped and fell face down in the snow. Karl grimaced, expecting a kick in the head. Instead, he felt a hand grab his jacket collar. The other lad pulled Karl to his feet and peered into his bloodied eyes. "Forget the lousy horse meat. We both need to get to school," the bigger boy said. "We'll finish this by ourselves tonight. This has been too good a fight to end with you slipping like that."

Stunned, Karl nodded acceptance of the temporary truce. They agreed to meet at the edge of the Tiergarten, near the Brandenburg Gate, that evening at five. Later that day, Karl recalled that he knew the larger boy as Ziggy. They had tussled several times before over cartons of vegetables.

5:00 P.M.

It was already dark and the snow had given way to a cutting winter wind. As Karl walked in the fading light across the Pariser Platz toward the Brandenburg Gate, he could recall better evenings just before other Christmastimes, when his father would bring home strudel and they would eat it after dinner with ice cream and hot chocolate. In the distance, he saw Ziggy, leaning with one hand on a park bench. As Karl approached, Ziggy stepped forward, his arms at his side. In a moment, they stood two feet apart. Neither spoke. Karl was about to utter a greeting when Ziggy's stinging right fist hit him squarely in the mouth. Karl crashed face down in the frozen snow, expecting Ziggy to pummel him. Instead, for the second time that day, Ziggy helped Karl to his feet and extended his open hand.

"Little Karl, it's time we introduced ourselves. My name is Klaus Ziegler. My friends call me Ziggy. I've just taught you a lesson, one you should never forget." Ziggy's resonant tone belied his fifteen years but told of an early addiction to stolen cigarettes.

"And what message is that, Klaus Ziegler?" Karl muttered through his bloodied lips. "Just this," Ziggy laughed, "never wait for the other fellow to start a fight. Once you know you'll be in a fight, hit first as hard and as fast as you can. It's been a rule of mine. That's why I don't lose fights. We both came to fight, so why fuss around? I hit first and you went down and that was that. This morning at the railhead, I couldn't apply the rule because you came at me from behind. Not very sporting of you, I must say. But I learned how much your punches hurt and that you have balls. You would never have started a fight with a kid who's almost a foot taller than you unless you had balls."

"Thanks."

"You're welcome." Ziggy clicked his heels, giving an honest smile.

"Do I owe you anything for the lesson?" Karl asked.

"Not one pfennig. I'd like us to be friends, or let's say partners. We would make a good team at the railhead. Who could beat the two of us? What's more, my father owns the Café Ziegler on the Mauerstrasse. Our customers are interesting people, though few are saints. We serve good food when we can get it and good beer. We're better than half-full every night. My father will pay you a fair wage. I asked him about it this afternoon."

Rounding his shoulders against the wind, Karl eyed Ziggy, then straightened up. "Good," he said, "we'll work together. I'd like that."

"Then things are settled between us?" Ziggy asked.

"Just one more thing," Karl said, smiling.

In that instant, Karl's windmill left hook struck Ziggy's right ear. Ziggy never saw it coming. Nor did he see the lightning right that sent him to the snow. Ziggy lay flat on his back, eyes closed. He remained unconscious for several seconds until he saw Karl's outstretched hand. Ziggy accepted the help and rose, spitting blood.

Karl put an arm around him.

"I owed you that one. Now we can be friends. Please understand."

"You son of a bitch – yes, I think we will be very good friends."

That night Karl arrived home late to tell his mother about his new job in another restaurant. He explained how the place was called Café Ziegler and how the son of the owner had befriended him. Karl reached into his school bag and gave his mother two fresh oranges from Spain, a gift from Ziggy's father.

9. SECOND AVENUE AND EAST 82ND STREET, MANHATTAN, MARCH 15, 1920

Otto Kerner walked to the small bakery on Second Avenue. He sat alone at a table adjacent to the window, preparing to savor the moment. The letter that had arrived in the mail that morning was from his sister, Marianna. He hadn't heard from her since September 1914, when she'd written to tell him of her husband's death.

Otto had come to New York some ten years before and earned a comfortable living teaching music to the smart sons of rich New Yorkers. He looked forward to reading the letter over his usual black coffee and freshly baked crumb cake, an indulgence he had pursued every Saturday morning since his wife's fatal heart attack three years ago.

Dorotheenstrasse
Berlin
March 3, 1920

Dearest Otto,

Please accept my sincere apologies for not having written you in so long.

Now I must write with my heart in hand. My health is failing due to severe influenza and repeated bouts of pneumonia. I must limit myself to a few piano lessons a week.
My son Karl, thank Almighty God, has a sharp mind and a strong body, just like his late beloved father. He's been a good student and hard worker. His school is one the best in Berlin. His grades have been among the highest in his class.

However, for the last several months, Karl has fallen in with the wrong people. He works at a restaurant frequented by some of the lower elements of Berlin society, like prostitutes and sellers of opium and cocaine. Some of his "work" involves stealing food to stock the restaurant. He does less and less homework, and his grades have fallen.

Karl needs a better environment and, I must say, a strong masculine hand.

So, my question is simple. May Karl come to live with you in America? He will not burden you, though his appetite is robust, and he always needs larger clothes.

Please respond as soon as you can. It would be wonderful if he could begin the autumn school term in New York.

Please also accept my apologies for this surprise.

With sincerity and love,

Marianna

10. 305 EAST 84TH STREET, MANHATTAN, MARCH 22, 1920

The thought of having a young man to help fill his lonely apartment appealed to the childless Otto Kerner. That afternoon he sat at his small kitchen table and wrote a letter.

My Dear Marianna:

I cannot tell you how good it was to hear from you.

I will accept the boy. I look forward to his bringing some life back to the place. The school where I teach music is one of the best in New York. Just as important, it has a policy that allows free tuition for the sons and immediate family of faculty members. It will afford him a sound general education in preparation for university studies and allow him to enjoy the companionship of boys from respectable families.

Please understand that he must behave and maintain good grades and that, for the sake of the boy, I must be in charge.

Please inform me of the details regarding the manner and time of his arrival.

Your loving brother,

Otto

11. MANHATTAN, AUGUST 20, 1920

Karl emerged from the entry center at Ellis Island with a knapsack on his back, having paid for his passage by working as a cabin boy on a British freighter out of Bremerhaven. At Marianna's behest, the headmaster at Karl's school in Berlin had arranged the passage through one of his students, who had immigrated to England before the Great War and become a shipping executive. Ziggy's father paid for the train that took Karl from Berlin to the North Sea port.

Otto Kerner recognized Karl as soon as he appeared in the Tyrolean suit, bought with money his mother had borrowed from a neighbor. Marianna had feared that somehow Otto and Karl would not be able to identify each other. She knew that such attire would make Karl stand out among the masses at the immigration center.

When they entered Otto's East 84th Street apartment, more than forty of Otto's neighbors and friends, along with their offspring, were there to welcome Karl. Most were German immigrants. Others were Italian or Irish, some German-Jewish. Everyone was either an immigrant or a first-generation American.

Karl at once became the visiting dignitary, answering questions with disturbing tales of the poverty, crime, and chaos in postwar Berlin. He amazed the guests with his crisp, streetwise answers. He was polite, responding with "Sirs" and "Madams." His table manners were impeccable, particularly for a boy who had apparently been exposed to the darker side of street life. He awed Otto's guests with his appetite for the knockwurst, bratwurst, Westphalia ham, red cabbage, and sauerkraut, most of which Otto's neighbors had prepared. Few such traditional German delicacies were readily available in Berlin at the time, even for employees and patrons of Café Ziegler.

The older people delighted in conversing with Karl in German. The younger among them, more Karl's contemporaries, spoke and asked questions in Americanized English. Karl had fun trying to answer in schoolboy English, which he spoke with a halting British accent.

After a healthy portion of vanilla and strawberry ice cream from Schrafft's, Karl went to the hallway closet to fetch his knapsack, which held a small photograph of his mother that Otto and his neighbors had asked to see. He saw that the knapsack was missing and began to search for it. A moment later, Karl saw his bag on the bed in a small bedroom off Uncle Otto's parlor. A boy who had been introduced to Karl as someone who lived in a place called "the West Side" had his hands in the bag. Karl rushed over to him, grabbed him by his necktie, and yelled at him in German: "What the hell are you doing in my bag?"

In an instant the bedroom filled with guests both shocked and curious. Uncle Otto held up his right hand. "Enough," he declared, his eyes fixed on Karl. In the silence that followed, Otto placed a hand firmly on Karl's shoulder and spoke in soft, slow German. "Karl, take your hands off this boy. He was trying to help you. I asked him to unpack your bag and put your things in the dresser drawers. He was doing you a favor."

Karl's eyes flooded. He began to cry but stopped himself. "I'm sorry, Uncle," he said, this time in English. "I thought . . . No, I have no excuse. I must apologize to my uncle and his guests." He turned toward the boy he had just threatened. "I especially apologize to you. I hope we shall be friends."

"We will be," the other boy replied. "In fact, we'll be at the same school starting in two weeks."

Karl was embarrassed. "Excuse me again," he said. "I cannot now remember your name."

"That's okay. You've met so many people today, but my name hasn't changed. I'm still Josh Greenberg. I hope you'll let me show you around town. We can start tomorrow morning if you like."

12. MANHATTAN, AUTUMN 1920

At school, some of the boys teased Karl about his accent. That was always a mistake. It often led to scuffles and a stinging punch in the face from Karl. That stopped the teasing. Learning English had it challenges, but Karl worked at it. Josh took time to help. It helped that Josh spoke German too. Uncle Otto was even more helpful. He decreed they speak only English at home.

Karl and Josh teamed up to compile a five-page bibliography on evolution, which earned them both an A in biology. Josh already had A's in lots of subjects. And for Karl, it would be the first of many. The two worked together on other projects and, at the same time, competed in a friendly way to see who could achieve the highest grade-point average.

Still, there were problems. While their fellow students learned quickly not to tease Karl about his German accent, they were less fearful of throwing anti-Semitic barbs at Josh. When Josh received the highest mark on a biology exam, young Malcolm Williamson III, whose father presided over one of the larger Wall Street law firms, failed to enjoy the moment. He accused Josh of getting help from his "Yid" school teacher father, a professor at the City College of New York. Karl took the matter into his own hands. In the locker room, a flurry of rights and lefts from Karl was enough to knock out three of Williamson's upper front teeth. The incident got Karl a week's suspension. It would have been worse if Otto weren't on the faculty.

After that, things were quiet at Uncle Otto's apartment. For a week, Otto said nothing to Karl. Otto scolded him with silence, and he kept it up.

13. MANHATTAN, DECEMBER 24, 1920, 3:00 P.M.

Otto's discipline continued. On Karl's first Christmas Eve in New York, there was neither a tree nor any presents, except for a card from Marianna Ludwig to her son. As the late December dusk gathered, it was Uncle Otto who broke the silence. "Karl, come sit with me at the kitchen table." Otto took a milk bottle from the icebox, filled two glasses, and pushed one across the table toward Karl. He then offered Karl a banana from a fruit bowl.

"Don't you understand, Karl," Otto began, "flying off the handle and throwing reckless punches at schoolmates, no matter how well deserved or intended, could get you expelled from a wonderful school, perhaps cost me my job, and make it necessary for me to send you back to Berlin?"

"Yes, Uncle," Karl replied, his head bowed. After a silent moment, Karl looked up at Otto. "Uncle," he said, "I understand now. I must hold my temper. I know you have been good to me. I don't want to leave you and my friend Josh and go back to Berlin. My mother, she worked so hard for me to get here. I cannot go back, not now."

Otto took hold of the boy, gave him a hug, and then stepped back to speak. "Yes, perhaps we will be able to send for your mother someday. But now we must have dinner – a true Christmas Eve dinner. Wash up and put on the suit you wear to school. We're going to Luchow's on 14th Street. I think you'll like it."

For the rest of the Christmas holiday Karl remained at home to study. At Uncle Otto's suggestion, be began writing long letters to his mother, reporting on his life in New York, his friend Josh, and what he was learning in his classes. Later, as he read Karl's letters, Otto could see that Karl had indeed been absorbing the subject matter from his classes. The letters to Marianna Ludwig would become a weekly exercise and kept Karl from forgetting his German. By June, Karl's grades had improved to straight A's. The next year he made the football team as a lineman, Josh as a running back.

14. MANHATTAN, MAY 1923

When it was time for college, Karl accepted a pre-med scholarship at Columbia. He dropped football because he knew the long practices and team meetings would take time away from study. For exercise, he joined the boxing team, which didn't demand as much time and allowed him to work out more on his own. Karl would go on to win the Ivy League middleweight championship in his sophomore and junior years.

Josh won scholarships to Princeton and Yale, but instead chose the publicly owned City College of New York, where there was no tuition. Besides, he knew that anti-Semitism was a fact of life at Ivy League schools. At CCNY he studied hard and excelled in the pre-med program.

Josh and Karl still met for trips to the Polo Grounds on summer afternoons. Sometimes they would go with Bobby Bellacosta and Tim Riordan, Josh's classmates at City College, both of whom were also leaning toward careers in medicine. Bobby, who lived on Mulberry Street in Little Italy, could always get free tickets to Giant, Dodger, and Yankee games through his well-connected older brother Vinny. Tim had an older sister who threw lively parties at her East Side apartment. Her friends were invariably attractive, well bred, and often compliant. The four friends often drank in Yorkville speakeasies and talked about girls, baseball, boxing, and medicine.

But more often than not, Karl and Josh sought each other out. They often talked over beer about the latest medical research on muscle and bone reconstruction. Sitting at Otto's kitchen table late one night in August, they decided to attend the same medical school, agreeing to accept the tuition scholarships that Columbia Medical School had offered to each of them.

15. IDEAL COFFEE SHOP, MANHATTAN, JUNE 1, 1926, 9:00 A.M.

Restless on his counter stool, Karl pushed away his half-eaten bowl of oatmeal and read the letter from his mother's doctor for the third time. She had died in her sleep two weeks before, her lungs having finally surrendered to repeated bouts of influenza. He had written and sent her what money he could spare, but there had never been the time or enough money to get back to see her in Berlin or bring her to New York. Uncle Otto's death three months before had been hard too. He missed the old man's strength, his silent disapproval if Karl consumed more beer than was prudent, and the pride his uncle took in his success in school, his scholarships, and his boxing.

And the reality was that, with Otto gone, there was far less household income. Karl had to pay the rent, buy food, and find money for the expensive books medical students needed. His scholarship covered only tuition. He would have to box more frequently, that was obvious. But the preliminary bouts he was able to get and have time to train for just paid pocket change.

He needed a job, not the usual student job as a waiter or tutor, but one that paid real money.

Karl grabbed a discarded copy of the *New York Times* from a nearby table and searched through the classifieds. Several firms needed salesmen for a new type of experimental printer called an "offset" machine. The ads said that knowledge of the new process was "a must." Karl tore the page from the paper, folded it into his vest pocket, gulped the last of his cold oatmeal, and rode the IRT to Hudson Street, otherwise known as Printers Row.

16. PRINTERS ROW, HUDSON STREET, MANHATTAN, JUNE 1, 1926, 10:35 A.M.

Karl surprised the stout middle-aged woman at the cluttered reception desk. He told her that he wanted to buy one of their new offset printing machines for his uptown employer which, he claimed, was a small publisher that contemplated entering the newsletter business.

"Pasquale!" she shouted, without looking up. Seconds later the owner appeared, a lean and curly haired Italian of about fifty. Pasquale led Karl to a back room that housed a machine the size of a car. After a one-hour technical presentation followed by questions and answers, Pasquale allowed Karl to operate the machine. Karl loaded and unloaded paper, removed and reinstalled the printing drums, and fixed paper jams. He promised to return the next day with a check to close the sale, assuring Pasquale that his boss would buy the machine and expect speedy delivery.

His playacting done, and armed with fresh knowledge of the offset printer, Karl walked down the busy street of printers and printing equipment shops in a light spring drizzle to the address of a printer that had placed a want ad for a salesman in that morning's *Times*. Karl's knowledge of the machine won him the job within thirty minutes. Over the next ten weeks, there was no more productive offset salesman on the streets of Manhattan than young Karl Ludwig. When classes resumed at Columbia that September, he had enough money for books and rent for the entire year. Boxing paid for food and beer. The print shop welcomed Karl back each summer vacation from medical school.

17. ROOM 40, THE ADMIRALTY, LONDON, MARCH 2, 1915

After graduating near the top of his class from Christ College, Oxford in 1913, Channing Brown began a career as a journalist with the Manchester *Guardian*. But the outbreak of war in August 1914 inspired him to enlist in the Royal Navy. High scores on geopolitical exams and language aptitude tests, plus the Royal Navy's need for intellectual horsepower, earned him a hasty commission as a lieutenant and placed him in Room 40, the intelligence nerve center of the Admiralty. He soon discovered that "intelligence" reports from Ankara, Brussels, Berlin, Paris, St. Petersburg, and other European centers of power were too often inaccurate, uncoordinated, or contradictory. Lieutenant Brown complained of the reports' inadequacies in a blistering memorandum to his section chief, who sent it on its way up through the naval bureaucracy.

Just minutes after the memorandum reached the desk of the First Lord of the Admiralty, Channing Brown felt a firm hand planted on his shoulder. "Don't get up lad. I'd like a word."

"Sir, I . . ."

Brown sat erect as the First Lord Winston Churchill pulled up a chair. Brown saw that Churchill held his memorandum.

"Lieutenant Brown, what you have here in this ill-advised critique illustrates two seemingly contradictory notions that I first encountered some fifteen years ago when we were battling the Boers down at the arse end of Africa. One notion is held by chaps in the head office, like those of us here at the Admiralty. We tend to believe with absolute certainty that the men out in the field haven't a bloody clue as to what they're doing. The other notion, held with equal conviction by those in the field, is that we blokes here in the head office, meaning of course the Admiralty, have no idea what we're doing. Now would you like to know the truth, Lieutenant Brown?"

"Yes, Sir, I would."

"They're both bloody right."

Churchill did not wait for his point to penetrate. "Your memo," Churchill said, "speaks from an ignorance born of having seen matters only from Room 40. You need more experience, something out on the line, lad. That's where you'll begin to grasp the dynamic of things, and learn to prepare for the absolute certainty that the unexpected *will* occur."

"I would be more than happy to accept such a posting, First Lord."

"Splendid. I am ordering you to sea duty as an intelligence officer on the HMS Prince of Wales. She's about to embark for Gallipoli. As you know from the documents you've been handling, our goal is to land troops and march on Constantinople and Ankara, enabling us to command the Dardanelles. Now make a good job of whatever you're ordered to do. I shall eagerly await a report."

18. GALLIPOLI, JUNE 9, 1915, 3:30 A.M.

Under a brilliant crescent moon, Channing Brown jumped from the small motor launch and set out inland across the sand, keeping south of the long narrow toehold the Allies had gained on the Turkish peninsula. His specific assignment was to confirm the location of what Intelligence believed to be a small but troublesome gun battery, estimate its ammunition stores and defense readiness up close, and return with the information not more than twenty-four hours later, when the launch would be waiting. If he wasn't there, the launch would return at the same time the following day. A company of Royal Marines on the same mission three days before had never returned. It was deemed that one man, acting alone, would attract less notice and would be able to report back without incident.

Brown took no chances in the early morning light, crawling eastward on his belly in the direction of where his map indicated the Turkish guns might be. Brown's shipboard commanders had not concerned themselves with his lack of combat or reconnaissance training. The order from Churchill had been clear: "Let the lad get a taste of battle, one that will stand him well in future days."

6:02 A.M.

There was a sudden stench in the close morning air, like nothing the young officer had ever smelled before. As he moved over a knoll he saw its source. Scores of dead British soldiers lay there in the dawn light.

He rose up on his knees to see more. He began to count, but stopped. There were too many shell craters, too many severed arms and legs strewn about. He would never forget the sight or the stink of it. He moved on to the spot where his map showed the approximate location of the Turkish battery. Arriving on the spot, however, Brown found nothing but sand. He put the map in his pocket and moved further inland.

8:03 A.M.

When he reached higher ground, Brown scanned the rolling sandscape in search of cover. He spotted a knoll with tall grass and a stand of Lone Pine just off to the east, a vantage point from which a scout could detect the arrival of an enemy force. When he reached the place, he climbed one of the pines to get his bearings. He didn't see a rag-tag battery with a cannon or two, which was what he expected. What he saw were many cannons — twenty by his careful count — protected by a long line of machine gun nests dug into the sand. Through binoculars he saw the bearded faces of his enemy. They moved about with dispatch and discipline. Each man had a rifle strapped over his shoulder and an ammunition belt. Then he knew he had seen enough. Marking the site on his map, he decided to wait until dark before returning to the launch. He knew the battery was well within range of the guns of the Prince of Wales and its sister ships. A saturation bombardment would wipe out the lot of them, men and guns, without a single British casualty. Off to the south, a short distance away, Brown spotted a small cluster of tall weeds that would provide the shade and concealment he needed until nightfall.

9:07 A.M.

He had not wanted to fall asleep but he did. They jumped him as he slept. He struggled for a moment until the butt of the Turkish rifle caught his jaw and knocked him unconscious.

19. GALLIPOLI, JUNE 27, 2:00 A.M.

A thin beam of light from a gas lantern came through the barred window of the cell. The air was filled with the stench of his own waste. The ceiling was too low for him to stand – and he was weak from lack of food. All his captors had given him was a stale piece of bread and brackish water once a day. He cursed the bad planning that put him where he was. He had given little thought to his survival and neither had anyone else, it seemed. He blamed himself for venturing into hostile territory without knowing how to get out. What had the blokes on the Prince of Wales been thinking when they sent him out on this mission? But regardless of what they had or hadn't done, he knew that he should have made his own escape plan.

The marks he'd been making on the damp dirt floor told him he had been in the cell for close to three weeks. Now it was too late to even think of escape.

When the iron door swung open, two guards pulled him up and threw a bucket of water in his face, then led him in the darkness to a long, candle-lit tent.

In a moment, he found himself standing before two men, both seated on a deep red carpet. One was in a Turkish Army officer's uniform. He had a larger than normal head and a strong jaw, his straight shiny hair combed back. The other wore western work clothes. He was a young man, not much older than Brown, with short reddish hair. Brown readied himself for a round of polite, softly spoken questions regarding the disposition of Allied troops and supplies, along with a veiled – but very real – threat of torture if he didn't cooperate. His all-too-short training on the Prince of Wales had taught him that much.

The guards gestured for him to sit down in front of the two men on the fine Persian carpet, next to a tray of flat breads and dates, a tin coffee pot, small ceramic cups, and a pitcher of water. The man in uniform spoke. "Lieutenant Brown, allow me to introduce myself. I am Lieutenant Colonel Mustapha Kemal, and at the moment I command our forces in this area, specifically the 19th Turkish Division. With me is Mr. Tallmadge McGruder. Mr. McGruder is an American from a place called Galveston. His country, in its wisdom, has chosen to stay out of the war."

Kemal poured coffee into a cup, gesturing for Brown to accept it.

"No thank you, Sir." Brown responded politely. "I'm your prisoner, not your guest. I dare say you would treat a guest a mite better than confining him to live in his own muck, without a proper lavatory or decent food for more than a fortnight."

Kemal smiled. "War imposes hardships, like having your country invaded."

"I know. I hear the Belgians, French, and Russians have rather the same complaint. Curious how touchy people can be."

Kemal fired up a cigarette, offering one to Brown, who declined with a jerk of his right hand. "You're quite flippant, young Britisher. I expected that," he said. "You're too young to know better. Now allow me to explain the purpose of this meeting. Understand, please, that we judge you to be unlike most of the Englishmen we have captured. You had only a pistol on your person, no rifle. Also, the men posted to guard your cell have observed that your arms are those of a man who works at a desk. So instead of beating you and reinforcing the notion that we Turks are barbarians, I will give you a message, one that I hope will reach your Prime Minister, your King, and the others who run your aging Empire."

"Is this something so terribly profound that I should take notes?"

"I choose to ignore your sarcasm."

"Please understand. Your hospitality has made me irritable."

Again Kemal offered the coffee, this time with bread. This time Brown accepted. He took and chewed some bread. He needed something in his stomach.

"I am prepared to listen," Brown said.

"Good. My message is simple. So is the one from my friend McGruder here."

Kemal nodded at McGruder. "I think it's better if I go first, Lieutenant, if that's okay with y'all," McGruder said in a heavy south Texas drawl. "Like Kemal said, I hail from Texas. I'm in the oil business, so to speak. But to be more specific, I'm in the geological survey business. We search for oil deposits. We started in Texas and went on to Oklahoma, where, as you may know, there's also a lot of real black gold. Folks need the stuff. Demand is growing and not just because of this war y'all are having. Back in the States, more and more people are buying automobiles."

McGruder paused for his message to sink in. Brown saw Kemal nod for McGruder to continue.

McGruder took a cigarette from his shirt pocket, giving himself time to light it from a candle and take a deep drag. "The problem, as my friend Kemal here knows, is that there's very little, if any, of the black gold in Turkey. It's just south of here, in a godforsaken place called Kurdistan. As you no doubt know, Kurdistan is part of a country now called Iraq. The fact of the matter is that Iraq and the desert lands to its east and south have oceans of black gold under all that white sand."

Now Kemal spoke. "We have many Kurds living here in southeastern Turkey. They have an affinity with their brothers to the south. Why should brothers live in different countries?"

"So you want to annex Kurdistan and its oil?" Brown asked.

Kemal smiled, choosing his tone and words with care. It would be best for the British not to interfere in my country's dealings with our brothers in Kurdistan. What you do in the rest of Iraq is your business. I want you British to give Turkey a free hand in Kurdistan."

"How, might I ask, does that involve me?"

"Agree to bring that message to your leaders, and I'll arrange for your safe passage through our lines."

"By what authority do you speak? With all due respect, Sir, you're merely a lieutenant colonel and command but one division."

"Just get my message to your government. I can bide my time. I don't expect a response until after my followers and I have taken power in Turkey. By then, the present war will be over. But you need not concern yourself with that. It will happen without your help."

"Your self-confidence is convincing."

"Thank you. You're an intelligent young man after all."

20. ABOARD THE PRINCE OF WALES, JULY 2, 1915

Rested and nourished, Brown sat at the small desk in his cabin, typing up a report to Churchill on and his conversation with Kemal and McGruder. It concluded as follows:

> *What I learned speaks to the need for having competent agents in places like Istanbul and Ankara – to ensure that His Majesty's government can keep closer tabs on the likes of Kemal and McGruder, and follow oil-related developments in the region.*

21. BAGHDAD, NOVEMBER 16, 1918, 7:15 A.M.

Re-energized by the war's end, a dozen British Tommies stood erect as they guarded the bridge over the River Tigris and directed the slow traffic of camels and small trucks. Talmadge McGruder, dressed in dusty cowboy boots and a light tan business suit, greeted Channing Brown with a strong handshake at the bridge's midpoint.

"It appears you survived the war, McGruder," Brown said.

McGruder smiled. "Well, I've been lucky. Some people in Washington thought it was more important for me to poke around here in the Middle East and in Oklahoma and Texas – in search oil deposits – rather than serve in the trenches in France. So I skipped all the fighting."

"So did I," Brown said. "After Gallipoli, I returned to a desk at the Admiralty."

"Now y'all didn't ask for this meeting for old time's sake. So tell me," McGruder asked, "why are we here?"

"It goes back to our meeting when I was Kemal's prisoner. I reported what he told me, which happened to coincide with what some of our own people knew about oil resources in Persia and northern Iraq. Since Turkey was on the losing side in the bloody war, it's lost any real claim to Kurdistan and northern Iraq. So London took hold of matters here. In fact, we now have a mandate to oversee the bloody place."

"Smart move, but Persia and northern Iraq are just part of what you could call a vast Mideast oil reservoir."

"Really?"

"You can bet on it. There's more oil in southern Iraq, near a place called Basra, and in the lands along the Persian Gulf, including the Saudi peninsula, clear down to the Gulf of Oman and the Arabian Sea. The same goes for the Caucasus Mountains and Caspian Sea basin."

Brown let McGruder's information sink in as the two men watched the dark waters of the Tigris flow under the bridge. After a minute, he responded. "What you say is most informative, and some of it is new enough to inspire continuing interest on the part of my superiors and others in high places at Whitehall. You see, McGruder, we have made rather thorough inquiries focused on you and your company, and we would like to establish an ongoing relationship."

Brown reached into his vest pocket and removed an envelope. "This, Mr. McGruder, is a contract. His Majesty's government wants a comprehensive geophysical survey of worldwide petroleum resources. We expect your completed findings within thirty-six months, according to the schedule specified in the contract. The contract provides payment of two million pounds sterling, plus all expenses for travel, necessary equipment, and administrative staff. It provides an additional half-million pounds for subsequent annual reports on the exploration, discovery, and refinement of oil, as well as its distribution in world markets."

McGruder opened the envelope and leafed through the seven-page contract, then returned his gaze to Brown.

"May I suggest that we find a quiet spot to talk this over," McGruder said.

As they settled into a dark, smoke filled café just off the Tigris embankment, McGruder spoke to the waiter in precise Arabic. The strong black coffee he ordered came quickly. "Now we can talk," McGruder said. "I have two questions."

Brown nodded. "Fire at will."

"First, why choose an American firm?"

"Simple, Mr. McGruder. His Majesty hires British and non-British firms alike. There are times when it can prove advantageous to use a firm that operates under a different flag. For example, prior to America's entry into the war just ended, we learned much about Germany from several American firms that had a presence there."

"Now for the second question," McGruder said, leaning over the table toward Brown. "Can you make that three million pounds sterling instead of two million?"

"Ah, my friend. Please understand that any attempt to increase the price would be most ill advised and put our otherwise promising partnership in jeopardy. Consider – this city is now occupied by 5,000 of His Majesty's best-trained, most battled-hardened troops, veterans of more than four years of combat in Belgium and France. On a less obvious note, also please consider that those officials who administer the British mandate in Iraq could easily require mountains of permits, registrations, and other paperwork before allowing you to search for another bloody drop of oil, here in Iraq or any other country under British protection. I don't think you want to do that."

"All right, Brown I get it. Y'all can't blame a guy for trying."

"It's like golf, Mr. McGruder. And you've just used your mulligan. Now let's get the hell out of this filthy place. I know a pleasant spot not far from here where my superiors have set up a sort of officers' club. There we can drink to our arrangement over a proper eye-opener."

22. THE ADMIRALTY, LONDON, JANUARY 6, 1920, 10:00 A.M. AND YEARS FOLLOWING

At his desk at the Admiralty one bright winter morning, Channing Brown opened a sealed white envelope to find that he had been assigned to a new agency, the Secret Intelligence Service, or SIS, within the Foreign Office. Established following the 1918 Armistice, the SIS coordinated intelligence gathered by the Admiralty, the War Office, the Foreign Office, and the newly established Air Ministry.

"You are to assemble all information gathered by the different military and diplomatic units, evaluate this information, and prepare a synopsis for the SIS Command on a weekly basis, more frequently if necessary," the transfer order said.

In his new post, Brown began absorbing reports from Europe and around the globe, information that he refined and communicated in crisp and prescient memos. He consolidated several disparate documents from British sources in Italy to alert the Foreign Office that an upstart newspaper editor named Benito Mussolini was likely to seize power in Rome. That earned him a transfer to the more prestigious German Desk at the SIS offices in London, and soon a posting to Berlin, from which he traveled throughout Germany. He talked with bartenders, shopkeepers, and journalists. His German, learned first at Oxford, became fluent.

Brown soon discovered that there were scant funds for the young SIS. What money there was went to strengthen another intelligence unit, the Government Code and Cipher School in London. Years later, Brown would understand the wisdom of funding the code school, which eventually moved away from the curious eyes and ears around Whitehall to a far more secluded site at Bletchley Park.

In Berlin, he met, courted, and married Jillian James, a bright young correspondent in the Berlin bureau of the *Times* of London. Brown's travels throughout Germany and the couple's mutual passion for what was happening on Continental Europe kept the marriage young. On SIS business, Brown monitored and reported on a seemingly endless run of conferences, which in turn produced a proliferation of treaties designed to ensure peace in Europe. According to one treaty, Italy would guarantee the security of Albania, Austria, and France. According to another, Czechoslovakia, Rumania, and Yugoslavia organized themselves w into the so-called "Little Entente."

The diplomats, Brown observed, loved the conferences and the empty treaties they produced. Foreign ministers promoted them. Heads of government took comfort in them. Brown believed that they did so at their peril. He found this especially true when he traveled to Locarno, Switzerland, for a conference that supposedly provided for the arbitration of disputes among

Germany, France, Belgium, Poland, and Czechoslovakia – a pact which, it was believed, would secure "the peace of Europe." Brown didn't believe it, especially after his time in Germany.

Alone in his hotel room on the final night of the Locarno conference, Brown savored the moonlit view, as fresh snow fell on the Alpine slopes. He sipped claret, uncased his portable Underwood, lit a fresh cigarette, and began writing.

CONFIDENTIAL

DATE: 1 DECEMBER 1925

TO: THE FOREIGN SECRETARY

FROM: CHANNING BROWN

The majority thinking here is that Germany has a genuine interest in abiding by frontier guarantees and dispute arbitration. The realities evident from my travels in Germany argue otherwise. My reasons are fivefold.

1. Fear of Russian Communism. German leadership, like our own, remains wary of the young Soviet Union. But the German trepidation is more immediate: They are much closer geographically to the Soviets, with only Poland separating them.

2. Fear of German Communism. Just as telling is what I learned during more than two years in Berlin and other cities. For example, I talked with a thirty-year-old ex-infantry sergeant who has worked only odd jobs since the war. He wishes he had the money to immigrate to Russia, where "the people have taken charge." Many Germans are just like him. They far outnumber the naïve left-leaning Oxford and Cambridge lads who parade through Whitehall.

3. German Resentment. Germany's defeat in the Great War remains a source of heartache for many Germans. An older man I talked to in a beer hall in Hannover remained deeply distressed by Germany's defeat in 1918. Believing my story that I was a teacher on holiday, he told me: "You can afford vacations because you won the war. That horseshit at Versailles, that won't happen next time. We will regain our honor."

4. The Prussian Factor. Equally worrisome are the career military officers, a sort of German upper crust that has been building and rebuilding armies since Caesar's time. The defeat in 1918 both humiliated and infuriated them. The Versailles Treaty has impeded their ability to rebuild the war machine. They need their tanks, aircraft, ships, and artillery – and the young men to use them. They're willing to support the new right-wing party of rabble-rousers called the Nazis, whose leaders insist that Germany must be strong.

5. Scarce Resources. Although German farms are productive, they're not producing enough food for a population growing faster than all its neighbors – and twice as fast as France. This situation could well rekindle Bismarck's old dream of an empire that stretches across the breadbasket of Eastern Europe and into the Ukraine. Even more significant is the fact that Germany – like Britain, France, Italy, and other "advanced" European countries – has not one cubic centimeter of oil, the natural resource that is fast becoming indispensable to economic growth and waging modern warfare. Germany will use military force to get the oil and food it needs.

I, therefore, respectfully recommend stepped-up and more aggressive surveillance of German rebuilding.

Brown addressed three envelopes. The original document went to the Foreign Secretary, and would go in the diplomatic pouch. One carbon copy was for insertion in his personal file back in London. And the other carbon went to the former First Lord of the Admiralty, then residing at Chartwell, his country retreat.

The memo earned Brown severe reprimands from the Office of the Foreign Minister. In meetings, Brown repeatedly heard the argument that communism was Great Britain's most formidable enemy. Just before he was to take some Christmas holiday leave, Brown received a memorandum from the Foreign Secretary.

MOST CONFIDENTIAL

AUTHORITY: OFFICIAL SECRETS ACT

DATE: 15 DECEMBER 1925

FROM: THE FOREIGN SECRETARY

TO: CHANNING BROWN

The Prime Minister has authorized me to inform you that he agrees with your assessment of Germany's potential resurgence. He has nonetheless asked me to point out to you that the problems you have identified may not be as pressing as those presented by the new Soviet Union.

It is the conviction of the Prime Minister and others in the cabinet and in Parliament that the Red Army of several million men poses a far greater threat to our security than do the right-wing hooligans of Bavaria.

Moreover, a resurgent Germany, while distasteful in several respects, could serve as a reliable bulwark against Soviet Russia. Many support that view.

Please restrict this memo to yourself.

23. LONDON, OCTOBER 15, 1932

Brown kept the December 1925 memo to himself for years. In 1932 another memorandum arrived on the Foreign Secretary's desk, this one from Paris.

BOB MACKIN

MEMORANDUM

DATE: *15 OCTOBER 1932*

AUTHORITY: *OFFICIAL SECRETS ACT*

TO: *THE FOREIGN SECRETARY*

FROM: *HIS MAJESTY'S AMBASSADOR TO THE FRENCH*
                         REPUBLIC

The French Foreign Minister invited me over this morning. Also present was Pierre Rousseau of the Deuxième Bureau, the French military intelligence unit. Rousseau, who runs French agents in Germany, informed me of a discovery by one of their agents in Berlin. This agent, one of their best, came upon a secret Soviet-German treaty signed in Rapallo, Italy, ten years ago – on 24 June 1922, to be precise. The Weimar Foreign Minister at the time was Walter Rathenau, who was well regarded among diplomats in the immediate post-Versailles years. According to Rousseau's agent, Rathenau slipped out of an economic-development conference in Genoa to talk with a Russian delegation in nearby Rapallo.

That meeting produced an until now top-secret accord in which the Soviets agreed to set aside large tracts of land where the Germans could develop and test new military aircraft, armored vehicles, tanks, and other military hardware in secret defiance of Versailles.

The French agent has obtained a carbon copy of the document. Rousseau informs me that his agent could have taken the original but received orders to leave it in the file and minimize the possibility that the Germans would discover it missing.

The revelation has shaken both the French Foreign Minister and Rousseau in no small way.

24. WHITEHALL, LONDON, OCTOBER 18, 1932

Brown was one of a select few in the SIS allowed to view the memo. Clearly the French agent in Berlin had scooped him. But there was a lesson in the experience. The French agent in Berlin had done more than observe. He had done actual prying and snooping, most likely in the dead of night. Brown's own present operatives in Germany were good men and should remain in place. But they were just observers, gatherers of conversational nuggets at diplomatic receptions and avid readers of newspapers and periodicals. He knew he needed more. He needed people willing to do things, difficult things.

He needed safecrackers, second-story men and, yes, a killer or two. He needed chaps who could pull the trigger, slip by frontier guards, and deceive officials – con men, beguiling women, actors. He resolved to recruit such operatives and have them work with others already in place.

Brown then typed up another memorandum to the Foreign Minister, this one recommending the "recruitment of extraordinarily competent individuals to serve undercover in various locations, to acquire information and undertake high-risk, proactive assignments . . . "

Brown stopped. "Why not?" he asked himself aloud. He added several words to the last sentence. Those words were: "and initiate forceful physical action aimed at changing the course of events."

He had made two carbon copies. He put one in his files and posted the other. He wrote "Personal and Confidential" on the envelope, addressing it to Winston Churchill, M.P., House of Commons.

25. WHITEHALL, OCTOBER 22, 1932, 9:00 A.M.

On a return visit to London to present a firsthand report to the German Desk on the upcoming German elections, Brown encountered Churchill at the entrance to the Foreign Office. The two had not seen each other since the war.

"You look fit enough, lad," Churchill said, eyeing Brown up and down. "I hear good things about your work, and I thank you for the information you've sent my way. Strong stuff there."

"Thank you, Sir."

Churchill flicked a cigar ash onto the pavement. "I'm on my way to my regular BBC broadcast. But lest we waste this fortuitous moment, let's have a spot of lunch. What say we meet at White's Club in St. James at noon?"

"Wonderful, Sir. I shall see you there."

26. LONDON, OCTOBER 22, 1932, NOON AND FOLLOWING

As Brown entered the barroom, he saw Ralph Wigram, First Secretary at the British Embassy in Paris, seated alone at the bar. Brown had long admired Wigram, a serious professional and a man even more wary than himself about German rearmament. "Winston rang me about your meeting and asked me along. Hope you don't mind, Channy. Winston's already in a private dining room upstairs."

"Not at all. By all means, let's join him."

Over a delicate Dover sole and a bottle of Chablis, the three discussed Germany, with Churchill and Wigram asking the questions and Brown answering. Brown surprised them by announcing that he had met with the editors of the *Economist*, with whom he discussed the possibility of joining the publication's editorial staff. Churchill responded with a knowing nod.

Relishing his last bite of tender sole, Churchill wiped his lips with the large white napkin tucked into his collar. "Channy, lad, the fact is that just after my BBC broadcast I had a telephone chat with both Prime Minister MacDonald and Stanley Baldwin, who at this hour holds the real power in Parliament. As you may know, I seldom see eye to eye with either of them, although both have agreed to an idea I proposed – that you should organize a discrete unit within the SIS, a unit along the lines sketched out in your recent memorandum to the Foreign Secretary, one that would perform both intelligence and espionage work. As you proposed, this unit would do more than gather information; it would undertake real actions. With Hitler gaining more political power every day, the PM agrees with us that this step makes sense. What you set up could well serve as a model for similar units in the future."

"And what, may I ask, Sir, is the catch? How did you pull it off?"

"A quid pro quo, Channy. I've agreed to help round up support for a bill to fund storm sewers, an expensive but necessary undertaking that will spur employment in both MacDonald's and Baldwin's home districts. I may not be in the cabinet, but I remain a Member of Parliament, and I still exercise some measure of influence – at least when it comes to sewers. "

"Before I accept," Brown said, "I must insist that I be allowed to recruit my own people and that I have adequate funds to make a proper job of it."

Wigram spoke up. "Do you have particular persons, or some specific amount, in mind?"

"I'll need at least twenty people to get started." Brown replied. "I will personally recruit all of them, and I do believe we should pay them well. After all, there will be risk."

"We'll find the funds," Wigram said in a low voice. "In fact, I can transfer money from my research budget, set up a sort of private slush fund, and bend a rule or two. Not quite proper, perhaps, but necessary if the operation is to be top drawer."

"Good of you, Ralph," Churchill said. "What do you say, Channy?"

"You shall have my answer this afternoon. Thank you both."

Brown stepped into the first red telephone kiosk he could find and called the *Economist*, telling them he had decided to remain in the service of the Crown. Then he called Jillian.

In the weeks that followed, he set up a new office at Whitehall and recruited young people with strong language skills as well as the necessary intellectual and physical resources.

Brown's recruits underwent extensive training at Thornbil Castle in Scotland, a remote Highland property long owned by the Crown and used for training special personnel. After long days of instruction, each of the twenty recruits could rattle off the names of Adolf Hitler's first and second cousins, identify every station stop on the Berlin U-Bahn, cite the price of eggs in Bavaria, and describe how Stalin plied subordinates with vodka while he himself drank mostly white wine to keep his wits about him.

One of Brown's recruits was Bonnie Peters, a lean brunette who had placed fourth in the women's decathlon at the 1932 Olympics in Los Angeles. Brown had known her father, a gunnery officer on the Prince of Wales at Gallipoli. Years later, the father introduced her to Brown at an Admiralty reception. Brown was impressed by the way the young woman carried herself. She was attractive, but not in a way that alienated other women. When Brown met her, Bonnie was working as a freelance sports journalist, which meant she needed the money that Brown could pay her.

Another recruit was Scotty North, lean and fit, with an I.Q. in the 97th percentile. A versatile actor, Scotty had occasional parts in Belfast theaters and in London's West End. He could play characters of almost any age or background and excelled at disguise and dialects. But the unsteady nature of theater work in troubled times inspired him to seek the treasures that awaited him in the townhouses of Mayfair, Belgravia, and Notting Hill. In the parlance of the Bobbies of the Metropolitan Police, who knew him well, North was a "gifted second-story man." Eventually caught in the act, North was serving a five-year sentence in Wormwood Scrubs when Brown recruited him. He entered the agency's employ in 1933 at the age of twenty-eight. Once on the job, North began German-language studies and soon perfected a Rhinelander accent. He also practiced impersonating different character types he might have to play in his new job.

There was also Jamie Creel, a still youthful Cockney at age forty-one. A native of London's Elephant and Castle neighborhood, Creel was a man of many talents, one of which was demolitions, a skill he had acquired during his service as a sergeant major in the Royal Marines. And Creel was as good as any man behind the wheel of almost any vehicle – on land or in water. During the Great War, Creel, a strong swimmer, had led three other Marines in an underwater swimming expedition to the German submarine base at Brugges. That operation – planned by the young Lieutenant Channing Brown after his return from Gallipoli to Room 40 – resulted in three destroyed enemy submarines and two damaged repair docks.

Another was Carolyne Wentworth, a career SIS operative with strong language and analytical skills. Trim and pretty at thirty-eight, her black hair was accented with long strands of scholarly gray. Wentworth had served in Moscow during the early Stalin years and monitored the strength of the early Soviet economy from her post as commercial attaché at the British Embassy. Brown recruited her on her return home in 1933.

Essential to the new unit's communications network was Edith Farrington, a professor of German at Cambridge. Widowed at age forty during the Great War, and bored with academia, she jumped at the opportunity to escape to a new life in Germany.

After a month in Scotland, Bonnie Peters received her first assignment — to travel in Germany as a journalist to identify potential recruits for Brown's unit. With the help of Scotty North, she became adept at disguise and at passing through border checkpoints.

After completing his training, Scotty North began using his well-honed burglary skills to commit a series of undetected break-ins at embassies and other guarded sites in Europe and the U.S. In an early assignment for Brown, North managed to break into the Italian Air Ministry in Rome and obtain documents on the production of plywood warplanes and on proposed air raids in support of a planned invasion of Ethiopia.

Under Brown's direction, Creel identified some twenty European and North American vendors willing to sell explosives, weapons, and "special" services to customers on either side of the law. Creel, whose German soon became fluent, later won a yearlong job in an aircraft parts plant, where he learned how a new tri-motored transport was ideal for carrying paratroopers.

Carolyne Wentworth needed little training. No sooner had she signed on with Brown than he dispatched her to Germany, where she applied for and won a post teaching economics at the University of Heidelberg. Brown soon realized that she had a knack for charming male acquaintances into letting their guard down at cocktail receptions at which some men could not resist the temptation to drop names and boast. As it happened, she had few scruples about sharing her pillow to learn what she needed to know. That's how she first learned of plans for German "volunteers" to go to Spain to help Franco in the Spanish Civil War.

Edith Farrington established herself in Berlin, working in quiet obscurity as a waitress in a bakery on Berlin's Friedrichstrasse. She became a vital asset for relaying the messages of SIS agents back to London through Stockholm and Berne.

While Brown's recruits enjoyed several successes, not everything went smoothly. During her liaison with a rising young SS Leutnant named Günter Jurgen, Carolyne reported to Brown on the sadistic anti-Semitism that drove him and his comrades. That was the easy part. Jurgen's need for rough sex tested her limits. The fighting skills she had learned at Thornbil served her well, although they seemed only to spur Jurgen's appetite. Ever suspicious that he wasn't the only man in Carolyne's life, Jurgen searched Carolyne's apartment and discovered that her treachery extended far beyond sexual infidelity. The evidence, though well hidden, was conclusive. Rifling through her apartment, he found a miniature camera, a pistol of British manufacture, and – what really set him off – a large package of condoms, all hidden behind a large bedroom mirror.

Only much later did SIS operatives learn that Carolyne had died after being brutally whipped by Jurgen in the interrogation chambers beneath SS headquarters on Prinz-Albrecht-Strasse in Berlin. Brown learned of her fate when a highly placed operative overheard Gestapo Chief Heinrich Himmler bragging about it at a cocktail reception at the Chancellery. After hearing the news, Brown left his office and sat for more than an hour on a bench in St. James Park.

Brown knew that attractive women could gain valuable information from even the wariest of men. After Carolyne's death, he realized that women often encountered more violence than men when caught. After that, he took it upon himself to select only the strongest female agents.

When Brown's clandestine travels took him to Heidelberg, he overheard a young woman engaged in an impassioned argument with a young man wearing a Swastika armband in a street café near the university. She was arguing with conviction that the Nazi campaign against Jews was counterproductive, causing some of Germany's most talented and resourceful citizens to flee the country. Brown observed that the young woman remained calm even as her companion kept shouting the Nazi line that Jews had undermined the German war effort in 1918. "Stop living in the past, Wolfgang," she said in a self-controlled tone. "Stop making excuses about why we lost the stupid war." Her calm infuriated the young man even more. Slamming down his beer mug, he bolted from the café. Brown rose and went to her table, offering to pay the bill.

"*Danke, mein Herr,*" she said with a smile. She didn't seem the least bit upset at being left sitting at the table alone. Brown learned that she was a native of the Obersalzberg and studying nursing. They talked for most of the afternoon. A few weeks later when the school term ended, she took her holiday in Scotland.

27. THE THAMES EMBANKMENT, LONDON, OCTOBER 22, 1934, 5:00 P.M.

Brown and Ralph Wigram walked along the promenade and stopped to watch a coal barge glide by in the autumn twilight. Wigram pointed to a nearby bench for them to sit.

"Tell me, Channy, can you come to Chartwell, Winston's country place this Sunday? Some of the usual chaps will be there. But we shall save the main conversation until after they leave. Then we shall retire with Winston to his study and have a chat."

"Any background?"

"As you have reported, the new German government has made striking progress in building a war machine. And what's far worse, it's a war machine that our sources in Berlin tell us is driven by an ill-tempered madman."

"How did you see my reports?" Brown asked. "I addressed them only to the Secretary."

"The fact is, Channy, most of your documents have come my way, as have the reports from others in Germany, including those from Churchill's closest friends. I saw the carbons you sent him. And he has friends, like me, with whom he has reviewed those reports, trusted advisors from his days as First Lord of the Admiralty and from his travels. He shares a great deal within a tight little circle, which could now include you."

Brown pulled up the collar of his suit jacket to fend off an autumn wind from the Thames.

"I accept your invitation," Brown responded. "Indeed, I'm a bit flattered." Wigram lit his pipe, cupping his hand over the bowl against the breeze. "Bring your wife," he said. "It must all appear quite social. Clementine Churchill has arranged for a ladies' tea on the dot of four. That's when we'll sit with Winston. If your wife would fancy a set or two of tennis, my wife, Ava, would be available."

"How do I prepare?"

"Well there is one matter you might want to look into . . ."

After several moments they parted, taking different paths, Wigram to Mayfair, Brown across Hyde Park toward Bayswater.

When Brown reached the end of the Mall, he stopped at a red kiosk to telephone Jillian, who had taken a job on the copy desk of the *Times* on their return from Germany. They agreed to meet in the Silver Swan, a pub at the corner of their street.

Like her husband, Jillian Brown was an avid reader. In the hours they spent together in the book-lined study of their Victorian home and over pints of lager in the local pubs, their nonstop conversations usually focused on political and international news. At the same time, he had learned not to trespass into her professional life, just as she had learned not to trespass into his. Talk of espionage and intelligence work was strictly taboo.

That evening they sat where they were most comfortable – at the bar of the crowded, smoky Swan. They had ordered a second pint of Whitbread's when Jillian mentioned that a rather loud parade of left-wing students from Cambridge had disrupted traffic around Trafalgar that morning.

"According to reports," she said, "the demonstrators were Cambridge students carrying pro-Soviet placards." Her left hand rested on Brown's forearm.

Brown savored a sip of Whitbread's then answered. "What these aristocratic young twerps don't realize," he said, "is that they wouldn't fare so well if a Soviet-style revolution should happen here. They would have to forfeit their ancestral castles to the proletariat, just as the Russian aristocrats have had to do."

"No fun there," Jillian offered. "No more debutante parties and black-tie dinners."

"Quite. I dare say that some union or people's committee would run the bloody Savoy. Now on the other hand, under the Nazis, the Adlon in Berlin remains a place where the elite gather to be seen in their finest."

"The *Economist* made just that point in an editorial earlier this week," she said, holding a cigarette for him to light. "Hitler is showing an affinity for wealth. He has embraced powerful industrialists like Krupp, I.G. Farben, and Frederick Wagner, from what I read."

"While we're on the subject of power, would you fancy motoring down to Chartwell this Sunday?" he asked.

28. CHARTWELL, OCTOBER 28, 1934, 4:00 P.M.

After a spare lunch of a clear mushroom soup and cucumber sandwiches, the men nodded and stood as the women left for the tennis court. The faces at the large round table were all familiar to Channing Brown. Guests included Sir Robert Vansittart, Permanent Undersecretary of the Foreign Office; Major Desmond Morton, who had a cottage just over the hill; Tory Anderson, an RAF Wing Commander troubled by Britain's lack of airpower; Rex Leeper, who headed the Foreign Office News Department; and Ralph Wigram. At Churchill's invitation, Channing Brown provided a brief but comprehensive report on the progress of his now two-year-old unit. Of particular interest was news from a well-placed veteran MI6 agent who had begun supplying information on German plans to manufacture a new generation of tanks and other armored vehicles.

As the other guests dispersed and went their separate ways, most back toward London, Wigram and Brown remained. They followed Churchill to a high-ceilinged room, where a man Brown judged to be on the far side of sixty sat waiting in comfort on a long Chesterfield, wearing a camel's hair jacket and black turtleneck.

Sir Crawford Ware rose and gave Brown a strong handshake as Churchill made introductions. Ware was a large man, well-built and bald, who gave the accurate impression of being a millionaire several times over. He had ample holdings in farmland, agricultural equipment, shipping, pharmaceuticals, and an international investment company. He was also a principal or "name" in a leading insurance underwriting syndicate at Lloyd's and a major financial backer of Winston Churchill's campaigns for Parliament over more than a score of years.

Churchill poured each of his guests and himself a half-tumbler of brandy from the crystal decanter on his desk, then turned to Wigram. "Ralph, please secure the lock," he said, pointing toward the curtained French doors and gesturing for them to sit down at the long uncluttered mahogany table. Churchill turned to Ware. "Crawford, can you start?"

Sir Crawford leaned forward. "We all know who it is we're talking about, so I'll get straight to it," he said. "The question before us isn't *what* we do about the bugger, but *how* we do it. Do I make myself clear?"

"Splendid," Churchill quipped. "Channy, tell us what's been tried so far, and what's failed."

"From what I know, it appears that previous attempts have been rather amateurish, careless, and ill-planned."

Brown went on to describe how a young Gypsy had his arm broken the very instant he reached for his pistol during a Nazi parade in Munich back in '31. Several Nazi thugs in the crowd were ready for just such a possibility. The would-be assailant was hauled away to an unknown fate.

Brown recounted that in another case, a clique of Nazi homosexuals in the SA, the so-called Brownshirts, frightened by violent queer baiting in the Party upper ranks, had hired a sharpshooter. They did so after Hitler had SA leader Ernst Röhm arrested and killed in July 1934. Röhm had been Hitler's right-hand man in the early days of the Nazi Party but fell out of favor when Hitler perceived him as a rival. These Brownshirts planned to assassinate Hitler with a high-powered rifle from a hidden perch on the mountainside overlooking the terrace of the Berghof, Hitler's home in the Obersalzberg.

But, Brown explained, the plotters talked too much. One evening, a drunken conversation between two of them fell on alert and curious ears. An hour later, a squad of goons loyal to Hitler hauled them off to an alley and shot them on the spot.

Brown also noted rumors involving old-school military men who had talked about killing Hitler, but lacked the gumption to follow through. And there had been at least one case where a bomb failed to explode.

Brown paused and sipped some brandy, allowing time for questions.

"Any recent attempts?" Sir Crawford asked.

"None since he won the election. Now that he's head of a sovereign government, the security around him has become close to bloody foolproof. The man himself, we understand from an agent close to him, is a fatalist, believing that if it happens it happens. Still, there are as many as five bodyguards with him at all times. Of course, a sharpshooter with a long-range rifle remains a possibility, but that raises multiple issues of logistics and concealment of the weapon."

"So much for idle speculation and hearsay," Sir Crawford quipped.

Churchill nodded and lit a fresh cigar. He rose and walked to the French doors, opening them to assure himself that there were no eavesdroppers. Closing and relocking the doors, he turned again to face his three guests. "It's quite obvious that none of us has a bloody clue where to begin." He looked at Channing Brown. "We need a specific person and a precise plan. And I'm asking you, Channy, and the people you work with, to come up with a plan that will bloody work."

Churchill frowned. He let his words sink in as he sat back down, and then resumed speaking. "Channy, we shall grant you our patience, but we need your focus. Most of all we need your discretion. We certainly don't need to read about this afternoon's conversation in the *Daily Mail*."

"Quite so," Brown agreed. "Now allow me to be blunt. We're talking about the murder of the constitutional leader of a sovereign power, a nation with which we are at peace. Let me remind you that we seek to avoid a war, not start one."

"Point well taken," Churchill said.

"I believe we should move in a very controlled way," Brown continued. "What we need is to put a competent agent in place, in a position where he can remain until actually ordered to strike. That way no one has any true criminal intent. And, of course, it should not be an operation directly associated with His Majesty's government."

"I quite agree," Churchill said, sipping more brandy. "Please understand that this enterprise would have no official authorization. Channy's work on the project would be in addition to his regular duties in intelligence and espionage, and off-budget. The same goes for his staff here and agents abroad."

"Right on point, Sir," Brown offered. "But what you ask will require a rather tidy sum."

"Winston told me you were a smart lad," Sir Crawford said, "one who would home right in on such a practical question. Let me assure you that adequate funding will be available. Tomorrow morning there will be a special account established in your name at the Royal Bank of Westminster in the amount of one million pounds sterling. That, of course, is only seed money. I'm taking steps to secure an additional ten million pounds. Some of that money will go to numbered accounts in Zurich. The amount will be finite, but more than adequate."

Brown thought for a second before speaking. "Then the game has begun. We'll start our search for the man to do the job as soon as the money is in place."

Wigram broke his silence. "Channy, I would rather not think of this enterprise as a *game*. I believe we all lean toward a nobler motive. We must kill one scoundrel to stop a war, a war in which many millions could die."

"Well, you're both right," said Churchill. "But let me make one point bloody clear. We are not planning to kill the bugger. We are instead planning to have a very competent person or persons in place to kill the bugger." Churchill sat back and slapped his palms on his thighs. "And that, gentlemen," he said, "is quite enough for this Sunday. Let's take our brandy and join the ladies."

29. ON THE ROAD BACK TO LONDON, OCTOBER 28, 1934, 7:15 P.M.

"How was the tennis?" Brown asked.

"Good. Eva Wigram gave me some stiff competition, but I won. The best came later, though. I had a brandy with Mr. Churchill just before we left Chartwell. You were huddled up with Sir Crawford and didn't notice."

"And what did you talk about? Any secrets?"

"We talked about his book on the Duke of Marlborough. When you said we were going to Chartwell, I dashed out and bought a copy and managed to read some of it. Mr. Churchill loved chatting about his ancestor John Churchill, the first Duke of Marlborough. He's an incredible history buff. You told me that long ago, and you were right. Too bad he's not in the cabinet and can't make much history himself just now."

When they arrived home, Channing Brown went directly to the study. He needed to think about two telephone calls he would have to make the next morning – one to New York and the other to Berlin.

30. LLOYD'S OF LONDON, OCTOBER 30, 1934, 12:15 P.M.

On the busy floor of Lloyd's, Channing Brown followed Sir Crawford Ware as they wended their way through rows of booths where insurance syndicate underwriters accepted shares of maritime, aviation, and other large risks that other insurance companies were unwilling, or unable, to cover in their entirety. Sir Crawford nodded to the brokers, who greeted him cheerfully by name. After they had passed several booths, Sir Crawford led Brown to a table stacked with copies of *Lloyd's List*, the world's oldest daily newspaper, one that reported on the location and day-to-day progress of ships as they plied the oceans.

"See here, Channy, it shows that, as of yesterday, the Matsui Maru, a freighter of considerable tonnage, was in the eastern reaches of the Indian

Ocean, near Christmas Island, bound for Perth." Sir Crawford then led Brown across the expansive floor to a large blackboard where clerks used white chalk to record shipwrecks, plane crashes, fires, and other catastrophes that could trigger insurance claims against Lloyd's syndicates. Sir Crawford gestured for Brown to observe what one clerk was writing. "Matsui Maru: total loss, crew and cargo, typhoon, forty miles south of Christmas Island; estimated insured loss: two million British pounds."

"Quite a loss," Brown observed in a low voice that only Sir Crawford could hear amidst the chatter on the crowded Lloyd's floor.

Sir Crawford put a hand on Brown's shoulder. "So it would appear. You see, Channy," he whispered, "the storm and the ship are both fictions, but the claim money is real." Brown responded with the subtle grin. "I knew you would get the joke," Sir Crawford said with a laugh. We have several similar 'losses' planned for next week. It will all tally up close to the promised amount. My Lloyd's syndicate will wire the proceeds from the losses to a numbered, meaning no-name, account at the Credit Suisse in Zurich."

31. SIR CRAWFORD'S EAST ANGLIA ESTATE, JANUARY 15, 1935, 11:15 A.M.

In the secluded comfort of Sir Crawford's mahogany-paneled study, Brown reported on his search for the man to do the job. At Brown's request, ten agents and several other SIS colleagues had joined the effort, although none received any information regarding the target. Brown had masked the enterprise as a general recruiting effort aimed at expanding his unit's "resources."

Long-distance sharpshooters, more than twenty of them, had been identified, interviewed, and rejected one by one. None of them, in Brown's judgment, would be able to conceal his weapon. He had explained this back at Chartwell. But the need to be thorough compelled him to continue searching. He rejected the idea of an assassin using a pistol. Many of the prospective sharpshooters were criminals, often too lazy to take the long hours required to achieve accuracy with a pistol, or lacking the finesse to get close enough to take a proper bead on the target.

Brown reported that he'd been equally unsuccessful in his effort to recruit chefs and waiters willing to use poison. Chefs were too temperamental; waiters, at least most of them, lacked the necessary imagination. Besides, the SIS Berlin desk had reported that Hitler's food was always pre-tested.

Brown's agents also interviewed explosives specialists but decided that planting a time bomb entailed unacceptable uncertainties. There was always too much chance that a bomb would fail to explode or would explode at the wrong time. Hitler had a habit of changing his schedule at the last minute, arriving late or leaving early, sometimes by design, sometimes on impulse.

"You need to broaden the search, lad," Sir Crawford said after Brown had finished. "We need more than a killer here – we need a bloke with the resourcefulness to remain undercover and survive in Germany while he waits for the order to strike, an order which might come only after a long delay." Brown knew Sir Crawford was right.

On his return to Whitehall, Brown sent a coded message to agents assigned to the search. "Progress," the message began, "unsatisfactory. Broaden your search. Please consider general resourcefulness. We need more imagination from each of you."

32. PALM COURT, THE PLAZA HOTEL, MANHATTAN, JANUARY 31, 1936, 2:00 P.M.

Frederick Wagner settled into his straight-back chair to think as he listened to the string quartet play "The Skater's Waltz." He had much to mull over, having spent the morning exchanging cables with London and Berlin. Just before lunch, he decided to cut his current trip short and to return to Berlin. Too much was happening there. Now, with Hitler entrenched in power and digging in deeper, Frederick needed to protect his several highly skilled Jewish engineers and chemists. These were men who had been with him since he was a fresh graduate of the Berliner Polytechnic – back when he first began running a family-owned tool plant with his father in the Berlin suburb of Wedding, shortly before what some now called the Great War.

Just that morning, Frederick had learned that Meyer Feinburg, his best tool-and-dye man, and Feinburg's wife were under arrest for possessing anti-Nazi pamphlets. Frederick believed he could do something but that he had to return to Germany to do it. He had given sizeable contributions to Rudolf Hess, the Nazi Party leader, who had brought him into the new Führer's inner circle, along with Krupp and Frick. He had become a skiing companion of both Hess and Hermann Göring.

As he enjoyed "The Skater's Waltz," his thoughts turned to Fern. He reflected on how she had grown into a beautiful woman and an accomplished professional. He took some pride in everything she'd achieved. He recalled the time when Fern and her mother had come to visit him in London, where he had settled in to learn the investment business after his time in a British prisoner-of-war camp. Shellfire from three British destroyers had damaged the propeller of the U-54 he commanded. The British fired on him just as he was about to launch a daring surface attack on two British merchant vessels in the shallow waters at the mouth of the Thames at first light on April 2, 1915. Frederick ordered the scuttling of the U-boat. He and his crew were fished from the water and taken prisoner as the submarine sank.

As a POW, his mechanical knowledge proved most useful in the repair of worn-down but essential tractors, trucks, and other farm equipment. After several months, he was transferred to a small prison encampment on the estate of Sir Crawford Ware in East Anglia, where he oversaw maintenance of all farm vehicles on the sprawling two thousand-acre property. Thanks to the improved performance of Sir Crawford's tractors, trucks, and plows, the estate's production of wheat, barley, and vegetables had increased 20 percent by the war's end. Sir Crawford convinced Frederick to remain in Britain after the war to learn more about the assembly-line manufacture of tractors. Sir Crawford's well-paid lawyers cut through the bureaucratic red tape, making it possible for a former prisoner of war – who under normal circumstances would have been returned to Germany – to stay in Britain. Two years later, at Sir

Crawford's urging, the young Frederick went to London learn the investment business.

After an internship, Frederick began to prosper enough to send funds to restore the family's Berlin plant to limited production.

As he began to establish himself in London, Frederick invited Hildy Wagner, the widow of his only brother – killed on the Italian front late in the war – and her daughter Fern to leave the uncertain environs of postwar Berlin for the comforts and security of England. He arranged to rent a separate flat for them not far from his own near Lancaster Gate and for a young unemployed professor, erstwhile of Cambridge, to tutor them in English, which Fern had already started learning in school. Six months later, mother and daughter moved up to Oxford, where Fern resumed undergraduate studies at St. Anne's College, and Hildy, attractive and engaging at thirty-eight, made friends among faculty members and the many bright young men who courted Fern. An avid reader, Hildy audited courses in international economics and political science, spending her evenings in robust conversations with the students while Fern applied herself to her studies.

On Fern's graduation with high honors, all three returned to Germany – Frederick with enough capital to expand the family business with profits from his small London-based investment enterprise, Fern with a letter of acceptance to the University of Berlin Medical School, and the widowed Hildy with a fresh lease on life.

Frederick's thoughts returned to the present when Fern arrived. He saw that she cut a stunning figure – tall, with shining chestnut tresses that curled at the shoulders of her camel's hair coat. She unwound her maroon scarf, kissed him on both cheeks, and grinned approvingly as the quartet played "Tales from the Vienna Woods," a favorite from her childhood.

Frederick knew it was time for a good family chat – and a farewell. *"Bitte Fern,"* he said as she sat down at the small table. She had loved Frederick since her childhood. A lifelong bachelor, he had many genuine friends, but no close family except for Fern and Hildy. Hildy now lived well in Berlin on a small pension, which Uncle Frederick supplemented as a responsible and generous brother-in-law.

Frederick poured hot coffee from the ceramic pot. "Fern, I know your time is precious." He offered no sugar. He knew Fern always took her coffee unsweetened and black.

"I thought of inviting Karl but wanted to have a family tête-à-tête," he said.

"No matter," she said. "Karl's so busy now. He's decided to do a few more professional fights – ten-rounders, so he's training much harder. No alcohol. And, as always, no smoking of any kind, better food, more sleep, more running, with lots sparring and gym work. He's doing it so that we'll have enough money to go to California. He'll do his advanced residency in orthopedics there at St. Francis Memorial Hospital while I begin my practice in plastic surgery."

"California?"

"Karl's always wanted to live there, and I've already had a wonderful job offer to practice there."

"Tell me more, Fern."

"St. Francis has a special burns unit, so I'll work there and have a further affiliation with Stanford University Hospital in Palo Alto."

She saw that Frederick's expression had become curious. "Naturally, we will marry. We're thinking of doing it a week after Karl's last fight. We'll have just a few friends and you, of course, if you're in New York."

He thought for moment before speaking. "I am sure that you will both enjoy great love and success. I, of course, cannot speak for Karl's future as a doctor, but I have seen him fight. His right can kill, and the same goes for his left hook. And best of all he's fast – lightning fast. Too bad he's not a heavy-weight. He would give Schmeling a go."

"That will never happen. He'll soon be finished with boxing." Fern grinned, savoring a lemon cake from the silver tray on the small table.

Glancing at his vest pocket watch, Frederick leaned forward. "We should speak German now," he said. She nodded with a frown, preparing for bad news. "I must return to Germany. I will be leaving tonight on the Bremen. Now that the Nazis have been in power for close to two years, they're tight-ening their grip. I must deal with Hitler in person, and I must do so soon."

"Sounds awful."

"It has its challenges. I have to deal with some rather rough customers, including my friend Hermann Göring, who's a boy at heart. He can be an interesting companion at times, an excellent skier, by the way."

Frederick lit his pipe. "Enough of Germany," he said. "I want to hear more about your career, your medical writing. We've had no time to catch up."

"Nice of you to ask," she beamed. "The University of Chicago has asked me to present a paper on burns and plastic surgery in February. And the *New England Journal of Medicine* has asked me to write another article, which will be my fifth piece for them."

"Any trouble writing in English?"

"Not really, thanks to the good foundation I got at Oxford. And Karl's English is perfect, like his German. But make no mistake, Karl would be happy never to speak another word of German."

"Yes, you've told me that. But why?"

"Several reasons, Uncle," she said. "For one thing, he's been here for fifteen years. And although he doesn't talk about it, I know he's embarrassed because we Germans have accepted a clown like Hitler. What's more, his best friend, Josh Greenberg, is Jewish. German-Jewish, but Jewish. His mother and father are both from Berlin, and German is his first language. But his parents insisted that he learn English and speak it well, just as they had learned to do. Josh and Karl have been friends since Karl arrived in America. Josh helped Karl with his English and taught him the rules of American sports. He showed Karl how to use the subway. Josh's friends became Karl's friends. Josh's parents took the two of them to baseball games, Broadway shows, and museums. Without Josh, Karl might have been just another tough immigrant kid in New York."

Frederick sat back, biting on his pipe. "But instead he became the perfect man, and you found him?"

"Karl is far from perfect. He has a tendency to get into fights. By now, though, he's learned that I won't stand for it. I've explained that he's a healer, a mender of broken bones, not someone who smashes and breaks them. He began to understand this after he shoved a waiter who tried to pad a bill at the Bavarian Inn. I was mortified. And then one evening on 86th Street, we came upon a young man, a big guy, who was trying to wrest a purse from an elderly woman. Karl grabbed him by the collar, threw him against a street lamp, and pounded his chest, stomach, and face. He stopped only after I started screaming at him. Lord knows what might have happened if Karl had kept hitting him. Thank God, the man ran away and Karl didn't kill him."

"Yes, it's true," Frederick said. "The law is quite harsh on boxers who use their fists outside the boxing ring. It's considered assault with a deadly weapon."

"Indeed, but more important to me is that Karl failed to control himself. Staying in control is fundamental."

"What did you do?"

"Actually, it's what I didn't do. After the second incident, I refused to speak to Karl for a full three months, wouldn't even acknowledge his presence when we would run into each other in the hospital hallway or the cafeteria, even in the operating room. I knew that I was hurting him, yes, hurting him enough that he would never forget."

"The poor lad must have died from the cold of it. 'Hell hath no fury,' as the man said."

"Karl needed a lesson he would never forget. He had to understand that I wouldn't tolerate his being a vigalante, no matter what."

"Tell me, Fern, how did this impasse come to an end?"

"Quite simply. I sent him a note, asking him to meet me for coffee in the hospital cafeteria. There I told him that I still loved him but that he had to grow up and learn to control his anger, no matter how righteous his cause. I reminded him of the oath we take as doctors to 'do no harm.' I argued that this oath even applies outside the practice of medicine and extends to a doctor's life in general. I told him that if he ever lost his temper and got violent with anyone, or even threatened it, I would stop loving him and start seeing other men."

"Stop loving?"

"Difficult."

"Yes, but not impossible. Did he accept your demand?"

"Yes, but only after he drew a certain line. He said a man could get into a dispute or fight he didn't start and that he had a right to defend himself and his friends. I told him that defending oneself or one's friends was one thing, but taking unfair advantage or bullying was quite another, especially for a professional boxer."

"Well, Fern, what about improper advances other men might make toward you? I imagine such instances would test Karl's patience, to say the least."

"Such instances have been rare. You see, dearest Uncle, one nice thing about having a professional boxer for a lover is that other men mind their manners. And on those rare occasions when a new doctor crossed the line at the hospital, I handled it. A threat to report them to the chief of medicine is usually enough put them in their place. I've had to do it twice, even though two other women doctors at the hospital advised me against making an issue of it. I never tell Karl when that happens."

"What about outside the hospital? I've been around long enough to know that men aren't saints."

"Actually, I asked Karl what I should do in those situations. What he suggested has worked wonders on the two occasions when I've had to defend myself – once, when a teenage boy with the worst garlic breath you can imagine started rubbing himself against me in a crowded car on the Third Avenue El. I gave him a quick knee where it hurt most. Karl taught me how."

The quartet changed from Strauss to Schubert. They listened, taking in the moment until Frederick peeked at his pocket watch.

"I'm afraid this is goodbye for a time," Frederick said. "Thanks to the miracles worked by my New York office, my trunk is packed and on the Bremen. My ticket and passport are in my jacket pocket. Of course, you're welcome to come see me off. The beer on the Bremen is the best in New York. Even better, the bar is stocked with wonderful Mosel and several brands of twelve-year-old Scotch. I must say, however, that the bon voyage parties on the Bremen aren't what they used to be now that Prohibition is over." He gestured for the check.

She saw him to a Checker taxi and waved as the cab turned onto 59th Street. Frederick directed the driver to the Wagner Industries offices at 50 Rockefeller Center. He saw that his secretary, Ingrid Trenner, a poised and efficient German expatriate, appeared ill at ease. At the sight of Frederick, she snatched up a telegram delivered just an hour before by a uniformed Western Union messenger. She had already exercised her authority to read anything addressed to Frederick not marked personal. Still in his overcoat, Frederick sank into a chair to read it.

"Here, take this," Ingrid said, offering him a snifter of brandy she had poured earlier and left on his desk.

"*Nein danke.* I need to think."

He stuffed his papers in his briefcase and said goodbye to his five-person New York staff.

He decided to walk to the 12th Avenue pier where the Bremen waited. The low winter sun made him squint as he headed west on 43rd Street. He let the senseless event described in the telegram settle in his mind. The reality was that his longtime friend and top chemist, Meyer Feinburg, was now dead. Feinburg had allegedly suffered a "sudden heart attack" under questioning by the Gestapo after his arrest for possession of pamphlets critical of the new regime's seizure of Jewish property. Like many men who were good at their job, Meyer could be headstrong. Frederick wondered whether he might have been able to do something had he been in Berlin.

In his stateroom, Frederick put Meyer Feinburg's misfortune aside. He had to make up his mind on another matter. He sat at the small desk and made a list of pros and cons on a page of Bremen stationery. Then he sat for some ten minutes before realizing what he had to do. He tore the paper into bits and placed them in the large desk ashtray, struck a match, and watched the little fire until it flickered out a moment later. Then he washed up and headed for the first-class bar and a very dry martini. The rest of it would have to wait until he returned to Berlin.

33. 125TH STREET, MANHATTAN, FEBRUARY 3, 1936, 9:00 A.M.

Jack Elwood's face lit up when he saw Karl Ludwig coming through the doorway of the men's clothing shop. Jack's store sold the best neckties, shirts, and suits in Harlem. Karl's visits gave Jack a chance to talk about boxing and about

Harlem and its kids. At Karl's suggestion, Jack arranged lunch meetings of Harlem merchants at the Hotel Theresa to raise funds for the boxing program at the Harlem Boys Club. The lunch became a monthly event after Karl suggested inviting Jack Dempsey to speak. To everyone's surprise, Dempsey accepted. Later Henry Armstrong, Jack Sharkey, Jim Braddock, and other boxing celebrities also took a turn as guest speaker. Karl served as master of ceremonies and began developing his public-speaking skills. The lunches yielded well over $1,000 a month. Many of the white merchants who owned shops in Harlem, as well as those from the German, Irish, and Italian neighborhoods – butchers, shoemakers, and restaurant owners – came and gave generously.

"Hey, man, what's up?" Jack asked.

"What's up is what's in my bag," Karl answered. He emptied a gym bag and a smaller cloth bag, both full of coins, one-dollar bills, and raffle ticket stubs. "It's about a hundred bucks, just from this morning's visits. We covered every open store on the north side of 125th, from Lenox to Second Avenue, between 5:30 and 7:30 this morning – all the coffee shops, cafeterias, and newsstands. And not one merchant refused to buy tickets. The boys and I celebrated with oatmeal at the Ajax Coffee Shop, just down the block from here, before I sent them running off to school."

"I think we can do the south side tomorrow when I don't have to be at the hospital."

"Karl, that makes over $21,200 you've raised for us this year. Doesn't it take away from your job at the hospital?"

"Not really. It's easier now that I've completed my residency and work regular staff hours. And the kids are helping me a lot. They hardly need me. They've learned not to talk about how the boxing program helps them. Instead, they talk about the radio we're giving away as the raffle prize, how having that radio behind the counter will help store owners attract customers with music or a ballgame."

"You got that right, Karl. I don't sell shirts. I sell a customer on how handsome he's going to look in that shirt. Back home in Charleston, I worked for a landscape gardener. He did real well seeding lawns. Sometimes I'd go with Old Ben on cold calls. Just before we rang the doorbell at one of the big old houses near Charleston Harbor, Old Ben would put his hand on my shoulder and say: 'Now Jack, don't forget, we're not selling our seed, we're selling their grass.' It worked every time."

34. LUNA RESTAURANT, LITTLE ITALY, LOWER MANHATTAN, FEBRUARY 13, 1936, 1:05 A.M.

A cold, driving rain splashed against the large front window of the restaurant, but inside, in the back, it was warm and dry. Over anisette and espresso, Channing Brown and Jamie Creel could hear the music of Verdi as they listened to the man with wire-rimmed glasses and curly gray hair, a man highly recommended by Sir Crawford.

"We won't disappoint you, Mr. Brown. Your generosity will enable us to take care of everything. But before we undertake the job, we need half a million in cash here tonight and another half-million deposited in the Bank of Messina one week after we complete our assignment."

"Tonight's installment is in the briefcase, under the table," Brown said.

"*Bene*," said the stout man with the large jaw who sat next to the man who had done the talking. He reached down for the briefcase, rested it on his lap, and examined the contents, counting the large bills. "It's all here, Charlie," he said.

"I told you we could trust these guys," said the man with the curly hair. "What the hell, they're as good as the Bank of England." He offered a handshake, which Brown accepted. They all stood to signal the end of their rendezvous.

Brown and Jamie took a taxi to P.J. Clarke's at 55th and Third. Brown knew the place would still be open. He wanted some Johnnie Walker Black and so did Jamie. He reckoned that they deserved a nightcap after concluding a million-dollar transaction with Charlie "Lucky" Luciano.

35. LUNA RESTAURANT, FEBRUARY 15, 1936, 11:00 P.M.

Luciano decided that no one else should be present for his meeting with Victor Minnelli. He was happy that the driving rain had kept the late crowd to himself and Minnelli. Still, he was careful to post bodyguards outside the door of the empty dining room.

Luciano stood to embrace the taller Minnelli, a handsome, well-built, twenty-six-year-old Sicilian with straight black hair and a one-inch scar over his left eye, the result of a knife fight in Palermo when he was ten. Minnelli had a tattoo depicting two pistols, barrels crossed, on the back of his right hand. The tattoo was a gift from one of Luciano's clients, who had been delighted by Minnelli's skillful use of a pistol to eliminate a competitor in the business of making book on horse races. Minnelli was also skilled with the garrote and with his hands.

"Victor, *bene*. It's a lousy night. Have some hot chocolate."

"Just what I need, Charlie. It's cold as a witch's crotch out there," Minnelli said, glancing over his shoulder, an instinctive move for a man who lived on the edge.

Minnelli sat as Luciano poured hot chocolate from a silver pot on the table. Minnelli declined Luciano's offer of butter cookies. He was ready to talk business.

"Okay, Charlie, what's up?"

"We have work to do, Victor, a major contract. It's going to require careful planning, but it'll make us a lot of money. It's no job for boy scouts. I want your muscle and your brains. Tonight we can begin the planning. After that, you can organize it and get it done."

The two men talked until the first rays of daylight came through the front window. Minnelli went to the pay phone on the wall and placed calls to four trusted individuals – the Mulberry Street wine importer Vinny Bellacosta; a corrections officer at Sing Sing Prison; an NYPD captain responsible for deploying police officers in a part of the city known as Manhattan North; and an ambitious young assistant district attorney for New York County. None minded getting an early-morning call from Victor Minnelli. Back at the table to talk with Luciano, Minnelli reviewed the notes he'd taken. Naturally, some of the details would have to be worked out later. When they said goodbye on the sidewalk, the rain had turned to snow. Luciano stepped into a chauffeur-driven Packard. Minnelli walked to the one-room apartment he kept on Mulberry Street.

36. SECOND AVENUE AND 79TH STREET, FEBRUARY 16, 1936, 5:10 A.M.

Karl had been running for more than an hour in the swirling snow, exhaling short white puffs in the frigid predawn air. He ran further every morning. He would warm up slowly, jog for a mile, walk for a minute, then begin to run, increasing his speed steadily for thirty minutes. He finished with sprints at hundred-yard intervals. At first he completed only three such repetitions, but now he was up to fifteen. It built his endurance and turned his legs to steel pistons. He turned east on 79th Street, then down Fifth Avenue, passing the early risers shivering as they waited for the double-decker bus. By his measure, he had run ten miles on this morning. He passed the Plaza Hotel, an Impressionist masterpiece in the falling snow, and then ran on to Stillman's Gym on West 54th Street.

Karl regretted that his training would soon end. He loved the early morning runs, the camaraderie among the fighters, and the inimitable New York characters at the gym. There he would spar, work the punching bags, and lift dumbbells. On this morning, he knew he had reached optimum conditioning. He doubted he would ever be in this good a shape again. For the next five days, he would taper off his training regimen, resting the day before the fight with only some easy shadow boxing. This would be the last of the ten-rounders he had agreed to fight. None of the previous fights had gone the distance. He had knocked out all of his opponents well before the fifth round, with Josh and Fern often treating the smashed noses and the shattered cheekbones.

Karl was bothered by nagging thoughts that he could really hurt an opponent, deprive him of some part of his brain, even his life. He had tried denial, but the thoughts always came back, sometimes just before a fight. At the same time, Fern worried about the boxer unlucky enough to be on the wrong end of his more bone-breaking punches. Just as disturbing to each of them was what might happen to his hands. He knew each punch could take its toll on the nimble and sensitive fingers a surgeon needed.

But there was no escape from the fact that each fight earned him five hundred dollars. Irv Levin had been good to his word, paying Karl with a roll of five crisp C-notes after each fight. The money would buy a Ford to take Karl and Fern to San Francisco. Karl's prior earnings would be used to pay for a small wedding party and help them lease and furnish a decent apartment, ideally one with a view of the bay. If they needed more money, they knew Uncle Frederick would help.

Once at the gym, Karl fixed his mind on the coming fight. His basic strategy was always the same: Karl let his opponent expend some energy, show his style, and reveal his weaknesses. He absorbed punches on the shoulders, chest, and stomach for three rounds, allowing his opponent to gain a false sense of confidence. Then Karl would machine-gun him with a sudden flurry of lefts and rights. That usually sent the opponent down.

After his morning workout, Karl showered in the grimy bathroom at the gym and headed for the automat on East 42nd Street, where he treated himself to orange juice, hot black coffee, and oatmeal. Then he strolled to the Third Avenue El for the ten-minute ride to the hospital.

37. OFFICES OF VINCENT BELLACOSTA, WINE IMPORTER, FEBRUARY 25, 1936, 11:00 A.M.

Since he seldom went there, the invitation to visit his brother Vinny's office came as a surprise to Bobby Bellacosta. Bobby didn't like to go there. He found the men who worked for his brother to be vulgar and profane. Still, the business had paid for college and medical school – and he loved his brother.

Entering the office, Bobby was happy to see that Vinny was dressed in a conservative gray double-breasted pinstriped suit. Bobby hated the flamboyant dress of Vinny's underlings. Vinny Bellacosta stood and moved around the desk to hug Bobby. "Glad you could make it down here. I know how busy you are. I just wanted a private moment to tell you that I leased that office space you liked on West End Avenue. Lots of rich old folks live up there. You should do great with the general medical practice."

"Vinny, that's more than you should have done."

"Forget it, little brother. And don't worry. I won't send you any non-legit business. This is strictly my present to you."

"So how's business?" Bobby asked.

"We have a big deal pending in Italy – Italian wines are becoming more popular all the time. Next week I'm off to Naples, Rome, and Florence. The idea is to get an exclusive contract to sell some top Italian brands here in the States. I leave Saturday on the Queen Mary. Come see me off. I'm having a little party on board."

"I may be too hung over to see you off. That's the morning after Karl Ludwig's bachelor party at the Bavarian Inn."

"Yeah, I read in the *Daily Mirror* that his last fight is on Friday. I know the manager at the Bavarian, so I'll see that you get a good table. We'll arrange for some good Champagne. And by the way, the whole dinner is my treat. Too bad about Karl's decision to quit fighting. He could've been a really great boxer. In fact, I know people who would be happy to finance a boxing career for him. I'm told he could have a title shot in sixteen months."

"Forget it. He's going to concentrate on medicine and marriage."

Vinny shrugged, the brothers embraced, and Bobby was off to the hospital to make his rounds.

After his brother had left, Vinny called the headwaiter at the Bavarian Inn to confirm the number of the table booked for Karl Ludwig's bachelor party. Then he made another call.

38. EN ROUTE TO THE BAVARIAN INN, EAST 86TH STREET, FEBRUARY 28, 1936, 10:15 P.M.

As predicted by both the *Mirror* and the *News*, Karl easily won his final fight with a knockout. It came with a fast left hook to his opponent's right ear, twenty-two seconds into the third round.

"Thank God you didn't kill him," Fern said as their cab crawled up Eighth Avenue from Madison Square Garden.

"I know. But at least now I won't have to do it again. Besides, boxing has always been too risky for me."

"Yes, darling, I couldn't agree more," she said, resting her head on his chest. "You don't need strong fists. You need a surgeon's gentle fingers." She took his right hand and held it to her cheek. "Let these hands do only good," she whispered.

"It could be a wonderful night for just the two of us," he responded, "but Josh and Bobby have both gone out of their way. By now they'll be itching to open the Champagne. Bobby's brother has offered to foot the bill."

She turned toward him, pressing her head against his chin. "After the party, come to the townhouse. Don't worry about waking me, just brush your teeth. I'll take your gym bag with me. You won't need it."

"Be careful with the bag," Karl said. "I keep a picture of the two of us inside. Now that I'm finished fighting, I'll let you have it. I've written a note on the photo. Just don't read it. I want to be with you when you do."

They shared a long and gentle kiss as the cab rolled to a stop in front of the Bavarian Inn. He stood for a moment on the pavement as the cab vanished in the Friday night traffic on 86th Street. Fern was what mattered now, Fern and their life in San Francisco. But now it was time to be with his friends, drink Champagne and eat a steak, one that was thick, juicy, and rare.

39. BAVARIAN INN, 10:35 P.M.

The downstairs room was filled with tobacco smoke and noise. Karl looked around at the faces — mostly German, but some Irish and Sicilian too. With the end of Prohibition, the place had become more popular than ever. Karl saw Josh waving to him from a table across the room. Josh, Bobby Bellacosta, and Tim clapped as Karl approached. On a signal from Josh, a waiter stepped up to open a bottle of Dom Perignon. Before speaking, they waited with anticipation as the waiter filled the four chilled Champagne glasses. His three friends had decided not to drink until Karl arrived – and now they were ready.

"*L'chaim*," Josh bellowed, climbing up on his chair to command attention. His shout hushed scores of conversations and stopped the clatter of dishes and beer steins. "Please everyone, a toast for Karl Ludwig, recently retired and undefeated as a boxer, and soon to be one of America's greatest orthopedic surgeons. And to his bride to be, the talented plastic surgeon Dr. Fern Wagner." Nearly everyone in the crowded room applauded.

Karl gave little notice to an adjacent table, where three men remained seated in silence. One was short and well built, with a shining bald head. Another, wearing a turtleneck and blue blazer, had a pockmarked face and a bouncer's physique. He wore a small but recognizable swastika pin on his lapel. The third had a strong, handsome face, straight dark hair, and projected a forceful presence. Karl noticed a tattoo of crossed pistols on the back of the man's right hand and an inch-long scar over his left eye. Karl took them for members of the German-American Bund, which was a strong presence in Yorkville. The Bund's ranks had been growing throughout New York City and the German-American suburbs of Long Island.

Karl rose to respond to the toast but never got a word out. The man with the swastika pin peered directly at him and began shouting: "You're not a real boxer. You don't fight real men. You only fight Jews and niggers."

"Ignore him, Karl," Bobby said. "He's drunk." Karl saw that Josh was making an effort not to react.

Karl again began to speak. "Let me . . ." Just then, the man with the pockmarked face slammed both fists on the table, rattling dishes. The room went silent. The man with the swastika pin spoke again in a loud threatening tone. "Max Schmeling would make sausage of you." He glared at Karl, straight into his eyes. Karl looked away.

"Look, dumbo," Bobby Bellacosta shouted, "Schmeling's a heavyweight. Karl's a middleweight."

"Easy, Bobby," Karl said trying not to raise his voice. "These louts are looking for trouble. Get a cop." Bobby bolted up the staircase.

The bald man shouted again. "So this traitor to Germany sends his friend running for help. Too bad there aren't any Jews or niggers for him to fight," the man growled through clenched teeth, his eyes fixed on Karl. Diners began leaving their tables and heading for the stairs.

"Karl, this guy's just itching to get you mad," Tim said.

"If he starts a fight, it won't be his first," Karl said in a tone low enough that only his friends could hear. Josh looked at Karl but said nothing.

40. EAST 86ᵀᴴ STREET, 10:36 P.M.

"Why can't you ever find a cop when you need one?" Bobby muttered as he scanned the crowded street in all directions. Then, through the steamy window of the Ideal Coffee Shop, Bobby could see two officers sipping coffee. He rushed inside.

"Excuse me, officers, there's trouble – a possible fist fight . . . in the Bavarian."

"Don't those Heinies have a bouncer?" Sergeant Sean O'Malley, twenty years Bobby's senior, asked.

"I think this could be serious," Bobby said.

"Serious, is it? Now isn't everything? Just run along. We'll be there in a minute."

"That could be too late, if you don't mind me saying."

"Look, Dago, truth be told, I *do* mind. Let me and my partner, Paddy here, finish our coffee. Then we'll come have a look. You run along now."

Bobby turned and ran from the coffee shop.

41. BAVARIAN INN, 10:41 P.M.

Bobby rushed back down the stairs of the Bavarian. The Bierkeller was now vacant, except for Karl, his friends, and their hostile neighbors. Bobby could see that all six were now on their feet.

"Look you guys," Josh said, "we just want to mind our own business."

"Shut up, Jew fuck," the bald man shouted.

Karl turned, looking for a waiter or policeman, but saw only Bobby, who had returned alone.

"Let's sit down and cool off," Josh said.

"I thought I told you to shut up," the bald man shouted with a spray of spittle.

"Let's get going," Karl said to Josh. "If we stay, they'll never leave us alone."

The man who looked like a bouncer eyed Karl. "I heard that. You want to run. You betray your Aryan blood," he growled, his teeth still clenched.

The bald man started shouting at Josh. "Why don't you put on a god-damn yarmulke like all your Jew friends on Mott Street? Hey, it's Friday night. Shouldn't a Yid like you be down there in a synagogue?"

Karl peered toward the stairway. *Where in hell were the cops? The waiters?*

The big man with the pockmarked face and swastika pin took several steps toward Josh.

"What are you guys trying to do, start a riot?" Josh said, straining to stay calm. "We could press charges."

"Well, press this," said the man with the scar over his left eye as he punched Josh in the nose, then drove a knee into Josh's groin, sending him to the floor.

Tim lunged to tackle the man with the scar, only to take a kick in the balls. As Tim doubled up, the man grabbed him by the collar and threw him against the wall.

Bobby took a swing at swastika man but missed by a foot. The man's counterpunch knocked Bobby out cold.

Karl looked again toward the stairs. The dark-haired man moved toward Josh, picked him up off the floor, stood him up against the wall, and began punching him in the ribs. Josh dropped to the floor a second time. Then the man started kicking him in the head and chest.

Karl exploded. He grabbed the man's black hair, turning him around to deliver a stinging left to the forehead, then a right that sent him over a table and to the floor in a mess of broken dishes and glass. Karl's next punch sent the bald man to the same glass-strewn spot on the floor, landing him atop his friend. Karl then spun around to face swastika man and sent him to the floor with a single sharp left hook. Only then did Karl see that the men in blue uniforms had arrived. Karl dropped his fists.

11:44 P.M.

"An ambulance will be here in a minute," Sergeant O'Malley said, motioning for Karl to sit down. He pointed to the three men Karl had knocked to the floor, and to Tim, who had begun to regain consciousness. "The medical people will tend to them," O'Malley said. "Now be a good lad and tell us what happened."

Josh and Tim left on stretchers as their three assailants staggered up the stairs. Bobby had regained consciousness.

After Karl told his side of the story, the police instructed him and Bobby to return home and not to leave New York. Karl walked with Bobby to New York Hospital, where they learned that Josh was in intensive care and that Tim appeared okay, although he was still getting X-rays. Bobby hailed a cab for home. Karl walked to Frederick's townhouse. Once there, he dismissed any thought of waking Fern. Too tired even to pour himself a glass of water, he kicked off his shoes and fell asleep on the drawing room couch.

42. 19TH PRECINCT HEADQUARTERS, EAST 67TH STREET, FEBRUARY 29, 2:14 A.M.

A desk sergeant with a square Irish jaw reviewed the paper work. The bald man and the man who had removed his swastika pin had just signed and sworn to official complaints as instructed by a lawyer who had been waiting for them at the precinct headquarters. They also signed documents authorizing the lawyer to handle all matters pertaining to any forthcoming procedures related to the indictment and prosecution of one Karl Ludwig for assault with a deadly weapon – an offense that could bring three separate ten-year sentences. The documents affirmed that each man would appear in court to aid the prosecution if necessary. The lawyer also had papers stating that a third complainant had given him power of attorney because this complainant had business commitments that required him to travel. The lawyer was well prepared and quite thorough.

2:51 A.M.

A car was waiting for the two men when they left the police station. One of Luciano's men, sitting in the back seat, presented each man with an envelope containing a thousand dollars in small bills, and a train ticket to Miami. From Miami they would travel by yacht to Cuba. Everything had been arranged. In Havana, there were good jobs waiting for them at one of the casinos.

43. ACROSS THE STREET FROM THE BAVARIAN INN, 2:52 A.M.

No one noticed as the white delivery van parked on the north side of 86th Street, across from the Bavarian Inn, began moving and turned south, driving under the Third Avenue El before crossing the 59th Street Bridge to Long Island. Eventually the van traveled east on deserted roads to Roosevelt Field in Garden City. On strict orders from Luciano, neither the driver nor the passenger beside him uttered a word during the trip.

As instructed, the van drove into an open hangar, where a twin-engine DC-2 sat waiting. The pilot greeted his passenger warmly. "Mr. Minnelli, good to see you again, Sir. There's a hot breakfast waiting in the cabin, bacon, eggs, and coffee. We'll be in Havana for lunch tomorrow, after we refuel in Jacksonville."

44. FREDERICK WAGNER'S TOWNHOUSE, 4:48 A.M.

It took several raps of the nightstick against the large oak door to wake him. Karl staggered from the couch and peered through the bay window to see three black-and-white police patrol cars, exhaust flowing from their tail pipes.

He opened the door to three policemen standing on the front steps. Fern heard the noise and came rushing down the long staircase, barefoot and tugging at the sash of her terry cloth robe. Then she went rigid, midway down the stairs, and listened.

"Are you Karl Ludwig?" the tallest of the three policemen asked.

"Yes."

"Then, son, you'd best come with us."

45. THE TOMBS, FRANKLIN STREET, MANHATTAN, FEBRUARY 29, 1936, 10:30 A.M.

There was no love in Fern's eyes as she stared through Karl, who sat on the wrong side of the glass partition.

"Josh is out of the coma, in a special critical-care unit. He's got a few cracked ribs and a punctured lung. Tim is badly bruised but resting at his folks' place on Long Island. Bobby called this morning to say that he's still a little stiff, but fine."

"But, Karl," she said, raising her chin and lowering voice, "how could you have been so stupid?"

"Look, the guy could have killed Josh. Believe me, Fern, I waited as long as I could for help from the cops. Then I had to jump in to save Josh."

"Did you have to punch them? Couldn't you have grabbed one of them and pinned him down? Something besides throwing punches?"

"You weren't there, Fern. I was. They would have killed him. I had to save Josh. I cooperated with the cops."

"Well then, my love, why are you in jail?"

"Frankly I'm not sure. Something about *assault with a deadly weapon.*"

"Well, as it turns out, that's precisely the charge, according to the newspapers. And it's all over the radio and the tabloids, which, I hate to tell you, have made it a front-page story. Have a look," she said, holding up copies of the *News* and the *Mirror.*

FIGHTING DOC IN BARROOM BRAWL

DOCTOR VS. BUND IN BLOODY YORKVILLE FISTFIGHT

"As you can see, the *News* and *Mirror* both love your story. The *Mirror* even has a full-page story based on what two waiters said after the fight and about the formal complaints filed by the men you beat up. They're all saying you could get up to thirty years. This is real trouble, Karl."

Karl looked away, over her shoulder, but said nothing.

"We'll need the best lawyers," Fern said. "I've tried to contact Uncle Frederick by trans-Atlantic telephone, but there's no answer at his apartment, his Berlin office, or at his place in the Obersalzberg. Frederick knows some good lawyers here in New York, but I don't know whether any of them specialize in criminal defense work. That's what you need now."

Karl was grateful that Fern hadn't made good on her threat never to see him again if he used his fists outside the boxing ring. "Look Fern, I had to do something," he said.

Fern listened and then spoke in a low voice with tears in her eyes.

"Forget what happened," she said. "It's done. Now we have to control the damage. You realize, don't you, that even if you get out of this, you'll have a hell of a time trying to salvage your career."

Karl said nothing. She looked down at the floor, then up at him.

"There's nothing more I can do here now," she whispered, leaning toward him. "I've asked to go on duty even though this was supposed to be my day off, you know – since it was just days before our wedding. But now with you in jail for God knows how long, I have time on my hands. So I'm off to the hospital. I need to get my mind off this mess."

And then she was gone. He knew there was no chance of getting bail, so he hadn't even mentioned it to Fern.

Just after Fern left, Bobby appeared on the other side of the glass partition to tell him that his brother Vinny had offered to provide a lawyer. With Fern not able to reach Frederick, Karl saw that he was in no position to refuse help.

Later that day, Karl Ludwig was arraigned on three counts of assault with a deadly weapon, with each count carrying a maximum of ten years. Judge Francis Xavier McGraw denied bail. At the arraignment, Dino Lamberti, a lawyer who worked for Bobby Bellacosta's brother, represented Karl at no charge.

46. THE FOREIGN OFFICE, LONDON, MARCH 1, 1936, 4:00 P.M.

Channing and Jillian Brown had a long-standing rule of not telephoning each other at work. The Foreign Office and his bosses at SIS were sensitive to the fact that Brown was married to a journalist. What's more, there were always too many interruptions during the day. On this particular Sunday, he would make an exception and telephone her at the *Times*. He told her he was preparing for a rare Sunday visit with the Secretary and needed to be up to the minute on all the breaking foreign news. Was anything happening in New York?

"Nice surprise to hear from you, Channy. Dull Sabbath at Whitehall? New York? I'll have look at the wires. Mind holding the line?"

Brown doodled on a long yellow pad as Jillian left the copy desk and walked a few strides to the row of news tickers. "Hi, Love," she said, returning to the phone. "It's a ruddy bore just about everywhere. Across the pond, New York is enjoying a quiet late winter weekend. It's been raining there. Things are awfully dreary, save for one item. The AP's New York bureau is moving several stories on some boxer who, according to the reports, beat the bloody hell out of some German-American Bund members late Friday night in a Manhattan restaurant. The wires also note that New York law takes a rather dim view of boxers who use their fists outside the ring, all tasty grist for the tabloids."

"Thanks, Jillian. Let's be sure to catch up over a pint or two at the Silver Swan. Meet you there at half-five?"

"See you then, Love."

Brown replaced the receiver of the candlestick phone and walked down the hallway to the U.S. desk. He learned from the junior aide, one unlucky enough to have pulled Sunday duty, that according to the British Consulate in New York, all ten of the city's daily newspapers carried not one but several stories about the young fighter and resident physician suddenly turned avenger. The *Herald Tribune* had even run a sidebar story insinuating that the young doctor had Jekyll and Hyde tendencies, reminding readers that Jekyll was a doctor too, albeit a fictional one.

Ten minutes later, Jillian called Brown again. The AP, she learned, had issued a more balanced report, one saying that the physician-boxer was also known for helping teenage boxers in Harlem and that he and his friends had been subjected to unprovoked harassment. The same story, she said, went on to explain that such harassment was an example of the mounting anti-Jewish sentiment among Bund members and other Nazi sympathizers.

All the news outlets reported on a statement by a New York County Assistant District Attorney, who insisted that the rule of law must prevail and that such a violent assault by a professional boxer demanded "justice and appropriate punishment, no matter how distasteful the provocation." An Associated Press story quoted the President of the New York State Medical Society, who said that the doctor's conviction could lead to "the permanent revocation of his license to practice in New York and make it unlikely that he could practice medicine in any other state."

Brown made notes, returned to his office, and grabbed the candlestick phone.

47. VISITORS ROOM, THE TOMBS, MANHATTAN, MARCH 2, 1936, 10:00 A.M.

Karl saw that the two men came from different worlds. At the arraignment, the police, clerks, and bail bondsmen had all addressed the first man, Dino Lamberti, by name – by his first name. Karl had met Dino – who was about thirty-five and always dressed in a double-breasted navy blue pinstriped suit – at a party in Bobby Bellacosta's Mulberry Street apartment several months before. The second man, of medium height, bald, and older by at least ten years, wore a charcoal gray three-piece suit. He introduced himself as Jordan DeWitt of Chapman and Chesterfield, a London-based law firm with offices on Wall Street.

After the introductions, Dino Lamberti moved directly to the specifics. "Karl, Mr. DeWitt and I will be working together on your case. The expenses have been paid."

"So Fern got her Uncle Frederick to . . . "

"Not exactly. The fact is, he happened to telephone her," DeWitt answered. "Something about securing his townhouse residence in view of her plan to marry you and move out West. But now, of course, that's out of the question. When Fern told her uncle what happened at the Bavarian Inn, he asked Mr. Lamberti's firm and mine to collaborate on your defense."

"What about bail? Does the judge's decision stand? I need to get the hell out of here."

"Sorry, Karl," Dino responded softly. "The judge let us know that he won't change his mind. He says the case has already received too much publicity."

Karl sat back, looking at them through the partition.

"Look, I threw some punches to save my friend. What was I supposed to do?"

"Nothing, Karl." Dino said. "You should have done nothing."

48. FREDERICK WAGNER'S TOWNHOUSE, MARCH 7, 1936, NOON

After a fitful sleep, Fern sat at the kitchen table. It was all such a nightmare. Jordan DeWitt had been keeping her up to date by telephone, but she was intelligent enough to realize that she didn't understand everything he said about Karl's bleak prospects if he stood trial.

She knew that she'd had been drinking too much coffee and had just poured herself another cup when the telephone broke the silence.

"*Liebchen.*"

"Karl. I hope you have some news, good news."

"Well maybe. Dino arranged for me to make a phone call so we could talk things over. I spent most of the morning with Dino and DeWitt. They'd just come from a meeting with the Assistant DA, a guy named Jason Prince. He's been assigned to prosecute my case. Dino and DeWitt both say that he's dead set on exploiting the trial to showcase himself. You know, the fearless champion of the people against the bully boxer. DeWitt says Prince is a white Protestant type bent on boosting his reputation with pro-Bund people and anti-Semites. At least that's the way Dino and DeWitt see it."

"What else did they say?" Fern asked

"That it would be a big mistake to go to trial."

"Really? Why? If you were trying to save Josh, surely there were witnesses."

"None that anyone can find," Karl replied. "All the other customers had left the restaurant by the time I got into the fight. What's worse is that the cops have affidavits from the guys I punched out."

"So what do the lawyers say?"

"That there's no way they could find impartial jurors, not after all the publicity. The reality, they say, is that we'll lose any trial and that a trial would only generate more headlines. They said Prince will likely go for the maximum sentence, which could be three ten-year terms."

"Karl, I'm no lawyer, but even I know that you could get considerable time off for good behavior and any lawyer Uncle Frederick hires should be good enough to persuade the judge to allow concurrent sentences. Now what do these lawyers think you should do?"

"They proposed a plea – meaning that I plead guilty to a lesser charge to reduce my prison time. They say I might end up serving only five years. After the publicity dies down, they believe I could be out on parole even earlier, especially since I have no criminal record and I've done lots of community-service work in Harlem."

"How long do you have to think about it?"

"The D.A. says I have until tomorrow morning at ten. That's his ultimatum."

"How kind of him. It sounds as if he just can't wait to go to trial and make a name for himself. I'd hate to give him that opportunity, but I can't stand the idea of having to accept all this."

"I can't stand it either. But if I do the plea, I'll do my best to behave in prison."

"Karl, I hate to be the one to tell you, but you're in all this trouble because you did not behave. If you had behaved at the Bavarian Inn, we wouldn't be living this nightmare."

"I had no choice. I couldn't let them kill Josh."

"Look, I need time to absorb all this. I need to say goodbye now. I'm going to the hospital to see how Josh is doing."

49. IDEAL COFFEE SHOP 86TH STREET, MARCH 11, 1936, 7:30 A.M.

The townhouse felt empty. Fern found that taking breakfast in the coffee shop made eating alone less of a chore, especially after many sleepless nights. Ernie, the huge Bavarian behind the counter, was always ready to talk about the events of day if she wasn't too tired. On this rainy morning, the shop had only two other customers, a well-dressed couple, sitting quietly at the far end of the long counter.

After trying to interest herself in the front page of the *Herald Tribune*, Fern pushed away her half-eaten scrambled eggs and gestured for the check.

"Hey, Dr. Fern, you got to do better than that if you want to eat here," Ernie said.

"I know. Zero appetite. Sorry."

Ernie took her money and returned with change. "No tip, please. I have a favor to ask," he whispered. "See that couple at the far end of the counter? They need a word with you. Hope you don't mind."

"Do you know them?"

"Yes, good people. From München. They've been in America for ten years. Nice family. Just go to a booth so you'll have some privacy."

Fern stood by a booth away from the counter as the couple approached. "Dr. Wagner, I am Fritz Mayer, and this my wife Ute. Please sit and talk with us. It won't take long."

Ernie delivered three cups of hot black coffee and left.

"Bitte, Herr Mayer, Frau Mayer."

Fritz Mayer pushed his coffee aside and laid his hand flat on the table as Fern took a seat opposite the couple. "Dr. Wagner, I know you're busy. And I am prepared to pay for what Ute and I are about to ask you."

"It concerns our son," Ute Mayer said.

"Has he been injured?"

"No, thank God," Ute Mayer replied. "He's healthy as a bull."

"Please go on."

"You see, Dr. Wagner, our son Jacob is a great student and a strong athlete. He's excelled in sports at DeWitt Clinton High School, near our home in the Bronx. He's an outstanding football player, a fullback. In fact, he won a football scholarship to Yale. He'll no doubt receive a fine education, one that will afford him great opportunities," Ute Mayer said.

"I earn a decent living as a marketing representative for the Ruppert Brewery," Fritz Mayer said, "and I could easily afford to send Jacob to a local college. But Yale and the Ivy League – well, such schools are out of the question without the scholarship."

"But you have the scholarship. So what's the problem?" Fern smiled.

"The problem, Dr. Wagner, is that we're Jews," Ute Mayer said, "and so of course Jacob is circumcised. He's already been subjected to locker-room ridicule from some of the Christian boys in his school. He's handled it well so far, but it could be worse at Yale. The university officials deny it, but we are realistic. Many Yale students are from anti-Semitic families. You know, they're in clubs that bar Jews, that sort of thing."

"I understand. I see it at the hospital. It's nothing like back in Berlin, but it's there. So what would you like from me?"

Fritz Meyer replied, both palms on the table. "Dr. Wagner, we don't want him to be harassed for his rather pronounced nose or because of his bareheaded penis."

Fern sipped her coffee. "Telephone me at the hospital this afternoon so we can schedule a get-acquainted visit and prepare for the required surgery. Easter vacation is coming up, Passover too. That should be a good time. We do a lot of nose jobs at the hospital, and the reverse circumcision procedure is performed many times more than you might expect. Actually, it's a procedure that dates back to ancient times."

"You're very kind," Fritz Mayer said. "What will all this cost?"

"The hospital will have its charges. After all, they have to keep the place running. But I like you both, and Ernie is a friend, so there's no fee."

"No, we must pay you something," Fritz Mayer insisted. "We didn't come here to beg. We came because Ernie said you were an exceptional doctor and a good person."

"I said I wouldn't charge a fee, and I meant it. But you can send a case of Ruppert to my home. I love the stuff. I'll give you the address."

In the weeks that followed, Fern performed five more reverse circumcisions on young Jewish boys, and two nose jobs on Jewish girls. She charged only a small fee. But the extra work helped keep her mind from slipping into the anger she felt for Karl and his failure to stay out of trouble. She scheduled the operations on her off days and put in more hours at the hospital. Still, she was lucky to get four hours of sleep, and her normally robust appetite remained absent. The unforgiving scale in the townhouse master bathroom told her she had lost twelve pounds in two weeks. She began to think of who could help. Not Josh, who was recovering but in no position to comfort her. Uncle Frederick had proved impossible to reach. His office said he was traveling on business. Desperate, she placed another trans-Atlantic call to him.

50. THE WHITE HOUSE, APRIL 14, 1936, 5:00 P.M.

Alone in the crowded East Room and feeling a little odd about it, Channing Brown broke into an uncertain grin when the tall black butler guided President Franklin Roosevelt's wheelchair through the gathering toward where Brown stood by a punchbowl. The President tilted his jaw upward toward Brown. "Good afternoon, Sir. I presume you're Mr. Channing Brown. I couldn't help but notice your handsome tweed suit. We don't have such high-quality wool here in the States, I must admit. Now just follow me. I have a place where we can talk."

Moments later they entered a smaller room, where the President gestured for the butler to close the door and leave. Roosevelt then nodded to acknowledge the presence of two other men, who rose from their seats at the round mahogany table.

"Mr. Brown, allow me to present Messrs. Harry Hopkins and Bill Donovan. Harry helps me run the store here in Washington. Bill practices law in New York, but helps me with overseas matters as well."

Roosevelt turned toward a tea cart that held a pitcher filled to the brim with orange liquid. The pitcher sat in a silver bucket full of chopped ice. "Shall I pour us each a whiskey sour?" Roosevelt asked. No one declined. He filled four long-stemmed cocktail glasses without spilling a drop. Brown could feel Roosevelt's charisma. It put them all at ease.

"Some liquid refreshment for Mr. Brown is definitely in order," Roosevelt said. "He's come a long way and through the good offices of Sir Crawford Ware, who dropped by the Oval Office for a tête-à-tête last Sunday afternoon. Sir Crawford exercises considerable influence in the London financial markets, where they buy a lot of our Treasury bonds. He asked whether Mr. Brown might stop by to tell us about a special project he's heading up. Mr. Brown leads a highly specialized cadre of intelligence and espionage agents within SIS. He's interested in hiring one of our own countrymen, an immigrant who's now a U.S. citizen and fellow New Yorker, a rather formidable young man all in all. Right now, that young man is my neighbor, residing as he does in Sing Sing Prison, less than fifty miles from my home in Hyde Park. His name is Karl Ludwig, and his case attracted considerable attention in the newspapers a few weeks ago."

"I've read about Ludwig," said Donovan, tasting the first sip of his sour. Hopkins had a yellow legal pad on his lap and began to write. "No notes, Harry," Roosevelt said, rolling his wheelchair back a few inches. "As you can see, Mr. Brown, you have our attention," the President said. "Tell us what you will."

Channing Brown took just five minutes to outline the project and identify the one man who Brown and his principals believed could achieve the objective. Brown's crisp presentation earned the cautious respect of the President and the others.

Roosevelt eyed Brown. "Mr. Brown, I think I understand your proposal. This Ludwig fellow appears to be a good enough chap who's been judged rather harshly in the press and by police and prosecutors. I can't help but think that a good New York lawyer like Bill here would have gotten him off the hook, but that's spilt milk. What's important now is to give Dr. Ludwig the opportunity to set out on the mission that Mr. Brown has described. That is, of course, if the doctor can stomach the risks."

"What do you think, Harry?" the President asked, turning toward Hopkins.

Hopkins looked back at Roosevelt then shifted his gaze toward Brown. "If this Ludwig fellow is foolish enough to take the job," Hopkins said, "then let's turn him loose and do what we can to make sure he's ready to kill the son of a bitch."

The President nodded.

"What about it, Bill?" Roosevelt said glancing toward Donovan.

"Harry's right, but it's still a big *if*. Ludwig will need all the incentives we can provide."

"Good point," Roosevelt said. "Although Mr. Brown is prepared to offer a generous financial award, there's much more than money at stake here – especially for a man with Ludwig's damaged reputation. He'll want a clean slate. I want a full pardon for him, so if he survives he can have a fresh start in his career. All this, of course, depends on his taking the job."

Glancing toward Hopkins, Roosevelt pointed to a phone on the table. "Harry, get someone at the White House switchboard to find Governor Herb Lehman up in Albany."

51. VISITING ROOM, SING SING PRISON, OSSINING, NEW YORK, APRIL 16, 1936, NOON

On her seventh visit to Sing Sing in three weeks, Fern told Karl the good news first. Josh was now out of bed and had begun walking the halls of New York Hospital in his bathrobe, recovering from surgery to repair his punctured lung. Bobby, with his brother's backing, would soon begin his office practice on West End Avenue in partnership with an established doctor. And Tim was on a round-the-world vacation, a present from his parents on completion of his residency.

Karl told Fern that he'd been working in the prison hospital. She mentioned the reverse circumcision she performed on a young man headed to Yale and how the work had won rave word-of-mouth reviews and several referrals. Such surgeries could, she told him, become a lucrative part of her practice.

On this visit, Karl noticed that Fern lacked the knowing grin she wore when she was happy, and now there was no life in her voice.

"I know you have something else to tell me, Fern," he said.

"Yes," she said, pressing her lips together. "I've been invited to teach at the University of Berlin, where Uncle Frederick is a trustee. I'd be teaching a course on the plastic surgery and treatment of severe burns. I've been told that I can publish my lectures as a medical school textbook once I put my notes together and refine them. The university will record and transcribe the lectures, so all I need to do is edit them to complete the book. The university's press will do the publishing. There's also an opportunity to be on the staff at Charité Hospital in Berlin."

He wanted to fall on the floor and beg her to stay. But he knew it was important not to hold her back, not to allow his jail time to slow her professional progress. He knew she wanted to go. Her ambition had always excited him, and it still did.

"Fern, this is a wonderful break for you," Karl forced himself to say. "You have to do it. It'll make me prouder of you than I've ever been, if that's possible."

"I wanted you to be a little heartbroken," Fern teased.

"That goes without saying."

"I have to leave in two days." Neither spoke for a moment.

"That soon?"

"Afraid so. Uncle Frederick has a good connection with the Deutsche Zeppelin-Reederei, so I can leave on the Hindenburg. I can get there early and prepare for the summer classes. Mother says I can stay at her house on the Tiergartenstrasse. Someday maybe we can visit there together."

"Yes, someday – after we're established in San Francisco we can go to Berlin on vacation."

She nodded *yes* and both fell silent for another moment.

"I think you should go now," Karl said, not meaning it. She put a finger to the glass partition and then blew a kiss.

She stood, turned toward the door, and left without looking back. That disappointed him. Moments later, outside the prison gate, Fern squinted in spring sunlight as she rushed to catch the train back to New York.

52. INMATES' RECREATION YARD, SING SING, APRIL 21, 1936, 2:35 P.M.

They caught him from behind. As he went down, Karl realized there were two of them – one who pinned him down while the other pummeled him. After two months of inactivity, Karl lacked the strength to fight back. It didn't matter much. It took the guard only seconds to break up the skirmish and separate the men. But the fight earned Karl a week in solitary.

53. SING SING, MAY 1, 1936, 7:55 A.M.

Karl had been out of solitary only two days when again two men jumped him from behind as he walked in the yard after breakfast. Two others quickly joined the fray – with three of them pinning him down while a fourth started kicking him in the face. He strained to throw them off, as before, but lacked the strength.

"What the hell do you guys want?" he gasped.

"Your balls, Kike sucker."

Karl had taken three kicks to the head before the guards intervened. He got another week in solitary.

54. SING SING, MAY 12, 1936. 10:00 A.M.

Karl was ready for them the next time they jumped him. There were three of them this time. When they came for him, Karl rolled with the tackle, grabbing the tackler by the belt, then standing and throwing his assailant to the ground before the other two took him down, one pounding his ear into the ground, the other punching his rib cage, turning him over and kicking his spine before the guard stopped it. This time Karl went to the infirmary on a stretcher.

55. SING SING, MAY 15, 1936, 8:00 A.M.

For the third straight day, Karl woke up stiff, with a pounding headache. Through the interior window he saw a prison guard posted outside his infirmary room. He'd started to drift back to sleep when he heard the familiar low-pitched voice of Dino Lamberti. Dino was standing next to his bed, Jordan DeWitt by his side. DeWitt waited for Karl to open his eyes before speaking.

"Sorry about your discomfort, Karl, but we're worried that this incident could kill any chance for early parole."

"Hell," Karl groaned. "I didn't do a damn thing. How much longer do I have to put up with this?"

"Not much, perhaps," answered DeWitt. "We'll explain."

Karl struggled up on his elbows. "Okay, I could use some good news."

"It seems," DeWitt continued, "that the Commandant of the U.S. Military Academy wants to improve the punching prowess of the Cadet boxing team. West Point isn't far, just across the Hudson, some twenty miles north of here.

"The Commandant has prevailed upon Warden Lawes to allow you to visit the Academy. The visit is scheduled for three weeks from now – early on the morning of June 6. You should have recovered by then. At West Point, the plan is for you to watch several intramural matches and share observations and pointers that will help the Cadets improve their boxing. The Cadets do their boxing early, between six and seven in the morning."

"I like being up early," Karl answered.

"Well it's good for us because no one else is paying much attention at that hour, especially since it will be a Saturday."

"So how do I get to West Point? I assume I'll travel under guard."

"You'll have two MPs from West Point, plus a driver," DeWitt went on. "Their military van will pick you up at the prison gate at five that morning. A prison guard will escort you up from your room here in the infirmary right to the prison gate. The Warden has received special authorization from Governor Lehman to take all steps necessary to keep you isolated here in the infirmary and under protective guard. There will be no slip-ups."

Karl was silent. He knew he had little to lose.

"Now comes the interesting part," DeWitt continued, his eyes riveted to Karl's. "Another man will visit you this morning, and we understand that he'll have a lot more to tell you. Neither Dino nor I know exactly what this man will propose. However, we know that if you do what he asks, you'll never have to return to Sing Sing. If you don't agree, all bets are off. You'll likely end up serving out your sentence here, plus whatever additional time you get for those three fights in the prison yard and for whatever else happens."

Karl grimaced. He didn't like DeWitt's tone but tried to suppress any signs of anger. A way out was a way out. He would grab it.

Then Dino spoke. "Nothing," he said, "comes without a price. You see, Karl, there are people who've taken a very active interest in your case. The man you're about to see represents those people. He can explain things."

"Okay, I'll see the guy. Now let me get some rest."

10:55 A.M.

One of the infirmary guards came to Karl's bedside to wake him and announce the visitor. Karl strained to throw off his sheet and blankets and dressed in a drab gray robe and slippers. He staggered on stiff legs as the guard led him to a small visiting room.

His visitor stood erect in a gray three-piece suit, a white button-down shirt, and a blue bow tie. He carried a slim leather portfolio. Karl felt immediate discomfort in the presence of this well-tailored stranger.

"Mr. Ludwig, my name is Channing Brown. Please forgive the intrusion." Brown gave Karl a firm handshake.

"Let's sit, Mr. Ludwig," Brown said, gesturing toward the small table under barred windows. His engaging British accent brought on Karl's first smile in days. Brown nodded for the guard to take his leave. "I'll be as direct as possible. I sometimes enjoy a bit of small talk before discussing important matters, but this is not one of those occasions. You see, Sir, I have a very serious proposition, one you may accept or reject on its merits – there'll be no salesmanship, no clouding of the issue on my part. Accept my proposition and you will gain release from this wretched place, not for one day but forever."

"Okay, I'm listening."

"My proposition would make you financially secure. I'm prepared to offer you one million British pounds, with an advance of half a million deposited in a numbered Swiss account. You'll receive the rest upon completion of the mission. We'll pay the balance even if we decide to abort the mission."

"What mission? So far, I don't get the joke. Somehow Sing Sing makes me lose my sense of humor."

"No joke, Mr. Ludwig. The risks you'll face are real. In fact, there are countless ways – many of them quite unsettling – in which this mission could result in your demise."

Brown offered Karl a cigarette from his pack of Camels. For the first time since he'd been a teenager back in Berlin, Karl considered taking one. He declined, knowing it would make him sick.

"Whatever you're asking me to do, how much time would it take?"

"Not possible to say, there are so many contingencies. Of course, there would be extensive training and planning before the hard part – the actual implementation, getting the thing done."

"Getting what done?"

"Killing someone, a specific individual."

"Well, Mr. Brown, you sure came to the right place. There are lots of killers here in Sing Sing. Just go to Death Row. There are guys there with nothing to lose. Not one son of a bitch among them who wouldn't jump at your offer. But not me. I'm no killer. I'm supposed to be a healer."

"None of your fellow inmates will do. You, on the other hand, are uniquely qualified."

"Me? I don't know a thing about guns."

"Perhaps not, Mr. Ludwig. But I have it from reliable sources that your fists can be as lethal as any gun. My colleagues and I have reviewed your record carefully. We've talked, discreetly of course, with various people around the boxing scene here in New York. We have several eyewitness accounts of your prowess. We've concluded that, given the right training, you would be quite capable of killing a man with a well-directed blow or blows to the neck, chin, nose, or head.

"As you'll no doubt recall," Brown went on, "six years ago in San Francisco, the German-American boxer Max Baer killed a lad named Frankie Campbell with a blow to the head that jolted Campbell's brain from its moorings. Campbell never woke up."

"Well, I'm no killer, Mr. Brown. But I'm curious, so tell me: Who is the lucky person you'd like me to kill with a hard right?"

"Adolf Hitler."

56. GRANT HOTEL, NEWARK, NEW JERSEY, MAY 15, 1936, 10:57 A.M.

Jamie Creel had just driven a Packard carrying three dozen sticks of dynamite over primitive back roads, from Ashland, Kentucky, to Newark, New Jersey, in thirty-two hours. Setting his hard suitcase down and writing a fictitious name in the hotel register, he spoke to the desk clerk in a well-practiced Kentucky twang. When Jamie reached the shabby fourth-floor room, Scotty North was already there, stretched out on one of the twin beds with his shoes off reading *Time*.

"Nice trip?" Scotty asked, looking up.

"A mite tiring, I don't mind telling you. Where's Brown?"

"Just rang in from Sing Sing. Said he's about to sign up the American bloke who would be our companion on the long voyage home. Brown says we should get some rest and be ready to move forward with matters at our end."

"Fill in the blanks for me," Jamie said.

Scotty sat up on the edge of his bed. "Brown worked it out tidy as can be with that chap Lucky and his henchman Minnelli. Tough blokes, those two. You wouldn't want to cross them, that's for sure. Brown and I spent the better part of two days going over things with them. Anyway, here's the bloody plan . . ."

57. SING SING PRISON, MAY 15, 1936, 11:21 A.M.

"Kill Hitler?" Karl said for a third time after several seconds of silence, raising his voice enough to make Brown wonder about who might hear. "Sing Sing, Mr. Brown, is a prison, not an insane asylum. I'm not crazy, not that crazy."

Channing Brown waited before speaking. "The real question, Mr. Ludwig, isn't how crazy you are but how smart you are. I dare say that you're smart enough to weigh the risk of remaining here, at the mercy of louts who take their recreation by beating you to within an inch of your life, against the risk of being the point person in a well-funded operation designed to eliminate an evil man and make you a very wealthy man."

"Yeah, one rich dead guy, the world is full of them."

Brown looked into Karl's eyes. Clearly the young man was not persuaded. "Consider also, lad, that should you choose to remain here, serve your time and, by some miracle, survive the punishment from your fellow inmates, you shall leave Sing Sing with only what you had when you arrived – precious little money, a revoked medical license, and an uncertain future. But accept our offer and you'll regain your license to practice medicine and the opportunity to earn a million pounds – not a bad place to be in this less-than-certain world."

Karl crouched forward, almost in a tuck. "What do I tell my fiancée? Will she know what I'm doing?"

"No. You must tell her nothing – for her protection as well as yours. She will believe, as will the rest of world, that you're quite dead. Part of our agreement will be that you cannot tell one living soul, especially her, until the fulfillment of your task."

"I don't know if I can do that."

"Then you can just settle in among the loving inmates of Sing Sing."

Karl eyed Brown. "Who's behind all this? Who in hell are you anyway? British? Australian? Or are you from somewhere else? Did you learn that accent in an English boarding school? An acting class? Believe it or not, I once spoke with an accent very similar to yours. That's the way I started learning it back in Berlin. You need to show me some credentials that prove to me who you really are. Right now I don't know anything or trust anyone, except what my lawyers tell me."

"You're quite right to be skeptical," Brown responded with sympathy. "You'd surely be the wrong man for the job if you were a trusting soul."

Brown showed Karl his SIS identification.

"That could be a phony ID."

"Quite right. But you did say that you trusted your lawyers, didn't you?"

Brown rose and stepped into the hallway, reappearing seconds later with Jordan DeWitt and Dino Lamberti. Brown nodded to DeWitt. "Please show Mr. Ludwig the documents," Brown said. DeWitt removed three envelopes from his briefcase and placed them on the table in front of Karl. "Our firm can vouch for these, Karl. They're authentic, all originals," DeWitt said, opening the first envelope.

DeWitt then placed a letter on the table, directly under Karl's nose. The stationery bore the word *Excelsior* in the Great Seal of the State of New York.

EXECUTIVE CHAMBER, ALBANY

May 15, 1936

By the authority vested in me as Governor under the Constitution and laws of the State of New York, I hereby grant a full pardon to Karl Ludwig for all crimes to which he pled guilty in Criminal Court, New York County, on March 31, 1936. This pardon shall take effect immediately and is irrevocable. Furthermore, I hereby reinstate the New York license to practice medicine of the same Karl Ludwig, effective the same date.

Herbert Lehman
Governor

DeWitt handed Karl another envelope. This one was from the White House. It contained a handwritten note.

THE WHITE HOUSE

May 15, 1936

Mr. Karl Ludwig:

I have met with the bearer of this letter, Mr. Channing Brown. I do hope you agree to what he proposes.

If you do agree, I assure you that I will take a personal interest in your progress.

FDR

His eyes fixed on the letters, Karl read each for a third time. Then he turned to Brown.

"Quite impressive, Mr. Brown. You promise wealth – wealth that I could never live to enjoy. My choice, as you present it, is whether to risk getting killed in this cage at the hands of anti-Semitic thugs or risk dying in some Nazi dungeon at the hands of German thugs, who, from what I've read, would very likely make my fellow inmates here seem like altar boys."

Brown nodded. "So what will it be, Mr. Ludwig?"

"You win, Mr. Brown. I'm in. Just give me a contract, one stipulating that the remuneration go to my estate should I fail to survive the mission, and naming Dr. Fern Wagner, my fiancée, as sole beneficiary."

Brown reached into his portfolio and produced a contract. "For reasons I'm sure you can understand, it's a bit vague," Brown said. "It states only that you are to perform 'a certain task.' We anticipated your insistence regarding the estate and your fiancée, so we've already included those provisions." Brown took a Waterman fountain pen from his suit jacket and unscrewed the cap as Karl pored over the document word for word. He wondered how they knew about Fern.

Karl read on. "Wait a minute," Karl said, "what's the Lloyd's Crawford Syndicate, Ltd.? Why am I contracting with a syndicate?"

"Very simply," Brown explained, "it's a private firm that has raised – or facilitated the raising of – the lion's share of the funds for this enterprise. In a sense, the Lloyd's Crawford Syndicate is your employer. Or, shall we say, your client. Please understand that, subject to change, this undertaking has no official connection to His Majesty's government, or, for that matter, to the government of the United States."

"Really? No official connection. What's that supposed to mean?"

"Quite candidly, it means that while I am indeed in the employ of His Majesty's government and head a special espionage-intelligence unit within the SIS, our conversations – and the enterprise I've identified – are not in any way official. The lot of it is off the record and off the books. And, if asked, I may have to deny that I ever heard of you."

Karl nodded and continued to read as Lamberti left the room.

"Before I sign," he said, "let me tell you one more thing. I have no intention of making this a suicide mission. My priority is to survive. Yes, Mr. Brown, I intend to stay alive and in one piece. Therefore, even though you'll train me and plan most of the mission, the final stage, the actual *coup de grâce* so to speak, will be up to me and only me. I alone must control the final execution of the plan – its time, its place, and everything that has to do with my survival. Use your fountain pen and write that down, right on the contract. Then I'll sign."

"All things considered, you make a reasonable request," Brown responded. He used the Waterman to add Karl's stipulation, then showed the amended document to Karl.

Karl signed the letter and handed it to DeWitt, who had remained in the room to witness the signing. "You're my lawyer. Make sure you keep this in safe place." He offered the pen back to Brown.

"No, you keep it. Let's call it a gift to memorialize the moment. Besides, in the months ahead, you'll endure many lectures, briefing papers, tutorials and, let us say, 'fieldwork.' You'll need to take copious, legible notes. I've always found that a fountain pen helps me to think better than I can with a pencil." Brown handed Karl yet another document. "Here, you should see this too," he said.

PRIVATE AND CONFIDENTIAL

The Executive Chamber
The Capitol
Albany, New York

May 15, 1936

Lewis E. Lawes
Warden of Sing Sing Correctional Facility
Ossining, N.Y.

Dear Warden Lawes:

Please allow inmate Karl Ludwig a special pass to visit the U. S. Military Academy at West Point on Saturday, June 6, 1936. Please also inform the Sing Sing correctional officers of Mr. Ludwig's plans and take all other necessary steps to ensure his safe passage and prompt exit through the main prison gate at 5:00 a.m.

The U.S. Army will transport Mr. Ludwig from Sing Sing to the Academy and will return him to Sing Sing by noon the same day. Mr. Ludwig will require no additional escort or assistance after he leaves Sing Sing.

Herbert Lehman
Governor of New York

Brown waited until Karl had finished reading. "I shall deliver this letter to the Warden in person before one o'clock this afternoon. The Governor has already telephoned him, telling him to expect me."

Back in his room, Karl saw a blue suit, white shirt, necktie, and black shoes laid out neatly on a table near the window. He put the clothes in a small closet and climbed back into bed. He knew he should have asked more questions but didn't yet know what they were. He also knew he needed to rest.

58. LUNA RESTAURANT, MANHATTAN, JUNE 6, 1936, 12:57 A.M.

Frankie Lenti and Lorenzo Polana finished stuffing themselves with lobster ravioli with marinara sauce and Chianti. Their next stop would be a brothel hidden in an old tenement building just off Canal Street. They looked up Mulberry Street for the parked Cadillac chauffeured by the young Enrico Donnelli, who helped them with the rough stuff on those who were slow to pay their debts. They decided to let young Enrico wait another hour while they took their pleasures. As they walked in the warm evening air, neither Frankie nor Lorenzo gave any notice to the black Packard parked on the far curb, away from the light of the corner lamppost.

Built like a fit middleweight, Frankie was a strong man and a sadistic intimidator. Just that afternoon, one poke from Frankie's middle finger into the ribs of an elderly Jewish tailor on Mott Street had been enough to persuade the old man to pay half of what he owed to Luciano's bookmakers. But that was just for openers. The real persuader was the punch in the stomach Frankie gave the tailor to remind him to pay the balance in three days.

Lorenzo was a rogue cop who had been on the pad for years, a precinct captain who gave Frankie, Enrico, and other friends of Luciano free rein south of 14th Street all the way down to Fulton Street. Lorenzo often accompanied Luciano's men on their rounds. For months, Lorenzo, Frankie, and Enrico had been skimming at least 5 percent off what should have been going to Luciano. What they didn't know was that Luciano's bookkeeper had done the math.

Anticipating fellatio and walking a few steps ahead of Lorenzo, Frankie took no notice as Minnelli slipped out from a darkened alcove. Less than thirty seconds, later the garrote slipped over Lorenzo's head and tightened around his neck. Frankie didn't hear Lorenzo drop dead softly to the sidewalk. By the time he heard the footsteps behind him and turned to see who it was, Minnelli gripped his head in an arm-lock and snapped his neck.

Enrico Donnelli remained in the Cadillac. He was already dead. Ten minutes before, Minnelli had forced him out of the car at gunpoint, then stepped up from behind and broke his neck.

In the dark alcove of a bakery, two of Minnelli's goons stripped the three dead men to the buff. They stuffed Frankie's body into fresh underwear, socks, shoes, and a blue wool suit of the kind given to Sing Sing prisoners traveling to court appearances. Minnelli's men dressed the other two in U.S. Army Military Police uniforms, complete with official identification and counterfeit dog tags.

1:21 A.M.

Scotty North jumped from the front seat of the Packard according to plan and helped Minnelli's men cram the three corpses into the trunk.

At the wheel, Jamie Creel flashed the headlights to signal Minnelli, standing in the doorway of Luna, that the first phase of the operation had come off without a hitch.

Back on the sidewalk, Minnelli paid the two men, giving them each a plain white envelope. "It's all there, you guys. Thanks for a clean operation – no mess, not a drop of blood. Our late friends were in the habit of visiting that whorehouse on Canal Street after dinner, so the ladies there expect some business. Let's not disappoint them."

59. NORTHBOUND ON ROUTE 9 NEAR YONKERS, JUNE 6, 1936, 1:31 A.M.

The drive north out of Manhattan was uneventful. Jamie Creel had driven the route twice earlier to make sure they knew the way in the dead of night. "Any trouble driving on the right side of the road?" Scotty asked.

"I had plenty of bloody time to get used to it on the drive up from Kentucky," Jamie replied. "Keeps a bloke on his toes, but then so does the fact that we've got three dead blokes in the trunk and enough dynamite to start a war. Try explaining that to a traffic copper."

Scotty turned on the radio and managed to find dance music broadcast from the Hotel Astor Roof Garden in Manhattan. They relaxed into the drive, Jamie staying under the speed limit.

60. BEAR MOUNTAIN BRIDGE ROAD, ON THE EAST BANK OF THE HUDSON, JUNE 6, 1936, 4:00 A.M.

Patrolling the winding, cliff-side road some two hundred feet above the Hudson, Trooper Jack Sweeney welcomed the order that came over the two-way radio from his headquarters in Newburgh. His orders were to end his predawn cruise and return to the barracks for a meeting. He paid little heed to the military van that passed him heading north.

61. BEAR MOUNTAIN BRIDGE ROAD, NEAR PEEKSKILL, NEW YORK, 5:30 A.M.

Jamie brought the Packard to a careful stop alongside the guardrail of the cliff-side road and turned off the headlights. Scotty stamped out his cigarette. They took several seconds to let their eyes adjust to the dark of the clear moonless night. Scotty jumped from the Packard and jogged to the place where the road took a sharp turn. Two nights before, after driving up from Newark, he had come to the same spot, one where the road took a sharp left-hand turn. With a wrench, he had loosened the bolt that held the guardrail. Now he took a moment to look down at the railroad tracks below, a two hundred-foot drop. He heard a vehicle approaching and fell face down on the gravel near the guardrail. When the car passed, he stood and trotted back toward the Packard and waited.

After ten long minutes, a military van approached, heading north and rolled to a gentle stop at the side of the road next to the Packard. In the van, Channing Brown sat next to the driver, who was dressed in the uniform of a U.S. Army corporal with an MP armband. In the rear of the van. another MP sat next to Karl Ludwig.

With the first hint of daylight to the east, Brown and Scotty North moved the still- warm corpses from the Packard to the idling van. They gently placed Frankie, dressed in a blue suit of the same make that Karl wore, in the rear seat of the van, then cuffed his hands behind his back and stuffed a wallet with Karl's prison ID in the vest pocket. They shoved Lorenzo's remains, dressed in an MP uniform, next to Frankie. The dead Enrico went right next to the driver's seat just before Jamie jumped in behind the steering wheel. Through the open window, Scotty handed Jamie the cluster of twelve sticks of Kentucky dynamite. Jamie placed them on the floor of the van and lit the fuse as Scotty ran to the Packard to join the others. No stranger to explosives, Jamie knew he had thirty seconds to do the rest of it.

5:35 A.M.

Jamie put on leather gloves and used a clean handkerchief to wipe any fingerprints from the steering wheel and dashboard. It took a little effort to ignore Enrico's uniformed corpse seated beside him at the wheel.

"Holy Mother Mary," Jamie whispered, blessing himself.

He shifted out of neutral, and slammed his foot on the accelerator from his cramped perch in the driver's seat. In three seconds, he had shifted up into second gear and opened the driver's-side door. The speedometer jumped to 30 mph. The tortured engine began to scream, and Jamie saw the guardrail speeding toward him.

He jumped to Mother Earth and rolled, a technique learned in the Royal Marines. He was still rolling when he heard the explosions, first the dynamite, then the crash of the van. He stayed down for all of five seconds to shield himself from the force of the blast, then dashed to the open door of the waiting Packard, which had already begun to move.

62. SOUTHBOUND ON ROUTE 9, APPROACHING MANHATTAN, 6:00 A.M.

They drove in silence in the early-morning light. By now Jamie had caught his breath, and Brown had made the introductions. The two uniformed MPs were, in fact, FBI special agents on assignment from Washington. They would accompany Brown and his companions to the Mandalay Star, a freighter scheduled to depart New York for Liverpool at 7:00 a.m. The agents would then return the Packard to the FBI motor pool in Washington. The FBI men, both young bachelors, were in the process of being transferred to a new South American intelligence unit, an assignment that would place them in the remoter regions of Brazil and Argentina for the next three years. They understood that what had transpired that morning would require no report, written or oral. It was a secret each would carry to his grave.

63. WEST POINT, 6:19 A.M.

The Commandant had just lathered his face to shave when the phone rang. He rushed to grab it, not wanting to disturb his wife. It was a desk sergeant at the Newburgh station of the New York State Police. There'd been a horrible accident, the sergeant explained. The van carrying Karl Ludwig from Sing Sing to West Point had somehow failed to negotiate a sharp turn on the Bear Mountain Bridge Road and crashed through the guardrail. No one had survived.

64. ABOARD THE MANDALAY STAR, LOWER NEW YORK BAY, 8:00 A.M.

As they passed Staten Island on the starboard side, the four men leaned against the ship's rail and maintained a watchful silence, each alert to the possibility that a speedy police launch could cut over the calm waters to intercept them. Channing Brown scanned the horizon through binoculars as the Mandalay Star passed through the Narrows between Staten Island and Brooklyn. Jamie, Scotty, and Karl also watched the horizon, each taking an occasional look back to assure himself that no police patrol boat or Coast Guard launch was speeding to catch up with them.

"We'll pass the three-mile limit soon, lads," Brown said. "Once that's behind us, let's find the galley and treat ourselves to a measure of Johnny Walker and some breakfast. Then let's get some sleep. We can reconvene at dinner tonight."

Once in the galley, Brown proposed a toast to Karl and the entire team. Then he saluted Jamie Creel for having "the stones" to do what he'd done on the cliff-side road. They drank a little and ate well — sausage, bacon, and fried eggs, with lots of bread. "Let's not even attempt serious discussion now, lads," Brown said. "We're all too tired to say anything intelligent." He saw that Karl had spoken very little and knew the young doctor needed some time to think.

After breakfast, Karl found himself alone in the bunk of his cramped cabin. Small though the cabin was, it was heaven compared to Sing Sing. He fell into a dreamless sleep.

65. BY THE ASSOCIATED PRESS, ALBANY, NY, JUNE 7, 1936

Governor Herbert Lehman announced today that he has directed the State Police to expand its investigation into the Bear Mountain Bridge Road crash of a military van that resulted in the death of Sing Sing inmate Karl Ludwig and two military policemen.

According to the State Police, questions about the accident remain. They said there is evidence that the van was carrying dynamite or some other explosive material. The van was totally destroyed by fire, and the passengers' bodies burned beyond recognition.

Ludwig, a physician and former prizefighter, had recently completed his residency in orthopedic surgery at New York Hospital in Manhattan. He pleaded guilty to three counts of assault with a deadly weapon following his role in a March brawl at the Bavarian Inn, a Yorkville restaurant. The fight reportedly involved members of the German-American Bund.

According to prison officials, Ludwig was en route to West Point, where he was to coach intramural boxing at the request of the Academy's commandant. West Point officials could not be reached for comment.

66. BERLIN, JUNE 9, 1936, 7:00 P.M.

Now that she'd begun to settle in, Fern spent most of her evenings either at the university doing laboratory work or talking shop with students and fellow faculty members over a light meal and a beer. On this night, however, she sat in her mother's spacious kitchen listening, over dinner, to Hildy Wagner's take on life in Berlin – the receptions and the new faces, mostly Nazi Party and military types, it seemed – when the telephone intruded. Hildy Wagner, tall and fit at fifty-three, rose from the table and hurried to the telephone, which sat on a credenza in the hallway. "It's for you, Fern. A Dr. Greenberg from New York."

"Fern?" The connection from New York was clear of the usual static and crackle that went with trans-Atlantic calls. As soon as he spoke her name, Fern could tell that Josh was nervous.

"Was that your mother? It's good that someone is with you."

"Someone with me? Why?"

"I have the worst possible news."

Fern stiffened. She knew it had to be about Karl. She sank into a small chair in the dark hallway.

"Fern, Karl's dead. It was an accident. A van he was traveling in crashed in upstate New York."

"No . . ."

"I'm afraid it's true, Fern. I'm so sorry."

She said nothing for a moment, her mind in denial, rejecting what she'd just heard. She had been so selfish. She had left him there in Sing Sing, and now he was dead.

"Are you there, Fern? Did you hear me?"

Fern's mind raced back to the Bavarian Inn, the Tombs, and her fare-well meeting with Karl at Sing Sing. Her fingers were ice. Karl dead. Unacceptable. Impossible. After several seconds of silence, she asked Josh to repeat everything.

Josh confessed that he had put off calling her for two days. He had finally summoned the courage to break the news to her. He worried that she might learn about it from someone else or see it in some news report. When she asked, Josh told her that Karl's remains had been burned beyond recognition and that he, Bobby, and some other friends were planning a memorial Mass.

Fern's mind raced ahead. She would return to New York as soon as she could book passage on the Zeppelin. Fern put down the receiver with a whispered goodbye.

Sensing that something was wrong, Hildy Wagner came into the dark hallway. She'd picked up the essence of the conversation from the kitchen. Her English was excellent. She led Fern back to the dining room, opened the liquor cabinet, and poured two large snifters of brandy. Fern stared at the wall, not saying a word. Since her return to Berlin, she had confided very little about Karl to her mother. After finishing her second brandy, she rambled on about what Josh had told her – and about Karl and their dream of going to California together. She didn't cry. She'd wait until she was alone to do that.

67. ABOARD THE MANDALAY STAR, NORTH ATLANTIC, WEST OF LANDS END, JUNE 12, 1936, 7:00 A.M.

Wearing an oilskin jacket the captain had lent him, Channing Brown gripped the starboard railing as the Mandalay Star sliced through the waves and foam of the North Atlantic. He felt a small measure of satisfaction at having pulled off the New York operation. Karl was out of prison and on the team. He'd even begun to eat well and take long, solitary walks on deck. Brown knew Karl needed time alone. He had given Karl that time since they had left New York. But now it was time to further educate Karl on the price of his freedom.

"What do you say we have a spot of breakfast in the galley?" Brown asked as Karl approached. "I've arranged with the captain for us to have some privacy this morning. He's been paid enough not to ask questions. Just for your information, I've told him we're all returning from work in the Oklahoma oil fields, where the pay was good. He seemed fine with that."

"He may not have any questions, but I sure do."

"Quite understandable. So let's eat and talk."

Once they'd finished their eggs and bacon, Brown poured them each a second coffee and looked around to make sure the cook was done cleaning up and had left them alone. "Let me tell you more of what's ahead."

"Shoot."

"I'll start with some good news. Beginning at nine this morning, Zurich time, a numbered account was opened for you with an initial deposit of a half-million pounds sterling. There's another account, in a different Swiss bank, in which we've deposited ample funds for, shall we say, 'out-of-pocket' expenses related to your mission. In time, we will put that money in a Berlin account, which you can access as needed."

Brown handed Karl a letter-size envelope. "A slip of paper inside has the number of each account," Brown told him. "Memorize them, and then burn the paper."

"Okay, Brown. I need to know more about who's depositing this money. Who the hell am I really working for?"

"Fair question. What you need to understand, Karl, is that you now belong to a special espionage team, a self-contained unit within SIS, His Majesty's Secret Intelligence Service. Sometimes referred to as MI6, SIS is concerned exclusively with foreign intelligence. Under its umbrella, our unit gathers information and makes mischief in foreign jurisdictions. Our unit is independent and self-directed. We leave no fingerprints and receive no accolades. As we discussed, your mission is in no way an official operation of His Majesty's Government."

Brown offered Karl a cigarette, which he waved off.

"We've recruited people from all over the world, but most of our operatives are British subjects. A few, like you, are native Germans," Brown explained.

"Okay, when do I start?"

"First you'll undergo some rigorous training and instruction. Then you'll be sent to Berlin, where you'll work to get close to Hitler."

"At least within punching distance," said Karl, "with no one else around and a way to survive."

"Yes, that'll be the trick of it," Brown said.

68. JOSH GREENBERG'S APARTMENT, JUNE 13, 1936, 9:00 P.M.

Josh tightened the sash on his cotton bathrobe and took in the view of the East River and the bridges stretching out to Long Island. Then he sat down at the small desk in his bedroom and began typing on his portable Smith Corona.

Dearest Fern,

First I'd like to tell you about the memorial Mass we held for Karl. You would have been proud. Just about everyone Karl knew from the hospital was there. There were several eulogies. Bobby and I each did one. And there was one by his old Irish landlady, Mrs. Hanrahan. She talked about how Karl got heart medicine for her from the hospital dispensary. I believe she thinks he stole the stuff for her. (I happen to know Karl paid for it!) Max Levin and a half-dozen or so of Karl's boxing friends showed up, including a young Irishman, one of the kids whose jaw I fixed back in the old days. So did Jack Elwood, the owner of the clothing shop on 125th Street, and several other Harlem and Yorkville business guys, including Ernie from the Ideal Coffee Shop. More than a dozen of the Negro boys who Karl shepherded through the youth boxing program also came. Elwood arranged for the Harlem Boys Choir to sing. It was all quite beautiful, not a dry eye in the church.

Hope you can get back to New York soon. Since I haven't heard from you, I presume you're having some trouble with your passport or something. From what I read, it's not that simple getting out of Germany these days.

As for me, I'm beginning to walk around the neighborhood more and feeling stronger every day. My punctured lung has healed nicely. So have my ribs. I still get headaches, but they go away faster now. I'm looking forward to long walks in the park with my new girlfriend, Nancy Corrigan. She's incredible. She's really helped me get back on my feet. She was assigned to me as a private-duty nurse the night of the fight at the Bavarian Inn. She came to New York from California and started at the hospital only last January. She never met Karl, but she remembers you from the OR. I'll write more about her later.

I'm going to skip the clichés about how life goes on. You know you have a friend in New York. I'm here if you need me.

Please stay in touch.

Love always,

Josh

P.S. I read your latest article on facial restructuring surgery in the New England Journal of Medicine – great information and insight.

69. LONDON, JUNE 19, 1936, 8:30 A.M.

Brown had sequestered Karl in the Green Park, a small Mayfair hotel on Half Moon Street – a brisk twenty-minute walk to Whitehall. Most of the other guests were business travelers with second-tier enterprises. Karl spent much of his time at the hotel reading reports Brown had given him – reports on Germany, on Hitler and the Nazis, and on a territory once known as German East Africa. Karl made careful notes with the Waterman pen Brown had given him back at Sing Sing.

Brown and Karl met for lunch every day, and the two men would question each other. Occasionally, Brown would invite Karl to Whitehall where there were special maps and reports which, for security reasons, had to remain on government property. On some days, Scotty North and Jamie Creel would join the discussion.

On his way to Whitehall one muggy summer morning, Karl observed a parade of students carrying pro-Communist placards exhorting workers to support the Loyalist cause in Spain. Once seated with Brown, Creel, and North at the small conference table in the library that adjoined Brown's office, Karl mentioned that the young men he had seen in the parade appeared well dressed – in marked contrast to the factory workers he'd seen at "Red Rallies" at Union Square in New York.

"They're down from Oxford or Cambridge on summer holiday with nothing to do," Brown explained. "Both places are a breeding ground for Reds and pro-Soviet types. Many today at Whitehall argue that we should not dismiss such students out of hand. Only five years ago there were fewer than 3,200 known Communists in Britain, most of them members of tiny cells.

Now, thanks to the worldwide Depression, along with Stalin and his louts in Moscow, we're up to our necks in them."

"So what are you doing about them?" Karl asked.

"Not much," Brown replied, "though we know they bear watching. Through SIS sources, we know that the Soviets are in no position to challenge us in any military way. Stalin, we've learned, has been purging his top military of all those suspected of disloyalty. Such purges won't strengthen the Soviet military. Germany, on the other hand, is getting stronger every day. The so-called Führer's popularity is growing, and he seems quite eager to play King of the Hill in Europe. He, too, has supporters right here in Britain. Many of them view German resurgence as a welcome bulwark against Red Russia. Of course, they'd go barking mad if they had even a hint of our little enterprise."

"Okay. Thanks for the education. I won't forget it. What's next?"

"A weekend off in London, lad. Lord knows you have one coming. Just relax. Do whatever you'd like, within reason of course. Just please don't get into any fights. And rest up for what's ahead."

"And what would that be? I've had my fill of surprises."

"Well here's another. At 5:00 a.m. on Monday a Royal Air Force driver will call at your hotel and take you to the aerodrome at Croydon. There you'll rendezvous with Scotty, who'll escort you."

"What should I bring?"

"Nothing," Scotty said. "A suitcase packed with everything you need will be waiting for you on the plane."

70. LONDON, JUNE 20, 1936, 1:45 P.M.

It was a muggy summer Saturday, and Karl walked on impulse toward the Theater District, where he bought a single ticket for a matinee performance of Noel Coward's *Tonight at 8:30* just as the curtain was about to go up. He needed a few laughs but soon felt quite alone among the giggling couples. No fun to laugh alone. He got up and walked out.

Back at his hotel, the desk clerk handed him his daily bundle of German newspapers. After washing up, he decided on a beer and sandwich in the hotel taproom, with the *Berliner Morgenpost* for company. Scanning the sports pages, he read with relish a feature on Max Schmeling and another on the upcoming Berlin Olympics.

Over his smoked salmon sandwich, he mused on what life might be like in his old hometown. He knew Fern would be there. He had been trying not to think about her. Just an hour earlier in the theater, he thought he heard her laughing. Of course, that was silly. But it wasn't at all silly to think of her in Germany. Was there some way he could let her know he was alive? See her on the sly? No. That would be far too dangerous for both of them. A more realistic but worrisome thought was that once he was in Germany, he and Fern could run into each other entirely by chance. Had Brown figured on the Fern factor? He must have. Yet Brown had said nothing of Fern. Had she gone back to America? Anything was possible. Karl knew that Brown was far too thorough to have overlooked a chance encounter that could wreck the mission.

A voice invaded his privacy.

"*Haben Sie eine Zigarette?*"

"*Nein.*"

"That's quite all right."

"Sorry," Karl said, looking up, "you startled me with the German." He saw a tall handsome woman standing over him.

"Please excuse the intrusion. I just thought you might be German," she said. "I noticed the newspaper. I haven't been there since I was little girl. Actually, I don't even smoke."

"Neither do I."

"Thank goodness. I loathe smoking. It's left a terrible taste in the mouths of some of the men I've kissed."

"And bad for the lungs," Karl added. He hadn't been this close to any woman, especially an attractive one, since that last day with Fern in the visiting room at Sing Sing.

As a precaution against such surprises, Karl introduced himself using an agreed-upon false name, just as Channing Brown had instructed. "I'm Karl Vollmer, from Madison, Wisconsin," he said, rising from his seat.

"Please sit. My name is Constance Crosby, and I'm off to meet some friends in a few minutes. We motored up from Cambridge to hit the pubs and catch some theater." Before he could respond, she explained that her friends were all staying in different hotels. "Poor planning, but I like this hotel. I always try to stay here. It's rather nice, tucked away as it is, don't you think?"

"Well it's not bad for a transient American. Many of my friends from the University in Madison stay here," he said. "Will you join me for an ale?"

"I'd prefer a pinot grigio, actually. I'm meeting my friends soon, so I have to dash off momentarily."

He let her ramble on about herself and learned that she was an assistant to a language professor at Cambridge. Her job, she explained, was translating nineteenth-century German documents. He described himself as an assistant professor of German at the University of Wisconsin.

They spoke in German. As far as Karl could tell hers was flawless, although she'd obviously learned it at an English school. She talked so much about herself that she never asked what he was doing in London.

Her goodbye was as quick as her hello. "Perhaps we'll run into each other again," she said, rising to leave. "I rather hope we do," she whispered, taking his hand in hers.

71. LONDON, JUNE 21, 1936, 2:00 P.M.

After a long sleep, a hot shower, and a late in-room lunch, Karl went straight to the empty hotel taproom, eased onto a bar stool, ordered a Whitbread, and lost himself in reflection. Since leaving prison, he'd spent nearly every waking moment when he wasn't alone with Brown and his people – except for the moment he'd spent yesterday with the woman who called herself Constance.

How in the hell had he gotten himself into this fix? And now that he'd agreed to work with Brown, how was he going to pull it off? Would he ever get back to medicine? To Fern? It might have been smarter to stay in prison. No, that was stupid. Someone had been out to get him there. But who? Why?

Brown had gotten him out of there. Now he was beginning to understand the price, which included being alone a lot. At least it was easier than trying to stay alive back at Sing Sing.

He was on his second sip of Whitbread when he felt her soft touch on his shoulder.

Constance Crosby slipped onto the bar stool beside him. "Last night was great fun. I should have asked you to join us. We really cut up a bit, the lot of us. Now I need some hair of the dog. Be a love and order me a glass of pinot grigio."

"You seem a bit out of sorts," she said, sensing his gloom.

"It's just the heat," he lied. "It never gets this hot in Wisconsin," he lied again, never having been there. She told him how she and her friends had done a pub crawl in the West End the night before. He was content to listen.

"I have a mind to suggest a change in scenery," she said. "It's too hot and stuffy here, don't you agree? I know a lively little bar just around the corner – on Waverton Street. What do you say we have a look?"

Constance was right. The pub on Waverton proved to be the perfect tonic, bright and cheerful, with attractive people three deep at the bar, all engaged in intense chatter. Karl had just handed Constance her second glass of wine when four well-dressed Americans, one striking woman and three men, entered the place and started working their way toward the busy bar. Karl recognized the woman as the actress Carole Lombard. He kept talking to Constance.

He found Constance stunning in the smoky afternoon light. As she spoke, she ran her fingers through her dark shoulder-length hair.

"You're a cool customer," she said. "Most men would have gotten all worked up seeing a star from the pictures up close. You barely noticed. I find that quite curious, rather charming as a matter of fact."

"Maybe it's the reserved German-Midwesterner in me."

Karl nursed his beer as Constance tossed down another glass of wine. She remained remarkably lucid, talking at length about Cambridge, her job, her friends. Finishing her third drink, she slipped her middle finger gently under his belt.

"It's crowded in here, isn't it?" she whispered. They left the pub and hurried toward the hotel as loud claps of thunder announced a sudden early evening thunderstorm. He followed her to her room. She said nothing as he followed her inside. Their kissing was gentle at first and soon he was rock hard. "It's been so long for me," he said.

"Wonderful," she murmured as she undid his belt buckle, unbuttoned his trousers, and began fondling him. Karl's arms fell to his side and she felt him go limp. Constance stepped back while Karl stared at the floor.

"What?" she began to ask.

"Not your fault, Constance. Please understand. I can't."

He expected a reaction, but there was none.

He rebuttoned his pants in the dark.

"Girl back in Madison?" she asked.

"Something like that," he said. She took a firm grip of his arm and led him back into the hallway. He could hear her throwing the bolt behind him.

In the morning, he asked the desk clerk whether he'd seen her and learned that she had already checked out.

72. ADLON HOTEL, BERLIN, JUNE 30, 1936, 6:00 P.M.

Under a wide-brimmed straw hat, Fern took a seat at the bar and removed her long white gloves. Feeling a tap on her shoulder, she turned to embrace her uncle.

"What's kept you from seeing me for so long?" she asked.

"Business for the most part," he responded.

Fern closed her eyes and forced a smile. "I'm trying to live with that, Uncle."

"I know – but the issue is *how*. I've talked with your mother. She tells me you're working too much, not having the fun a beautiful young professional woman should be having in Berlin, especially now that summer's here."

"Fun is for later. Right now I feel as if I have to throw myself into my practice. I'm affiliated with the Charité Hospital and, thanks to you, I teach at the university. That's in addition to preparing the lectures, which you arranged for me. The work keeps my mind off Karl. To twist a phase from Karl Marx, 'Work is the opiate of the grieving class.' Exercise, too. I've been playing a lot of tennis with Mother."

"Well," said Frederick, "let's have a martini."

"I'd love to," she whispered. "This will be the first strong drink I've had since the night I learned of Karl's death, when I drank brandy with Mother until I went numb and got sick. What a hangover I had! And speaking of Mother, she seems to have found a lot of new friends among government and military people. It's quite a circle of high-ranking generals and Party officials, I'm afraid."

"I can take some credit – or blame – for that, I think," Frederick said. "I've introduced your mother to many of them. She's been showing some old-fashioned Berlin hospitality to her new friends, many of whom are from Bavaria, you know, longtime Nazis."

The arrival of the martinis interrupted Frederick.

"Well," Fern said, savoring the bite of the gin on her palate, "your friends have made a quite an impression on her."

"Oh?"

"Yes, she appears enthralled and far too impressed. Last week I received a letter from Josh Greenberg, a friend of Karl's and mine from New York. Naturally, his name and address were on the envelope. Mother was afraid the concierge in our apartment building would report us for receiving mail from an American Jew. She believes the Gestapo may have actually read the letter and may have been listening to my telephone conversation with him."

Frederick fixed his eyes on Fern and saw with relief that the people scattered around the bar were out of earshot and caught up in their own gossip. Still, he lowered voice.

"I'm afraid I share your mother's concerns," he said. Fern nodded to let him know he had her attention. "Listen to me, Fern. I know what's going on in Germany these days. It's not like what you've grown accustomed to in New York. Understand this, my dear," he said lowering his voice even further. "This is *not* the time to be corresponding with a Jewish friend in New York."

"*Gott im Himmel*, Uncle," Fern said through clenched teeth. "I can hardly stop Josh from writing! Remember, this was Karl's best friend. I just lost Karl. Can't I get a letter from his friend?"

"I remember Josh. A free spirit. But no matter. We all need to be careful."

"One letter?"

"Let me be blunt, Fern. You must let Josh know that getting such letters could jeopardize your well-being here. In fact, it would be better if you dropped him altogether."

"It's that serious?"

"Indeed it is. I don't know everything, of course, but it's entirely possible that someone opened and read your letter, especially since there was a Jewish name on the envelope. The Nazis want to know everything. The Gestapo has taken over the municipal police here in Berlin and just about everywhere else. They're tightening their grip on everyone and everything – and that includes letters from New York and the people who receive them."

"Letters are something they can use against you if they want to," Frederick went on. "Phone calls too. Eavesdropping on telephone talk is easy, and then there are the billing records. Believe me, they will monitor your phone calls. You see, Fern, the trouble isn't just with the police. It's with nearly everyone – the people at the telephone exchange, neighbors, your mother's new friends, and yes, even the concierge in your mother's apartment building."

"Go on, Uncle, I'm listening," Fern said, closing her eyes and nodding.

"The Nazis are pervasive. It's in their nature. They've got block captains who gather information about people. Information on a woman like yourself, someone who's spent several years living in America, who has a Jewish friend writing to her from New York – all that is irresistible to block captains, concierges, and other busybodies eager to feed tidbits to the Gestapo."

"Okay, Uncle Frederick, you know a lot. Tell me, how much are you mixed up with the Nazis?"

"There's no way for someone in my position to avoid getting involved with them. Years ago, when I returned to Germany after building a business in London, I saw that certain German firms had tremendous investment potential – manufacturers of aircraft, auto parts, farm tractors, radio tubes, and pharmaceuticals. They all needed capital. So that's where I put my money. At the same time, I had to be a realist. I knew that without help, any firm that I might invest in could never compete with giants like Krupp, I.G. Farben, Messerschmitt, and Bayer. So I took a train down to Munich and met with a fellow I'd known since 1912, an aviator who made a name for himself during the war and went into politics afterwards. His name is Hermann Göring. I'm sure you've heard of him. Shortly thereafter I became a financial contributor to the Nazi Party. Yes, Fern, I paid my dues, and I've done very well for myself, and for your mother and you. Say what you will about the Nazis, they take care of their friends."

"Sounds dreadful," Fern said, being careful to keep her voice low.

"That may be, Fern, but it's the reality. What you need to do now is settle in and become a good German. Make some new friends. Keep on with your career and become important in your field."

"Will I be allowed to participate in international medical conferences?"

"Perhaps. But for the time being, you should forget about jumping ship or leaving Germany for good. If you were to defect, there's no telling what would happen to your mother."

"You mean I'm stuck here? That idea gives me what the Americans call 'the creeps.'" Fern finished her martini with a long determined swallow. Frederick decided on another round of drinks and signaled the bartender.

"Fern, I don't mean to frighten you, but you must listen. What I haven't told you yet is that Reinhard Heydrich, the man second only to Himmler in the Gestapo, called me this morning. He and I do some fencing from time to time at the Berliner Sportverein, a club frequented by the Nazi brass. He wanted me to know the real reason your request for passage on the Hindenburg was denied. He said that as a doctor you're an extremely valuable resource to the Reich, and that there's too much risk that you'd stay in America and not return to Germany – which, he assured me 'would not be in the best interest of you or the Reich.'"

"You mean I should have done as Karl said and become a U.S. citizen?" she said staring into her drink.

Frederick said nothing, but gave a gentle affirmative nod as she looked at him. He gestured to the bartender and paid the bill. After a curbside hug, he put Fern in a taxi for her mother's apartment. The night air had become pleasant and he decided on a walk to refresh himself. Confronting Fern with what she did not want to hear had drained him.

73. POLICE HEADQUARTERS, BERLIN, JUNE 30, 1936, 11:30 P.M.

Chief Detective Hans Krebs let the unlit cigarette dangle from his tired face as he typed out a report.

From the corner of his right eye, Krebs could see Otto Geissler, his new boss and a Gestapo man, seated smugly at his corner desk beyond the glass partition. Geissler's presence at the station was part of Reichsführer Himmler's move to centralize control of law enforcement agencies throughout the Reich. Hans stuck to his work. Fifteen years of police work had taught him to see, hear, and speak no evil.

A veteran of the Marne and Verdun, Hans had killed ten Frenchmen in a single day – six with his rifle and four with a pistol. He liked being a detective in Berlin, working in the Zitadelle, a district that included the Reichstag, the Foreign Office, the prestigious Adlon Hotel, and most of the city's major embassies, including the American.

At six foot two, Hans Krebs was an instantly recognizable figure in cafés and shops all over the city, equally well known among Wilhelmstrasse bureaucrats and Berlin underworld characters. Years before, as a young beat cop, he had acquired a reputation for his deadly accuracy with a handgun. He had shot his way to notoriety in gunfights with bank robbers and in armed conflicts with rabble-rousers in the unrest following the Kaiser's war. A long list of dead criminals attested to his prowess as a marksman.

Since his promotion to detective, he was best known for cracking the toughest cases – homicides, drug rings, high-profile burglaries, bank robberies, and tracking down hard-to-find suspects. His list of informants was the best in Berlin.

Hans ripped the sheet from the typewriter, read it carefully, and walked it over to Geissler. "It's all here," Hans said. "Two of my men have been tailing her since she got that overseas telephone call from New York. She left her apartment at five thirty in the afternoon. She walked straight to the bar at the Adlon, where she met a man who looked to be in his late fifties. It has all the trappings of her having an affair with some rich older guy. But guess what, Geissler. When they asked the bartender if he knew the man, they found out it was Frederick Wagner, head of Wagner Industries. This guy's part of Hitler's inner circle. And we learned that the lady is Herr Wagner's niece. Wagner put her in a taxi. Our guys jumped in another taxi and followed her to a home on the Tiergartenstrasse. She went straight in and didn't come back out that evening. The lady lives there with her mother. She returned to Germany recently after an extended stay in America."

Geissler put down his cigar and read the report. "I had expected more," he grunted. "I need more information on her. I'm leaving for a meeting now. See that the clerk files this properly." Krebs weighed Geissler's instructions as the Gestapo man strode out the door. Glancing back over his typescript, Krebs ambled over to Felix Strasser, the desk sergeant. "Felix, be a good cop and file this," Krebs said. "On second thought, put it where no one can find it, then forget about it."

Krebs rubbed Felix's head, messing his straw-like hair. "Hey, our shift's nearly over. Let's get out of here. I'll buy you a beer."

74. BERLIN, JULY 10, 1936, 7:00 P.M.

Fern indulged herself in a long yawn as she opened the apartment door after an exhausting day. She had been rising early every day to prepare her lectures.

As Fern stepped into the sunken living room, she was surprised to see that her mother had a guest. "My dear," Hildy said, "please meet General Martin Haber, a good friend. He's been transferred recently to the General Staff here in Berlin. He's just back from the fighting in Spain."

"Herr General," Fern said, remembering Frederick's counsel and extending her hand. "It's a great honor to have you in our home. Mother, have you served the General the Mosel I bought last week?"

"It's iced and ready," Hildy said. "I was about to get it."

The General, Fern noticed, had chiseled Prussian features and thick snow-white hair. Hildy came in with a teacart, on top of which were three stemmed glasses and the open bottle of wine in an ice bucket.

"Let's toast to the Führer," Hildy said raising her glass.

Fern felt her stomach turn. "To Führer and Fatherland," she intoned loudly. "How good it is to be home!"

The General nodded vigorous approval. "Tell me, Doctor, how are you finding life in Berlin? The changes, I mean."

"It's exciting. I left Germany six years ago, when there still were breadlines. Now there's so much activity everywhere. It's wonderful to be part of it."

Hildy and the General sat on the long leather couch. Fern took a seat opposite them in a large upholstered chair.

"You must be a very strong woman, Doctor. Your mother was just telling me about the series of tragedies that befell the young man you intended to marry. I understand he was an excellent boxer."

"Yes, he would have been an even greater orthopedic surgeon."

"The General here knows several eligible officers," Hildy Wagner said, leaning toward her daughter.

"I'm sure the Doctor has no need of my help in that regard."

"Please understand," Fern said, "My fiancé has been dead only a month."

"I respect that," Haber replied. "I dare say that few of the eligible officers I know would be worthy of you. Still, you shouldn't spend too much of your time alone. May I suggest that you join your mother and me at the Taverne for dinner tonight? I would be flattered to dine in the company of two of Berlin's most beautiful women."

Fern accepted. She did not want to appear aloof.

75. DAR ES SALAAM, TANZANIA (FORMERLY GERMAN EAST AFRICA), JULY 11, 1936, 9:00 A.M.

Karl and Scotty emerged from their musty two-story hotel into the burning sun, each carrying a briefcase slung over his shoulder. The thermometer on the shaded cement wall read thirty-nine degrees Celsius. They walked under the large palm trees that sheltered the dusty street, their shirts soaked with sweat.

"Makes a guy yearn for the March winds sweeping across the exercise yard at Sing Sing," Karl muttered.

Scotty put his hand on Karl's damp shoulder. "Take heart, lad. All this trouble could prove useful someday when your life bloody well depends on knowing the town you're supposed to have lived in as a lad. Lots of German colonists returned to the Fatherland after the Armistice in 1918. If you're unlucky, you could bump into some of them back in Berlin – then you'll have to chat it up about old times in Dar es Salaam. Now you've at least seen the place, and you'll soon learn more."

Scotty led Karl to a one-story clapboard structure. "This house is where, according to the records, the real Karl Muller lived with his parents. A right proper neighborhood, from the look of it," Scotty said.

The two men slogged through the stifling heat, snapping pictures of houses and shops with a Kodak Brownie, the camera favored by tourists. They wended their way up and down the streets, attracting no attention. As fatigue slowed their pace, they decided to sit on the shaded terrace of a street café near the rebuilt Government House. "The Colonial Office chaps say they still serve a decent lager here," Scotty said. "There's also supposed to be an old Boche waiter who may have a helpful memory."

A tall man with a white apron and a round, bald head soon appeared before them as they sat down. Karl judged him to be on the far side of seventy. "*Kann ich ein Bier?*" Karl asked. "I'm afraid we have only local beer," the old man replied in perfect German.

"But please be assured it's of the very highest quality. The Germans who stayed after the English took over have been operating the brewery. The Englanders like it, not that they know anything about beer."

"Then we'll each have one," Karl told him. The waiter returned quickly with two steins brimming with creamy white foam. "Can you sit with us for a moment?" Karl asked. "You seem like you know this place."

The old man shrugged and took a seat. He was pleased to hear his native tongue spoken so well, not the clumsy tourist German he usually heard. At the busiest times of day, sitting with customers would have been strictly *verboten* – but now with the place half-empty it appeared acceptable. "I'm happy to sit with you, but I can't drink anything. My Englander boss forbids drinking with the customers. So what can I do for you?"

"We understand that a family named Muller lived here some years ago," Scotty said in his Bavarian accent. "We've lost touch with them."

"Ah, there were several families named Muller here in the old days, when Dar es Salam was German, before the English invaded," the old waiter answered.

"Were there any children?" Scotty asked.

"Yes, one of those families had a boy, an only child I believe, who was about nine when the war broke out," the waiter told them.

"We need to confirm that," Scotty said. "You see, as luck would have it, this boy has come into a sizeable sum – life insurance money from his grandfather, who recently passed away back in Essen. We represent the Hannover Insurance Company, which will pay a sizeable claim in this matter." Scotty and Karl both flashed their false credentials. "Naturally, we're prepared to pay for the information. Let's say a bank draft for a hundred British pounds?"

"Cash only," the waiter said. Opening his billfold, Scotty removed five twenty-pound notes and passed them to the waiter.

"My eyes aren't that good anymore," the waiter said in a raspy voice. "From what I can see, though, your money is real, so I'll tell you what I know."

Karl took a small notebook from his shirt pocket.

"Well," the waiter began, "the Mullers lived on this street. The father owned an apothecary not far from here. Like many others, they fled inland when we came under siege from the British warships. I didn't know Mr. Muller, but from what I heard he was a good man, made money in quinine."

"What happened to them?" Karl asked. He already had a page of notes.

"People say he died not long after the war. Mrs. Muller went home to Germany. At least that's what I heard."

"What about the boy?"

"Lost in the war."

"Dead?"

"Probably, but who knows?"

"You've been extremely helpful," Scotty told the waiter.

The old man excused himself to wait on a young couple at a nearby table.

"A loyal German," Karl said once the old waiter was out of sight.

"But a right talkative bloke," Scotty said. "Our questions gave the old boy a new lease on life. And it all fits into our creative biography of Karl Muller. Now let's have another pint and some lunch before getting the afternoon train for the high country."

76. KIGOMA, EAST AFRICA, JULY 14, 1936, NOON

Karl recognized the gurgle of phlegm from deep inside the small chest of the five-year-old girl who lay naked on a straw mat. He'd heard the sickening sound before – from deep in his own mother's chest back in Berlin as the war ended, and later in patients from Harlem. He knew tuberculosis when he heard it. Karl had been hearing the same cough in African children in other huts they'd visited. Few, if any, would live another year, he guessed. In this hut, the mother had three other children to care for, and all three had the same cough. Karl gave her several small packets of the powdered sulfa drug he had brought from London and, with several hand gestures, instructed her to boil the brackish water that came from the well near her hut.

Scotty stood waiting outside the hut. "Had enough?" he asked.

"That makes seven huts I've visited, sick kids in all of them. I'm ready for the next."

"No, Karl, you've seen all you need. Everything else you need to know is in the documents compiled by doctors and missionaries who've been here before. Brown has all this material tucked away for the book you'll write when we get to Scotland. He also has lots on Tabura and the high country. That's where we go to next."

"A book?"

"Yes, a book. This Karl Muller will be quite an accomplished bloke."

77. NEAR KIGOMA, EAST AFRICA, AUGUST 2, 1936, 8:00 A.M.

Lake Tanganyika sparkled in the morning light. From the grassy hill where they sat, Scotty and Karl could see the rolling green hills of the Belgian Congo across the lake. "So this, Karl, is where young Dr. Muller has been practicing medicine. You started out treating accidental gunshot wounds of the idle rich who came here on safari, mostly Brits, a few Yanks. Soon you saw the need to improve sanitary conditions for the indigenous people. As Brown imagines him, our Dr. Karl Muller is a white supremacist with a social conscience. Nothing like a hint of compassion to lend credibility to your character."

"The time we've spent in these villages," Karl said, "will help me put flesh and blood on the medical data and get that book written. There's so much to do here, there's no real sanitation. The death rates from cholera and dysentery must be very high."

"No time for that now, lad, we need to get moving," Scotty said, checking his watch. "There's a seaplane down on the lake waiting to take us to Johannesburg – another place where Dr. Karl Muller has spent time."

78. JOUBERT PARK, JOHANNESBURG, AUGUST 5, 1936 8:00 A.M.

After a long walk in the park, Karl and Scotty found a secluded wrought-iron bench.

"Orders from Brown came through in the diplomatic pouch." Scotty said. "The old boy wants you to get some burglaries under your belt."

Karl smiled. "I didn't know you guys hired me to be a burglar."

"The fine art of breaking and entering without stirring a fleck of dust is a skill you may bloody well need in the job ahead – and it's not something they teach at Oxford. I learned it from one of the best, an old pro who worked Mayfair and Belgravia, quit while he was still ahead, and retired to Paris.

Today we'll begin by visiting Witwatersrand University Hospital – that's where Karl Muller studied medicine and did his residency. We'll spend the early evening there."

"Don't tell me were going to burglarize the drug dispensary."

"Quite to the contrary," Scotty replied. "We intend to *give* them something."

79. SUNNYSIDE PARK HOTEL, JOHANNESBURG, AUGUST 5, 1936, 2:15 P.M.

In their hotel room, Scotty reached into his briefcase and removed two metal nametags.

"Take one, lad," Scotty said. "These identify us as staff doctors, blokes who work at the University Hospital but happen to be off this evening. Have a look in the closet and you'll find that while we were at breakfast an SIS operative dropped off the white coats and stethoscopes we'll need to complete our costumes."

80. WITWATERSRAND UNIVERSITY HOSPITAL, JOHANNESBURG, AUGUST 5, 1936, 6:00 P.M.

"See, lad, there's nothing to it," Scotty whispered. They had gained access to the immense room full of filing cabinets with ease. Once inside, Scotty used a small flashlight to read the markings on the file drawers.

There it was, just as that afternoon's SIS report had indicated – a drawer marked "Interns and Doctors in Residence, 1926-1932." From his briefcase Scotty took a worn manila folder containing Karl's forged professional documents. Thanks to scrupulous research, the typeface on Karl's file label exactly matched the other labels in the drawer, and the papers in the file showed the same degree of wear. Scotty slipped the folder carefully in its proper alphabetical niche.

Hearing voices, Scotty closed the file drawer without a sound. Listening in the darkness, they both heard it now, a faint but familiar sound – heavy breathing coming through the closed door to an inner office, some twenty feet from the filing cabinets. The breathing was getting louder. Scotty nodded toward the exit.

Moving quickly toward the door, Karl didn't see the standing ashtray. His hand brushed against it with just enough force to send it crashing to the tile floor. They froze and listened again but heard nothing. Seconds later they were alone in an elevator headed for the ground floor.

"What now? What about that noise?" Karl asked.

"You mean the passionate moans you heard from the back office? Relax, Karl. Whoever was involved was sneaking one on the side. Otherwise, why the office? They aren't likely to report anything, if you ask me."

81. JOHANNESBURG STAR, AUGUST 12, 1936

BENIGN BURGLAR STRIKES AGAIN

JOHANNESBURG – Police reported last night on a third bizarre residential burglary in the Braamfontein neighborhood near Witwatersrand University. "What makes these break-ins unusual is that no money or items of value have been taken," Constable Ernst Kriss of the Johannesburg Police said. "All residents were away from home when the break-ins occurred," the Constable confirmed.

At each home, the Constable told reporters, the intruders left a distinctive calling card. "All of the householders," Constable Kriss explained, "discovered that their front door was unlocked and slightly ajar when they returned home from dinner or the cinema. Each also found an empty beer bottle and two soiled glasses on the kitchen table. Otherwise, they would have had no idea that a break-in had occurred."

One homeowner, a diamond company executive, characterized the intrusion as a "prank," most likely, he speculated, committed by restless youths wanting to see if they could break into a home and get away with it.

82. OXFORD, SEPTEMBER 10, 1936, 4:09 A.M.

Karl sat over the black coffee he'd just brewed on a rusty hot plate that rested on the windowsill of his cramped room. On the desk near the drafty window was a three-inch-thick red loose-leaf binder on the life of Dr. Karl Muller, the man he would soon become.

He had read the contents twice the previous afternoon. When he finished his third reading of the section titled "German East Africa," he reread an old SIS report on the history of the country before, during, and after the Great War. Many of the report's statements were supported by precise footnotes. In the margins, Karl made careful notes on places he had actually visited in the old German colony. He also wrote down questions he thought he might encounter in his counterfeit life, along with what he thought would be plausible answers. Next came a binder on Berlin. It contained street maps of the city and the U-Bahn railway network. He began memorizing the network, line by line, station by station, and testing himself by drawing his own maps.

83. HALL OF INTERNATIONAL POLITICS, OXFORD, SEPTEMBER 10, 1936, 7:30 A.M.

With the red binder under his arm, Karl entered the small brick building that housed Oxford's Hall of International Politics. He anticipated a breakfast of tea and scones with Channing Brown and some Christ College dons with expertise in African affairs. He had questions for them.

To his surprise, the interior of the building was dark and silent. He groped his way up an unfamiliar staircase in the half-light and found his way into a second-floor conference room Brown had told him about the evening before. A sudden voice broke the silence.

"*Guten Morgen, Herr Muller.*"

"Morning," Karl answered tentatively.

"*Sprechen Sie Deutsch!*"

A spotlight snapped on, illuminating an enormous black, white, and red swastika flag pinned to the wall behind him.

The same voice, now louder, commanded him to sit. The spotlight beam guided him to a wooden desk on his right.

Then several voices began shouting in German at the same time. A flashlight caught his eyes and held them. "What the...," Karl grumbled as a rope fell over his chest, tightened by someone who had come up from behind him unnoticed. "What?" he gasped again.

A figure stepped from the dark and slapped him hard in the face. *"Sprechen Sie Deutsch!"*

Another man stepped up from behind. "What's your name?" he shouted in German.

"My name is Karl Muller."

"What's your nationality?"

"German."

"Where were you born?"

"Dar es Salaam, in East Africa."

"When?"

"January 8, 1905."

"You say you're German. Why were you born in Africa?"

"My father was born there too. His parents were German colonists."

"Your mother's maiden name, what was it?"

"Volkert."

"Her first name?"

"Inga, Inga Volkert."

"Do you have papers that verify what you say?"

"Only carbon copies."

"Where are the originals?"

"British warships destroyed the City Hall, right at the start of the Great War."

"What was the name of this British warship?"

"There were two: the Pegasus and the Astraea."

"Only a spy would have such detailed information. Are you a spy?"

"No, I'm Dr. Karl Muller. The war, needless to say, was a major event. How could I not remember the name of the ship that destroyed our Government House and other important buildings? It's one reason why I hate the British."

"Why have you come to Germany?"

"Because I like what's happening in Germany. Our Fatherland is getting stronger – and someday East Africa will belong to Germany again."

"You seem to remember the war in East Africa. Tell us about it."

"The English attacked from the east, from ships in the Indian Ocean. The Belgians invaded from the Northwest, from the Congo. My parents and I moved from Dar es Salaam to avoid the shelling and the imminent British occupation. We took the railway inland to Tabura. My parents helped run a field hospital there. My father was a pharmacist. It was hard because everything was in short supply, including drugs, soap, and clean water. Then in September 1916, the Belgians and their Negro mercenaries took Tabura. They plundered everything. There were many rapes."

"You've given me nothing but generalities. Be specific."

"Well, one morning, in front of our small house, a black-skinned sergeant asked a local man 'where the nuns were hiding.' When the man wouldn't answer, the sergeant shot him through eyeball."

"What did they do to your family?"

"Nothing."

"Why nothing?"

"Because my mother stood up to them."

"How did she stand up to them? Give us some details."

"One day a Belgian officer and more than twenty of his black troopers appeared at the front door of our house. The officer, a captain, told my mother that we had to leave the house, that they were seizing it so they could billet troops there. My father was at the field hospital at the time. My mother informed the captain that she would not vacate the house. The captain repeated his request, and my mother repeated her refusal. I could see and hear everything through the open doorway – the captain with all those black soldiers, all of them standing at attention. The sweat from their armpits showed through their dirty khaki shirts. They all stank, even from several feet away. The captain stared at my mother, and she stared right back. He repeated his demand. My mother refused. After a long silence, maybe about thirty seconds, the captain turned and led his troops away."

"Then what happened?"

"Nothing to us, but many women were raped by soldiers. At a house only half a kilometer from ours, a woman killed her three young daughters rather than risk having them fall into Congolese hands."

The light blinked off and then came on again, this time brighter, illuminating Karl's face and eyes.

The voice grew louder. "Go on with your story."

"The British took control of the colony after the war. We migrated back to Dar es Salaam. My parents heard that the British had started a good school there. I learned English and did well in school. My father was able to open a small pharmacy back in Dar es Salaam. He prospered mainly through the sale of quinine – both to individual colonists and to clinics. The income enabled my parents to send me to Johannesburg for further education. I stayed there through medical school and my internship, working as a staff physician. After that I returned to Tabura, where I practiced general medicine. I kept a diary, which has served me well when writing on public health in eastern and southern Africa."

"Where are your parents?"

"Both are deceased."

"What kind of medical practice do you plan to establish in Berlin?"

"I've purchased an existing practice from Dr. Ernst Heiden, who had a significant general practice in Zehlendorf."

"Where did you get the money to buy the practice?"

"I have money from my father's estate and from royalties on my book about public health in East Africa. My father invested in South African diamond mines. I inherited those stocks and later sold them at a good price."

"We know you're lying to us, that you plan to infiltrate the Reich and spy for the English, the Russians, or maybe both."

"You're the experts. Examine my documents. They're authentic. Reject me and you'll harm the Reich. If the Fatherland is to regain its greatness, it will need a powerful military. Armies need doctors, and so do the citizens of a healthy Germany."

"Will you join the Party?"

"It would be my honor if the Party would accept me. I can work for the Party and practice medicine at the same time. The Party is the engine that drives German resurgence."

"In your medical practice, will you treat Jews?"

"I might treat some."

"What do you mean 'some'? That could well violate the Reich's policies."

"The policy of the Reich is to build a strong Germany. Suppose a Jew comes to me with syphilis. I'd do my best to cure him so that he couldn't infect Aryan women."

"If the Gestapo requested specific information, regarding a Jew or any other patient, would you give it to them?"

"Of course. After all, the Gestapo has an important job to do. I respect that."

"According to your papers, you were baptized in the Catholic Church. Do you sill practice your faith?"

"Not since I saw the suffering in the last war."

"You're nearly thirty-two. Why aren't you married? There's no place for faggots in the Reich."

"I am not a homosexual. I'm too busy for courtship and marriage right now. And there were very few eligible white women in the African bush, and even fewer who were Aryan."

In the next instant, the bright light in his eyes went dark and the lighting in the room returned to normal, revealing the presence of Channing Brown and a smiling Scotty North, pleased with his performance as inquisitor.

"On the whole," Brown said with a nod, "you did quite well. You know your part in our little play. You've definitely done your homework, lad. As you know, there was a family named Muller in Dar es Salaam. This Muller boy apparently fled Dar es Salaam during the British occupation and most likely perished in the bush. In any case, he was never heard from again. As luck would have it, his name really was Karl."

"Okay, what's next?"

"Two more weeks of study and interrogation here at Oxford," Brown responded. "Then we're off to Scotland, where you'll actually write that book. You'll also be getting back into fighting shape – and encounter some rather new challenges."

84. NEW YORK, SEPTEMBER 16, 1936, 8:00 P.M.

Josh Greenberg settled over the portable typewriter on the living room desk of his new East End Avenue apartment, which he had rented with his girl-friend Nancy.

Dearest Fern,

I'm back at work and this is my first day off.

Nancy Corrigan has helped me regain my health. Let me tell you more about her. She's originally from California and studied for her RN at University Hospital in San Francisco. She's been part of the New York Hospital staff now for close to a year. As I think I mentioned before, Nancy assisted you in the OR several times before you left for Germany. We've just moved into a new apartment on East End Avenue. It has a great view of the East River. Our new address is on the envelope.

Nancy is very active in the workers' rights movement and is busy organizing a nurses' union, against the wishes of the hospital board. That means we spend less time together than I'd like.

How are you doing, Fern? What's going on in Berlin? I thought that by now you might have written about the Olympics there. Did you see any of the games? Jesse Owens's four gold medals are cause for great happiness on this side of the Atlantic.

The press here reported that Marty Glickman, a New York runner from Syracuse University, lost his spot on the four hundred-meter relay. The American coaches reportedly did not want to embarrass Hitler by having a Jewish athlete win a gold medal.

That leads me to another, related subject. Friends should always be candid with each other, so I must confess that I'm concerned about not hearing from you for so long. Nancy and I have been talking to Jewish couples and other immigrants recently arrived from Germany – and most are relieved to have gotten out while they could. Many of the Jews we talk to had to leave money and possessions behind because of the Nazi crackdown. The Daily Worker, *a newspaper that Nancy reads, always has a lot of terrible news about what's happening to the Jews in Germany.*

Nancy believes the Nazis are up to no good, particularly since their march into the Rhineland last spring. She says that they're stoking political unrest in Spain by sending "volunteer" combatants. The Worker *is making a very big deal about that too.*

From here, it does not appear that Europe is the place to be. So why don't you get the hell on the Hindenburg and come back here? You could be here in no time. I'll drive out to where it lands, in Lakehurst, New Jersey, to meet you. We have a guest room in the new apartment and you could stay with us until you get your bearings.

Love,

Josh

85. BERLIN, SEPTEMBER 21, 1936, 9:00 P.M.

After working late at the hospital, Fern crossed the Oberbaum Bridge, her eyes fixed on the calm black waters of the Spree. Her mood was as dark as the river. The denial that had persisted for weeks had left her. Karl's death was now a reality that pervaded her every thought. She contemplated the flat water and wished she was someone else, one of those who believed they could escape reality with a simple leap into the river and a forgiving death. But she knew she wasn't that other person. She understood that she could not escape.

She knew her soul, her talents, perhaps even her grief demanded more of her, even though the pain might never go away. Looking up and away from the river, she hailed a taxi and rode to her mother's home on the Tiergartenstrasse. If Hildy was still up, or wasn't busy entertaining one of her new Nazi friends, well then perhaps they could talk over some schnapps.

86. HILDY WAGNER'S HOME, 9:35 P.M.

Hildy Wagner was waiting for Fern in the half-light of the hallway.

"Dear, we have to talk," Hildy said, leading Fern to the sitting room. "You had a caller this afternoon. He was a policeman."

"So, what did he want?"

"He asked several questions."

"Such as?"

"Whether you had a Jewish lover in New York."

"Oh, for God's sake."

"Fern, it shows that they've been reading your mail, maybe even listening to our telephone conversations. You know, with one of those listening devices. I'm afraid they know things, and what they don't know they'll imagine. It frightens me, and it should frighten you too."

"Well, it doesn't frighten me."

The telephone rang. Fern picked it up and listened. "Yes, I can be there in thirty minutes," she said and hung up the phone. "The police," she said, turning toward Hildy, "they want to question me. The officer seemed polite enough. He invited me to come down to the Alexanderplatz. Don't worry, Mother. I can handle this."

87. ALEXANDERPLATZ, BERLIN, 10:15 P.M.

At the police reception desk, a stout woman was banging away without letup on her ancient typewriter. Fern found the station tidy in the usual German way – two rows of neat wooden desks, each with a sturdy black Seidel & Naumann typewriter, but no paper cluttering the desktops. A tall blond man in a red turtleneck waved to her from behind a glass partition.

As she walked toward him, she was surprised to see that he was smiling.

"I apologize for the inconvenience, Dr. Wagner. Please have a seat."

After a long pause he spoke. "My name is Hans Krebs, Chief of Detectives here. You can relax. This won't take long."

"Are you telling me that you're Gestapo?"

"Yes, I'm with the Gestapo. But I'm a real cop, too. As you must know, the Gestapo has recently taken over all police work in Berlin. They've got their noses in everything, including what I do – and what you do."

Fern couldn't help but notice the Mauser pistol in the shoulder holster lying on Hans Krebs's desk blotter. The ashtray was empty, but soiled from frequent use. In fact, the place stank of stale cigarette smoke. "I hope I didn't frighten your mother," he said, leaning toward her.

"Perhaps a little. She's extremely wary of the police, of the Gestapo, of anyone who might be snooping. But she tries to hide her concern. Please be assured that I am not like my mother. I don't frighten so easily. And I don't believe there's anything wrong with receiving letters from a friend in America."

"Who said anything about letters from America? You must know it's a mistake to volunteer information, even accurate information."

Fern nodded. "I'll try to remember that, Herr Krebs. Now please, can we do our business so I can go home and get some sleep? My patients and students expect me to be at my best in the morning."

Krebs leaned back in his swivel chair, taking his measure of Fern. "It's refreshing to hear a woman speak her mind these days," he said. "But it might get you in real trouble."

"Why? Because I object to questions about an innocent letter and a telephone call?"

"Dr. Wagner, nothing – and no one – is innocent in Berlin. And besides, I haven't asked you any questions yet."

She looked around the room. The woman at the reception desk had stopped typing and the room was quiet. Fern coughed.

"I apologize for the air in this place," he said, lowering his voice. "Most of the Gestapo detectives who work here smoke too much. They're gone now, off to destroy the office of some underground newspaper. It's great fun for them."

Krebs kept speaking in a low voice. He could always sense an eavesdropper. Still not typing, the big receptionist was making a show of reviewing her work.

"It's getting late," he said. "Could we finish this interview somewhere else? There's a good café nearby."

Sensing that Krebs wanted some privacy, Fern broke into a smile. "Yes, let's get the hell out of here," she said.

88. ROMANISCHES CAFÉ, 11:05 P.M.

At a small table near the sidewalk they talked over steins of beer.

"It seems to me, Chief Detective Krebs, that you must have more important things to do with your time than interrogate me about letters and telephone calls I receive from New York."

"Perhaps. But I don't want to see you get into more trouble than you can handle, especially since you've been away from Berlin for so long. Beyond that, I know you're related to Frederick Wagner. That in itself warrants special treatment."

He paused to let her reflect on what he'd said. "Busybodies, like the typist back at the police station, are everywhere these days. The Gestapo gets much of its information from the so-called block captains. Frau Klaus, the concierge in your mother's apartment building, is a block captain. Watch out for her. She reports everything to the typist you saw back at headquarters. Believe me, these people have little to do except report choice tidbits, like your getting a letter from a Jewish friend. It makes them feel important.

"Let me tell you something, Dr. Wagner: I've read a photostat of your friend Josh's letter."

"So?"

"Some of what he said could get you in trouble."

"Rubbish."

"Believe what you want, Dr. Wagner. The truth is I want to help you. It may surprise you to learn that I can't stand Gestapo types and neighborhood spies. There's nothing noble in what they do. I don't like busybodies. Now they're running my city – and ruining it."

He took a long drink of beer and went on. "I remember what a great place this used to be before the war. There were painters, writers, and actors, just like Paris. And yes, every so often there was a sensational murder case or bank robbery. But even in the worst of times, right after the war, the struggle for survival brought out our people's resourcefulness. Now a gang of louts is running the place."

When they finished their beers, Krebs signaled the waiter to bring two more. "I don't think I want another," Fern protested.

"Believe me, you'll need one."

"Really. Why?"

Krebs leaned forward. "Just this morning, we arrested one of your neighbors, a school teacher who was receiving letters from a former student, a Jewish boy who'd moved to Austria. Sound familiar? Of course there are differences between your cases. This school teacher actually wrote back – a very bad idea. So far, you've received two letters from a Jew in America, the country where you spent the last several years. That feeds the Gestapo's paranoia. They like to add two and two and get two hundred."

"I think I will have that second beer," Fern said, resting her chin in her palm, eyeing him directly. "Thanks for the warning. But I'm curious, why are you doing this?"

"Actually," Krebs said, his unshaven face breaking into a grin, "I'm returning a kindness."

"How?"

"Five weeks ago you treated several teenage girls who suffered burns in a chemistry experiment at school. Some ended up in your hospital. One girl had an ugly burn on her cheek. You stayed with her for an extra half-hour, making sure the bandages and dressing were just so, reassuring her that everything would be all right. That girl was my daughter. Our family physician, Dr. Heiden, removed the bandages only yesterday, and there's no hint of a scar. He told us you did a remarkable job. My daughter has written you a thank you letter. She admires you very much."

"I remember the letter, of course, and your daughter. She's very pretty, a blonde like you, pure Aryan, as they say. Her name is Gretchen, isn't it? We talked about how much she likes science. I followed up with Dr. Heiden, by the way."

"Did you know that Heiden is about to retire? He's sold his practice to some young doctor who's moving here from East Africa."

"I wonder why in hell anyone would come to Berlin now," Fern said, glancing at her watch. "It's getting late. You've been very kind, Detective Krebs, but now I need some sleep. I go on duty at the Charité Hospital tomorrow morning at six. Should we meet again, I won't be calling you *Detective* or *Chief Detective*. I'll address you as *Herr Krebs* instead. That way I won't feel as if I'm under investigation."

"Please call me Hans."

She finished her beer and rose from the table. "Well, Hans, good night." He escorted her to a taxi, clasping her arm. Fern was at ease on the ride home. It had been some time since she'd felt the touch of a gentle man.

89. NEW YORK, OCTOBER 5, 1936, 10:15 P.M.

Josh buttoned his trench coat against the rain. No matter how hard he tried, he couldn't stop thinking about what Fern had told him the night before on the telephone.

When he reached 84th Street and Second Avenue, he took shelter in Cassidy's, a local pub with few customers that night. Sitting at the bar over a beer, he mused on their strained conversation. Her message had cut him to the quick. She'd decided to stay in Germany and practice medicine there. So much was happening in her homeland. And "all things considered" – yes, she'd actually used those words – it would be better if he did not write or telephone.

Yes, Karl was dead. And the Fern he had known was as good as dead. Nothing he could do about it. He gulped his beer, left half of it, and walked home. Nancy would be off at midnight. He would wait up for her.

90. ROMANISCHES CAFÉ, BERLIN, OCTOBER 8, 1936, 5:00 P.M.

Fern let the white-coated waiter guide her to a table on the terrace of the Romanisches Café. She ordered a glass of white wine and let the gentle afternoon breeze refresh her face. She'd left the hospital early to shop for clothes.

Using part of a cash gift from Uncle Frederick, Fern bought herself several fine woolen suits imported from London. She also found two ski outfits for the Christmas holiday in Garmisch that Uncle Frederick had promised.

She needed new outfits because she had begun receiving social invitations. She had dined twice with a young engineer who worked for Uncle Frederick before realizing that he would never do – he was far too insecure about seeing his boss's niece. There were also two eligible young doctors at the hospital. One, unfortunately, espoused all that "master race" nonsense, while the other was far too aggressive sexually.

She discovered that it wasn't a good idea to attend receptions with her mother and General Haber, which put her in the company high-ranking Nazis, like Goebbels and Bormann, both of whom were shameless womanizers. She realized how lucky she had been back in New York, where men kept their distance once they knew she was "Karl Ludwig's girl." She realized it was unlikely that she would find another Karl Ludwig, but she nonetheless felt the need for someone who would inspire trepidation in other men, a man who would be content just to spend time with her, who wouldn't force himself on her. So far, though, none of her would-be suitors met those specifications.

91. THORNBIL CASTLE, SCOTLAND, OCTOBER 10, 1936, 5:00 A.M.

An autumn nip was in the air as Karl and Channing Brown walked the craggy hillside paths near the main sentry post, one of several that guarded the castle's perimeter.

"I thought we might share a candid moment to discuss a few episodes where your performance showed a need for improvement," Brown said, waving for them to a halt near a rock.

"Sure."

"Let's start with two mistakes."

"In London, you came close to consorting with a woman about whom you knew nothing, except what she told you of herself. Very dangerous, that. As you know, pillow talk has been a bountiful source of intelligence since Delilah beguiled Samson. Similar episodes crowd the files of intelligence agencies around the world. We'd know about even more of them if the dead could talk. That woman who said her name was Constance Crosby was in fact one of our own top people, Bonnie Peters. We had to test you. And yes, we had to test your devotion to Dr. Wagner."

"Nothing happened."

"That's no assurance of how you'll behave in the future. Men think with their peckers. That's why attractive women often have an advantage in espionage. The Germans are making effective use of lady spies, just as we are."

"Okay I'll watch out. She practically threw herself at me, you know."

"Bad excuse, lad. Others may do the same. Just keep it buttoned up if you fancy staying alive."

Karl nodded.

"Now let's turn to another matter, the ashtray you knocked over in Johannesburg. You managed to create a tell-tale mess. Credit your escape not to your own resourcefulness, but to the dim-witted hospital security. Those in charge of security at any similar facility in Berlin will be far more alert, quite possibly with the assistance of some hungry Dobermans."

Karl knew Brown was right. "Point taken. So what now?" he asked.

"What you need now is more training in the fine art of burglary. You also have to get busy writing your book on public health in southern Africa. And you'll start a rigorous physical regimen emphasizing readiness for the unexpected. Perhaps most important, you're going to learn how to strike a special blow, a potentially fatal punch we refer to as Jackhammer, after the code name we've assigned to your mission."

92. THORNBIL CASTLE, OCTOBER 22, 1936, 5:07 A.M.

Channing Brown watched the driving autumn rain splatter on the picture window of the library, then added a fresh log to the fireplace. He read the story on page four of the Glasgow *Daily Record* with satisfaction. According to the report, "the Kitchen Burglar" had struck again – the seventh such incident in a fortnight. Police said that in each case the burglar had picked the front door lock, entered the kitchen, and helped himself to whatever beverage was in the icebox, usually a bottle of beer or some milk. Police also noted that the burglar always left a typewritten note saying that he had been there and thanking the household for its involuntary generosity. The burglar's note – always the same – entreated members of the household not to be afraid, and reassured them that he would not return.

Warming himself by the fire, he buttoned up the thick wool cardigan Jillian had given him three Christmases before. He sat at the table, uncapped his black Waterman, and took the legal pad from the briefcase at his feet. His mind worked best in the early morning and he wanted to give serious thought to Karl and his upcoming mission.

Brown already knew what came first. Karl, in the person of Karl Muller, had to be credible – a reputable citizen of the Reich, a man of substance and courage. He would have to overcome the curiosity and skepticism that were sure to arise when someone appeared out of nowhere. In bold capitals at the top of the clean page he stroked the word CREDIBILITY.

As Brown ruminated on the mission, he heard staccato bursts of typing from Karl's bedroom down the long hall. Karl was an early riser, like Brown, and would finish the manuscript soon. There was no question that Karl had to write the book himself. Only then would he be able to field questions posed by medical colleagues, Africa buffs, and the "friends" he was about to make in Germany. A respected London publisher had agreed to issue the book and distribute it to medical libraries. All sales agreements had been negotiated and executed in advance. Brown even arranged for a favorable review in the *Proceedings of the Royal Society of Medicine*. Royalties from the book would help Dr. Karl Muller gain the respectability he needed to access the upper echelons of the Third Reich, a key step to the success of his mission.

Access to Hitler was essential, of course, and problematic. Karl would have to cultivate relationships with people who were close to Hitler to gain access to the Führer himself. Brown wrote down several names. Karl would have to establish credibility with each of them. Brown made a note to search Karl's background for talents beyond boxing and medicine, talents that would help Karl win entrée to the German Chancellor's inner circle.

Karl would need to be in Hitler's presence several times to ensure that the Chancellor was at ease with him. That would present its own challenges. Karl's insistence that he alone would plan the final steps – the actual killing and subsequent escape – could present its own challenges. Brown made a note that read: CREATE AND DEVELOP SPECIAL PROJECTS.

Brown then focused on the deed itself – delivering the actual blows or punches that would put Adolf Hitler's lights out forever. Since arriving at Thornbil, Karl had made great strides toward recovering the fitness and boxing skills he would need, but there was still much more he needed to learn. Karl, Jamie, and Scotty took a brisk run every afternoon at three, looping around the expansive Castle grounds, increasing their speed and distance every third day. They'd been at it now for five weeks with only Sundays off. To no one's surprise, Karl soon proved the strongest runner of the three. Starting today, Brown would insist that Karl run five miles in thirty minutes or less. After each run there was mountain climbing, followed by three rounds of boxing or weight lifting on alternate days. Now it was time to step things up. Brown wrote: ENHANCE FIGHTING SKILLS AND FITNESS – PROCEED WITH SPECIAL BOXING TEST SOON.

There was yet another high-risk factor that would require aggressive management: Fern Wagner's presence in Berlin. Brown knew he had to minimize the chance that she and Karl would run into each other. Brown believed that Karl posed the lesser risk because he at least knew that Fern was alive. On the other hand, Fern's reaction to a chance meeting, whatever form it might take, could derail the mission completely. Brown wrote: MINIMIZE RISK THAT KARL AND FERN MEET BY CHANCE.

That thought led Brown to another ongoing dilemma. There was no question that Karl would be eager – perhaps too eager – to get the job done. Lack of patience on Karl's part could lead to disaster. Then there was the impatience of Sir Crawford and Churchill. Each man expected results on his own timetable. Both were likely to become impatient if the mission proceeded at too deliberate a pace. And Karl would likely encounter people and situations in Germany that would test his patience. Brown wrote: INSTILL PATIENCE – IN KARL AND OTHERS.

There was one last factor to consider, Brown realized. Karl had done a fine job studying current events in Germany. But he needed a better understanding of history and international geopolitics, of shifting and uncertain alliances, and the fact that what happens one day could be ancient history the next. Brown wrote: FURTHER EDUCATE KARL RE GEOPOLITICAL ISSUES THAT COULD AFFECT MISSION.

93. THE LIBRARY AT THORNBIL CASTLE, NOVEMBER 10, 1936, NOON

Karl sat in silence as Brown finished reading the 300-page manuscript. The book reported on the lack of sanitation and potable water in the tribal villages of eastern and southern Africa and described the deadly and dreaded diseases spawned by such conditions. It chastised the British colonial government for its negligence.

"Good job, Karl," said Brown. "It's very readable for an academic book."

"The researchers you hired provided strong documentation," Karl said. "With their help, the book almost wrote itself. What about the German translation?"

"Our chaps back at Oxford will take care of that. They'll also show it to various doctors and public-health experts. We're making certain that the book receives a thorough vetting."

94. THE LIBRARY, NOVEMBER 12, 1936, 5:30 A.M.

Gesturing for Karl to sit, Brown poured them both fresh hot coffee and pointed to a thick orange binder.

"More required reading for you, lad. You've already absorbed hundreds of pages on Hitler – his background and habits, the radio speeches, intelligence reports on his trench warfare experience, his temper, and his curious sex life. His behavior, as you know, is quite erratic, and his moods change."

"I can almost smell his bad breath," Karl quipped.

"Well, this new material isn't about Hitler, but rather about the people closest to him, individuals you'll need to know in order to get close to Hitler. Each is a formidable personality. And they're all in there," he said, pointing to the binder.

"Okay, help get me started. Tell me about a few of them."

"First is Rudolf Hess, the Nazi Party boss and Deputy Führer. The binder includes ideas on how you can get close to him, based on his need to raise funds for the Nazi Party. Most interesting to you, perhaps, Hess is a skier."

"Who's next?"

"Martin Bormann, Hess's deputy. Never mind that Bormann works for Hess. Hitler, we are told by one of our better agents, pays little attention to organizational charts and that sort of thing. Bormann, mind you, is a competent, well-organized chap, but not liked by those seeking Hitler's attention. Many are envious of Hitler's high regard for Bormann, and there's little doubt that Hitler relies on him. At a recent reception, one of our diplomats overheard Hitler say something that may explain his esteem for Bormann: that Bormann doesn't just come to him with problems, as so many others do. Instead, Bormann always offers practical recommendations on how to address the problems he identifies. That sort of assistance is invaluable to any leader."

"A no-nonsense guy," Karl surmised.

"Not necessarily. Please note – and the binder explains this in some detail – Bormann can never quite wait to get his pants off. Not only will he screw any tart he can get his hands on, he's managed to keep his wife pregnant. He's already sired six little Bormanns."

"Hermann Göring is another key figure," Brown said. "He's ubiquitous, never misses an opportunity to get his picture in the newspaper. He's a self-indulgent man with a great fondness for fine food, toy trains, and expensive military hardware. Despite his boyishness, he's very well organized, always thinking. And despite his portly build, he's an avid athlete. Once in Germany, you should definitely polish your skiing skills. That will help you get close to both Hess and Göring."

Karl leafed through the binder, glancing over the photographs and typed SIS reports, newspaper and magazine clippings. He knew he'd have to spend many hours with the files, making notes and preparing questions.

"Okay, I've got my work cut out for me. Anything else?"

"A lot, actually. One of the most important people in your new life isn't profiled in the binder. That person is Frau Inga Frick. She's been Dr. Heiden's nurse-assistant for several years. She knows that a Dr. Karl Muller has purchased Dr. Heiden's home and his medical practice, and she's offered to stay on. As luck would have it, she happens to be quite active in the Nazi Party, which presents both challenges and opportunities."

"Are there notes on people I should avoid?" Karl asked.

"Indeed. Frederick Wagner is one of them because he knows you from America. And, of course, you must avoid his niece. That, I believe, is obvious."

"It is."

Brown turned the page and sipped his coffee.

"Well, there are two other chaps you may not be able to avoid: Heinrich Himmler and Reinhard Heydrich. Both can be nasty. Himmler's in charge of the police and counterintelligence. He runs the Gestapo, the SS, and the SD, a new counterintelligence arm of the SS that's becoming more important every week. The SD could eventually rival the Abwehr, Germany's military intelligence. Bear in mind that your arrival in Germany could well arouse the suspicion of any or all them. Be aware that Heydrich, although he's Himmler's titular deputy, does much of the real work. Our Berlin sources tell us his ambition knows no bounds."

"They sound pretty formidable. Anyone else?"

"Dr. Theodor Morrell, Hitler's personal physician. He treats the Führer for stomach cramps and eczema, among other ailments. We've learned that he has a penchant for injecting Hitler with serums of his own creation. Bormann and Göring are reportedly wary of him. And one of our Berlin operatives reports that Göring has described Morrell as 'needle happy.' Of course, there are other doctors who treat Hitler. But Hitler depends on Morrell, so be careful. He could show up at an inopportune moment."

95. THE GYMNASIUM, THORNBIL CASTLE, NOVEMBER 12, 1936, 2:30 P.M.

The clang resonated through the cavernous, high-ceilinged room, which once served as a grand banquet hall. Now it served as a training gym, complete with barbells, punching bags, and an elevated, regulation-size boxing ring, all specially installed by the Royal Marines.

Karl moved forward with confidence in the ring. Six weeks of intense training – running, weight lifting, and boxing – had begun to restore his strength and punching speed.

Unknown to Karl, several new opponents had arrived at Thornbil that afternoon fresh from the Royal Marines Boxing Club. All were well-trained and sworn to silence about their activities at Thornbil.

At the bell, Karl opened with a flurry of punches to his opponent's mid-section, backing him into the ropes. In the next instant, Karl felt a stinging punch to the back of his head. He spun round to face a second boxer. Then a third Royal Marine boxer, unseen at first, hit Karl in the nape of the neck.

"Holy shit," he grunted through his mouthpiece. Karl bobbed and weaved fast enough to keep all three men in his field of vision. Moving toward the man on his left, Karl forced him to retreat and turn, then hit him with a left hook that knocked him unconscious against the ropes. Then Karl's original opponent charged directly toward him. Karl stopped him with a lightning fast left-right combination that put the Marine face down on the canvas. Seconds later, Karl felt a piercing pain in his shoulder blade from a punch delivered by the third boxer. Karl could see that the third opponent sensed an advantage. Not waiting for him seize it, Karl threw a windmill left hook, then a piston-like right, sending the third man to the floor just as the bell sounded. All three opponents were out cold.

Channing Brown climbed through the ropes and into the ring. "Hope you didn't mind the surprise, lad," Brown said, wrapping a towel around Karl's shoulders. "We had to see how you'd handle multiple opponents with no forewarning. You did well indeed. You just prevailed against three of the best boxers in His Majesty's Royal Marines. You moved quite fast and thought just as quickly, feigning weakness then springing to surprise your adversary. From now on, you'll face three men in each boxing session."

"Good trick, Brown. Next time I'll be ready."

Brown nodded and frowned, not wanting to tell Karl about his next surprise.

96. THE GYMNASIUM, THORNBIL CASTLE, NOVEMBER 14, 1936, 4:15 P.M.

The opening bell of the first round had barely rung when the third of Karl's Royal Marine opponents gave him a pendulum-style kick to the groin that sent Karl to his knees, doubled over in pain. Karl caught a second knee to the face, and a third to the back of his head, sending him down to the canvas. One of the Marines tried to leap on top of Karl, but landed on the canvas as Karl rolled out of the way, a move he recalled instinctively from his youthful adventures at the Friedrichstrasse rail yard.

Karl sprang to his feet and ducked a fast left hook as he regained his footing. He knew he had to reassess his strategy. He backpedaled just long enough to let his opponents think they had the advantage. Then he charged ahead, aiming a flurry of punches at one opponent as another hit him with a stinging right from behind. When he saw the first man go down, Karl spun around to catch the second with a knockout right to the sweet spot of his jaw. As that opponent fell, the third Marine rushed at Karl with a flurry of punches. Karl retaliated with furious series of lefts and rights to the man's chest and stomach, sending him to the canvas too. Brown rang the bell and a fresh contingent of four marines jumped into the ring to attend to their mates with smelling salts and cold water. Brown handed Karl a fresh towel. "All that took forty-two seconds," Brown told him, glancing at his pocket stopwatch. "Next time you'll need to do better."

"I know. Speed has been my greatest asset. I have to be even faster," Karl said.

"Yes," Brown replied, "a lot faster."

97. THORNBIL CASTLE, NOVEMBER 21, 1936, 7:00 P.M.

A fire crackled in the hearth as the four men – Karl, Channing Brown, Jamie Creel, and Scotty North – gathered for dinner in a small room off the main hall of the castle. They had helped themselves to pints of lager from a tap behind the unattended bar and settled onto wooden stools as Brown began to speak.

"Cheers are in order, lads," Brown proclaimed. "Karl has given us and the Royal Marines an amazing display of his fighting skills. Even when outnumbered three to one, and with the Marquess of Queensberry rules suspended, Karl prevailed."

"Never forget," Brown resumed, addressing Karl directly, "that the Gestapo and the Nazis will not play fair. Kicks, head butts, knees to your jewels – you need to be ready for all of it. Henceforth, your training sessions will differ from a street fight only in that you'll continue to wear boxing gloves as a precaution against injuring a hand, and quite possibly killing one of His Majesty's young Marines. And of course you will keep wearing that all-important protective cup."

"You're honing me into physical and mental shape to withstand just about anything," Karl said. "But there's one problem. How in the hell am I supposed to stay in this kind of shape once I'm in Berlin?"

"Actually, you'll find several excellent athletic clubs in Berlin. You'll join the Berliner Sportverein, an exclusive club frequented by Party members and Nazi brass. SIS has already compiled a list of high-ranking Party men who take their exercise there. But more on that later. Let's drop all this blathering in English."

In a seamless shift to German, the conversation turned to Berlin, and reports by several SIS intelligence operatives, whose information was based on "snippets of facts" about the comings and goings of Nazi leaders, including Hitler.

After shepherd's pie and lager, the three Brits peppered Karl with questions about everyday life in Berlin, like getting from one district to another by U-Bahn and the price of beer and bread. They talked about the food served at the best restaurants, the procedures at different hospitals, Karl's book, and how he came to write it. The conversation then shifted to Karl Muller's childhood in East Africa.

The after-dinner talk ceased when Brown held up a hand and asked Jamie to switch on the shortwave radio, which was tucked among the Scotch bottles on the shelves behind the bar. They all listened as Hitler addressed a Nazi Party rally in Munich. At first, the Führer's voice was quiet, almost conversational. Soon, however, Hitler's shrill voice soared to a frantic pitch as he focused on the Communist menace to the east and within the Reich.

"Well, lads," Brown said once the speech was over, "there's some truth in what Hitler says. Stalin has successfully recruited agents in Germany, just as he has here in Britain. Oxford and Cambridge are producing young men who want to save mankind from capitalist oppression. We're reasonably sure that some of them have obtained critical posts in the Foreign Office, and even in SIS. The problem is, we don't know who or where they are."

"Enough politics for now, gentlemen," Brown said, pushing his chair back from the table. "Let's repair to the billiards table."

Focusing on the game, Karl failed to notice a Royal Marine enter the room behind him. Nor did Karl see the Marine's flattened hand rise slowly and strike suddenly into the soft tissue where his neck and shoulder met.

They used smelling salts to revive Karl.

"Sorry, lad," Brown said as soon as Karl had recovered enough to understand. "Thought you'd like to know firsthand how the Jackhammer works, especially when it hits you by surprise. You may well find it a rather handy addition to your arsenal."

"When do I start practicing?"

"Right now. There's a guard at the main gate to the castle grounds. Do him first. But remember, he's carrying a Lee-Enfield rifle and a sidearm. Jamie and Scotty will be around to offer assistance should anything go wrong."

Knowing a plea for time to prepare would show weakness, Karl said nothing. Moments later, after Scotty and Jamie had positioned themselves nearby and out of sight, Karl crept to where the Royal Marine sentry stood at parade rest, the barrel of his Enfield resting on his gloved right hand. Karl's swift silent blow put him down with a thump. Karl later practiced the blow on other sentries, all of whom were sworn to silence.

As winter approached, bringing down the curtain of dusk earlier each evening, Karl began spending more time in the gym. He worked to improve the speed of his punches, which Channing Brown's stopwatch timed with unforgiving precision. In the boxing ring, Karl survived more no-holds-barred onslaughts against fresh trios of Royal Marines. The bouts now resembled street fights, except that Karl and his opponents wore boxing gloves. Brown began cutting back on the frequency of the fights, knowing that Karl needed to conserve strength for the next phase of training.

98. GARMISCH, GERMANY, DECEMBER 20, 1936, 7:45 AM.

Morning sunlight filled the expansive dining room of the Pension Alpenhoff. At the elaborately set table, Fern and Frederick savored the scent of fresh fruit and black coffee. A week of skiing had done wonders for both of them. "You're almost like your old self, my dear," Frederick Wagner said, tipping his glass of orange juice toward her.

"You're so right, Uncle. I haven't been skiing since Karl and I went to Vermont two years ago. I'm a little stiff, but I can feel the strength returning to my legs now. See if you can you keep up with me today."

"I'll try. But a man my age must know his limits on the mountain, though I know a fellow who may be able ski right off your shoulder. He arrived last night, and I've asked him to join us for breakfast. I hope you don't mind. Ah, here he comes now."

Hermann Göring, larger than life in a forest-green ski suit, smiled and extended a hand to Fern. *"Guten Morgen, Doktor Wagner, Frederick,"* Göring bellowed, anticipating Frederick's proud introduction of his niece. "I see now that you're as beautiful as Frederick has boasted, proud uncle that he is," Göring said, seating himself across from Fern. "I hope you'll be so kind as to allow me to join you and Frederick on the mountain."

Fern laid her palm flat on the table. "Well, Reichsmarschall, if you're as good a skier as Frederick says you are, we shall have a wonderful day. It would be our honor to have you ski with us."

"It is I who am honored, Dr. Wagner. Your work in America and now in Berlin, not to mention all your writings, has attracted considerable attention. As an old *Luftstreitkräfte* pilot, I'm aware of the seriousness of burns and scaring. I myself have endured some very painful injuries. But, please, let's not waste this beautiful morning on such topics. Tell me, Doctor, did you learn to ski in America?"

"No, not in America, though I did ski there with my late fiancé and Uncle Frederick. American ski resorts are rather primitive compared with what we have here in Germany. I learned to ski as a schoolgirl, right here in

Garmisch. My mother's here with us now, but she's sleeping late this morning. I believe you've met her through General Haber."

Frederick beckoned for the waiter so they could order breakfast. He was relieved that Fern had decided to be gracious.

"I understand from Frederick that your late financé left Germany for America and became an American citizen," Göring said, once the waiter had taken their order. "Many Germans have done that. We need to keep our talented young people, like you, here in Germany. Do you believe we can do that, Dr. Wagner?"

"Yes," Fern replied, returning her coffee cup to its saucer. "I believe that more and more Germans living abroad will return to the Fatherland once they realize what you and your colleagues have accomplished here."

"I applaud your insight," Göring said, as the waiter served breakfast.

99. ALPSPITZE MOUNTAIN, GARMISCH, 12:35 P.M.

Fern saw that Göring was indeed an excellent skier, faster and more graceful than his portly figure suggested. It was a challenge for her to keep up with him. They were now on the fourth run down the mountain. Frederick, although skilled, often needed to rest and catch his breath. "I think Frederick spends too much time in his office and his factories," Göring said to Fern as they waited for her uncle halfway down the mountain. "He needs more exercise."

As they saw Frederick resume his downhill path toward them, Göring spoke again. "Fern, please telephone my office and make an appointment after the New Year holiday. There's something important I need to discuss with you, an opportunity for you to serve the Reich."

What, Fern asked herself, could Göring want? The thought of seeing Göring again bothered her, but she knew Frederick wanted her to behave.

"*Wunderbar,*" she said. "I shall telephone you as soon as I return to Berlin."

"Excellent. Once Frederick joins us, let's race to the bottom and get some lunch. Then I must get the afternoon train to Berchtesgaden."

100. WINSTON CHURCHILL'S TOWNHOUSE, MORPETH MANSIONS, LONDON, DECEMBER 31, 1936, 10:48 A.M.

Winston Churchill answered the doorbell and, without a word, led Channing Brown to a small drawing room, where he poured them both half-snifters of brandy. Thanks for responding so quickly to my invitation," Churchill said from deep in his chest. "Ralph Wigram is dead, quite possibly by his own hand. Ava Wigram discovered him this morning sprawled across the hardwood floor of his study. Damn bloody shame."

"Indeed, Sir. Ralph had been down in the mouth for some time and wrongly blamed himself for allowing Hitler's march into Rhineland last spring."

Churchill downed the brandy and turned his gaze to Brown. "Understand me, Channy, Ralph's death shall not go unanswered."

101. THE AIR MINISTRY, BERLIN, JANUARY 4, 1937, 1:00 P.M.

Hermann Göring strode across his spacious office to greet Fern, guiding her to a chair facing his enormous mahogany desk. Outside, a cold winter rain splashed against the window. "January in Berlin," he muttered, "no snow, just bone-chilling rain."

"A far cry from that wonderful morning on the mountain," Fern said, as she took her seat.

"Indeed," Göring sighed, "although I confess that I find it exciting to be back in Berlin. I had dinner with Frederick last night, and he talked a lot about you, as he always does. He's proud of your medical achievements, and he's hardly alone in his admiration of your work. I've just read a report from the Health Ministry that describes the innovative procedures you performed on some girls who were burned in a school chemistry lab fire here in Berlin. You did remarkable work there."

"You're very kind, Air Marshall. But why have you asked to see me?"

"I'll get right to the point. We're establishing a Luftwaffe hospital in Munich with a special burn-treatment and plastic-surgery unit. I'd like to appoint you head of that unit. The pay would be 20 percent more than you currently earn as a staff physician and professor here in Berlin. You would be assigned to the Luftwaffe as a Special Medical Officer."

Since she was familiar with the growing medical literature on disfigured combat pilots, Fern hardly needed to ask why the Luftwaffe needed a special burn-treatment unit.

Fern accepted Göring's offer of a small chocolate from the jar on his desk but held the candy in her hand. "Air Marshall, I will consider your offer," she said. "It sounds like a wonderful opportunity."

"It's a once-in-a-lifetime opportunity, Fern. We've already sent a sizeable Luftwaffe contingent to Spain to help Franco fight the Communists. So far, we've sustained very few casualties. But that could change. The fighting is extremely fierce. Volunteers are arriving from all over the world. American, Russian, and English volunteers have come to fight Franco. The Führer is committed to helping him. This will be the Luftwaffe's first great test."

Biting into the chocolate and savoring it, Fern chewed carefully while considering her response. "You're very persuasive, Air Marshall Göring. As it happens, I am just now winding up my lectures and completing a monograph. Once I have fulfilled those professional commitments, I'll inform you of my decision. In any event, I hope we can see each other again soon."

"Yes, we must do that – hopefully in celebration of your acceptance of this important position."

102. THE LIBRARY, THORNBIL CASTLE, JANUARY 5, 1937, 5:15 A.M.

"No running or boxing today," Brown told Karl. "Today you're off to Debden for some accelerated RAF flight training."

"RAF? Debden? Flight training?" Karl said, surprised and not knowing what to think. "What about my staying in shape?"

"That will proceed, except now we'll be slowing down the pace. You'll continue running and weight training, but only every other day. On the off days, you'll focus on flying. No boxing for a bit. You'll receive training in both single and multi-engine aircraft."

"You're forever surprising me, Brown, but I understand," Karl said. "I saw in my briefing binders that many of the Nazi brass enjoy flying. In fact, they seem to consider it a form of recreation. Among the elite, Hess and Heydrich are both skilled aviators, and Göring was a decorated combat pilot in the Great War. Flying will put me in the 'club,' so to speak."

"Precisely. As a doctor who's spent most of his life in Africa – with its poor roads and vast distances – you would be expected to know how to fly a small plane."

103. TIERGARTENSTRASSE, BERLIN, JANUARY 9, 1937, 7:00 A.M.

Standing on the enclosed terrace of her mother's home, Fern looked out over the sun-bathed blanket of snow covering the Tiergarten and contemplated Göring's job offer. Her first instinct had been to turn him down, but now the thought of being in Munich, and away from Berlin, pleased her. The Luftwaffe hospital would have its grim military side, but she would be helping young men who needed her specialized skills. She also felt the need to get away from her mother at least for a while.

After a Saturday morning breakfast of fried eggs and sausage, Fern told her mother that she would accept Göring's offer. She fully expected her mother to urge her to remain in Berlin, but Hildy's response surprised Fern.

"Bravo, Fern. This offer presents an incredible opportunity. I'm so proud. Hermann Göring is the second most important man in the Reich. You'll be quite stunning in Luftwaffe blue, and you'll meet important people. We should have some schnapps to celebrate, just the two of us."

"Mother, it's too early."

"Nonsense."

Hildy poured shots of Rumplemintz into their breakfast coffee. "I'll miss having you here with me, Fern, but you must move on with your own life. I wanted to play matchmaker and find you a young up-and-coming officer. But most of the officers in my circle are General Haber's age, fine for me but not for you."

"Tomorrow," Hildy continued, "let's go shopping for your new Munich wardrobe. We can ask Frederick to come with us."

"I don't think so, Mother. For one thing, it would bore him to death. And I'm a big girl. I'd rather buy my own clothes."

104. ROYAL AIR FORCE BASE, DEBDEN, ENGLAND, JANUARY 18, 1937, 4:05 A.M.

Shutting off the unwelcome clang of the alarm clock, Karl reached out to turn on the gooseneck lamp, happy he'd been able to sleep in comfort. The brick walls of what would soon be the flight officers' quarters for an RAF aerodrome provided more protection against the cold than did the ancient castle stones at Thornbil.

After climbing into sweatpants and an RAF-issue turtleneck, Karl sat down at the small bedside desk and studied his RAF training manual, taking notes and jotting down questions as he read. Then he went back over everything, making sure that his notes were tidy and legible and that they clearly identified what he did and did not understand.

5:15 A.M.

He put the manual aside and retied the laces of his sneakers, pulled a hooded sweatshirt over his head, made a scarf of his bath towel, and left for a predawn run. He passed four new hangars under construction. The clear winter air refreshed him. His legs felt sturdy and strong while his arms and shoulders welcomed the respite from the no-holds-barred training at Thornbil.

6:25 A.M.

After a quick shower, Karl went to the officers' mess where Brown had arranged for him to take his meals under a new assumed identity. According to the cover story, Karl was an executive with Brewster Aeronautical, an American aircraft manufacture that was developing new training manuals for test pilots. All of his work was "top secret," which precluded almost all conversation.

The immaculate new mess hall was serving breakfast to a handful of test pilots assigned to early-morning training sessions. Unable to adjust to the British preference of tea with milk, Karl asked the corporal behind the counter for tea with lemon. As advised, he again took no solid food in the morning before a flight.

Karl sipped his tea and thought about flying, trying to review everything he had learned. This was his twelfth consecutive day of training, and tomorrow would his first solo flight.

105. OVER DEBDEN, JANUARY 25, 1937, 8:10 A.M.

With his solo training in lighter aircraft behind him, Karl banked his single-engine Hurricane into the wind. His heart raced with the engine. Pulling back on the throttle, he soared to 10,000 feet. Through the canopy of clouds, he could see the town of Saffron Walden to the east as he listened for instructions on the two-way radio.

"Take her down to 1,000 feet," the voice at ground control commanded, "then pull up hard – and be sure to keep your mouth shut."

Don't think about it, Karl told himself, easing the stick forward and putting the Hurricane's nose on a steep collision course with the planet below. The needles on the control panel danced and the earth rushed toward him, closer every second. He waited until the plane was at 900 feet before pulling up on the stick. He soared sharply upward before leveling off. Minutes later, he set the Hurricane down on the flat grass runway. He was getting hungry.

Karl removed his leather helmet as he entered the officers' mess, ready for a light breakfast. The slightly built Captain Neville White was waiting for him.

"Congratulations, Karl. Good go of it in the Hurricane. That was a splendid dive from what I saw."

"I'm starting to enjoy it."

"Well then, lad," said White, "you'll be happy to learn that there's more to come. Your twin-engine training starts now. That means twice as much can go wrong. Meet me here in an hour and we'll have a go in one."

106. NEAR DARVEL, SCOTLAND, JANUARY 30, 1937, 3:00 P.M.

With Channing Brown as a passenger in the co-pilot's seat, Karl guided the Lockheed Hudson to a perfect three-point landing and taxied to the cement-block hut that served as an office for the small airfield. A driver from SIS waited outside the hut next to a Crossley staff car, rubbing his hands together against the damp highland chill. Brown had not briefed Karl on the nature of their trip, except to say it was the result of some thinking he'd done while Karl was at Debden.

Ten minutes later, Karl and Channing Brown stood in the doorway of a white thatched-roof cottage overlooking a wide grassy meadow. Before Brown could knock, Dr. Alexander Fleming flung open the wooden door and led them toward a fireplace that warmed the sitting room of his cottage.

"Mr. Brown, thank you for coming," Fleming said with only the hint of Scottish burr. A man of fifty-some years, Fleming had a gentle handshake. Brown introduced Karl as "Dr. White." He had already told Fleming "Dr. White" was about to embark on a risky enterprise.

"Dr. Fleming, we at SIS have been following your work," Brown said. "We understand that you've discovered a very promising new drug that may help Dr. White win new friends where he's going."

Fleming responded with an understanding nod and gestured for them sit on a sofa near the fire. Both accepted Fleming's offer of a sherry. "I hope that what I'm about to show you proves helpful," Fleming said. "It's a drug that my associates and I have developed. Some very capable people are working to refine it for the commercial market. But I think you'll understand better if I start from the beginning."

Fleming told them the story of how several years before, in his laboratory at St. Mary's Hospital in London, he happened upon a new drug that appeared to have unparalleled efficacy as an antibacterial agent.

Fleming poured each a second sherry. "Let's take our drinks to the basement," he said. "I'd like to show you my laboratory. It's small, but it allows me to tinker when I'm away from St. Mary's."

They went down a narrow stairway into the well-lit laboratory, in the center of which stood a large table covered with Petri dishes of different sizes. "Here, in these little dishes, are the spores that produce the drug," Fleming said with a grin.

"So how did you happen to discover this drug?" Karl asked

"Blind luck, as it were," Fleming responded. He told them that some years before, when he'd had a bad cold, a drop of his nasal mucus fell into a bacteria culture. He'd been upset with himself at first, thinking that he'd ruined a well-prepared culture. Soon enough, however, he discovered that the stuff from his nose had killed the bacteria. Intrigued, he began more experiments.

"I didn't get very far at first. The active agent I had isolated proved too weak to kill the kind of bacteria that cause serious illness. But then six years later, luck intervened again. After a window had been left open all night, I noticed that some of the staphylococci colonies I was cultivating were covered with a mold that was killing them. It was a rare mold called *penicillin notatum*, one that produces a very potent antibacterial agent."

"Then a doctor who knew what he was doing," Karl ventured, "could use small quantities of this antibacterial substance to perform what might appear to be miracle cures. Is that so?"

"Indeed he could."

"Does the substance require refrigeration?" Brown asked.

"No," Fleming said.

"Wonderful. So tell us, Dr. Fleming, how much of this antibacterial agent can we have?" Karl asked.

"I have a dozen vials that I don't really need. Take them," Fleming said.

"Thank you, Doctor," Brown said. "But I'll also need samples of the bacteria your penicillin kills – specifically the kind that cause bronchitis or other respiratory infections. Do you have any such bacteria?"

"No, but such bacteria can only be stored in well-insulated metal containers. As you must know, such substances pose grave health risks."

"That, of course, is why we need them," Brown replied. "We would, however, be happy to accept whatever samples of your miracle drug you can spare. We'll have to look elsewhere for the nasty bacterial agents."

107. CHANNING BROWN'S OFF-SITE OFFICE, HALF MOON STREET, MAYFAIR, LONDON, FEBRUARY 5, 1937, 9:00 A.M.

Karl sat reading and rereading the SIS briefing papers that Brown had recently added to his binder. He made notes in the margins and silently tested himself on the material, making sure he retained and understood everything. By now he knew every stop on the Berlin U-Bahn and the precise locations where he could drop and pick up messages.

Most important was what he was learning about his target, a former vagrant and political rabble-rouser who had somehow risen to become the leader of a great nation. In private meetings and public speeches, Hitler referred ad nauseum to his identification not with the Prussian elite, but with the common foot soldier, the man in the muddy trenches. Karl learned that Hitler himself had suffered serious wounds that had temporarily blinded him during the Great War.

Karl marveled at how this failed artist and bohemian drifter had built the Nazi Party into an awesome political juggernaut. He reflected on how Hitler used classic political spectacles, like parades and mass rallies, while at the same time successfully exploiting twentieth-century technologies like cinema, radio, and the airplane to make his presence known – and felt – in every corner of Germany. Karl reflected on what he'd learned about the Nazi Party, how it penetrated all aspects of daily life, from the workplace to the kitchen table – and how families with barely enough money to buy food would nonetheless contribute regularly to the Party.

Karl stood and stretched to clear his mind, then thought about those closest to Hitler – Bormann, Göring, Hess, and the others. Thanks to information in the briefing binders, much of it based on a deep undercover operative in Germany, Karl knew about their talents, proclivities, and vices. He knew their mothers' maiden names, where their grandparents were born. He quizzed himself about each man relentlessly – his exploits, his accomplishments, and his habits. At last Karl felt he knew all he could about these men without ever having met or talked with any of them.

108. CHANNING BROWN'S OFF-SITE OFFICE, MAYFAIR, FEBRUARY 8, 1937: 9:00 P.M.

"Karl Ludwig is dead," Channing Brown said, "and the life of Karl Muller is about to begin.

"Karl Muller's papers include documents showing the fictitious itinerary that will bring him to Germany. Those documents show that he left Cape Town by freighter on 4 January bound for Liverpool by way of Funchal, Madeira. From Liverpool, he came straight to London by train, arriving today to meet with his London publisher.

"Muller will stay for two nights here at Coleridge's and then hop the ferry from Folkston to Calais. There he will entrain for Gare du Nord in Paris. And from there, luggage in hand, he'll take a taxi to Gare de l'Est and catch another train, which will take him to the border checkpoint at Aachen, Germany. We're taking steps to ease his passage into Germany. If all goes according to plan, Karl will be in Berlin within seventy-two hours."

Brown stopped using the third person and addressed Karl directly. "Scotty or someone else from the unit will drop in on you from time to time as needs arise. And remember, we already have people in Germany. You'll be alone, but you'll have friends close by."

Brown removed a packet about three times the size of a wallet from his briefcase. "This packet contains more than twenty doses of Dr. Fleming's remarkable serum as well as several tightly sealed vials of illness-inducing bacteria concocted by a chemist at St. Mary's Hospital. Used properly, these should come in rather handy in working miracles and helping you to win friends in high places."

Karl told Brown he would tuck Fleming's miraculous serum and the bacteria with the new dress clothing he had just acquired – three tailor-made suits, a navy blazer, and a tweed jacket, all from Savile Row.

The expensive clothing concerned Brown. It might draw undue attention. Many Germans, even fairly well to do ones, hadn't bought a tailored suit for years. Then again, Brown thought, as a newly successful author from rural East Africa, Karl might be expected to display some *nouveau riche* tendencies.

"Jillian's after me to cut back on the cigarettes," Brown said, lighting the pipe his wife had given him for Christmas. "Now for some final plans that Jamie, Scotty, and I worked on while you were soaring though the clouds over Debden. Each will demand your unique talents and knowhow, and should bolster the credibility you'll need to gain access to Hitler."

Brown took three envelopes from his desk and handed one to Karl. "This one concerns the work you'll be doing for the Nazi Party once you've settled into you medical practice. Please open and read it."

Karl slit open the first envelope, which bore the inscription "Green Mark," and read the two-page memo. "Okay, this will present some challenges, but it's doable."

Brown handed Karl the second envelope, which bore the inscription "Matador."

Karl sat back after reading the one-page memo. "Pretty imaginative," he said. "But how will I . . ."

"It would be better not to know more now," Brown said. "Just keep in mind that the first time you hear the word 'Matador' you'll know that it's on. We'll tell you everything you will need to know then, but not before."

Brown handed Karl the third envelope, in which Karl found only a blank sheet of paper.

Brown did not wait for a question. "Yes, lad, it's blank. You've made a point of telling us that you and you alone must plan and execute the final phase of the mission. We intend to stick by that bargain. That, of course, is not to say we can't come up with new ideas as needs arise."

Brown reached into his desk again and this time took out a fifth of Johnnie Walker Black. "Incidentally, should you require any additional incentive," he said pouring out ample measures of Scotch into two tea cups, "your personal Swiss account has accumulated nearly nine months' worth of interest. In the event of your death, it's payable to Fern Wagner's account at the East River Savings Bank in New York."

"Cheers to that," Karl responded, sipping his Scotch. Brown nodded. "We could both use some rest," Brown said, savoring the bite of the Scotch on his palate. "You'll need to be at Victoria station tomorrow morning at five forty-five to start your journey."

"I suppose you've chosen my arrival in Germany to coincide with Mardi Gras?" Karl laughed.

"Right you are, Karl. As you know, the Germans call it *Fasching*. Aachen isn't New Orleans, but people will be having a rousing time of it and may have their guard down at Passport Control."

"Thanks, Brown. I know you guys have done all you can. I'm ready."

109. VICTORIA STATION, FEBRUARY 9, 1937, 5:25 A.M.

Standing in the cavernous station, Karl was unsurprised to see Channing Brown striding toward him. Brown was looking directly at Karl with something close to a grin, his soiled trench coat slung over his shoulder. Karl noticed that Brown was unshaven and wearing the same suit, shirt, and bowtie as the night before, although the tie now was unknotted and his collar dirty and unbuttoned.

"The Scotch kept me up. I tried to nap on the office couch, but it was no use. So I thought I'd trot over here for a second farewell and a . . . "

". . . last word?" Karl interrupted with a quizzical smile. He patted the vest pocket of his double-breasted blue pinstriped suit to assure himself once again that he had his forged passport and wallet full of fresh Reichsmarks.

"There's something I neglected to mention last night," Brown stammered. "Don't rush any part of this job. That will only tempt failure. Also, never forget that your precise orders are to get yourself in position to strike, and then to wait for the final go-ahead. You must wait for the order. Only after receiving it should you proceed with the final phase of the mission and your escape – all on your own, of course."

Karl nodded as he handed his two bags and a five-pound note to a porter. At train side, the two men shook hands. Then Karl leapt onto the train without looking back, and Brown disappeared in the flow of early-morning commuters, not in the least sure that he would ever see Karl Ludwig again.

110. CHURCHILL'S TOWNHOUSE, MORPETH MANSIONS, LONDON, FEBRUARY 9, 1937, 8:30 A.M.

Despite his beleaguered appearance, Brown decided to report immediately in person to Churchill. Clementine Churchill answered the door, greeting him with a warm smile.

"Good morning, Channy. Winston is anxious to see you." She took his coat and hung it carefully in a hallway closet, leading him up the carpeted stairs. "You may think you've caught Winston indisposed, but he often receives visitors this way. Don't be embarrassed."

Brown followed Clementine Churchill to the top of up the staircase and down the hall to a half-open bathroom door. "Winston, it's Channing Brown," she said, just loud enough for Churchill to hear.

Up to his nipples in warm soapy water, Winston Churchill sat in the tub scrubbing his back with a long-handled brush. He looked to Brown like an aging but cheerful cherub.

"Good to see you, lad." Brown half expected an apology, but Churchill appeared unfazed. "I hear you have something to report, and I presume you didn't want to use the usual channels."

"I wanted to let you know that I saw our man off this morning."

"Splendid. How soon will he be ready to strike?"

"That depends on how quickly he can establish personal and professional credibility. It won't happen overnight, that's for certain."

"Pity," Churchill said as he stopped scrubbing. "Keep after the lad."

111. THE FOREIGN OFFICE, WHITEHALL, FEBRUARY 9, 1937, 9:30 A.M.

Brown returned to his Whitehall office, where a visitor was waiting for him in the reception area. Bill Donovan rose to reintroduce himself.

"Pardon the surprise visit, Mr. Brown, but I was just calling on the Foreign Secretary and wanted to have a word with you."

"May I suggest then that we quit this dreary place where the walls have ears and walk in the morning air down to the Thames Embankment?"

112. THE THAMES EMBANKMENT, FEBRUARY 9, 1937, 9:47 A.M.

They stood at the railing of the Embankment while Brown gave Donovan a thorough oral report on Karl's training and departure for Germany.

"Should be boarding the ferry for Calais about now," Donovan surmised.

"Yes. We prepared the lad as much as we could. But, of course, one never knows."

"I'll be frank, Mr. Brown," Donovan said. "Preparation isn't the same as a plan. It will puzzle President Roosevelt when I report to him what you've told me. He'll want to know why there isn't a precise, step-by-step plan for completion of the mission, right through Ludwig's escape."

"I can respect that. I realize you Yanks like to plan ahead. So do we Brits, but we're somewhat different. Rather than come up with a precise plan, we create situations, try to exploit them, and seize the opportunities as they may to arise."

Donovan took out his pipe and managed to light it despite the wind. "Brown, I defer to your expertise in these matters. You guys have done all the work. Just accept that our President is a curious fellow. He'll have me, or someone else, checking up on this mission from time to time. He's also concerned about a foul-up. He has enemies in the press and Congress and has to keep his guard up."

113. EAST END AVENUE, MANHATTAN, FEBRUARY 9, 1937, 12:30 P.M.

The passion of the previous evening stirred anew in Josh as Nancy slept beside him, her dark hair covering her almond-shaped eyes. They'd had a rousing time drinking at Cassidy's with friends from the hospital. Josh wanted Nancy to wake up and make love again. She was totally giving of herself, and fellatio came naturally to her. In that respect, she was different from all the other Irish-Catholic girls Josh had known. There were certain things they simply didn't do. Josh liked the fact that Nancy kept her religion to herself without being shy about it. She often went to Sunday Mass at St. Catherine of Siena. He knew the church because it was where Karl and Fern had planned to marry. That was a memory now, part of the past.

Nancy was part of the present. She was alive, not only when she was with him but in everything she did, like organizing a fledgling nurses' union at the hospital and writing letters to the editor of the *Daily Worker*. Yes, something else made Nancy different from the other Catholic girls he'd known. Nancy was a Communist.

Josh slid out of bed and into his robe and slippers. The chronic headaches that had plagued him since the beating at the Bavarian Inn nearly a year before had mostly subsided. As he waited for the coffee to perk, he leafed through the *Sun* and a two-day-old copy of the *Daily Worker* that Nancy had left on the kitchen table. Moments later she appeared in the kitchen and rubbed his head to say good morning.

"What's the *Worker* got to say?" she asked, fastening her terrycloth robe.

"There's a lot about Spain. It seems you Commies are taking your lumps there."

"What can you expect," she yawned, "with the Germans bombing whole villages? Someone has to help the defenseless people that Franco and his German thugs want to destroy. I'm donating five dollars to the Spanish Loyalist Children's Relief Fund. Care to match that donation, my love?"

"You're getting to be expensive company."

"You're a capitalist doctor, you can afford it," she said resting her chin on his shoulder. "There's something else you can do," she said, sitting up, "and it won't cost you a cent, only a little time."

"What's that?"

"There's a Party rally to support the Spanish Loyalists next Monday night down at Union Square. I'm going to post a flyer on the bulletin board. I want you to come."

"You know I have no interest in that stuff."

"Josh, I love everything about you, but I don't understand your blasé attitude toward the Party and the changes it can bring for workers."

Having learned not to escalate arguments, he rejected the temptation to ask if she'd ever heard of the New Deal. "What's important to this worker is what I do at the hospital. That's where I fix broken bones."

Nancy climbed on his lap and wrapped her hands around his head. "Josh, at times like this I think your skull is so thick you must be Irish. You don't like Communists. But you say you love me, and I'm a Communist. I love what's happening in Russia. I hate what's happening in Germany. I hate the war in Spain, and so should you. There are probably thousands of injured children there thanks to Franco and his Nazi pals."

Josh moved to kiss her, but she placed a hand over his mouth. "Wait," she said, "I have more to say. I've never made a secret of my politics." She laid her head on his chest and then sat up to face him. "Do you know what it was like to see strikebreakers, I mean real goons with lead pipes? They cracked my father's skull wide open and left him lying on a San Francisco dock. No help came and he bled to death, Josh, right before my eyes. My mother and I were right there with him." She had told the story many times before, and he knew she had to get it out again. He held her for long moment before getting up to pour them both some coffee.

Nancy held her cup in both hands and looked up at Josh. There were no tears, just uncompromising resolve.

"You *do* hate the Nazis, don't you?" she asked, her dark-blue eyes fixed on his.

"You know I do."

"Well then, while the rest of the world grovels before them, the Communists are the only people with the guts to stand up to them in Spain. Ever think of that?"

"*Touché*. Let's get out of here and take a walk."

"Good, I'm ready for some breakfast."

A continent away, a man whose passport identified him as Karl Muller was carrying two suitcases as he entered the Gare de l'Est in Paris, where he asked a porter for directions to the evening train to Berlin.

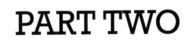

PART TWO

114. HOTEL KOBLENZ BIERKELLER, AACHEN, GERMANY, FEBRUARY 9, 1937, 9:00 P.M.

Among the thousands of revelers in the Bierkellers on the Bahnhof Platz, none was happier than young Franz Faber. Although his legs were feeling a little shaky, he was having the time of his twenty-two-year-old life. But hell, Franz reasoned, it was *Fasching* – and he would have all of Lent to repent for the sins he would commit on this night.

The sins Franz most wanted to commit were with a tall *Mädchen* with long honey-blond hair and short bangs. She had slipped her arm into his and introduced herself as Inga Keller. She'd told Franz that she was staying in Aachen for *Fasching*, en route to Hamburg to keep house for an aging aunt.

Challenging Franz to keep pace with her beer drinking, she jabbered on about how lucky she'd been to meet someone with an important job like the one he had at Passport Control. "What a shame that you must return to your post. It's always this way when I meet a handsome man," she said, tugging at his belt buckle.

"I'll be at the Bahnhof for another hour," he said. "I can meet you back here."

"I have a better idea," she said. "Walk with me to my hotel room." She led him up the stairs, opened the door, and handed the key to him. "Come back soon," she whispered in his ear. A gentle tip of her tongue on his ear punctuated her farewell.

Moments later, drunk and late for work, Franz hurried through the crowd in the Bahnhof as he heard the whistle of the incoming train.

115. COMPARTMENT 4B, PARIS-TO-BERLIN EXPRESS, FEBRUARY 9, 1937, 10:19 P.M.

Karl heard a man's voice speaking German on the train's public address system: "All passengers must disembark with their luggage and proceed directly to Passport Control."

With his new suit, freshly shined black shoes, and wool topcoat draped over his shoulder, Karl got off the train. He didn't mind standing out as the best dressed among his fellow travelers. The border guards, Brown had told him, rarely questioned the most conspicuous passengers.

Karl opened his suitcase at the customs cage where Franz Faber was in charge.

He could smell beer on the young man's breath as Franz rummaged through the neatly packed underwear, shirts, and suits. He saw Franz's eyes latch on to the shoebox. "They're wingtips from Harrods in London. Would you care to see them?" Karl asked. "*Nein, danke,*" Franz said in a rush.

Five more passengers were in the queue behind Karl. Franz squinted at the strange passport that identified Karl as a resident of British East Africa and stamped Karl into the Reich. "*Willkommen in Deutschland, Herr Muller,*" he mumbled.

On his way back to his first-class compartment, Karl noticed a tall woman in a fur hat with long gray hair and wire-rimmed glasses entering the neighboring compartment. He'd noticed her in the line of passengers boarding the train.

Closing the door to her compartment, Bonnie Peters drew the curtain and removed her gray hairpiece, which she stowed in her shoulder bag, next to a shoulder-length blond hairpiece with bangs. She was thankful that she'd cut her dark brown hair very short back in London. It made it easy to change wigs.

In his own compartment, Karl saw that the porter had opened his bed. He undressed to his shorts, pulled the crisp white sheet and fresh wool blanket over himself and slept the rest of the way to Berlin.

As the train pulled away from the Aachen Bahnhof, Franz hurried through the crowded Platz, back to what was an empty second-floor hotel room.

116. FRIEDRICHSTRASSE BAHNHOF, BERLIN, MARCH 20, 1937, 11:00 A.M.

Hans Krebs handed Fern the claim check for her trunk as she tried to make her voice heard over the clamor of baggage carts, locomotive whistles, and loudspeakers. "Still a half-hour till departure," she shouted. "Let's sit somewhere."

They found seats in a crowded café not far from the gate where Fern would board the train for Munich.

"Hans, you're an angel for helping me."

"My reward is another half-hour with you."

She knew Hans did not want her to leave Berlin and that he would miss her.

"I've enjoyed the time we've spent together, especially our chats over beer," she said. "I can't talk to Mother much anymore. She goes on forever about how wonderful it is that the streets are clean thanks to Hitler and the Nazis. Believe me, Hans, the sight and smell of a Manhattan street strewn with discarded orange peels, day-old newspapers, and dog droppings would do me good right now."

Fern rested her chin on her right fist and watched as Hans lit a cigarette. "One final thought about Mother," she said. "She's spending inordinate time with General Haber. He's always there for dinner. I suppose he'll stay through breakfast now that I'll be in Munich."

Hans shrugged. "That's just the gossip your mother's concierge, Frau Klaus, would report to the Gestapo or the SD. They love to keep an eye on generals and their ladies. A guy named Heydrich keeps files on nearly everyone. But don't worry. I'll see that anything Frau Klaus reports about your mother gets misfiled and forgotten."

"You're a dear, Hans. Mother and I need you to keep us out of trouble."

The loudspeaker announced the arrival of the train from Aachen in two minutes. Seconds later, it announced that the express train for Munich was ready for boarding.

"Come back to Berlin for a weekend as soon as you can," Hans said, touching Fern's arm.

"I'll try."

They made their way to the platform where the Munich train was waiting. Fern wondered what she would say when they parted. She found Hans appealing enough in a down-to-earth way. They'd been to the opera once, met several times for drinks, and dined out twice. Conversation between them had always flowed easily.

Hans hoisted her bags onto the overhead rack in her first-class compartment. She hugged him warmly, offering her cheek.

"What a dear you are, Hans. I'll buy you dinner when I get back."

"It's a date," he said, as he left the train, happy for the offer but wanting more.

117. ZEHLENDORF DISTRICT, BERLIN, APRIL 13, 1937, NOON

Karl relaxed in his back garden, which was awash with spring sunlight. As he waited for lunch, he thought about how he would gain access to Hitler. He had only recently finished setting himself up in the handsome stucco house where Dr. Heiden had lived and practiced medicine for three decades.

During his first weeks in Berlin, Karl had called and introduced himself to each and every patient who had a telephone. The others he called on in person, in their homes. He wanted Dr. Heiden's longtime patients to know that he, Dr. Karl Muller, was now available to treat them.

On most evenings he dined alone at home, though sometimes he visited one of the small neighborhood restaurants or Bierkellers. He shopped for groceries at the local markets, where he greeted his neighbors cheerfully. He asked them about their jobs, their children, and their grandchildren, always careful not to appear too inquisitive. On more than one occasion, he took the U-Bahn into the center of Berlin to go shopping or enjoy a beer in the sunlit street cafés amid the low-rise buildings that provided an ambiance very different from the canyons of Manhattan.

To his delight, he found that Dr. Heiden had left a robust practice and a well-organized office. As Brown had indicated, Frau Inga Frick came with the purchase of the practice. Forty-four years old, she was slender, energetic, and competent, both as a nurse and as a secretary. She ran a tight ship – answering the newly installed telephone and keeping scrupulously accurate files and books. She also brewed strong morning coffee that was far better than any coffee he'd tasted in the local restaurants.

Anticipating a simple lunch, he considered how relatively uncomplicated his life had been since his arrival in Berlin and how all that was about to change. As Brown had told him, Frau Frick was a committed member of the Nazi Party. He made sure that there was nothing in the house that could reveal his true identity or purpose, with the exception of the new drug and the tightly sealed vials of illness-inducing bacteria. He had taped these items to the underside of the bottom drawer in the large mahogany desk in his office.

Karl now delegated as much work as he could to Frau Frick. She kept his schedule and made all patient appointments. She even ordered medical supplies – an important task that Dr. Heiden had always kept for himself. The added responsibility thrilled Frau Frick. A month after his arrival, Karl gave Frau Frick a 10 percent increase in her weekly pay.

On this morning of routine office visits, mostly with elderly patients, Karl suggested to Frau Frick that she prepare them some sandwiches for a lunch in the garden to celebrate her raise. Lunch with Frau Frick usually consisted of shoptalk. This lunch would be different.

"I wonder whether I might ask you an important question," Karl said to Frau Frick as he finished a ham and Muenster cheese on thick dark bread.

"Why, of course, Dr. Muller."

"As you know," Karl began, leaning back in his seat, "I've been focused mainly on establishing the medical practice – and with your invaluable help we seem to be doing quite well. But I haven't come all the way from Africa only to practice medicine. I've come because of the rebirth of Germany under the Führer. I want to contribute to what you and others are doing here in Germany. Tell me, if you would, how I might go about joining the Party?"

Inga Frick beamed. "I'd be honored to have you join our local Party group here in Zehlendorf. We have some very prominent members in the Zehlendorf group, Reinhard Heydrich among them. A bright young man named Walter Schellenberg is also one of us. Although they're neighbors and members of our group, I must say they don't come to our meetings very often and aren't active at the neighborhood level. Too busy, I suppose."

Karl concealed his relief. He didn't want to encounter Heydrich or Schellenberg so soon.

Frau Frick began gathering the dirty dishes from lunch. "I should begin making preparations for your afternoon patients," she said. "The first is a lovely sixteen-year-old young lady named Gretchen, who was a patient of Dr. Heiden all her life. She has a bad case of what may be bronchitis. She was last here a few months before your arrival. She had received facial burns in a school fire, and came to see Dr. Heiden after receiving treatment in the hospital. Her father, Hans Krebs, is bringing her in at 3:30 this afternoon. He's a detective with the Berlin police."

118. KARL'S OFFICE, 3:30 P.M.

Hans Krebs led his daughter into the office. Gretchen was a curly-haired blonde with bright brown eyes and a healthy complexion, which minimized the appearance of the tiny scar on her left cheek, just below the ear. Examining her, Karl found significant pulmonary congestion and a high fever.

"Dr. Heiden took excellent care of Gretchen, as I am sure you will," Hans said. "She does well in school, but I don't want her to miss many more days. Exams are coming up next week, and she needs to be healthy to prepare."

"May I speak on my own behalf?" Gretchen asked in a respectful but impatient tone.

"My father forgot to mention that he's competing in the police pistol marksmanship championship this weekend in Stuttgart. I'd like go with him if I'm well enough."

"I already told her that won't be possible," Hans said with paternal authority. "She would need to feel much better than she does now, especially with exams coming up."

Gretchen sat up. "What my father doesn't understand, Doctor, is that I've already prepared for the exams. I've been in bed with my books for three days with nothing else to do."

Gretchen eyed Karl. "Papa has a good chance of winning the championship for the third year in a row. In fact, he can't miss. He's that good. And I want to be there to see him win."

Karl looked at Hans, who wore an exasperated expression. Karl led Gretchen and Hans into an adjoining examination room and then excused himself. Returning alone to his office desk, he could hear Frau Frick engrossed in a telephone conversation at her desk in the outer reception area. He pulled out the bottom drawer and removed a vial of Dr. Fleming's precious serum.

Karl filled a syringe with a small dose. "With your permission," Karl said turning to Hans, "I'm going to give Gretchen an injection in her bottom – that's the most effective place to inject this new medicine. Tomorrow when she wakes up, her temperature should be back to normal. And in two days the congestion should be gone. She should be able to accompany you to Stuttgart – and take her exams, of course. If, for any reason, she doesn't feel much better in two days, please call me."

As Hans and Gretchen were preparing to leave, Karl offered a parting remark: "I understand from the file that Gretchen suffered a facial burn in a school fire earlier this year. It appears to have healed."

"Very well, yes," Gretchen said. "In fact, I have only one small scar – here," she said, indicating the quarter-inch discoloration on her cheek.

"Whoever treated you did a fine job," Karl said.

"That was Dr. Fern Wagner," Gretchen said. "She's my father's girlfriend."

119. GIDEON PUTNAM HOTEL, SARATOGA SPRINGS, NEW YORK, MAY 2, 1937, 7:30 A.M.

Nancy emerged from the bathroom in her blue terrycloth robe brushing her dark hair. Her moist good-morning kiss and mint breath got Josh thinking. He tugged at the sash of her robe, but she pointed to the breakfast tray that had arrived while she was in the shower.

"After breakfast, darling. You won't cool off, but the coffee will."

They read the local *Saratogian* while eating their scrambled eggs. Extracting the sports section, Josh saw that the Giants had beaten the Dodgers 4-3 on a home run by Mel Ott at the Polo Grounds. The two teams would be playing again that afternoon, with a doubleheader the following day.

Nancy perused the main section of the newspaper. "German bombers blast Barcelona," Nancy read aloud. "Bastards."

Josh was not distracted. "You know, if we leave for New York early enough tomorrow, we could get to the Polo Grounds in time for both games."

"Not so fast. I'm not spending the last morning of my honeymoon racing to watch baseball. There will be times when it's me or baseball."

"You'll win every time."

"I sure hope so," she smiled. "But let's drop the small talk for a minute, Josh. We need a serious *tête-à-tête*."

"I know," he said. "It's Spain, right?"

"Yes, Spain. And all the good we could be doing there."

Josh leaned back, thinking. He'd heard it all before, and had already used his best arguments against going. They were both earning good money, far more than most couples their age. They could save, buy a house, and have children. Then again, all that could wait. Why rush? Besides, Nancy wanted to go to Spain. She brought it up again and again.

"Hey, partner. Are you here?" she asked.

"I've made up my mind," he said, leaning across the table to kiss her on the forehead and take her hands in his. "Here's the deal. It's in three parts. First, we make mad love until lunch. Second, we get out of here at dawn tomorrow and drive to the Polo Grounds to catch the Giants-Dodgers doubleheader. Third, after giving a civilized notice, say thirty days, we'll leave our jobs, sublet the apartment, and take our asses to Spain, where we'll find a hospital that needs us. I'm sure there are plenty of them there."

"Deal," she said, tugging at the sash of his robe.

120. THE FRICK RESIDENCE, ZEHLENDORF, BERLIN, MAY 2, 1937, 6:00 P.M.

It had stunned Karl at first to see Frau Frick and her husband in their tan Nazi Party uniforms. Now he sat at the table in their immaculate kitchen, having accepted an invitation to Sunday supper before attending his first local Party meeting, where Frau Frick and her husband would introduce him to other Party members. Karl found Wolfgang Frick, a skilled mechanic and owner of the largest auto-repair garage in Zehlendorf, to be a gracious, amiable host, pleased to meet his wife's new boss. The three shared of a chilled bottle of Piesporter.

Over a single-dish dinner of beef, potatoes, peas, and carrots, Karl listened to the couple's stories about the Party, how it hadn't been very strong in Berlin before the Nazis came to power. Their stories confirmed what Karl had read in the briefing papers he'd studied back at Oxford and Thornbil Castle. He recalled reading that the Nazi Party had won only 33 percent of the vote in Berlin in the federal elections of 1933. Frau Frick and her husband were among that 33 percent. They hadn't climbed on any bandwagon. They'd joined the Party because they actually believed in it. They knew how important it was for the Party to grow and stay strong for the Nazi regime to secure its hold on Germany.

After dinner, the three took a delightful walk to the Dresdener Bierkeller, where the Sunday-evening meeting of local Party members was about to get underway. Fifteen men and three women, all wearing tan Party uniforms, were seated at a long wooden table. Karl and the Fricks took their seats next to the local chairman, Kurt Mannheim, a stout man of about forty with thick blond hair combed straight back. After some brief welcoming remarks, Mannheim spoke of the need to raise more money for the Party. He wanted to see the Berlin Party become as strong as in Munich. Mannheim also spoke of the need to print more Party leaflets to boost turnout for a speech the Führer would be giving at the Olympic Stadium, still a focal point of Nazi pride one year after the 1936 Olympics. At end of his talk, Mannheim mentioned the upcoming door-to-door collection drive, which would help the Party purchase medical supplies for the brave men of the Condor Division fighting the Communists in Spain.

Chairman Mannheim introduced Karl as a prospective Party member. After scattered applause, Karl gave his first Nazi salute. He thanked Mannheim and the Party members for allowing him to attend and paused to let the silence work in his favor before resuming slowly in a low, respectful tone.

"I want you to know how honored I am to be here in your company. As members of the Nazi Party, you were fighting Communists in the streets while I was enjoying the simple life of a backcountry doctor. You faced hunger and bitter cold winters in the years after the Armistice while I enjoyed the sunshine of East Africa, where I was born under a German flag. I dream that our new flag will fly over that land one day soon. I promise to work with you and the Party to make that happen. What I've heard here tonight is that, despite your best efforts and many generous donors, the Party remains in critical need of funds, especially here in Berlin. I ask most respectfully that you allow me to join you in raising money for the Party. I hope you will accept my offer."

Chairman Mannheim leaned forward on his elbows. "Your words, Dr. Muller, are like Brahms to our ears. The Party needs money. So we welcome you, Dr. Muller, and we thank Herr and Frau Frick for bringing you to us."

9:10 P.M.

After accompanying the Fricks back to their house, Karl decided on a long walk to gather his thoughts.

A few blocks away, Chairman Mannheim sat at the typewriter in the kitchen of his modest home. He was putting the finishing touches on his Party meeting report, which he would deliver in person to Prinz-Albrecht-Strasse early the next morning.

121. LUFTWAFFE HOSPITAL, MUNICH, MAY 17, 1937, 4:00 P.M.

A warming afternoon sun filled Fern's second-story office. In the courtyard below, four wounded young men sat playing pinochle. A petite young nurse with slender arms held the cards for one airman, whose burned arms and hands were swathed in bandages.

Considering the scene outside her window, Fern laid aside reports from the Condor Legion's medical headquarters near Madrid. She headed down to the courtyard. Approaching the table, she was pleased that she could recall each airman's name.

Kurt Huber, a nineteen-year-old from Frankfurt, had suffered severe facial burns during an aborted takeoff. She had operated on him for three hours, and the bandages had come off only the day before. He was still black and blue, but Fern was reasonably sure his features would be restored.

Walter Grosse, twenty-six, from Cologne, had sustained serious burns over half his body when his ME-109 got caught in a swarm of Russian fighters and crashed near Madrid. Fern minimized the facial scarring.

The young man with bandaged hands was Willy Trenner, twenty-four. It would be another month at least before they knew whether he would regain the use of his fingers.

Not all patients at the facility required plastic surgery or treatment for burns. Josef Kramer, thirty, from Heidelberg, had broken his left leg in three places when a Condor Legion aerodrome near Seville came under surprise attack. The leg had to be rebroken and reset in Munich.

Josef was the first to see Fern approaching. "Please join us, Doctor. We've made a solemn pact – the winner of our little game will propose marriage to you."

"Thank God. I was afraid you were going to let me remain a spinster forever," she said with a wink.

"We hear your boyfriend is a Berlin cop and that scares us," Kurt laughed. "It wouldn't be healthy for any of us to get fresh with a cop's girlfriend."

"Suicide," said Walter, "goddamn suicide."

Fern responded with a grin. "Lottie," she said to the young nurse, "could you do us all a big favor? There are two bottles of Mosel in the refrigerator in the officers' mess. Both have my name on them in red crayon. Please bring them here, along with a corkscrew, which you'll find on top of my office bookshelf. You'll find some glasses in the doctors' lounge."

Lottie completed the task with haste but declined a drink.

"Smart girl, Lottie," Fern said. "I wouldn't trust these rascals not to squeal on you."

Lottie blushed. She was a trainee, only seventeen years old. She'd thought to bring a straw for Willy Trenner, whose bandaged hands couldn't lift a wine glass.

Fern uncorked both bottles and removed the pins that held her hair in a bun. "Okay, my friends," she proclaimed shaking out her hair, "I receive regular reports from Spain, all of which are censored and tell me very little. I need to know what's really happening there, and I need your help. There don't seem to be many German casualties," she added almost as an afterthought.

"Our planes are much better than theirs," Josef said. "They have mostly Russian planes, made by Communist factories."

"One thing I know for sure," Walter said. "I wouldn't want to be on the ground where our bombs are landing."

"It's true," Josef added. "The war is giving us a chance to test our planes and combat skills."

"But it's a crazy place," Walter said, holding up his bandaged hands. "On our side of the line, anyone even suspected of being a member of a labor union can be shot. And the few Spaniards who fail to attend Sunday Mass are branded Marxists."

"It's no better on the other side," Kurt interrupted. "I heard that after we bombed Valencia, the Loyalists retaliated by herding more than two hundred Nationalist sympathizers into an open field where they machine gunned them. I've also heard about priests being forced to dig their own graves before being buried alive."

"Well," Fern responded, "all this is as horrifying as it is informative. But I need to know how our medical people in Spain are doing."

Kurt cast a backward glance, concerned that someone might be listening.

"Please understand," Fern said, "I want to improve conditions in Spain. I can take up these issues with Air Marshall Göring without mentioning any names. Remember, Göring was himself wounded as an airman and still suffers from his injuries. He wants to know what's really happening. Most important, he has the ear of the Führer."

Kurt nodded and was about to respond when Josef spoke up again.

"You can listen to us all you want in this lovely Munich courtyard, on this beautiful spring afternoon, but that won't help you understand life in the war zone. War, Doctor, is shit. You've got to get up close and smell it for yourself."

They all sat in silence for a moment, sipping Mosel.

"Well put," Fern said. "Thank you for your candor, Josef."

That evening, in her spartan apartment near the hospital, Fern received a telephone call from Frederick. He would be in Munich the following day and had a proposition for her: If she would mix him a martini, he would take her to dinner. After everything she had heard that afternoon, it would be good to see Frederick and get his thoughts about what was happening in Spain.

122. ZEHLENDORF, BERLIN, JUNE 29, 1937, 10:00 A.M.

Karl sat at his polished mahogany desk examining the ledger on which he recorded the money he'd raised for the Nazi Party. Although his training had included much about the Nazi Party's constant hunger for funds, it nevertheless surprised Karl to see that, despite all the power the Nazis had amassed, their fundraising efforts remained quite primitive. Following Party protocol, he went door to door and family to family soliciting donations, usually on Sunday evenings. He kept precise records on the people he'd met and those who hadn't been home so he could return the following week.

He always spent time talking with Frau Frick over lunch to learn as much as he could about the people he planned to call upon. He sat with donors in their gardens on early summer evenings, sipping a beer or a glass of wine. He played with their children and grandchildren, whose names he memorized. His efforts paid off. In two months, donations among the families he visited regularly had more than doubled.

Then, with the blessing of Herr Mannheim, Karl went in search of bigger game. He began seeking more – and larger – donations from local business people and professionals. He started by making his own donation of ten thousand Reichsmarks. He couldn't ask prospective donors to do what he had not done himself. He started with bakers, butchers, green grocers, tailors, barbers, and hairdressers. After a time, he approached factory owners, engineers, dentists, and most important, fellow doctors.

Frau Frick used the telephone to set up appointments for Karl to meet with prospective donors over lunch, dinner, or cocktails. She was proud to help. Most prospective donors were happy to meet with the newly arrived doctor from Africa and to accept an autographed copy of his new book. Every donor received a handwritten note of thanks.

He began receiving letters from Party leaders commending his efforts. One was from Rudolf Hess, Deputy Führer and head of the Nazi Party. There was also a letter of praise from Reinhard Heydrich. Karl remembered something Brown had told him – that Heydrich kept files on just about everyone who came to his attention.

Karl used the newly installed intercom to invite Frau Frick into his office so he could ask her advice on "an important matter." He knew it was time to build on the momentum he had already established.

"If I am to serve the Party better," he said once she was seated, "I must know who can authorize me to expand my fundraising efforts. Obviously, the Führer is far too busy to deal with Party fundraising. Hess, I suppose, is also very busy, though he may be approachable. What do you think?"

"As you know," she said, "Deputy Führer Hess spends much of his time in Munich."

"I could write and ask to meet with him there." Karl sat back, weighing his thoughts. "I read recently that Hess is a member of the Berliner Sportverein, which he visits often when he's in Berlin. And that reminds me – I need to start exercising more regularly. May I ask you to secure me an application for the club?"

"Of course," she said. "How exciting! My husband and I have met Deputy Führer Hess on several occasions."

123. HILDY WAGNER'S HOME, BERLIN, JULY 1, 1937, 8:00 A.M.

Fern arrived at her mother's home after a fitful sleep on the night train from Munich. She had telephoned her mother from the Munich Bahnhof to say she was coming to Berlin for an appointment at the Air Ministry and a restful weekend, apologizing for the short notice. It had been difficult to get her mother on the telephone. She seemed never to be home.

A smiling Hildy Wagner held the door open and led her daughter to the kitchen, where Fern was less than surprised to find General Haber seated at the breakfast table.

"You look wonderful in Luftwaffe blue, Fern," Hildy said cheerfully. "It's your best color." Fern saw that her mother was not the least bit embarrassed about the General's presence.

The General rose and greeted Fern. "It's wonderful to see you, Fern. I've heard nothing but praise for your work in Munich. I understand that you're overseeing a thoroughly modern burns facility there. Won't you join us for coffee?"

"I'll sit and talk, but no coffee, thanks. I need to nap for at least an hour before my noon appointment at the Air Ministry."

"Tell me, Fern," Haber said, "what do our young heroes have to say about Spain and the enemies we're fighting there?"

"Actually," she said, "they're remarkably honest in their assessment of our capabilities – they understand that we're fighting a weak, under-equipped enemy. But our boys are valiant warriors, very courageous. Some, however, have been impaired for life. Just yesterday I treated a young man from Westphalia who's been blinded for life. He'll never see a pretty girl again."

Fern accepted a large Kaiser roll with butter and a glass of milk from Hildy, consuming both quickly.

"Have your nap now, dear," Hildy said. "But first let me tell you some good news. The General and I have decided to marry. He'll be moving in with me here and will use our library as his study. That way I can keep an eye on him – and keep him away from the pretty young stenographers at the General Staff offices."

"How wonderful, Mother. Of course, I'm not surprised. I've seen how much you two enjoy each other."

Fern thought she might grow to like General Haber as a man, but not his uniform. And she was sure that the uniform was what mattered most to her mother.

124. THE AIR MINISTRY, BERLIN, JULY 5, 1937, 9:15 A.M.

The whirring of a large floor fan reverberated through the room. Erhard Milch, special aide to Air Marshall Göring, the man who ran day-to-day operations at the Ministry, escorted Fern to a table near an open window that looked out over the Wilhelmstrasse. Despite the heat and high humidity, Milch's uniform jacket was buttoned to the neck.

"Air Marshall Göring apologizes that he cannot see you today," Milch said in his pleasant yet stern tone. "He was called to attend a special meeting at the Reich Chancellery. However, the Air Marshall wanted me to inform you that he has granted your request for an assignment in Spain. In fact, your request pleased him very much, not least because it coincides with the Führer's decision to increase German support for Franco. You'll be in charge of a field hospital unit on the Madrid front."

"Please thank the Air Marshall for granting me this honor," Fern said. "Tell me, do you know how many doctors I'll have on staff? In my posting request, I asked for ten doctors and twenty nurses, plus ample quantities of sulfa drugs, morphine, and medical supplies."

Milch stared at the folder in his hands for a long moment. "Unfortunately," he said, "according to this report, you'll have only two doctors and four nurses. As for medicines and drugs, our resources remain limited."

Fern stood and walked to the window, then spun around to face Milch. "I know that qualified doctors are in short supply. So are medical supplies," she said in a low clear voice. "But pilots are also a precious resource. When a good pilot is wounded, we need the capability to treat him without delay. That requires skilled medical personnel and ample supplies of modern drugs."

"Give me a detailed list of what you need," Milch said curtly, "and I'll submit your request to the Air Marshall."

"I've already provided the list," Fern said. "If you've lost it, I'll send a carbon copy. I'll also be sending a copy of the request to my Uncle Frederick, who encouraged me to seek the assignment in Spain. His pharmaceutical company can supply the drugs I'll need. You get me the doctors."

Fern turned and left the room, not waiting for Milch's response.

125. MADRID, AUGUST 15, 1937, 1:00 P.M.

Josh wended his way around the craters that pocked the Plaza Mayor as he walked back to the hospital after lunch. It was the fourth day in a row that his midday meal consisted of a slice of stale brown bread and an orange, which he ate in the apartment he and Nancy had taken off the Calle del Arenal. He stopped to tighten his belt. He'd already lost ten pounds. When he arrived back at the hospital, a nurse rushed him to the operating room, where a four-year-old girl needed to have her leg amputated. Once he'd finished that procedure, he splashed cold water on his face as two stretcher-bearers arrived carrying a middle-aged jeweler suspected of passing information to the Nationalists. The stretcher-bearers told Josh that Loyalist militia had castrated the jeweler and left him to die on the steps of the Palacio Real. Josh managed to stop the bleeding, but the man died twenty minutes later. Josh closed his eyes and looked up to see a badly burned boy, barely school age. He would take no break that afternoon.

126. HOFBRÄUHAUS, MUNICH, AUGUST 16, 1937, NOON

The air in the beer hall was thick with the odor of tobacco smoke, beer, and sausage as Karl waited at the bar for Rudolf Hess. He had just taken his first sip of beer when he was startled by the presence of a stunning young woman whose prematurely gray hair was tied back. She wore a black skirt and a gray jacket with a swastika armband.

"*Heil Hitler*, Dr. Muller. My name is Greta Heppler and I work for Rudolf Hess. Your letter to the Deputy Führer was referred to me. Herr Hess and I have discussed it. He extends his apologies for not arriving on time. He's been delayed by a telephone call from a top Party supporter in Berlin and sent me to greet you. I suspect he won't keep us waiting long."

Karl stood, extending his hand. "The Deputy Führer is eager to meet you," Greta Heppler said, standing at the bar. "In fact, he asked me to tell you that he knows you've come all the way from East Africa – and with the success of your book and the way you've been helping the Party . . . it's all quite remarkable, really. Herr Hess has reviewed your letter and, needless to say, will be happy to accept all the money you can raise, especially from educated supporters in Berlin and northern Germany where the Party needs to grow stronger."

An unsmiling Rudolf Hess arrived only moments later. "*Heil Hitler*, Dr. Muller," Hess said, giving a fast Nazi salute. He sat down before Karl could rise to greet him and then waved for his two bodyguards to stand down and take seats at a nearby table. "*Drei Biere*," the Deputy Reichsführer barked to the bartender.

"Thank you for coming, Dr. Muller. I hope that Fräulein Heppler has conveyed our appreciation for all your efforts on behalf of the Party. I understand that Frau Frick is in your employ in Berlin."

"It was on Frau Frick's advice that I asked for this meeting."

"I've known Frau Frick and her husband for five years," Hess said, with a trace of a smile. "Both are committed National Socialists."

With one hand, the bald bartender placed three beers on the bar in front of them. Hess downed his stein in several gulps.

Karl ignored his beer and looked at Hess. He'd been planning exactly what he would say for several days.

"Thank you for meeting with me, Deputy Reichsführer," Karl began. "What I'm considering, if you don't mind me getting straight to the point, is to travel throughout the Reich speaking to small groups of prominent professionals – doctors, bankers, insurance executives, and industry leaders. My thought is that the surest way to gain these men's financial support is to first gain their emotional allegiance. So I'll start by telling them some jokes and amusing stories about growing up as a German boy in East Africa, reminding them what a privilege it was to bring German culture and civilization to that part of world. Then I'll remind them how everything changed in Africa after 1914 – how Negro conscripts from the Belgian Congo butchered and raped German women."

"A sound emotional approach, but how will you relate that to what is happening now?"

"I'll tell them that we Germans must continue to grow strong so that such things can never happen again. A strong Nazi Party, I'll remind them, means a strong Reich, which will overcome the rape of Versailles and overwhelm the ranting of Communists here in Germany, in Spain, and everywhere else in the world."

"You make your case well," Hess said, leaning forward with interest.

"But how will you arrange for these presentations?" Greta Heppler asked.

"Well," Karl said, "I would rely on your Party operation here in Munich to open doors and book engagements for me. Frau Frick can do the travel and hotel arrangements. If necessary, I can save time by flying myself to important engagements."

"Ah, so you're a pilot as well," Hess said.

"Flying is necessary to traverse the vast distances of Africa."

"It appears, Dr. Muller, we have more in common than our love of the Party. You see, I too am a pilot. Perhaps we shall fly together one day soon."

"I look forward to that. In fact, I'm planning to join a flying club in Berlin to keep up on my flying skills."

"Excellent," Hess said. "I hope we can enjoy some free time together soon – hopefully in celebration of your successful fundraising."

127. EL TORO BAR, MADRID, AUGUST 17, 1937, 7:42 P.M.

Josh and Nancy sat at a table near the bar in the smoky cantina. The evening shelling had not yet begun. They had just finished their dinner of canned salmon, tomatoes, and weak local beer when a man approached their table.

"I see that you're Americans. May I join you? It gets lonesome in a crowded place when you don't know anybody. And none of my pals has shown up tonight," the man said, removing his wire-rimmed spectacles. He was a tall, well-built man with a neatly trimmed mustache. His dark hair showed strands of gray. Josh sensed a presence about him.

"Sure, sit down and have something to eat," Josh said, offering the man bread and olives.

"I'm Josh Greenberg, and this is my wife Nancy. We work at the hospital near the Prado. I'm an orthopedic surgeon, and Nancy's a nurse."

The man settled opposite Josh. "My name is Ernest, Ernest Hemingway. This is a hell of a place to meet such a good looking young American couple."

"Thanks," Nancy said. "We know your work. I've read *A Farewell to Arms* and loved it, especially Catherine Barkley, the nurse."

"So did I," the writer said. "But that's another story. I'd like to talk about you instead. I need some fresh anecdotes for a piece I'm doing for *Colliers*. It's due in two days, but the story just hasn't come alive for me yet. It needs more flesh-and-blood stuff about what Americans are really doing in this war – and not just the guys doing the fighting, but the ambulance drivers, the doctors, the nurses – people like you."

"We're not looking for glory," Nancy said. "The hospital where we work is the real story. That's where you get to see severed limbs, gangrene, and disfigured faces – the real horror of war."

Reaching into a side pocket of his gray cardigan, Hemingway took out a notepad and pencil. Then he waved to the old waiter, a rail-thin man well into his seventies. "Let's have the best red you've got," the writer said in Spanish.

"I hope General Franco doesn't interrupt us with his regular evening bombardments," Nancy said with a nervous laugh.

"Don't worry," Hemingway said. "Forget Franco and his Nazi pals. Tell me about your hospital and the little kids you've treated there. Tell me about the wounded civilians and the old people."

"There's one thing I do every day that never gets any easier," Nancy offered.

"What's that?" Hemingway asked.

"Closing the eyes of a dead child."

128. BERLIN, SEPTEMBER 22, 1937, 6:00 P.M.

The next time he was in Berlin, Rudolf Hess responded with enthusiasm to Karl's invitation to work out with him at the Berliner Sportverein. Karl had been a member of the prestigious men's club for several weeks. The club had recently rid itself of homosexuals, who had formed much of the pre-Hitler membership. Karl had told Hess to invite a guest if he wanted, so it was no surprise when Hess arrived in the company of a stocky man named Martin Bormann, his deputy.

"It's an honor to meet you Herr Bormann," Karl said. "I hope the club proves adequate." Hess and Bormann were both dressed in well-tailored single-breasted suits of light gray wool.

"Exercise will do us all good," Bormann said. "Keeping the Führer on schedule leaves me little time for recreation."

"It's a privilege to host two men so close to our Führer."

"The privilege is ours," Bormann said. "One doesn't often have an opportunity to meet a man who's a serious author and a formidable fundraiser. It's an interesting combination."

"Karl, it may please you to know," Hess said, "that I brought up your fundraising achievements during this afternoon's meeting with the Führer. He was very interested in your success and chided me for not using you to greater advantage."

In the weight room Karl held back, lifting less than a quarter of the weight he usually did. Hess proved fit enough, especially in the pool, where he swam twenty laps without interruption. Bormann did some light swimming then opted for a massage.

Later, in the half-light of the club barroom, the three men sat at a circular table and ordered steins of pilsner. "Rudolf, Martin," Karl said, pushing his stein aside, "I realize that there are many demands on the Führer's time. But I was wondering whether you gentlemen could arrange for me to meet with him."

"I wouldn't press for it now," Bormann counseled.

"I agree," Hess said flatly. "You might catch him in a bad mood. You don't want that, Karl."

Bormann nodded. "Every meeting with the Führer requires a specific purpose. He has no patience for idle talk."

"I respect your advice, gentlemen," Karl said. "I withdraw my request and will buy you both another beer." Since there was no waiter in the small barroom, Karl walked to the bar and ordered another round, interrupting the bartender's perusal of the football scores in an afternoon newspaper. Glancing back at the table, Karl saw that Hess and Bormann were sharing a laugh and not looking at the bar. The bartender placed three fresh drafts in front of Karl and returned to his newspaper. Karl reached into his jacket pocket and uncapped a vial of the bacteria Brown had given him, emptying its contents into one of the steins. Back at the table, he pushed that stein under Bormann's chin. He was content now to let his two guests do most of the talking, interrupting only to suggest that they adjourn to the Taverne, a popular Italian restaurant where dinner would be on him.

129. THE TAVERNE, SEPTEMBER 22, 1937, 8:30 P.M.

They took a corner booth in the crowded, noisy restaurant. "It's a pity we didn't meet sooner, Dr. Muller," Bormann said. "We might have enjoyed an evening on the town while my wife and children were in the Obersalzberg. In case you haven't noticed, Berlin has more than its share of beautiful women and, of course, foreign journalists." He nodded toward a packed table in the back of the room, noting the presence of William Shirer, the American CBS radio correspondent, and Martha Dodd, daughter of the American Ambassador, along with several others, all engaged in animated conversation.

"I've been so absorbed in my practice and with Party fundraising that I haven't had much of a chance to get out on the town," Karl responded.

"Then by all means, Doctor, when time permits, I'll have to show you where to find some female companionship." Hess stiffened in his seat. He was far too dedicated to the Party and the Führer to entertain any thoughts of womanizing.

Over a platter of Bavarian sausage and sauerkraut, Karl listened as Hess and Bormann reminisced about the Nazi Party's early struggles. Just before coffee, Bormann excused himself, saying that he felt feverish.

"As you may know," Karl said as Bormann rose to leave, "I've taken over Dr. Heiden's practice in Zehlendorf. Please call me tomorrow if you still feel ill." Karl handed his calling card to Bormann.

130. THE BORMANN RESIDENCE, BERLIN, SEPTEMBER 24, 1937, 9:15 A.M.

"Doctor Muller, welcome. Herr Bormann is expecting you." The short, white-haired housekeeper who answered the door guided Karl to the master bedroom on the second floor, all the time explaining that Frau Bormann was out shopping with four of her six children, while the other two were in a basement playroom.

Karl found Martin Bormann clad in a blue woolen robe, sitting upright in a straight-back chair.

"Ach, Karl Muller, thank goodness you're here," Bormann said, coughing into a handkerchief. Karl reached into his black bag for a thermometer and placed it in Bormann's mouth.

"My God, Martin you have quite a fever, over thirty-nine degrees," Karl said reading the thermometer. "Perhaps I should call the fire brigade." Karl then listened to Bormann's breathing with a stethoscope.

"Shit, Karl, I'm to meet with Hess and the Führer to go over his speech for a Party rally in Munich this weekend. The Führer will go crazy if I stay home."

"Well, Martin, like it or not, you dare not go to work. Based on what I've heard, the Führer is very protective of his health. He wouldn't want to catch whatever is in your system."

"True. But I'm afraid he'll send Dr. Morrell, his crazy personal physician, over here. All Morrell does is administer weird injections, what you might call a 'cocktail' of different drugs. I don't like the guy. I think his injections make the Führer nervous."

Beads of sweat were forming on Bormann's furrowed brow. "Martin," Karl said in a firm voice. "I can help, but it will require an injection. You'll have to trust me."

Bormann paused. "At this point I have little to lose, so let me have it." He began rolling up the right sleeve of his robe.

"No, Martin, this injection won't go in your arm. I have to put it in your buttock. Now just lower your pajama bottoms and lean over the bed."

Bormann didn't flinch as Karl administered the injection. "Now stay in bed today," Karl advised. "I'll come by to see you first thing tomorrow morning."

As Karl was leaving, Bormann used a bedside telephone to call the Chancellery to explain his absence. Hanging up the telephone, he pulled the quilt up around his chin and fell asleep.

131. THE BORMANN RESIDENCE, SEPTEMBER 25, 1937, 3:20 A.M.

Bormann awoke to find that his chills and fever were gone. He rose and pulled on his robe. With his wife still asleep, Bormann put on slippers and crept down to his study, where he began poring over a set of architectural drawings.

At dawn, he dressed and telephoned for his chauffer, who drove him to the office.

132. ZEHLENDORF, BERLIN, OCTOBER 8, 1937, 10:30 A.M.

There was still more than an hour before lunch, and Karl had already seen five patients. He enjoyed immersing himself in the day-to-day routine of general practice, even though he missed the specialized orthopedic work he'd done back in New York. He sat at his desk reviewing the neatly typed schedule, prepared by Frau Frick, outlining the remainder of his day. There was a Party function in Charlottenburg that evening. Mannheim and the other local leaders wanted him there. And, thanks to Hess, there was a meeting of business leaders that evening in Potsdam.

There was a knock at his office door. Before he could rise to answer it, Frau Frick entered the room with an envelope in her hand. "This just arrived," she panted with excitement. "A messenger drove up in a black Mercedes. It's marked for your 'Personal and Immediate Attention.'"

Raised printing on the envelope indicated that it had come from the "Office of the Chairman and President, Wagner Industries." Karl slit the envelope open, trying to hide his apprehension. He hoped that Frau Frick would interpret any visible anxiety on his part as being due to Frederick Wagner's eminent position in the Reich.

WAGNER INDUSTRIES HEADQUARTERS
BERLIN
OCTOBER 7, 1937

My Dear Dr. Muller:

As a man concerned about Germany's future and one who believes that the Nazi Party must play a vital role in that future, I commend your recent fundraising efforts on behalf of the Party.

In that regard, I have something very specific to request. I discussed this idea with the Führer and Air Marshall Göring over dinner last night. The Air Marshall agreed with the idea and will be available to discuss it with you at five o'clock this afternoon. He has reserved a table for that purpose in the cocktail lounge at the Hotel Adlon.

Reply only if you are unable to attend this meeting. I regret that business in Hamburg will make it impossible for me to participate.

In light of your diligent efforts, I feel compelled to offer a token contribution of my own. Enclosed please find a bank draft made out to the Party in the amount of 100,000 Reichsmarks. I trust you will accept it with my respect and admiration.

Very truly yours,

Frederick Wagner

Karl smiled at Frau Frick and showed her the bank draft.

133. HOTEL ADLON, BERLIN, OCTOBER 8, 4:50 PM

Wearing a brown tweed sport coat and a black turtleneck, Hermann Göring attracted little attention as he tapped his right foot gently in step with the string quartet's Strauss waltz. He feigned interest in the newspaper, a defense against any passersby who might impose on him.

Göring liked the bar at the Adlon, an elite watering hole where he could take the measure of this Karl Muller. Whatever Muller had done, it had lit a fire under Hess, and that was good. And if this idea of Frederick Wagner's worked – well, that might ease some of the pressure on Frederick, Krupp, I.G. Farben, and the other industrial giants that the Party was always asking for funds.

Glancing at his wristwatch, Göring saw that Dr. Muller should arrive within ten minutes. It bothered Göring that Frederick was in Hamburg and wouldn't be on hand to present his own idea to Muller. But, as Frederick had put it: how could anyone dare say 'No' to the Commander-in-Chief of the Luftwaffe? Göring thought about what Frederick had said on the telephone that morning: "Send this young doctor to Spain as a medical officer attached to the Condor Legion. Let him do good work there and bring him back as a hero. Then his fundraising speeches will be even more compelling. Instead of these tales of a simple backcountry doctor from East Africa, he can recount glorious adventures with the Condor Legion and its fight against the Spanish Communists." As always, Frederick had been quite persuasive.

There was, of course, another benefit of sending Muller to Spain. As Frederick had observed, Muller appeared to be a natural leader as well as a good doctor. He could replace Fern Wagner in Spain, freeing her to return to Munich, where she'd be out of the war zone and have a bigger staff and more equipment.

Looking up to see Karl standing before the table, Göring rose to greet him. Karl shook Göring's hand firmly. "Please join me, Dr. Muller. Would you like a Bavarian beer?"

"A beer would be wonderful," Karl responded, easing into a seat.

"Strangely enough, Dr. Muller, I had just been thinking about a fellow member of your profession, Dr. Fern Wagner. As you know, I'm in close contact with her Uncle, Frederick Wagner. Do you know Dr. Wagner?"

"Only by reputation," Karl lied. "In fact, I've read some of the articles she's published in medical journals. And I believe I heard something about her being appointed to a hospital in Munich."

"That was some time ago. Now she's in Spain with the Condor Legion. I must tell you, Dr. Muller, she is a very attractive woman and a highly accomplished physician. You should meet her someday."

"I look forward to doing so, Air Marshall."

Karl listened as Göring outlined the plan. Karl would spend six months with the Condor Legion near Madrid, where he would replace Dr. Wagner, who was doing a magnificent job but whose skills would now be more valuable back in Munich. While in Spain, Karl's main mission would be to acquire medical experience in a combat zone. Such experience, Göring explained, would enhance his credibility among professionals and business leaders once he returned to Germany and resumed fundraising for the Party. The sky-blue Luftwaffe uniform with its Hauptmann insignia wouldn't hurt either.

"With all due respect, Air Marshall, I'm still settling into my practice here in Berlin. My patients are just getting used to me."

Göring smiled patiently. "The Luftwaffe will pay you a salary equivalent to your current income. Naturally, you can return to your practice at the conclusion of your service in Spain. And we'll see that your patients get the very best treatment during your absence. Think about it: serving in Spain can only benefit your practice in Zehlendorf. Many of our top government officials are your neighbors and may soon be your patients. From what I hear, you're a superb doctor. Bormann never shuts up about how you helped him."

Karl decided that he'd shown reasonable resistance.

"I am, of course, humbled by this incredible opportunity to serve the Reich and the Party. I shall be proud to wear the blue uniform of the Luftwaffe."

"Splendid. I shall inform Frederick and the Führer. The Führer will be especially pleased."

"I would be honored to meet with the Führer."

"So Bormann has told me. The Führer's schedule is incredibly demanding. Seeing him will almost certainly have to wait until after your return from Spain."

The remark relieved Karl. He knew he wasn't ready.

"Naturally," Karl said, "I find the idea of meeting the Führer to be quite exhilarating. But I also know it would be better to wait until after I've completed my service with our brave men in Spain. Then I can stand before him as a fellow soldier."

"Well put, Karl. The Führer has great respect for combat veterans, including pilots, I'm happy to say."

"The Air Marshall should know that I too am a pilot."

"Where did you learn to fly?"

"In Africa," Karl lied, and then added, truthfully, that he was currently honing his skills with instruction in multi-engine aircraft at Berlin's

Templehof Airport. "I already have ten hours of twin-engine training," Karl told him.

"Wonderful. I'll recommend you for membership at my flying club here in Berlin. Hess is also a member. He's a very enthusiastic aviator."

"I can see that you're a man of many interests," Göring said, savoring the last of his beer. "So am I. When you return to Germany, perhaps we can go flying together. And if you're a skier too, so much the better. Frankly, that's what I love to do when I can get the hell away from Berlin in winter."

"I'm eager to learn the sport," Karl said, lying again.

"Excellent," Göring said, rising to leave.

134. CONDOR LEGION AIRFIELD, THE MADRID FRONT, OCTOBER 10, 1937, 5:30 P.M.

To his SS colleagues, thirty-year-old Leutnant Günter Jurgen seemed destined for rapid advancement. He had already completed a stint as a volunteer-observer with the Condor Legion during the infamous Operation Rugen – an air raid on the northern city of Guernica. During that raid, Heinkel He 111 bombers killed more than sixteen hundred and wounded another nine hundred, nearly all of them civilians. After that, Jurgen served with a special SS group that spearheaded ground offenses for Franco-led forces near Malaga and Bilbao. Jurgen became a hero in that operation, crawling around a Loyalist machine gun nest on his belly and then jumping the two enemy soldiers who manned the emplacement from behind, knocking both unconscious with his fists. That he was good with his fists came as no surprise as Jurgen was undefeated in the SS boxing program.

On this autumn afternoon, Jurgen sat alone at a table in the tent that served as the officers' mess. His tour was nearing its end, and he had just bullied his way through the red tape to reserve a seat on a Luftwaffe tri-motor back to Berlin and a new posting at SS headquarters on the Prinz-Albrecht-Strasse.

Alone and anticipating the pleasures of nightlife in Berlin, Günter finished his fourth bottle of beer. He knew there was a good brothel three miles down road, though he hardly considered it worth the bother. That place would furnish him only with a Gypsy or some other dark-skinned slut. What he craved was a fair-skinned Saxon beauty, the kind he could find at Salon Kitty, which catered to SS officers and other elite clients in Berlin.

As the last beams of autumn sunlight shone through the tent, he noticed a woman sitting alone at a nearby table. He moved closer to where she sat, though she seemed oblivious to his presence.

"Need some company?" he asked. "I'm Leutnant Günter Jurgen." Even in the late-afternoon dusk – no one had lit the lanterns yet – he could see the finely sculpted features of her face.

"I'm Dr. Fern Wagner," she said as he moved closer to where she sat.

"Can I get you a beer?" he asked.

"*Nein, danke,*" she said, raising her hand to decline the offer.

"Are you sure?"

"*Ja,* but you go ahead. I have to look in on some comrades of yours in a few minutes." When he returned with another beer, Fern did what she always did to put a man at ease: She asked him about himself, a ploy she'd learned from her mother.

"So, Leutnant, where are you from?"

The Leutnant's father, she learned, had worked as a tailor in a Munich men's shop owned by a Jew. His mother had been an obedient *Hausfrau,* a devout Roman Catholic. The Jewish shop owner had fired his father during the days of hyperinflation, and he never worked again. The father spent his days cursing Jews and the weaklings in the postwar Weimar government. His mother never worked outside the home. "She just kept saying the rosary, going to Mass, but nothing ever changed for us," Jurgen said.

Jurgen told her how, as a teenager, he started running errands for Nazi Party leaders in Munich – Hess and a few others – though he had never met the Führer.

"And what about a girlfriend?"

"No time for one," he answered, finishing his beer.

"But time for lots of them. I know your type."

"Are you sure you don't want a beer?"

"Again, no thank you."

"Tell me, Dr. Wagner, what do you think of our Condor Legion?"

"Well, it's doing a pretty good job of killing people, if that's what you want to know, Leutnant. Of course, I'm hardly qualified to evaluate the military. I'm far too busy trying to put our aviators back together once they're wounded or shot down."

Jurgen offered her a cigarette, which Fern declined.

"I've heard about you – you're the doctor that lived in America," he said.

"Yes, I lived in New York."

"It must have been horrible, far too many Jews."

"Well, there are more now than there used to be. So many Jews have fled Germany."

"If history tells anything, these Jewish vermin are likely to take over New York, and the rest of America too."

"Well, that might not be so bad for America," Fern said. "They make good scientists and writers."

"Are you sure you don't want a beer?" He had begun to slur his words. She saw it was time to leave.

"No thank you. I've got to meet with my colleagues and get started on the evening rounds."

"Do you have dinner plans?" he asked. "I know a good bistro nearby."

"You haven't been listening, Leutnant. I have patients who need my attention. Please excuse me."

"I'll walk you to your quarters."

"There's no need, really."

"I insist." He took her arm at the elbow.

My God, he's really going to try something, Fern thought.

She knew what to do. Moments later, at the entrance to her tent, Jurgen wrapped his strong fingers around her shoulders.

"No need to be so aggressive," she whispered in a softened tone that both surprised and pleased him. "Just because I didn't want a beer doesn't mean I'm not interested in something else."

He pressed himself against her.

"Where would you like me to start, Leutnant?" He guided her hand to where he was hard. "Get your legs further apart. I want to make sure it's hard," she whispered in his ear. He closed his eyes, surprised by her sudden compliance.

Fern's swift right knee to the groin made his knees buckle as he gasped for air. Then he doubled up, collapsing to the dirt groaning.

"Now will you leave? Or should I start screaming?" she snapped, delivering a stinging slap to his face before he could get up. "You had better pray to God that I don't report this."

Jurgen struggled to his feet and staggered away. Fern knew he wouldn't bother her again. Thank God for Karl. He had taught her well.

135. CONDOR LEGION FIELD HOSPITAL, NEAR BRUNETE, SPAIN, OCTOBER 23, 1937, 5:00 P.M.

By her own reckoning, Fern had been on her feet at least twelve hours every day for the past three weeks when Robin Baxter appeared at the field hospital. Once a barn, the building now housed some twenty beds, half of them occupied by Condor Legion aviators recovering from surgery. Baxter, a journalist with the London *Times*, had become a regular visitor to the wounded. He would often take the time to play pinochle with those well enough sit up and use their hands. Fern and her patients enjoyed his consistent good humor.

Fern felt sure that the youthful British journalist was intent on seducing her. To his credit, though, he was never obvious or hurried about it, and he was actually helping to advance her career. The articles he'd written for the *Times* describing her surgical mission with the Condor Legion were making Fern the subject of growing international acclaim. And she was honest enough with herself to admit how important that was to her.

On this late autumn afternoon, Baxter approached wearing his usual laundered khaki uniform. He stopped about a foot from where Fern was standing, his even white teeth holding her attention. "Dearest Fern, please permit me, as one of your most ardent admirers, to invite you to dinner this evening. I've reserved a table at a little bistro near the plaza in Pozuelo at half six. It's up in the hills to the west – away from the bloody war. I have procured a rather quaint little Volkswagen to get us there."

"I'm too old for you, Baxter."

"Rubbish. You remain in the full splendor of youth, and far too fetching. Besides, rumor has it that you're about to return to Germany. The pity is that I may never see you again."

"You win, but I'll drive. I've seen how much you drink. A road accident would be messy."

136. EL BISTRO ISABELLA, POZUELO, OCTOBER 23, 1937, 10:00 P.M.

In the back of the café, near a large fireplace, they finished their second bottle of local red wine before even giving a thought to ordering dinner. Despite having drunk most of the wine himself, Baxter remained lucid. It was their third dinner together in a month, and each new conversation was deeper and more animated than the one before. They talked of literature – Dickens, Trollope, and Mann – medicine, and journalism. He was curious about New York and America, about unemployment, and the talk of bread lines. Did the unions have any real political strength? Did Americans really understand what was happening here in Spain? Or in Germany and Russia?

Fern regaled him with stories of life in New York – the subways, department stores, theaters and, yes, Prohibition. She assured him that Americans didn't give "two figs" about what was happening anywhere in Europe, especially Spain. Baxter proved a good listener, peppering the conversation with questions, even when she talked about her surgical work in the field hospital. The salty, garlic-laced fish stew helped sober them up for a time. Baxter ordered more wine. He could obviously hold his booze.

"Fern, I know that you're extraordinarily bright, that you've accomplished more than your share of surgical wonders and done an outstanding job organizing the Condor field hospital. Yet I feel as if I've learned nothing about the real you beyond your professionalism, brain power, and smashing good looks."

Fern knew that she was about to let her guard down but had tired of keeping it up. What's more, a rather handsome young Englishman wanted to know more about her and was not forcing himself on her. Nor was he asking whether she'd received mail from a Jewish friend in New York or questioning her loyalty to the Third Reich. She nodded for Baxter to pour more wine.

"My dear handsome young Englishman," she said, leaning forward, taking a long sip of wine. "Since my tour of duty here ends next week, I might as well spill my guts. You see, Baxter, my story is that I've been victimized by what the Americans would describe as 'The Fickle Finger of Fate.' Instead of *victimized*, the Americans use the past participle of a more familiar verb beginning with the letter F."

Eyeing their half-empty wine bottle, she poured herself another glass. "Damn you, Baxter, you're going to get me to spill it all – the whole damn mess of the last two years."

Fern broke off a large piece of bread and chewed it carefully before speaking again. In a low tone, she told Baxter of her life in New York with Karl – beginning with how he'd helped her perfect her English grammar to his sudden violent death. She spoke of her regret about not becoming an American citizen, her return to Germany, and how her uncle had introduced her to Göring.

"I've been lucky enough to have an uncle who knows people in high places. That, Baxter, has helped me to survive this hell."

"That, my dear, is no small achievement. To assure your continued survival – and despite what we agreed on earlier – I shall drive you back to the field hospital, at least as far as the sentry post. From there I'm sure some Aryan superman can escort you to your quarters. Frankly, I wouldn't trust myself to remain a gentleman in the company such an alluring woman, especially one who's just confided so much and happens to be tipsy."

"Your taking advantage of me wouldn't become you," Fern slurred. "You like women, but you're not a cad. And even in my present state, I can see that you're a gentleman, a chap in control of himself. Years from now, we may find ourselves wondering what might have happened if you had decided to press your advantage."

Putting down the pipe he was about to light, Baxter took the frayed cloth napkin and wiped a tear from Fern's cheek.

"Please keep everything I've told you to yourself, Baxter. I don't want to read about it in the Sunday papers."

"You have my pledge."

He managed to maneuver the Volkswagen down the bumpy dirt road and back to the field hospital. She kissed him quickly on the forehead as he entrusted her to the young German corporal at the sentry post.

When he returned to his cramped room in the bomb-damaged inn down the road, Baxter went straight to his portable Smith-Corona and typed out a full report, which the people in Moscow wanted from him every day.

Five days later, Fern boarded a plane for Munich. With a month's leave due her, she gladly accepted her Uncle Frederick's invitation to join him on an extended business trip to Paris, where Wagner industries had just bought two auto-parts plants.

137. GESTAPO HEADQUARTERS, PRINZ-ALBRECHT-STRASSE, OCTOBER 26, 1937, 2:05 A.M.

Working by the yellow light of a gooseneck lamp, Reinhard Heydrich was halfway through a thick file labeled "Unusual Incidents/Border Control Points." The folder contained records of all incidents going back to the first of the year. Heydrich noted several instances where border guards had been lax. One such lapse had occurred on the night of Fasching, when a young border guard returned to his post drunk after his dinner break. When questioned later about his behavior, the young man broke down and confessed that he had been distracted by a woman. Heydrich lit a cigarette, inhaling deeply, savoring the smoke as he exhaled. The file revealed that the border guard resigned his post out of embarrassment a week after the incident, joined the German Navy, and was now on a U-boat somewhere.

Heydrich then examined the list of train passengers who had entered Germany through the Aachen border control on that night. Soon enough, he came upon the name of Dr. Karl Muller. In a conversation just several weeks before, Heydrich's boss, Heinrich Himmler, had mentioned this same Dr. Muller as someone who was distinguishing himself as a fundraiser for the Party. Heydrich recalled that he had received a letter from a local Party leader named Mannheim praising Muller for his fundraising efforts and had himself written a brief congratulatory note to the doctor.

Yes, Heydrich concluded, it was time to start a file on Dr. Karl Muller.

But he needed help. If only he could persuade Hans Krebs to come on board as his special assistant. Krebs would learn what Muller was up to in no time. But Heydrich was a realist. He knew Krebs would resist a move to the Prinz-Albrecht-Strasse, and it made no sense to try and persuade him. Krebs was far too independent. It was what made him such a clear-thinking detective.

Heydrich went to his file cabinet, removed a folder, and returned to his desk. He maintained extensive files on the most promising up-and-coming SS officers, those already fanatically dedicated to the new Reich and to the Führer, and those he could cultivate – men whose primary loyalty would be to Heydrich himself, young officers who would obey his orders without question. Heydrich scanned his lists, realizing that most of the men were too young for the job he had in mind. He wanted someone in his early thirties, a man close in age to Dr. Muller.

Heydrich soon came upon the name of the right man. He was an athlete, a fine boxer with lightning-fast punches. And he had served with some distinction in Spain. Yes, Heydrich decided that the job of keeping an eye on Dr. Muller would be a suitable next step for Leutnant Günter Jurgen. They were about the same age, and Jurgen's athleticism gave him something in common with Dr. Muller. At a recent Chancellery reception, Heydrich had learned that Dr. Muller was in the habit of taking long runs in the Tiergarten and that he exercised regularly at the Berliner Sportverein. He would see that Jurgen became a member there.

138. LINDENER SQUARE, HANNOVER, NOVEMBER 9, 1937, 11:00 A.M.

The morning sun warmed the café terrace where Karl was drinking coffee with Rudolf Hess. Both men leaned over the typescript of the speech Karl would deliver that evening before the Hannover Medical Society.

Karl's basic fundraising speech now included anecdotes about medical research he had conducted in East Africa, a light touch of Nazi jingo, and the need to regain Germany's hold on the African continent and its vast mineral resources. That speech had worked quite well before some fifteen audiences.

"Karl, this will be the most prestigious audience you've addressed so far," Hess said. "We have arranged for three doctors in the audience to rise, one at time, and pledge monetary gifts to the Party. But things will be a little different this time." He told Karl that he had arranged for Hermann Göring to make an "impromptu" appearance. Göring would report on the glorious achievements of the Condor Legion, then announce that Karl would soon be joining their ranks as a medical officer.

Karl saw that Hess was still pensive. "Forgive me, Rudolf, but you seem preoccupied."

Hess nodded, gratified by Karl's sensitivity. "Karl, I fear you'll be working for Göring soon. The Party is no longer the political center of gravity. There's a shift away from the Party in Munich and toward the government and military in Berlin. My deputy Bormann understands this, and finds more and more reasons to be with the Führer in Berlin."

Karl sensed that Hess wanted him to disagree. "I think you're wrong, Rudolf. In the months and years ahead, the Führer will need the Party more than ever. He'll need the Party to marshal popular support, especially in the event of a war."

Hess shook his head. "In a war, the Führer and the Fatherland will need steel, petrol, food, planes, tanks, and fighting men as well as doctors to treat the wounded. Why do you think Göring is gracing these doctors with his presence this evening? It's about setting an example for other doctors to follow."

"Well, Rudolf, I must admit that I'm quite eager to meet the Führer."

"I understand. Perhaps I'll put Bormann on it," Hess responded, biting his upper lip.

Karl sat back. "Let's go over the speech one more time."

"Why? What do you want to change?"

"Maybe the closing, just to make Göring feel even more important."

Karl eyed the last paragraph and added several words. Hess read them and nodded approval.

"Excellent flying weather," Hess said, looking up at the clear sky.

"Let's not just talk about flying," Karl said. "Let's do some."

"You mentioned that you've done multi-engine training."

"Yes, in fact, I've now logged more than fifteen hours in multi-engine aircraft. Göring let me fly one of his new Messerschmitt Bf 109s a couple of weeks ago – a magnificent airplane."

"There's a Luftwaffe base only a few miles out of town. Perhaps the commandant can loan us two Messerschmitts for a couple of hours."

"I'm sure you can persuade him, Rudolf."

139. OVER HANNOVER, NOVEMBER 9, 1937, 2:00 P.M.

The two Messerschmitt 109s soared steeply, climbing through banks of high white clouds. Being the more experienced pilot, Hess let Karl set the pace. "Try this, Rudolf," Karl laughed over the two-way radio, taking his plane into a barrel roll.

"Your instructors have taught you well, my friend," Hess shouted, completing his own barrel roll.

"Remember, I learned to fly in Africa, where there are real mountains and strong updrafts," Karl lied. He was getting good at it.

"Then try this," Hess bellowed, pulling hard on the throttle and putting his plane into a steep 70-degree dive. "Follow me, if you can." Karl stayed on his tail until Hess flattened out at 500 meters and then dropped to skim the treetops.

"Had enough, Doctor?" Hess's voice crackled over the two-way radio.

Karl resisted the temptation to show off. "I know when I've met my match, Rudolf. Now I know I've flown with the one of the best pilots in the Reich."

140. HOTEL BISMARCK, HANNOVER, NOVEMBER 9, 1937, 8:00 P.M.

In the smoke-filled Bierkeller, Karl slowed and softened his voice as he neared his concluding remarks. He wanted his words to have an impact on all the doctors seated at the six long tables.

"We cannot have a strong Germany without a strong Party. The Party must be the backbone of a renewed Germany, a Germany strong enough to face the Red menace in the East and the decadence in the West. Only through the Party can we build a future for our families."

He paused, letting his eyes wander over the audience.

"And if any man among you doubts that Germany needs to be strong to protect this and future generations of Aryans, then let him travel back in time with me to East Africa, where Congolese mercenaries, in the pay of the Belgians and the British, raped German nuns in our schools and German wives in their homes and robbed food from German children. I could show you the exact spot where shells from British warships killed the fathers and mothers of my schoolmates. That must never happen again."

He paused again.

"And that is why I have left Africa to come home to the Fatherland and live among you, to serve our profession, and build a stronger Nazi Party and a stronger Reich. I have but one request – that you join me in making an annual pledge in the name of our Party, our Reich, and our Führer."

Karl finished to rousing applause. On a prearranged nod from Hess, a tall slender man rose to his feet and extended his right arm in the Nazi salute. "*Heil Hitler.* I am Dr. Franz Keller, and I have been practicing obstetrics here in Hannover for fifteen years. I served in the Kaiserlich Marine from 1914 to 1918. I hereby pledge five thousand Reichsmarks to the Party."

Then a small, balding man with a black eye patch stood. "I am Dr. Paul Stutz," he said, giving the Nazi salute, "and pediatrics is my specialty. I was in the infantry at Verdun, and I pledge twenty thousand Reichsmarks . . ." Next, the only woman in the group rose. "I am Dr. Monica Strauss. I was a nurse during the war, and now I'm a surgeon here in Hannover. I pledge two thousand Reichsmarks a year." Before she sat down, six more doctors were on their feet.

"Fellow members of the medical profession," Karl said, raising his arms to quiet the crowd, "your contributions have inspired me. The man whose Condor Legion warplanes are destroying the Red menace in Spain has further inspired me. Only our Führer has done more for Germany than this brave aviator and statesman." Karl pointed toward the back of the Bierkeller as the unmistakable figure of Hermann Göring emerged into the light. A hush swept the room, then a spontaneous applause. As the applause crescendoed, Göring raised his arms in a plea for silence. He needed no podium. He simply stood among them, dressed in a simple gray business suit.

"Physicians of Hannover, please forgive me for imposing on your hospitality. But since I was in your beautiful city and learned that both my old friend Rudolf Hess and my new friend Dr. Karl Muller would also be here, I couldn't forsake the opportunity to share some important news with you."

Göring paused to let silence settle over the smoky room. "My announcement tonight will bestow great credit on your profession. Dr. Karl Muller, whose stirring speech you've just heard, has volunteered to serve as a medical officer with the Condor Legion in the war against Communism in Spain."

As Göring tilted his head toward Karl, the audience sprang up to applaud. Dr. Stutz, the pediatrician, began the chant of *"Sieg Heil,"* which quickly swept through the room and grew louder with every repetition.

141. CAFÉ LAFAYETTE, RUE CADET, PARIS, NOVEMBER 25, 1937, 7:20 P.M.

Fern stood at the bar sipping a Burgundy, refreshed by an afternoon nap and some window-shopping on Boulevard de la Madeleine. Frederick's invitation to join him at his suite in the Ritz provided the perfect respite after three months of war in Spain. To her delight, she had run into Robin Baxter in the hotel lobby only an hour before. He was on a break from the Spanish war and had just left some friends at the Ritz Bar. She readily accepted his invitation to meet at the Café Lafayette after he attended to some errands.

On her last day in Spain, Fern asked a nurse assigned to the Condor Legion about Baxter and learned that he was in fact married, which made him at once more intriguing and perhaps safer. But she felt she needed some fun before returning to Germany, and Baxter had proven himself a perfect gentlemen and a terrific listener.

Baxter arrived wearing a black turtleneck and a brown tweed jacket, a pipe clenched securely in his teeth, which were remarkably straight for an Englishman.

In fluent French, Baxter asked the frowning bartender for a Glenlivet, which he poured from a dusty bottle that looked as if it hadn't been touched for years. Fern was already halfway through her Burgundy.

"I hope you don't mind meeting here. Thought you might fancy this place – it's a haunt for businessmen, bankers, and insurance types. Now let's go somewhere we can talk. There's a little restaurant up in Montmartre called Chez Frances, one the tourists don't know about."

As the taxi crept along in early evening traffic, Fern folded her arm into Baxter's. How good it felt to talk with a man and not have to worry that he might report you to the SS or the Gestapo. Baxter left Fern alone with her thoughts.

"What a lovely evening," she said at last. "It's so warm for November. Back in America they call it Indian summer. How I love autumn."

At the restaurant, Robin ordered a bottle of cabernet from Frances, the young proprietress and chef who greeted him as *Monsieur Robin*. They accepted her suggestion of roasted *agneau* and a *salade verte*.

"What bloody luck it was to run into you here, Fern," Baxter said, raising his glass. "Tell me – what's it like to wake up in the Ritz?"

"Delightfully decadent, especially after living in a tent on the Madrid front. But let me tell you, Robin, if you ever wake up in the Ritz, it won't be with me. The only reason I get to sleep there is because I have a wealthy uncle who's in Paris to instill our German work ethic on what he calls a 'lazy Marxist workforce' at an auto plant he just bought."

They climbed the steps to *Sacré-Coeur*. Fern was certain Baxter would try to kiss her, but instead they stood together taking in the view. How she wished she could have seen the same view of Paris with Karl. When a taxi stopped to drop off another couple, they jumped in and headed for the Ritz.

In the lobby Fern extended her hand to Baxter. "Call me tomorrow at noon," she whispered, offering her cheek. "I'll need to sleep until then."

Baxter returned to his room on the Rue du Rivoli to type up another report.

142. CONDOR LEGION FIELD HEADQUARTERS, THE MADRID FRONT, SPAIN, NOVEMBER 27, 1937, 7:37 A.M.

The moment Karl arrived at his field hospital office, a young Luftwaffe sergeant handed him a sealed envelope marked "For Dr. Muller, from Dr. Wagner." Karl turned to make sure he was still alone. Once a schoolroom, this room had been Fern's office just a few weeks before. It was empty enough now, except for the bookcases with neat rows of medical books and the movable typewriter table standing against a cracked plaster wall. He looked around the room again, scratching his unshaven face. He sniffed the air, then the envelope itself, hoping to catch some scent of her. He let his finger run over the envelope a third time without opening it, not wanting the moment of discovery to pass too soon, even though he knew the contents would be routine and businesslike.

He opened the envelope, and he pulled out two stapled documents – one much longer than the other – as well as a short note in Fern's handwriting. He began reading after pressing the note to his lips.

October 28, 1937

Dr. Muller:

Please provide the best treatment possible to the young men who are here now or will soon come under your care. My experience has been that they have the capacity to face their injuries and endure pain with great bravery. I understand that your professional background is in general practice and orthopedics, while mine is in plastic and cosmetic surgery. Both skills are needed here, even though casualties remain light. You will find Dr. Werner Ott, who served as my deputy, to be a thoroughly competent physician. He took care of all administrative details, which allowed me to devote myself to the wounded. I recommend that you take advantage of his abilities.

I believe that you will find the other doctors and nurses on staff to be quite knowledgeable. Please read the two attached documents carefully. Good Luck.

Sincerely,

Fern Wagner, MD

He ran his fingers across the paper one more time and then read the first of the other two documents, both typewritten.

To All Medical Personnel Assigned to Condor Legion Field Hospital, Madrid Front:

October 27, 1937

My three and a half months here have provided me with enough combat-related experience to draft written procedures that, once tested, may prove helpful in future Luftwaffe field hospitals. I ask that each of you inform me in writing of any errors or misstatements in the text, including specific recommendations on how to correct them.

Fortunately, the number of German casualties remains low. Nonetheless, the severity of some airmen's wounds – especially those involving loss of vision, amputation, or disfigurement – can be psychologically devastating for the wounded individual and have a negative effect on morale. I know you will continue to do your best to make such patients as comfortable as possible – in body, mind, and spirit.

Please review the attached draft procedures document carefully. And please share with me in writing your thoughts and reactions within the next two weeks. I will compile and condense what you send me and include it in a final draft for Luftwaffe Commander-in-Chief Göring.

Heil Hitler.

Fern Wagner, MD

A slender blonde nurse approached Karl. *"Willkommen, Hauptmann Muller.* My name is Trudy Gretzler, and I'll be your surgical assistant. It will be an honor to work under you. I've heard so much about your book and your work for the Party. I'd love to talk more, but right now I must escort one of our patients, Leutnant Karp, to the medical tent, where we're putting a new dressing on his eye. I have a new black patch that will give him a dashing appearance."

143. THE TIERGARTEN, BERLIN, NOVEMBER 29, 1937, 8:00 A.M.

Martin Haber had accepted Frederick Wagner's invitation to mount up for a ride under the tall Linden trees. Both were skilled horsemen, trained from their youth in the Junker tradition. On this brisk autumn morning, they were galloping along the bridle path when Frederick raised his arm to signal a respite.

"I need a word with you, Martin," Frederick said. "Shall we dismount?"

"Of course, Frederick," Haber said, gesturing toward the statue of the Amazon on Horseback.

"Several of my engineers have just returned from Spain. They've prepared glowing reports on the performance of our new Panzers in Spain."

"Yes, I understand they've done quite well. We'll soon start training more Panzer crews."

"That's wonderful to hear, Martin, but I need a military man's evaluation. My engineers are good, but they have no combat experience. I wonder if you could fly down to Spain and have a look."

Haber was quick to nod yes and began looking forward to several days away from his paperwork.

144. CONDOR LEGION ENCAMPMENT, MADRID FRONT, SPAIN, DECEMBER 8, 1937

Karl returned to his office tent to find Dr. Werner Ott waiting for him. "I have exciting news," Ott said. "General Haber is flying in for an extensive inspection. The rumor is that he wants to see how well the new Panzers perform. But he'll mask the true nature of his mission by visiting various field hospitals, this one included."

"There's nothing for us to worry about. Everything here is in order."

"Tell me," Ott said, "what about your beard? You haven't shaved since you got here. There may be photographs taken for the newspapers back in Berlin."

"Well then, I'll get a sharp pair of scissors and trim it a bit, but the beard stays."

145. THE RITZ HOTEL, PARIS, DECEMBER 20, 1937, 11:30 A.M.

Using the bedside telephone, Fern ordered breakfast and coffee from room service. Then, rising from her bed, she slipped into a warm white robe and slippers and sauntered into the sunken drawing room. Glancing toward the coffee table, she expected to find a note from Frederick about plans for a long-anticipated dinner at La Tour d'Argent that evening. Instead, she saw her mother.

"I hope I haven't shocked you, dear," Hildy said in soft, confident voice. "Martin had to leave for Spain. As luck would have it, Frederick telephoned to say that he was returning to Paris, and invited me to accompany him on his plane. He's such a thoughtful brother-in-law! So I asked myself: what self-respecting German mother would allow her daughter to go shopping alone in Paris just before Christmas? I think we should shop ourselves into poverty! I love the shops on Rue du Faubourg Saint-Honoré and the Avenue Victor-Hugo."

"I haven't done any shopping, Mother, only sleeping and taking quiet walks."

"Well, I'm dying to hear about Spain. Martin says you performed quite well there. Your name also came up at a recent Chancellery reception I attended – Hermann Göring couldn't stop bragging about your work with our wounded pilots. You must tell me everything."

"Frederick said we'll be dining tonight at eight sharp," Hildy continued. "Leave it to him to be so precise. He told me that you'll be on the arm of a young English journalist. You must tell me about him, too."

"Mother, it's not what you think. My journalist friend is just that – a friend. He's quite young, only twenty-five."

"I remember his type – a university man, chivalrous yet dangerous."

"And I might say very bright, very handsome, and very married."

"All the more reason to look him over."

146. LA TOUR D'ARGENT, PARIS, DECEMBER 20, 1937, 9:00 P.M.

At a round table near a picture window with a view of Notre Dame, the party hosted by Frederick Wagner consumed Champagne and *Canard á l'Orange*. Baxter fit in well with the Wagner family. Frederick moved the conversation to Spain. He wanted to hear about Baxter's wartime experiences as a correspondent.

Hildy offered that her husband, General Haber, was eager to witness operations on the front. "I believe he's somewhere near Madrid," Hildy said.

After dinner, Fern and Baxter hurried off for a Left Bank rendezvous with some of his journalist friends.

"That Baxter's a very clever man, a wealth of information, don't you think, Frederick," Hildy chirped. "Too bad he's married."

"My dear sister-in-law, please recall that Fern lived in my New York townhouse for several years. She had many admirers and managed to keep them all at arm's length, all except for Karl that is. She can handle Baxter. Think about how much she's been through. She's lost Karl. She's had to adjust to a new life in Germany. And she's endured several months of front-line duty in Spain. I'm happy enough to see her have some fun."

Frederick hailed a taxi that would take Hildy back to the Ritz. He stood on the sidewalk as it rolled away and breathed the fresh December air. He thought of Fern, how her life had changed. He stopped at the steamy window of a café on Saint-Michel, went to an inside table and drank three cognacs. Then he walked back to the Ritz, sober as a stone with Fern still on his mind.

147. THE MADRID FRONT, DECEMBER 21, 1937, NOON

Karl took his lunch of watery chicken broth in a small café across the dusty plaza from the church. He'd eaten at the same café twice before since arriving in Spain, and made the acquaintance of several Condor Legion officers there.

The officers helped Karl get the commandant's permission to accompany a small infantry group on night patrol. So far, he had been out on three such patrols.

He was finishing his watery soup when he noticed a hunchbacked nun stumbling across the plaza, headed straight toward him. Karl stiffened. He had no coins to deposit in the woman's wicker basket, but gave her a crumpled five-peseta note, hoping it would send her away.

But the nun paid him no heed and bowed her head toward the café floor. "*Señor*, I ask only that you open your heart to the crippled children," she said in deliberate, high-pitched Spanish., In the same instant, she dropped to her knees and only then did Karl hear a masculine voice. "Can't you spare a few more pesos, lad?"

Karl recognized Scotty North's voice and sly grin. "Take the paper that's in the basket," Scotty said, "and put it in your pocket. Commit it to memory, and then bloody burn it." Karl knew enough not to speak, just to do as he was told. "These instructions are straight from Brown," Scotty said, remaining on his knees. "It's about Matador, the caper planned in Scotland. Some if it is in the memo Brown gave you when you left London, some of it he didn't tell you about. And some of it we'll just have to improvise. We need you to provide a foolproof map of the officers' quarters in your encampment – building by building, room by room, and tent by tent – including all areas where they have parked vehicles and posted sentries. Deliver it to me here tomorrow at noon."

"How the hell did you know I'd be here?"

"We have our sources, lad. We know this plaza is the only place around here where a man can have a decent meal – and we knew you'd been here before. We figured you had to show up again sooner or later. I've actually been watching for you, perched up in the belfry of the church tower, with field glasses. Been here two bloody days. Got my gear and some food stashed up there. Not the Ritz, but it'll do. I flew into Madrid on a Hudson with Red Cross markings and crossed to this side of the line by night. We also know about General Haber's imminent arrival."

"You guys always have your surprises. Now what about tomorrow?"

"Look for an older bloke, no cane but struggling to walk. Just be here – alone – with the bloody map."

148. THE MADRID FRONT, DECEMBER 23, 1937, 12:50: A.M.

Under the blanket of a cloudy night, Scotty North crept thorough both the Nationalist and Loyalist strongholds to reach the shabby hotel he'd taken in Madrid's outskirts. He ate the last of the food in his ration kit – some dried fruit and crusty cheese – and then drew the curtains and set his portable alarm for ten in the morning. That would give him a good night's sleep and leave time to fashion a detailed plan using the maps Karl had given him, and for a decent meal before he met up with the eight Royal Marines who had flown with him to Spain in the Hudson with Red Cross markings.

Thanks to arrangements Brown had made through the Foreign Office, Loyalist officials at the airport were happy to cooperate in exchange for badly needed medical supplies. In addition to housing the Hudson, the Loyalists provided the British with the services of Captain Elian Sandoval, a Madrid native who had spent two years defending the city.

Scotty had crossed the same front lines the night before, but now taking eight fully armed Marines across unseen multiplied the risk.

149. THE MADRID FRONT, DECEMBER 25, 1937, 3:00 A.M.

Captain Sandoval had proved his value. In the pre-dawn of Christmas Day, he led Scotty and the Royal Marines along an obscure winding pathway free of landmines and tank traps to a spot just outside the perimeter of the Condor Legion encampment and field hospital. Sandoval had done it all before. At age thirty, he was a hardened warrior. He had crossed into unfriendly territory many times, and killed five men in hand-to-hand combat along the way. Scotty North, who respected few men and trusted even fewer, trusted Sandoval as much as he could trust any man.

Before they crossed over into "no man's land" at dusk the night before, Sandoval had given a five hundred peseta note to the guard at the final checkpoint. Sandoval promised the guard another note of equal or greater value if he could ensure their safe return back through the Loyalist line. "Please understand, amigo, we'll be returning in an ambulance," Sandoval whispered to the guard. "If you're not here to let us back through the checkpoint, you will receive orders to return to Madrid, where your assignment will be to disarm unexploded bombs. That means you'll likely be dead by the New Year." Scotty knew Sandoval was bluffing, but that his words would inspire obedience.

3:42 A.M.

Their eyes now accustomed to the dark, Scotty and his party slipped in silence past the two-man sentry post on the outer perimeter of the Condor Legion encampment.

"Look, *Señor*," Sandoval whispered, pointing across the barren field toward the encampment. Peering into the darkness, Scotty North and the Marines saw two machine gun nests, two Panzers, and a Mercedes ambulance with prominent Red Cross markings. Everything appeared to be just as Karl had mapped it out. Scotty hoped that the key would be in the ambulance's ignition as Karl said – a practice designed to assure that the vehicle would be ready the instant it was needed.

3:48 A.M.

Scotty whispered for the Marines to advance toward the encampment. They obeyed without turning a pebble.

Sandoval cut the barbed wire and let Scotty North go in first. Now on their bellies, the eight Marines followed, with Sandoval bringing up the rear. The ten men crawled to a spot where they could see the lone German guard milling about near the barracks. They watched as he stepped behind a tree to relieve himself of his Christmas beer.

On Scotty North's hand-signal, two Marines stole toward the distracted guard without stirring a leaf. As the guard was re-buttoning his trousers, one Marine rose up and slipped a garrote around his neck. No one heard the German boy kicking the night air before the Marines eased his lifeless hulk to the ground.

Scotty North waved again, signaling his team to advance beyond the parked ambulance to the barracks tent where, as Karl's map indicated, the off-duty Condor Legion guards would be sleeping.

Sandoval checked his watch. Scotty, flanked by two Marines, entered the adjacent tent, which bore the word "Haber" on the map provided by Karl. *"Guten Morgen, General,"* Scotty whispered, jamming the barrel of his Webley revolver into Haber's thick, snow-white hair just above the right ear. "Now just get up and get dressed, *schnell,*" Scotty hissed in German. Three Royal Marines stood guard as Haber complied, calm and composed.

Scotty proceeded to Karl's to tent, where he found Karl wide awake and already dressed. "Karl, just listen. The curtain's up on act one. Remember your part, lad. Now play a proper Prussian."

At gunpoint, Scotty and Sandoval led Karl and Haber to the ambulance. "This is a field hospital," Karl said indignantly in German-accented English. "And I am a doctor here. I demand that you release us."

"Shut up," Scotty snapped. "Get in the bloody ambulance."

Scotty ordered Haber and the eight Royal Marine guards to board the ambulance through the rear door. "You, Hauptmann Doctor," he barked at Karl, "you ride in the front where I can keep an eye on you." Sandoval slid behind the steering wheel, relieved to find the key in the ignition. "Now get us the hell out of the here, Captain," Scotty yelled as he jumped in on the passenger side, the barrel of his Webley jammed into Karl's ribs.

The burst-away speed of the ambulance took the outer-perimeter guards by surprise. They fired hurriedly, but Sandoval raced the ambulance through the checkpoint and onto the shell-pocked dirt road leading toward the Loyalist line.

"Shit," Sandoval shouted in English as he caught sight of a new TU-4 Soviet tank hidden among the trees on the crest of a small knoll. Clenching his teeth, Sandoval gunned the engine and prayed that the tank crew would respect the ambulance's Red Cross markings.

4:40 A.M.

In the back of the ambulance, Haber kept his composure. "Where are you taking us?" he asked the Marine sitting next to him.

"We only work here, guv," the Marine replied with a shrug.

Up front, Sandoval kept his eyes on the road ahead. Karl noticed that all of the road signs were down. It hardly mattered – Sandoval knew the way to Madrid.

150. HANGAR NUMBER ONE, BARAJAS AIR TERMINAL, MADRID, DECEMBER 25, 1937, NOON

After their captors took mug shots, Karl and Haber found themselves locked in a small room. Karl peered through an interior window that looked out on the expansive airplane hangar. Haber lit the last of his cigarettes and joined Karl at the window. Two Royal Marines, each armed with Enfields, stood guard near a Hudson with Red Cross markings.

"Perhaps they'll fly us to England," Haber speculated. "They want to learn what I know about the Reich's military strength and planning, which, I am afraid, is a great deal."

"Why go to all that trouble when they could ask the same questions here?" Karl responded.

"Not that simple. The British want the information for themselves. If they interrogate me here, they might very well have to share what they learn with the Spanish Loyalists. The British aren't stupid. They know the Loyalists would relay what they learn straight to Moscow."

"Can they make you talk?"

"Over time, yes. But not by torture. They can be far more subtle. They could take me to some stately country mansion – provide me with intelligent company over lunch, tea, and dinner. There could be a billiards table and a tennis court. They might accompany me on quiet walks down country roads, perhaps even on horseback rides – all quite civilized. Over days and weeks, they're bound to learn things. Their methods are far more refined than the rather brutal methods Himmler and Heydrich use in the basement of the Prinz-Albrecht-Strasse. You may not believe this, but Heydrich once told me that he admired the way the British went about their intelligence-gathering, and that we Germans have much learn from them."

Haber stomped out his cigarette. "All this has a purpose Hauptmann Muller, a specific purpose. I'm sure of it. If general intelligence was all they wanted, they could simply interrogate prisoners and take aerial photos. Consider also that we sailed right through the Loyalist lines without even having to stop and answer the most basic questions. This entire operation appears to be quite well planned."

"No matter, General Haber," Karl said, "the issue now isn't how we got here or where they're taking us, but how to get the hell out of here."

They heard the door unlock. Two Loyalist guards entered. The taller of the two pointed the barrel of his rifle toward Haber's chest.

"Come with us, General," he said in English. Haber stood as they blindfolded him and marched him away.

151. HANGAR NUMBER ONE, DECEMBER 26, 1937, 1:42 A.M.

Karl was stretched out on the hard wooden bench trying to rest when the door sprang open again and two Royal Marines entered the room.

"Come with us, Hauptmann. No bloody tricks, mind you," one barked.

Karl expected that they'd blindfold him, but they didn't.

They marched Karl toward the Hudson. When they reached the portable stairway that led up to the passenger cabin, a third Marine, with the chevrons of a sergeant major, appeared. Karl recognized him from the night before. The sergeant major jabbed the barrel of his pistol into the base of Karl's spine. "Inside with you, and hop to it," he growled in a thick Scottish burr.

Instead of the usual rows of passenger seats, the plane's cabin was furnished only with a central table surrounded by six seats. There was also a small cocktail bar, but no whiskey bottles or glasses. Once inside, Karl saw Scotty North through the open door of the pilot's cabin.

"Thank you, Sergeant Major," Scotty said, stepping out of the pilot's cabin. "Secure him to his seat, and make a tight fit of it." Scotty dismissed the sergeant major once he had tied Karl to the seat.

"Sorry, Karl, but I asked the Sergeant Major to play up the rough stuff. All in a day's work." Scotty then slid a small Swiss Army knife into Karl's right hand. "Now let's just review a few next steps," he said.

"Our lads are roughing up General Haber right now," Scotty said. "That means you need to get a touch of the same treatment." In that instant, Scotty punched Karl just above the left eye with a hard right. Karl didn't react. He'd been expecting the blow but didn't know when it would come. It was a well-aimed punch. There was no blood, but it was sure to produce swelling around the eye.

"Nothing personal, lad," Scotty said. "Now that I have your attention, are you ready to start punching?"

"We'll soon see. Remember, I haven't thrown a punch since Thornbil, close to a year ago. My only practice has been on a punching bag in a Berlin athletic club."

"Well lad, you dare not appear too professional. The only person you have to fool is General Haber, and he won't even see it happen."

"It's just as well. He's already seen enough. Did you guys ever consider that kidnapping Haber could trigger a big-time diplomatic incident?"

"That won't happen, Karl. The good general isn't even supposed to be here. All the Germans in Spain are volunteers, here to fight the bloody Reds. It would be idiotic of them to admit that a high-ranking General Staff member was touring Spain, taking notes. Trust me, lad, there won't be a peep from Berlin on this."

4:10 A.M.

General Martin Haber stumbled aboard bleeding from a cut above his left eye, escorted by the sergeant major and a corporal. The Marines tied the half-conscious Haber to a seat next to Karl. The rope was tight enough to numb Haber's limbs. Two uniformed pilots in RAF flight gear came aboard just as the Marines finished tying Haber to his seat.

The pilots ignored Haber and Karl as they climbed into the cockpit and signaled for a Marine to hand-crank the propeller.

Scotty nodded to Karl and ordered the sergeant major and the corporal out of the plane. "Now it's all yours," Scotty whispered. "Do what you have to with the pilots. Once you're airborne, fly six miles due south, toward Getafe. Look for a monastery on a hill, and you'll see a small Condor Legion airfield nearby. Make sure to find the Luftwaffe frequency on your radio so you can identify yourself to them."

With a wink at Karl, Scotty scampered out of the Hudson and down the stairway, leaving the door ajar. He headed to a room that housed a large fuse box.

Back in the Hudson, Karl cut his own hands free before cutting the rope that bound Haber. "Wake up, General," he shouted into Haber's ear. "I've untied you." Haber blinked.

With no time to explain things, Karl darted to the cockpit, where the pilot had just signaled for two Royal Marines to remove the wheel blocks. Karl's fast Jackhammer to the nape of the pilot's neck blacked him out. As the co-pilot turned, Karl's left fist cracked two of his ribs, while a lightning-fast right knocked him cold. Karl grabbed both men by the belt, dragging them out of the cockpit one at a time, and heaved each out of the cabin onto the stairway, which he then kicked away. Karl locked the cabin door and scrambled back to cockpit, shouting for Haber to join him.

Haber, fighting a pounding headache, began to wake up. He stood on shaky legs and struggled into the co-pilot's seat. Karl flashed the Hudson's wing lights on and off just long enough to get a good look at the flat grassy field that served as a runway. Karl inched the Hudson forward, toward the open hangar door. He could see Loyalist troops, rifles in hand, rushing toward the plane. Several were kneeling to take aim as the hangar lights went out.

A Loyalist flare lit up the sky, allowing Karl to catch sight of the wind-sock, which indicated a strong westerly wind that would boost their take off. He opened the throttle, gaining speed over the bumpy grass and into the wind. He took the Hudson to seven hundred feet, well out of the range of the Loyalist shooters. No sense wasting time just to gain more altitude. That would only give the Russian fighters time to swarm. He killed the cabin and wing lights. The black night sky was their friend.

4:19 A.M.

Karl switched the radio to the Luftwaffe frequency and executed the final stage of the plan, heading for the Condor Legion airfield near Getafe, just inside the German lines, south of Madrid. He handed the radio microphone to Haber. "Identify yourself, General, before our friends start shooting at us."

Now alert, Haber spoke in a clear voice. "This is General Martin Haber, Wehrmacht General Staff, Berlin. I am approaching Getafe and need clearance to land in a British Hudson with Red Cross markings. I am with Hauptmann Karl Muller, who is piloting the aircraft. We were captured by British mercenaries but have escaped in their plane. I repeat, we seek clearance to land at Getafe. Repeat. We seek clearance to land at Getafe. We are not armed."

Karl switched on the Hudson's navigation lights and dipped the plane's wings, first left and then right, the international signal that the aircraft was friendly and intended no harm.

4:21 A.M.

They saw a searchlight beam. "That could be Getafe," Karl shouted over the engines. "Let's hope they heard your message and that they believe you. The light will either guide us to our friends or help them shoot us down."

Haber kept repeating his message as the airfield came into view. The searchlight swept the sky, then fixed on the Hudson.

Karl dipped the Hudson's wings again. They could see Condor Legionnaires waving as they lit the oil lanterns on the grass runway. Karl brought the Hudson to a perfect three-point landing.

After an exchange of radio messages with Berlin confirming their identities, Karl and Haber were escorted to a medical tent, where the duty nurse dressed their cuts and bruises. They had barely finished cleaning up when a half-dozen Condor pilots burst into the tent with schnapps, hot coffee, and fresh bread.

152. UNIVERSITY CITY HOSPITAL, MADRID, DECEMBER 26, 1937, 7:40 A.M.

Following Scotty's direction, the RAF pilots told the American doctor who examined them that they'd gotten into a fight with two Russian pilots over a pair of senoritas they'd met in a Madrid bistro.

"Bullshit," Josh laughed. "The last time I saw jawbone injuries like this was when a professional boxer did the punching." Josh's fast reaction surprised the old man who served as a Loyalist intelligence stenographer.

After Josh reset the co-pilot's jaw and treated the pilot's sore neck, both boarded a Hudson bound for a military hospital in Saffron Walden, Essex. There they would remain in forced isolation until spring, when they would both receive postings to an RAF base in Singapore, where their story of what happened in Madrid would take a long time to travel to London.

153. THE CHANCELLERY, BERLIN, DECEMBER 28, 1937, NOON

Adolf Hitler snapped his fingers, a clear sign of his anger, as he reprimanded Martin Haber. "Have we come this far for nothing?" Hitler shouted. "To have one of our top generals playing like a schoolboy on a camping trip? Why was I not informed of your trip to Spain?" Göring squirmed. Keitel lowered his head. Martin Haber stood his ground.

"As the Führer himself has so often said," Haber began, "officers must experience enemy fire to understand what their soldiers face. Otherwise, we're little boys playing with toys. I went to Spain because I'm a soldier. I believe that the short time I spent there was very informative. I'm proud to report that our men's morale is high, and their resourcefulness remarkable. Hauptmann Muller's initiative in engineering our escape illustrates my point.

Had I stayed longer, I might have been able to complete my mission – to present you, *mein Führer*, with a firsthand report on the performance of our Panzers on the primitive Spanish roads."

Hitler reflected on Haber's rejoinder, "Someday," he said, reclining on his chair, "I must meet this Dr. Muller. Hess and Bormann have spoken highly of him."

154. CONDOR LEGION FIELD HOSPITAL, MADRID FRONT, DECEMBER 29, 1937, 6:00 A.M.

A half-dozen Condor Legion pilots joined Karl at a long table in the mess hall tent. His escape from Madrid with General Haber had made him a celebrity among the pilots. Many had questions about the Hudson. Word had it that the British had purchased many of them from an American company called Lockheed.

Karl was about to get up for a second cup of the excellent Spanish coffee when a corporal approached. "Hauptmann Muller," the corporal said with deference, "Oberst Zimmer has asked me to escort you to his office."

It was a short walk. "Hauptmann Muller, you may remain standing," said Oberst Zimmer, a seasoned officer who had led several Condor Legion bombing missions. "I must tell you that your recent exploit has given a major boost to our pilots' morale. For that I congratulate you. That said, I must tell you also that Berlin has instructed me to deliver a message to you in person and see that you obey it to the letter." He handed Karl a single sheet of paper. "Read it, Hauptmann. Read it aloud so there will be no question of your missing the point."

Karl took the paper, glanced over it, and began reading.

Reich Air Ministry
December 28, 1937

To: All Condor Legion Officers and Volunteers Serving on the Madrid Front

Despite the praiseworthy heroism surrounding General Haber's daring escape from Madrid, there must be no further discussion – oral or written, direct or indirect – concerning the General's recent visit to Spain.

This order shall take effect immediately. Any violation of this order should be reported to me directly and without delay. Violators will be subject to severe punishment.

Hermann Göring

Reich Minister of Aviation

"Hauptmann, do you understand?" Zimmer asked.

"I'd be a fool not to," Karl answered, standing at attention.

"Good," Zimmer said, "I'll inform our men at Getafe. The Hudson's surprise landing there aroused considerable curiosity."

"If you will permit me, Oberst Zimmer," Karl said. "This instruction may have unintended consequences. It might tempt the men to come to me with questions, even innocent questions, and any failure to answer will only stimulate their curiosity. It may lead to more talk off base, in cafés and other places where outsiders could be listening."

"You're quite right, Hauptmann," Zimmer replied. "But what in the hell do you propose we do about that? Have you a specific solution in mind?"

"I do."

"So let's have it."

"Since so much of this talk focuses on me, it might be a good idea for me to get away for a while, perhaps a month serving with a combat unit. Without me here to answer questions, the talk should die down."

"Why would I do that when I could simply send you to back to Germany?"

"I should remind the Oberst that I serve here at the request of Aviation Minister Göring. If he wanted me to go home, he would have so ordered. Two weeks with a bomber squadron and another week or two with an infantry unit would allow this talk of the Haber incident to die down – and at the same time give me invaluable combat experience, which will generate more substance for my Party fundraising speeches. That's the real reason why I'm here in Spain."

"I understand. But who would run the field hospital?"

"Dr. Ott is quite capable of handling things here. My predecessor, Dr. Wagner, organized the hospital very well. And as you know, casualties remain quite light."

"All right. Tell Ott he's in charge for the next thirty days. That's how much time I'll give you. Then report to Hauptmann Manfred Braun. He's a resourceful young officer with a fine infantry company. His men know what they're doing. You'll be responsible for transporting yourself and your equipment to their quarters. After that, you can spend some time with one of our bomber units."

155. THE HABER-WAGNER RESIDENCE, TIERGARTENSTRASSE, BERLIN, APRIL 22, 1938, 6:15 P.M.

General Martin Haber had at last been able to clear his desk in time to host a small dinner party with his new wife. Hildy loved to entertain. She delighted in sharing elaborate meals and good wine with her family, her new husband, and his colleagues. Of course, there were nights when Martin had meetings to attend. But, as Hildy advised, if he organized his work properly, he could keep such meetings to a minimum. Hildy had transformed the library into a well-appointed study with new bookshelves and ample wall space for maps.

For Hildy, this dinner party was indeed a special occasion. Fern was up from Munich for a conference at the Air Ministry. She had taken a room at the Adlon but would be joining them for dinner. Frederick, whom neither Hildy nor Fern had seen in months, would be there too. Haber was also pleased that his old friend Erwin Rommel, now a Wehrmacht colonel, would be joining them with his wife Lucy. During the damp frozen winter of 1915, in the Argonne near Binarville, then-Hauptmann Haber and then-Leutnant Rommel had taken turns bailing the rain and snow out of the four-foot-deep dugout they shared. Haber was looking forward to an after-dinner brandy with his old friend, eager to discuss the rebuilding of the German military. Haber knew there was much he could learn from Rommel, whose books and papers on tank warfare and mobile tactics inspired much of Haber's own military planning.

Fern arrived first, striking in a navy blue wool suit and pink blouse. Haber greeted her warmly as Fern offered both cheeks.

"You look wonderful, my dear. My compliments on that fine-looking suit."

"Thank you, General. It's one of my extravagances from Paris."

After the Rommels arrived, the guests enjoyed a brisk conversation about skiing in Austria, speculating about how popular it might become now that Austria was part of the Reich. Over Hildy's pork roast, the talked turned to Fern's time with the Condor Legion, which won compliments from both the Rommels. But it was Haber's capture and escape from Madrid that inspired the most passionate conversation.

"I too should like to meet this heroic young doctor," Rommel said.

"So would I," said Frederick. "And I hope to do so when he returns from Spain. Right now, however, I have a practical question for Colonel Rommel: I want to know what he thinks about the performance of our new tanks in Spain."

Rommel sipped Rumplemintz while choosing his words. "The new Panzers have performed extremely well against the Russian tanks in Spain. But they use too much petrol. We either need to design tanks that can go further on less fuel or get more access to crude oil and the means to refine it."

Everyone nodded, and Fern fixed her eyes on Rommel and Haber in turn. "Our Panzer crews will also need medical support," she said. "Tank casualties are among the most severe, especially the burns. When a shell hits, the men inside can burn to death within seconds."

"This is a terrible business," Rommel said. "But from what I've heard, Doctor, your work in Spain was magnificent."

"I did what I could."

After Frederick and the Rommels left, Haber led Hildy and Fern into the drawing room. "You should be very proud of this daughter of yours, Hildy."

"You know that I am," Hildy responded, "and that I love her dearly. Right now, though, I can't stay awake another minute." Kissing Haber quickly on the cheek, Hildy left the room. Haber turned to Fern. "Have another schnapps with me."

"I guess one more couldn't hurt," Fern said, accepting a replenished pony glass of Rumplemintz and glad for the opportunity to learn more about this man who had become her mother's husband. Their conversation went on for more than an hour – about Berlin, Spain, and Dr. Muller. Fern realized the General and her mother might insist that she meet this Dr. Muller once he returned from Spain. Fern knew she would have to avoid that at all costs.

156. POLICE FIRING RANGE, BERLIN, DECEMBER 2, 1938, 11:15 A.M.

Hans held his Walther with a gentle firmness, as if the handgun were priceless crystal, fixing his eyes on the target thirty meters away. He squeezed the trigger with calm deliberation: another bull's-eye – his sixth in a row – for a perfect score. Three colleagues who had gathered to watch applauded enthusiastically. Hans Krebs was at home on the firing range. It was where the good cops hung out. For reasons he could never quite figure out, the "Gestapo types" he knew didn't spend time on the firing range.

After practicing their marksmanship, Hans and his colleagues would usually adjourn to the Romanisches Café for cop-talk – homicides, hookers, and heists. After washing up and adjusting his worn necktie, Hans walked toward the exit to meet his friends. He had often fantasized about finding Fern there, waiting for him. He heard that she'd returned from Spain, but she hadn't been in touch.

But today she was actually there, waiting for him, stunning as ever in a brown pinstriped suit that showed off her strong, finely curved calves. She wore her deep chestnut hair in a tight bun. She kissed Hans on the cheek and gave him a long hug.

"I went to the station first, but they said I would probably find you here. I hope you don't mind."

"Mind?" he said, breaking into a grin. There was no way he could restrain his joy. "We ought to have a drink, but if we go to the Romanisches we'll be surrounded by cops. Great guys, but I'm not in the mood to share you."

"Let's go the Adlon instead then. It's just a short walk. Since mother has married her General, I stay there when I'm in Berlin. I see that much has changed since I left for Munich and Spain," she said, taking his arm.

"Everything's busier – the factories, the shops, the people. And people have a little money in their pockets. Not too much, perhaps, but more than before."

As they crossed the Pariser Platz and entered the expansive splendor of the Adlon dining room, Fern told Krebs that she had been able to secure a good table there because Hildy was on good terms with the *maître d'*.

"Ah yes, Frau Haber's daughter," the *maître d'* said with deference, escorting Fern and Hans to a corner booth, where they both ordered steins of pilsner. Fern spoke before taking her first sip. "So how's the police business these days?"

Hans studied the ceiling. "I've learned at least one thing – that Heydrich is obsessed with gathering dirt on people. He wants to have the drop on anyone who might get in his way."

"How do you know this?"

"I'm a detective, Fern. I watch and I learn."

"I should have known," she said, tipping her glass in his direction.

"I mention Heydrich because there's talk that he wants me to be his special assistant in the SD, the relatively new internal security unit. It's my punishment," Hans said sarcastically, "for being such a good cop. If I work under Heydrich though, I'd have to spy on some decent people who haven't done anything wrong, except perhaps to attract police attention for being out of step with the new Germany."

After finishing the cold Norwegian salmon with capers and a thick potato soup, Fern covered her mouth to yawn. "I've had too much to eat," she smiled. They ordered coffee. The Adlon had the best in Berlin.

"I thought of you often when I was in Spain. And of course I wanted to write, but I refrained from doing so out of fear that someone like your friend Heydrich, or some other Nazi busybody, might read my letters. But now I can say what's on my mind. So please listen."

"When have I ever been less than attentive?"

"Never. That's why I'm here today," she said, leaning toward him. "I have a lot of questions and very few answers. Are you, dear Hans, the man for me?" She put a finger to her lips to show that she didn't want a response. "Neither of us knows. Do I love you? Not yet. Might it all work out for us? Perhaps. Am I still grieving for my dead fiancé? Yes. I haven't even begun to get over him. Should I start dating eligible Nazi bachelors? I don't think so. But General Haber, who's now my stepfather, is after me to meet this Nazi doctor who replaced me in Spain. But I find him repulsive, even without meeting him. He raises money for the Nazi Party, for God's sake. How could I stand to be with someone like that?"

"Fern."

She clasped his right hand, tightening her grip. "Please, Hans, hear me out."

"What are you trying to tell me?" he asked.

"That I want to have dinners and wonderful conversations and share confidences with you, that I want to hug you good night – but not spend the night together. That we just have to see what happens."

He nodded, as if he were about to speak.

"Please let me finish, Hans. My real surprise is yet to come. I know it's incredibly selfish of me to say so, but your presence in my life has made it easier to fend off the Luftwaffe officers and Nazi Party creeps with beer, sauerkraut, and tobacco on their breath. Being with you makes it easier to refuse so-called opportunities to meet creeps like this Dr. Muller."

"You know that I'd gladly take care of any creep that bothers you. But how much can my presence in your life do any good if you're in Munich and I'm here in Berlin?"

"Hell, Hans. Soon, I won't be in Munich or Berlin. I wanted to speak to you before I leave Germany."

"Leave for where?"

"Washington. It's all arranged. I'm going lecture at the Georgetown School of Medicine. Göring wants the Americans to know that we Germans are making major advances in burn treatment. He has some twisted notion that what we're doing Spain will be perceived as a benefit for all humanity. Stupid, yes, but it'll get me out of Germany for a few months. I'm scheduled to lecture during the spring, summer, and fall sessions. I'll be leaving Germany right after the New Year."

"Your lectures are sure to highlight German medical advances – but they'll also focus American attention on the horrors the Luftwaffe are inflicting."

"Too bad for Germany. For me, getting out of Germany was impossible to resist. Uncle Frederick has arranged for me to stay in an apartment one of his companies maintains in Washington – a neighborhood called Capitol Hill."

Hans looked away.

"Fern, one minute I hear you saying that you want us to be some kind of couple. And the arrangement you describe, even if it's not my first choice, could work with both of us here in Berlin, or even with me here in Berlin and you in Munich. But then you say you're going to America?"

"Which leads to my next question: Do you want to come with me? We would live separately, of course, but still see each other all the time."

"I need some time to think about this."

"Of course," she said, nodding toward the waiter. "Lunch is on me. Or rather, it's on mother. She has an account here."

157. ROMANISCHES CAFÉ, DECEMBER 2, 1938, 5:10 P.M.

Hans crumpled the empty cigarette pack and asked the waiter for some still water. His lunch with Fern had left him anxious. If he didn't accept the invitation, he might as well forget her. She was sure to find someone else there, either an American or a German-American, like her dead fiancé. But how could Hans Krebs, or any man, compete with a ghost? Hans knew he had to stay close to Fern if he had any chance of winning her. That meant he had to join her in America and would need a well-paying job there.

Then there was Gretchen. She'd already decided to prepare for medical school. Before long, she'd be out of his apartment and attending university. So there was nothing stopping him from going to America.

He needed work that would keep him close to Fern. The answer was both easy and hard. The easy part would be getting the job. Heydrich had long wanted him in the SD. The hard part would be working for Heydrich. But Hans prided himself on being practical. He drank his water, left some coins on the table, and walked to a sidewalk telephone kiosk to call Fern. He couldn't wait to tell her his decision. He would telephone Heydrich in the morning.

158. PRINZ-ALBRECHT-STRASSE, BERLIN, DECEMBER 3, 1938, 9:30 A.M.

Hans decided to be candid with Heydrich, who listened carefully before responding. "So," he said at last, "the fetching Dr. Wagner has inspired you to see the light, Krebs."

"What can I say?"

"Well Hans, it proves you're human. Still a son of a bitch, but at least a human son of a bitch. Yes, go to America. There you can be my son of a bitch. You can work out of our Washington embassy, just as you've requested. You can work under the guise of a commercial attaché while serving as an SD operative. From your home base in Washington, you can easily make trips to Long Island, New York. I am told that the German-American Bund is quite strong there. I want to know if that's true. They may just be a bunch of goose-stepping assholes, but you might find some useful informants among them. Report on them within a month of your arrival – and every month thereafter.

"More important, I'll also need reports on what the Abwehr is up to. We can't play second fiddle to that old fart Admiral Canaris and his dead-ass Abwehr. The SD must become Germany's primary intelligence organization. And you, Krebs, can help make that happen."

"I'll need some time to gear up for all that and arrange my passage."

"Fine. Don't worry about reporting to the embassy until January 15."

Thanking Heydrich, Hans rose to his feet and snapped a *Heil Hitler* salute, a gesture he rarely bothered to make. Heydrich walked Krebs to the door.

"One more thing, Krebs. I don't want you getting tangled up in all our bureaucratic horseshit when you return from America. Just understand that you're working for me as my special deputy. You'll report only to me. Understood?"

"Understood."

Heydrich counted to ten before hitting the intercom switch. "Hans Krebs has just left my office. He'll be working with the SD. I've assigned him to a temporary cover as an SD liaison attached to our embassy in Washington. Inform all appropriate parties that once Krebs arrives in America I want a report of his whereabouts and activities on my desk first thing every morning."

159. LOYALIST ARMY INTELLIGENCE HEADQUARTERS, MADRID, DECEMBER 6, 1938, 11:00 A.M.

Josh squirmed in the cold metal chair in the flickering light. The electricity was out, the power station having taken a direct hit during the shelling the night before. The lone candle on the table showed Josh the young face of Loyalist Captain Jorge Alvarez.

"Please relax, Doctor," the Spaniard said.

Josh's mood lightened when he saw that Alvarez was making a genuine effort to be courteous. "Dr. Greenberg, I'll get right to the point. We have questions about the Nazi capture of the British Red Cross Hudson last December. You examined and performed surgery on the co-pilot. You said that the co-pilot's injuries resembled those inflicted by a professional fighter. How would you know such a thing?"

"Look, that was almost a year ago."

"Paperwork takes time, especially when you're trying to not to be killed by shellfire."

"Well, I've got no secrets," Josh said. "In the past I performed emergency surgery on several boxers. A close friend of mine was a boxer, and several of his opponents suffered that kind of bone-shattering injury."

"You say 'a friend.'"

"Well, the doctor I'm referring to worked in the same hospital with me in New York."

"Are you aware that the man who escaped with the Nazi general was a doctor?"

"No, but the doctor I mentioned is dead. And I've heard that one of the assailants piloted the Hudson. My friend didn't know how to fly."

"Is there anything else you want to add to your statement?"

"No," Josh said just as another shell exploded. "I need to get back to the hospital."

160. HOFBRÄUHAUS, MUNICH, DECEMBER 15, 1938, 12 NOON

Hans sat at a table along the wall of the smoky Munich beer hall with his daughter Gretchen and a half-empty stein of Löwenbräu.

Hans was happy that Gretchen and Fern got along so well. Thanks to Fern's advice, Gretchen would continue her education at a Catholic boarding school for girls near Leipzig and begin her pre-medical studies at the university there in the autumn.

When Fern arrived she took a long swallow from Hans's beer stein. "Now our Christmas holiday has officially begun," she said.

"I agree," said Hans, taking a swig himself and ordering another around from the plump serving woman.

"Tomorrow," Fern said, "we'll take the train to Garmisch, where Gretchen and I will ski with Frederick and Reichsmarschall Göring. And you, Hans, will have time to study your English. I don't think you're in shape for skiing – too many cigarettes and too much beer. Target practice with a Walther hardly counts as exercise."

Fern then told them the rest of her news over lunch. "When I spoke with Göring this morning and told him that you two would be with me, he invited us to a Christmas Eve party at his home in Berchtesgaden. It should be quite an event. I'm told that the Führer himself will be there. Uncle Frederick will be there, too, along with Krupp and others from the

Wilhelmstrasse, including General Haber and mother. Uncle Frederick will send a company plane to take us from Garmisch to Berchtesgaden, where we can stay at his pension."

"Are you sure I'm invited?" Hans asked. "Hardly sounds like my kind of party."

"Indeed you are," Fern intoned. "I spoke to Göring about it."

161. LOYALIST ARMY INTELLIGENCE HEADQUARTERS, MADRID, DECEMBER 16, 1938 2:00 P.M.

Captain Alvarez sat in the bomb-scarred airplane hangar pounding on an ancient Underwood. He had to bear down hard on the keys because the ribbon was old and dry and there was no replacement to be found. His fingers and wrists ached. He had already chain smoked his way through ten reports now many months overdue. Alvarez was nearly finished with the one on Dr. Josh Greenberg when the shelling resumed.

He had just typed the words: "*. . . merits further investigation because the blows to the head of the co-pilot were, according to Dr. Greenberg, of a force that only a professional prizefighter could inflict. Little is known about Hauptmann Karl Muller, the German doctor who the pilots identified as their assailant. It appears that Dr. Muller piloted the aircraft during the escape because we know that General Haber is not a pilot.*" Alvarez was reading over what he'd written when the building jumped underneath him. A split second later, a falling steel beam crushed his skull.

162. NEAR THE GREENBERG APARTMENT, MADRID, DECEMBER 17, 1938, 1:00 A.M.

Josh walked through the rubble on the Calle del Arenal. The Loyalists' inability to defend Madrid was now clear. The city was little more than a dumping ground for Franco's live artillery shells. Smoke stung Josh's eyes as he made his way through the rubble. The flickering orange flames from the burning buildings helped him navigate through knee-high chunks of stone and cement. It was warm for December, and the overpowering stench of rotting flesh filled the night air. He turned into the narrow alley where he and Nancy had taken an apartment and climbed the building's outer stairway.

As he entered the candlelit apartment, he saw Nancy sitting on the frayed loveseat.

"Couldn't sleep?" Josh asked.

"Nope. If you're hungry, there's some bread and an apple I took from the hospital." She got up and walked with him into the kitchen, setting the candle on the table. Their district had been without electricity for a week. "Josh, we need to talk."

As she moved closer, he took her head in his hands and kissed her nose. She glanced at the floor for a moment, then back at his face.

"You only came here because of me. Now I've got to get us out of here."

"We can't leave now, Nancy, just because things are getting tough."

"You know I'm not a quitter, Josh. But this isn't tough," she said, tucking her head under his chin. "Tough is slogging through Macy's at Christmastime or an extra busy night in the emergency room. *Tough* is easy. This is broken bodies. Corpses everywhere. *This is goddamn hell!*"

Josh put his hands on her shoulders. "We've survived so far. I don't see why we should change now," he said

They shared a brief kiss. He moved to kiss her again, but she withdrew.

"We need to think about what's going to happen if our Loyalist friends lose this goddamn war."

"Considering everything he owes to Hitler, Franco would be happy to turn over all the Jews who've been fighting him here in Spain. God only knows what Hitler will do with them. Remember the news reports on how his thugs smashed up Jewish shops in Germany back in October? And what about all the terrible stories about Jews being beaten and killed in those parts of Spain controlled by the Nationalists, which is now most of the country?"

Josh took a last bite from the apple, wrapped the core in newspaper, and tossed it toward a wicker wastebasket. It flew in a perfect arc through the candlelight and landed in the basket.

"How about that?" Josh said with smile. She admired his ability to relax in the middle of an argument even though it frustrated her.

"All right," she said. "I've lost the *we're-losing-the-goddamn-war* argument. That's strike one. I've also lost the *big-trouble-for-the-Jews* argument. Strike two. Let's see how I do with my last-ditch effort."

"Okay, take a swing at it."

"Josh, I'm pregnant."

Josh stared at the ceiling, his head turning slowly as if he were watching the flight of an imaginary baseball.

"Home run. You win. Let's go to bed. We'll make our getaway plans in the morning." The shelling started again as they made their way to the bedroom.

163. GARMISCH, DECEMBER 18, 1938, 11:00 A.M.

Having completed his yearlong tour of duty in Spain earlier in the month, a clean-shaven Karl decided to postpone resumption of his medical practice until after the Christmas holiday. He flew to Munich on a Junkers tri-motor transport and telephoned Frau Frick from the airport, instructing her to prepare the office for his return in the first week in January.

In Munich he outfitted himself for skiing, then traveled by rail to Garmisch, where he took a room at the base lodge. Once he felt that he'd regained the necessary strength and skiing skills, he telephoned Hess and invited him to the mountain.

Hess proved to be an excellent skier, just as Channing Brown's briefing books had indicated.

Atop the Zugspitze, the snow sparkled against the blue December sky. Karl waited for Hess, who had left to relieve himself. "I just ran into Göring in the water closet," Hess said when he returned. "He's here with Frederick Wagner. They're skiing with Frederick's niece and her boyfriend's daughter. Hermann was in a hurry to rejoin them, but invited us to lunch once we finish this run down the mountain. See, there they are, all four of them," Hess said, pointing down the slope. Karl saw that Fern was skiing with her usual grace.

"Let's try and catch them," Karl said, lowering his goggles. He disappeared down the mountain, skiing the fall line in a full tuck, knowing his sudden burst of speed had taken Hess by surprise. Racing over a knoll, he came to a halt. Looking back up the mountain and into the sunlight, he was relieved to see that he was out of Hess's line of sight. He dropped to the snow and began massaging his right thigh with both hands.

"My right quadriceps is cramped," Karl said, his face contorted as Hess skied to a stop next to him. "I may be dehydrated. Drank too much beer with you last night. So it's better if I skip lunch and get a massage if I want to ski with you this afternoon. Please apologize to Hermann and the Wagners."

11:44 A.M.

At the base lodge, Karl stored his skis, leaving his goggles down and the woolen skullcap on his head. Passing the wide restaurant entranceway, he could see Hess and Göring alone at a corner table. In the next instant he realized that Fern, Gretchen, and Frederick were walking straight toward him. Both women had their eyes on Frederick, who was saying something about skiing the fall line. All three walked right past him without noticing. Not sure where they were headed, he decided to take refuge in the massage room, where he had a rubdown and tried, without success, to stop thinking about Fern. He knew there was nothing in Brown's briefing books to help him do that.

Emerging after one o'clock, Karl made his way back to the restaurant entrance. He scanned the room and saw Hess and Göring still seated at the large corner table, but no sign of the Wagner party. He decided to join them.

"Rudolf here tells me that you're quite a good skier," Göring said as Karl approached the table.

"I probably overdid it this morning," Karl said. "But I look forward to getting back on the mountain this afternoon. Tell me, where is the Wagner party?"

"Frederick said that his niece and her boyfriend, Hans Krebs, had an appointment to complete some travel documents. Krebs's daughter and Frederick went with them," Göring said.

"Let's get back on the mountain," Hess said, glancing at his watch. "Will you join us, Hermann?"

"I'm eager to get back on the mountain, too. But first I'd like to invite the heroic Dr. Muller to a Christmas Eve party at my home in Berchtesgaden." Göring put his hand on Karl's shoulder. "Rudolf will be there, of course. Come to think of it, Frederick and his niece will be there. So you'll have an opportunity to meet them. Even the Führer has given his solemn promise to join us. I've reserved rooms for all my guests at the new Berchtesgadener Inn. I'll make sure one is set aside for you, Karl."

"That's very kind of you, Air Minister. I am honored to accept your invitation."

"Then it's settled," Hess said. "Karl can fly with me to Berchtesgaden on the morning of the twenty-fourth. Flying over the mountains is spectacular in the clear December air."

164. THE KREMLIN, DECEMBER 24, 1938, 1:02 A.M.

The porcelain lamp on Joseph Stalin's desk provided the room's only light. Lavrentiy Pavlovich Beria handed Stalin a freshly translated, single-spaced one-page report. Only the month before, Stalin had appointed Beria chief of the NKVD. Despite its designation – the People's Commissariat for *Internal* Affairs – the NKVD played an active role in foreign intelligence.

The Soviet leader held the report up to the lamp, scrutinizing every word. After a long pause, he looked up at Beria. "So Lavrentiy Pavlovich, this document bears the date December 16. Why is it coming to my attention only now, so many days later?"

"Because of the relentless shelling of Madrid, Comrade Stalin. Our Loyalist friends discovered the original document in the rubble of a bombed-out hangar in Madrid. It arrived here this very evening on a diplomatic courier plane. Loyalist troops recovered the body of the man who wrote the report, a Captain Alvarez. They found him dead in the wreckage, his skull crushed, the report still in the roller of his typewriter."

Stalin reached into his desk drawer for the vodka he always kept there. Two glasses were already on the desk. He poured generous portions into both glasses, took a sip from one and pushed the other toward Beria. "I commend your people in Madrid for their thoroughness," he said in a throaty tone. "I seem to remember a related report, Lavrentiy."

"Comrade Stalin is referring to the information supplied by the young English newspaper correspondent who covered the war from Franco's side of the line. This young man won the confidence of the German woman doctor assigned to the Luftwaffe. Her name is Fern Wagner."

"Ah yes, this Dr. Wagner was a woman. There was something in her past."

"Indeed," Beria said. "According to our young Englishman, Dr. Wagner was engaged to a man named Karl Ludwig, also a doctor – a German-American, no less. He was a boxer too. Ludwig perished under very unusual circumstances: he died a car crash while serving a prison sentence."

Beria sipped his vodka and went on. "Apparently this Dr. Muller, the Nazi who helped General Haber escape from Madrid, displayed remarkable physical prowess. One blow in particular was quite devastating, as noted in the report, which cites the testimony of a certain Dr. Josh Greenberg. Greenberg's an American Jew who – and this we've learned from sources in Berlin – was a close friend of the Luftwaffe doctor, Fern Wagner, when they worked together at the same hospital in New York."

"That could be pure coincidence," Stalin said. "New York is up to its ass in Greenbergs."

"True," Beria replied. "But what compels my further interest is that this Dr. Greenberg examined the injured British pilots who were thrown off the plane during Haber's escape. Greenberg is quoted in Alvarez's unfinished report as saying that the blows these British pilots suffered appear to have been inflicted by a professional boxer. And that raises questions about this Nazi doctor, Karl Muller: Just *who is he?* He seems to have come out of nowhere, East Africa to be exact. And all the sudden he's some sort of Nazi hero."

"Lavrentiy Pavlovich," Stalin said, leaning back and biting the stem of his pipe, "you're grasping at circumstantial straws."

"Perhaps," Beria said. "But don't you see? It's possible that these two doctors—the Nazi Muller and the American Ludwig – are the same person. With that in mind, and with all due respect to Comrade Stalin, allow me to point out yet another compelling reality."

"Let's have it," Stalin sighed. "You've gone this far. Why should I stop you now?"

"As far as we can determine, the raid in which General Haber and the German doctor were captured wasn't authorized by any Loyalist officer. The airplane was an American-made Hudson, guarded by a contingent of British Marines. It would impossible to steal such a plane – unless, of course, the miraculous escape was an elaborate charade."

Stalin stood and walked to the window. A frigid night held Red Square in its grip. Stalin shook his head, his back to Beria. "All right, indulge your curiosity and pursue this matter further. Get word to the young Englishman to stay on the case. Even more important, get word to your special Berlin operative, the one you say is the best agent in Berlin. Have them both look into this."

Before responding, Beria let a final sip of vodka linger on his palate and trickle down his throat. "There are two other people who could help us clarify this business of Dr. Muller's identity. One is the Luftwaffe doctor, Fern Wagner. She happens to be the stepdaughter of Martin Haber, the Nazi general that Muller rescued. She's also the niece of a prominent Nazi industrialist. But she would never talk to us. The other is this Jew doctor, Josh Greenberg. He's accessible to us in Madrid. If our Berlin operatives can obtain a photograph of Dr. Muller and show it to Greenberg, then Greenberg could tell us whether Muller and Ludwig are the same person. It's that simple."

"Do you think Greenberg will cooperate?" Stalin asked.

Beria put down his empty vodka glass. "We have every reason to believe he will. We've been keeping a file on him for some time. His wife is a Party member. She's published letters in the *Daily Worker* and helped organize a hospital union in New York. By all accounts, Dr. Greenberg is agnostic when it comes to the Party and politics. But he did volunteer to go Spain, probably to please to wife."

Stalin relit his pipe and leaned toward Beria. "Then they won't mind coming to Moscow for questioning. If you want to get to the bottom of all this, let's bring the Greenberg couple to Moscow. If she's a genuinely loyal Party member, she'll jump at the opportunity."

"But they're needed in Madrid."

"The way things are going in Spain, this Jew doctor and his wife will soon be prisoners of the Nationalists or the Germans. We'll lose our last opportunity to question them if we don't act soon."

"I'll send a message to Madrid immediately."

"Do it. You've got my attention now, so don't fuck this up."

165. RED BRIGADE HEADQUARTERS, MADRID, DECEMBER 24, 1938, 4:52 A.M.

"What? On Christmas Eve?" Red Brigade Corporal José Cardozo asked indignantly as he stamped out his cigarette on the cement floor.

"That's right," said Sergeant Julio Martinez. "And remember, a good comrade doesn't give a rat's ass about Christmas, especially in this case. Do I need to remind you that this order comes straight from Moscow? They have firing squads for soldiers like you, Corporal," Martinez barked.

Corporal Cardozo knew Martinez was right. Discipline was harsher than ever now that Franco's Nationalists had stepped up the pressure on Madrid. Martinez used the telephone on the wall to issue the order: four soldiers were to join him and Corporal Cardozo to find and detain Dr. Josh Greenberg. It wasn't an arrest exactly, just an invitation to answer some questions.

166. LANDHAUS GÖRING, BERCHTESGADEN, DECEMBER 24, 1938 4:00 P.M.

Karl wended his way through the chatter and good cheer, seeking refuge on the second-floor balcony, an ideal vantage point from which he could observe every guest's arrival. He could also see the main hall of the ground floor, where a model electric train at the foot of the Christmas tree circled a gingerbread replica of the Brandenburg Gate.

Karl took in the faces. There was Bormann, holding forth in an animated conversation with several men Karl recognized as senior-level functionaries from the Wilhelmstrasse. Karl spotted another man he recognized from newspaper photographs as Heinrich Himmler. Himmler was frowning as he listened to a younger man with a long thin face. Karl surmised that the younger man was Reinhard Heydrich, head of the SD.

Karl kept reminding himself not to gape at Fern when she arrived. He told himself that he would have to know where she was at all times but avoid even the slightest hint of eye contact. He decided his best strategy would be to engage someone in close conversation. He hoped the well-groomed beard he had started back in Spain could help keep Fern from recognizing him should she glance his way. He knew there was no leaving the party. He had to stay to hold Bormann to his promise to introduce him to Hitler. As he glanced out over the balcony at the merriment below, he sensed the presence of someone behind him. "Dr. Muller, so nice to see you."

"Trudy Gretzler, now this *is* a surprise. You helped during those surgeries back in Spain. Together we saved several of our boys from losing their legs. What brings you to Landhaus Göring?"

"I'm a neighbor of the Air Marshall and the Führer. In fact, I grew up in Berchtesgaden. My father's a civil engineer. He helped Martin Bormann build the Kehlsteinhaus."

"Yes. Bormann has told me about the Kehlsteinhaus. It's quite a project, I understand."

"You should ask him to show it to you."

When a waitress passed with a tray of wine glasses, Trudy quickly emptied her glass and took a fresh one. She gave Karl a smile that showed her even white teeth. Her honey-blonde tresses fell straight to the shoulders of her Tyrolean holiday dress. Karl thought she seemed unusually friendly as she sidled up next to him along the balcony rail. Yes, he decided, she was the cover he needed. As long as he kept her engaged in conversation, he could look over her shoulder and survey the main entrance. No one would question his behavior. After all, he was an eligible bachelor. Why shouldn't he chat with a pretty girl?

Looking over Trudy's shoulder at the reception line on the ground floor Karl caught sight of Fern, erect and stunning in a bright raspberry dress, her hair in a fashionable upsweep. Fern's hand was on the arm of Hans Krebs. Hans's daughter Gretchen, alive with young excitement, was beside them. Behind them were Frederick Wagner, General Haber, and a handsome woman Karl guessed was Fern's mother.

Noticing that Karl was distracted, Trudy also focused her attention on the scene below, just as Adolf Hitler arrived, resplendent in a double-breasted white blazer. Hitler glanced upward toward the balcony, and for an instant Karl felt as if Hitler were looking straight at him. But when Hitler raised his arm to wave, it was clear that Trudy was the object of his attention. She waved back. Hitler then shifted his attention to the guests clustered around him. For the second time in three days, Karl had to cope with the reality of Fern's presence.

"So, Trudy, our Führer waved to you," Karl said, fighting off the impulse to stare at Fern.

"I've known him since I was fifteen," she said. "He's been coming to Berchtesgaden for years. I waited tables in a restaurant near the Bahnhof. Hitler would come there often for lunches with Nazi Party officials who arrived by train."

Unnoticed by Karl, Martin Bormann arrived on the balcony. "Trudy, so good see you," Bormann said. "You're in good company with Karl. But I must borrow him for a few minutes."

"You may do so only if he promises to hurry back."

Bormann placed a hand on Karl's shoulder. "The Führer wants to meet you, Karl. He's in Göring's study. Come now."

Bormann led Karl down the stairs to the ground floor, then along a short hallway where five SS guards stood at attention. Karl could hear Göring laughing on the other side of the closed door.

"The Führer will see you in a moment, Karl," Bormann said. "Who's with him now?" Bormann asked one of the SS guards.

"It's a rather large party," said a youthful corporal, standing tall in his dark SS uniform. "Air Marshall Göring, General Haber, and Frederick Wagner are there. So are three others – Dr. Wagner, the Berlin detective Hans Krebs, and Krebs's daughter."

"Of course, we must wait our turn," Bormann responded. He gestured for Karl to sit with him on a bench in the hallway.

Karl braced for the worst, trying his best not to appear anxious. If Fern saw the ghost of her dead betrothed, there was no telling how she might react – and Karl would just have to let that happen. He knew he couldn't feign illness like he had on the mountain.

"You look pale, Karl," Bormann said.

"Just a little nervous about meeting the Führer," Karl lied. "You see him every day. It's different for me."

The door flung open and the SS guard clicked his heels and led Karl and Bormann into the study.

With Göring beside him, Adolf Hitler was standing next to a brown leather chair. To Karl's relief, there was no one else in the room. Hitler stepped forward, not waiting for a formal introduction, his bright eyes fixed on Karl's.

"Dr. Muller, you have honored me and the Reich with the bravery you demonstrated in Spain."

Despite catching a whiff of Hitler's musty breath, Karl relaxed and smiled. He saw that Fern and the others must have left the room through a second door, one behind the desk where Hitler now stood.

"*Mein Führer*, I was lucky," Karl said, at ease now that the threat of facing Fern had passed – at least for the moment. "I simply saw an opportunity, and I seized it."

Hitler pointed to the well-stocked bar in a corner under a photo of Göring piloting a tri-wing aircraft. "Hermann, please bring the doctor here some of that beer you have on tap and a near beer for me. It's not often that we're in the company of a man such as Karl Muller," Hitler said. "Bormann's been after me to meet you."

"*Mein Führer*, I am honored to be here, especially since you speak with the authority of an experienced soldier who served at the front in the war against Britain and France. You know what it was like to endure damp, moldy trenches and to risk blindness, disfigurement, and death."

Hitler gave Karl an understanding nod.

"If the Führer and Air Marshall Göring will forgive me," Karl went on, sensing the power of Hitler's gaze, "the Western press and our own Berlin newspapers have paid attention so far mostly to our airmen. They are coura-geous warriors. No one can deny it. But not enough credit is being given to the men on the ground in Spain."

"Please go on," Hitler said.

"If it would please the Führer," Karl said, "I'd be happy to prepare a report highlighting the accomplishments of our ground forces in Spain."

"I'd be pleased if you could do so, Doctor. You could present it at the Chancellery."

Karl smiled to let Hitler know that he was pleased by the prospect of a future meeting. Hitler rose and extended his hand to Karl a second time, a clear indication that the meeting had come to an end. "I must return to Hermann's guests," Hitler said. "Then I'm off to the Berghof for a dinner with Frederick and his family."

Hitler slipped out the back door.

Returning to the party, Karl scanned the scene with care. Much to his relief, Fern was nowhere in sight. With Martin Bormann by his side, Karl found Trudy chatting with Frau Bormann near a ground-floor picture win-dow. After introducing Karl to his wife, Bormann placed his right hand lightly on Trudy's forearm. "I've known this young lady for some time, Karl. Her father gave invaluable assistance on the Kehlsteinhaus. And now, thank God, it's almost done."

"Then by all means, I must see it," Karl said.

"How about tomorrow? I can't think of a better way to spend Christmas morning," Bormann responded. "Let's say nine o'clock. Our children will be busy playing with their new toy trains and soldiers. I'll pick you up. After that you can join us for dinner."

The Bormanns saw Heydrich approach as Karl and Trudy excused them-selves for the dance floor.

"Martin, Frau Bormann," Heydrich said, "please allow me to wish you and your six beautiful children a joyful Christmas. Will you have time to meet me in your office once we're both back in Berlin, Martin?" Heydrich asked, drawing Bormann aside.

"Yes, of course."

"I need to discuss a delicate matter, one better suited for your office in Party headquarters on the Brienner Strasse in Munich, than mine on the Prinz-Albrecht-Strasse in Berlin."

"Very well," Bormann said. "Why don't call my secretary and set something up for the first week of January? I'll be in Munich then."

"Excellent. I'll see you then, Martin. Enjoy your holiday."

7:10 P.M.

Karl led Trudy off the dance floor and away from the other guests. "These parties can be such a bore," she said. "You've made this one fun – a nice start to a promising evening."

"Trudy, I ought to tell you that I promised Rudolf Hess that I'd have dinner with him and his family later this evening. I accepted the invitation weeks ago, and I must honor it."

"Of course you must. I would expect nothing less of you, Karl. Just be sure to let me know the next time you're next in Berchtesgaden," she said, squeezing his hand. "Can I drive you to the Hesses' place?"

"Thanks, but Rudolf invited me to ride with him, and he's getting ready to leave."

As Hess and Karl walked toward the car, Karl wondered about Trudy and whether she was working for Reinhard Heydrich – or for Channing Brown.

167. KEHLSTEINHAUS, BERCHTESGADEN, DECEMBER 25, 1938, 10:00 AM

Bright beams of a winter light shone through the towering trees as Martin Bormann maneuvered his Mercedes convertible up the narrow corkscrew mountain road. Eager to show his Kehlstein project in all its winter splendor, Bormann kept the top down, as a cold wind reddened their cheeks.

"Now you can see how the Party has spent the money you've been raising," Bormann said. Karl had been expecting a bumpy ride, but the roadway was freshly paved. After a heavy snowfall two days before, the road was now plowed and clear.

When they reached the end of the road, on a ledge of flat land a half-mile above the tree line, Bormann eased the Mercedes into a tunnel entrance built of arched granite blocks. A sentry in a black SS trench coat snapped to attention. Bormann nodded and drove some hundred meters into the tunnel, then stopped at the open door of a waiting brass elevator carriage.

"Are you taking me to the Pearly Gates, Martin?" Karl asked as the lift sped upward.

"This will be as close as you or I ever get," Bormann replied with a smile.

When the elevator door opened, another SS guard saluted, leading them into a well-appointed octagonal room, with oversize chairs, a large round table, and a fireplace. Karl took it all in, gravitating toward a window that looked out on the snow-capped peaks.

"Let's step outside," Karl said, noticing a door leading to the patio. He let Bormann precede him onto a long narrow patio with a stone floor. Karl remained silent, absorbing the view.

"It's not the Pearly Gates," Bormann said, breaking the silence, "but a fine view of planet Earth."

"You've created a masterpiece, Martin. Tell me, has the Führer seen it yet?"

"In the spring, I'll present it to him officially as a present from the Party on the occasion of his fiftieth birthday, though he's already been here several times. To be honest, though, he has a fear of heights – so he's not as enthusiastic about the place as I'd hoped."

"Still," Karl responded, "he must realize that a place like this will impress the hell out of foreign dignitaries."

"Yes, he understands that. He wanted to show it to Chamberlain when he was in the Obersalzberg last September, but the tight schedule made it impossible."

"Nevertheless, Martin, the place has endless possibilities for important meetings away from the day-to-day distractions of Berlin."

"Well, let's forget Berlin for now. I believe this mountain air should give you a good appetite for the roasted duck Frau Bormann is preparing for Christmas dinner."

168. MADRID, DECEMBER 27, 1938, 7:00 P.M.

Josh fastened the top button of his overcoat. The dusty café off the Plaza Major had no heat. He could see his breath as he talked with Jack Courtney, the tall wiry man who identified himself as the top representative of what remained of the U.S. State Department mission in Madrid. Most embassy personnel had relocated to the safer quarters in Valencia.

"Good thing you found me, Josh," Courtney said, scratching his bald head. "If you had tried to skip town without the proper papers, the Loyalists would probably have shot you and your wife as deserters – no questions asked. On the other side of the line, Franco and his Nazi pals believe it's only a matter of days before they take Madrid and end this goddamn war. If they're right, the shelling and bombardment will stop, but there will still be plenty of hatred left on both sides. And the killing will go on, at least for a while."

"Some things won't change," Josh said. "I'm a Jew, with the circumcised pecker to prove it."

"Well, be aware that the Nazis have started doing pants-down inspections to spot Jews trying to sneak out of Germany. Why wouldn't their Loyalist pals do the same thing here in Spain?"

Nancy walked into the café, exhausted. Josh could see that the early months of pregnancy and the cold air had dried her face. Once she sat, Josh and Courtney repeated the gist of their conversation.

"Have you told Mr. Courtney that I'm two months pregnant" Nancy asked.

"I was about to get to that," Josh said. "What happened, Courtney, was that the Loyalists hauled me in on Christmas Eve and offered us a one-way trip to Moscow. Moscow in the winter? I flat out refused, and they let me go.

Then two more of them, one a captain, came to the hospital this afternoon and repeated the offer."

"Look, Josh," Courtney said, "you're the doctor. You know Nancy's condition. And, Nancy, I know you're tough. But Moscow? With the anti-Franco fronts collapsing, all Spain is becoming a giant trap, ready to snap shut on escaping Loyalists."

"Okay, Courtney," Nancy said. "Our passports are still valid. Where, may I ask, are the Marines?"

"They're here, guarding the embassy, for what it's worth. There's also a detachment of Marines guarding a State Department plane at the municipal airport."

"State Department plane?" Josh asked. "The U.S. has a plane here in Madrid?"

"Yup," Courtney said. "It's tucked away in a hangar, where so far it hasn't attracted attention. It's a Grumman Goose, an amphibian bearing the seal of the U.S. State Department. It flew in via Lisbon yesterday. It's here to transport documents and a few diplomatic personnel out of Spain. That doesn't include you guys."

"You could change that," Josh said.

"I could put in a word. But I don't think it would do much good."

Nancy stared at her husband. "Are you thinking about telephoning New York, Josh?" It was half question, half command.

"If I can find a telephone that works," he said, putting his hand in Nancy's.

"Look, Courtney," Josh said. "The obvious question is: How can we get on that plane? And if not that one, the next one."

"There won't be any next plane, Josh. They've let us know this one will be the last. It takes off tomorrow at dusk – around four in the afternoon – when there's just a little light. Then it'll disappear into the night sky over the Pyrenees on its way to Bordeaux."

Josh looked around and saw that there was no one in the café except the three of them and the old bartender. "Listen Courtney," Josh said, still glaring at the State Department man, "I need to use your phone. I need a safe, working phone."

"Okay, Josh. You can try to telephone from my office," Courtney responded. "Let's do it then. There's no shelling at the moment, so I suggest we get the hell out of here now."

169. PRINZ-ALBRECHT-STRASSE, BERLIN, DECEMBER 29, 1938. 9:45 A.M.

Heydrich ground out his cigarette and motioned for Günter Jurgen to sit at the conference table.

"Listen, Jurgen, we need to know more about this Dr. Muller. One of our men has told me that Muller met with the Führer at Göring's Christmas party. I've already started a file on him. He's a recent émigré from East Africa. I find his decision to repatriate into the Reich intriguing. In the brief time since he took up residence in Berlin, he's become a top Party fundraiser and performed some rather remarkable heroics in Spain. It's all in this file," Heydrich said, pushing a folder across the table to Jurgen.

"I'll do what I can, Sir," Jurgen said. "I never met Muller in Spain. But from what I've heard, the men liked him. He wasn't afraid to leave the safety of his medical tent and go out on patrol with our infantry and Panzer units. He even flew a few bombing missions."

"So you knew him only by reputation?"

"*Ja*, only by reputation."

"Well, I want you to learn more about him, much more. You'll start by flying to Dar es Salaam, in our former East African colony. You'll travel undercover, posing as a correspondent for the *Berliner Morgenpost* doing research for an article on the achievements of German émigrés. I want you to find out whether this Karl Muller is who and what he says he is. You'll report only to me. And you're to tell no one else about this mission. That includes Reichsführer Himmler. He has more important things on his mind."

Heydrich opened a second folder. "Here are your counterfeit papers, including your passport and press credentials. If anyone asks me about your whereabouts, I'll simply tell them that you're on a special mission. When you get back to Berlin, I want you to befriend Muller. To that end, I've secured you a membership at the Berliner Sportverein, where Dr. Muller often goes for exercise. Your membership will help you train for this year's SS boxing tournament in Munich."

"You want me to gain his confidence?"

"Yes," Heydrich said, barely parting his lips. "I understand that will take time. When you see him at the club, strike up a conversation. Invite him out for a beer. He's bachelor. Perhaps you two could go on the prowl together."

Heydrich leaned back in his chair, keeping his eyes on Günter Jurgen. "Do you understand, Günter? This is a very delicate assignment."

"Yes, Sir. I understand."

"Good. I wish you luck then. Report to me as soon as you return."

170. THE CHANCELLERY, BERLIN, JANUARY 31, 1939, 8:05 A.M.

Hitler pushed aside the remains of his breakfast roll and marmalade and came out from behind his desk. He gestured for Karl to sit at the conference table before the fireplace, beneath the large oil portrait of Bismarck that dominated the German Chancellor's expansive office.

"It's kind of you to join us, Dr. Muller," Hitler said. Hitler introduced Karl to the three generals: Karl Rudolf Gerd von Rundstedt, Wilhelm Keitel, and Alfred Jodl. Karl was hardly surprised by their presence but would have preferred to meet with Hitler in private.

"I know the Führer is busy, so here is a ten-page brief that summarizes my assessment of the character of German fighting men in Spain. As the Führer knows, the best weapons in the world are worthless if they're not in the hands of courageous, loyal, well-trained personnel."

Hitler nodded for Karl to go on.

"The German soldiers and airmen I knew and treated in Spain were brave and resourceful," Karl said. "Allow me to present an example. Last August, I accompanied a Condor Legion scouting patrol. The enemy had launched a counteroffensive that trapped our patrol unit on a narrow road that ran along-side a steep cliff. Our goal, of course, was to return to our base, but we were boxed in.

"We moved cautiously through the stifling heat listening to a Loyalist loudspeaker that kept saying all 'fascist hirelings' would be annihilated – a very real prospect given that we were almost out of ammunition and had only a dozen or so grenades. As night fell, our point man spotted four Russian-made tanks lined up on the road ahead. There was no way to sneak by them in daylight.

"At sundown, our commander, a young Leutnant from Dresden, came up with a plan that called for us to wait until first light. That was when one of our corporals crept silently to a position just behind the lone sentry guarding the lead tank. Sneaking up behind the sentry, our corporal wrapped his arm around the man's mouth and sank a knife into his back. Then, after he gave a birdcall whistle, we all crawled on our bellies toward the tanks. Four of our men removed their boots and waited in the dark. Each shoeless man mounted one of the tanks, straddled his way along the barrel of the tank's cannon, pulled the pin on a grenade, and shoved it into the barrel. In the next instant, he dropped to the ground and scrambled away.

"Seconds later, the grenades exploded, rendering the tanks' big guns use-less. Of course, the noise woke the tank crews. But as they emerged from the tanks our bayonets made quick work of them. Forty minutes later we were back at the field headquarters enjoying breakfast.

"Some of you may have seen other, more routine reports of this action. But having been there, I can assure you that our young commander's clear thinking under pressure – and his men's courage and split-second execution – made all the difference. Our men did what they had to do, working together as a unit, without a misstep. No mistakes, no casualties, no prisoners."

Karl sipped water, making sure he still had Hitler's attention.

"I should add that in the course of my deployment, I also witnessed count-less examples of courage and clear thinking on the part of our airmen, who must proceed on instinct alone. Here I believe that our Aryan character and our German training serve us well. With Reichsmarschall Göring's approval,

I flew in the Heinkel bombing raids on Valencia and Barcelona. Taking part in those actions, I could readily see that our German pilots outflew, outgunned, and outsmarted their Russian and Spanish counterparts.

"Please note, gentlemen, that I have emphasized *courage* this morning. With your permission, I would like to expand upon the meaning of this word."

"You have our permission, Doctor," Hitler said. "The rest of you should listen with care to what Dr. Muller has to say."

Karl placed both hands on the table, taking care to speak at a thoughtful pace. "Gentlemen, of all the German military men I treated in Spain, not one whimpered or whined about the pain he had to endure. And based on every-thing I saw and heard, the few men who did die of their wounds met death with courage and dignity. What you have built, *mein Führer*, with the help of the men in this room, is a superb fighting force."

Karl paused for few seconds before continuing.

"Now I'd like to recount another incident, one that occurred soon after my arrival in Spain. It concerns an infantry unit that lost its way while return-ing from an engagement near Brunete. I learned about this incident when treating one of the survivors, who told me that their Hauptmann deviated from the return route he'd been ordered to take.

"The young Hauptmann chose another route home because a Loyalist prisoner he'd interrogated several days before had told him about a brothel tucked away on a side street off the main plaza in Brunete. The Hauptmann thought that visiting the brothel would reward his men for the courage they'd demonstrated fighting the Loyalist militia. It proved to be a terrible mistake.

"The trouble was that Loyalist snipers were inside the brothel. When a dozen of the Hauptmann's men reassembled outside the brothel after taking their pleasure, the snipers gunned them down."

Karl noticed Hitler looking down at the table in front of him.

"The Hauptmann reported to his superiors only that he and his men had come under fire in an ambush just after entering Brunete. He didn't say a word about the brothel – and indeed no official record of the incident exists. As I said, I learned about it only because I treated the survivors."

Hitler eyed Rundstedt, Jodl, and Keitel, nodding for Karl to continue.

"Disciplinary action should have been taken in this case," Jodl interrupted. "I will investigate further."

"*Ja*," Keitel chimed in, "we could launch a thorough inquiry."

"You both need to shut up and listen," Hitler said, breaking his silence. "I believe that the doctor's point is about much more than discipline. Continue please, Dr. Muller."

"Let me be blunt," Karl said. "We Germans sometimes lack moral courage. With General Haber's authorization, I was able to review the records of the Hauptmann who led his men to the brothel. He had performed heroically in previous combat engagements. His men also had displayed great courage. Yet he failed to muster the moral courage needed to own up to his mistake."

Karl noticed that only Hitler did not frown.   In the long silent moment that followed, Adolf Hitler rose from the table and clasped his hands behind his back. "Dr. Muller makes an important point, one we're all aware of but never discuss," Hitler said, staring at the military men. "But we must address this issue. You and the men under you need to own up to mistakes. Is that understood? We are in your debt, Dr. Muller."

"I fear that I've intruded for too long on the Führer's precious time," Karl said. "Unless there are questions, I will return to my medical practice in Zehlendorf."

Hitler surprised Karl by escorting him out the door, through the reception area, and into the hallway. "You're an extremely perceptive man, Dr. Muller. Hess and Bormann speak highly of you. Now I begin to understand why."

After shaking Hitler's hand, Karl walked out of the Chancellery and took a deep breath of winter air.

171. ABWEHR HEADQUARTERS, 74-76 TIRPITZUFER, APRIL 2, 1939, NOON

Frederick often visited his old friend Admiral Canaris. As young naval officers in the days before the outbreak of war in 1914, they had spent much time together and shared an interest in the evolving nature of naval strategy.

Canaris shipped out on the cruiser Dresden in the early days of the war, and Frederick assumed his post as a U-boat commander. Their friendship resumed when Frederick returned to Germany after achieving his financial successes in London. He respected the sharp-witted and well-traveled Canaris, whose organizational skills had built Germany's far-flung military intelligence network.

During his visits with Canaris, Frederick tried to learn as much as he could about the Abwehr, particularly what the Abwehr had discovered regarding weapons and scientific advances by Germany's enemies and potential enemies.

On this morning, Canaris shared with Frederick a report from a longtime Abwehr agent working undercover as a hardware store clerk in Garden City, Long Island.

The report showed that a man called Norden had developed a bomb-sight that would improve the effectiveness of high-altitude bombing and that another Abwehr agent had stolen a paper showing the design of the instrument.

Canaris further confided to Frederick that an agent in the Pacific Northwest had revealed that a long-range, four-engine bomber called the B-17 was in the early stages of production in a factory near Seattle.

Frederick made notes. "I trust that you've sent a digest of these reports to Göring."

"Sent them last night," Canaris said. "But to tell the truth, I hate to let this kind of thing out my office. Anything that goes to the Wilhelmstrasse will find its way to Heydrich. He and his SD operatives have been sticking their noses into military intelligence."

172. HANS KREBS'S APARTMENT, WASHINGTON, D.C., MAY 10, 1939, 6:00 P.M.

Hans sat in his shirtsleeves at the kitchen table of the Washington apartment he had taken near Embassy Row, not far from DuPont Circle.

Hans ate dinner with Fern as often as he could. On this night he planned to meet her at a snug little café they had discovered in Georgetown.

But first he had some thinking to do. After washing up, he sat at the small secretarial desk in the sitting room, gathering his thoughts about his most recent trip to New York. Once again, the Bund meeting had been a crashing bore.

But it wasn't his SD job that occupied most of his mental energy. It was Fern. And the thought of her set him to thinking about Karl. Fern had told him about the bar fight that landed Karl in prison. On a trip up to Sing Sing several weeks before, posing as a German reporter, Hans learned only that Karl had gotten into scuffles with more aggressive inmates.

On another occasion, Hans used Frederick's Packard to drive to the New York State Police barracks near Newburgh. There he learned that the state trooper who arrived on the scene of the accident that killed Karl had retired and left the country for a lucrative security job in a Havana casino.

Hans knew he could never conjure up an excuse for traveling to Havana. Still, his curiosity about Fern's time in New York had become an ongoing obsession. He knew he was snooping in places where no one had invited him. But, he thought, *What the hell.*

173. THE COSMOS CLUB, WASHINGTON, D.C., MAY 11, 1939, 10:13 A. M.

At ease in the sun-filled dining room, Frederick laid aside the *Washington Post* and lit his pipe. His meeting at the U.S. Department of Commerce was still two hours away. At last, after several appointment-crowded days in New York City and on Long Island, he had time to think. He had wanted to visit Fern but learned she was lecturing at Johns Hopkins in Baltimore. Now he was most interested in learning more about Hans Krebs's and Fern's relationship. Frederick had a favorable impression of the detective when they had met at Göring's Christmas party. Based on what Fern said about him, and from Frederick's own discreet inquiries, Hans Krebs appeared to be a man of quiet competence. His unaggressive yet steady courtship of Fern struck Frederick as most honorable.

Hans's decision to accept a position under Reinhard Heydrich in order to be close to Fern while she was in America seemed somewhat curious. From the little Fern had told him, Frederick wondered how Hans could work for a man like Heydrich. It was time, Frederick decided, to get closer to this Hans Krebs.

Frederick went to his room in the club's residence wing to retrieve some papers, then telephoned the German Embassy just down the street on Massachusetts Avenue.

174. GERMAN EMBASSY, MASSACHUSETTS AVENUE, WASHINGTON, D.C., MAY 11, 1939, 10:15 A.M.

Hans had just finished typing his report to Heydrich on the Bund. He knew its contents were insignificant.

Hidden in Hans's apartment, and far more important to Heydrich, were his notes on Abwehr operations in Washington and New York. He had spent a lot of time on Long Island talking to German immigrants employed at the Grumman Aircraft Engineering Corporation, Republic Aviation, and Sperry Corporation, all of which were major military contractors. Sperry had just begun making the state-of-the-art Norden bombsight.

Hans was about to ask his secretary to reserve him a seat on the afternoon train to New York when his telephone rang. His secretary told him that Frederick Wagner was on the line.

Less than an hour later, Frederick and Hans were sitting on a bench overlooking the tranquil Potomac.

Frederick set his briefcase between them on the bench. "Take this when you go," he said. "It will give Heydrich some concrete information on the extent of Abwehr activity in the United States, specifically about the Sperry plant on Long Island. These documents prove that the Abwehr has acquired designs for an advanced new bombsight called the Norden. An Abwehr agent, a German immigrant working at the Sperry plant, pulled it off months ago. Make no mistake: this is a major intelligence coup. Heydrich won't rejoice in the Abwehr's success, but he's professional enough to appreciate your work."

Hans frowned. "Why are you doing this?"

"Consider it a favor from Admiral Canaris. He's an old friend. And his Abwehr people *want* Heydrich to know about this. They think it'll upset him, and they're probably right. Boys will be boys."

Frederick looked toward the Jefferson Memorial. "Germany is now manufacturing bombsights based on the stolen plans. They'll be installed in of our new Heinkel bombers."

175. CAFÉ DU TROCADÉRO, PARIS, MAY 14, 1939, 4:00 P.M.

Nancy removed her wide-brimmed straw hat and turned to bathe her face in the warm light of the Paris spring. Here on the terrace, in full view of the Eiffel Tower, Nancy exulted in their escape from Madrid and safe arrival in Paris. Now seven months pregnant, she placed her purse on the empty chair to her right, just as she'd been instructed, and ordered an apricot tart. She was hungry all the time now.

Nancy delighted in how quickly Josh had made himself at home in Paris. He was working at the American Hospital, and she would have the baby there. They would stay in Paris as long as they liked, recharging their batteries and building up their bank account. Neither was in a rush to get back to New York.

Nancy also wanted to make room in her new life for the Party. Just as she and Josh were leaving Madrid, a Party operative at the hospital had slipped her a Paris telephone number. She had called the number just that morning and arranged today's rendezvous.

She'd finished reading her copy of the *Herald Tribune* and was scanning the front page of *Le Matin* when a young man with curly brown hair, dressed in an open-neck polo shirt and brown corduroy jacket, approached. She judged him to be in his mid-twenties.

"Mrs. Greenberg, I presume," he said, bowing politely. "My name is Étienne Prouxlanger. I'm honored to meet you." Taking a seat, he signaled a waiter for two coffees.

"You look fit enough for a woman who's just spent a year in Madrid and is with child," he said with the rasp of a heavy smoker.

She was about to thank him for the compliment, but he kept talking. "I've heard of your work in Madrid and about organizing the hospital workers in New York. We could have room in our little cell for someone with your talents. May I ask how long you plan to stay in Paris?"

"Indefinitely," she said. "And please understand, I won't rest on my laurels. I'm ready to prove myself."

Prouxlanger nodded. "We expect no less, *Madame*."

"Good," she said. "But my baby is due in less than nine weeks. So for the moment, I'm pretty much anchored to my apartment."

"I've already spoken to the editor of *l'Humanité*, the Party's daily paper here. He has read the letters you contributed to the *Daily Worker* in New York, and he'd be happy to consider articles based on your experiences in Madrid. You could recount, from your own perspective, the fascist atrocities, such as the German bombing of schools and hospitals. Your byline will attract readers – you've already won a certain celebrity thanks to the article Mr. Ernest Hemingway wrote on you and your husband in the magazine called *Colliers*. I believe that *l'Humanité* will accept what you write and pay you a fair sum for your trouble."

"Wonderful," Nancy said. "I'll do it. I can do the writing in my apartment on Rue Hamelin."

"Remember, though, this isn't America. Certain people are bound to take strong exception to what you say. The fascists are far stronger here than in New York."

"Don't worry about it, Prouxlanger. Remember, I worked in a tough neighborhood called Spain."

"Why don't you meet me right here at the same time a week from today? Perhaps by then you'll have a rough draft for a first article and some thoughts on future pieces. You can write in English. The editor will have his staff translate."

"How about if I translate the articles into French myself?" Nancy said. "My husband and I have been speaking it as much as we can since we got here. But thank you, by the way, for speaking English today. In the future perhaps we should switch to French."

"Whatever you wish, Madame," Prouxlanger responded. "Now I'd like to touch on a more delicate matter: your husband. I understand that he's not a Party member."

"You're right, and forget about trying to convert him. But he's Jewish, which makes him a natural enemy of the Nazis. Isn't it the Arabs who say *the enemy of my enemy is my friend?*"

"*Touché, Madame.* But still, may I be candid?"

"Of course, why not?"

"You need to drop the *berg* from your last name."

"Are you kidding? I caught hell from my Irish mother for marrying a Jew. Must I endure the same from a French Communist?"

"Simply a precaution, Mrs. Greenberg. If a pro-Nazi regime ever comes to power in France, your Jewish name would expose you, your husband, and even your unborn child to severe harassment."

"Anything else?"

"One thing only: If you give birth to a boy, don't have him circumcised."

"Stop right there. Of course I'll have him circumcised – and baptized. What's wrong with him having it both ways?"

"You're quite headstrong, very self-assured. The Party needs people like you," Prouxlanger said, lighting a cigarette. He appeared completely unperturbed.

Nancy fell silent for a moment. "Look, I'm sorry if I overreacted. Once you get to know me, you'll see that I'm very practical. I'm a dedicated Party member, but I knew when it was time to hightail it out of Madrid."

Prouxlanger nodded and stood, dropping his cigarette to the pavement and stamping it out. "I must go now. See you here one week from today. *Adieu, Madame.*"

"One more thing," Nancy said. "Stop calling me *Madame* and *Mrs. Greenberg.* It makes me feel old. Just Nancy or Comrade will do."

"Très bien," Prouxlanger smiled. She watched as he walked away and descended into the Metro.

176. NKVD HEADQUARTERS, MOSCOW, JUNE 1, 1939, 4:00 A.M.

In the yellow light of the banker's lamp on his desk, Lavrentiy Beria polished his pince-nez with a soiled handkerchief and pushed aside the one-page report from Paris. So the young American doctor and his wife had surfaced in the City of Light. Now, Beria thought, if only Dr. Greenberg could be shown a photograph of Karl Muller, the African immigrant to the Third Reich. Greenberg would be able to say for certain whether Muller was the same man as Ludwig, the German-American who went to Sing Sing and allegedly died when the van he was riding in went over a cliff. Beria dipped his pen in the inkwell and wrote brief instructions for his agent in Madrid: *Obtain a photograph of Dr. Karl Muller, the Nazi physician who escaped from the British in Madrid with the German General Haber. This may prove difficult but should not be impossible. There is an excellent chance that the Loyalist authorities at the Madrid Airport took mug shots of Dr. Muller when he was captured in December 1937.*

177. WHITE'S CLUB, LONDON, JUNE 2, 1939, 3:00 P.M.

The high ceilings and hardwood floors in the White's Club library provided Baxter with the sanctuary he needed. He was here to receive instructions from an undercover comrade, Guy Burgess of the Foreign Office.

After spending so much time in Spain, Baxter was relieved to be back in London and enjoying a proper martini before starting his new assignment in the Paris bureau of the *Times*. The two men's long-stemmed martini glasses rested on a teacart as they sat opposite one another in matching Windsor chairs. The young and portly Burgess looked about and rose to close the large oak door.

"So Robin, old chum," he said, returning to his chair, "it was grand of the *Times* to give you a brief holiday. I have some things to share with you. It seems that our friend in the East has become a trifle obsessed, his energy spawned in part by your intelligence reports from Spain. He's rather curious about what you learned from that German woman doctor, specifically the stories about her dead fiancé. A source in Berlin has informed him that General Haber was captured on a visit to the Madrid front – and escaped – with another man, a Nazi doctor. According to reports, this doctor displayed remarkable physical prowess during the escape. Indeed, the report indicates that the injuries this doctor inflicted on the plane's co-pilot are suspiciously similar to those a professional boxer might inflict."

"Guy, there's many a bloke who can throw a punch or two."

"True, but there's more to this story. I did some snooping around to see if any of our SIS lads might have had a hand in the escape. I got into the travel office files and discovered that an operative named Scotty North was in the vicinity of Madrid at the time. North works for a special unit, a top-secret operation with an official address in Whitehall, but mostly run out of a small clandestine office in Mayfair. The cerebral horsepower behind the unit is a seasoned hand named Channing Brown, formerly of the Royal Navy. Brown has longstanding connections in the Admiralty and with Churchill and Sir Crawford Ware. Lately, this group has been more focused on events in Berlin than in Moscow."

Baxter didn't respond at first. He took a tobacco pouch from the pocket of his maroon corduroy jacket and fired up his pipe.

"So tell me, Guy, what instruction for me is there from our friend in Moscow?"

"Once you get to Paris, you're to find out as much as you can about a certain American doctor and his wife, both of whom have turned up there recently. His name is Josh Greenberg. His wife, Nancy, is a Party member. Both were in Madrid as medical volunteers at the time of the Haber incident. There's a chap named Prouxlanger in Paris who can help you connect to the wife."

178. GOVERNMENT HOUSE, DAR ES SALAAM, EAST AFRICA, JUNE 15, 1939

Günter Jurgen coughed from the dust on the library shelves holding the Dar es Salaam birth records dating back fifty years. It took him only ten minutes to find the right volume. According to the ledger, a Karl Muller was born in Dar es Salam in 1905. Jurgen wasn't surprised. He had fully expected to find a record of Muller's birth. What got his attention, however, was a notation indicating that someone who'd given an address in Hannover, Germany, had checked the same record only three years earlier. He used a miniature camera to photograph the record and returned it to the reference desk, where he placed a five-pound note in front of the clerk, a woman of about sixty.

"Thank you for your help," Jurgen said in German. "You've done a marvelous job maintaining these records."

She looked up from her month-old copy of the *Berliner Morgenpost* and smiled. "That's very kind of you to say. Can I be of any further help?" she asked with a Berlin accent.

"Perhaps," Jurgen said, glancing at his notebook, glad to have met a fellow German so far from home. "I notice that someone else reviewed Karl Muller's birth records only three years ago. Do you recall anything about that?"

"I do remember," the woman replied. "Actually, there were two men. One had a distinctly British inflection in his voice but spoke fluent German. The other man appeared to be German, but said very little."

"Any idea where they were staying?"

"No, but most foreign visitors stay at the King William House. It has a well-shaded outdoor café where guests can socialize. There's an old German waiter there, from Hamburg I believe, who prides himself on his memory. He likes to talk, from what I hear, and remembers conversations with guests who stayed there years ago."

Ten minutes later he was sipping a beer on the café terrace. The old German waiter, he learned, would arrive for work in about an hour. Günter Jurgen was happy to wait.

179. BERLINER SPORTVEREIN, JUNE 28, 1939

A large ceiling fan did little to cool the rank indoor air. Karl paused to wipe the sweat from his neck and face. Outside the temperature was well above 38 degrees Celsius, which Karl reckoned was the Berlin equivalent of a 100-degree Fahrenheit scorcher in New York. Inside, it was even hotter. Air conditioning had not yet come to the Berliner Sportverein. Karl could not help but notice the man working the speed bag. He seemed to be a light heavyweight, and Karl saw that he was very fast. These days, Karl used the speed bag only when no one was around to see how good he was.

Karl was lifting barbells. Six months of workouts since returning from Spain had restored his lean muscle tone. The running also helped. On most mornings, he ran five miles, followed by ten fifty-yard wind sprints in the Tiergarten. It had begun to trouble him that, except for the escape in Madrid, he hadn't thrown a real punch since his days at Thornbil Castle.

The man working the speed bag stopped and toweled himself off, then turned and stepped toward Karl. "I'm a new member here at the club. Allow me to introduce myself. My name is Günter Jurgen."

180. THE GREENBERG APARTMENT, RUE HAMELIN, PARIS, JULY 14, 1939, 5:00 P.M.

With the baby due any day, Josh and Nancy decided not to risk venturing onto the streets on Bastille Day. Instead, they hosted a small party at their apartment. They invited some dozen of Josh's doctor and nurse colleagues from the American Hospital. With Josh's consent, Nancy had invited Étienne Prouxlanger.

Josh fixed pitchers of white wine over ice to ease the heat of the July afternoon. The party reminded Nancy of the gatherings they used to have back in Manhattan during what she now thought of as the "old days."

Josh was at the kitchen sink, opening another bottle of white wine when Prouxlanger approached. "Dr. Greenberg, I need to speak with you in private. Could we step outside, perhaps onto the roof?"

Josh led the way up two flights of stairs to a door that opened onto a roof-top view of the Eiffel Tower.

"I have something to show you," Prouxlanger said. "It's a mugshot taken six months ago of a prisoner of war in Spain." He handed Josh the photo. "Do you recognize this man?"

Josh stared at the blurry snapshot, which showed a bearded man in a Condor Legion officer's field uniform. Josh had seen many such photos used to identify dead patients or wounded soldiers. But this was different because of the man in the picture. Despite the terrible quality of the photo, he could see that it was Karl Ludwig. No doubt about it.

Several long seconds passed. "No one I know," Josh lied. "Why? Is this someone you want to recruit for the Party?"

Prouxlanger held the snapshot up to the sunlight. "No," he said. "Some believe this man was a doctor in New York, in fact a friend of yours. Of course, you know I could show this picture to your wife."

Josh concealed his anger and let a few seconds pass before speaking. "There was a doctor in New York who was a close friend of mine, but he never met Nancy. He'd left the hospital before she started working there – and he's been dead for three years."

"You're sure?"

"Of course, I'm sure. Actually, it's a long story. I fell in love with Nancy while recuperating from injuries I received in a fight, a free-for-all that started an awful chain of events that led my friend's death. But why the interest?"

"It's Party business. I hope you don't mind. Let's just say that certain people are curious. It's not unusual."

They returned to the party, where several couples were jitterbugging to a Glen Miller record on the wind-up Victrola. Josh would have been happier if they all left. He wanted to think. If it *was* Karl in that photo, did that mean he was alive? And if so, what in hell was he doing in Spain? Could it be a twin brother? Karl had never mentioned a twin, or any sibling, even though he had spoken often of his boyhood in Berlin.

Nancy came and kissed Josh on the nose, handing him a glass of wine and a cracker smeared with Camembert. Prouxlanger and one of the nurses from the American Hospital were jitterbugging to "Pennsylvania 6-5000." Josh tried to put the photograph out of his mind.

181. THE BERGHOF, AUGUST 10, 1939, 4 P.M.

After a painstaking review of Case White, the plan for Germany's rapid conquest of Poland, Adolf Hitler gestured for Martin Haber and Erwin Rommel to accompany him to his private study. The other participants – including Keitel, Jodl, and Rundstedt – left with some twenty others.

"I wanted to thank you both," Hitler said to Haber and Rommel. "You're the ones who've done the real work and whose views I respect the most."

Both nodded, pleased by the recognition.

"Erwin, I've already told Rundstedt that you'll accompany my party as we follow the invasion force into Poland. I want you to provide me with daily tactical briefings on the deployment of our Panzers and keep me informed on how well we're adhering to the plan elaborated by Martin. And Martin, I look forward to reviewing your next plan."

Hitler stood to signal the end of the meeting. Neither Rommel nor Haber spoke as they left the room.

182. BERCHTESGADEN, AUGUST 15, 1939, 7:30 A.M.

Karl woke to the sound of church bells, having slept well on the firm bed in the Berchtesgadener Inn.

After a shave and shower, he dressed in a wool turtleneck to guard and against the autumn chill, which he knew came early in the mountains. He walked down the two flights of stairs from his room and out into the town square, where he took a seat on the terrace of a café and ordered coffee. Across the square, the clock in the church tower told him he had thirty precious minutes to think before Trudy arrived. When he had telephoned her from Berlin earlier that week and asked if she could show him around town, she had welcomed the opportunity. Only the stepped-up frequency of his fundraising speeches and the demands of his medical practice, he explained, had kept him away.

As he savored his coffee – far better than he was accustomed to in Berlin – Karl understood why Hitler came to the Obersalzberg so often. As both Hess and Bormann had explained, it was here in the mountains, away from the unrelenting pace of Berlin, that Hitler felt at ease and at home. He could enjoy the spectacular views from the Berghof, his mountain retreat of many years, work in his private study, and entertain in the home's well-equipped dining facilities. Security was also abundant at the Berghof. Several hundred fiercely loyal SS troops were billeted in a barracks only a few dozen yards away. Karl knew that any attempt on Hitler's life at the Berghof would be suicide.

The retreat that Bormann was building atop the Kehlstein also presented challenges. Although security there wasn't as heavy as it was at the Berghof, escape down the steep mountain would prove treacherous in the extreme – even worse with SS guards and Dobermans in hot pursuit. Just getting Hitler up to the Kehlsteinhaus would be difficult. As Bormann had admitted, Hitler had shown little enthusiasm for the place.

Karl saw a man in a black SS uniform standing nearby. "Dr. Muller isn't it?" the man said, approaching Karl's table. "We met at the Berliner Sportverein several weeks ago. My name's Günter Jurgen."

"Of course, Gunter, the expert on the punching bag. Sit down and have a coffee with me."

"Are you sure I'm not intruding?"

"Not at all. I'm just biding my time, waiting for a friend. Actually, I'm happy to have company. What brings you to Berchtesgaden?"

Jurgen snapped his fingers to get the waitress's attention. After ordering his coffee, he leaned forward to address Karl.

"The SS brass has assigned me to our barracks near the Berghof. There's an excellent *Sporthalle* there that I've been using to train for the SS boxing championship in Munich in a few days. I'll be defending my light heavyweight title."

"Munich sounds pretty festive – lots of and beer and many women. How will that mix with your boxing?"

"No women or beer for me until the boxing is over," Jurgen said.

When the coffee arrived, Karl couldn't help but notice how Jurgen stared at the buxom server's cleavage.

"I've been to Munich only once," Karl said. "I was there briefly for a lunch meeting with Rudolf Hess."

"Munich comes alive at night," Jurgen said. "If you have occasion to be in Munich and I win the light heavyweight championship, I invite you to celebrate with me. Reichsführer Himmler will be there along with his deputy, Reinhard Heydrich."

"That's very gracious of you, Gunter. I'd love to come, even though I know very little about boxing."

"Well, I have a sparring session in thirty minutes," Jurgen said, rising from his seat. "Perhaps I will see you in Munich."

With Jurgen gone, Karl's thoughts turned back to Trudy. He had found her to be pleasant enough company during their two most recent encounters. The first was in the early spring, when she'd come to Berlin for a conference on advanced surgical procedures and invited Karl out for a beer. The second time she had come to Berlin to visit friends and invited Karl to join her for dinner. Their discussion had focused mostly on his medical practice. In these encounters, she displayed none of the sexual aggression that seemed so evident when they had met at Göring's Christmas party. Karl reasoned that whoever had trained her to keep an eye on him had done a good job.

Trudy Gretzler arrived only moments after Jurgen's departure and slipped into the same chair the SS man had vacated. "*Willkommen in Berchtesgaden,* Karl. I hope you're enjoying your time here."

"With your arrival, it's just become even more enjoyable."

"Well, my job is to help you relax now that you're away from your medical responsibilities and Party activities. Your life must be very stressful, what with all the trouble over Danzig and the talk of war in Berlin."

"Yes, I came here to relax, but all the war talk over Danzig makes that difficult."

"I think I can help. I'm off work today. It's the feast of the Assumption, a legal holiday in Bavaria. Let's start with a home-cooked breakfast back at my place. Then let's take a long hike in the mountains. You look as if you're in shape for it."

"A walk on the roads around the Kehlstein would suit me well."

"That'll give me a chance to tell you about my new job. I'm going to be head nurse at a hospital the Führer is having built here in Berchtesgaden. It's going to be called the Eckart Hospital after one of the Führer's early supporters. But let's go my place. It isn't far."

183. SS BARRACKS, BERCHTESGADEN, AUGUST 15, 1939, 11:45 A.M.

Heydrich sat at the desk speaking to Rudolf Hess in cordial tones on the candlestick telephone. Günter Jurgen stood ramrod straight by the side of the desk. Heydrich ignored Jurgen for the moment, focusing instead on his telephone conversation.

"Hess, my good fellow, Reichsführer Himmler and I are quite impressed by your Dr. Muller's fundraising efforts on behalf of the Party. The Reichsführer has asked me to make sure that you and Dr. Muller both attend a dinner party he's hosting at the Palace Hotel in Munich three evenings from now. We'll be there for the SS boxing tournament. Perhaps Dr. Muller can regale us with stories about his time in Spain. After dinner, we'll go to the arena to see our friend Günter Jurgen defend his SS light heavyweight title. I look forward to seeing you and Dr. Muller in Munich."

Smiling, Heydrich replaced the receiver in its cradle. Seconds later, the telephone rang. "Thank you," he said after listening for several moments. "I shall not forget this favor." Hanging the telephone up again, he turned his attention Günter Jurgen, who remained at attention.

"One of our men in the Foreign Ministry has just informed me that the Reich is likely to conclude a non-aggression pact with the Soviets in the next few days. This pact should prove extremely useful. It will give us a virtual free hand in Poland if we proceed with the planned invasion. What's more Jurgen, it means a special assignment for you. Once this boxing tournament is over, you'll move from the SD to command a special unit of the Waffen-SS. It's a great opportunity for you, another step forward in your promising career." Jurgen straightened his stance.

Pausing, Heydrich leaned back in his chair. "Your unit will advance into Poland several days behind the Wehrmacht and the other Waffen-SS units. No combat. Your unit and others like it will have a special task – to round up potentially troublesome civilians in German-occupied territory. I'm talking about teachers, intellectuals, high-ranking bureaucrats, pastors, and, of course, Jewish leaders. Once in Poland, you'll receive orders on what to do with them. If you perform well, we'll form similar units for future campaigns. There's no telling how far you can go."

Heydrich saw that his news pleased Jurgen.

"And one more thing, Jurgen: that was an excellent report you submitted on your mission to Dar es Salaam. I have some ideas about Dr. Muller. We can discuss them at length after your fight in Munich."

184. TRUDY GRETZLER'S HOME, BERCHTESGADEN, AUGUST 15, 1939, 4:35 P.M.

Toward the end of a day of hiking, Karl mentioned his fascination with the house atop the Kehlstein. Karl recalled that Trudy's father, an engineer, had contributed to the design of the Kehlsteinhaus. Perhaps she could show him some of the architectural drawings. It was likely that such drawings were in the house she shared with her father, who was away on business.

Trudy led Karl into her father's basement office, unlocking a flat file drawer and pulling out several blueprints. Karl eyed the blueprints carefully, focusing on the one that featured the Great Hall, its adjoining terraces, and the access to them from the Hall.

"It's time I started fixing us some dinner – that is if you want to stay."

"I'd love some wine and dinner, but after that I have to catch the nine o'clock train to Munich. I have a meeting with Hess there first thing tomorrow morning."

Karl noted that Trudy showed no disappointment. She simply nodded. "Then I'll hurry up and get dinner started upstairs."

"Good. I'd just like to take a moment more to admire you father's work. I'll put the blueprints back when I'm done."

Alone, Karl removed a miniature camera from his pants pocket, turned on all the lights, and took several photos of the plans for the Great Hall and the long narrow south terrace.

Later, after pork chops and sauerkraut, they went into the sitting room. Trudy rested her head on Karl's shoulder.

"Don't fall asleep on me," Karl whispered. "What about some beer and schnapps."

"Love some," she yawned.

When he returned from the kitchen he saw that her eyes had shut. He covered her with a quilt and went in search of her key ring. He compared the keys on her ring to the spare keys he'd noticed in a small basket near the breadbox. He found the matching key within seconds, and tested it in the front door. It worked and he slipped the spare key into his pocket.

Then Karl took a sheet of the stationery from the sitting room desk and wrote Trudy a quick note thanking her "for a wonderful day, a delicious dinner, and superb company," promising to telephone her soon. He slipped out of the house and returned to his room at the inn, where a telegram from Hess confirmed their arrangements for the next day. He caught the train to Munich with but a minute to spare.

185. MUNICH SPORTSPALAST, AUGUST 24, 1939, 7:30 P.M.

The amber smoke in the packed arena triggered Karl's memories of his New York boxing days. As he sat with Hess, Himmler, and Heydrich, he found it hard to believe that more than three years had passed since his last professional fight. He was glad to be in the arena, especially after Himmler and Heydrich had picked his brains about Spain and Africa over an endless dinner. He couldn't help but notice how the questions annoyed the pensive Rudolf Hess.

"We're just in time for the light heavyweight match," Heydrich shouted over the din. "Do you follow boxing?" he asked Karl.

"Not really," Karl said. "We didn't do much boxing in East Africa. Of course, I'm a fan of Max Schmeling. Every German knows about him."

"We're all fans of Schmeling," Heydrich agreed. "In fact, he's sitting just across from us, on the other side of the ring. Too bad he got beat by that American nigger, Joe Louis."

Karl stiffened. Would Schmeling recognize him from Stillman's Gym? Not likely, but possible. He avoided looking in Schmeling's direction.

Günter Jurgen stepped into the ring, his well-muscled torso shining in the smoky light. Karl realized how much he missed the adrenalin rush that peaked as he stepped into the ring just before a fight.

The clang of the bell brought the crowd, mostly SS men, to its feet. Within seconds, Jurgen landed a hard right to his opponent's jaw and a stinging left to his head, confirming Karl's earlier observation that Jurgen was a lefty. He watched as Jurgen moved straight toward his opponent, an SS sergeant from Hamburg. Jurgen kept on the attack, delivering a flurry of alternating rights and lefts to his opponent's head and chest. The only question in Karl's mind was how long Jurgen would toy with his opponent before finishing him off. Jurgen brimmed with confidence. He danced in, with another flurry of punches, this time to the stomach. His opponent staggered. Forsaking any defense, Jurgen delivered a fresh salvo of punches. Blood oozed from the sergeant's swollen left eye.

The black-shirted SS crowd began to sense a quick knockout. Their cheers filled the arena, and Jurgen moved in to finish off his stunned opponent. But the sergeant rallied with a sudden burst of lefts and rights. Karl saw it coming. Too intent on moving in for the kill, Jurgen had a dropped his guard and allowed the still-game sergeant to surprise him. Jurgen absorbed a series of blows, staggered, then backpedaled to recover his balance. Karl saw that Jurgen was focusing on the sergeant's wounded left eye. Moving in, Jurgen delivered several left jabs to the eye, then a devastating right hook to the face, sending the sergeant down on one knee.

Not waiting for the referee's count, the sergeant scrambled back to his feet, bleeding now from both eyes and the mouth. He came straight at Jurgen, landing a quick left to the nose and a series of rights to the stomach. Karl thought it was time for Jurgen to back off and reassess his opponent. Instead, Jurgen countered with an undisciplined flurry of rights and lefts, sending his opponent against the ropes, his arms limp. Jurgen continued pounding the sergeant's bloodied face. A New York referee would have stopped the slaughter. But here, the crowd cheered the punishment, even though the helpless sergeant was one of their own. As the crowd screamed for more, Jurgen caught his opponent's jaw with a lightning-fast left uppercut. The sergeant dropped like a rock. Günter Jurgen leapt in triumph. As the referee counted to ten, Karl saw that Schmeling was standing but not cheering.

186. LÖWENBRÄU HAUS, MUNICH, AUGUST 24, 1939, 11:00 P.M.

While Hess and Himmler were engrossed in Günter Jurgen's blow-by-blow recap of the fight, Karl glanced at the large cuckoo clock in the wall, then at Heydrich.

"With the current trouble over Danzig, everyone's priorities must change. We've transferred Jurgen to a special SS unit," Heydrich said, raising his voice to be heard over the noise of the beer hall.

"Yes," Karl said, "and it's time I joined a military unit again. It would enhance my ability to raise funds for the Party, just as my Spanish service did." Hess nodded agreement but said nothing.

Heydrich ran his fingers around the rim to the beer stein, studying Karl. "If you want to join one of our special units," he said, "I can make the arrangements. How soon can you be ready? And how long a commitment can you make?"

"It should take me a week to arrange for all my patients to get the care they need. And I have a fundraising speech next weekend in Dresden. After that, I'll be ready to serve if there's a war."

"Excellent," Heydrich said. Karl noticed how pleased he seemed.

187. THE KREMLIN, AUGUST 25, 1939, 5:00 A.M.

Lavrentiy Beria sat at his desk as dawn broke over Moscow. He liked to start the day early, before the inevitable interruptions. His early morning work habits dated from the days when he was a rising young Bolshevik in Georgia and the Caucasus. Each morning, he made a neat list of everything he wanted done that day. The list identified who would do what and provided notes about when, where, and how each task was to be carried out. This diligence and attention to detail played no small part in enabling Beria to run the NKVD, with its far-flung intelligence and counterintelligence operations. Beria's diligence had also made him invaluable to Stalin and had helped him gain precious personal access to the Soviet leader. Being a fellow Georgian didn't hurt either. Many years earlier, when Stalin moved north to St. Petersburg and later Moscow, Beria assumed responsibility for the care of Stalin's elderly mother – a good turn that cemented his relationships with the man who now ruled the Soviet Union.

Earlier in his career, as Georgia's Communist Party leader, Beria had proven his loyalty to Stalin time and again. He displayed the same ruthless talent for purging dissidents and perceived enemies that had enabled Stalin to rid the Red Army of hundreds of suspect senior-level officers. By the time Beria arrived in Moscow to assume his current NKVD duties, he had become one of only two men who had direct access to Stalin, at least on occasion. The other was Foreign Minister Vyacheslav Molotov.

Only a few days before, Stalin had listened as Beria and Molotov argued that it was in the Soviet Union's best interest to remain on good terms with Adolf Hitler and sign a non-aggression pact with Germany. Beria and Molotov both believed that the pact would give the Soviets time to strengthen their defenses against rising German military power. With so many senior military officers eliminated in Stalin's purges – purges he had helped to engineer – Beria knew that the Soviet Union was far from ready for war with Germany. And if such a war were to break out, Beria and Molotov had no illusions about their own – let alone Stalin's – prospects for survival in the wake of a German victory.

Beria turned to the pile of reports that had come in via the diplomatic pouch. His best agent in Berlin had once again provided vital military intelligence. The agent's report included astonishing detail on the Wehrmacht's planned invasion of Poland. From what Beria could see, the plan was a good one, ruthless but thoroughly professional. He looked at his desk telephone but decided against making a call. Someone could be listening. Instead he went directly to Molotov's office.

188. FREDERICK WAGNER'S TOWNHOUSE, MANHATTAN, AUGUST 28, 1939, 7:00 P.M.

Hans had come back to New York for a Bund meeting. Though he usually refrained from doing so, he decided to take Frederick up on his offer to help himself to the well-stocked liquor cabinet.

He poured himself a generous measure of Johnnie Walker Black over ice and carried the drink upstairs to the bedroom, anticipating a good night's rest. Kicking off his shoes and turning on the tall electric fan, Hans opened his shirt collar and eased himself onto the Chesterfield. He savored a gentle sip of Scotch as he let his mind drift to thoughts of Fern. Hans liked Manhattan. But he liked it more when Fern was there, even if it meant he had to take a hotel while she stayed at the townhouse.

He guessed that he was in the same room where Fern and Karl would have slept together when Frederick was away. The thought made him restless.

Putting his Scotch on the dresser and snapping on the radio, he heard the American correspondent William Shirer broadcasting from Berlin. Shirer told his American audience that the newspapers in Danzig had devoted more space to an upcoming football match than to the question of whether Danzig and Poland's land corridor to the Baltic should, as Hitler insisted, become a part of Germany. Shirer reported that Poland had mobilized and Berliners were lining up for ration cards for soap, textiles, and shoes.

There was a good chance, Hans thought, that he would soon get orders to return to Germany. He might not get back to the townhouse for a long time, if ever. He finished his drink and began packing his suitcase with the few personal items he had stowed in the top drawer of the dresser – fresh shirts, socks, and underwear. Then, as an afterthought, he checked the other drawers. He might have put something in one of them. The bottom drawer was empty except for a large brown envelope marked *"Verschiedene Artikel"* – miscellaneous items – hand-written in Fern's careful German script.

He opened the unsealed envelope and emptied its contents onto the bed. There was a U.S. citizenship application, which Fern had started but never completed, theater and baseball ticket stubs, and a handful of black-and-white glossy photos of various sizes. One photo showed Fern speaking at a podium. Another showed Frederick and Fern posing before a Christmas tree. A third was of Fern with her arm around a man wearing boxing trunks. The inscription scrawled across the photo told him more than he ever wanted to know. "To Fern, a true knockout and the love of my life . . . Karl."

The photo defied denial. The man in the boxing trunks was the same man who'd treated his daughter Gretchen, the émigré doctor from East Africa. Karl Ludwig wasn't dead. He was alive and well, and practicing medicine in Zehlendorf – and his name was Karl Muller.

He put the picture and everything else back in the envelope and closed the drawer.

The townhouse closed in on Hans like a stone trap. He grabbed his jacket and fled into the late-summer dusk, the honking taxis, and hurried pedestrians. His heels bore into the pavement as he strode toward Park Avenue. He needed to think but realized that his anxiety made thinking impossible. He walked south on Park as far as 72nd Street, then turned east, toward Second Avenue, then north, stopping at a newsstand to buy a pack of Camels and the early edition of the *Daily Mirror*. Stopping to light a cigarette, he opened the paper and glanced at the Danzig headlines. Nothing new. He dropped the paper in a garbage basket and resumed walking until he came to Cassidy's, a pub on the corner of 82nd and Second. He needed a bar stool and a beer.

Except for Sean, the thin Irish bartender he knew from prior visits, and a young couple in flirtatious conversation at the far end of the bar, the place was empty on this Wednesday night. Hans laid a dime on the bar and ordered a

Rupert, downed it, and ordered another. Questions, options, and consequences swirled through his mind. Could it have been some coincidental likeness? No, goddamn it. It was Karl Muller in the photo. Exposing Karl was one option. *But exposing him as what? Why had Karl changed his identity? And why in hell was he in Germany?* Exposing Karl would surely win him enormous favor with Heydrich and Himmler, at least in the short run. As a consequence, Karl would be subject to endless interrogation in some dark room beneath the Prinz-Albrecht-Strasse.

Under torture, Karl would likely spill all manner of information. In their thoroughness, his interrogators would look into his time in New York and learn about his relationship with Fern. Someone would be sure to remember that Fern received letters from and exchanged telephone calls with a Jew in New York. Any interrogation of Karl would also raise questions about Fern's mother, General Haber, and Frederick Wagner. It would also kill whatever chance he had of winning Fern. Finishing his second beer, he pushed his glass away.

And what chance did he really have with Fern? The time they'd spent together in Washington and New York had been pleasant, but without passion. For weeks now he had begun to accept that he had little chance of winning her heart. Now he knew he had none. The realization brought relief. He shrugged, almost laughed. It had been rough enough fighting the ghost of Karl when he thought Karl was dead. How could he fight a ghost that was alive? He had no answers, only questions.

189. FREDERICK WAGNER'S TOWNHOUSE, 11:15 P.M.

From the street, Hans could see that the first floor of the townhouse was awash in light. Through the picture window, he saw Frederick standing alone in the drawing room, bent over the Philco floor-model radio. Edward R. Murrow was broadcasting from London. Frederick turned down the volume.

"Sorry, I couldn't warn you that I was coming," Frederick said. "I was in Washington meeting with the *chargé d'affaires* at the German Embassy about liquidating some of my American assets. With all this talk of war, I need to get back to Germany. I had to charter a plane and landed at Flushing airport just an hour ago. Fern is flying in from Washington first thing tomorrow. She had to finish up a few things at Georgetown. Göring wants her back in Germany straight away, as you've probably guessed."

Frederick turned up the volume on the Philco so they both could hear the news as

Murrow reported on distribution of gasmasks to Londoners. When Murrow's broadcast was over, Frederick switched off the radio. "Let's go to the kitchen and have a beer," he said with soft-spoken authority. Frederick opened the refrigerator and filled two pint-size ceramic steins with beer, gesturing for Hans to take a seat at the kitchen table. "Let me be frank, Hans. The Reich Consulate telephoned me here just fifteen minutes ago. The Bremen is in New York but won't remain for the usual day or two. Instead, it'll be heading straight back across at Atlantic. It won't take on new passengers – except for Fern and me. It's a special accommodation. Both Hitler and Göring believe it's safer if we don't fly. She's meeting me at the foot of the gangplank early tomorrow.

"Well," Hans replied, "I expect I'll get called home."

"Not necessarily. You might be critical to the Reich's efforts here in America. I'm sure the SD will want to know what the Americans are thinking."

"I was going to head back to Washington tomorrow morning. But now I think I'll stay to see you and Fern off at the Bremen."

"You can see us off, just be discreet about it. As I said, the Bremen isn't supposed to be taking passengers. So don't bring flowers. Neither of us will be carrying luggage. My New York office will have some traveling clothes placed in our respective cabins. Now I say we both get some rest."

190. ZEHLENDORF, AUGUST 30, 1939, 10:30 A.M.

A telephone call informed Karl that he was cleared to serve as a medical officer in Günter Jurgen's special Waffen-SS unit. Karl was at ease with the idea of Frau Frick managing things in his absence. With him having been away so much, she had learned what to do. She excelled at managing the inevitable complaints about his frequent and lengthy absences. She would explain how Dr. Muller was working on behalf of the Party and the Reich. No one complained about that. As for emergencies, she had made a list of doctors more than willing to see Karl's patients when the need arose.

Now, sitting in Karl's office, Frau Frick expressed shock over that morning's headline proclaiming the Reich's non-aggression pact with the Soviet Union. "I hate those Communists," she said. "The Führer stood up to them here in Germany. So why is he signing a pact with Stalin?"

"I must tell you, Frau Frick, I believe that our Führer has made a brilliant move. He's signed this treaty with the Soviets so Germany doesn't have to wage war on two fronts. If we assert our God-given rights with regard to Danzig and the Polish Corridor, we risk war with Britain and France, both of which appear committed to Poland. Now thanks to the Führer's pact the Stalin, we don't have to worry about the Russians opening a second front against us." Frau Frick nodded but said nothing.

191. CAFÉ DU TROCADÉRO, PARIS, SEPTEMBER 1, 1939, 9:22 A.M.

Prouxlanger met Nancy on the crowded terrace of the Café du Trocadéro. Both stared beyond their breakfast dishes at the special edition of *Le Monde* proclaiming the German surge into Poland.

"What in the hell's going on, Prouxlanger? Now we have a new war, one made possible by our comrades in Moscow. Yes, the Soviet Union – the workers' paradise – facilitated war when it signed the non-aggression pact with Hitler and let him have Poland for lunch. Don't you get it, Prouxlanger? We went to Spain because the Communists were the only people on this godforsaken planet with the balls to stand up to the fascists."

"Nancy, allow me to . . ."

"Please shut up. Don't you understand that it's taken all my effort – and all my wits – to get my husband to put up with my involvement in the Party?

What can I say to him now that Stalin has jumped into bed with Hitler, whose thugs beat up Jewish shopkeepers and smash their windows?"

Prouxlanger folded his arms but didn't respond. Seeing the teardrops on her cheek, he handed her a napkin. He had no desire to upset her further. He lit a cigarette and waited. After all, it was a beautiful morning, and she had only recently given birth to a baby girl.

Prouxlanger leaned back, took a drag on his cigarette, and looked past Nancy toward the Eiffel Tower. "Rest assured, Nancy, that you're not the only Party member who's unhappy about the non-aggression pact. Was it not Marx himself who foresaw situations like this? He knew that there would be occasions when the Party and its leaders would have to do the expedient thing. The pact will give our Soviet brothers and sisters more time to rebuild the Red Army, an army that will be stronger than ever now that Comrade Stalin has purged it of malcontents and revisionists who would compromise the revolution."

"What about the Poles? What does it do for them?"

"The day will come when the Poles and all Europeans will live under Communism. Read *Das Capital*."

"Look, Prouxlanger," Nancy said, "I joined the Party to help workers' families eat more than beans for supper. I didn't join to read some dead man's book or cheer on Stalin and Hitler as they forced a *ménage à trois* on Poland."

"Nancy, let's not argue. You have your point of view and I've given you mine. On a more pleasant note, here's a check for the articles published in *l'Humanité*," Prouxlanger said, pulling an envelope from this jacket. "The editors were quite pleased. Apparently the response from readers was extremely favorable."

Her mood brightened visibly and she flashed an impish grin. "*Merci*, Étienne. This will pay for a baby carriage."

192. WHITEHALL, SEPTEMBER 1, 1939, 3:10 P.M.

Brown was just wrapping up a telephone conversation with Jillian, who'd been at the *Times* international desk since four that morning. She'd been helping to cover the deluge of news about Germany's invasion of Poland and briefed her husband on everything she knew. Brown had just put down the receiver when the phone rang again. It was Churchill.

"Some good news on this bad day," Churchill said. "I believe that Chamberlain is about to ask me to join his war cabinet. I shall once again be First Lord of the Admiralty. I wanted to share that with you, Channy."

"Wonderful news, Sir."

"Keep your lips sealed, though. I suspect the news will break soon enough. Remember, everything you've done with Jackhammer thus far is strictly unofficial. The less I know the better. Jackhammer remains an unsanctioned and unauthorized project. Now that I'll be back in the cabinet, we need to maintain the utmost discretion."

"I quite understand, Sir."

193. ABOARD THE BREMEN, SEPTEMBER 3, 1939, MIDAFTERNOON, SOUTHWEST OF ICELAND

Frederick gripped the rail on the promenade deck and took a deep breath of salt air. He had loved the waves and white foam that came with September on the Atlantic since his early days as a U-boat commander in 1914. Frederick needed time to think, particularly about Fern. Her life had changed so much – with her return to Germany, her work with Göring, and her friendship with Krebs. Fern had arrived only minutes before the Bremen had set sail, leaving her little private time with Hans Krebs. Their final embrace, Frederick noted, was warm but hardly passionate.

As Frederick breathed the fresh salt air, he felt Fern's presence next to him at the rail. "I just bumped into the first mate," she said. "He wanted me to tell you that the ship has received a radio message from Berlin – the Führer has refused to yield to Chamberlain's demand that Germany withdraw its troops from Poland. There's no comforting me, Uncle," she said, shrugging off the hand he had placed gently on her shoulder. "I know our situation. We're on the Bremen – a big, fat, slow-moving target on an ocean soon to be crowded with trigger-happy submarine commanders."

"At least the Bremen is a passenger ship," he responded.

"So was the Lusitania."

194. FREDERICK'S STATEROOM, 7:07 P.M.

Frederick was washing up for dinner when he heard a knock at the door.

"Good evening, Herr Wagner," Captain Ahrens said. "I wanted to tell the news in person. I won't be joining you and Dr. Wagner at dinner this evening. We just received a wireless that one of our U-boats has sunk the Athena, a British passenger ship. We must assume that the British will consider the Bremen fair game for retaliation."

"Thank you for telling me, Captain. May I ask what your plan is? As an old sailor myself, I'm curious."

"Of course. Berlin has ordered us to set a course toward the northern coast of Norway and then on to Murmansk."

"Just how dangerous will that be?"

"We'll know better when we see our first iceberg – or encounter a British submarine."

195. WAR ROOM, THE ADMIRALTY, LONDON, SEPTEMBER 4, 1939, 10:00 A.M.

The two men leaned over the large table with its embossed chart of the North Atlantic. "Sir, she's ours if we want her," Commander Reginald White told First Lord of the Admiralty Winston Churchill.

"Keep watching her," Churchill said. "Where's that passenger list from New York?"

"It's due any moment, Sir."

Churchill puffed on the stub of his cigar then ground it in a tabletop ashtray. "We need to know who's on board and what she's carrying. The Lusitania provided Britain with a propaganda coup, exposing the Huns as bloodthirsty killers of innocents. The sinking of the Athena could do the same. If we sink the Bremen, we forgo that advantage. In any event, I must await instructions from the PM. I've telephoned him and expect a response at any moment."

10:07 A.M.

Commander White took the call from Number 10 Downing Street. "Our people in New York say there were no passengers on the manifest. They're checking with Naval Intelligence in Washington to see whether the Americans know anything more," he reported.

"Don't they bloody well understand that Washington is still tucked in, fast asleep?" Churchill said, reaching into his vest pocket for a fresh cigar. "It's an hour before dawn there."

Channing Brown entered the room without fanfare and handed Churchill an envelope. Churchill ripped it open, glanced at the single sheet it contained, and handed it back to Brown. An alert SIS agent in New York had staked out the Bremen's departure. His assignment had been to see whether any possible war materiel was being taken on board. His effort included taking photographs, one of which showed a man and woman scurrying up the gangplank just before the ship departed. They carried no luggage, although the woman had a small black bag slung over her shoulder. Examination of the photos revealed the two to be the German industrialist Frederick Wagner and his niece, Dr. Fern Wagner.

"Precious cargo, eh Channy?"

Churchill turned toward White. "I shall counsel the PM that we take the high road in this case and *not* retaliate directly for the Athena. We'll avenge her in our own way and in good time. We shall simply follow the Bremen and try to learn where she's headed."

196. THE KREMLIN, SEPTEMBER 5, 1939, 2:00 A.M.

Stalin read the one-page report from Beria's best Berlin operative, then pushed it aside, and addressed Beria in a pensive tone. "So Lavrentiy Pavlovich, the Bremen is northeast of Iceland and, from what we can tell, bound for

Murmansk. If the British are too timid to sink the Bremen, what are we going to do with a German ship?" Stalin asked, puffing on his pipe.

"We can provide the asylum of a neutral port, seize the cargo, detain any passengers, and learn what we can from them."

"That's fucking nonsense," Stalin barked, pounding the desk with his fist. We've just signed a non-aggression pact with Hitler, which you and Molotov assured me was the right thing to do. Now we have to live with it. And speaking of Molotov, he phoned minutes ago to say that he'd just met with the German Ambassador, who carried a special note from Ribbentrop himself. Apparently the only *passengers* aboard the Bremen are Frederick Wagner and his niece, Dr. Fern Wagner. The Germans have asked that we receive them with every courtesy and assure their safe passage back to Germany should the Bremen reach Murmansk. I don't think we should question them unless we want to piss off Hitler."

Beria nodded, unsettled by Stalin's outburst.

"So can I count on you to facilitate Frederick and Fern Wagner's return to Germany?" Stalin asked. Beria nodded. He knew it wasn't a question.

197. THE ADLON, BERLIN, SEPTEMBER 15, 1939, 9:45 P.M.

Karl sat at the bar reading the *Berliner Morgenpost* as he waited for Bormann. The paper featured several stories on the German advances into Poland. Karl realized that this new war meant that Hitler and Bormann were soon likely to forget his and General Haber's heroic escape from Madrid. And serving as an SS medical officer in Poland might enhance his credibility with Hitler.

Karl looked up to see Bormann enter the bar with the American radio journalist William Shirer. Karl rose from his seat and Bormann introduced him to the journalist.

"I hope I'm not intruding," Shirer said. "I saw Herr Bormann speaking to Frederick Wagner, who's dining on the terrace with his niece, General

Haber, and Frau Haber. I was hoping Herr Bormann could introduce me to the Wagners. There are rumors that they were on the Bremen, which left New York before the war started. And now they're here. It could be quite a story."

"Go ahead, Martin. I'll wait here at the bar," Karl said. He watched as Bormann and Shirer made their way through the crowded cocktail bar and onto the terrace. He paid the bar tab, realizing that he might have to make a hasty get away.

9:55 P.M.

When Bormann returned, he glanced back over his shoulder to make sure no one was listening. "The Führer wants us to be nice to American journalists so their country stays out of this war. Of course, introducing Shirer to Frederick Wagner was close to a fool's errand. Frederick listened to Shirer's request, but refused him. Frederick knows that there's to be no talk of the Bremen. I'll alert the press censors. They review Shirer's broadcast scripts and will censor anything he plans to broadcast about the Bremen."

"So Herr Wagner and his niece are none the worse for their experience?" Karl asked.

"They're fine," Bormann said. "The Soviets provided them with excellent accommodations and decent food, what little of it there is in Murmansk. By the way, I'd be glad to take you out on the terrace to say hello. I'm sure General Haber would like to see you. And, of course, you've heard of Dr. Wagner. She's a very fetching woman."

"I know of her. She was my predecessor in Spain."

Karl changed the subject. "Martin, I'd love to meet Fern Wagner and her mother – and say hello to the General – but I have no time tonight. I asked to meet you because I'm leaving for Poland in a few hours. I've volunteered to serve as a medical officer for thirty days with a special SS unit there. I received my orders only this afternoon. It's all Heydrich's doing."

"I'm sure that will delight the Führer," Bormann said. "You know how much he values service at the front."

"I look forward to meeting him again soon."

"I'll work on it, though I can't promise anything."

198. LODZ, POLAND, SEPTEMBER 28, 1939, 6:00 P.M.

In his SS field uniform, Karl was about to eat his evening field rations when the screeching brakes of a motorcycle shattered the calm. He recognized Günter Jurgen, helmeted and in combat dress, as he strutted from the sidecar toward the tent.

"*Heil Hitler*, Günter. What a surprise."

"I thought you might be getting bored," Jurgen said, surveying the empty cots in the medical tent.

"I was about to go off duty. The Luftwaffe and Wehrmacht have been doing such a good job that I'm not getting much business."

"Then join us for some action. It shouldn't take more than an hour. Afterwards, we'll have dinner."

Moments later Karl and Jurgen climbed aboard an open truck with about a dozen troopers.

"We have an important task ahead," Jurgen said, slapping Karl's knee.

The truck rumbled over a shell-pocked dirt road for what Karl judged to be about three miles, stopping at a small farm with a thatched-roof stucco cottage and barn. A dozen men in black SS uniforms and armed with submachine guns were guarding the barn.

Leaping off the truck, Jurgen motioned for Karl to follow him to the wide barn door, which he ordered a sentry to open. The air inside the barn was rank with mildew and cow dung. But it was what Karl *saw* there that turned his stomach. Standing in a freshly dug pit some five feet deep and twenty-five yards square, Karl counted fifteen men and four women, all naked and shivering. Six armed SS men stood around the perimeter of the pit. Karl felt a clammy chill as his feet went numb.

Jurgen spoke in a low voice so that only Karl could hear. "Our unit is under special orders from Reinhard Heydrich. We now have an opportunity to carry out those orders. I thought it might divert you from the boredom of your field hospital."

"What we have here," Jurgen said, gesturing toward the ditch, "is the mayor of Lodz, his top deputy, and their wives. We also have the headmaster of the local elementary school, two journalists, five rabbis, two Catholic priests, a lawyer, and two of the areas' largest landowners and their wives."

"No Communists?" Karl asked.

Now Jurgen spoke in an even lower voice. "Our orders do not include rounding up Communists. Or, for that matter any Americans unlucky enough to be in Poland – even if they're Jews. The Führer doesn't want to piss off either Stalin or Roosevelt."

"What's this about?" one of the priests called out. "You have no right to treat us this way." Jurgen tilted his head toward the SS sergeants standing over the prisoners. The sergeant's machine gun burped and the priest collapsed in a heap.

"Now, does anyone else want to speak up?" Jurgen asked. There was no response.

One of the SS men climbed aboard a tractor equipped with a large earth-moving blade. Karl could taste his own stomach acid, but forced himself to swallow it. He nodded to feign approval, sensing that Jurgen expected some sort of reaction. Jurgen ordered his men to the edge of the ditch. "Fire at will," he barked.

When the guns fell silent seconds later, Jurgen approached the trooper on the tractor and gestured toward the mound of dirt. "You know what to do, Sergeant. Make neat work of it. Come on, Karl. I know where we can get some dinner."

199. SS FIELD HEADQUARTERS, WARSAW, OCTOBER 8, 1939

In a building that had been a bakery before the German onslaught, Günter Jurgen sat at the expansive table that now served as Heydrich's field desk and listened as Heydrich spoke.

"Bravo, Jurgen, well done. Your work here may well serve as a model for more extensive operations in the future."

Heydrich stood, went to the window, and gestured toward the small park across the street. "Magnificent autumn colors, don't you think, Jurgen?"

Günter Jurgen laughed. "Does it matter? I can't believe you've called me here only to praise my service and comment on the autumn foliage in western Poland. Are you expecting my report on Dr. Karl Muller?"

"Yes, let's have it."

"Well, Muller either is who he claims to be, or he's an exceptionally well-trained undercover agent," Jurgen said. "When we executed those nineteen Poles the other day, he showed no discomfort. I dined with him in the officers' mess in Lodz immediately afterwards and he had a hearty appetite."

"In other words, he acted just as a well-trained agent would in the company of his enemy. I've long admired the planning and preparation the British put into training their agents," Heydrich said. "This Dr. Muller could be such an agent."

"Then I should continue my surveillance?" Jurgen asked.

"By all means. Put Muller at ease. Socialize with him. Drink with him. Test him."

"I'll do my best."

"I'm sure you will. But keep this between you and me: Not even Himmler must know of our suspicions regarding Muller. Right now, this Dr. Muller has all the makings of a hero. Those in high places see him as capable and utterly loyal to the Party. No one can know that we've been snooping into his background. It might appear that we envy his celebrity."

Jurgen nodded, pleased that Heydrich had made him his confidant.

200. HOTEL BRISTOL, WARSAW, OCTOBER 13, 1939, 9:00 P.M.

Karl accepted Jurgen's invitation to join Heydrich and ten SS officers for a dinner party in Heydrich's penthouse suite in the Bristol, a hotel that had suffered only minor damage in the bombing. After three weeks of subsisting on field rations, Karl was ready for some real food and good wine.

Heydrich seemed more relaxed than Karl remembered him being during their previous encounter at Landhaus Göring the previous Christmas. As his guests sipped their after-dinner coffee, Heydrich gave a short talk explaining how the special work of the SS in Poland had been a masterpiece of planning and execution. He became more animated and emotional as he went on.

"We have great plans for the Reich's newest territorial possession," he said. "Now, with much of the local leadership eliminated, there should be little resistance to this forced migration. You and your men will play a critical role in the relocation of the Jewish and non-Aryan population. Eventually we'll transport them in small groups to Germany, where the healthy ones can be put to work. As you're no doubt aware, Oberleutnant Jurgen has led you in this effort to eliminate potential troublemakers and undesirables in Lodz. This operation could serve as a model for operations elsewhere. In recognition of his efforts, we are promoting Oberleutnant Jurgen to the rank of Hauptmann effective immediately."

When Heydrich finished, Jurgen rose to thank him for taking the time to address the SS men. He was excited not just by the promotion but because Heydrich had singled him out.

"Every man at this table is ready to serve the Führer," Jurgen proclaimed.

Heydrich looked toward Karl. "Would the esteemed Dr. Muller care to say a few words?"

"As your guest tonight," Karl began, sensing the need to respond without hesitation, "I want to say that we in the medical service stand ready to serve our soldiers, our Fatherland, and our Führer any way we can."

Heydrich squinted. "Well said, Doctor. It's our honor to host a hero of the Spanish victory. I thank Hauptmann Jurgen for inviting you. Now that our campaign here has succeeded, I shall be returning to Berlin. A Luftwaffe transport awaits me." Everyone sprang to attention and shouted *"Heil Hitler!"*

Heydrich paused in the doorway. "Give our Luftwaffe flyers credit," he said. "As luck would have it, they've left some of the city's best brothels unscathed. On that note, I have made some arrangements. I ask only that you behave as gentlemen. Any reports of misbehavior on the part of anyone in this elite unit might well offend the sensitivities of our Führer." Heydrich turned and left the room. A few scattered chuckles followed.

"Let us proceed then," Jurgen said. "I have the address. It's only a short walk from here. And Karl, you're invited to join us of course. Will you come?"

Karl saw no way out. "It would be my honor."

The stench of decaying human flesh drifted through the night air from beneath the rubble, though no one said a word about it. But minutes later, on a street of mostly undamaged buildings, they arrived at a five-story townhouse with the traditional red light over the front entrance.

Madame Waleska greeted her guests and ushered them into a parlor furnished with fine antique chairs and settees. She wore an emerald gown and had long, straight gray and black hair that fell to her shoulders. In better days, the red-carpeted parlor had welcomed a wealthy clientele that included diplomats from around the world and the cream of Warsaw society.

Madame Waleska exuded mature warmth that set men thinking, though not with their brains. She assured the visiting SS that her girls were clean and that hers was a reputable house. Of course, she had an ample supply of condoms for those who wished to use them. There would be no charge – Heydrich had taken care of everything, tips included.

She guided her patrons to the foot of the winding staircase. "Gentlemen," she said, "I ask only that you be gentle with my girls. Some of them are new to the profession and quite young. Each awaits you in a private room. I believe there are twelve of you," she said, counting heads. "I had assumed there would be only eleven – one girl to a customer. Unfortunately I have only that many girls working tonight. I would of course be happy to make myself available should one of you have an interest." Madame Waleska scanned the room and fixed her eyes on Karl. "You appear to be a more mature type. Would you find me acceptable, Hauptmann?"

"Indeed, I would prefer you, Madame."

"Then I shall not disappoint you. I'll meet you in Room Five in ten minutes."

Karl climbed the spiral stairway behind Günter Jurgen and Otto Kremer, a young Leutnant from Berlin.

"Do you have any cigarettes, Kremer?" Jurgen asked. "I'm fresh out. Sometimes these young whores lack passion. A cigarette usually helps." Kremer shrugged and gave Jurgen three cigarettes.

201. MADAME WALESKA'S, ROOM FIVE, 10:42 P.M.

Madame Waleska closed the door behind her and took a seat on a leather-upholstered chair. She took a moment to examine Karl. "I hope your companions enjoy themselves. But you're not like them, are you Hauptmann? You seem different . . . Are you?"

"Not so different. I'm a German and a Nazi Party member, but not an SS man. I'm a doctor. That makes a difference, I suppose. At least it should."

"Your accent is different from most of the Germans who've come through here recently. Are you from Berlin?" Her curiosity surprised Karl.

"Yes, but I'm East African by birth. I resettled in Germany two years ago," he said, wanting not to elaborate.

Madame Waleska approached Karl, running a finger over his belt buckle. He moved her hand away gently.

"Believe me, Madame, I would enjoy it. But I have a girl back in Germany. I didn't really plan to be here tonight. I just sort of went with the crowd."

"I quite understand. Shall we drink some wine then?" She poured them each a glass of red from a bottle on the teacart.

"To good wine and good company, Hauptmann." She, too, seemed relieved, more interested in talking than in empty copulation.

"My pleasure, Madame."

"So tell me more about Berlin. What does one do for pleasure there these days, now that you Germans have started another war?"

He never had a chance to answer. A shrill scream brought Karl and Madame Waleska to their feet. A second scream propelled them to the hallway. A third told them that the disturbance was in Room Seven, just across the hall. Madame Waleska inserted her passkey, pushed the door open, and gestured for Karl to follow.

In the half-light from the hallway, Karl could see the girl kneeling on the carpet, frightened, blood seeping from her mouth.

"This bitch turned out to be a Jew," Günter Jurgen muttered. "She tried to bribe me to help her get out of the country." Karl turned toward the girl, fighting his impulse to comfort her. Instead he turned toward Jurgen.

"Well, Günter," Karl laughed, "I hope you got a good piece for your trouble."

"Actually, she was tight and dry. The cigarettes worked wonders, though. No Jew-bitch wants cigarette burns on her face."

Kremer and the other SS men were gathering in the hallway, their fun interrupted. Madame Waleska escorted the weeping girl down the stairs, where she gave her an ice bag and a fresh white towel.

"Gentlemen, please return to your pleasures," Jurgen said. "Hauptmann Muller will be leaving now by automobile. Cars to take the rest of us back to our quarters will be here within the hour. It's all been arranged."

202. ZEHLENDORF, BERLIN, NOVEMBER 1, 1939, 2:45 P.M.

Medical consequences of the Warsaw night on the town came to Karl's attention not long after he resumed his daily practice in Zehlendorf. Already, three of the SS officers who visited Madame Waleska's had come to Karl complaining of the same symptoms – a yellowish discharge and terrible pain when they urinated. Karl diagnosed gonorrhea in each of them. It came as no surprise that Madame Waleska had lied about her girls being clean. The Madame herself, it turned out, was missing.

Karl gave each man an injection of penicillin. He knew that the antibiotic would work against the clap, but was worried because his supply was growing short.

The latest victim of the brothel adventure was none other than Günter Jurgen, who had called for an appointment that morning.

After giving Jurgen the injection, Karl broached a subject that had been on his mind.

"Günter, I'd like to enlist with your unit again. Serving at the front gets me away from treating old people, women, and children, who are all that's left in Berlin these days. I want to be somewhere I can help the Reich win this

305

war. Besides, my time in Spain and Poland helped my credibility as a Party fundraiser. Still, I always need fresh experience."

"I'd be happy to speak to Heydrich," Jurgen said, "but I may not have a chance anytime soon. I'm leaving Berlin later this afternoon. My unit has been ordered back to Poland."

203. CAFÉ SELECT, PARIS, DECEMBER 21, 1939, 7:30 PM

Nancy sipped Burgundy as she waited for Prouxlanger. She was sitting at a warm inside table toward the back of the smoke-filled café on the Boulevard Montparnasse. By now she had adjusted to motherhood. The arrival of Little Nancy made this new war seem somehow remote, at least compared to Madrid. Here their lives seemed almost normal. Josh was happy working at the hospital. A middle-aged woman who lived down the hall and had lost her husband at Verdun was happy to babysit Little Nancy for a few francs. That gave Nancy and Josh time to enjoy an occasional restaurant dinner or a twilight walk together along the Seine embankment.

Now that *l'Humanité* had paid for her articles, published as a five-part series, Nancy wanted to celebrate by buying dinner for Prouxlanger. She was toying with the idea of writing a book based on her own and Josh's experiences in Spain. She wondered what Prouxlanger would think and began anticipating the evening ahead. Things might get interesting, she mused, because Prouxlanger had promised to bring along a young British journalist who had also been in Spain, covering the war from the fascist side.

Étienne Prouxlanger arrived, self-assured as ever, and introduced the young journalist as Robin Baxter.

"Let's warm up, have some wine, and get acquainted," Prouxlanger suggested. He ordered a large carafe of Burgundy.

"Right you are," Baxter declared, taking a pipe from his worn tweed jacket. "I'm partial to Scotch, but red wine seems more appropriate for December in Paris."

Nancy eyed Baxter with caution. "Since leaving Madrid, I've read several of your dispatches from Spain, Mr. Baxter. I must say that our views

– yours and mine – couldn't be further apart. Your reports had a distinct fascist slant."

"You've judged my work quite accurately," Baxter said.

"My friend's writing has a distinct right-wing tone that's altogether intentional," Prouxlanger said as the Burgundy arrived. "It makes him less suspect."

"Well, Mr. Baxter," Nancy said, "since you were in Spain covering the war from the other side, you might enjoy talking to my husband. He's an American doctor, a fan of Franklin Roosevelt, the New Deal, and the Democratic Party. We have a strong marriage, but we disagree on politics, particularly about my membership in the Communist Party."

A waiter took their dinner orders. Prouxlanger was ready for a more purposeful discussion. "I invited my friend Baxter to join us because it appears that you two have a mutual acquaintance, a German doctor named Fern Wagner."

"I know her only slightly," Nancy said with surprise. "She was engaged to my husband's best friend back in New York. I met my husband – in fact, he was my patient – not long after his friend was arrested and went to prison. I worked with Dr. Wagner in the OR a few times. As far as I knew, she'd returned to Germany after her fiancé was killed."

Baxter laid aside his unlit pipe. "I met and befriended Fern in Spain. Although she never said so directly, I got the distinct impression that she'd never gotten over her fiancé. And there are some questions surrounding the circumstance of his death."

"Yes, my husband tried to look into Karl's death – that was his name, Karl Ludwig – but ran into a roadblock of police bureaucracy. It was a difficult time for Josh because he was still recovering from serious injuries he'd sustained in a barroom fight, the incident that got Karl Ludwig in trouble in the first place."

Prouxlanger blew a perfect smoke ring. "Nancy, does Josh ever speak of his friend Karl?"

"Hell, he never shuts up about him and the great times they had growing up together in New York. He talks about Fern Wagner sometimes, too. Apparently she considered it prudent to stop communicating with Josh once she returned to Germany."

They washed down the fresh grilled trout with a carafe of pinot gris, making it hard for Nancy to believe that there was a war going on. "We certainly didn't eat like this in Spain," she said, glancing at Baxter.

"No, but that could change rather quickly," Baxter intoned. "Germany's like a well-trained athlete primed for a major event. It can hardly wait to flex its muscles again. Spain and Poland were but previews of what's next."

"You certainly talk differently than you write," Nancy said, rolling her eyes. "I'm almost ready to believe Étienne when he says you're one of us."

"In contrast to Germany," Baxter said, "our Mother Russia is not yet in fighting shape. We can see that from her sluggish and thus far failing effort to invade Finland, despite the fact that she outnumbers and outguns them. In the larger picture, that non-aggression pact with Hitler bought Comrade Stalin some time," he said matter of factly. "Stalin knows full well that Hitler covets the Soviet Union's land and resources, especially Ukrainian grain and oil from the Caspian Basin. In other words, Stalin knows, or suspects, that Hitler will eventually attack Russia. Thanks to the pact, Hitler got Poland on the cheap – at least for the short term. What Hitler didn't expect was that Britain and France would finally have the gumption to stand up to him on Poland. He failed to grasp the shift in British public opinion after Germany violated the Munich agreement and seized what was left of Czechoslovakia – you know, the part he didn't get in Munich. Now Hitler must defeat Britain and France before taking on the Soviet Union, which he's itching to do."

"Interesting," Nancy said. "You make it sound like a tennis tournament – Germany against the West. The winner gets to fight Russia."

After coffee, Baxter picked up the check and they went their separate ways. Prouxlanger escorted Nancy to the door of her apartment building and then headed home. Baxter took a taxi to his hotel and wrote another report.

204. SS HEADQUARTERS, PRINZ-ALBRECHT-STRASSE, JANUARY 30, 1940, 8:00 P.M.

Returning to his austere office after that evening's Chancellery gala, Heydrich perused the file marked "Karl Muller." That file now included Günter Jurgen's detailed report on his visit to Dar es Salaam, based on what the old waiter and the librarian had told him. It also included another agent's authentication of Karl Muller's Cape Town medical school records. He pondered the curious incident with the drunken border guard the night Dr. Muller entered Germany and the miraculous escape from Madrid with General Haber.

The telephone rang. It was Günter Jurgen, calling to report that Karl Muller had left the reception in a great hurry. Heydrich thought for a moment, then made a note to review the guest list.

205. FREDERICK WAGNER'S TOWNHOUSE, MARCH 24, 1940, 8:55 A.M.

Hans Krebs's orders were to return to Berlin forthwith. The telephone call from the ambassador's secretary came as no surprise. His soft embassy duty was over. It had been a week since Heydrich had received his lengthy final report, which described how the Bund was an embarrassment to the Reich and the Nazi Party, and how pro-German sentiment among Americans was close to zero.

Hans learned that he would have only three days to close down his Washington apartment and get back to New York. The German Embassy, he learned, had already booked him on the Pan Am Clipper from New York to Lisbon. From there, he would fly Lufthansa to Templehof Airport in Berlin.

206. GENERAL STAFF HEADQUARTERS, BERLIN, MARCH 24, 1940, 5:05 P.M.

Erwin Rommel tapped a knuckle on the clear glass interior window of Haber's small office in the General Staff headquarters. Haber beckoned his friend to enter and take a seat.

"Erwin, you appear quite fit, as do the units under your command. I watched some of their drills near Aachen several days ago. Tell me, what do you think of our plans?"

Rommel sat across the desk from Haber, reflecting for a moment, choosing his words with care. "I like it. But we'll only know how good it is once we've begun to implement it. So much can happen in the heat of battle."

"Surely," Haber responded, "it makes sense to secure our far northern flank by taking Denmark and Norway, ensuring our continued access to northern Sweden and its iron ore. After that, our feint into Holland and Belgium will encourage the Allies to think that we're refighting the last war, using a variation on the old Schlieffen Plan. That two-front encirclement strategy almost worked in 1914, so it's logical to think we might try it again, especially now that German forces are highly mechanized and able to cover ground quickly."

"True, but what I like most about your plan is the element of surprise. It calls for a rapid-fire strike in the Ardennes where they won't expect it. From there, we can break through to the west with a clear path across France. Our radio-equipped tanks give us a strong advantage. The Abwehr reports that the French Army is unprepared in the extreme. Their tanks have no radios, no way to coordinate with each other."

Declining Haber's offer of a cigarette, Rommel continued. "But our victory will be tactical, not strategic. And that victory will prove very expensive. It will tax us tremendously since we'll have so much territory to occupy. Eventually, resistance will develop – and we'll need a significant occupying force simply to cope with that resistance. Yes, we'll acquire agricultural resources, but not enough. And we'll gain some mineral resources, but not enough. Most important, this plan will not get us the petrol for a long, mechanized war. The oil we need isn't in France and the Low Countries, but in Arabia and the Caspian Basin."

Haber sipped ersatz coffee, which was now tepid and more bitter than usual.

"Well, Erwin, there's much more to think about. The Führer is concerned that if we commit too many forces in the west, it will tempt Stalin to attack us in the east, at our rear. That's why our westward action must be swift and decisive. A stalemate there could prove disastrous."

"I have a meeting with my Panzer commanders in a few minutes," Rommel said, glancing at this watch and standing to leave.

They parted with a firm handshake. Haber felt invigorated. There was something refreshing about talking candidly with such a capable man, an intellect and visionary who was also a man of action – an unusual combination. Being with Erwin Rommel, Haber reflected, was a lot like being with Karl Muller.

207. NEAR BERCHTESGADEN, MARCH 30, 1940, 3:15 P.M.

Heydrich had provided speedy approval of Karl's request to serve a second tour of duty with Günter Jurgen's unit and to train in the mountains with Jurgen's men. Karl needed such training to learn more about how *his* body – arms, legs, and shoulders – would respond to the stress of climbing mountains and rappelling down cliffs.

"Shall we race to the top?" Karl shouted as he threw the grappling hook then yanked hard on the rope, tugging again to make certain it was secure. "But, of course," Günter Jurgen replied.

Karl held back just long enough to allow Jurgen to reach the ledge first.

"You perform quite well for a man of science . . . for a doctor, I mean. Are you sure you've never done this before?" Jurgen asked, catching his breath.

"Well, I try to stay in shape. I did some mountain climbing in Africa, though I've never had to contend with the ice and snow you have here."

As the last of his men gathered on the summit, Jurgen checked his watch. "Now every man must reach the bottom of the cliff in less than two minutes and then run the three miles back to the SS barracks in eighteen minutes," he barked. "After that, we'll shower, eat some dinner, and find some women."

As the men checked their equipment, Günter drew Karl aside. "Not a word to anyone, but tomorrow our group flies to Kiel. It's top secret."

"So that's where we're going?"

"No. That's where we embark for where we're going."

208. SS OFFICERS' BARRACKS, BERCHTESGADEN, MARCH 30, 1940, 9:10 P.M.

To Karl's surprise, Trudy was waiting in the reception area when he returned to the barracks after dinner. Jurgen was busy making his usual rounds of the local Bierkellers with several other SS officers.

"Some friend you are, Karl, not to call when you're in town." He kissed the cheek she offered.

"Our training here is secret, Trudy. I couldn't break security."

"I've missed you. Do you have time for a walk?"

They sauntered to a lamppost, where she stopped and put her face on his chest.

"Tell me, Karl, can you come to my place for dinner tomorrow night?"

"Sorry. We're out of here at dawn tomorrow. My gear's already packed."

"Where to?"

"Don't know. Can I call you when I get back?

"You'd better." She kissed him on the forehead and climbed into her car. Karl watched as she drove away, wondering again about who could have sent her. Brown had no idea that he was in the Obersalzberg, so it could hardly be him. Heydrich, of course, knew precisely where he was. Karl realized that he needed to stay on good terms, and on guard, with Trudy.

209. CAFÉ DU TROCADÉRO, PARIS, APRIL 9, 1940, 10:15 A.M.

Nancy scanned the front page of *Le Figaro*, which was filled with the same stories she'd just been hearing on her kitchen radio. Somehow there were Germans in Norway and Denmark. She glanced at the baby carriage to make sure her daughter was sleeping soundly, but it was *Le Figaro* that held her attention. She read that the Germans had taken Copenhagen in less than an hour and were advancing briskly toward Narvik and other Norwegian cities. Suddenly she realized that someone was talking to her.

"Such ugly news rather ruins the splendid spring morning, does it not?" The Oxbrigde accent was familiar. Looking up from her paper, Nancy did not, at first, recognize Robin Baxter in his military uniform, now required of war correspondents.

"Baxter?" she asked, with a squint. "Sit down, if you have a moment. I'm meeting an old friend from New York who should be here soon."

"Of course, my pleasure," Baxter said, signaling the waiter for a coffee just as Vinny Bellacosta arrived. Vinny was dressed in a double-breasted gray pinstriped suit and was carrying a black leather briefcase.

Nancy rushed through the introductions. "Vinny's a chum from New York," she confided. "His brother worked in the same New York hospital as Josh, my husband. Vinny's been a real friend when we've needed him most. He used his clout to see that we got on a U.S. government plane out of Madrid."

After they ordered coffee, Vinny recounted how he had met Nancy while visiting Josh in the hospital after the disastrous barroom fight. Vinny also talked about Karl Ludwig, the nightclub brawl that had sent Karl to prison, and Karl's fatal accident. Baxter listened. Vinny's story was consistent with what Fern had told him in Spain.

Baxter excused himself as soon as they'd finished eating. "I fear I may not be seeing you for a while, Nancy. The *Times* has assigned me to cover the British Expeditionary Forces stationed near the French-Belgian border. My train leaves this evening. Let's get together for lunch when I get back."

Vinny beckoned the waiter for more coffee and leaned forward. "We were lucky to get you out of Madrid, Nancy. We had to wake up a congressman at four in the morning to jump-start the State Department bureaucracy. We might not succeed a second time. Remember, there were only a handful of Americans in Madrid just before it fell. There are hundreds, maybe thousands of Americans in Paris – and they'll all be hell-bent to get out of here if the Huns get close."

"You'll need to explain this to Josh."

"Already have. Surprised him at the hospital early this morning. Figured we should talk man to man. No offense. He knows you want to stay, so he wants to stay."

"Listen, Vinny, I'll talk to Josh tonight. Maybe he should go and I should stay. Maybe it would help if you were there. Your presence might keep things grounded, so to speak. Why don't you come for dinner?"

"I can't, Nancy. I'm on the afternoon train to Bordeaux to make sure that $2 million worth of wine remains headed for our family-owned restaurants and liquor stores in New York. The good French stuff is getting harder to come by every week."

Vinny kissed Nancy on the cheek and dropped a few francs on the table to cover the check. She watched as he crossed the Place Trocadéro and disappeared into the crowd. There were still five minutes before Prouxlanger would arrive for their regular weekly meeting. She inhaled the sweet spring air and looked down into the carriage where her daughter slept.

210. GARE DE LYON, PARIS, APRIL 9, 1940, 3:05 P.M.

Victor Minnelli was standing near a newspaper kiosk, reading *Paris Soir*. Looking up, he recognized Vinny's rapid New York stride.

"Let's get an espresso," Minnelli said. They sat in a busy train station café, taking a moment to watch the comings and goings, the reunions and farewells.

"It's in the suitcase," Vinny said, "all ten grand, in three different currencies – Yankee greenbacks, Italian lire, and French francs.

"*Grazie.*"

"*Bene*, Victor. You did good work."

Not only had Vinny bought a large shipment of premium French wine, he had closed the deal at the right price. Emile Broussard, owner of a Paris-based wine exporter, had at first resisted the below-black-market prices the Bellacosta firm was offering. Like everyone else, Broussard knew that wartime shortages meant higher prices, the simple logic of supply and demand. Unfortunately for Broussard, logic had overcome his usual good judgment.

Now Broussard was dead. Three nights earlier at about ten, Minnelli had caught up with him on the Avenue Kléber, where Broussard kept a high-end retail shop on the ground floor, just below his office. The weather had been perfect for Minnelli – a driving rain, not a soul on the street, all the office and apartment windows shuttered. Minnelli knew the car, a lemon-yellow Pierce-Arrow sedan, which glistened in the driving the rain. Minnelli drew a bead on Broussard as the wine merchant fumbled for his car keys. The silencer on Minnelli's Beretta muffled the shot. Blood spouted from Broussard's temple as he lay dead on the cobblestones and Minnelli strolled toward Place de l'Etoile in the spring rain.

No one discovered Broussard's remains for several hours. But by noon the next day the papers were filled with pictures of the lanky corpse. That afternoon, with funeral arrangements to make, Broussard's grieving staff expedited a large wine shipment to Vinny Bellacosta at a reasonable price.

5:00 P.M.

Vinny reached into his vest pocket as the loudspeaker announced the imminent departure of the train for Rome. "Here's a new Italian passport and a ticket all the way to Palermo," he said, handing Minnelli an envelope. "You shouldn't have any trouble at the border unless Italy jumps into the war. Get yourself a decent place to hide in Palermo and rest up. Lay low, but stay in fighting shape. We'll be in touch. With the war and everything else that's going on, I'm sure we'll have more work for you soon."

211. EAST OF NARVIK, NORWAY, APRIL 17, 1940, 4:15 A.M.

In the light of a campfire, Karl pounded his boots in the deep snow to fight the numbness in his feet. A red rim of light framed the mountains to the east. He'd been in those mountains with Jurgen and his men for two days. They had scaled icy cliffs and trudged across vast glacial expanses in search of their prey – a half-dozen potential Norwegian "troublemakers" who had fled Narvik in dog sleds just before the Germans occupied the town the week before.

Now Günter Jurgen and his special SS unit were camped out on a plateau next to railroad tracks that led to Sweden. Karl heard Jurgen's thick voice behind him, a voice he'd been hearing every waking moment for over two weeks. Jurgen had been up all night interrogating two captured Norwegian boys, both of whom had learned enough German in school to grasp Jurgen's uncompromising message. They responded with stone-like silence.

"You're both very brave and very stubborn. But let me tell you something – if you persist in your silence, there will be consequences. Maybe you don't care about your own life. But what about the life of your friend? If one of you refuses to tell us what we need to know – where you were going and whom you were about to meet – we'll kill your friend, right here, on the spot, in a most unpleasant way, buried alive in the snow. Do you understand?"

Karl inched closer to where the two boys were kneeling, ten meters apart, their gloveless hands tied behind their backs. Abruptly, Jurgen stopped ranting. He moved to the taller boy, most likely the older to the two, and pointed at his companion.

"If he doesn't talk, we'll bury you right here," Jurgen said without patience. "Your silence only strengthens my conviction that you both know exactly where your friends are hiding." Neither uttered a sound.

Jurgen motioned for two nearby SS guards to untie both boys and handed the taller boy a shovel.

"Start digging," Jurgen ordered. "I'm told that the snow here is fifteen meters deep. Your friend will suffocate under the snow, which you will shovel over him. His corpse won't see daylight until summer, when his rotting flesh will befoul the air and make a fine meal for rats and field mice. You will survive. You'll go to Dachau with the memory that you sent your friend to an agonizing death."

The smaller boy couldn't help but hear and began to cry. He pointed to a peak off to the northeast. "We were to rejoin them over there. It's about ten kilometers," he sobbed.

"And who are they?"

"My schoolmaster and his wife."

"Who else?"

Jurgen waited as the younger boy spouted off several other names. Jurgen knew they were the people he sought.

"Now let's get rid of these two," he snapped at the SS sergeant standing nearby. "But let's not waste any ammunition. We've learned all we can from them. Tie them up, gag them, and bury them in the hole the taller one has dug."

Karl had thought nothing would shock him after Poland. He walked toward the ditch where Jurgen's men were shoveling snow over the two mute, squirming boys. He forced himself to move closer and watch. He needed to be sure that what he was seeing was real.

The Arctic sun peeked over the mountains as Karl and the SS contingent waited for the train that would take them to Sweden, then home to Germany. Karl tasted the bile rising in his throat and listened to Jurgen on the field telephone ordering another unit to pursue the fugitives whose whereabouts the boys had disclosed. As the train rumbled through the mountains toward Sweden, he tried to purge the two boys from his mind. His only comfort came from the thought that by now they were both dead.

He found a seat on the train and rested his head against the cold window and remembered that he had not slept for twenty-eight hours.

Her back was toward him, but he knew it was Fern. She was peering out the window of the railway car as Jurgen's men shoveled snow over the icy gravesite. Karl was about to tap her shoulder when she turned toward him, as stunning as ever in her field-green Luftwaffe uniform. He tried to speak but his tongue wouldn't move, too weak at the sight of her to muster a syllable. He moved to hold her but could not lift his arms.

"I saw you from the train," she whispered. "You disappoint me, Karl. You're so quick with your fists, but you just stood there with your hands in your pockets while those thugs buried two boys alive in the snow. How weak of you, Karl. Now I know you for the coward you are." He tried to look into her eyes but she had turned her head. As he strained to put his arms around her she vanished.

The poke in the ribs from Günter Jurgen woke him. "We've just arrived at the Swedish border. The guards want us to get off so they can check our identification and inspect the train."

212. THE TAVERNE, BERLIN, MAY 8, 1940 8:00 P.M.

Karl sat at the bar, nursing a beer while waiting for Günter Jurgen, who had invited him out for a drink. He hadn't seen Jurgen since they'd returned from Norway. He couldn't help but notice how few patrons there were in this usually popular establishment. Even now, at the dinner hour, the big round table in the corner was vacant. On a normal night, that table would be full of foreign correspondents, William Shirer among others, engaged in robust conversation.

Karl was glad Jurgen was late. It gave him a moment of solitude, time to think. That morning he'd taken a long run in the Tiergarten and completed a rigorous workout at the Berliner Sportverein after closing the office. Jurgen's tardiness also gave him time to glance over the headlines from the afternoon papers, all telling of anticipated British "aggression" and Churchill's desire to expand the war. Karl knew Goebbels was pushing this storyline for a reason.

He was less than happy that he hadn't had any contact with London for more than two months. His orders remained the same as when he first entered Germany three years before: *Establish credibility, gain access, find a position from which to strike, and wait for the order.* He'd made some progress, but things were advancing slowly. The preliminary work, the ongoing task of maintaining access to the Nazi brass, was going well enough. The escape from Madrid, the tours of duty in Poland and Norway, and the fundraising efforts for the Nazi Party had enhanced his credibility and access to those closest to Hitler but provided scant access to Hitler himself. Karl still had to overcome the difficulty of getting a private audience with the man he would have to kill.

The remote Kehlsteinhaus seemed like the kind of place where he could get the job done. But he needed to get Hitler up there alone, and he needed the go-ahead from London. He was about to order a second beer when he noticed a man standing at his side.

"Excuse me, aren't you Dr. Karl Muller?" the man said, interrupting Karl's reverie. "I believe you treated my daughter several years ago. My name is Hans Krebs."

"Of course, I remember," Karl said. "She had a bad case of bronchitis. How is your daughter now?"

"Very well, thank you. She's in school in Leipzig, preparing for a career in medicine." Hans and Karl eyed each other with caution for several seconds.

"Berlin feels quite empty this evening," Hans said at last. "Or perhaps it's just that I'm a little lonely. I saw my girlfriend off at the Bahnhof Zoo early this morning. She's a doctor assigned to the Luftwaffe. Her name is Wagner, Fern Wagner."

Karl's fingers grew cold. He nodded. "Ah yes, I've heard many good things about Dr. Wagner. She was my predecessor in the field hospital on the Madrid front. I remember also that your daughter mentioned her."

Hans stood next to Karl and ordered a beer, which he now sipped while deciding whether to elaborate. "She plays a rather important role with the Luftwaffe, reporting to Göring. The Luftwaffe depends upon her expertise with severe facial burns and reconstructive surgery, the kinds of things one doesn't normally talk about in public."

"You must be very proud of her," Karl said, "but if you don't mind, I think I have to use the men's room for a moment." Karl stood before the men's room sink throwing cold water on his face. Hans's sudden appearance was most unwelcome. So was the talk of Fern. But he knew he had to roll with the punches.

"Are you sure you won't have another beer?" Hans asked once Karl had returned to the bar.

"Quite sure."

"Well then, I'll have another. It's been a long day," Hans said, just as Jurgen appeared. Karl was about to introduce the two men when Hans interrupted him. "We both work for Reinhard Heydrich. We met several days ago when I returned from an overseas assignment."

"You were in Washington and New York, weren't you?" Jurgen asked.

"Both interesting cities," Hans said. "Very different from each other and from Berlin. The beer in New York isn't nearly as bad as you might expect."

"What about the women?" Jurgen asked. "Doesn't all that intermarriage between the races produce some hideous results?"

"Just the opposite," Hans responded, "There's a lot of intermarriage among Italians, Irish, and Germans in New York, and the women there are stunning – tall and slender with sculptured legs."

Hans wondered how Jurgen and Karl knew each other. "Gentlemen," he said at last. "I don't know what you have planned for the evening, but may I suggest that we all dine together here at the Taverne. Since the place is nearly empty, we can talk openly about the war without fear of being overheard by press people. Indeed, the absence of military men and foreign press tells me that something big is about to happen."

Karl liked the idea. Anything, he thought, was better than spending time alone with Günter Jurgen. Besides, he wanted to learn more about Hans, even if that meant hearing more stories about Fern. It would be dangerous, he realized, to allow Hans Krebs, a trained investigator, to determine the course of the conversation. Better if he led the conversation.

"It must be difficult for you," Karl said, "with your girlfriend away on military assignment."

"Well, I've gotten used to living alone. My wife died from influenza in 1922. But what about you, Doctor? How are you finding life in Berlin?"

"As you may remember," Karl began, "I settled here just three years ago and spend most of my time practicing medicine. I've also raised funds for the Party and volunteered as a special medical officer."

Jurgen listened, trying to discern what might interest Heydrich. Hans also listened as Karl told his story and revealed little. To learn more, Hans realized, he'd have to do what he did best – be a detective.

213. THE FÜHRER TRAIN, AT THE DUTCH-GERMAN BORDER, MAY 10, 1940, 5:32 A.M.

Fern looked up into the gray dawn. She'd taken Göring's advice and risen even earlier than usual on this Friday morning. A boyish private escorted her to a spot near Hitler's private railway car, named – by some bizarre twist – *Amerika*. From fifty meters away, she could see Hitler and his entourage atop a grassy knoll. She recognized Göring, who was holding his air marshal's baton. Keitel, Jodl, Rundstedt, and Bormann were there along with several others she didn't recognize. Even at that distance, she could hear Hitler's shrill voice, as he reprimanded someone who had miscalculated the time of sunrise by more than twenty minutes – an "incredibly idiotic blunder" she could hear Hitler yelling. The error had delayed the invasion, wasting precious daylight. Fern nodded to the young private, indicating that they should move away from the train and out of earshot. So, Fern reflected, this mistake – or was it Providence – had given the people of Holland and Belgium a few extra minutes of sleep before the Luftwaffe burned and crippled and killed them.

The drone of aircraft coming in from the east was faint at first but growing louder. She'd heard this sound before, in Spain, but it had never been this loud or lasted this long. Soon she could see them – a few at first, then many more – tri-motored Junkers flying low, each with its cadre of Aryan warriors, ready to pounce on their Dutch cousins. Fern could hear the small group clustered around Hitler begin to applaud the airborne armada. How in hell, Fern asked, had she allowed herself to become part of all this?

Fern realized that she was likely acquainted with more than a few of the young men flying those planes. Soon enough, some would again be her patients, this time in one of the new field hospitals she planned to establish in the coming fortnight. When the applause ended, Hitler's entourage walked back to *Amerika*, to await reports.

PART THREE

214. LONDON, MAY 10, 1940, 6:02 A.M.

Channing Brown answered the ringing telephone on his nightstand. It was Jamie Creel in Amsterdam. By some miracle he had managed to get an operator and an open line.

"It's no cakewalk here. We're up to our balls in exploding bombs," Creel shouted. "There is some good news, however. Van Cleef and the others are getting their industrial diamonds to me. I should have them in an hour. Then I'll make a dash for the coast . . ." Brown had sent Creel to Amsterdam five days before, after intelligence reports of an imminent German push into the Low Countries.

Brown waited for Creel to go on but soon realized that the line was dead. An hour later, in his Whitehall office, Brown was on the telephone with the Admiralty talking to one of Churchill's stenographers. The First Lord, she said, wanted Brown to write a memorandum containing "a definitive recommendation regarding the special operation code-named Jackhammer," and Brown was to deliver the memo in person no later than nine o'clock that morning. He was to return to the Admiralty at half seven that evening, at which time Brown and the First Lord would discuss the matter in detail.

Hanging up the candlestick telephone, Brown collected himself and rolled his chair to the typewriter table with the old Underwood and began the memo he had long wanted to write.

Scotty North arrived in the office just as Brown was removing the second and final page from the roller. Scotty reviewed the memo, and Brown accepted several word-smithed revisions. Brown read the revised memo aloud and retyped it with care, making two carbon copies.

"If Churchill says yes, Scotty, you'll have to slip into Berlin and talk to Karl face to face, just the two of you. Nothing less will do. No paper, no coded wireless message, nothing susceptible to interception."

215. THE ADMIRALTY, MAY 10, 8:05 P.M.

As he left Churchill's inner office, Brown strained to remember the name of the pretty Wren typing at her desk. Her nameplate saved him. "Daphne, please let me use the most secure line you have." He made three calls: the first to the Admiralty motor pool; the second the Croydon RAF base; and the third to Scotty North in his undercover Half Moon Street office. Brown knew it was getting late. He prayed that Scotty North hadn't left the Mayfair office for his Knightsbridge flat. If he was in the tube it might take forever to reach him.

"North here."

"Scotty. Jackhammer is *go*. You must leave tonight. A car from the Admiralty motor pool should be there in three minutes. It'll take you home to fetch whatever you need then take you to Croydon. From there, one of our Hudsons will fly you to Berne."

"Splendid. I'll catch a Berlin train from there. If I get on a sleeper tomorrow night, I should be in Berlin late Sunday night. By the way, I've just tucked the two carbons of your Jackhammer memo to Churchill in our office safe here."

"One more point, Scotty. Churchill wants it all to happen soon – right away if possible."

"No surprise there," North said. "But Karl won't be rushed."

"No rush, just all deliberate speed. Tell Karl we'll give him all the support we can."

Brown headed for the waiting Admiralty car, which would take him to his Bayswater townhouse where he and Jillian would sit on the sofa and listen to Chamberlain's farewell speech on the radio. Scotty heard Chamberlain's swansong in the chauffeured car on the way to Croydon. On his lap was the canvas travel bag he always kept packed and ready.

216. ZEHLENDORF, MAY 15, 1940, 9:15 A.M.

Taking a seat at Karl's desk, Frau Frick couldn't wait to tell Karl the news.

"I just received a telephone call from a Dr. Nordencrantz," she said. "He told me that he met you when you spoke in Hannover. Now he'd like to make a sizeable donation to the Party. He wants to give you the bank draft in person. He's in Berlin, staying at the Adlon, and requested that you meet him there in the main dining room for coffee at eleven. I've already changed all your morning appointments to after lunch."

"Thank you, Frau Frick."

217. THE ADLON LOBBY, 10:48 A.M.

Karl entered the lobby from the Pariser Platz and made his way directly to the restaurant, where the *maître d'* recognized him. "Ah, Dr. Muller. There's a Dr. Nordencrantz waiting for you. As Karl arrived at the table, a man in a dark brown three-piece suit and a pince-nez rose to greet him.

The disguise fooled Karl, but only for a moment.

"Nordencrantz" handed Karl an envelope, explaining that it contained a check for 20,000 Reichsmarks from the Bank of Hannover account belonging to Ernst Nordencrantz.

Karl opened the unsealed envelope, examined the check, and nodded. "Nordencrantz" filled Karl's cup from the silver pot of ersatz coffee and addressed him in English. "Nice work, don't you think?"

"What, Scotty, the bank draft or your disguise?"

"Both, I dare day."

Karl looked over Scotty North's shoulder.

"No need to worry," North said. "The place is ours, at least for the moment. I've checked under the table. And there's no one else in the room, not even a waiter."

"Okay, I'm listening. What's up?"

"Jackhammer is a go. Straight from Churchill. Brown wanted me to tell you in person so there wouldn't be any misunderstanding. Now the question is *when*."

"Tell Brown," Karl said after a moment's reflection, "that I understand the message and to stay tuned. Remember our deal. I pick the time to do it and means of escape – and keep all that to myself. It may test your patience to learn that the final phase will require very precise planning to get the fellow alone, without his entourage of generals and security louts. Now that I have the green light I can figure out the specifics."

Back on the Pariser Platz, Karl waited to make sure that no one appeared to be following Scotty North and then returned to his office.

218. ZEHLENDORF, MAY 16, 1940, 4:00 A.M.

Karl had gone to bed while it was still daylight and slept soundly for nine hours. Instead of taking his usual early-morning run, he wanted to think. He concentrated first on the *how* of the matter.

So much, of course, depended on *where* he would do it. The place Bormann had built on the Kehlstein presented the most promising venue. Sure, there would be security guards to contend with, but nowhere near as many as at the Berghof or the Chancellery. Still, the steep and unforgiving mountain would make a clean getaway next to impossible.

Thinking back to his time in Scotland, he recalled that Brown often spoke of being prepared to seize opportunities. So far he had succeeded in getting close to Haber, Göring, Hess, and Bormann. Then there was Günter Jurgen, a sex-crazed sadist. But where was the opportunity?

Then, in an instant, he knew what he had to do. It was so simple. Still, it would demand all his skills.

He returned to his desk and made notes. Each step of the plan was risky. None would be easy. He needed some things – and he could get them from an old friend, whose place of business he would telephone that very morning.

He reviewed his notes a second time, and then a third, committing everything to memory before tearing the paper into what Josh and his other friends back in New York might call "smithereens." Then he flushed it all down the toilet.

Back in the kitchen, he cut himself a generous slice of pumpernickel, one of the few things that tasted better in Berlin than in New York.

219. NEAR DINANT, BELGIUM, ON THE MEUSE RIVER, MAY 17, 1940, 11:07 A.M.

Fern sat in the corner hurrying to finish her paperwork at a wooden desk commandeered from a nearby schoolhouse. There were more than twenty empty cots in the hospital tent. Causalities had been light, and the few wounded men inside the tent had withstood their pain with barely a wince or a groan, just as they'd done in Spain.

Fern saw a young nurse rushing toward her. A high-ranking officer, a general from the 7th Panzer Division, needed several shell fragments removed from his face, just below the right eye. "I'll attend to him myself," Fern told her.

Fern waited as Erwin Rommel visited with a wounded corporal before taking a seat in the upright camp chair. Rommel recognized Fern. "I guess today's my lucky day, Doctor. You may recall the evening Frau Rommel and I spent in your mother's home on the Tiergartenstrasse. She's a wonderful hostess."

"Of course, I remember that evening," Fern said, applying a damp cloth and a strong antiseptic to Rommel's cheek. Rommel never flinched. She placed a small bandage where she'd removed the shell fragments and asked him to lie down.

Some twenty minutes later, Rommel woke to the touch of Fern's hand on his forehead. "I believe we've removed everything. Now all you need is a little more rest."

"Sorry, Doctor, neither I nor my men have time for rest," Rommel replied. He rose from the cot and checked his watch. "In just over an hour, my Panzers will attack across the Meuse, a full day ahead of schedule."

"Well, please do everything you can to keep the wound clean."

"Thank you, Doctor. I shall try." Rommel sprang from the cot, bowed toward Fern, and strode to a waiting staff car. Fern could hear him reprimand the driver for leaving the motor running and wasting petrol.

220. CAFÉ ZIEGLER, BERLIN, MAY 17, 1940, 6:05 P.M.

Ziggy sat at a table by the iron railing that separated his café from the sidewalk and enjoyed the onset of a magnificent spring evening. The air no longer carried the Baltic chill that made his half-foot ache, the foot that had been crushed when a rail switch snapped shut near the Friedrichstrasse Bahnhof in the winter of 1920.

Ziggy's face lit up in a bright grin as Big Julius, his number one man, took a seat opposite him. Ziggy's damaged foot and Big Julius's 270 pounds had kept them each out of military service. Big Julius reached into his vest pocket and removed a single sheet of paper, which he handed to Ziggy.

"So we have a new customer," Ziggy said, "most likely a burglar from the look of his list. Any idea who it is?"

"Only that he uses the name Herr Kraus."

"I presume you'll deliver the goods at one our safe apartments," Ziggy said, taking a sip of real coffee. He horded the real stuff for himself and a few special customers and friends.

"*Ja*," Julius responded, "probably the one off the Alexanderplatz."

"Use one of our taxis – and have the driver wait for you in case you need to get away fast. This could be a Gestapo trap, and a good right-hand man is hard to find these days. Too many of you clever fellows have been drafted. Good thing you couldn't make the weight."

221. ALEXANDERPLATZ, MAY 17, 1940, 6:55 P.M.

Karl entered the apartment building and identified himself to the concierge as Herr Kraus. "A man named Julius is expecting me," he said to the wiry man who looked to be in his sixties. Karl sensed that the concierge was on good terms with the Gestapo but probably on Ziggy's payroll as well.

"He said to send you right up," the concierge said with no change of expression. "He's in apartment 4B."

The door opened before Karl could knock. "Ah, yes, Herr Kraus. Come in." Big Julius had a soft voice and a large bald head, which shone in the glare of the shadeless floor lamp. The room was empty except for a dusty card table, an ashtray, and two metal folding chairs. There were no introductions, no small talk. Julius opened a large Wertheim shopping bag and dumped its contents on the table.

"It's all here, Herr Kraus," Julius said. On the table were a crowbar, a lock pick, several black woolen skull caps and ski masks, a dozen pairs of black leather gloves, a half-dozen sets of brass knuckles, and four ounces of cocaine.

"Have a snort," Julius said with a knowing smile, seeing that Karl was eying the cocaine.

"Never use the stuff. I'll take your word that it's good."

"No need to worry, Herr Kraus, we're professionals. When you live on the edge, you learn how to walk a straight line."

"You don't have to tell me that Ziggy's a professional. His reputation is legend."

"You know Ziggy?"

"I'll pay you for all this now," Karl said, ignoring the big man's question.

"It's all yours for what you agreed to pay on the telephone – 10,000 Reichsmarks, cash," Julius said with a smile.

Karl spread the money out on the card table so Julius could see that it was the right amount. "Quite a sum," Karl said.

"Someone has to buy retail," Julius laughed, as he put the items back in the shopping bag. If any of your purchases are less than satisfactory, just give us a call and ask for me, Big Julius." Handing the bag to Karl, he said, "Now you can take the U-Bahn home and look like a normal shopper."

"*Danke*, but I have one more request, a big one. I need a furnished ground-floor apartment. It should be in the rear of a building, in a busy neighborhood where people have no time to gossip. It should have easy access to the street, and the concierge shouldn't be too nosy. I'll pay up front, in cash, to cover a year's rent. I don't want a lease, nothing in writing."

"Berlin apartments where you can avoid the prying eyes of the concierge and other, shall we say, interested parties are in short supply," Julius replied. "But my boss does have a few buildings where the concierge works primarily for us, not the Gestapo."

"Here's two thousand Reichsmarks for the apartment," Karl said, taking the money from his jacket. "Let me know if you need more, but don't be greedy – I don't want you asking for more money for at least a year."

Julius took his time counting the twenty hundred-mark notes Karl laid on the table.

"I hope I've established my credibility," Karl said in an even tone.

Big Julius smiled and gave Karl a strong handshake. He recognized a good customer and knew when not to ask questions.

"When do you want to see the apartment?" he asked.

"I'll call you tomorrow afternoon. I hope that gives you enough time. I want something in a busy neighborhood, not far from the center of Berlin – a place where people won't gossip about a new neighbor they don't see often and who comes and goes at odd hours. I'll be back here tomorrow evening at seven. You can give me a piece of paper with the building address and the apartment number, along with the necessary keys. I'll visit the apartment in my own time. If I don't like it, I'll let you know, and you can get me another."

"Sounds like a deal," Big Julius responded.

Karl returned to the Alexanderplatz, which was still full of pedestrians despite the blackout. Walking past a man on a bench reading a late edition of the *Berliner Morgenpost*, Karl glimpsed a headline about the German breakthrough at Sedan. Seeing an idle taxi, he jumped in. In a taxi, no one would ask what he'd purchased at the Wertheim Department Store.

Once home, Karl went straight to the pull-down ladder that led to the spacious attic, where he kept all the things he didn't want Frau Frick to see. Back in his bedroom, he set the alarm for five a.m. He needed to get up early and take a good run.

222. STRAUSBERGER PLATZ, BERLIN, MAY 20, 1940, 9:40 P.M.

A heavy suitcase in hand, Karl stepped into his newly rented *pied-à-terre*. Big Julius had found him the perfect place. If it was too late to travel back to

Zehlendorf, he could hide out here unnoticed by the concierge or curious neighbors, coming and going in the dead of night through the ground-floor window at the back of the building. He unpacked the clothes he'd brought – two business suits, some freshly laundered shirts, underwear, socks, ties, black shoes, and a pair of sneakers that he'd dyed black, arranging the items neatly in the dresser. A new, fully stocked shaving kit went into the bathroom medicine cabinet.

Before leaving, Karl checked the apartment for hidden microphones, running his hands under the tables and around the electrical fixtures. Finding nothing suspicious, he decided to leave behind some of the tools he'd bought from Big Julius, locking them in a suitcase, which he placed in a bedroom closet. Taking a book of matches from his pocket, he carefully stood one match against the far side of the suitcase. Anyone who moved the suitcase or tried to open it would surely knock over the match. He placed three more matches against the closet doors.

He reviewed the checklist he had prepared that morning, then made some more notes. The place needed more coffee and canned food, just in case. The kitchen was already stocked with dishes and cooking utensils. The bedroom closet held ample linens and blankets.

Satisfied, he slipped out the bedroom window and into the Berlin night, making his way to the U-Bahn.

223. NUMBER 12 GELLER STRASSE, BERLIN, MAY 26, 1940, 11:05 P.M.

Taking a deep swig of Rumplemintz from a silver flask, Karl swished the schnapps around in his mouth then spit it out onto the pavement. He put the flask back in his jacket pocket and resumed walking with the faintest tilt and weave, just another drunk who'd wandered down the wrong street.

Karl stopped to scan the facades of the baroque townhouses, now divided into flats, but the moonless night and the blackout made it hard to read the addresses from any distance. Then he found the house he was he was looking for – Number 12 Geller Strasse. He climbed the stoop, looking up and down the dark street and saw no one. Günter, he had learned, would be at the Salon Kitty all evening and would not return until very late. Still, he had to be quiet. The slightest sound could arouse a sleeping neighbor.

He slipped his pick into the lock of the outer door. It worked. He pushed it open, thankful that it didn't squeak.

Karl crept up the dark staircase, feeling his way with his hands and feet. At the fourth landing, he squinted to read the nameplate on the door – "Apartment 4C, Günter Jurgen." Again, the pick worked.

Inside the pitch-black apartment, Karl slipped off his shoes. His flashlight probed the small sitting room, then the bedroom, where he found a well-ordered cedar closet with several neatly hung uniforms, three business suits, and two sports jackets. Three sets of boxing gloves occupied a deep chest-high shelf on the right side of the back wall of closet. Karl probed the underside of the shelf with his gloved fingers.

From his jacket pocket Karl removed a set of brass knuckles, which earlier that evening he'd rubbed in mud and scraped on concrete to show use. Then, resting the flashlight on a lower shelf, he used black friction tape to attach the knuckles to the underside of the shelf holding the boxing gloves. Karl was betting that Günter wouldn't clean his drawers or paint his closets for some time. Karl had lived as a bachelor long enough to know the risk was minimal. He used the flashlight to see that the knuckles were secure and out of sight. It had all taken less than ten minutes, but he had more to do.

He closed the closet doors without a squeak. His flashlight scanned the bedroom, keeping the beam as low as he could. The three-drawer secretarial desk in the corner would be perfect for the last part of his night's work. He tested each drawer to make sure it opened and closed smoothly, then removed the mostly empty bottom drawer, which contained only a few pencils and paperclips. Using the black tape, he fastened a large white envelope filled with cocaine to the underside of the drawer; then, after replacing the drawer slowly, opened and closed it twice to make sure the envelope didn't catch.

From the bay widow, he scanned the blacked-out street below. Geller Strasse seemed deserted except for a lone man standing at the bus kiosk. Then, suddenly, he saw and heard a couple about to enter the front door of the building. Using his flashlight, he hurried to find his shoes, tied them, and made his way out of the apartment and into the hall, locking the front door of the apartment without a click. Karl kept his back to the wall and listened until the giggling couple entered a second-floor apartment below him.

Ten minutes later he was five blocks away, far enough to stop and hail a taxi for Zehlendorf.

224. JARDIN DES TUILERIES, PARIS, MAY 28, 1940, 10:00 A.M.

Rocking Little Nancy in her new baby carriage, Nancy enjoyed the sun-drenched warmth of another beautiful spring morning. But the weather offered little consolation for the news of the German invasion of France. Nancy still rejected the idea of leaving Paris. Prouxlanger had told her of the orders he'd received from Moscow – their group was to "remain together in Paris."

Josh arrived on time, his starched white medical coat looking scruffy after a night's work. They kissed quickly and sat down together on a wrought-iron bench.

Josh sat back, stretching his legs. He'd just worked an extended shift, attending to some of the most seriously wounded men brought in on the hospital train from the east. "A thought occurred to me," he said out of the blue. "We're U.S. citizens. Even if the Nazis take Paris, they're not likely to rough us up. They don't want to anger Washington. They want America to stay out of this war."

"Josh, wake up." Nancy said. "The Nazis won't give two figs that we're Americans. Now that doesn't mean I want to leave. The Party wants me to stay put. Let's go get some breakfast and talk this over some more."

"Sorry, no time. There were hundreds of wounded on the last train. We weren't ready for so many. I have to get back."

225. BERLIN, JUNE 10, 1940, 7:45 A.M.

Frau Inge Lenz, still vigorous at age seventy, tightened her grip as Wolfie, her young German shepherd, howled and strained at the leash. Wolfie pulled her forward and then to the right, leading her into a long narrow alley off the Bellevuestrasse. The dog led her twenty yards down the alleyway to a beaten and bloodied, but still-breathing, hulk of a man in the dark uniform of an SS major. A lifelong Berliner, she was not easily shocked – but the man's bloody face sent her scurrying for help.

A middle-aged policeman used smelling salts to revive the SS man and ordered Inge to stand by while he found a telephone and called an ambulance.

226. CHARITÉ HOSPITAL, BERLIN, JUNE 21, 4:00 A.M.

The night of carousing to celebrate their return to Berlin from Norway had ended badly for the two SS colonels, Klaus Frank and Joachim Heinz. Both now lay on cots in the Charité emergency room. They'd been blindsided while strolling toward the Pariser Platz, where they hoped to hail taxis to their respective apartments. The attacker had come from behind and delivered devastating blows to each man where his neck joined the shoulder. A flurry of punches followed. Frank had a fractured jaw; Heinz a badly cut cheek and a classic black eye.

A nurse was about to transport them to a double room for the night when Reinhard Heydrich arrived. "They can rest later," Heydrich told her. "I have questions for them."

Colonel Heinz appeared to Heydrich to be the more alert and attentive of the two, but he could remember next to nothing after the blow to the neck.

"No face? Nothing about his size?" Heydrich asked, trying to control his frustration.

"Well, only that I was about to light a cigarette. I'd just struck a match, and in the flicker of light I saw – or thought I saw – a shadow on the pavement. There must have been someone behind me, but I didn't see him. Then, before I knew what was happening, I was being pummeled and everything went dark. It all happened too fast."

"Say absolutely nothing about this once you're released from the hospital. Word of these attacks *must not* get out," Heydrich snapped. He gave both men the *Heil Hitler* salute and left the room. He didn't bother interrogating Frank, whose broken jaw made it impossible to speak.

227. OUTSIDE THE NOLLENDORFPLATZ THEATER, JULY 6, 1940, 12:13 A.M.

The three men had just seen an evening showing of the American film *Gone with the Wind*. Hauptmann Manfred Klaus led the way as he and two companions strolled in the summer night. The three SS officers had thoroughly enjoyed their assignation with the compliant ladies at the Salon Kitty the previous evening. With his twenty-seven-year-old libido at peace, Klaus had suggested that they spend the next-to-last night of their leave at the cinema before returning to France for occupation duty.

Klaus felt that he needed some wholesome activity he could write about to his mother back in Essen. His companions had similar obligations.

The assailant who crept up behind them in the blacked-out street not far from the theater cast no shadow. His first blow fell at the base of Klaus's neck. An hour later, a policeman discovered all three men lying unconscious on a side street, their faces badly bloodied.

228. PRINZ-ALBRECHT-STRASSE, JULY 13, 1940, 10:45 A.M.

Heydrich led Hans Krebs to a chair beside the desk. "So, Krebs, I've read your report on the Bund. It's very informative, though I must tell you that Goebbels will be disappointed. He thought the Bund would help sway American opinion in Germany's favor. And, speaking of the Americans, I want to thank you again for informing me about the Abwehr's theft of the plans for that American bombsight. It shows how hard we must work to outdo the Abwehr and Canaris."

Hans reminded himself to keep quiet. He didn't like being drawn into the rivalry between Heydrich and Canaris. He knew that Canaris was close to Frederick. The information Frederick had given him about the Norden bombsight proved that.

"With that in mind," Heydrich continued, "I have several new projects for you now that you're back in Berlin. One concerns a growing black market in medical supplies. Another involves underworld cocaine sales. The background files on these cases will be on your desk in an hour."

"Fine. I'll get started right away."

"Good. But first I need to tell you of another more urgent matter, one that you'll no doubt find intriguing and worthy of your skills as a detective. It seems there's been a rash of assaults lately against SS officers on the streets of Berlin. So far, about a dozen men have been attacked and badly beaten. All the attacks have occurred at night. And all the victims have been found unconscious, often discovered by passersby in the early morning."

"What do the police say? Do we have anything to go on?"

"Only that the attacks are being directed exclusively at SS officers, that they occur only at night, and that the assailant appears to be someone quite skilled in hand-to-hand combat. He wears some kind of ski mask and probably uses brass knuckles. He has attacked as many as three men at a time."

"I'll get on it," Krebs said.

"If you come up with any leads, anything at all, report to me – and only me – at once. This must remain top secret. We don't want the foreign press getting wind of it. That would embarrass all of us."

229. CAFÉ DE LA PAIX, PARIS, JULY 15, 1940, 8:00 A.M.

Fern finished her croissant and *oeufs au plat* made with real eggs and thought about what she needed to accomplish on this sun-filled summer day in Paris. She was glad to be back in Paris after a month spent organizing Luftwaffe field hospitals in Normandy. Göring had arranged a suite at the Ritz for her. At his request, she had come to Paris to inspect a number of hospitals, to identify those facilities best equipped to treat severe burns in the event that Britain didn't quit the war. Dressed in a plain gray cotton suit, Fern planned to walk or take the Metro from one hospital to another. She had rejected the idea of an escort and a fixed schedule of visits, knowing that she'd learn more simply by showing up unannounced. Her Luftwaffe identification card and the letter of introduction from Göring would provide universal access in what was now Nazi-occupied Paris.

In one sense, the city seemed to have changed little. The shops and cafés were as busy as ever. At the same time, German armored cars were a conspicuous presence on the streets and bridges. So were the German soldiers in their field-gray uniforms. Sipping her coffee, Fern found it hard to believe that she'd grown accustomed to drinking the crude ersatz served in the Luftwaffe mess halls in Belgium and Normandy.

At first Fern took no notice of the three men in white lab coats, probably doctors at the American hospital, seated several tables away. One was obviously a Frenchman, about fifty years old, but the younger two looked and sounded like Americans. As a waiter served them coffee, one of the doctors, Frank Rizzo, an expatriate from Springfield, Ohio, cast his gaze over the crowded terrace.

"Don't turn around now," he whispered, "but that's one smashing lady sitting over there. A German, from the look of her. Hey Josh, you said you spoke German. Here's your chance."

"Not me Frank, I'm happily married. Remember?"

"Nor I," laughed LeBrun, the Frenchman and a native Parisian. "I'm not about to fraternize with a Hun, no matter how beautiful she is."

"She's all by herself, Josh" Rizzo said.

"Forget it, Frank. I'm a Jewish boy from New York. What do I want with a German girl?"

By now LeBrun had taken his mandatory glance. "Josh, Frank is right. She's what you Americans call a knockout. Do yourself a favor and at least take a look."

Josh turned and saw Fern, then bolted to his feet, spilling coffee on his white lab coat. He turned away quickly.

"For Christ sake, Josh, don't overreact," Frank said.

"Shut up, Frank. Let's get the hell out of here."

No wait, Josh thought. *It wasn't that simple.* After all, Fern hadn't been the first girl to drop him because he was Jewish.

As Josh rose to leave the café, Fern recognized him. She sprang up, slung her purse strap over her right shoulder and fixed her eyes to the floor. She wanted to bolt from the café, to avoid Josh at all costs. Surely that was what Frederick or her mother would advise. *No, Fern Wagner, you're not that kind of coward, at least not yet.* She looked up to see Josh's unshaven face not two feet from her own.

"Josh."

"Fern," he said, "what in hell?"

"What in hell, yourself?" she responded.

"I'm with some colleagues from the hospital, the American Hospital," he said. "We just finished an all-night shift and figured that we might as well treat ourselves to a decent breakfast before the Germans eat all the real eggs left in Paris."

Fern's mind flashed back to the day she'd broken off their correspondence but decided not to bring it up.

Seeing Fern's striking face for the first time in so many years, Josh recalled the Bastille Day talk he'd had with Prouxlanger and the picture the young Communist had shown him. Was Karl still alive? Did Fern know anything about it? But Josh held his tongue – he would keep all that to himself, at least for now.

After excusing himself from his colleagues, Josh sat down at Fern's table. They hurried to exchange the missing chapters of their lives, but neither had time for details. He decided that it made no sense to dredge up her decision to end their correspondence. That was four years ago. Despite any misgivings, he was happy to see her and invited Fern to join Nancy and him for dinner at their flat that evening.

230. BERLIN, JULY 18, 1940, 6:12 P.M.

The thumping sounds of marching bands and hysterical shouts from the sidewalks filled the humid summer air as Berliners hailed the parading conquerors of Continental Europe. Karl worked his way through the crowds toward the Chancellery. Once inside, relieved to be off the street, he gave the ticket Haber had sent him to the guard, entered the large chandeliered ballroom, and joined the long receiving line. Hitler had convened the event to honor military officers who had distinguished themselves in the Blitzkrieg across Belgium and France, Erwin Rommel not least among them.

Karl realized that he would have to stay in the queue for a long time simply to shake Hitler's hand. The excuse to get out of the line came when Martin Haber tugged on his arm.

"Karl, Hildy and I will be dining with another couple at the Adlon this evening. Won't you please join us?"

Karl arrived at the Adlon barroom to find the Habers and their friends already seated at a corner table. "Dr. Muller," said Haber, rising from his seat, "allow me to present my bride, Hildy, and my dear friends Erwin Rommel and his wife Lucy." Rommel too rose from his seat to shake hands with Karl, who bowed in the direction of Mrs. Rommel.

"I've heard much about you from General Haber," Rommel said as they sat, "especially your adventures in Spain. I know you haven't received public commendation for saving General Haber, but you deserve it."

Karl nodded, showing respect.

When Karl's beer arrived, Haber proposed a toast. "To Dr. Karl Muller, for getting me out of Spain in one piece. And to my friend and colleague Erwin Rommel, who smashed through enemy lines in Belgium and France. Two of the bravest men I know."

"Did you know," Hildy said, after they'd all clinked their glasses together, "that General Rommel's men were the first to cross the Meuse?"

"I didn't know that," Karl said. "Now I'm all the more honored to be in his presence."

"Enough about me," Rommel interrupted. "I'm intrigued by Dr. Muller's exploits. From what the Habers tell us, you were quite a hero in Spain."

"An opportunity presented itself," Karl said.

"The point," Rommel said, "is that you seized the opportunity – that's the essence of success in any struggle. And for that I salute you, Karl."

"I understand that Dr. Muller is also an author of some renown," Lucy Rommel said. "He's published a highly regarded book on public health in Africa. I understand it's been selling quite well in America. I should add that Erwin has published a very important book on infantry attacks. How fortunate we are to be in the company of two such accomplished men!"

"My good friends," Hildy said, raising her glass, "let's drink to you both!" Turning to Karl, she said, "I've read General Rommel's book. I thought it would help me become more conversant with my husband and his colleagues."

"My dear Hildy," Haber said, "you're fast becoming one of the most well informed of all Wehrmacht wives, except of course for Lucy."

"Enough about books and the war," Rommel said. "I understand that Dr. Muller is an excellent skier . . ."

231. HANS KREBS'S BERLIN APARTMENT, JULY 26, 1940, 7:00 P.M.

Alone at the desk in his small study, Hans Krebs reflected on what he'd learned in the past two weeks. He had been following Karl as much as his work schedule allowed. He had seen Karl dine with the Rommels and Habers, speak to business groups and factory workers around Berlin. He had seen Karl enter the Berliner Sportverein and disappear for long runs in the Tiergarten. To all appearances, Karl Muller was leading an exemplary German life – with perhaps an overemphasis on being physically fit. He realized he had been following Karl mostly in the daytime. Only twice had he followed Karl at night – once to the Taverne and once to the address on the Geller Strasse. And now that he had been assigned go get to the bottom of the beatings of SS men, more night work was in order.

Hans reviewed the notes he'd made since he began tailing Karl. Yes, circumstantial evidence suggested that Karl could well be the person responsible for attacking SS officers on the streets of Berlin. Who but a professional fighter in top physical condition could carry out repeated sneak attacks on two – and more recently, three – SS officers, attacks that left the victims unconscious within seconds? Of course, there was no hard evidence, nothing to link Karl directly to the attacks. Hans's old-school police discipline demanded forensic evidence. Indeed, some of the facts argued against Karl's involvement. In the earliest incidents, the masked assailant had attacked by stepping out of some dark corner and punching his victims in the face, chest, and stomach. More recently, though, the assailant was sneaking up on his victims from behind, striking them with sudden sharp blows to the soft tissue where the neck joined the shoulder. Why, Hans wondered, would a trained boxer attack that way?

Hans was thankful that Heydrich had been preoccupied in the past several weeks with the management of his growing SS and SD empires, both in Germany and in the occupied territories. He'd been too busy to bother Hans for reports on his investigation of the beatings. Hans's instincts told him that Heydrich would soon want the name of some suspect, or suspects.

From his notes, Hans saw that the attacks tended to occur in clusters – and that there had been no attacks during the previous two weeks. He'd made numerous calls to Karl's office and found that Frau Frick was always happy to tell him when the Doctor was in town to see him for his nagging lower back problem. But as far as Hans could tell, Karl had been in Berlin when each of the attacks took place.

One thing was certain: if Karl *was* the assailant, he and whomever he was working for hadn't gone to the trouble of faking Karl Ludwig's death and establishing Dr. Karl Muller's presence in Berlin – and in the Nazi Party – just to rough up a few SS officers. And the heroic escape from Madrid? If true, how had Karl pulled that off? It could have been staged. That would have required careful planning and a well-financed team. More than likely, a foreign government was involved, perhaps the British, the Soviets, even the Americans. But why?

Hans stood and looked out at the Oberbaum Bridge. Then he telephoned Ziggy.

232. ROMANISCHES CAFÉ, JULY 29, 1940, 11:45 A.M.

Hans checked his watch. It was almost time. He surveyed the café patrons who had settled on the terrace for an early lunch. None of them looked to be Gestapo, at least none that he recognized. Two of Heydrich's SD goons had been tailing him. He managed to lose them while crossing the Leipziger Strasse.

He paid his bill and headed toward Unter den Linden, checking his watch yet again as he reached the curb in front of the Café Bauer. He saw the taxi waiting – on time to the minute. He recognized the license plate number as the one they gave him when he'd asked for the meeting.

Hans climbed into the back seat where Big Julius was on his left. They'd known each other for fifteen years. "Get on the floor and stay down, Hans. We'll be gentle," Big Julius said, "but we have to take certain precautions, especially when a cop asks for a meeting."

Big Julius handed Hans a black ski cap. "Pull this over your eyes, *schnell*. We don't want you to see where we're going. Someday Heydrich might try to beat it out of you."

The taxi swerved through the noontime Berlin streets, its occupants silent. Hans tried to count the number of times the car turned, and in which direction, but there were just too many.

Hans figured they'd been driving for about twenty minutes when the car made a final sharp right turn and came to a stop. He heard what sounded like a large door swing open. Then the taxi moved forward again, stopping after a door banged shut behind them. He smelled petrol.

Someone pulled the cap off Hans's head and he squinted in the sudden light. He was in a garage – a large, high-ceilinged space with a skylight and two repair pits, a petrol pump, and long shelves filled with batteries, oilcans, and tires. Several gray-haired men in mechanics coveralls were repairing taxis.

Three baby-faced young men – all under the age of twenty, Hans guessed – emerged from the shadows in the rear of the garage. Then the man he expected to see came limping toward him with the help of cane.

"Good to see you, Hans. It's been a while," Ziggy said, extending his hand. "Nice trip?"

"A little dark and uncomfortable, perhaps."

"We have to be careful, Hans." Ziggy pointed at the three young men. "Meet some friends of mine They're all Jews. Right now, they eat, work, and sleep underground – right here in this garage. There've been others like them. We hope there will be more."

Ziggy introduced them, by first name only, as Isidore, Abe, and Howie.

"Isidore here drove the taxi that just picked you up," Ziggy said, pointing to the tallest of the three, a handsome boy with curly dark hair. "We let him drive because he has a straight nose."

"How'd you find these kids?" Hans asked, leaning against the taxi, stretching his cramped legs.

"They found me. All of them were unlucky enough to be born Jewish, but lucky enough to be from well-to-do families, and smart enough to know they needed help. I fenced their considerable assets – jewelry and other valuable items their parents had hidden away before being carted off to resettlement camps in Poland. Isidore's father was a teacher, his mother a painter. Abe's parents were both doctors. Howie's father was a journalist and his mother a good German-Jewish *Hausfrau*. There's been no word from any of them."

Ziggy then turned toward Julius and the three young men. "Why don't you guys go smoke a cigarette and let my friend and me talk in private."

Ziggy then led Hans to a small office that occupied one corner of the main garage. "They're all good boys, and now they're in hiding and work hard," he said. "They work and eat right here in the garage. And they sleep in a crawl space over this office. Guys I like who need a place to hide have been using my crawl space for years. You cops don't catch everyone."

"Ziggy gave Hans time to light a fresh cigarette before going on. "So tell me, Hans, why do you come to me now?"

"Because I need information."

"So ask."

"Have you sold brass knuckles, burglary tools, and ski masks to anyone in the past several weeks?"

"Actually, yes. Big Julius made a delivery like that not long ago. The guy paid cash, of course. We have no idea who he was."

"But Julius actually saw him?

"Met him face to face. Julius said he kind of liked the guy."

"What else?"

"We found a furnished apartment for him."

"Really? Where?"

"That's as much as I can tell you, Hans. In fact, I've told you too much. You know I have to protect my clients."

"Fair enough. Can I talk to Julius? I'd like to know what this guy looked like."

Ziggy shouted for Julius. "That guy who bought the burglary tools and the other stuff, what did he look like?" Ziggy asked, as Julius appeared in the office doorway. "Hans here wants to know."

"He was tall, with dark brown hair," Julius said. "Not a bad looking guy, and well dressed, too. More refined, I'd say, than our usual clients."

"Did he buy anything besides the burglary tools and the brass knuckles?" Hans asked "Anything unusual?"

Ziggy looked at Julius. "Go on, Julius, tell him. You know we can trust Hans."

"He bought some cocaine," Julius said, looking directly at Hans.

"For himself?"

"No, I don't think so. He seemed like the kind of guy who took care of himself. Wouldn't even sample the stuff."

Ziggy slapped his thighs and looked at Julius, then at Hans. "You're looking into the beatings of SS officers?"

"Who said anything about beatings?" Hans asked.

"You didn't have to, my friend. We heard about the SS officers that have had the shit punched out of them by someone using brass knuckles and wearing a ski mask. We trade in information just like you do. You surprise me, Hans. You know that we work with people in the hospitals, people who dress gunshot wounds, people who have access to drugs. People who know things, like where the beaten-up SS officers are being treated. They tell us what they know. And lots of times that's how we help you."

Hans fought to keep his mind from racing ahead too fast.

"That's enough for now, Ziggy. Can I get another free taxi ride out of here?"

"Of course," Ziggy smiled. "But Hans, I may want to see you again soon."

"Just name the time and place, and I'll be there."

233. NUMBER 12 GELLER STRASSE, JULY 31, 1940, 10:55 P.M.

Hans stood in the bus kiosk on Geller Strasse and took a deep drag on his cigarette. He had changed trains twice on the U-Bahn to be sure that Heydrich's goons weren't following him. Recently, he'd checked the city address directory and saw that Günter Jurgen lived at number 12 Geller Strasse.

Hans had been watching as Jurgen turned off the lights and left the apartment just ten minutes earlier. Using a lock pick, he was inside the building, up the stairs, and inside Jurgen's flat. Having searched many apartments, Hans knew right where to look. Using his flashlight, he located the brass knuckles taped under the shelf in the cedar closet. And although it took him a few minutes, he found the envelope taped under the bottom drawer of the desk in the bedroom. He didn't disturb it. Thanks to the information Julius had given him back in the garage, he knew what was inside. The envelope full of cocaine and the other planted items all pointed to a frame-up. But why? What was Karl up to? Hans slipped out of the apartment, locked the door behind him, and reached for the stick of white chalk he'd taken from the office.

234. THE TIERGARTEN, BERLIN, AUGUST 2, 1940, 9:13 P.M.

It was only a two-minute walk along the gravel path to the public lavatory. As Hans relieved himself, Ziggy entered and limped up next to him. Having emptied their bladders without speaking, the two men took turns using the worn washbasin, walked outside, and scanned the scene. Satisfied that they were alone, they sat down on a nearby park bench.

"So what's the quid pro quo?" Hans asked. "I assume that's why you wanted to meet me here."

"My sources in the Gestapo," Ziggy began, "have told me about the Star of David inscribed in chalk on the front door of a certain Günter Jurgen. Don't try and tell me you didn't do it, Hans. I know it was you. One of my men tailed you two night nights ago, first to the Geller Strasse, then to other addresses. We know you shook the Gestapo tail, as you always do, clever cop that you are. But my guy stayed on you. He saw you enter three other apartment buildings. We later learned there was an SS officer living in each of those buildings – and each of these officers ended up with a Star of David inscribed on the front door of his apartment. So, my friend, we had to conclude that you're trying to pin the SS beatings on some shadowy band of Jews."

Hans frowned. "Good work, Ziggy."

Ziggy stared down at the gravel walk. Hans could see that his friend was unhappy.

"I had to force things a bit, Ziggy. I don't have much time. Heydrich wants me to crack this case sooner rather than later. I have to face Heydrich. You don't."

"Sorry Hans, but I don't buy your horseshit. You can handle pressure. What's the real reason?"

"Can't tell you."

"Well, you must have a good reason," Ziggy said. "I respect that. But understand that I too have a reason for what I'm about to ask."

Ziggy turned and looked behind them, then from side to side. It was getting darker. The Tiergarten was deserted except for a few meandering couples.

"It's getting late, Ziggy. Let's have it."

It's about the three boys you met in the garage. You can help them, Hans."

"Okay, how?

"I need help getting them out of Berlin. Out of Europe, in fact."

"Now how do you propose to do that?"

"First the easy part," Ziggy said. "Thanks to some creative pilfering at a Kriegsmarine supply depot and a highly skilled Jewish tailor now in hiding as a dishwasher at my restaurant, I am in possession of several Kriegsmarine officers' uniforms, the type junior officers wear when they're training for U-boat duty. So I have well-fitting uniforms for all three of the boys. They already have the necessary papers and documents, all forged by an experienced Jewish printer, also in hiding. But as you probably noticed back in the garage, two of my three boys have rather pronounced Jewish beaks. And they're all circumcised. In case you haven't heard, German border guards now routinely conduct full-body searches of all men leaving the Reich."

"So you need a doctor?" Hans asked.

"Yes, we need a skilled plastic surgeon. I know you've been seeing someone who'd be perfect for the job. This is the price you have to pay if I'm going to keep my mouth shut about these beatings, if I'm going to let you blame some underground band of Jews."

"You mean Dr. Fern Wagner?"

"Yes, of course. I understand that you two are quite an item. We need her for this job."

"She's in France right now."

"Get her back here, Hans. Do that, and I'll do what I can to calm down the Jewish leaders. As you might imagine, they're pissed that Jews could be blamed for these beatings."

"I'm worried about that, but the Jews would get the blame no matter what," Hans said.

"Regardless, Hans, you need to make amends. And I just told you how you can do it. I'll be speaking to some of the rabbis this week, and hopefully they'll listen. I'll do what I can to see that they don't overreact."

235. SUB-BASEMENT OF THE CAFÉ ZIEGLER, AUGUST 3, 1940, 4:10 A.M.

Seated at a long table near the refrigerators, three bearded men – a rabbi, a surgeon, and a former department store owner – told Ziggy what he expected to hear. Word of the beatings of SS officers had spread through the Jewish neighborhoods. The stories had grown more sensational with each telling. According to the rabbi, on one occasion the assailant had taken on as many as five SS officers, then opened a sewer cover and thrown each of them into the stench. On another night, the assailant stripped his SS victims of their trousers and threw the men into the Spree, or so the story went.

"I'm impressed by such tales," Ziggy said, "happy to hear them. But now let me tell you why I invited you here. As it turns out, I have a contact in the SD, someone I've known for years. He used to be a very good police detective before circumstances forced him to take a job with Heydrich. Believe me, he's no Nazi. He let me know that some unidentified Jewish underground gang could soon get blamed for the beatings."

The department store owner's right hand became a fist. "If that's the case, we must retaliate. We could set fire to Gestapo headquarters. We still have some men who are good at that sort of thing." The surgeon nodded. "What do we have to lose? Enough is enough."

The rabbi was about to speak when Ziggy raised a hand to stop him. "All that, gentlemen, is *dreck*," he said. "Retaliation would yield the worst of all possible results. For one thing, it would inspire the Gestapo to send more of your people to the camps that are springing up in the East. And retaliation might prompt Heydrich to beef up what is now just a one-man task force investigating the beatings."

Ziggy paused to eyeball each of the three men, waited a second and then resumed. "My SD contact doesn't want that to happen. He hasn't told me this, but I believe he doesn't want the person or persons doing the beatings to get caught. He's keeping his reasons to himself. I can only tell you he's a good man and a resourceful detective. He can help me get more of your people out of Berlin – with your cooperation. Do you all understand?"

There were no words, only nods of agreement.

Later that morning, after a short nap on his office couch, Ziggy telephoned Hans to tell him that everything had turned out the way he wanted.

236. THE ADLON, AUGUST 5, 1940, NOON

Frau Frick recognized Dr. Nordencrantz's voice the moment she picked up the telephone. Could Dr. Muller meet him for lunch? There was little doubt in her mind that a meeting with the generous Dr. Nordencrantz augured another large donation for the Party.

The menu proved sparse, featuring what turned out to be a weak lentil soup and black bread. Four uniformed Gestapo officers were seated just two tables away, killing any hope of a candid conversation. Instead, Karl and Scotty North – in the guise of Dr. Nordencrantz – made small talk in German, voicing their conviction that the British would soon come to their senses and respond to Germany's overtures for peace. Karl accepted Nordencrantz's five thousand-mark draft on the Bank of Hannover. That, he knew, would be sure to please Frau Frick, not to mention Hess. After an ersatz coffee, they agreed to stroll around the Pariser Platz.

They walked toward the Brandenburg Gate under gray skies, striding briskly to evade curious ears. "London needs a progress report, Doctor. The PM wants to know when you can strike."

After they'd walked for a moment in silence, Karl said, "I've chosen the spot where I can pull it off. I think I know how to get away with it. The trouble is getting our man to meet me there under circumstances I can control, completing my mission, and getting away with it. What can you tell me about an SS man named Günter Jurgen?"

"Brown knows a few things about this Günter Jurgen chap. Some years ago, he killed Carolyne Wentworth, one of Brown's best agents. Sources tell us that Jurgen enjoys a sterling reputation as an officer on the rise and as a confidant of Heydrich."

"I suppose so," Karl said, "though how 'sterling' his reputation is depends on your point of view. Jurgen's in Paris now, planning the eventual extermination of Jews and potential resisters. He'll start when the Nazi brass decide the time is right."

"The most recent reports I've seen," Scotty said, "indicate that the Germans in Paris are now model house guests, comporting themselves as gentlemen even in the brothels – and that the orders to behave well have come directly from Hitler."

"Really?" Karl said, breaking into a wide grin. "That gives me an idea, Dr. Nordencrantz. Please come with me to the Romanisches Café for a drink. Let's find a quiet table and I'll explain."

237. LE CHABANAIS, 122 RUE PROVENCE, PARIS, AUGUST 14, 1940, 11:00 P.M.

In the blue light of Room 5A in a brothel favored by SS officers, the Abwehr, and the Luftwaffe, Collette Dublanchet, all of eighteen years old, complied with Günter Jurgen's every demand for prolonged oral foreplay. Collette did her job well. She had come to know Günter, who'd been in Paris since June. She found Günter to be a bore. She much preferred the company of young Luftwaffe pilots on leave from Normandy. They were courteous and appreciative and sometimes gave her lovely little gifts of perfume and chocolates.

On this particular summer evening, however, Collette did not even attempt to hide her disdain for Jurgen's fetishes and hurried him to an early ejaculation and its consequent letdown. Disturbed by her lack of interest, Günter dressed hurriedly while she sat on the edge of the bed, her eyes fixed on his image in the mirror. She watched as he adjusted his collar and pulled up the dark trousers of his SS uniform.

"*Cheri*," Collette said, "do you want to know why I rushed you so tonight?" He looked over his shoulder, awaiting an explanation. "It's because you're such a lousy fuck. I just wanted to get it over with."

As Günter spun around to face her, Collette jumped to her feet. "The other Germans who visit me here make me come. They know how to treat me. You don't." She felt a sharp sting on her cheek from his slap. She spat in his face. Two punches to the stomach put her on the floor.

"You're still a lousy fuck," she yelled, spitting at him again. Then Jurgen kicked her in the mouth and left her lying on the rug, bleeding.

As he signed out at the desk, he made no mention that the young woman in Room 5A would require assistance. No matter, he'd be leaving Paris and returning to Berlin the next morning.

238. CAFÉ LAFAYETTE, RUE CADET, AUGUST 15, 1940, 8:00 A.M.

Collette chewed her croissant after dipping it in warm milk. Her cheek was sore and swollen, though nothing was broken and she had all her teeth. She wasn't surprised when an elderly man took a seat at the next table. Neither said a word. The man ordered an espresso and a cognac, downing the cognac in one lusty swallow before perusing the front page of *Le Matin*. He then turned toward her, folded the paper neatly, and handed it to Collette. "Perhaps Mademoiselle would like to read the news."

"Bien sûr, Monsieur. Merci."

Three minutes later, Scotty North was on the Metro headed for the Gare du Nord. Collette was in *les dames*, where she opened the folded newspaper and counted the 20,000 francs she'd earned. Leaving the bathroom with the money secured in her bra, she returned to the brothel and reported the incident with Jurgen to the Madame, who in turn reported it to the Paris *gendarmes*. Collette then arranged to meet her brother in the café near the munitions factory where he worked. With the money she received from Scotty North, they would bribe their way into the *zone libre*.

239. WAGNER INDUSTRIES HEADQUARTERS, BERLIN, AUGUST 23, 1940, 7:15 A.M.

Frederick Wagner picked up the candlestick telephone. He'd asked his switchboard operator to keep the line open to accept a call from France, knowing that Fern would return his call as soon as she could.

"Uncle Frederick?"

353

"Sorry to call so early, Fern. I know your time is precious, so I'll get right to the point. It's Hans — he's experiencing severe chest pains. He contacted me because he knows I can get through to you faster than he could. His doctor, Karl Muller, is off giving a speech in Frankfurt. And Hans, being rather stubborn, says he won't see any doctor but you. I can send our company plane to fetch you and have you here at Tempelhof by late this afternoon. I've already taken the liberty of speaking to Hermann about it. He has no problem with your leaving."

"Can you tell me anything more about Hans, Uncle Frederick?"

"Only that he's resting at home. He's refused to let any SS doctors examine him, and was adamant about seeing no one but you."

"It's not like Hans to be so stupid. But of course I'll see him. Just tell him to rest until I get there."

240. HANS KREBS'S APARTMENT, BERLIN, AUGUST 24, 1940, NOON

Hans was sitting at the kitchen table reading the *Deutsche Allgemeine Zeitung* when he heard Fern open the door, which he'd left unlocked for her. He rose to greet her.

"Shouldn't you be in bed?" Fern asked, setting her black leather medical bag on the table. "Let's get your shirt off and see what's wrong."

Hans held up both hands. "Fern, stop. The fact is I'm fine. There never were any chest pains. I got you here on a pretext — there's something important I need you to do."

"This had better be good, Hans," she said, frowning as she settled into a chair. "You have no idea of the pressure on us back in Normandy. There's a disturbing rumor going around among the Luftwaffe officers. Last weekend, they say, two Heinkels flew over London and dropped bombs right in the center of the city. The story is that they lost their way — but it's still a major foul-up. So far, London has been off limits — only English military installations have been targeted. Hitler, reportedly, was beside himself, screaming and yelling over the phone from Berlin. If the rumor's true, it was a terrible blunder. It gives Churchill license to retaliate against Berlin."

Fern walked to where Hans was standing. "I'm certain of very little these days, Hans, but I know you wouldn't lie to me unless it was important. So tell me what it's about."

"Understand one thing right from the start – the less you know about this the better. Then again, there are some things you *need* to know."

Hans explained about the three Jewish boys and what Ziggy proposed. Fern kicked off her shoes and listened. When he'd finished she remained silent. He knew she was weighing the risks, so he walked onto the terrace, leaving her alone. She had to decide without his help. Hans inhaled the humid summer air. Looking out on the Spree, he watched the slow progress of a coal barge until he felt her hand on his arm.

"Of course I'll do it," she said.

"Good. I never doubted that you would, but it had to be your decision. Now here's what we need to do . . ."

241. HANS KREBS'S APARTMENT, BERLIN, AUGUST 25, 1940, 2:00 P.M.

Hans made a pot of Chase & Sanborn coffee he'd brought back from America. Pouring himself a large cup, he picked up the telephone on the kitchen wall, gave the operator a number, and counted five rings.

As planned, someone picked up after the fifth ring. Rather than saying "hello," Hans simply started talking, taking care to mask his voice.

"The delivery's here now, on schedule, and should arrive at three-thirty this afternoon." It was a precautionary lie. He had arranged with Ziggy to provide a time an hour earlier than his actual planned arrival, a safeguard against the possibility of a tapped telephone or a trap. If there were a trap, it would be sprung before he and Fern arrived – and they would postpone the procedure.

After hanging up, Hans went to the den, settled at his desk, and began jotting notes. Their first obstacle would be to evade the two goons who, Hans knew, Heydrich had staked outside his apartment building to observe his comings and goings.

In the bedroom, Fern began dressing in a crisp while tennis outfit, white sneakers, and a light-blue cotton sweater that Hans had bought for her the previous afternoon.

"You look pretty terrific," he said. "Now just make sure to take everything you need."

She checked the surgical instruments in her shoulder bag, then slipped the shoulder bag into a larger canvas tennis bag that Hans had provided. The tennis bag already held a racket and several balls. Finally, she took several long swallows of the warm black coffee that Hans had left on the dresser.

"Okay, what now?" she asked.

"We have to get out of here without being followed. Since I began working for Heydrich, two SD agents try to follow me pretty much all the time. They're downstairs on the street right now. Easy to recognize – two guys standing around doing nothing. When they see you leave the building, they could get curious and ask some questions.

"But they won't suspect anything if you approach them. Just go up to one of them and ask how to get to the Olympic Park tennis courts on the U-Bahn. Just be natural. If they ask, say that you're from Hannover and are here visiting your sick grandmother, Ute Koenig. Ute's a nice old woman who lives down the hall and never leaves her apartment.

"Meanwhile, I'll leave through a ground-floor in the back of the building, where there are lots of bushes and fir trees. I'll give you a three-minute head start. Take the U-Bahn to the Lehrte Station. Here's the address and apartment number. It's not far from the station. If the concierge asks any questions, tell him you're a friend of Mr. Ziegler, the restaurant owner and that he's expecting you. If you see me on the U-Bahn just ignore me."

242. ZIGGY'S FLAT, AUGUST 25, 1940, 4:30 P.M.

After introducing himself to Fern, Ziggy led her to a long dining table covered with a thin mattress and a fresh linen bedsheet. Fern pressed down on the table and tried to shake it, but the strong chestnut legs didn't creak or budge.

When Hans arrived a moment later, Ziggy showed them the pile of clean white sheets and towels he'd stacked on a buffet table. He'd sent his wife and two teenage daughters to the Café Ziegler for an early dinner, after which they would see *Stagecoach*, a Hollywood Western playing at a cinema near the Potsdamer Platz. After the movie, they would return to the café for dessert, as was their habit. All that would leave just enough time for Fern to perform the surgeries and for Ziggy to clean up the apartment. If there were any unforeseen delays, Ziggy would call the café and have Big Julius make some excuse to detain his wife and daughters.

Fern went to the kitchen and used the largest pot she could find to sterilize her instruments. She instructed Ziggy to keep a pot of water boiling so she could re-sterilize the instruments after each surgery.

Her preparations complete, Fern returned to the dining room and found herself face to face with the three young men, all of whom were trying to mask their nervous fear. "Here's your doctor, boys," Ziggy said. "No formal introductions, no names."

At the window, Hans parted the heavy drapes and peered out. There were no signs of a Gestapo stakeout on the Königstrasse, three floors below.

Fern needed more light, even after the young men had brought all the lamps in the apartment into the dining room and removed their shades.

"Do you have any extension cords, Ziggy?" she asked.

Ziggy nodded yes.

Fern then turned to the three young men. "Now I want each of you take a hot shower with lots of soap and water. Be sure to rinse well with cold water. Pay special attention to your faces and genitals."

After washing her own hands and laying out her sterilized surgical tools on a fresh white towel, Fern asked Ziggy to reposition the lamps for the best possible lighting.

One by one, the boys had returned to the dining room, each clad in a white towel.

"Ziggy, you can scrub up and assist me at the table," Fern said. "You're about to become an anesthesiologist." Gripping the ether dispenser Ziggy had procured for the evening, she doused a clean towel with the colorless liquid, seeing the apprehension in the boys' faces. "Relax, my young friends.

You're going off to dreamland. You, on the left. You're first. Get on the table and lie on your back."

Following Fern's instructions, Ziggy placed an ether-soaked towel over Howie's mouth and nose. On Fern's command, the young man started counting backwards from fifty. He was under at the count of forty-four.

8:00 P.M.

Exhausted after two nose jobs and three reverse circumcisions, Fern washed her instruments a final time and slipped them into her small black shoulder bag, which she placed inside the larger tennis bag.

Ziggy proffered an envelope, which, she presumed, contained an ample quantity of Reichsmarks.

"*Neine, danke,*" she said, looking at Hans. "Hans wouldn't have asked me to do this if it wasn't important. Give it to the boys. They'll need it more than I do."

The three patients were still unconscious, wrapped in clean white sheets, lying on the living room carpet. "They'll start waking up in half an hour," Fern advised.

"Do you have a clean, safe place for them to hide, and a way to get them there?" Hans asked.

"Hans, this is Ziggy. Do you really think I would neglect to plan for such a thing? Someone will be arriving shortly to transport them to a safe apartment. Just don't ask me where."

"My friend, I don't even want to know."

"Just a few quick points before I go," Fern said. "They should rest as much as they can for at least a week. Ice will help reduce the swelling. I trust you have a doctor who can check on them for any possible post-surgical infection. And remind them not to masturbate or have any sexual activity until the swelling and inflammation have completely subsided. Also, they'll have some itchiness but must refrain from scratching themselves. A doctor or a competent nurse should see them every day to change the bandages and make absolutely certain everything stays clean and that there's no infection."

"It's all arranged," Ziggy said. "Thank you, doctor. It's my honor to assist you."

Ziggy telephoned a trusted driver to transport the three young men to the home of a physician he'd known for many years. Then he called the café and asked Big Julius to detain Mrs. Ziegler and his daughters for another hour. He needed more time to tidy up and air the place out.

Hans and Fern took separate taxis back to his apartment building. Fern, still in her tennis outfit, again exchanged pleasantries with the Gestapo agents who had earlier directed her to the U-Bahn station. She entered through the front door only moments before Hans crawled in through the unlocked hallway window on the ground floor.

243. HANS KREBS'S APARTMENT, AUGUST 25, 10:05 P.M.

"It looks as if our precautions paid off," Hans said. "We've made it there and back with no one following us. Let's have a beer."

"Good idea."

Hans expected Fern to be on edge after being dragged into the Berlin netherworld with hardly any preparation. He was wrong. She made room for him on the sofa as they sat together with their beer.

"Thank you, Hans. It's been such a long time since I've used my skills in a wholly good cause. It's different in France. There my skills are used to patch up the airmen so they can go out and drop more bombs on English children.

"Sometimes I cringe when I realize that I'm German. If only I'd never come back. Germany's a trap – and so now is most of Europe. You're the one truly decent person I've met in the past few years, Hans – the only person I can be candid with, and tonight you showed me how I can do something worthwhile. Let's do more of the kind of thing we did tonight. There must be others who . . . "

"No, Fern. It's nice of you to offer, but *no*. It would only be a matter of time before both of us were caught. And that would have devastating consequences for your family and mine. It would be worse than if you'd defected."

Fern fell asleep still dressed in the tennis garb. Hans removed her sneakers, covered her with a blanket, and poured himself another beer.

11:50 P.M.

Just as he began to undress for a night on the couch he heard a faint hum in the night air. At first he thought it was the whir of the electric fan, but it grew louder by the second. Stepping out onto the terrace, he saw searchlight beams crisscrossing the night sky and heard the thump of anti-aircraft guns. Fern appeared on the terrace fastening the sash of Hans's bathrobe. Their eyes followed the searchlight beams, which revealed the squadron of Lancaster bombers off to the west but getting closer. On the street below, pedestrians scurried to find bomb shelters. Hans and Fern heard explosions and watched as fires ignited across the cityscape. The sound of sirens blended with the flak guns.

"Churchill didn't wait very long to respond, did he?" Hans sighed.

"This puts an end to any wishful thinking that the British lack resolve, and that this war is going end soon," Fern said, placing her arm in his.

244. GENERAL STAFF HEADQUARTERS, BERLIN, SEPTEMBER 9, 1940, 5:00 P.M.

Many in the German military elite had strong reservations about Operation Sea Lion – the proposed cross-Channel invasion of Britain, but General Erwin Rommel was not among them. He had often expressed his conviction that the assault was worth the risk. He arrived in Berlin late that afternoon from Normandy, where his men were training for Sea Lion, and proceeded directly to General Staff headquarters. There he met Generals Haber, Keitel, and Jodl as well as Frederick Wagner. General Rundstedt had declined to attend, but asked General Friedrich Paulus, the methodical but indecisive Deputy Chief of the General Staff, to take his place.

Over a map of southern England spread out on the conference room table, Rommel presented his tactical plan: his forces would cross the Channel and land near Rye, then make a quick thrust inland toward Hawkhurst. Rommel explained how the well-paved English roads would facilitate a swift invasion using tanks and other motorized vehicles with a minimum of wear and tear.

When Rommel completed his presentation, General Paulus turned toward Frederick and began peppering him with questions about the durability of his Panzers. Frederick had prepared for the onslaught. He knew what the Panzers he built could and could not do. He also suspected that Paulus was less interested in the roadworthiness of the new Panzers than in keeping an eye on the man who would be commanding them.

"Don't you think, Herr Wagner," Paulus asked, "that a mission like Operation Sea Lion might overtax our Panzers? Repairs and replacement parts will be an issue. Remember, at Dunkirk we had to halt operations and refit dozens of tanks, thus allowing thousands of British and French soldiers to escape. Can you assure us that won't happen again?"

Rommel sat up straight and held his tongue. Everyone present knew that Rommel's Panzer Division had been nowhere near Dunkirk. Instead, they'd been racing across northern France to reach Cherbourg, ignoring orders to halt and regroup. Paulus had asked the question to remind everyone of Rommel's independent nature.

Frederick had been expecting the question, or one like it. "In the end, General Paulus," he said in measured tones, "we must realize that our Panzers, good as they are, cannot think for themselves. Brave soldiers inside those Panzers, commanded by courageous field officers remain indispensable."

245. REINHARD HEYDRICH'S ZEHLENDORF HOME, BERLIN, SEPTEMBER 15, 1940, 11:00 AM.

Heydrich sat in his shady garden waiting for Admiral Canaris and his family to arrive for their regular Sunday morning croquet game. Like the lunches they frequently took together, the lawn game provided Heydrich and Canaris an opportunity to maintain family social ties while exchanging intelligence updates and gossip. It was their way of paying lip service to the "Ten Commandments," an informal agreement forged to manage the rivalry between Heydrich's SD and Canaris's Abwehr, keeping each man off the other's turf. Though neither would admit it, both took the commandments as a joke.

Canaris had called earlier to say that Frederick Wagner would be joining them, if Heydrich didn't mind. Frederick had told Canaris that he needed to bring some sensitive matter to Heydrich's attention.

Heydrich and Canaris played their first round of croquet with characteristic competitive zeal. Frederick asked to take on the winner, who, as it turned out, was Heydrich. Heydrich accepted the challenge and soon prevailed over Frederick.

"You're a great competitor, Reinhard," Frederick exclaimed, "but that hardly surprises me." Before they rejoined Canaris, Frederick asked to have a private word with Heydrich on "a delicate matter, one outside the Admiral's sphere of interest." The two men sat together in the shade of a large elm. "This matter," Frederick resumed, "relates to war production at one of our munitions factories in Paris, which, as you know, is one of my primary responsibilities."

Heydrich nodded. He was well aware that Frederick oversaw production quotas in the Paris factories.

"As you also know," Frederick went on, "we're trying to get as much work as we can out of the French labor force, but it's a constant challenge. While most of them are glad to have a job, they've grown lazy over the years under the protection of leftist trade unions. The slightest provocation can trigger a slowdown, sabotage, or even terrorist acts."

"Worker discipline is your purview, Frederick. How does this concern me?"

"It becomes your concern when one of your top aides, a Hauptmann named Günter Jurgen, beats up a whore in a Paris brothel, and the girl's brother – a munitions-plant worker in Paris – tells his co-workers. Many of them have been Communist Party members and would rather stage a slow-down than build bombs for the Luftwaffe. By now, word of the despicable act has spread beyond the plant. Our Paris assembly line's been jammed three times in the past two weeks after errant pieces of metal somehow found their way into the machinery. These aren't *accidents* if you ask me."

Heydrich folded his arms. "I understand, Frederick. I'll request a full report from Paris. I had high hopes for Jurgen, but he's clearly prone to excess and bad behavior where women are concerned. Rest assured that I'll do all I can to resolve this problem. Now let's rejoin the Admiral."

As soon as the Canaris family and Frederick were gone, Heydrich's thoughts returned to Günter Jurgen. He had put Jurgen on the fast track in part because he admired the younger man's athleticism. Jurgen had several useful talents. His surveillance of Dr. Karl Muller had been exemplary. So was his quick disposal of the British woman who had been spying on him early in his career. And Jurgen's devotion to the Führer and the Fatherland was indisputable, perhaps even excessive. What's more, Jurgen seemed to glory in his relationship with Heydrich.

But as useful as Jurgen was, Heydrich realized that the Hauptmann was a sadistic bully and an abusive sex addict. These messy brothel incidents – first in Warsaw and now in Paris – could upset Adolf Hitler.

Indeed, the Führer's sexual proclivities were the subject of countless hushed conversations by men close to him and by others who didn't know what they were talking about. No matter. Heydrich knew he had invested too much in advancing his own career to suffer for Jurgen's indiscretions. It could only be a matter of time, Heydrich realized, before word of Jurgen's deeds reached Hitler's ears. It was not possible to predict how Hitler would react – and such uncertainty was not acceptable to Reinhard Heydrich.

246. HEYDRICH'S VACATION COTTAGE, FEHMARN ISLAND, ON THE BALTIC SEA, SEPTEMBER 20, 1940, 8:00 A.M.

The Baltic tide was at its lowest. Günter Jurgen and Reinhard Heydrich had just finished a three-mile run and ten wind sprints on the long stretch of flat gray sand at the water's edge. Their faces were red from the sharp wind. Heydrich suspected that Jurgen had purposely finished just behind him in each of the sprints. Although he was a well-conditioned thirty-six-year-old who excelled at fencing, riding, and skiing, Heydrich knew that the younger man, who'd undergone extensive training as a boxer, could have beaten him.

As they emerged from the sea after a quick dip in the foaming surf and were jogging toward the small vacation cottage, Heydrich told Jurgen to remain in the cottage and keep his wife, Lina Heydrich, company that afternoon.

"I need to attend a meeting at the Café Frida," he said to Jurgen. "I'll call you when I'm done, and you can meet us for a drink. The café isn't far from the cottage."

247. CAFÉ FRIDA, FEHMARN ISLAND, 5:00 P.M.

As Jurgen walked up to the bar, Heydrich greeted him with a hearty slap on the back. Being in Heydrich's presence always made his spirits soar. Jurgen felt especially honored as Heydrich introduced him to Major Walter Schellenberg.

"Walter specializes in foreign intelligence," Heydrich told him. "Someday, with his help, we'll be as adept at espionage as the British."

Schellenberg extended his hand to Jurgen. "Reinhard has many good things to say about you, Hauptmann. He tells me you're a diligent officer and an excellent boxer."

"I thought the three of us should have a martini," Heydrich said. "By the way, did you find Frau Heydrich to be pleasant company?" Heydrich asked Jurgen as the three men sat at a table near the bar.

"Yes, I did," Jurgen answered. "We had a tasty lunch of lentil soup."

Heydrich handed Jurgen a martini in a tall stem glass.

"And what else happened, Hauptmann?"

"Not much else."

"Not much else?"

"We talked."

"What about?"

"The war mostly."

Heydrich raised his voice enough to get the attention of the half-dozen other uniformed officers at the bar.

"Now wasn't there more to it, Hauptmann?" Heydrich's tone turned shrill. Schellenberg excused himself for the men's room.

"You took a swim in the Baltic, didn't you? Admit it, Hauptmann."

Jurgen realized that Heydrich could have assigned someone to spy on the cottage and the grounds, someone who might testify to anything Heydrich wanted, regardless of what had really happened – or not happened.

"Well," Jurgen said, tentatively, taking several quick sips of his drink, "we went swimming before lunch."

"Well, what else?

"Nothing," Jurgen stammered.

"Admit it, Jurgen – you tried to force yourself on my wife. For God's sake, be a man about it."

"All we did was have a swim, eat lunch, and talk."

"You expect me to believe that! From you of all people! A man with a reputation for screwing any woman he can get his hands on . . . a man who bullies prostitutes. Please understand how serious this is, Hauptmann. I should inform you that the martini you appear to be enjoying contains a lethal poison, a slow-acting, highly effective toxin fatal in even the smallest doses. Should you decide to come clean and admit that you tried to fuck my wife, I'll give you the antidote. The choice is yours, Hauptmann."

Shocked and shaken, Jurgen looked at the floor. His head was spinning – maybe Heydrich *had* poisoned him. Heydrich snapped his fingers while looking toward the bar. In the silence that followed, the SS men who'd been drinking there retreated to a table in the far corner of the café.

Motioning to a waiter, Heydrich snapped his fingers again and the waiter returned with another martini as if on cue. Heydrich shoved the fresh drink toward Günter Jurgen.

"Never mind," he said. "Here's your second martini, one that contains the antidote. Drink it now and return to Berlin to await your new orders. Don't bother going back to the cottage to pick up your things. We'll have them sent to you. Schellenberg will arrange for your transport back to Berlin."

Minutes later a military staff car pulled up outside the café. Schellenberg barked orders to the driver and again extended his hand to a glassy-eyed Günter Jurgen. "Don't take it too hard, Hauptmann. The son of a bitch tried the same thing on me."

"Was my martini really poisoned?"

"Who knows? I'm alive and so are you."

Jurgen sat frozen in his seat on the long trip back to Berlin.

"Thanks for helping me get rid of Jurgen," Heydrich said as Schellenberg re-entered the Frida. "Now he can resume his work in the SS, though I don't really care what he does. I don't need to see him again."

248. BERLIN, GERMAN GENERAL STAFF HEADQUARTERS, OCTOBER 20, 1940, 2:35 P.M.

In staff meetings and other high-level gatherings, Hitler had begun ranting about his mistrust of Stalin and his fear of an attack from the Eastern Front. And that fear only added to his misgivings about any prospective cross-Channel assault against Britain. Now Haber had a new assignment: to draft a comprehensive plan for the invasion and destruction of the Soviet Union. Knowing that he needed privacy to write, Haber won clearance to work on the assignment from his home, away from the day-to-day distractions and intrigues in the General Staff offices.

Still, much of his work required him to be at General Staff headquarters, where he could consult with others, gather information, and get advice.

Frederick Wagner's unexpected arrival in Haber's office provided the general with a welcome interruption. "I can tell by the look on your face that you've heard the news," Haber said, rising to greet Frederick.

"Yes, Martin, I'm afraid I have. It's just as we feared. Jodl telephoned me to request plans for railroad cars that would fit the wider gauge track the Russians use. Why don't we get some fresh air?"

249. CHANNING BROWN'S BAYSWATER RESIDENCE, OCTOBER 30, 1940, 3:42 A.M.

In the small den that served as his home office, Channing Brown pored over reports. Since the evacuation at Dunkirk and the French collapse, Brown had been concentrating, as best he could, on maintaining his network of operatives on the Continent, managing to keep most of them alive, in place, and productive. There had been the inevitable setbacks. His unit had lost three agents since Dunkirk. All told, SIS had lost some twenty agents in the same period. Brown spent a fair amount of time worrying about the Soviet agents who had infiltrated SIS – no one knew how many there were or what information they were relaying to Moscow.

He had worked through that night's air raid, which, by the sound of it, was concentrated in the Docklands. A terse call from Churchill that afternoon had compelled Brown to work long into the night. The Prime Minister wanted another progress report on Jackhammer, which was his way of reminding Brown that it had been six years since they had chatted at Chartwell.

In a response that would fail to satisfy Churchill, Brown could only say that the challenge of getting Karl and Hitler together in a private meeting was proving far more difficult than anticipated. Brown's reminder that rushing matters could be dangerous – or even counterproductive – had not sat well with Churchill, not when Londoners were sleeping in the Underground and some believed that the Wehrmacht would arrive before winter. At the same time, there were tantalizing reports from reliable agents that Hitler had postponed a cross-Channel invasion and was focusing instead on plans for a German invasion of the Soviet Union.

Brown was about to light the last cigarette from his pack of Players when he felt Jillian's gentle fingers massaging the back of his neck.

"For heaven's sake, Chan, please come to bed. Between work and the air raids, I don't think you've slept more than three hours any night this week."

Brown squeezed Jillian's soft hand and rose without speaking. Jillian followed him into the bathroom, putting her arm around his waist as he splashed water on his unshaven face. "Is there anything you want to talk about?" she whispered.

"No, except to say that I've managed to put a thoroughly decent chap in a totally horrid position – and now I have to help him."

"Must you go to the office tomorrow to do it?"

"No, I suppose not. I could work here. Might help me think, might even be a bit more secure," he muttered, toweling himself off.

"Fine, I'll telephone in the morning to say you're ill," Jillian said a moment later. Brown was already asleep.

250. CHANNING BROWN'S RESIDENCE, OCTOBER 31, 1940, 6:00 P.M.

The bedside clock told Brown that he'd slept through the day. He put on his robe and slippers and went downstairs. Jillian was at her desk in the den. He saw the neat pile of typescript pages at her elbow, the top page showing bold strokes from a grease pencil. Colleagues at the *Times* called it her *deadly weapon*.

"Busy?" he asked.

"Rather," she hummed, feeling his boney left hand on her shoulder.

"What did you tell the office?"

"I spoke to Jamie. He was rather delighted that you wouldn't be there to bother him. Then I phoned my office and told them I'd be working here, your being ill and all. That way, I'd be able to answer any phone calls on the first ring, so it wouldn't disturb your sleep."

"And your office believed it?"

"Well, it's not exactly a tall tale. You *were* in desperate need of rest. And I needed to stay here to use my own books to fact-check a series we're running on how the Germans were able to run us off the Continent last spring. We may have trouble getting some of it past the military censors. Those chaps must have a look at it, but I'm sure the paper will publish it. The writer is a Cambridge military scholar. He contends that just as the machine-gun and fixed-position defenses were the prevailing facts of life in the previous war, lightning-fast offense – meaning tanks and warplanes – is now proving decisive. The trouble with the piece is that it's all about machines and numbers and says almost nothing about the motivations and personalities of Hitler and his generals. What can you tell me about them without violating security?"

Brown pulled up a chair to sit next to her. "Well, I can say we've known for some time that Hitler takes credit for every military success and blames others for anything that goes wrong. He doesn't suffer rivals. You'll recall that back in '34, the year after he came to power, Hitler had his longtime colleague Ernst Röhm killed along with a number of Röhm's friends and allies. And Röhm had been instrumental, some say indispensable, in building the Nazi Party. But Hitler and some of those around him believed that Röhm had ambitions of his own. It was a true bloodbath. So it'll be interesting to see how Hitler handles other potential rivals, especially any that might emerge in the wartime military."

"But it seems to me," Jillian said, "that Hitler doesn't mind when that rather sizeable fellow Göring gets press attention. Doesn't that undercut your theory?"

"True," Brown said, "Göring does get a lot of attention – and a lot of credit. But our top agents in Berlin inform us that Göring – although he's utterly ruthless, greedy, and highly ambitious – is content to defend his number-two position in the Reich. In other words, he would never pose a direct threat to Hitler. Göring loves his titles and the trappings of power but appears content to limit himself to defending what he's already achieved. He takes skiing holidays, plays tennis, and spends time with his electric trains. Hitler knows that Göring won't challenge him for the top position."

"A bloke named Rommel also appears to be getting a lot of press coverage in Germany and America, though not so much here in Britain," Jillian said, pointing to an open folder and a pile of clippings at the corner of her desk.

"Ah yes, Rommel," Brown sighed. "There's no disputing Rommel's success. His Panzers chased the French all the way to Cherbourg. It's no secret that Rommel is quite capable, even a bit daring. In fact, he's too daring in the eyes of some colleagues. At the same time, he's a German soldier – loyal to a fault. He does, however, have critics among the upper echelons of Hitler's high command. They question Rommel's methods. His critics think that he violates a long-established military doctrine , which says that a general should stay behind the front lines. In France, Rommel was often in the lead tank. He's been known to leap out of a staff car to spur on a team of engineers repairing a bombed-out bridge so that his tanks can cross a river. At times, he even directs infantry and artillery fire. He has a reputation for altering established strategy based on a hunch."

"How does Hitler view Rommel then?"

"No one really knows, not yet anyway. I think it's fair to say that Hitler now sees himself as a player on the world stage. So you could conclude that he might well resent Rommel's growing renown, inside and outside Germany. But that's only a guess, mind you."

"God," Jillian said, "I'm famished. Isn't it time we had a proper supper? Would you like a Scotch?"

"Not tonight. My head feels quite clear after all that sleep. Maybe I'll just have a sandwich and get back to work."

After coffee, Brown closed the blackout curtains, sat at his desk, and tapped the eraser of his pencil on the blank yellow pad. How *did* one get a chap like Hitler alone? If Karl had figured that out, he wasn't telling anyone. Karl's insistence that he alone plan the mission's final stages complicated matters but did not stop Brown from entertaining his own ideas.

His talk with Jillian earlier that evening stuck in his mind. Men like Hitler had an instinctive fear of rivals. The bigger the bully, the thinner the skin. The more powerful they became, the less secure they felt. Most of those close to Hitler, Brown realized, were classic Yes Men. But this fellow Rommel might be different. He appeared to have a real flare for the dramatic, not unlike Caesar.

Brown recalled a report from the code breakers at Bletchley Park. Rommel and one of his Panzer Groups, the report said, would soon be going to North

Africa to bolster Mussolini's beleaguered legions, which were failing in their attempt to take Egypt and choke the British jugular at Suez. From North Africa, Rommel might well break through to the Levant and perhaps on to the Saudi Peninsula. Or he might continue northeast into Iraq, Persia, and the Caspian Basin. These were barren lands with one thing in common – the promise of untapped oil deposits.

What did Hitler hope to accomplish by sending Rommel to North Africa? How much trust did he place in Rommel? And how could Karl exploit that trust or lack of trust?

Brown made some notes, then called the Foreign Office switchboard. He stayed on the line while the operator found the number and placed a call to Galveston, Texas. While he waited, Brown opened a fresh pack of Players.

9:03 P.M.

After a productive conversation with an old acquaintance, Brown heard the familiar wail of air-raid sirens. He declined Jillian's invitation to join her in their Anderson Shelter, motioning for her go on alone. He needed to do some more work and reached for his portable typewriter.

11:31 P.M.

Brown read over the draft he had typed in a single two-hour sitting. He was pleased that it captured many of the ideas he'd been mulling over that evening. Nonetheless, it was an initial effort. To refine his idea, he needed to consult with an authority on geostrategic issues.

251. OFFICE OF SIR JOHN DILL, CHIEF OF THE IMPERIAL GENERAL STAFF, HEADQUARTERS OF THE IMPERIAL STAFF, NOVEMBER 1, 1940, 7:45 A.M.

Brown sat up straight in his chair as Sir John read the six-page typescript. Chief of the Imperial General Staff since the German breakthrough at Sedan, Sir John had a reputation for uncanny strategic insight.

"Well, Brown," Sir John said, pushing the typescript aside, "I dare say that you've produced a rather provocative report. If the Germans were to follow your line of reasoning, they might just win this bloody war. Of course, we know from intelligence sources that they already have a somewhat similar scheme, Plan Orient, which envisions a giant pincer movement with a force from Africa and another from southern Europe eventually coming together to capture the Caspian region."

"I know of Plan Orient," Brown said. "The combination of northern and southern forces is a military planner's wet dream."

Sir John nodded. "What I like about your plan is that it emphasizes the southern thrust, making the northern operation all but unnecessary. It would achieve the same results as Plan Orient at less cost and make any potential incursion into Soviet territory unnecessary."

"I'm glad you think so," Brown said. "Rest assured, Sir, that your assistance has been extremely valuable."

252. BROWN'S MAYFAIR OFFICE, NOVEMBER 1, 1940, NOON

That morning, Brown borrowed an Olympia typewriter from the German desk at MI6. He also procured a dozen sheets of German General Staff stationery, pilfered by a deep-cover agent and preserved with loving care at Whitehall. With Scotty North at his side, Brown translated his report into German, writing in longhand. Then, with extra assistance from Jamie Creel, they took turns typing the report in German script, making sure that every passage conformed to the style of the German military.

Once they'd finished, Scotty tucked the typescript into a padded envelope and headed off to Whitehall, where he would pick up his tickets and foreign currency. He'd be flying first to Zurich. After a brief stay over at the British Embassy there, he would entrain for Berlin disguised as Dr. Nordencrantz and deliver the report to that wonderful bakery on the Dorotheenstrasse. Brown had his own travel plans. He would fly first to Lisbon, where he would board the Pan Am Clipper for New York.

253. THE WARWICK HOTEL, MANHATTAN, NOVEMBER 5, 1940, 9:00 P.M.

Brown recognized McGruder the instant the Texan opened the door to his penthouse suite. McGruder was still lean and straight, but his face was now weathered by years in the sun, and his curly red hair was laced with gray. For Brown, seeing McGruder brought memories of Gallipoli, of the damp jail cell, of the man who called himself Kemal, and of his meeting with McGruder in Baghdad after the first war. Kemal, later known as Atatürk, had risen to become an effective of leader to the Turks before dying of a heart attack in 1937.

Now Brown needed something that McGruder could provide – hard facts to back up the claims he'd advanced in the memo, which Scotty North had recently put in the hands of a highly placed operative in Germany.

Brown knew that the interwar years had been good for McGruder. McGruder Geophysical had become the leading firm specializing in oil exploration and refining – discovering new crude oil deposits and then figuring out the most cost-effective means of drilling and refining that oil for consumption. And consumption had grown astronomically in recent years: gas-thirsty cars and trucks, and now battleships, tanks, and war planes. His firm had its headquarters in Galveston and offices in New York, Berlin, London, Budapest, and Baghdad. Shares of the firm traded on the New York Stock Exchange.

Brown accepted McGruder's offer of a Johnnie Walker Black over ice and followed McGruder through the open French doors onto a balcony. The clear air of the Indian summer evening and the Manhattan lights invigorated Brown, weary after months of blackouts and bombs.

After a moment, McGruder suggested that they retire to the suite's drawing room to focus on the matter at hand. They sat at the table and McGruder took a map of the Middle East from his briefcase. Once unfolded, the map covered most of the table. McGruder used a red Crayola crayon to mark specific sections of the map as he responded to Brown's questions.

An hour later, the two men were strolling east toward Fifth Avenue, enjoying the evening air, which had just begun to cool. At McGruder's suggestion, they stopped into the Oak Bar at the Plaza Hotel, where they took a corner booth and ordered another Johnnie Walker.

"You're asking me to cowboy up to a big risk," McGruder said. "I could end up in the basement of the Prinz-Albrecht-Strasse."

"I work with men and women who take that chance every day."

"And you want me to join them?"

"Quite so," Brown said, "because you have the credibility to support what's already been said in a separate but highly sensitive document, which one of my best agents will soon place before curious eyes in Berlin."

"How much?"

"A one-time payment of a million pounds sterling, over and above the annual retainer we agreed on back in Baghdad. Plus expenses for personnel, equipment, and insurance. The million will go into in a numbered Swiss account – half when you sign and the balance on delivery of the final report we discussed back at the Warwick."

Brown knew that this was no time to argue price with the Texan. He reached into his vest pocket for the contract, printed on the stationery of a Swiss banking corporation whose letterhead identified Sir Crawford Ware as Chairman and Brown as Chief Executive Officer. Brown wrote in the amount of the fee.

After McGruder signed, they sealed the deal with another Johnnie Walker.

254. WHITE'S CLUB LONDON, NOVEMBER 9, 1940, NOON

Channing Brown sat in a comfortable Chesterfield chair enjoying the sanctuary of the White's Club coffee room and admiring portraits of the club's more accomplished members, all dead. He sipped strong black coffee, a much-needed elixir. An air raid the night before had robbed him of all but two hours' sleep. He had just begun feeling a surge of energy when his guest arrived.

Chip Egan, London Bureau Chief of *Life* magazine, was a lean twenty-eight-year-old from Columbus, Georgia. His straight dark hair had already begun to thin and turn gray, and his right thumb and index finger were stained yellow from nicotine.

"Y'all said on the telephone that this wouldn't be an ordinary interview," Egan said in a raspy Georgia drawl. "In exchange for my not asking questions about the nature of your work, you'll give me an exclusive story idea I can pitch to my boss in New York. Is that right?"

"Quite so," Brown said.

"Okay, Mr. Brown, let's have it. In less than an hour I've got to meet a photographer who's shooting the bombed-out row houses in Lambeth."

Though he hated being rushed, Brown knew that Egan was working under punishing deadlines. "I understand your hurry, lad, so here's the fast version. We have reason to believe that a prominent German industrialist would be willing to cooperate in an exclusive picture story about his plants, which are producing planes, tanks, and other materiel for the German war effort. We're quite sure this industrialist will cooperate."

"Why?"

"Because Hitler and Goebbels want the world to believe that the RAF bombing raids on Berlin are having little effect on their weapons production. And they especially want the Americans to believe that."

Egan took a deep drag on his freshly lit Camel. "We've been trying to get a story on German war production since the goddamn war began, but we always get turned down by that little shit Goebbels. Didn't want us snooping, I figure. Probably thought we'd be spying for y'all."

Brown nodded. "And that's quite understandable from his perspective. But matters have changed now that we British are dropping tons of explosives on Berlin almost every night, which Goebbels and Göring once boasted would never happen. So now Goebbels needs to show the world that Nazi war production continues apace despite the bombing."

"I suppose," Egan mused, not convinced. "The Germans have been quite secretive about the precise locations of their plants."

"Don't worry. We know where they are."

Egan ground out his cigarette in the ashtray. "Okay, I'll telephone New York on this as soon as I get back to my office. I'll need their green light."

"I'm afraid not," Brown said. "Your office poses too great a risk. Come to the SIS office in Whitehall at half-seven this evening, the very heart of the business day in New York. I'll see that you're shown directly to my office, where you can telephone on a secure line."

"Anything else?" Egan asked.

"Yes, one rather critical matter. As it happens, there's a Wehrmacht Panzer Corps Commander who emerged as something of a hero during the German blitzkrieg in France last spring," Brown said. "We'd also like your Berlin bureau to do a brief accompanying story on this commander – what I believe you journalists call a 'sidebar' – one that plays up his leadership ability, initiative, and heroism. And the heroism angle would in no way be a contrivance because there's so much evidence to back it up. Indeed, this commander – his name is Rommel, Erwin Rommel – is renowned for getting up on the line himself and taking charge of matters. His story would be the perfect complement to your story on tank production."

"So the piece on Rommel would be the quid pro quo for your greasing the skids on the factory scoop."

'Right you are, Mr. Egan."

"Okay, see you at seven-thirty," Egan said as he rose from the table. "It sounds like a decent spread for *Life*. Now if you'll excuse me, I have to leave for Lambeth."

"Off with you then, lad. I know that you Yank reporters are keen on protecting your sources – so remember, the factory story and the sidebar are *your* idea."

255. THE SPREE EMBANKMENT, BERLIN, NOVEMBER 15, 1940, 3:10 P.M.

They stared at the flat water in the gray afternoon light. Karl listened as Scotty North, disguised as Dr. Nordencrantz, spoke. "Karl, this is straight from Brown. He knows you've established credibility with Hitler, but we all know you haven't been able to gain the access required to get alone with the bugger and finish him off."

"So?"

"Well Karl, Brown has thought on the matter and has an idea that just might get you that opportunity. He's already set matters in motion."

"Hold it, Scotty. That's not our deal."

"Hear me out, Karl. If Brown's scheme works, you'll have something you don't have now – a reason to be *alone* with Hitler, with no generals, security guards, or flunkies around. How you bloody well handle things once you're in the meeting remains your affair."

Karl looked away toward the river. "Okay, Scotty, I'm listening."

256. THE HABER RESIDENCE, TIERGARTENSTRASSE, BERLIN, NOVEMBER 21, 1940, 7:00 P.M.

Karl arrived at the Haber residence promptly at seven, having received an invitation by telephone only that afternoon. General Haber greeted him with a warm handshake and led Karl directly to his study.

"Good to see you, Karl. Hildy's gone to the cinema with some friends, as she often does. She has so many friends that I can't keep track of them all. I was hoping that you and I might catch up on a few things. I went horseback riding with Frederick Wagner in the Tiergarten this morning, and he mentioned that he wants you to address the workers at his suburban Wedding factory. With that in mind, he thought this might give you some idea of what's happening at his factory there," Haber said, handing Karl a copy of the latest of *Life*.

"It's an American magazine, very popular I'm told. Frederick brought it back from Stockholm. Look inside."

Karl leafed through the magazine until he got to the photo spread on the armaments factory.

"I showed the article to the Führer this morning," Haber said. "It says that Frederick's plant in Wedding is assembling record numbers of tanks despite the British air raids."

Karl perused the four-page spread, which featured black-and-white photos of smiling workers, gleaming Panzers fresh off the assembly line, and a lively interview with Frederick Wagner, who praised his workforce for their ability to maintain such high levels of productivity in the face of stepped-up British bombing.

"Now turn the page and look at the next story," Haber said.

Karl flipped to the page featuring two photos of Erwin Rommel, one a simple headshot and the other showing Rommel, in uniform, on the turret of a Panzer as it drove down a rubble-strewn street in Cherbourg. Under the headline "A New Breed of German General: Erwin Rommel, Maestro of the Blitzkrieg," the article began: "If Adolf Hitler's Wehrmacht reaches London, Generalmajor Erwin Rommel and his 7th Panzer Division may well be the first to rumble down Piccadilly. At once a highly disciplined Prussian officer and an intrepid opportunist, Generalmajor Erwin Rommel . . . "

"Now let me tell you what happened at this morning's briefing at the Chancellery," Haber said. "Rundstedt, Paulus, and Goebbels were all there. Frederick had suggested that I show the article to the Führer, so I did. The Führer was happy enough with the first story, but when he saw the Rommel piece, he threw the magazine across the table. German victories, he shouted, were the result of our soldier's collective bravery, not their generals' tactical vision."

Karl continued to look at the magazine, fighting a sudden instinct to read more about what was happening in America.

"I could tell," Haber went on, "that the Führer's anger delighted Paulus and Rundstedt, who find Rommel's unorthodox tactics unacceptable. Perhaps I should have spoken up on Rommel's behalf, but I didn't. It would only have intensified the Führer's rage and inspire him to question Erwin's loyalty. You must understand why our Führer has a deep fear of generals who become too strong or too popular. That's why every general, in fact, every German soldier, must swear an oath of loyalty to him."

After a silence lasting several seconds, Karl directed his gaze toward Haber and spoke in a deliberate tone.

"Allow me to offer a suggestion, General."

"Please, Karl, what is it?"

"Assign me to the 7th Panzer Division as Rommel's chief medical officer."

"Watch what you ask for, Karl. Although Rommel doesn't know it yet, he'll soon be leaving the lush farmlands of Normandy for the arid sands of northern Africa to assist our Italian allies. But, tell me Karl, what do you hope to accomplish by serving with Rommel?"

Karl feigned surprise at the news of Rommel's imminent assignment to Africa, even though Scotty North had already told him about it when they met on the Oberbaum Bridge.

"Serving with Rommel," Karl said, "will enable me to verify his loyalty to the Führer. When I return to Berlin, I can report my findings in a private, confidential meeting and put the Führer's mind to rest."

"Rommel is a fellow officer and a good friend," Haber said. "I don't like the idea of spying on him."

"It wouldn't be spying," Karl responded. "We both know that Rommel is loyal. But we also know that Hitler might suspect otherwise, especially since – based on what you've told me – some of the officers in the Führer' inner circle are visibly disgruntled by Rommel's imaginative approach. The Führer needs to know he can trust Rommel, and he needs to hear that from someone who's spent time in Rommel's presence."

"I'm not so sure," Haber said, looking directly at Karl.

"I quite understand your reluctance, General. But after serving with Rommel in Africa I'll have grounds to testify to his absolute loyalty to the Führer."

"I have no doubt of that. Still, I don't like it. Erwin's my friend."

"Look at it this way, General Haber: Since the article in *Life* has triggered the Führer's suspicions, the Führer might well ask someone *less* friendly to Rommel to check up on him – and those scenarios could spell trouble for Rommel."

Haber folded his arms and turned toward the picture window that over-looked the Tiergarten. Karl waited to let Haber absorb what he'd said.

"Have you anything else to say, Karl?"

"Only that assigning me to serve with Rommel is the best way to reassure the Führer of Rommel's loyalty. Hitler has already shown confidence in me. And since I'm not a career military man, I have no ax to grind, no motivation to report anything but the truth. Most important, perhaps, what I tell the Führer will be based on firsthand battlefield experience."

Karl noticed that Haber still seemed skeptical.

"My report would be for the Führer only. It would be a confidential meeting – and no one would have to know except you, me, and Hitler."

Haber nodded.

"And since I'm not attached permanently to any unit, I'm no one's prop-erty, so to speak. Assigning me to serve with Rommel can be accomplished with a minimum of red tape – just as Göring sent me to Spain and Heydrich sent me to Poland and Norway."

"I see, Karl. I'll try and discuss the matter with the Führer tomorrow eve-ning. Hildy and I will be attending a reception he's hosting for Count Ciano, the Italian Foreign Minister."

"Good. Then I'll prepare to take another break from my practice and fundraising activities."

257. WHITEWALL, NOVEMBER 23, 1940, 4:00 P.M.

Brown stepped into the smoky cocktail reception and its sea of familiar faces. The event's purpose was to introduce a bright young recruit. He was one of those who'd been able to escape from Dunkirk, a former journalist with a reputation for insight and resourcefulness. He'd seen war firsthand as a cor-respondent in Spain and more recently in Belgium and France.

SIS chief Stewart Menzies greeted Channing Brown with a firm hand-shake. "Channy, you know just about everyone here, but let me introduce you to our newest man. Menzies led Brown to a handsome young man with a strong jaw. "Channing Brown, meet Robin Baxter. He's recently left his job at the *Times* to come aboard here at Military Intelligence, Section 6 – or MI6, as we're now often called."

"I've heard much about you, Mr. Brown," Baxter said, "including that you run several of our best agents on the Continent. Please let me know if I can be of help there. I know both France and Spain quite well."

"Let me think about that, lad," Brown said, glancing at his watch. Brown liked to do his own recruiting. "There are risks to the enterprise, as you know. Think I'll make it an early night tonight, if you don't mind. I want to have dinner with my wife."

"Well," Baxter said, undeterred, "do say hello to Jillian for me. She was a colleague at the *Times* when I reported from Europe. She proofed my copy on any number of dispatches."

In the taxi on the way home, Brown decided to ask Jillian what she knew of this Robin Baxter.

258. THE THAMES EMBANKMENT, 8:13 P.M.

Baxter sat down on the bench and ran his hands along its wooden underside. No message had been left for him. He took a white envelope from his vest pocket and used a thumbtack to fasten it, and the coded message it contained, to the underside of the bench. He remained on the bench for several minutes, alone with his thoughts. All in all, he reflected, things were going well enough. He was now part of MI6 and was sending real intelligence to Moscow.

259. THE CHANCELLERY, BERLIN, NOVEMBER 25, 1940

Karl had telephoned Bormann earlier, saying he wanted to thank Hitler in person for agreeing to Haber's idea concerning surveillance of Rommel.

On his arrival in the large red-carpeted dining room, Karl found Bormann in a pleasant mood. Of course, there was a spot for Karl at the table. Bormann was thriving on his growing authority as the Führer's de facto gatekeeper, all but replacing Hess, who stood alone at a tall window that looked out on the Chancellery garden. Karl saw that the gathering included no military or high-ranking industrial types like Frederick Wagner, and only a smattering of Party officials, smiling and chatting on the day's news and gossip.

A hush fell over the room as Hitler arrived. Bormann went straight through the cluster that had formed quickly around Hitler. He whispered and nodded toward Karl to approach as the crowd of hangers-on dispersed. Hitler drew Karl away, behind the long as yet unoccupied luncheon table.

"Ah, Karl," Hitler muttered, making sure he was not overheard. "Rommel. Africa. It must be a wretched place, all sun and sand."

"Well, I hope my being close to Rommel will serve the Führer. I look forward to an evening when the two of us can be alone together, and I can tell you what I've learned."

"Alone, of course," Hitler said. "We must be discreet. No one must know I have concerns about Rommel. The truth is I like the fellow – smart but impulsive. Seldom does he tell his superiors what he is about to do. I must know that I can count on his loyalty, and I'm not sure of that now. This should be job for the SD or the Abwehr, but they have more than they can handle in the occupied territories."

"So you will report to me in person. Speak to Bormann as to the time and place," Hitler said, turning to the nearby Bormann, who gestured toward the luncheon table.

260. BOULEVARD MONTPARNASSE, PARIS, DECEMBER 8, 1940, 10:00 P.M.

Relaxing with an after-work glass of red wine, Josh noticed a tall thin man standing before him in the café.

"You're just the Yank I want to see."

Josh looked up and saw Jack Courtney. "Let's have some more wine on me, Josh," Courtney said, as Josh motioned for him to sit. "I'm a commercial attaché based here in Paris."

"What gives, Courtney? Are you working part-time for the Gestapo?"

Ignoring Josh's attempt at a joke, Courtney ordered a carafe of Burgundy and two glasses. As they caught up on each other's lives since Madrid, Josh learned, not to his surprise, that Courtney was thoroughbred prepster – Choate, Yale, and graduate work at Princeton.

When they started on their second glass of wine, Courtney got down to business and pushed an envelope toward Josh. Tearing it open, Josh removed two documents, which he found hard to read in the smoky café.

"I'd light a match, but that might attract unnecessary attention," Courtney said. "Instead, I'll tell you what the papers say. What you have in your hand is an authentic diplomatic passport for an American doctor named Enzo Galifano. The other document is a letter on State Department stationery that identifies you as a U.S. Embassy staffer, a sort of special medical attaché whose name just happens to be Enzo Galifano. Most important, the letter certifies that you have diplomatic immunity. Together, the passport and the letter give you the freedom to go almost anywhere, to visit virtually any city on the planet, as long as America keeps out of this goddamn war."

"So tell me, what do I have to do for all this?"

"We'll get to that tomorrow evening. All you need to know for now is that I'll pick you up in at your apartment tomorrow at 9 p.m. sharp."

261. HOTEL GEORGE V, PARIS, DECEMBER 9, 1940, 9:08 P.M.

Bill Donovan opened the door to his fourth-floor hotel suite and greeted Courtney with a nod and Josh with a firm handshake.

Donovan led them to a dining room table and gestured for them to sit. He didn't offer them a drink.

"Since we've just met, let me tell you a bit about my background," Donovan said. "I'm a practicing lawyer, originally from Buffalo, but now I work mostly in New York City. My cover here is Paris is that I represent a

New York investment firm whose American clients hold stock in companies with properties in Occupied France.

"At the invitation of President Roosevelt, I also dabble in what some people call intelligence gathering. In its present form, however, intelligence might be more aptly labeled calculated guesswork. Most of our so-called intelligence is based on a few strands of knowledge, some of it right, but much of it wrong or irrelevant. We Americans are still a long way from getting the hang of it. Anyway, at the request of the White House, Courtney and I have been keeping close tabs on you and your wife since you left Spain."

"Since I'm married to a member of the Communist Party, your interest hardly surprises me, Mr. Donovan."

"Courtney here tells me that you're quite canny, in your way," Donovan said with a smile. "He knows a lot about you, and he's told me most of what he knows. Your life story combines two seemingly contradictory behavior patterns, both pretty interesting."

"Do tell."

"Back during your residency, you performed a number of complex orthopedic surgeries without informing the hospital and without charging a fee. These were brave, perhaps even commendable acts. In fact, though, you were goddamn lucky to get away with it. You could have been fired and lost your license to practice."

"How did you guys find out about that?"

"We tracked down a couple of the fighters whose broken jaws you fixed. They had only nice things to say about you. We also know about the noble and courageous work you did in Spain. We read Hemingway's piece in *Colliers* that described how you performed surgeries under constant shelling, staying on your feet for thirty-six hours at a stretch. We even doubled-checked his sources. All that we put on the plus side of your personal ledger."

"There's a non-plus side?"

"Well, you do have a long history of getting involved with people whose motives and associations are questionable, to say the least. I suppose your wife and all her Communist Party friends are Exhibit A. But let's not forget your links to the Bellacosta brothers. How do you explain all that?"

"I don't know what there is to explain, especially when it comes to Nancy. You see, gentlemen, I'm stuck on her. Loving her is the driving force in my life. She's a born Red, and the Party wants her to stay in Paris and lie low. Being a Communist is more important to her than anything except our daughter. Even our marriage comes second. I've learned to live with that. As for the Bellacostas, it's pretty simple. Bobby Bellacosta and I were in medical school together. Then we interned and did our residency at the same New York hospital. The connection is real and, truth be told, it's been a big help."

"We appreciate your candor," Donovan said. "Very refreshing. I need people who are honest – honest with themselves and honest with me. In this line of work, there's no room for bullshit. If you're interested, I have a job for you."

"Is it here in Paris?"

"Hell no," Donovan said. "You need to put some distance between yourself and Paris. And you need to do it soon."

"I keep hearing that," Josh said. "But I'm still here. So far, the German occupation seems pretty civilized."

"You're lucky you're not in Warsaw," Donovan said, "where they're already herding Jews into concentration camps, separating families, and beating the shit out of the older ones. You can ask Courtney here for the details."

"You're telling me Paris isn't safe for me and my family, even though we're Americans?" Josh said.

"Exactly. And you can't count on America staying out of this war forever," Courtney said. "And if that happens, every American in Paris will be at risk, especially the Jews."

"Where am I going then?"

"Moscow."

"Why Moscow?" Josh asked.

"We'll tell you when you get there," Donovan said.

"And why me?"

"Because of your wife – she gives you the credibility you need in Moscow," Donovan said.

"And what if I say no?"

"We got you and Nancy out of Madrid. And if you take this job, we'll get you – and your family – out of Paris, if it comes to that. Otherwise you're on your own."

262. PRINZ-ALBRECHT-STRASSE, DECEMBER 10, 1940, 9:07 A.M.

Heydrich spoke to Hans in a hushed tone. "Last night, three of our best SS men in Berlin were beaten up near the Kroll Opera House. Three nights before that, two other SS men were assaulted on a side street near Unter den Linden. All were left bleeding and unconscious on the sidewalk, right out in the open for any citizen of Berlin to behold. Tell me Krebs, how is it that we can conquer most of Europe, but we can't stop our best men from getting mauled in the streets of our capital?"

Heydrich eyed Hans. "Enlighten me, Krebs, when can we expect an end to this embarrassment?"

"Soon," Hans said.

Heydrich responded in a shrill voice. "A detective of your caliber ought to have cracked this case by now. I want results, and so does Himmler. Now get back to it."

Hans turned and retreated to his office. He knew that Heydrich could have chewed him out more harshly. He was thankful for small favors.

263. HEINRICH HIMMLER'S OFFICE, PRINZ-ALBRECHT-STRASSE, BERLIN, DECEMBER 12, 1940, 10:05 A.M.

Hans's three-page report said that an underground Jewish gang operating in Berlin appeared to be responsible for "most, if not all" of the attacks on SS men, and for the Star of David chalk markings on the doors of their residences.

"So," Himmler said, eyeing Heydrich, "I don't find this very credible. What's worse, Krebs hasn't come up with one member of this so-called gang."

"I know," Heydrich said, "terrible police work, especially for someone of Krebs's reputation. But, if I may say so, it's quite acceptable. Our own people tell us there are close to 100,000 Jews still in Berlin. It's reasonable to assume that there could be one, even several organized groups among them."

"True," Himmler acknowledged, "but wouldn't the leaders of any such gangs be smart enough to understand that attacks on SS officers would only trigger retaliation, with more of their people being shipped off to the East?"

"So what?" Heydrich responded. "The Jews are the logical villains here. We've surely given them enough reason to attack SS officers. And our Führer has blamed them for everything else that ever went wrong in Germany. So why not blame them?"

Himmler nodded. "I agree. Should the foreign press learn of the beatings and start asking questions, we can blame a Jewish gang and cite Krebs's report. After all, Krebs enjoys a fine reputation. This Krebs, is he giving this case his best effort?"

"I can't say, Reichsführer, though I share your curiosity. We've been tailing him and he knows it. I regret to say that thus far he's proven himself a master at shaking the tails we put on him. He's good at the game of hide-and-seek and loves to play it. He's done so well with all the other cases I've assigned him, so I'm surprised he hasn't made more progress with this one. Just after he returned from America, I asked him to investigate the unauthorized sale of narcotics to badly wounded Luftwaffe flyers. He broke that case in two weeks. He also cracked a case involving black-market cigarette sales and coffee smuggled in from Sweden. Then there was that Norden bombsight stolen by the Abwehr. We would never have known about that if it weren't for Krebs. He's an asset and we must treat him as one."

264. THE CHANCELLERY, BERLIN, DECEMBER 22, 1940, 3:00 P.M.

More than two hundred military planners and SS officers were already gathered for the briefing when Adolf Hitler, accompanied by Martin Bormann,

entered the theater-style meeting room. The surprised participants, led by
Rundstedt, Keitel, Haber, Himmler, and Heydrich all sprang to their feet in
a rousing *Sieg Heil*. No one had expected the visit.

"Be seated, gentlemen," Hitler said. "Today I've authorized you to proceed with the further planning of what I believe will be *the* decisive campaign
of the war – the destruction of the Soviet Union. This campaign will win for
us the great eastern breadbasket along with the region's mineral resources.

"Once we've killed the Russian bear, we'll be free of the threat to our back
and free to concentrate our force against the English bull. Then we will bring
Churchill to the peace table or crush him. The choice will be his.

"Gentlemen, allow me to be candid. This Russian operation is not for
the faint of heart. In the early days of the campaign, we'll be advancing
rapidly over vast tracts of land. We could well encounter serious resistance
from troublemakers, partisans, and guerrillas in the territory we have taken.
Understand me – I want any such resistance crushed before it starts, just as we
did in Poland and Norway, and will soon do in France and the Low Countries.
Special SS units will round up anyone who might resists our occupation –
local political leaders, teachers, intellectuals, and journalists as well as all Jews
– and dispose of them immediately."

Hitler nodded toward Himmler, then toward Heydrich. "I should mention another vital matter. Our friend Reinhard Heydrich here, along with several others, has been working on a master plan for the Reich, the final version
of which Reichsführer Himmler and I will present at a later date. I've already
seen a preliminary draft and would like to share its vision with you today.

"The plan foresees a vast expansion of the present territory of the German
Reich – extending throughout Poland, the eastern Ukrainian breadbasket,
and into the rich oil fields of the Caucasus Mountains and the Caspian Basin.
We will populate these regions with German settlers of every kind, from
farmers to petroleum engineers. Our plan envisions modern six-lane highways
and extensive new rail lines, which will connect the new settlements with each
other and with Berlin and other cities throughout the greater Reich. Make no
mistake, we will *purify* this new land. We will relocate current inhabitants,
pushing them further east, where they will have to resettle and make do. The
land they leave behind will be ours forever."

The applause started slowly as the officers absorbed Hitler's message. Then it picked up and fed upon itself, ending in a climax of *Sieg Heils*.

As the military planners filed from auditorium, Hitler turned to Heydrich. "I heard this morning about the latest attack – this one on three SS men just a block from the Kaiser Wilhelm Bridge. All were badly beaten, and one had his jaw completely shattered."

"We think it's the work of a Jewish gang," Heydrich replied. "That's the preliminary finding of the detective I have on the case."

"I don't care about your preliminary *finding*," Hitler spat, shoving his hands into the side pockets of his gray military blazer. "These beatings have been going on for too long. I want the people responsible rounded up and punished. Now. Your failure to catch these hooligans reveals an incompetence I find intolerable." Hitler then dismissed him.

Heydrich snapped a salute. He had expected a dressing down. He knew he would have reacted in exactly the same way if he were in the Führer's position.

265. AMERICAN EMBASSY, MOSCOW, DECEMBER 24, 1940, 3:15 P.M.

Peering out a window that faced across Red Square, Josh watched the swirling snow blend with the December dusk. He sat down at the typewriter, stared at the blank white page for a moment, and began to type a letter to Nancy, telling her he had arrived safely in Moscow and apologizing for his hasty departure from Paris.

Josh addressed the envelope by hand, marked it for the diplomatic pouch, and was putting it in his out-basket when Jack Courtney appeared in the doorway.

"There's a little office Christmas party getting started down the hall. The ambassador has just left for a reception that Molotov is hosting at the Kremlin, so we can all let our hair down a bit."

"Hell, Courtney, I didn't know *you* were in Moscow."

"Get used to it. As it turns out, I'll be overseeing your real assignment, which Donovan conveniently failed to elaborate on back in Paris. Once I introduce you to everyone and we've enjoyed some Yuletide cheer, I'll fill you in on your job here."

266. THE CABINET WAR ROOMS, LONDON, DECEMBER 24, 1940, 10:00 P.M.

Studying the wall map of Britain's coastal defenses, Winston Churchill glanced over at the stenographer, who sat at a small, uncluttered desk, grateful for the respite after more than an hour of the Prime Minister's rapid-fire dictation. Churchill relit his half-smoked cigar, a signal that he was about the resume. "Now let's do a memorandum to Channing Brown."

"To Channing Brown," he began. "Given the distinct possibility of a cross-Channel invasion by spring, or early summer at the latest, the timely completion of Jackhammer is now more critical than ever. The success of that operation could well deter any such enemy initiative. Spare no expense in completing this operation as soon as possible. My best to you, Jillian, and your colleagues in this Christmas season, difficult though the times may be. WSC."

267. THE RECEPTION HALL, AMERICAN EMBASSY, MOSCOW, DECEMBER 24, 1940 7:00 P.M.

Josh worked the room, introducing himself and mingling with the embassy staff. He hadn't been to anything close to a real party since his Bastille Day *fête* in Paris in the summer of '39, and he'd never been to anything quite so fancy. The Italian red wine went down smoothly, and the plentiful hors d'oeuvres kept him sober. As the crowd thinned out, Jack Courtney approached with a handsome woman at his side.

"As you may have noticed, Josh, I've saved the most interesting introduction for last," Courtney said. "Josh Greenberg, a.k.a. Dr. Enzo Galifano, please meet Dr. Victoria Crane. Vicky's on a leave of absence from Georgetown, where she teaches international studies. Her cover is that she's my personal secretary, but in fact she's one of the State Department's top experts on the Soviet Union and international geopolitics."

"Charmed to meet you, Dr. Galifano," she said with a southern lilt. Looking at her clear, healthy complexion and dark hair parted in the middle, Josh guessed that she was in her late thirties.

"Vicky will try to give us a sense of where this war is going and how that might affect the U.S.S.R., Europe, and the U.S."

Courtney guided Josh and Vicky back to his office. He motioned for them to sit at a small conference table and poured them each a healthy dose of Hennessy. "I'm going to let Vicky do most of the talking," he said.

"Let's all start with a panoramic perspective," Vicky said, folding her hands together and looking at Josh. "As we move into 1941, the war is beginning to look more and more like a standoff. Hitler certainly won the first few rounds – taking Poland, Norway, and much of Western Europe. But he hasn't delivered anything close to a knockout punch. He could try for a decisive victory in the spring, but only if he mounts a cross-Channel invasion – a costly, high-risk venture, to say the least, and one he appears unwilling to take at the moment. The German Kriegsmarine, with its fleet of U-boats, has been an effective force against merchant vessels in the broad expanses of the North Atlantic. But it would prove no match for the Royal Navy fighting in the English Channel to stave off an invasion of the home islands. Hitler doesn't have the naval savvy or enough surface warships to take on the Brits.

"I've seen the cross-Channel adventure played out at the Naval War College in Newport. Hitler's chances of establishing a secure beachhead are about three in ten. If he tries and fails, he risks losing the power and prestige he gained from the victories last spring. Repelling a German invasion would give Britain a major victory, comparable to its defeat of the Spanish Armada in 1588.

"Even if a cross-Channel invasion were to succeed – and the Wehrmacht occupied Britain – that wouldn't necessarily end the war or lead to a decisive German victory. The Brits would likely fight on from Canada and other

Commonwealth countries. And that no doubt would bring the U.S. into the war, which Hitler definitely does not want. Such contingencies, we believe, make Hitler reluctant to opt for a cross-Channel invasion. Remember, and this is crucial, he also has the Russians at his back."

"In fact, one of our State Department operatives in Berlin," Courtney chimed in, "heard from an informant that Hitler will move against Russia by spring. The British have just heard the same thing from another source. Hitler's plan to invade the Soviet Union must be the worst-kept secret of the war."

"He's wanted to do this all along," Vicky said, "expand his Reich in the east."

"Has any one told the Russians?" Josh asked.

"Not to our knowledge," Courtney said. "But we need to find out exactly what the Russians *do* know – or what they think they know. President Roosevelt thinks it would be a good idea to tell them at least some of what we know. That, Josh, is where you come in."

268. ROMANISCHES CAFÉ, BERLIN, DECEMBER 24, 6:00 P.M.

Trudy had telephoned Karl to invite him out for a drink. He found her sitting in the back of the café, a half-empty glass of red wine on the table.

She offered Karl her cheek as he took a seat across from her and ordered a glass of wine. She told him that she'd been working at the Charité Hospital in Berlin for the last two months.

"You must think I'm terribly aggressive," she said, changing the subject. "After all, I practically threw myself at you twice – during Göring's Christmas party and again in Berchtesgaden just before the war. Then I wrote you a letter, but you never answered."

"Sorry, Trudy. It's the war."

"Karl, you don't have to make excuses. I'm here to tell you a secret. You and I are on the same team. I asked Brown if I could come clean with you before I leave Germany."

"Brown?"

"Yes, Channing Brown," Trudy whispered, relieving Karl of the need to ask questions. "I work for him too, have been since he recruited me in a Heidelberg Bierkeller back when I was a student. After tonight's air raid, a purse with my ration card and driver's license will be found in the rubble. It's not a foolproof plan, but it'll buy the time I need to escape. Later tonight I'll board a flight for Stockholm dressed as a nurse, assisting an elderly Swiss gentleman. The gentleman, of course, will be Mr. Scotty North. He's quite an interesting fellow, don't you think? With any luck, I'll be in Brown's London office in two days' time."

"So you've been one of my minders all along?"

"Too long a story for now. Maybe someday."

"Fair enough, I suppose. Give Brown my regards. What about your father, though? If the Gestapo discovers the truth about you, he could be in for a rough time."

"He's in Tokyo now, working on the expansion of a naval shipyard. As soon as I'm safe in Britain, Brown's people will reach out and tell him that I'm alive and offer him a way to defect. If he wants to, that is."

"What about the house in Berchtesgaden?"

"It's empty. I know you have a key, Karl. I saw you take it that night when you thought I'd fallen asleep. Feel free to use the place if you need it. I don't know what your mission is. Scotty keeps a tight lip. I should be going. I've still got to pack my bag and dress in my nurse's uniform."

269. LUFTWAFFE AIRFIELD, PAS DE CALAIS, DECEMBER 24, 1940, NOON

Fern could see Hitler approaching out of the corner of her eye. Göring was at his right, and the two men were striding along the line of Luftwaffe pilots standing at attention. Fern saw the pilots' smiles. She knew that their good cheer had less to do with Hitler and Göring's surprise visit than the fact that they wouldn't have to face the English anti-aircraft guns, Hurricanes, and Spitfires over London that night.

The receiving line moved quickly. In no time, Göring was introducing Fern to Adolf Hitler. Fern mentioned to Hitler that they had met once before, at Göring's home in the Obersalzberg two Christmases ago.

"Of course, I remember," Hitler said. "You were quite stunning in that red dress. Hermann's forgotten that we had a private visit with you and your family. I am honored to meet you again, Dr. Wagner. Hermann has told me of your fine work here."

Moments later, Fern saw Hitler and Göring speeding away in a heavily armed Mercedes toward the next airfield. Fern left soon afterward and boarded a train for the Gare Saint-Lazare to spend Christmas in Paris with Nancy.

270. THE HABER RESIDENCE, BERLIN, DECEMBER 25, 1940 4:15 P.M.

Karl and the Rommels accepted the Habers' invitation to Christmas dinner, which, they assured him, would be a modest affair. The General told Karl that Fern's duties in France made it impossible for her to attend. The Habers had also invited Frederick Wagner, but he'd come down with the flu.

Despite the food shortages plaguing Berlin, Hildy had prepared a feast – pork roast, fresh carrots, and asparagus commandeered from the officers' mess at General Staff headquarters. Karl savored the scent from the kitchen. It brought back memories of the dinners Fern had made for them on East 86th Street.

Karl enjoyed Hildy's company. Despite her obvious affinity for the Nazi generals, he saw that she was much more than a *Hausfrau*. Like Fern, she was bright, strong willed, and well informed. She amused everyone with snippets of gossip gleaned from her gossip with other generals' wives and mistresses. Over Champagne, Hildy's regaled her guests with accounts of Fern's medical work in France, information she'd gathered from uncensored portions of Fern's letters.

After a dessert of Black Forest cake and homemade vanilla ice cream, Hildy and Lucy Rommel repaired to the kitchen. Haber invited Karl and Rommel into his study for a brandy. He gestured for his guests to take the comfortable leather chairs opposite the desk and poured them each a snifter of Napoleon brandy, a Christmas gift from Fern.

Karl didn't mind being the silent third person in the conversation. He listened with attention as the charismatic Rommel and the studious Haber recalled their time in France and on the Italian front in the previous war. Karl grasped Rommel's use of surprise, for doing what he believed his enemy least expected, then hitting him with all the strength Rommel could muster.

Karl's mind raced back to the Friedrichstrasse railhead, then to the smoke-filled arena in Munich. "What you say reminds me of boyhood scuffles in Dar es Salaam and an evening I spent at the SS boxing championship just before the war. A good boxer can set up a stronger opponent with a feint and beat him with a good left or right hook or a punch to the jaw – if the opponent doesn't expect it. In other words, the boxing ring can be a microcosm of the battlefield."

"It's always been so," Rommel said. "Surprise is essential."

"Most interesting, Herr General," Karl said. "I know your mind will be on more serious business. But I hope we have time to talk once we are in Africa."

"It's all arranged, Karl. I learned this morning that you'll be joining Rommel's new unit at their base near Munich and accompany them to Africa."

The ring of Haber's telephone interrupted them. Karl was closest to the phone, and Haber asked him to pick it up. He heard a long-distance operator with a French accent informing him that Paris was calling. A second later Karl heard Fern's clear, unmistakable voice.

"Hello there," she said, testing the connection. "I hope you're all having a splendid Christmas . . ."

271. FERN WAGNER'S SUITE AT THE RITZ, PARIS, DECEMBER 25, 1940, 5:40 P.M.

Fern put down the telephone and looked at Nancy. "Strange," she said. "No one responded for a long moment after I said hello. There was dead silence until General Haber picked up."

"So?" Nancy shrugged.

"So nothing, I guess."

"Pour me some more Champagne, Fern."

Nancy's eyes took in the elegance of suite. "Your friend Göring has excellent taste in hotel rooms."

"You should see the suite he's taken for himself. It has a music room with a grand piano, two bedrooms, and a dining room with magnificent chandeliers."

"I still find it hard to believe you know the Nazi brass, Fern."

"My uncle, Frederick Wagner, has real access to Hitler and his gang, including Göring. Uncle Frederick's a survivor. When I returned to Germany, it shocked me to learn how tight he was with the Nazi bigwigs. Frederick, mother, and my friend Hans all advised me to keep any anti-Nazi sentiments to myself, and that's what I've done."

Fern decided not tell Nancy of the operations she'd performed in Ziggy's apartment. She would keep that to herself.

"It comforts me to know you're not a good Nazi. And I must not be a very good Communist," Nancy said, swigging Champagne. "I'm about to suggest that we open another bottle, whose delicious contents were produced by oppressed French grape-pickers who toiled in the vineyards for little pay."

"Listen, if it's on the Third Reich, what the hell," Fern laughed. Then with Prussian efficiency, she used a white linen napkin to uncork a second bottle of Champagne.

As they drank, their conversations turned back to the Spanish war.

"Josh and I sometimes used to do it during the shelling. The explosions excited me. It was fantastic."

"I'm afraid I can't relate to that part of life anymore," Fern admitted. "Hans and I, well, we're good friends. I tried, but the chemistry isn't there."

"Are you saying that Hans has committed the unpardonable sin of not being Karl Ludwig?"

"Something like that."

"Then how about another glass of Champagne? What the hell, it's Christmas."

272. KARL'S RESIDENCE, ZEHLENDORF, DECEMBER 25, 1940, 11:00 P.M.

He locked the door, drew the blackout curtains, and sat at his kitchen table in the dark. Her voice hadn't lost its wonderful clarity. It had stayed with him since he picked up the telephone in Haber's apartment.

For too long he had fought off thoughts of Fern. Now he let the rich memories roll – East 86th Street, the Bavarian Inn, the cafeteria at New York Hospital. How could he have known that the damned mission would take so long? It was nuts, all of it. How had it all happened – Sing Sing, the whole godforsaken mess? It was an enterprise into which some quixotic Brits had sunk millions. He knew he had no alternative, no way to quit. He let some minutes pass, then stood and turned on the lights. How could be face Brown to tell him he wanted out? And how – if he ever had the chance to talk to her again – could he ever tell Fern?

273. PRINZ-ALBRECHT-STRASSE, JANUARY 2, 1941, 11:42 A.M.

"No, I *will not* take a call from Hauptmann Jurgen," Heydrich spat into the intercom. "How many times must I tell you? Hauptmann Jurgen is persona-non-grata. I don't care how much he wants to see me."

Since the incident in the Café Frida the previous September, Heydrich had shunned Günter. Although his access to Heydrich and other higher-ups was now severely restricted, Jurgen's career was not entirely ruined. He was still training special SS squads that would weed out troublemakers and Jews once the planned invasion of the Soviet Union was underway.

Banished from the Prinz-Albrecht-Strasse SS headquarters, Jurgen was too embarrassed even to visit that neighborhood, where he feared bumping into Heydrich or other SS brass. Most days, when his work was done, he returned to his apartment on the Geller Strasse and kept to himself.

274. GORKY PARK, MOSCOW, FEBRUARY 2, 1941, 10:30 P.M.

Josh stood in the falling snow, his legs numb to the knees. He had arrived early on purpose. He needed time to review the improbable sequence of events that had unfolded since Christmas – the vodka-drenched New Year's reception at the Kremlin and the round of meetings at the Moscow Medical Academy, where he'd met Dmitri, the man who arranged the rendezvous that was about to take place.

Dmitri managed the distribution of surgical supplies for the Medical Academy and several other major hospitals in Moscow. That was his day job. Dmitri spoke flawless, Oxford-accented English and had taken an immediate interest in Josh, realizing that the American doctor's medical expertise could help elevate the level of orthopedic care in Moscow's understaffed and equipment-starved medical facilities. Josh's Spanish experience was of special interest to Dmitri, not just the work he'd done in the field hospital, but his near-miraculous escape before Madrid fell to Franco's forces and their German allies.

Josh's mission was simple enough. As Courtney had put it: "President Roosevelt wants to know how well prepared the Soviets are for a Nazi invasion. One of your jobs will be to find out whether the Soviets have the capacity to treat mass casualties in the event of all-out war. How, for example, would Moscow endure the kind of bombardment inflicted on Madrid or London? Your time in Spain and Paris qualifies you for the job. How well prepared are Moscow hospitals for shortages in medical staff, food, medication, and anesthesia?"

On Courtney's instruction, Josh had responded to Dmitri's friendly overtures, drinking shots of vodka with him in a bar near the Moscow Medical Academy. Josh reported back to Courtney and Vicky after each meeting with Dmitri. All three soon concluded that the Soviets were woefully unprepared for the onslaught that Hitler could inflict. But for whatever reason, Dmitri was courting Josh. "Let's exploit his curiosity and see where it takes us," Courtney advised.

That morning, during a rendezvous in a restaurant near the Kremlin, Dmitri had revealed his real job. He was a senior counterintelligence officer for the NKVD, and there was someone he wanted Josh to meet.

Josh's teeth were chattering when the snow-covered limousine pulled up to the park entrance, not twenty feet from where he was standing. Dmitri, wearing a black skullcap, emerged from the rear door and motioned for Josh to climb in. Closing the door behind Josh, Dmitri then climbed into the front seat next to the driver. Removing his cap, Dmitri turned to face Josh and the large man sitting next to him on the back seat. "Josh, allow me to introduce Lavrentiy Beria."

275. THE KREMLIN, FEBRUARY 5, 1941, 4:00 A.M.

Josef Stalin stood in the doorway of his Kremlin apartment to meet Beria. There was no handshake, no exchange of pleasantries. Stalin led Beria to the study, gesturing for him to take a seat before the large desk. The air was thick with tobacco smoke. Stalin remained standing.

"So tell me about this American Jew," Stalin said, relighting his pipe with a long wooden match, "this doctor who uses a fake Italian name."

"This doctor, Josh Greenberg, is a man of candor and professional competence, Comrade Stalin. He revealed his true identity to us right away, which bespeaks either his forthrightness or his naïveté. Of course, we already knew who he was from Prouxlanger, our man in Paris. Prouxlanger is a confidant of Greenberg's wife."

Stalin started pacing around the room. "Keep talking, Laverentiy."

"From the report we received just before Madrid fell to the fascists, Greenberg's work in Spain was exemplary, both from a professional and political perspective. He proved himself to be an excellent orthopedic surgeon, performing scores of complex operations even while his hospital was under attack. He and his wife abandoned their bourgeois life in New York to live with the rats in a Madrid slum and treat victims of the fascist war machine. His wife, Nancy Greenberg, has been an active Communist Party member since her university days in San Francisco. She's agreed to remain in Paris and work for the Party under young Prouxlanger. As instructed, our people in Paris are keeping a low profile, at least as long as our pact with Hitler remains in effect."

"So much for the background," Stalin sighed. "What do you propose?"

"That we cultivate a relationship with him."

"Why?" Stalin asked, easing into his chair.

"Two reasons," Beria said.

"First, despite his jovial and relaxed demeanor, this Josh Greenberg shows an inner toughness. He's already seen more blood and suffering in Spain than most men see in a lifetime.

"Second, and perhaps more important, he's in love with his wife. Young Prouxlanger confirms that their relationship is a strong one. With her and their half-Jewish daughter in Paris, Greenberg is unlikely to do anything to jeopardize their safety. In other words, he wouldn't dare work against us. And someday, perhaps, he might even work for us."

"Then let's keep him close to us," Stalin said and poured Beria a glass of vodka.

276. ROMMEL'S COMMAND POST, TRIPOLI, MARCH 1, 1941, 10:00 A.M.

Karl found Rommel to be in high spirits, seated in his command tent at the portable folding table that served as his desk. Neither man bothered to salute. "Sit down, Karl. I received your report an hour ago but haven't had a chance to read it yet. Can you summarize it for me?"

Karl knew enough not to waste Rommel's time. The main focus of the report, he told Rommel, was how the desert temperatures, which varied by as much as forty degrees Celsius from day to night, affected the men's health. Such variability, he said, heightened their susceptibility to severe colds, even pneumonia, especially since most were sleeping outdoors and in tents. Proper nutrition and vigorous exercise were essential. Karl further noted the need for abundant water, quinine, and lightweight clothing to protect them from the Sahara sun.

Rommel let a moment pass before he responded.

"I agree, Karl. Nearly everything I need to sustain my soldiers is in short supply.

There's another shortage that concerns me almost as much – the acute shortage of petrol. Shipping petrol to Africa has proven extremely difficult, thanks to British submarines and aircraft based in Gibraltar and Malta."

"What does Berlin propose to do about it?" Karl asked.

"My orders are to maintain a defensive posture, but I'm inclined to disagree. I've ordered a probe toward Benghazi tomorrow. We'll learn then how strong the enemy really is. If I'm right, and they're as weak as I suspect, we shall attack in force the following day.

"Once we've made the thrust toward Benghazi, I'll be leaving for Berlin. I'm going to plead for the petrol and other supplies we need for an extended campaign toward Suez."

277. AMERICAN EMBASSY, MOSCOW, MARCH 13, 1941

Jack Courtney's shoeless feet rested comfortably atop his desk as he motioned for Josh to take a seat.

"We've been receiving more choice intelligence about the possibility of Hitler attacking Russia," Courtney said, removing his feet from the desk and sitting upright. "I, for one, never believed it. Secretary of State Hull was skeptical. So was the President. Yet the President ordered this intelligence to be passed along to the Soviet Ambassador in Washington. The Soviet Ambassador was grateful at first. We later learned that he never believed it either. In fact, he characterized our report as 'disinformation,' a ploy designed to help the Brits by getting Stalin to suspect Hitler of foul play."

"So you want me to tell the Russians something we've already told them, which they refuse to believe?"

"That's right."

"Why?"

"Because they just might just believe *you*. They think you're an honest broker since your wife is basically under their protection in Paris. Besides, we've changed our minds — we now believe with some conviction that the Nazis *are* preparing to attack to Soviets. The Brits have observed flows of German heavy equipment toward the east and construction of new airfields in the same area. The MI6 people in London believe the invasion is set for mid-May."

"Beria is still not likely to believe it. He might think you're using me."

"That's his problem. We just need to be on record as having told the son of a bitch."

278. THE KREMLIN, MARCH 14, 1941, 10:14 A.M.

Josh had been waiting for more than half an hour when Dmitri, all smiles, strode out of Beria's office and into a reception area.

"Good morning, Josh. I'm sure this is important."

"It may surprise you to know that I'm here on official embassy business. In fact, I'm here on orders from the White House."

A moment later, Beria welcomed them into his office and led them to a small sitting area. Beria listened with contained impatience.

"I've been hearing this rumor for weeks," he said. "I know you're new to this kind of work, Josh. I must tell you, however, that Comrade Stalin and I both believe that the British are spreading such rumors to divide the Soviet Union from the German Reich. You can thank your President Roosevelt for taking the initiative to inform us. We will weigh it in the context of the strong relationship we now enjoy with Germany and its Führer. Beria stood, ending the brief meeting. "And next time, Josh, bring me something I haven't heard before."

279. THE ADLON, BERLIN, MARCH 19, 1941, 5:57 P.M.

The quiet comfort of the cocktail lounge in the grand hotel could not relieve Erwin Rommel's frustration. He had pleaded with Hitler, Rundstedt, and Paulus for more men and supplies, especially petrol, confident that once reinforced, his Panzers could take Cairo and Suez. But Hitler, hoarding men and materiel for Operation Barbarossa, had been noncommittal, promising only to send Panzer Division to Africa at some point in May.

Rommel was grateful that Frederick Wagner had telephoned him earlier that day to invite him out for a drink. Frederick hadn't been there when Rommel met with Hitler, but Haber had told him about Rommel's disappointment.

Frederick Wagner arrived promptly at six. To Rommel's surprise, he wasn't alone. With Frederick was a tall man – at least three inches taller than Frederick – with curly reddish-gray hair and dressed in a gray business suit and black cowboy boots. Once he introduced Rommel to Tallmadge McGruder, the two men shook hands. Frederick ordered a bottle of chilled Mosel, while Rommel and McGruder took the measure of each other.

"Erwin," Frederick said, "please accept my apologies for this surprise. I know you're a man who likes to seize every opportunity, so when Mr. McGruder let me know he was in Berlin, I thought you'd want to meet him and hear what he has to say. It could have a direct bearing on your assignment in North Africa. Mr. McGruder is an American from Texas, and his company has an international reputation for locating, extracting, and refining crude oil. He's prepared a report you'll want to read," Frederick said as McGruder handed Rommel a twenty-page document with a soft blue cover.

Frederick and McGruder sipped their wine while Rommel leafed through the report, then eyed McGruder.

"I'll read this later," Rommel said, slipping the report into his briefcase. "But tell me what it says now."

"General, what y'all have here is what we in the business call a geophysical document. It's a report based on what our top geologists tell us about oil reserves in the Middle East. It says that there are enormous deposits of readily accessible crude oil in the Saudi Peninsula, Iraq, and Iran. And when I say enormous, I mean unlike anything we've seen before. What's more, these deposits aren't that far from the General's current position in the Sahara. In fact," he said, "they're about as far from your present position as you were from Cherbourg when you started your advance last spring."

"Interesting," Rommel responded. "Unfortunately – or should I say ironically – I don't have enough petrol to reach those oil deposits you mention. And notwithstanding their obvious strategic importance, our Führer appears to have other priorities."

Rommel checked his watch. "Thank you for the report, Herr McGruder. I'll study it in detail tonight on my flight back to Tunis."

280. THE CHANCELLERY, MARCH 20, 1941, 8:00 A.M.

Frederick arrived early for the meeting, well before anyone else. It was to be a special presentation – he would be briefing the General Staff on the durability of the improved Panzer III and its ability to negotiate the unpaved roads of western Russia.

He looked at the forty briefing binders his office had prepared and sent over to the Chancellery the previous evening. The binders lay unattended on a long credenza in the meeting room. Each bore the name of a meeting participant. As he waited for the others to arrive, Frederick opened each binder to make sure it contained all the necessary materials and that nothing had been omitted through some clerical mistake. He took special care with one binder.

12:07 P.M.

Sitting at the desk in his Chancellery office after Frederick's presentation, Bormann opened his briefing binder for the first time. Since he always took notes during meetings rather than relying on prepared materials, he hadn't opened the binder until now. He intended to take a quick look and then store the binder in a secure place.

When he opened it, he noticed an additional typescript several pages long, clipped to the first page. Clearly this typescript was separate from the official document, which was secured in a three-ring loose-leaf binder.

The top page of the extra document was printed on General Staff stationery, which looked somewhat faded. His first impulse was to look for a name on the document, but there was no name. Looking up to make certain his office door was closed, Bormann began to read.

CONFIDENTIAL DRAFT – NOT TO LEAVE OFFICE – DO NOT COPY

PROBLEMS WITH BARBAROSSA AND A PRACTICAL ALTERNATIVE
We believe that Operation Barbarossa, the proposed German invasion and conquest of the Soviet Union, is an ill-conceived plan that is destined to fail. The purpose of this memo is to identify specific flaws in Barbarossa and to propose a military alternative capable of achieving all the major strategic objectives of Barbarossa at a fraction of the cost.

GEOGRAPHIC CONSIDERATIONS
The current plan does not take sufficient account of the challenges posed by the sheer size of the Soviet landmass. Operation Barbarossa calls for initial thrusts deep into Soviet territory with the aim of cutting off, surrounding, and defeating the Red Army in the early days of the campaign. Our forces would then advance to the Urals and go on the defensive. In all probability, however – given the potential of strong Soviet reserves in Siberia – we would need to advance much further, perhaps all the way to the Bering Sea, to secure our grip on Soviet territory, all the while maintaining supply lines stretched over millions of square miles. We also need to recognize that our forces are more than likely to encounter guerrillas fighting on their home territory.

Challenges posed by the Soviet rail system also require further consideration. Soviet trains run on wider gauge track than those in the rest of Europe, and this will likely cause significant delays in the eastward transport of men, equipment, and supplies. We also face the probability of corresponding delays in shipping Russian resources – oil, grains, and other materials – back to the Reich.

TIMING AND WEATHER
The current plan, which proposes that we launch an attack in mid-May 1941, is barely feasible, especially in light of the size of the landmass that needs to be conquered before the onset of the unforgiving Russian winter.

Other factors requiring more consideration include the current Italian misadventures in Greece and the ongoing strife in Yugoslavia, either or both of which could require German military intervention that might, in turn, delay Operation Barbarossa. Such developments could postpone Barbarossa for at least a year, or even until we have defeated the British.

OTHER STRATEGIC CONSIDERATIONS
Our Japanese allies, although they might like the idea of the Russian Bear being engaged with an enemy to the west, might not welcome the possibility that the Army of the Third Reich could be sitting at their back door in Siberia.

A more immediate consideration, however, is the potential trouble that could erupt in France, where both the Abwehr and the SD report that a formidable Communist underground has been sitting on the sidelines. Reports indicate that Stalin has ordered the French Communist Party to stand down following our non-aggression pact with the Soviets. But once we invade Russia that will almost certainly change. Our "peaceful" occupation of France will come to an end, and we'll need to commit significant forces to combat subversion, sabotage, and terrorism.

Even if German forces do successfully conquer the whole of the Soviet landmass, what then are we to do with the place? Its size is many times that of the considerable area we already occupy. In addition to requiring enormous manpower, any occupation of the Soviet Union would consume exorbitant military and transportation resources, and have a decisively negative impact on our war in the west against Britain.

Beyond the considerations outlined above, what makes Barbarossa especially unwise is the existence of a simpler, more productive alternative, one that will enable us to acquire the same resources with less risk and at far less cost.

AN ALTERNATIVE FOR HIGH-LEVEL CONSIDERATION

The Reich can acquire enough petrol to fuel our war effort and support the civilian economy well into the next century. And we can do so for only a fraction of the cost – in men and materiel – of Barbarossa.

In essence, this alternative plan focuses on capturing resources and territory in North Africa and the Middle East. The campaign would be spearheaded by revitalized and reinforced Panzer Divisions, which would smash through the undermanned and poorly equipped British and Australian forces in North Africa to capture Suez and the oil-rich lands beyond the Sinai.

The puppet princes who rule (or claim to rule) this region have neither the political will nor the military muscle to thwart our advance. Even a robust rear-guard action by well-trained British forces could do little to impede our advance. If properly supplied and manned, our Afrika Korps could easily overrun Suez, cutting the British jugular. From Suez, our forces could advance across the Saudi Peninsula and into Iraq and Iran in less than ninety days.

There are oceans of crude oil underneath the desert sands of these easily conquered territories. Once we control North Africa and the Middle East, the vast oil resources in the Caucasus and the Ukrainian breadbasket would be within easy reach. A recent report by a reputable American firm, McGruder Geophysical, documents the abundance of those deposits and identifies the most expeditious manner of refining the crude oil into petrol.

407

TIMING
In order to succeed, the alternative plan outlined above needs to be set in motion as quickly as possible – but with significantly greater resources than are currently allocated to our African forces.

Timing is critical. Enemy forces in Africa and the Middle East region are currently quite weak. The Reich should be able to defeat these forces with relatively small expenditures of manpower and materiel. Our Luftwaffe has the edge over the RAF, at least for the moment. Although British forces in Africa and the Middle East are now weak, Abwehr reports indicate that they are being reinforced from India, Australia, and New Zealand.

We must allocate more resources to our African forces as quickly as possible.

Bormann used a fresh handkerchief to wipe the sweat from his brow. Hitler, sequestered in his inner sanctum with Jodl, Keitel, Rundstedt, and Frederick Wagner, would surely not welcome any interruption – but Bormann knew that he had no choice. Not to act would put him at risk of being discovered in possession of the incriminating document.

Moments later, Bormann was in Hitler's office, explaining how he had come into possession of the document. As Hitler read it, Bormann readied himself for the inevitable tirade. But Hitler rose from his seat and walked calmly to the window, staring outside for several seconds before speaking.

Hitler recounted the gist of what he'd just read to Frederick, who nodded and skimmed over the memorandum that Hitler handed him. "Without question," Hitler said, "someone is out to disrupt our planning for Barbarossa. The proof is right here. The question now is what we do about it."

"Should I alert the Abwehr and the SD?" Bormann asked, relieved that Hitler was angry but not enraged.

"May I offer a suggestion?" Frederick asked. Hitler nodded.

"An order to investigate," Frederick said, "would only launch a witch hunt, and more nonproductive competition between the Abwehr and the SD. Word would spread that there are high-level misgivings about Barbarossa.

And that might give Himmler and Heydrich cause to send some high-ranking officers to Dachau."

"So you recommend that we keep this to ourselves?" Bormann asked.

"Yes," Frederick said. "Whoever produced this document expects the Führer to react. Instead, we'll surprise him and do nothing. This document is an original typescript. We don't even know if there's a copy."

Hitler broke his unaccustomed silence. "I think I already know who wrote this. And while I have great respect, and even admiration, for Generalmajor Erwin Rommel, I don't think it's a coincidence that he was here with us in Berlin only yesterday. As head of our North Africa forces, he would clearly stand to gain the most from this so-called alternative to Barbarossa."

As the meeting ended, Frederick drew Hitler aside. *"Mein Führer,"* he said, "you were smart to approve General Haber's idea of sending Dr. Muller to Africa to spend some time with Rommel. From all I've heard, this Dr. Muller is a highly resourceful fellow. I look forward to meeting him."

"Yes, I'll want to hear what our Dr. Muller has to report," Hitler said.

281. ROMMEL'S SCOUT PLANE OVER CYRENAICA, MARCH 22, 1941, 5:45 A.M.

As the sun peeked over the distant sand dunes, Karl banked the single-engine Storch to the east and glanced toward Rommel. Rommel signaled for Karl to fly over the advanced British positions. General Alfred Gause, Rommel's savvy chief of staff, sat behind Rommel. Earlier, a Wehrmacht foray near El Aghelia had resulted in the German takeover of the town and the capture of valuable British petroleum stores.

"Our men did well," Rommel said, "confirming my suspicion that the British aren't nearly as strong here as the Italians led us to believe. From here, we can launch raids toward Egypt within forty-eight hours."

"As the Field Marshall well knows," Gause said, raising his voice above the drone of the engine, "we're under strict orders to await the arrival of the 15th Panzer Division before we attack."

"Back in Berlin," Rommel said, "I was told that those Panzers wouldn't arrive until mid-May. By then, the British will have regrouped and resupplied their forces. Why wait for them to grow stronger? We attack in two days."

282. OVER EL AGHELIA, MARCH 30, 1941, 4:14. P.M.

"Are we going to refuel soon?" Gause asked Rommel, as the Storch circled over the battle. General Rommel was preoccupied, peering through a pair of field glasses, watching the western horizon.

"We have them on the run," Rommel shouted. "No time to refuel. We must cut off their retreat while there's still daylight."

"We're bound to have casualties," Gause said, his voice steady.

"Our wounded will require medication, including morphine," Karl said, raising his voice above the engine. "Supplies are already short."

"No stopping now. We have the advantage," Rommel said. "The faster we move and get the job done, the fewer casualties we're likely to sustain. The British find it more difficult to hit moving targets."

283. KNIGHTSBRIDGE, LONDON, APRIL 3, 1941, 8:00 A.M.

Auburn tresses covered the fine features of her face as she slept. Watching her, Robin Baxter contemplated further fornication before facing the day ahead. He knew that once he nudged her, Melissa Farnsworth's long-limbed body would respond with passion. But he also knew it was better that she slept. He had work to do and not much time to do it. Moscow had grown impatient. Three weeks had passed since Baxter had first called at the Bond Street offices of Biddle & Company, an estate firm that managed sales and rentals in Mayfair and where Melissa worked as an agent. He had perhaps been spending too much time with her.

Back during his first weeks at MI6, Baxter noticed Brown's frequent long absences from his desk. On several occasions he followed Brown, who took various routes, all of which led to a Half Moon Street townhouse that was divided into flats. On evenings when he followed Brown to the building, Baxter noticed that someone, most likely Brown himself, would always draw the black drapes in the fourth-floor window. Baxter was curious. Brown wasn't the type to keep a tart on the side.

Baxter met Melissa during his first visit to the offices of Biddle & Company on Piccadilly. He had introduced himself as a dry goods salesman from Plymouth in search of a short-term lease on a comfortable flat, something well-furnished in a good neighborhood where he could entertain prospective clients – at least to the extent that entertaining was possible when Luftwaffe air raids were a nightly occurrence. When Melissa responded to his question about a proper pub where he might have lunch, Baxter was quick to ask her to join him, an invitation she was thrilled to accept. Over a bowl of lamb broth and bread, he learned that her husband, an RAF Hurricane pilot serving in Singapore, had been gone now for more than a year.

In the half-light of the pub, they talked about the bombing and about how Melissa had become an avid reader now that her husband was away. She told him she was halfway through Daphne du Maurier's novel *Rebecca*. Over tea with a dash of brandy, Baxter lied about how he'd fought on the losing side in the Spanish Civil War and suffered a severe leg wound that prevented him from serving in the current conflict. Halfway through tea, Baxter excused himself to make a telephone call "confirming an upcoming appointment." He returned to tell Melissa that his customer had postponed the meeting for two days. It was a disappointment, but perhaps the afternoon would not go to waste if Melissa could show him some vacant flats. Ever efficient, Melissa kept several passkeys in her purse at all times, and as luck would have it, her afternoon was free. Since the onset of the bombing, the estate business in London had been dreadfully slow.

A gentle rain was falling as they left the pub. "I need a place that's quiet, with no children around," Baxter said. "A flat with business offices nearby would be best because it would be quiet in the evening. A friend tells me there are such places on Half Moon Street. If that's so, I would very much like to have a look at one."

"By the luck of it, we do have such a place on Half Moon Street," Melissa said, clasping Baxter's arm. "It's a nicely furnished flat that was once part of a townhouse. It's a short walk from here."

"What's the number of the apartment we're going to see? Just so I don't forget," he lied.

"It's number 5A," she said, looking at him curiously.

"I must write the number down as soon as we get inside," Baxter said. "My boss in Plymouth is a stickler for detail. Tell me, how long might I have the place?"

"As far as I know, you can have it for as long as this bloody war lasts. A wealthy widow holds the lease, but she's off in New York, sitting out the war on Park Avenue. Actually, quite a lot of money has gone into improving the flat, making it very cozy indeed. There's a well-stocked bar, some tasteful pictures of the English countryside, an enormous fireplace, and a magnificent four-poster in the master bedroom." Melissa turned the key with a soft click.

Melissa was right. The bar had an ample supply of twelve-year-old Scotches and French and Italian red wines. Baxter was quick to announce his love for the place and promised Melissa that he would sign all the paperwork first thing in the morning.

"Why not a small celebration?" he suggested. "Surely the old lady in America won't mind if we borrow a bottle of claret."

That night the bombs fell to the west, over the docklands. Baxter and Melissa left in the morning.

284. THE CHANCELLERY, BERLIN, APRIL 12, 1941, 10:00 A.M.

Martin Haber saw the Führer standing at the conference table, his fists pressed against the edge of the large map of North Africa. Keitel, Jodl, Rundstedt, and Paulus stood opposite Hitler.

"So Haber," Hitler snapped, "your friend Rommel is on the offensive in Libya. You and I both know that his orders were to remain on the defensive for now."

Hitler raised his palms to indicate that he wasn't interested in a response. "Listen to me," he shouted. "I don't want to say this again. *Forget* Libya. *Forget* Egypt. North Africa is a sandbox for children and their toys. We have more important things to do. Now," he shouted, fixing his eyes on Haber but still addressing the group, "what is the disposition of our Panzers for Barbarossa? We should be ready to launch an attack no later than May 15. That means we must consign all available petrol supplies to Barbarossa. Do I make myself clear?"

"Surely, we can reserve *some* petrol for Rommel's African Division," Haber ventured.

"Only what we can spare," Hitler said. It was the kind of vague directive he was in the habit of issuing when he faced competing priorities. Hitler fixed his gaze on Haber then turned toward Rundstedt and Paulus. "Perhaps it would better serve our cause if General Paulus went to the desert to observe Rommel's operation firsthand. This discussion ends now," Hitler said, folding his arms.

Haber knew that this wasn't the time to remind the Führer that Karl was already in Africa for the same purpose.

285. ROMMEL'S HEADQUARTERS NEAR BENGHAZI, APRIL 23 1941, 7:00 P.M.

Seated at the small table, Rommel gestured for the young corporal to fill two glasses with riesling as he and Karl prepared to dine on the same field rations given to the men under his command.

"You fly the scout plane well, Karl, just like a Luftwaffe pilot. But in most other ways you're very different from the military men around me."

"Well, as the General knows, I'm a doctor first and a pilot second."

"It's more than that, Karl."

"Well, I've spent nearly all my life in Africa, not Germany."

"So I'm told."

"But enough about me and my past," Karl said. "May I suggest that we speak of the present engagement and discuss what the Field Marshall has planned for tomorrow?"

"Tomorrow we'll begin a second thrust toward Tobruk. I've committed nearly all our Panzers to this operation, so the British will have their hands full. The Abwehr reports that they've had to send a large contingent of troops and equipment, including Panzers and planes, to Greece because the Führer has decided to intervene there again to save our Italian allies."

Rommel looked around to make sure the corporal was out of earshot and lowered his voice, knowing that sound traveled far in the desert.

"More than likely," Rommel said, "these interventions in Greece and Yugoslavia have forced the Führer to postpone Operation Barbarossa for several weeks, or even a month. That could prove disastrous."

"Why disastrous?"

"Because the rain-soaked Russian roads will turn to mud by September and then to ice-bound death traps by early December. If we don't defeat the Red Army before the first snows fall, the Wehrmacht may well suffer a calamity of Napoleonic proportions. A key element of Barbarossa calls for a German army based in Russia to sweep through the Caucasus and capture the Soviets' rich oil resources – a prize to be sure, but one that may be impossible to achieve given any delay."

Rommel paused. Karl saw that Rommel was mulling over just what he would say next.

"The truth," Rommel resumed, "is that with adequate reinforcements we can capture all the oil we need to win with this war without the risk of Barbarossa." So, Rommel had actually studied the paper Scotty North described on the Oberbaum Bridge. It had turned Rommel to thinking of a rational alternative to the Russian adventure.

Karl felt a sense of relief. Despite the arrangement he had made with Haber, Karl did not intend to ever meet with Hitler to report on Rommel's loyalty. He would finish off Hitler before that. But now, should things somehow not proceed as Karl had planned, Rommel had provided him with just the sort of statement he needed. Of course, Karl could have concocted the same utterance, putting the alternative to Barbarossa in Rommel's mouth. But after seven years of lying, it would be easier to tell the truth, even if it meant betraying a man he had come to respect.

286. PAS DE CALAIS, MAY 10, 1941, 4:00 P.M.

A brisk afternoon wind blowing off the English Channel had cleared the air of spring pollen. Fern's eyes no longer itched and watered as she walked under the camouflage net that concealed the twin-engine Heinkels that would be dropping incendiary bombs on London that night. That meant more burned faces, more dead, and more wounded – both among the Luftwaffe airmen and their victims on the ground. Each German air raid sent more young men to the advanced burn-treatment facility she had established in Paris.

Fern wondered if she had a counterpart in London. Were the Royal Air Force doctors now stretched as thin as she and her Luftwaffe team?

Fern followed her usual early-evening routine. She retreated to her cramped but tidy office in the field hospital to sign a score or so of death certificates, many for young men in their late teens and early twenties. Then she washed her hands and face and saw in the small mirror how her thirty-six years had begun to show around her eyes. A plastic surgeon, she decided, should never look in the mirror.

Fern then made her rounds in the converted red-brick schoolhouse that served as a field hospital. During rounds, she checked bed charts and tried to joke with the healthier patients. Then she ate dinner in the barn that was the officers' mess. She might even permit herself a glass of white wine. Other doctors often joined her, and their camaraderie would always remind her of her medical school days in New York – and of Karl. After dinner she would return to her tent, where for five minutes, no more and no less, she indulged in her grief for Karl – memories of their days together in New York and their dream of moving to San Francisco. She napped on her cot for half an hour. Then she washed up again and walked back to the schoolhouse, readying herself for the job ahead, a job that helped her put her heavy baggage away for another night.

5:17 P.M.

Fern had just reached the door of the mess hall when a staff car approached. "Dr. Wagner!" called the handsome young driver, a corporal, as he jumped from the car. "I have a message for you from Herr Frederick Wagner. He's in Calais and requests your presence for ninety minutes. I am to take you to him then return you here in less than two hours. Everything's been cleared by the base commandant."

6:00 P.M.

Frederick led Fern onto the terrace of his hotel suite. They embraced and stood at the railing, watching the whitecaps spawned by the gusty wind.

"I'm only here for the night," Frederick said. "I thought I might offer you some company. I spent much of the day in a hangar discussing the performance of the Heinkel HE 111 with some of our pilots. The new British Spitfires are giving them more trouble than we expected."

Frederick saw that Fern had folded her arms, fighting the wind. "Come inside, it's warmer," he said, gesturing for Fern to step into the small dining room, where a table of cold meats and cheeses and a carafe of red wine awaited. He poured them each a glass.

"I heard some of the pilots talking about being transferred to new bases in Poland," Fern said. "What do you know about that, Uncle?"

"It's true. We'll need them there should we invade Russia."

"Now why in God's name would we do that?" Fern said indignantly. "The war was supposed to be over – and now the Führer wants to expand it. Why, for God's sake?"

"We need the oil and the wheat. Besides, the Führer believes that once we eliminate the Soviet threat, the British will at last get the point that Germany is invincible and agree to peace on our terms."

"Invincible? The wounded and dead in our field hospitals seem far from invincible to me, Uncle."

Frederick rested his chin on his right fist. "I know," he said. "The truth is that the Luftwaffe has failed to accomplish its mission. It did not destroy the RAF, as Göring promised. And we've exacerbated matters by bombing London instead of concentrating on more rational military objectives. The only thing we've accomplished has been to rally the British population against us."

"How utterly predictable," Fern sighed. She knew from the mounting number of Luftwaffe dead and wounded that the war was not proceeding as planned. But she'd clung to the hope that somehow it would end soon. Now she had begun to see there was no end in sight. She nibbled on some cheese and shook her head to decline Frederick's offer of more wine.

Frederick poured her a coffee instead. "I'll take advantage of being away from Berlin and try to get some sleep tonight," Frederick said. "One can't get much of that in Berlin these days with bombing raids almost every night."

"Yes, Uncle, I suppose it must be like London."

287. MELLISSA FARNSWORTH'S FLAT, KNIGHTSBRIDGE, LONDON, MAY 10, 1941, 10:50 P.M.

The leisurely Saturday evening dinner on the Strand accompanied by two bottles of vintage claret had worked as planned. Melissa now lay in a drunken slumber. Baxter called her name aloud for the third time to make sure she was sleeping. Easing himself from the bed, he found her purse atop the dresser and removed the passkey.

It was Saturday night. She wouldn't notice the key's absence until Monday morning – and by then he would have returned it. He put on his trousers, shirt, and tweed sport jacket, checking to see that he had the miniature camera and that it was fully loaded. Then he sat down at the secretarial table to pen a tidy note saying he would telephone her about an early dinner rendezvous the following evening. The orders from Moscow that morning had been clear. His performance was not considered satisfactory, especially compared to a certain unidentified Berlin operative. Baxter knew he had to do better, and soon. Chatting with Channing Brown earlier that day, he learned that Brown and Jillian were planning a Saturday night at the cinema. Brown wouldn't be in his Mayfair office.

When the sirens started to wail, Baxter was striding at a fast clip along Kensington High Street through the Saturday night pedestrian flow. The sirens — and the anxiety they provoked — more than suited his needs. The imminent air raid would provide ideal cover for the task ahead.

Baxter had reached Green Park when he heard the distant scream of a falling bomb. Based on the sound of the explosion, way off toward the southwest, he reckoned it had fallen well beyond Marble Arch. He cut under some trees, then over a long stretch of grass and crossed Piccadilly.

Melissa's passkey opened the street-level door on the Half Moon Street house. The building rattled as a bomb landed several streets away. Baxter was no virgin when it came to air raids. He'd endured intense shellfire and near-constant Luftwaffe bombing before in Spain, Belgium, and France. As he climbed the circular stairway, a nearby blast jarred the building and threw him back onto the first-floor landing. On instinct, he reached for his pocket camera. From what he could see — which was very little in this dim light — his fall hadn't damaged the camera. Back on his feet, he climbed the winding stairs to the fourth-floor apartment. He took several deep sniffs of air and breathed easier. He couldn't smell any smoke. He still had time.

12:01 A.M., MAY 11, 1941

He slid the passkey into the door of the flat. Once inside, he used a pocket flashlight to find his way around. He saw that Brown had fashioned the small flat into a spartan office. The main room was equipped with three desks, a hot plate, a radio, and several candlestick phones. There were no papers or folders on any of the desks. Opening a closet door, he found the first object of his search: a large steel safe, the only place in the flat where files and papers could be stored securely. Looking back over his left shoulder to make sure the blackout curtains were drawn, he flipped on the closet light, thankful that the electricity was still working.

The combination lock proved a greater challenge. He spun the dial and listened. He knew he had to be patient. The exploding bombs kept breaking through his concentration. He waited for a lull. Years earlier, foreseeing just this kind of endeavor, Baxter had paid out of his own pocket for tutorials from one of London's most accomplished safecrackers. A keen ear and gentle hands were the trick of it. On this night, the investment proved productive – he had the safe open within five minutes.

Inside the safe was a file cabinet with three drawers of neatly alphabetized folders, the first of which was labeled "Asian Access." A quick glance inside revealed that it concerned an anti-drug operation in Hong Kong. The second folder was marked "Beethoven" and concerned a spy station in Vienna. Baxter wasted no time on either. He kept leafing through folders until he came to a hefty binder labeled "Jackhammer."

Baxter rummaged through the pages of neatly pasted newspaper clippings and black-and-white photographs, all of which concerned a boxer identified in photo captions as Karl Ludwig. There were stories about a nightclub brawl, a Sing Sing prison sentence, and a fiery death under suspicious circumstances. Baxter's mind darted back to his dinner conversation with Fern in Spain.

There was more: One of the Jackhammer files included a photograph of Fern – no doubt that it was she – with a handsome young man, presumably Karl Ludwig, both in ski outfits. There were also letters and memoranda on the stationery of both the Crown and the White House as well as some twenty pages of minutes from various MI6 meetings. One memo caught Baxter's eye. It described a step-by-step plan for the capture and escape of General Haber from Madrid. Another, from Channing Brown to Winston Churchill, dated May 10, 1940 – precisely one year ago – summarized Karl Ludwig's real mission. Then Baxter smelled smoke.

Three successive blasts rocked the building. The Luftwaffe was dropping more than just incendiary bombs. Baxter knew he had little time. Patience, concentration, and steady nerves were now his only friends. He arranged what he believed to be the most important papers on the floor. Then he went down on his stomach to avoid the accumulating fumes, removed the camera from his jacket pocket, and began photographing the documents, one page at a time. The jolt of another blast knocked the miniature camera out of his hand.

He retrieved it and kept shooting even though his eyes were tearing up. He photographed several of the pages two or three times to make sure he had them. Finished, he scooped up the pages of the Jackhammer file, and returned them to the binder, taking precious seconds to ensure they were in order before returning them to the safe. Breathing as little as possible, he slammed the safe shut, investing several more precious seconds to double-check that it was locked and wiped clean of fingerprints.

Thick smoke choked the stairway. Closing his eyes and holding his breath, Baxter reached for the banister to guide him but found it too hot to touch. Slowing himself, he placed a soiled handkerchief over his nose and mouth and descended one step at a time. He fumbled in his jacket pocket to make certain the tiny camera was still there. When he reached the ground floor, another bomb shook the building, throwing him to the floor in the foyer. He bolted through the doorway. The night air, cold for the time of year, was full of smoke. He took several steps toward Piccadilly but couldn't resist looking back. The townhouse that contained Channing Brown's satellite office collapsed in a burning heap.

He wended his way through the fire trucks and hoses toward the Thames Embankment. Away from the heat of the fires, he shivered and turned up his collar. To his left, toward the City, he could see multiple searchlight beams and puffs of flak as bombs kept exploding. He'd been though many air raids, but nothing as intense and prolonged as this. Was it, perhaps, a prelude to the long-anticipated invasion?

He stopped in the doorway of a small bookshop and glanced about to make sure that no one was close enough to see him remove the film from his camera and place it carefully in an envelope.

Sirens screamed everywhere. His pace was deliberate, not fast enough to attract undue attention. At the Embankment, he saw that the bench he used as his regular pick-up and drop-off point was still there and, thank goodness, neither on fire nor occupied. Hearing more explosions off toward the Docklands, he took a small notepad from his vest pocket and jotted down a short, cryptic message, which he stuffed into the envelope alongside the film cartridge. Again, he looked around to be sure he hadn't attracted anyone's curiosity.

Seeing no one close by, Baxter took a small packet of thumbtacks from his jacket pocket and fastened the envelope to the underside of the bench. He didn't know *who* would come to retrieve the envelope, or when, but he knew for sure it would happen soon. Baxter stood, pulled up his jacket collar against the cold night air, and walked toward his Kensington flat, exhausted.

288. HOTEL CLERCY, PAS DE CALAIS, MAY 11, 1941, 10:38 A.M.

The ringing telephone caught Frederick just as he was about to leave his room, suitcase in hand. It was Göring, and what he had to say surprised Frederick.

"Thank you for letting me know, Hermann," Frederick said, sitting down on the bed and loosening his tie. "Yes, I'm sure he's in a terrible mood. And who can blame him? No wonder he doesn't want to meet with any of us this evening. I'll stay here and return to Berlin tomorrow."

289. LUFTWAFFE BASE, PAS DE CALAIS, MAY 11, 1941, 11:15 A. M.

Frederick found Fern in a hospital tent, where every bed was occupied. He led her outside, into the morning sunshine. "I see you're busy, so I'll be quick," he said. "Keep this to yourself – Hermann just telephoned me from the Obersalzberg with awful news. Hess took off in one of the new reconnaissance planes from the Messerschmitt plant in Augsburg, flew across the Channel. He left the Führer a note saying he planned to parachute into Scotland. Needless to say, the Führer is beside himself."

"Thanks for confiding that to me, Uncle, but as you can see, we're rather busy here. I haven't had any rest since I saw you yesterday. From the rumors I hear, last night's raid was the last one on London, at least for a while, thank God." She looked at the rows of occupied beds, then back at Frederick. "I have leave coming, and I'll take it. I'll visit mother in Berlin, stay at the

Adlon, and have a dinner or two with Hans. Then I'll spend some time resting in my apartment in Munich, where I can look in on the Luftwaffe hospital."

"You might as well spend some time in the Obersalzberg, too," Frederick said. "Feel free to use my chalet there."

"I'd love to, but only if you're coming down there to join me. We could play tennis and have long talks, just like in the old days in New York. You look as if you could use some rest, too."

"I'll let you know."

"Uncle, you must. It will be some time before I have another leave. If the invasion of the Soviet Union proceeds, I'll probably be sent to the front."

290. BERIA'S OFFICE, THE KREMLIN, MOSCOW, MAY 13, 1941, 9:00 A.M.

In the bright yellow light of his gooseneck desk lamp in the otherwise unlit office, Lavrentiy Beria examined the photographs and documents he'd received from Baxter.

Beria nodded with respectful admiration. So, the wily British had recruited an American boxer, an immigrant from Germany, to kill Hitler. *What balls*, he thought, smiling to himself. Who would ever believe it? But there it was, spelled out in the documents he had photographed, including forged medical school records from East Africa. Churchill and Roosevelt were both up to their ears in it. The files contained the boxer's new German identity and outlined his plans as a Nazi Party fundraiser. There was even a planning memo detailing the contrived escape of General Haber from Madrid.

It all checked out, all the way back to the suspicions noted in the unfinished typescript left by the dead Loyalist Captain Alvarez in Madrid.

What seemed farfetched not so long ago was now very real – and all the more interesting in light of Greenberg's arrival in Moscow. This Greenberg was on more than a medical mission. If medicine were his sole concern, the

American Embassy would never have selected him to relay information about an impending German invasion.

But that was old news. Beria had been hearing about a possible German invasion for months from a variety of Western intelligence sources. His best operative in Berlin had recently provided him with copies of maps of the proposed German battle plan. Even more recently, there'd been reports of brazen German reconnaissance flights over Soviet territory, and of troop buildups and construction of airfields in eastern Poland.

Beria couldn't see a silver lining in any of it. A successful German invasion would spell his own doom and very likely be the end of the Soviet Union. Even if he managed to survive the invasion itself, Beria realized, he would surely be among the first rounded up by Heydrich's death squads.

Ever the realist, Beria knew that the Red Army wasn't ready to repel a large-scale invasion. Stalin's purges of the 1930s had decimated the leadership cadres, robbing the Army of many of its best generals. Some of the new generals were capable professionals, but they needed more time to build a disciplined fighting force. Buying that time was one of the main reasons Beria and Molotov had argued for the non-aggression pact. Stalin wouldn't forget that. Even worse, Stalin had placed Beria's NKVD in charge of setting up defenses on the new frontier with German-occupied Poland. Progress there had been slow thanks to Stalin's insistence that the original fortifications, on the old Polish border, be moved west. Stalin favored the slow pace because he feared that too rapid a buildup might provoke the Germans. Stalin's strategy – like that of Beria and Molotov – was to buy time.

Against that backdrop, the American named Josh Greenberg remained a curiosity. So why not test him?

11:10 A.M.

Beria's secretary announced by intercom that the American had arrived. Beria arranged the material Baxter had sent into a logical display, one that would be easy for Josh to grasp. Then he pressed the intercom button. "Tell the American to come in."

291. THE CHANCELLERY, MAY 15, 1941, NOON

Rundstedt and Paulus waited as Hitler pored over Paulus's report on Rommel. Presentation of the report had been delayed by more than ten days because of the intense planning for Barbarossa. Paulus's report turned out to be a blunt sledgehammer of a document that portrayed Rommel as a stubborn commander whose strong will might prompt the General Staff to act against its better judgment and reinforce the Afrika Korps at the expense of Barbarossa. Paulus anticipated a positive response from the Führer – perhaps even a decision on Hitler's part to replace Rommel. But Hitler merely nodded as he finished the report. Rommel, he said, had gotten results. That was what counted. But although Hitler didn't mention it, it was Rommel's loyalty – not his competence – that was in question.

292. AMERICAN EMBASSY, MOSCOW, MAY 15, 1941, 11:05 P.M.

Jack Courtney looked up from the two-page memo from Josh, which reported on everything Josh had learned about the London documents during his visit to Beria's office earlier that morning. Beria had shown Josh everything that Baxter had photographed on Half Moon Street.

"I knew Beria's guys were good," Courtney said, "but who knew they were that good? Great work, Josh I'll let Washington know that the Russians are wise to Dr. Muller. The President can decide what to tell the Brits."

293. THE WHITE HOUSE, MAY 16, 1941, 9:07 A.M.

In the sanctuary of the Oval Office, Franklin Roosevelt read the memo from the American Embassy in Moscow. It took but a few seconds. Bill Donovan, now Roosevelt's top intelligence man, stood by waiting for the President's reaction. Donovan didn't have to wait long.

"Thanks for getting this to me right away, Bill," Roosevelt said, looking up and turning his chair to face Donovan, "Let's try to hook up with our friend in London."

294. ROMANISCHES CAFÉ, BERLIN, MAY 19, 1941, 10:00 A.M.

The elderly man removed his field cap, which showed that he'd served in the Imperial German Army during the Great War, and set it down on the table as if were a precious artifact. He fixed his eyes on the *Morgenpost* and never looked up until Dr. Karl Muller, in a single-breasted, charcoal gray suit, took a seat at the next table. They remained silent until Karl saw the waiter and asked for an ersatz. Both looked around to make sure no one could hear them.

"So *mein Herr*, what does the paper say about the German advance into Greece?" Karl asked.

"We're about to chase the British from another part of Europe," the old man replied. "Perhaps now they'll give up. They're fleeing Greece like the cowards they are."

Karl nodded in agreement and signaled the waiter. "Another ersatz for my friend here." Karl invited Scotty North to move to his table. Scotty checked under both tables for any hidden listening devices and then nodded for Karl to speak.

"I can get it done in the next thirty days," Karl said in hushed German. "We shouldn't meet again until it's over. I won't respond to further attempts to reach me. Understood? "

"Karl, my good fellow, you have expressed yourself with great clarity."

295. PRINZ-ALBRECHT-STRASSE, BERLIN, MAY 20, 1941, 9:15 P.M.

Hans stood in Heydrich's office next to a young SS Leutnant with a heavily bandaged head. The beam of Heydrich's desk lamp was trained directly on the man's face. Hans and the Leutnant both stood at attention as Heydrich spoke.

"So Leutnant, you obviously ignored last night's curfew even though the order was quite clear. Your defiance is an insult to your comrades, who at this very moment are fighting and dying in the Atlantic, over Britain, and in the Balkans and the African desert. Your behavior has sickened Reichsführer Himmler, just as it sickens me. You've distracted me from important work for the Fatherland.

"What you need, Leutnant, is the discipline you'll learn only by being demoted to the rank of private. You'll spend the next thirty days in Spandau prison. No visitors. No pay. After that you'll report back to me for reassignment to one of our special squads in occupied areas. Now get out of my sight."

The young Leutnant clicked his heels, gave the Nazi salute, turned, and left the room.

"So Krebs," Heydrich said once the young officer had left, "let's get down to business. The beatings have resumed. What new information do you have for me?"

"We have strong evidence that our assailant – if there is only one – is left-handed."

"What about your underground gang of Jews?"

Hans thought carefully before answering. "All I'm saying is that there's a strong indication that the assailant or, if you will, one of the assailants, is left-handed."

"Go on, Krebs. Give me the specifics."

"In nearly every case, the most devastating blow has been to the victim's right eye. In fact, all the victims have more damage on the right side of the face, indicating that the assailant landed his heaviest, most direct blows from the opposite side – in other words, with his left fist."

"But in a street fight," Heydrich responded, "blows can come from all sides, and land on either side of the face. Or anywhere. Isn't that right, Krebs?"

"Yes, that's true, but only in a sustained fight, one where both men land blows helter-skelter over a period of several seconds. Or in a prolonged boxing match, or any fight with lots of moving around. But that's not what we're looking at here. The victims of these assaults don't remember much. But from what they tell us, in every single case the assailant launches a surprise attack, stepping out from an alley or a doorway. Or else he attacks from the rear, with a hammer-like stroke to the base of the neck. There is flurry of punches from the attacker, with the victim having no chance to fight back. These *fights*, if we can call them that, last only seconds. There's no real exchange of blows. In every case, the victim goes down before he has a chance to fight back."

Hans paused, letting Heydrich absorb what he was hearing.

"As for the blow from behind," Hans resumed, "they all land at the junction of left shoulder and neck. That's precisely where any left-handed assailant who wanted maximum impact would aim his punch."

"I've heard enough talk, Krebs. I need a suspect – and I need one soon."

Heydrich lowered his head to indicate their discussion was over.

Once out on the Prinz-Albrecht-Strasse, Hans began to wonder why Heydrich had been so patient with him, while at the same time showing such contempt for the likes of Günter Jurgen and the beaten-up SS Leutnant.

296. MARTIN BORMANN'S OFFICE, THE CHANCELLERY, BERLIN, MAY 21, 1941, 10:15 A.M.

The morning after his return from the desert, Karl sat in Martin Bormann's outer office. Karl had learned of Rudolf Hess's flight to Britain only the night before when he was on a tri-motor Luftwaffe transport from Africa. A fellow passenger, a Luftwaffe Oberst with one arm in a cast, had confided to him about Hess's escapade. Now, with Hess in Britain, Karl was all but sure that Bormann had total control over who saw Hitler. Satisfied that he had cultivated a strong relationship with Bormann, Karl knew it was now or never.

After an hour's wait, Karl entered Bormann's office, offering a firm handshake. "Hold all my calls unless it's the Führer himself," Bormann barked into the intercom. "I want time to talk to my friend." Bormann gestured for Karl to sit in the straight-back chair opposite his well-organized desk.

"Karl, the desert appears to agree with you. You look quite fit."

"I lost twelve pounds thanks to the Afrika Korps field rations and the exercise I took with the infantry, good men who don't get enough credit. I look forward to telling the Führer about them, which I hope to do soon. I'm also eager to report on a pressing matter that I know he'll find of great interest."

"The present distraction in the Balkans has kept the Führer occupied for days now," Bormann reported. "It even diverted him from Barbarossa, which he had to postpone."

"But doesn't he expect me to report on what I learned in Africa?"

"Africa? Karl, surely you know that the Führer now sees the African front as little more than a sideshow."

"I realize that, Martin."

"Be careful, Karl. Our Führer's in no mood for that."

"Well Martin, that's why I need to meet with him in private, somewhere away from Berlin. I don't want to put him – or myself – on the spot in front of others, especially the generals. That's why I'm proposing a confidential meeting on the Kehlstein."

The intercom sounded. Adolf Hitler wanted Martin Bormann in his office. It was Karl's signal to leave.

9:00 P.M.

With Hitler secluded in the adjoining conference room, pouring over maps of western Russia, and with Hess gone, Bormann took a moment to assess his own situation. The job as Hitler's gatekeeper was his, and his alone, but he knew he could not rest on that. He had the job. Now he had to keep it. Bormann knew he still had rivals and that they would not go away. There was Himmler, and especially there was Heydrich, who long ago had let him know he had information on Bormann's sexual adventures, information that could well unsettle the Führer.

Bormann had not forgotten that Himmler and Heydrich had helped engineer the demise of Ernst Röhm, once Hitler's close crony. That, of course, was ancient history. What was not ancient history, Bormann well knew, was that others had showed signs of resenting his growing influence over access to Hitler – Göring, still defensive over his failure to bomb the British into quitting the war; Goebbels, Hitler's old friend from the early days of the Party; and the architect Albert Speer, whom Hitler saw as an artistic colleague. Bormann knew he could not afford to underestimate of any of them. He rose from his desk to view the vacant and blacked-out Wilhelmstrasse. Yes, Bormann knew he had enemies. He needed a friend. So if Karl Muller wanted to see the Führer, then Martin Bormann would make it happen.

297. BERLINER SPORTVEREIN, MAY 24, 1941, 6:00 P.M.

Karl spent several days searching for Günter Jurgen. He had received no response to the telephone messages he'd left at the Prinz-Albrecht-Strasse switchboard or to the note he'd mailed to Jurgen's home address on the Geller Strasse. Karl at last found Jurgen pummeling the heavy bag and invited him out for a beer.

On their walk to the Taverne, Karl noticed that Jurgen displayed none of his previous swagger. "So, Günter, you seem to be keeping yourself in top shape," Karl said as they stood at the bar. Jurgen shrugged, slumped his shoulders, and downed his beer in quick gulps.

"You're angry about something, Günter. Want to talk about it?"

"You noticed?"

"If you were okay, you wouldn't be drinking so fast. And you'd probably be encouraging me to join you at the Salon Kitty."

"The hell with whores."

"So tell me. What's bothering you? We haven't spoken in a while."

"It's that fuck, Heydrich."

"So what? Everyone knows he's a prick. Tell me what he's done to you" Karl said, signaling for a second round of beers.

"He's cut me off. I can't speak with him."

"Why's that?"

"I got rough with some French whore in a Paris brothel. I slapped her around a bit and caught hell for it. All of us on occupation duty were under strict orders to behave well in France. But what the fuck?" Karl smiled to himself, glad that his idea to entrap Jurgen in the Paris brothel had worked.

"Not long after that," Jurgen went on, "Heydrich accused me of making a pass at his wife."

Karl resisted the temptation to ask if the accusation was true. It didn't matter. He sensed Jurgen's desperation.

"Why'd he accuse you of making a pass at his wife?"

Jurgen looked up from his beer, shrugged again, and recounted what had happened that day at the Café Frida.

"It's obvious he wanted to rid himself of me. Now I'm on his shit list, even after all the special work I did for him in Poland and Norway."

Karl pushed another beer under Günter Jurgen's chin. "You don't have to convince me, Günter. Remember, I was there in that barn outside Lodz and in the mountains near Narvik. You deserve special recognition for that work."

Jurgen said nothing.

"Let me work on this, my friend," Karl said. "Perhaps I can make your life more promising. I might even be able to get you a meeting with the Führer. Just the three of us. Would you like that? There's an event in the works."

Jurgen frowned. "Heydrich would go crazy. Remember, I'm still under his thumb. Just got orders to rejoin my SS unit, something about special duty in the East."

"Blame me. Say that I arranged the introduction as a surprise. I don't answer to Heydrich. But make sure this remains our secret until it happens. Can you do that?"

"Don't worry. I'd be crazy to talk about it."

"This could be great for you, Günter. If you get to know the Führer, maybe you can get out from under Heydrich's abuse. I'll telephone you once I've set it up."

Karl left Jurgen sitting at the bar but froze in his tracks as he approached the door. Off to his left were Frederick and Fern walking behind the headwaiter, who was leading them to a table. Although they weren't ten feet away, both were looking in the other direction, their eyes fixed on the waiter. Karl looked down and darted onto the street, escaping into a taxi that took him straight home to Zehlendorf. He didn't see Frederick turn back toward him as he went through the doorway.

298. THE CHANCELLERY, MAY 25, 1941, 9:14 P.M.

After a working dinner in Hitler's office chambers, Bormann rose from his seat and closed the heavy blackout curtains. The drone of several electric fans filled the room. Sitting in a leather chair, Hitler had been addressing his generals without interruption for nearly thirty minutes, mostly about the importance of Operation Barbarossa.

Frederick Wagner was there to answer questions about fuel consumption of the tanks and aircraft produced in his factories. He sat and listened, as did Göring, Keitel, Jodl, Rundstedt, Paulus, and Bormann. When Hitler finished, Göring reported on casualties incurred during the air raids over Britain, as well as on operations in Greece and Yugoslavia.

"That's enough for now, Hermann," Hitler said. "We all know the British have been making a fight of it, and this distraction in the Balkans has disrupted our plans. But we must launch Barbarossa soon. The absolute launch date is June 22."

"As the Führer knows," Frederick said, turning toward Hitler, "Goebbels has received informed inquiries concerning Barbarossa from several foreign newspaper and radio correspondents stationed here in Berlin. It's no secret that there have been leaks, which are perhaps unavoidable in light of the size of this operation. But that makes it imperative to keep the launch date secret."

Hitler nodded. "And how do we that?" he asked.

"We let it be known," Frederick answered, "that the Führer will spend a relaxing weekend in the Obersalzberg from Friday, June 20, until the following Monday.

That will minimize suspicion that the invasion will begin that weekend."

"No!" Hitler said. "I will remain in Berlin, in communication with my generals."

The room remained silent until Hitler spoke again. "Gentlemen, we stand adjourned." Frederick lingered until only he, Bormann, and Hitler remained in the room.

"May I have an additional word, *mein Führer?*" Frederick asked.

Hitler gave Frederick a condescending nod. "What is it?"

"With all due respect," Frederick began, "I ask that you reconsider your decision about the weekend in the Obersalzberg. It would be an ideal time to receive Dr. Muller and hear his report on Rommel away from the generals and the busybodies here at the Chancellery."

Hitler frowned. "I *do* want to hear what Dr. Muller has to say about Rommel. His desert operations have made him into something of an international celebrity, particularly in the American press. It would interest me greatly to know whether Rommel mentioned that foolish paper proposing an alternative to Barbarossa."

"Very sensitive issues indeed, *mein Führer,*" Frederick said. "You certainly don't want to learn about Rommel's views from some American magazine, or from gossip here at the Chancellery."

Bormann turned to Hitler. "Dr. Muller himself has mentioned that the Kehlstein would be an ideal place for such a meeting."

"Besides which," Frederick added, "your meeting with Dr. Muller in such a prestigious setting will no doubt enhance his fundraising efforts for the Party."

Bormann nodded agreement. "And if we schedule it right, you could still return to Berlin in time to receive the first field reports on the invasion."

Frederick saw that Bormann had Hitler's attention. "Of course," Bormann said "we'll need to conceal the fact that you're conducting a private meeting with Dr. Muller by hosting a slightly larger group. It'll be a relaxed gathering of friends. You and the doctor can slip away without calling any attention to yourselves."

"All right," Hitler said at last. "I'll meet with Dr. Muller at the Kehlstein on June 21. And I like Martin's idea of a somewhat larger gathering. We should also invite someone from Mussolini's government," he said, looking at Bormann.

"Of course," Bormann replied. "We need to be able to say we invited at least one representative of the Italian government."

"I certainly don't want to offend our Italian allies," Hitler said, "especially since Rommel is supposed to be serving under their command."

299. THE FRIEDRICHSTRASSE, BERLIN, MAY 26, 1941, 6:31 A.M.

A driving spring rain splattered against the window of the small café-bakery. Frederick motioned to the approaching waitress, who was humming "The Skater's Waltz," their prearranged signal that it was safe to talk. Frederick ordered a Kaiser roll and ersatz.

"As usual, your ersatz is good, better than most places these days. Tonight I'll be traveling to Stockholm on business. I'd like to have real coffee while I'm there. Do you know a place where I might find some?"

"I know of a wonderful café called Johannson's, which I believe is the owner's name," the waitress said. "I have an aunt who lives in Stockholm. She's mentioned it in her letters."

"Thank you. I'm arriving by plane in the early morning, so I'll be in the mood for a good cup of real coffee," Frederick replied. He ate the roll, drank his ersatz, and left the bakery.

300. STOCKHOLM, MAY 27, 1941, 7:45 A.M.

The man Frederick had arranged to meet in Johannson's was sitting alone at a table near the window, hunched over his tea.

"Frederick, punctual as ever," Channing Brown said in German. "It's a bit loud in here, isn't it? There's a quiet park just down the street with a statue of King Charles XII near the entrance. Meet me there in ten minutes."

A spring drizzle had just begun as Frederick and Channing Brown met in front of the statue. Both men took it as a blessing — with the rain, there was no one there to eavesdrop.

"You wanted to see me," Brown said, "so I'll shut up and listen."

"We have a problem and no small one," Frederick said. "In fact, it could wreck Jackhammer — almost did so just a few nights ago."

"What in blazes happened?"

"Our friend Karl and my niece came within seconds of running into each other at a Berlin restaurant. I was there, so I was able to distract Fern."

"Any chance that either one saw the other?"

"I don't think so. But a near miss like that shows us the risk of a chance encounter between Karl and Fern. We could abide that risk when they were in different cities. Now things have changed. They're both in Berlin, and both will soon be in the Obersalzberg — Fern and I will be attending a little reception that Hitler is having atop the Kehlstein on 21 June. It's the very meeting you directed me to arrange. As I see it, this will be the occasion when our friend Karl is likely to carry out his plan."

Brown reached down to pick up a pebble and tossed it away. "Have there been any other close calls?" he asked.

"A few, yes," Frederick responded, but he did not not elaborate.

Brown's eyes searched the gravel. "Anything else?" he asked.

"Thus far, we've succeeded in keeping them apart — putting them in Spain at different times and keeping Fern out of Berlin when Karl was there. But we can only machinate so much. Now Karl, Fern, and I are all in Berlin, and soon we'll all be in the Obersalzberg — at the worst possible time."

"Any chance she could handle the shock of seeing Karl with no warning?" Brown asked.

"Very little, I think. After all, she doesn't even know he's alive. It might prove disastrous."

Brown gestured for them to start walking. "A wise man once told me to listen to those in the field and not make their decisions for them," he said. "So tell me, old friend, how will you minimize the risk?"

"By letting her know that Karl Ludwig is alive in the person of Karl Muller," Frederick said. "She'll also have to know he's working for you Brits, as I am. And she must learn all this sooner rather than later."

Brown walked a few more steps before speaking. "So, my friend, you must jump to it. See that she learns only what she needs to know – and not a syllable about Karl's actual mission."

301. ZEHLENDORF, MAY 31, 1941, 6:00 P.M.

Karl sipped a beer at his kitchen table. He would be staying off the streets of Berlin tonight. His shoulder ached after three consecutive nights of lurking about on the darkened streets and attacking seven more SS officers. Now he wanted to rest up for a morning run in the *Tiergarten* and a workout at the athletic club. He was about to reheat the sauerbraten that Frau Frick had been kind enough to prepare for him when a knock on the front door surprised him. He went to the sitting room, pulled back the drape, and saw a black Mercedes idling at the curb.

The man at the door wore a gray chauffer's uniform and cap. Karl knew he'd seen the man before but couldn't recall where. "Dr. Muller," the man said with a polite smile, "my name is Max Ulrich. My employer would like to see you. He requests that you accompany me now."

"Excuse me," Karl said, stepping outside the house, "but I'd like to know who is extending this unexpected invitation."

"I've been instructed to withhold his name, *mein Herr*. But I can tell you that you and he met some years ago in New York."

"Impossible. I've never been to New York. Tell your employer I must decline."

"He anticipated that you'd say that. He said you'd accept if I mentioned a certain word – *Jackhammer*."

Karl fetched his suit jacket without saying a word. Minutes later, with Karl in the back seat, the Mercedes rolled out of Zehlendorf and headed west.

8:45 P.M.

After leaving the autobahn, Max turned onto a bumpy unpaved road that wound its way through a thick forest of pines until the Mercedes rolled to a stop at a small lakeside cottage. A tall man emerged in the fading daylight.

Frederick Wagner opened the car door. "Karl, good to see you after all this time. Sorry to bring you so far."

Karl nodded with a half-smile but said nothing. Suspicious, he looked over Frederick's shoulder but saw no one. Well, he thought, if the Gestapo or SD were around, there was very little he could do about it.

"It's a modest spot," Frederick said, pointing toward the cottage. "I come here occasionally for some reflection, reading, and walks in the forest. There are no other cottages for five kilometers in any direction. Best of all, it's a bit of a dump. Forgive me, but who would believe that Frederick Wagner owned such a place?"

Frederick led Karl inside the cabin and gestured for him to sit at the bare wooden table. Max remained outside. "So, Frederick," Karl said at last, "you seem to know something of what I'm doing."

"I know all of it, but that's not why you're here. You see, I've recently returned from a rendezvous with our mutual friend Channing Brown."

"Brown? You know Brown?"

"Yes, long enough to have shared an adventure or two with him."

"How can I be sure, Frederick? The Gestapo or the SD could have learned the code word. You could be working for them. Hell, they could be listening in the next room. There could be more of them in the woods. That wouldn't surprise me."

"Brown trained you well, just as he did me. Tell me, does he still work in the library at Thornbil at all hours of the day and night? Does he still fancy a Johnnie Walker Black before dinner and a game of pool afterwards? Ask yourself, Karl: Why would I go to all the bother of getting you out here if I were working for the Gestapo or the Abwehr? Why wouldn't I simply let them know your true identity once I'd seen you in person? Don't you realize that we've almost run into each other several times, most recently at the Taverne?"

"You could have your reasons. Maybe you're working for both sides."

"And you'll just have to live with that possibility."

"So why are we meeting now?"

"We're here because I wasn't sure how you'd react to what I'm about to tell you."

Frederick told Karl of his meeting with Brown in Stockholm. "You see, Karl, for all these years, we considered it safer to keep Fern from knowing that you were alive, much less what your mission is. We've been able, for the most part, to keep you and her in separate locations. Now that you're both in Germany, hobnobbing with the Nazi elite, and frequenting many of the same places, it's just too risky to go on as before."

"I know," Karl said. "I saw you and Fern at the Taverne and got the hell out of there as fast as I could."

"It was then that I knew I had to reveal myself to you, especially since you and Fern will soon be together in the same place."

"Where?" Karl asked.

"Hitler's reception at the Kehlsteinhaus on the evening of 21 June. The Führer, you see, was kind enough to invite Fern and me to the event."

"How come?"

"There's no time for that now. You need to let Fern know you're alive. The risk of doing nothing is unacceptable."

"So what do you want me to do?"

"Just go and see her. Tell her you're working for the British – that's essential. Believe me, Fern's no Nazi."

"She'll have questions."

"Don't answer them. Brown insists that you say nothing about your mission. Just let her know you're alive and working for the British. We don't want her to bump into a ghost on the Kehlstein."

Karl sat fixed in his chair. His mind raced back over the mountain of lies. How could be ever tell Fern the truth or, as Frederick demanded, the half-truth of it? Why in hell couldn't Frederick tell her? No, that wouldn't work. There was a good chance she wouldn't believe Frederick, and even if she did, there was no telling how she would react.

Karl leaned forward. He knew Frederick was right: Fern had to know.

"Okay," he said at last, "I'll tell her. Any idea how I should do it?"

"Yes. She's in Munich now, on leave. I'll telephone her there and say I'm coming to Bavaria on business for several days. I'll ask when I can drop by her place for a drink and take her out to dinner. We'll fix a date and time. She'll be there waiting, but I won't show up. You will."

"Sounds easy, though it probably won't be," Karl said. "Anything else?"

"Not tonight. You should get going. Max will drive you back to Berlin and return for me tomorrow. No sense in our being seen together."

302. MUNICH, JUNE 2, 1941, 6:15 P.M.

Karl's wristwatch told him he was fifteen minutes early. Fern's apartment building had a stucco façade and faced the green expanse of the Englischer Garten. He decided on a short walk.

On the train ride from Berlin, Karl had thought of nothing but Fern, what he could and couldn't say to her. How would she react? His feet numb, his fingers cold, his mouth sour. Minutes passed. It was time.

6:29 P.M.

In her spartan third-floor apartment, Fern had fixed two of what Frederick called her industrial-strength martinis. Each chilled long-stemmed glass held two generous ounces of the Gordon's gin she'd hoarded since the war started.

She had just put some cashews, also hoarded, in a small bowl when the buzzer rang. The concierge announced that a Herr Wagner had arrived. She took one of the martinis to give to Frederick as she opened the door, knowing he'd like that.

Once on the elevator, Karl found himself hoping that Fern's flat would be at the far end of the hallway. But the open apartment door was opposite the elevator. Fern stood facing him in the half-light, martini in hand, stunned at the sight of Karl.

In the longest instant of their lives, they rushed into a frantic embrace. Then, as his strong arms and hands tightened around her, she froze and squirmed away, then bolted into her apartment, the martini wasted on the carpet. She stared through the open window, her back to him. He tried to put a gentle hand on her shoulder, but she jerked free.

"It's really me, Fern." She said nothing but turned to face him.

"Really who?" she said. "Are you the Karl Ludwig from New York, the fairytale land with a neighborhood called Yorkville, the Bavarian Inn, and the 86ᵗʰ Street Brauhaus where they sang the *Schnitzelbank Song*? Are you from that fantasyland where we stayed in a gorgeous Victorian townhouse on 85ᵗʰ Street, a place for parties and to make love on rainy Sunday mornings?"

"Fern . . ."

"Shut up," she said, her teeth clenched. "You see, I had to forget all that – forget the doctor who worked in the freezing cold to save children burned in a Christmas Eve tenement fire, forget the prizefighter who raised money for little boys in Harlem. That Karl Ludwig is dead."

"Fern I'm still that person. Let me explain."

"Explain? How can you explain? I know who you are," she said. "The truth of it kills everything I loved about Karl Ludwig and our life in New York. I know all about the renowned Karl Muller, the doctor so many Nazi big shots have wanted me to meet. He's the savior of General Haber, the skiing buddy of Hermann Göring, the heroic Nazi Party fundraiser. He's even served with the SS in Poland and Norway. You're famous. You're Karl Muller. I've heard more about Karl Muller than I ever want to know."

"Fern, believe me. I know how you feel."

"How in the name of God could you know how *I* feel? What claim do you have to know anything about me? The person you knew in New York was a naive resident doctor. Now she works for people who drop bombs on mothers and fathers, grandparents, and little kids in Warsaw, Rotterdam, and London – all for the greater glory of your Nazi Party, your Fatherland, and your Führer."

She looked away from him, gathering her thoughts. "Karl, you didn't die in that crash. But my love for you died when I learned that you lost control of yourself and used your fists in that barroom fight, even after swearing to me that you'd never let that happen again. And now look at us."

"Fern."

"Stop, I'm not finished. You see, Karl, you're not the only one who's dead. I died too. I died when I said goodbye to you at Sing Sing. I died again when I returned to this nightmare called the Third Reich, and when I abandoned our best friend Josh because he made the unforgivable mistake of being a Jew. And I die again every night when I'm in my bed trying to sleep."

"Fern, let me . . ."

"I said shut up. I've just started. Whoever you say you are now, the Karl Ludwig I knew would never have allowed the woman he loved to believe he was dead – not for seven years, not for a single godforsaken second. Karl Ludwig was a real man, and real men don't lie. And you can bet your sweet ass they don't lie to the woman they intend to marry."

He moved toward her.

"Keep the hell away from me. I mean it."

He stood where he was.

"I hear you, Fern. I've got it coming. But soon I'll be able to explain everything. For now, just let me say that I had to get out of Sing Sing. But that's a long story. What you need to know now is that I got out because I accepted a mission – one that involved becoming Dr. Karl Muller."

"That's splendid, terrific, very Hollywood. Was your mission to be the all-star fundraiser for the Nazi Party? " she asked, denying him eye contact.

"No, Fern, that's just part of it. Spain was another part."

"And helping my mother's husband escape from the Communists in Madrid? Was that part of it too?"

"Yes. That was part of it, too."

"Part of what? Tell me, for God's sake . . . On the other hand, no. Forget it. None of that interests me now. But goddamit, Karl," she said, stepping toward him, "how could you not tell me you were alive?"

"The people I work for deemed it too risky."

"I'm not talking about them, Karl. I'm talking about you and your seven-year lie, a lie of silence. Have you nothing to say about that, even now?"

"Only that Muller will be my name for only a little while longer. But that's how you must address me whenever we're together in public."

"Together in public? Are you kidding? I won't be seeing you at all if I can help it. Tell me Karl, why did you seek me out now?"

"Because the people I work for thought there was too great a risk of our bumping into each other – and that would blow my mission. They knew a chance meeting would upset you and call attention to us. Then you would be in trouble too."

"This gets worse, Karl, doesn't it? You didn't just betray our love, you put my life in danger, knowing I might be exposed to the Gestapo or SD."

"I always thought you'd return to America. If you had become a U.S. citizen, you could have gone back for good."

"Don't dig yourself in any deeper, Karl. None of this is my fault. It's your fault, one hundred percent your fault."

He stepped toward her. "Let's stop all this bickering and go have some dinner."

"Dinner? Eat by yourself. You must have gotten used to it after seven years. And in case you're too thick to have noticed, Karl Ludwig, this *mission* stuff doesn't impress me at all. It means nothing to me. What matters to me is that you lied, that you betrayed me."

She rose from the couch and walked to the little breakfast bar where the second martini remained untouched. She took a long gulp and handed the glass to Karl. "Here, you may need this more than I."

Karl finished it.

She looked him in the eye. "And what about Frederick? He must be involved in all this. Otherwise, he wouldn't have set me up like this."

"Yes, but you'll have to ask him."

"You can bet I will."

She went to the window that overlooked the Englischer Garten. "It doesn't appear that anyone followed you here. Gestapo agents are pretty clumsy when it comes to tailing people. I learned that from my friend Hans Krebs. You must know him. You're his family doctor. I believe you've treated his daughter."

"I know him."

"He's a wonderful man. I enjoy his company, and I intend to continue seeing him."

"Fern, I . . ."

"No use, Karl. We're done. I mean it. You killed it. Please know that if you telephone me, I'll hang up. Should we run into each other, I'll be polite, but read nothing into it. And rest assured, I won't be foolish enough to blab about this meeting to anyone – not Hans, not Mother, no one. I know enough not to take that risk. I'd be too embarrassed."

He reached out to take her hand, but she snapped it back. "Don't ever touch me, not ever. Just remember this," she said, as her windmill slap stung his cheek.

He stepped back, his left cheek stinging. She turned toward the window, shoulders arched forward, her face in her hands.

"Go now," she said.

Karl didn't wait for the elevator. He rushed down the stairway and walked as fast as he could to the Bahnhof. He knew she meant every word she'd said and that she hated him.

At least he was sure she would keep his secret. He had to force her out of his mind. Now he had to concentrate on staying in shape and completing his mission. He still felt the sting of her slap. All he could do was keep on walking and pray that he might somehow win her back.

7:05 P.M.

Fern stood rigid at the kitchen sink. She poured herself a second martini. No vermouth. She flashed back to the night five years before, when she'd gotten drunk because Karl was dead. Now she was about to get drunk again because she had just felt his strong arms and hands and knew he was no ghost. Why hadn't he told her about his mission in the beginning? And why, for God's sake, had she left him in Sing Sing and returned to Germany? There was so much she didn't know or understand. She took a sip then poured the rest of the martini down the drain.

A moment later she left the apartment and walked toward the café where she had made a dinner reservation for Frederick and herself. She would explain that her companion's plans had changed and that she would dine alone, away from other customers, hopefully at a corner table. Once seated, she would enjoy a glass of dry white wine before dinner. She needed time to think because things had changed. *Karl was alive.*

303. PRINZ-ALBRECHT-STRASSE, JUNE 4, 1941, 11:00 A.M.

Reinhard Heydrich pushed his chair away from his desk and indulged in a satisfying stretch. The job of policing Western Europe had challenged him. And now that the beating of SS officers had resumed, things were proving difficult right here in Berlin. There had been four beatings in the previous fortnight. He shut his office door and examined the scant reports of each episode.

Using graph paper, he transcribed the time, date, location, and a brief description of each attack. All of the assaults had occurred at night, on Berlin's blacked-out streets. More often than not, the assailant leapt from a doorway, an alley, or an alcove. Heydrich noticed the sporadic nature of the attacks. There were sudden bursts of activity, with several attacks in the course of a single week. Then nothing. And despite the fact that there had been as many as three victims in a single attack, none could say for certain that there had been just one assailant.

Heydrich picked up the telephone and demanded a list of known thugs, athletic club members, and current or former boxers and wrestlers, professionals and amateurs – men with the skills to inflict such severe injuries. He further ordered several junior SD staffers to find out who, among the SS and SD, had actually been in Berlin on the nights of the attacks, demanding a report within forty-eight hours.

As for Krebs, Heydrich was sure that the otherwise competent detective was covering up for someone. But who and for what purpose?

304. PRINZ-ALBRECHT-STRASSE, JUNE 6, 1941, 2:15 A.M.

Heydrich's eyes burned from too little sleep. He reread the reports for the third time. Most of the men on the list were too old to have inflicted injuries as terrible as those suffered by the victims of the recent beatings. There were three over-the-hill boxers on the list as well as a former Olympic gymnast nearing his sixtieth birthday. The younger men on the list were, of course, in the military, and information on their whereabouts on specific dates wasn't readily available, except when it came to members of the SS, the SD, and special units like the one still headed by Günter Jurgen.

305. THE HEYDRICH RESIDENCE, ZEHLENDORF, BERLIN, JUNE 6, 1941, 6:00 P.M.

Hans emerged from the black Mercedes he'd taken from the SD motor pool that morning. He recognized the melody on the violin, something by Bach. He saw Heydrich, playing in the shade of a large umbrella. Hans kept his distance until Heydrich put the instrument down.

"Ah, Krebs, thank you for allowing me to finish," Heydrich said, returning the violin carefully to its case. "The violin is my passion, my escape from day-to-day aggravations. Fencing used to be my passion, but I have no time for it these days. Please sit with me."

Hans sat and stretched his legs.

"Krebs, I must apologize for neglecting you these last several weeks. Policing a territory the size of the Reich is no easy task. I apologize also for my impatience at your failure to solve these beatings, a frustrating case to be sure."

"No need for apologies. You're the boss, and you have your priorities."

"There have been three more beatings this week. Himmler and the Führer find this troublesome. If we're to rule Europe, we can't keep losing good men like these, even for a few days. So tell me, Krebs, have you learned anything new?"

"Evidence continues to mount that underground Jewish groups and their sympathizers are active here in Berlin."

"Yes, your discovery of the safe apartment appears to support that theory. Still, I'm not entirely convinced."

"I appreciate that."

"Good. So I'll get right to why I asked you here this afternoon. I am embarrassed to say that we must start to keep a closer eye on our own men. The SS and SD aren't altar boys, after all. Just between you and me, Krebs, some of them are Neolithic brutes, capable of almost anything. That's why I'd like to keep your sharp eyes on two particular individuals . . ."

Hans took a small memo pad from his vest pocket and began making notes.

306. WHITEHALL, JUNE 12, 1941, 9:00 P.M.

Channing Brown and Jamie Creel listened as Scotty North reported on his six-week continental sojourn. He'd crossed the Channel only the evening before in a fishing boat captained by a Breton skilled at eluding German coastal patrols. Scotty saved for last what he'd learned from Karl during their meeting on the Spree embankment: Karl would strike soon; remain incommunicado until he had completed the job and secured his own survival; and request that London initiate no further communication with Frederick Wagner, in order to protect Frederick and his family.

"It's his show now," Brown said, "just as he wanted it."

Once he had given his report, Scotty learned that the Half Moon Street office had been destroyed in a bombing raid.

"Quite a loss," Brown said. "But now lads, I have even more troubling news. You'll recall that we took some comfort in the fact that our office safe and its contents survived the fire-bombing of the Half Moon Street house. But I received a coded message from our friend Bill Donovan in Washington. An American agent has irrefutable evidence that the Soviets know Karl's true identity and the objective of his mission. Beria himself has photocopies of our Jackhammer documents. Beria told this American agent that the Soviets have a spy who's infiltrated MI6. The spy must have broken into the house, photographed the Jackhammer documents, and sent his film to Moscow."

"So Beria knows everything? Scotty asked.

"In short, yes," Brown said, laying his hands flat on the table. "We recovered the locked safe in the rubble. That means someone trained in safecracking, someone professional enough to cover his tracks, got into the safe before the building burned to the ground. And how did that someone even know about the location of our Half Moon Street office? Just more evidence that we're up to our balls in Soviet agents."

"What should we be doing about it?" Jamie asked.

"Nothing, for the moment," Brown said. "It's up to Karl now. If anyone tries to stop him, it won't be the Russians. Given all the rumors of an impending German invasion of the Soviet Union, Beria and Stalin would rather fancy the idea of a dead Hitler. And let's not forget — all these rumors about an attack on Russia could be a clever ruse. Hitler may be about to launch a cross-Channel invasion now that the warm weather is upon us."

A stenographer rushed into the office without knocking and put a note under Brown's nose. He gave it a quick glance and bolted to his feet.

"I'm off to the Cabinet War Rooms. Something urgent from the PM."

307. CABINET WAR ROOMS, BENEATH WHITEHALL, JUNE 12, 1941, 9:15 P.M.

Winston Churchill gestured for Channing Brown to take a seat at the small desk.

"Good to see you, Channy. Feel free to smoke. You'll need a cigarette, or something stronger, when you hear what I'm about to tell you."

Churchill waited for Brown to light up. "It appears that the rumors we've been hearing are true: Hitler is about to make an epic blunder and invade the Soviet Union. His mistake should provide us with a strong ally. Think of it, the German leader is giving us a bloody present – an ally with limitless natural resources and an enormous army."

Churchill paused, taking a bright-eyed bead on Brown. "And we must do nothing to stop Hitler's Russian adventure. That, Channy, means we must abort Jackhammer. I've been mulling this over for some time but just decided on it this evening."

"Abort?"

Churchill saw Brown's jaw tighten. "Yes, a bloody shame, but we have no choice. If Jackhammer succeeds and Hitler ends up dead, his generals might well have the sense to scrub Barbarossa and resume preparations for invading us. The Huns could be in our lap by midsummer, perhaps sooner."

Brown leaned forward. "Sir, there's something you should know. It's too late to tell our man Karl to stand down. He's cut off all communication and is poised to strike."

"I can't accept that, Channy. Consider the bigger picture here. We no longer want Hitler dead. We want the bugger alive, at least for now. This is a direct order, Mr. Brown: You are to take immediate steps to stop your man from carrying out his mission, whatever the cost."

Brown knew this was no time to debate Winston Churchill. "I quite understand, Sir. Is that all?"

"Indeed. Go and do what you must, Channy. And let me know in person when you start to move the matter forward."

Brown walked in the fading twilight back to his Whitehall office and sat alone, staring at the wall. He cursed himself for dallying. Churchill had given him no time for contemplation. He reached for the candlestick telephone and asked the switchboard operator for a secure line to New York. The call took ten minutes.

He knew the people in New York were professionals. They asked the right questions and knew what to do, how to work out the details. A quarter of a million pounds would be fine. They appreciated the business. They assured him they had the right man for the job, their best. He was already in Europe, hungry for a payday. Brown had a deal.

Brown put down the phone. He'd carried out his order and that was that. He wiped sweat from his forehead. Soon he'd walk back to Bayswater and meet Jillian at one of their locals and get very drunk. *No. It wasn't that simple. There had to be something more he could do.*

Recalling that Churchill wanted an in-person confirmation that Brown had initiated the matter, he left his office and headed back to the Cabinet War Rooms. He had an idea.

308. PALERMO, SICILY, JUNE 13, 1941, 10:00 P.M.

For Victor Minnelli, the handwritten message waiting at the front desk of the hotel near the Quattro Canti came as a welcome surprise. He'd been spending his days alone, and his evenings with the wife of an Italian Army captain stationed in Africa. She came to him most nights after putting her children to bed and always left before dawn.

The message was clear:

Call us in New York as soon as you receive this. Major job awaits. Urgent. Will pay $100,000 on completion.

Minnelli grinned. The money would go straight into his Zurich bank account, where he'd already stashed at least a million dollars. It would be enough to retire to his mountain chalet near Davos. He'd become a ski instructor and enjoy the company of firm-breasted Swiss girls who worked at the nearby resorts.

Minnelli decided not to use the phone in the hotel lobby. Once back in his room, he checked to make sure his Beretta was loaded, put the weapon in his ankle holster, and hurried down the stairs. He took a short cut through crooked back alleys to the train station where he knew there was a good telephone kiosk, one he used for important calls when the people on the other end were paying the toll. He waited for an international connection, thankful that the station wasn't crowded. Even though he always carried forged discharge papers, he didn't want the police questioning him about why he wasn't in the military.

The familiar voice on the other end of the line told him that the job was important and the time factor critical. He had to leave immediately for Rome, where he would learn more.

309. VIA DEL CORSO, ROME, JUNE 14, 1941, 11:45 P.M.

A bright yellow light was shining on the back-room table of the café where Minnelli sat with the others, five of Luciano's best men in Rome. They had been there for more than two hours drinking espresso, focusing on an impro-vised diagram of the facility atop a far off mountain called the Kehlstein. The British were all but certain this would be the location – and that the attempt would take place on June 21. They knew the name of the man Minnelli was to kill and provided him with a precise description. Minnelli was attentive but relaxed, happy for the respect he was getting.

Luciano had made himself very clear on the telephone. Minnelli was to approach the job with even more caution than usual, and take no unnecessary risks. He was to wait until the target made his move on Hitler. Only then should Minnelli fire his Beretta and kill the assailant. That way, Minnelli would survive and be recognized as a hero, having gunned down the man who was about to assassinate the German Führer.

After the kill, Minnelli was to leave the Kehlstein as soon as it was feasible, saying that he needed to report forthwith to Il Duce in Rome. He'd be long gone before the Gestapo, SS, and SD began tripping over each other with questions.

"One more thing, Victor," said the lean bald man who'd been doing most of the talking. "And this is critical. If, by any chance, the target never makes his move against Hitler, you're to do nothing – just relax, enjoy the party, and get your ass off the mountain when it's over. It means someone has reached out to the target and persuaded him to stand down. That would be fine. Remember, Hitler's survival is what our client wants."

310. BILL DONOVAN'S RESIDENCE, WASHINGTON, D.C., JUNE 12, 7:07 P.M.

Newly commissioned to build up America's fledgling intelligence capabilities, Bill Donovan was now in daily communication with the White House. Still, it surprised him when he answered the telephone just before dinner and heard the unmistakable voice of Franklin Roosevelt. Donovan scribbled a few quick notes on a legal pad.

The President's message was an urgent one. Churchill had just called to say that Jackhammer was being aborted, that Hitler was now more useful alive than dead. The Brits wanted him alive so he would persist in his folly of invading Russia. Unless someone could reach Karl and persuade him to abort the mission, an assassin would kill him. The contract on Karl's life had already been issued.

Donovan also learned that Channing Brown had persuaded Churchill to give the Americans a chance to intercept Karl.

On the telephone, Roosevelt had been unequivocal: "I'm counting on you, Bill. Let's save this young man. And don't blame Churchill and the British. They've got enough on their hands. Indeed, this invasion of Russia might be just the break they've been hoping for."

Donovan knew of only one person who could stop Ludwig. He picked up the phone.

311. BORMANN'S OFFICE, JUNE 15, 1941, 9:00 A.M.

Karl entered Bormann's office, refreshed by an early morning run in the Tiergarten.

"Martin, I want to thank you again for everything you've done to make the Kehlstein meeting possible. I dropped in to tell you that I'll be leaving for the Obersalzberg tomorrow. I'll take a few days off and stay at the Berchtesgadener Inn. I have lots to tell the Führer, and I need some time to think it over."

"Excellent, Karl. You know how much the Führer appreciates a well-prepared presentation. But we need to discuss security."

"Security?"

"Yes. Five SS security guards are with or near the Führer at all times."

"You realize that my report on Rommel is for the Führer's ears only?"

"So?"

"So I have an idea, one I believe will satisfy your security needs. But it has to be strictly between us."

312. KARL MULLER'S OFFICE AND RESIDENCE, ZEHLENDORF, JUNE 16, 1941, 9:04 A.M.

Frau Frick had just finished rescheduling Karl's appointments. The doctor had told her that this would be his last day in the office until July 1. Frau Frick, now adept at reshuffling Karl's appointments and keeping patients content, didn't mind. After all, the doctor was doing important work for the Führer. She was typing a revised schedule when the phone rang.

"Ah, Herr Krebs. *Heil Hitler.* Good to hear your voice. Would you like to see Dr. Muller?"

"Yes," Hans responded. "Nothing critical, mind you, but I think it's time I had a thorough checkup. I've been feeling a bit tired, not sleeping much. Can I make an appointment to see Dr. Muller, or is he off on one of his speaking tours? If he is, I can wait until he returns."

"Well, he does have an important meeting coming up in Berchtesgaden. He's going there for several days. Suppose I put you down for 11:00 a.m. on July 2?"

"That would be wonderful, Frau Frick. *Heil Hitler.*"

313. HANS KREBS'S DESK, PRINZ-ALBRECHT-STRASSE, JUNE 16, 9:07 A.M.

Hans sat up when the switchboard operator told him he had a call from Berchtesgaden.

"Hans, when are you going to join me?" Fern said. "I only have a few days' leave remaining."

"Tell me, are you getting the rest you wanted?"

"Yes. I've been doing absolutely nothing except taking long hikes in the mountain air and playing tennis with Uncle Frederick. But I miss our conversations. Besides, I'm sure you could use some time off."

"I'll be coming down soon, staying in the officers' quarters at the SS barracks. It sort of goes with the job. Heydrich arranged it."

"Bring your best suit. The Führer has invited us to a reception at the Kehlstein this Saturday evening, the 21st. I need an escort, and you're it."

314. MOSCOW, JUNE 16, 1941, 11:00 P.M.

Josh was brushing his teeth before bed when the embassy switchboard operator rang to say that a man named Dmitri was on the line. Dmitri's message was simple enough. Josh got dressed and left to see Beria.

Minutes later, a uniformed NKVD guard led Josh down three flights of stairs to a cavernous basement room, where a bright yellow light shone into the bloodied face of a man bound to a chair. Two uniformed guards stood at attention on either side of the bound man. Beria, standing in front of the man, wore a sweat-drenched sleeveless undershirt that revealed a physique more muscular than Josh would have expected. He was holding a two-foot length of lead pipe in his right hand.

"I received your message, Josh," Beria said. "So you're being posted to Berlin. I find that interesting since your country suspended diplomatic relations with Germany last month. Berlin will present its challenges. I thought I'd put you in touch with someone there who might be helpful. You never know what might develop. You may need a friend there someday."

Beria handed the lead pipe to a guard and wiped his face, neck, and chest. "Excuse me for exposing you to this unpleasant situation, Josh. This scum in the chair is a former friend. In fact, he once had a very promising career. He was a major in the Red Army until just three hours ago. Then I learned that he's been sleeping with a German national, a young secretary in their embassy here. He gave us the typical bourgeois excuse that he'd fallen in love. He says she confided to him that there are rumors of an imminent German attack on the Soviet Union. So not only has he been careless in consorting with a foreign national, he told his fellow officers what she said. He thus helped to spread a lie, despite clear orders not to repeat unfounded rumors. Tomorrow he'll be on a train to the Gulag. Ten years there should help him build character."

Turning toward the prisoner, Beria hit the man across the mouth, sending part of a tooth skittering across the floor. Then Beria struck two blows to the man's chest. There was no cry of pain. The young major was out cold. He would be lucky, Josh thought, to die right there.

Beria nodded toward the two guards, who remained at attention. "Take him to his cell. Give him fresh clothes to replace the uniform he's disgraced."

Beria toweled himself off again and put on a white dress shirt that hung over the back of an empty chair.

"I want to share something with you, Josh. I confess that I knew you were right several weeks ago when you told me of an imminent German invasion. Some of us in the Kremlin have known about these German plans for some time, but the information was always very general. Now we have the specifics – the launch date, the battle orders, everything – right from our best agent in Berlin. So come to my office. We'll have some vodka, and I'll show you."

"Wait," Josh said. "Didn't you just accuse that guy downstairs of spreading disinformation about an attack?"

"Indeed, I did. Such disciplinary actions will show our faith in the pact with Hitler, and that we're not the ones breaking this solemn agreement. That's what Comrade Stalin wants, and that's what he gets. Any word that we're preparing for an attack might just provoke Hitler into striking sooner. I'll confide to you that we're far behind in our preparations – any time we can buy is valuable. Now let's drink," Beria said as they reached his office.

After downing his shot in a single gulp, Beria handed Josh a slip of paper with a number scribbled on it. "Call this number when you get to Berlin. This person is a mere intermediary but can arrange a meeting with the important individual I mentioned earlier."

Josh stuck the paper slip in his wallet. "Okay, what else can you tell me about the invasion?"

"Only that we have a deep-cover agent who has informed us that the Germans will attack in less than a week – at three in morning on Sunday, June 22. Is that specific enough for you, Josh?

"Tell your superiors in Washington that Comrade Molotov and I appreciate President Roosevelt's willingness to share with us what he knows of the coming attack. It has been of great help, and we'll need more American help very soon. Now if you'll excuse me, I must see Comrade Stalin."

Once back at the embassy, Josh accepted a sealed envelope from the Marine guard at the reception desk. He had a one-way ticket on an early-morning flight to Berlin.

315. BLETCHLEY PARK, ENGLAND, JUNE 17, 1:12 A.M.

Hard at work in her glass-enclosed cubicle, Daphne Walker-James had just deciphered an intercepted message from Berlin to Rome – something about a reception at a new facility atop the Kehlstein in the Obsersalzberg. Now she found herself working on a related message, acknowledging a reply from Count Ciano, the Italian Foreign Minister. The message identified an Italian naval officer who would be attending the reception representing Il Duce.

316. THE ADLON, BERLIN, JUNE 17, 8:00 A.M.

Josh sipped ersatz in his room at the Adlon and read the front page of the *Morgenpost*, which said that the fighting in the Balkans was coming to an end – a smashing victory for the Wehrmacht. The ringing telephone startled him.

"Josh, it's Vicky. I'm in the lobby. Can you meet here in ten minutes?"

In the lobby, she hugged Josh and whispered into his ear. "Courtney is sure your room is bugged. Let's go feed some pigeons in the Tiergarten."

"Tell me, Vicky, what in the hell am I doing here among all these Heinies?" Josh asked as they strolled under the Brandenburg Gate and Vicky took a firm grip on his upper arm.

"It's simple," she said as they kept walking. "But it won't be easy. Your job is to find Karl Ludwig – a.k.a. Karl Muller – and stop him from killing Hitler."

"Why should I stop Karl – or anyone – from killing the son of a bitch?"

"Because the Brits, bless their hearts, now believe that killing Hitler isn't in their best interest. What's more, FDR agrees. They know Hitler's about to invade Russia, and they *want* him to go ahead with the attack because that'll drive the Soviets to ally with Britain.

"Hitler has to be alive for the invasion to proceed. With Hitler dead, there's an excellent chance his generals would call off the invasion. The Brits are serious about this, Josh. They've contracted for a hit man to stop Karl."

"Okay," Josh said, "how do I figure in all that?"

"We want you to talk Karl out of it, to save his life."

Josh looked away. "Talk him out of it? Now just how am I supposed to do that, Vicky? First I have to find him. And he might not even listen to me. Remember, we haven't seen each other in more than seven years."

"No offense, Josh, but the President of the United States wants this done and has ordered you to do it."

"So where the hell is Karl now?" he asked.

"We don't know."

"So where do you suggest I start?"

"At the U.S. Embassy. As you know, the President recalled our ambassador last December. But we still have a competent staff running the store."

317. AMERICAN EMBASSY, BERLIN, JUNE 17, 11:52 A.M.

Courtney was waiting for them in his new office. He didn't wait for Josh to ask questions. "The good news is the Brits have learned of a reception Hitler is holding on the Kehlstein this Saturday evening, June 21. The bad news is that they've almost certainly alerted their hit man, and that's where he's headed. Since Roosevelt recalled Ambassador Wilson, we don't receive many invitations from Hitler, or from anyone else in the Nazi government. The only way we can save Ludwig is for you, Josh, to get your ass to Berchtesgaden and find Ludwig before the hit man does. The Brits are cooperating, hoping that we can get to Ludwig first. They've informed us that Karl will be staying in the Berchtesgadener Inn."

"I'll find him at his hotel," Josh said, "If not, I'm sure I can intercept him at the reception."

"First you'll need an invitation," Courtney said.

318. WASHINGTON, D.C., JUNE 17, 8:15 A.M.

With Donovan on the line, Franklin Roosevelt placed a fresh cigarette in the long ivory holder. He thought about what Donovan had just proposed – sending a letter to Adolf Hitler, through the German Foreign Minister, requesting that he invite an American doctor already employed by the State Department to a Saturday evening reception being held on the Kehlstein. Roosevelt inhaled smoke, savoring the intrigue of the moment.

"Okay, Bill, let's do it. I'll put a White House stenographer on the line. You dictate the letter. If I approve the text, I'll have it translated, coded, and teletyped to Leland Morris, the Chargé d'Affaires running our Berlin embassy."

8:52 A.M.

Roosevelt telephoned Secretary of State Cordell Hull and read the letter to him for the sake of protocol. Technically, this was still a diplomatic matter best handled through State. Roosevelt then told Hull to make two trans-Atlantic calls – one to inform Jack Courtney that the letter Courtney had requested was on its way, and the other to the German Foreign Minister, Joachim von Ribbentrop. Forty minutes later the translated letter arrived at the U.S. Embassy in Berlin.

319. AMERICAN EMBASSY, BERLIN, JUNE 17, 4:15 P.M.

Jack Courtney read standing up, squinting through his wire-rimmed glasses.

"This should get the Krauts' attention," he said, turning toward Josh. "Let's go over to the Foreign Ministry and deliver it in person. Secretary Hull just telephoned Ribbentrop, so we're honoring diplomatic protocol. Hull got Ribbentrop to give us five minutes. Hull believes that Ribbentrop is accommodating us because he's one of the few Nazis who still think America will stay out of the war. Leland Morris, the Chargé d'Affaires, can come with us. Let's go to his office, and I'll introduce you."

320. THE FOREIGN MINISTRY, BERLIN, JUNE 17, 4:45 P.M.

Josh sat between Leland Morris and Jack Courtney on the bench in the high-ceilinged hallway outside Ribbentrop's office. A black-uniformed SS guard stood at attention at the doorway to their left.

"I have an idea," Josh whispered.

"Okay," Morris said. "We could use a fresh thought about now."

"Instead of just handing Ribbentrop the letter," Josh said, "what if I read it to him aloud? My German is still pretty good. Since the letter's about me, that might have more impact than if we let Ribbentrop read it to himself."

"What do you think, Jack?" Morris asked, keeping his voice low even though he was sure the sentry knew no English.

"It's crazy," Courtney answered, "but it shows the kind of balls Ribbentrop might respect. And what the hell, the meeting is about Josh, so let's have him make the pitch."

321. FOREIGN MINISTER JOACHIM VON RIBBENTROP'S OFFICE, 4:48 P.M.

The formal introductions were brief. Chargé d'Affaires Morris, who'd dealt with the Foreign Minister before, spoke first, introducing Jack Courtney and Dr. Galifano as new attachés to the U.S. Embassy.

"Foreign Minister Ribbentrop," Morris began, "we're most grateful for this opportunity to meet with you. We're carrying a letter for the Führer from President Roosevelt. I respectfully request that Dr. Galifano read it to you now." Ribbentrop nodded his consent. His rigid aristocratic demeanor revealed the faint trace of a smile as Josh began to read.

June 17, 1941

Adolf Hitler
Chancellor
The Chancellery Berlin

Dear Chancellor Hitler:

In the interest of peaceful relations between our two governments, I have appointed Dr. Enzo Galifano to serve as Special Envoy to Germany.

In addition to being an accomplished orthopedic surgeon, Dr. Galifano is fluent in German and well-versed in international relations. He has the confidence of both Secretary Hull and myself. Dr. Galifano's most recent posting was in the U.S. Embassy in Moscow. His experiences there may well interest you. As Special Envoy, Dr. Galifano is authorized to act as a confidential courier, facilitating the exchange of sensitive information outside normal diplomatic channels.

This letter requests that you meet with Dr. Galifano, in person, at your earliest convenience. Toward that end, allow me to offer a course of action, one that would demonstrate your desire to improve relations between our two governments.

I ask that you accept Dr. Galifano as my personal envoy at the private party you are hosting on the Kehlstein on Saturday evening, June 21. Your affirmative response to this request is extremely important to me.

Most cordially yours,
Franklin D. Roosevelt

Ribbentrop took the letter. Who *is* this young man? Ribbentrop asked himself. And why is he presenting himself to us now? Does Roosevelt at last see a German victory as inevitable? If his arrival was too good to be true, it was also too tempting to ignore. What did he have to lose by granting Roosevelt's request?

"Young man," Ribbentrop said, looking Josh directly in the eye, "I shall see the Führer this evening and will personally deliver your President's letter to him at that time."

322. PRINZ-ALBRECHT-STRASSE, JUNE 17, 5:59 P.M.

Gazing out over the Prinz-Albrecht-Strasse, Reinhard Heydrich watched the office workers scurrying toward the U-Bahn. Was there, perhaps, something to be said for the simple life these people had chosen or were forced to pursue? But what did it matter? He had chosen another path, and it was too late to change now.

Returning to his desk, Heydrich picked up the list of athletic club members, ex-boxers, and others who had been in Berlin on the nights when the attacks took place. As he expected, the list was extensive, more than three hundred names, many of them members of the Berlin elite. There were Party members and military officers on the list. As he already knew, Günter Jurgen and Karl Muller were on the list – and the two men had been spending a great deal of time together lately.

The telephone interrupted. It was an operative in the Foreign Minister's office whose primary allegiance was to Heydrich, not Ribbentrop. This man had proven himself effective in unearthing valuable information about unusual goings-on and reporting them to Heydrich without delay. Heydrich listened and hung up.

Why, Heydrich wondered, would the Americans want a specific individual to attend the Führer's reception at the Kehlstein? Heydrich would have to see for himself. After all, it was high time that he inspected the Berchtesgaden SS barracks. The special political action units bound for the Soviet Union were gathering there to receive their final orders, Günter Jurgen's unit among them. Heydrich would recommend to Himmler that they both arrange to get invitations to this curious gathering. Heydrich remembered that Krebs had requested a few days off for a holiday in the Obersalzberg. Well, Krebs would just have to mix business with pleasure. Heydrich called the detective and ordered him to keep a distant but careful eye on Jurgen and Muller.

323. ROME, JUNE 17, 10:00 P.M.

The pretty dark-haired stenographer's moist lips promised more, but Commander Carlo Malzone decided to postpone her favors. He needed to catch the 6:00 a.m. train to the Obersalzberg. Earlier that day, the youthful

Malzone learned from Ciano's office in the Ministry of Foreign Affairs that he was to attend a special reception at Hitler's mountaintop retreat in Germany. The occasion required Italian representation since there might be some discussion on the war in North Africa. His thoughts wandered back to his evening with the navy stenographer as Minnelli's garrote slipped around his neck.

10:24 P.M.

With slow quiet strokes, Minnelli rowed the dinghy to middle of the still waters of the Tiber. Then he pulled up the oars and let the boat drift in the moonless night to a spot where he couldn't see either bank. Taking the rope at his feet, he fashioned a noose and slipped it around the neck of Malzone's naked corpse. He pulled the noose tight, looping the other end of the rope through a concrete block. With a muted grunt, he hoisted Malzone's lifeless body overboard and let it slip into the Tiber with barely a ripple. He'd done it before.

324. NUMBER 10 DOWNING STREET, JUNE 18, 1941, 8:25 P.M.

"What exactly have you instructed the Sicilians to do?" Churchill asked Channing Brown. "I need you to tell me."

"To stop Karl Ludwig at all costs," Brown said. "The man they're sending will wait for Ludwig to make a move before cutting him down. Only then can he claim to have saved the Führer and escape with his own skin. Their man, like ours, wants to survive at any cost. But if someone can get to Ludwig first and stop him, well, I have to tell you, Sir, that would answer some prayers."

"It's a bloody shame that your man's got this far only for us to have to stop him," Churchill said. "But tell me, what's being done about contacting him to call the thing off?"

"The Americans have jumped to it," Brown said. "We're reasonably sure that Ludwig is in the Obersalzberg, staying at an inn called the Berchtesgadener. We've passed that along to the Americans. They've found an old chum of Ludwig's, another doctor as it happens. They're hoping the chum can reach him before he moves against Hitler."

Churchill rose and poured them both a brandy. "So the matter hinges on who gets to our man first: the old chum or the assassin. Heavy burden on the chum, if you ask me. Do you know anything about him?"

"The Americans say he's quite the free spirit and that he's unlikely to be fazed by the presence of Adolf Hitler. Officially he's a State Department employee, assigned most recently to Moscow, but he actually works for Donovan's new intelligence network."

"Don't you think his chances of success are minimal at best?" Churchill asked.

"Perhaps, but sometimes you go with what you've got. And with Hitler and company wanting America to stay out of the war, the Nazis should treat him well."

"What about our friend Frederick?

"I'm sure you'll agree that he's too valuable an asset to risk. We simply cannot afford for him to have any further contact with Ludwig. Indeed, Ludwig understands this. He's asked that we not try to reach Frederick in this final phase of the operation."

325. THE BRENNER PASS JUNE 20, 1941, 10:05 A.M.

Fit and handsome wearing the still-fresh white uniform of the Italian naval commander he'd just murdered, Minnelli ordered coffee and breakfast rolls as the train sped through the Alpine landscape. Minnelli had slept well in his first-class compartment. So far everything had gone according to plan. He reviewed the notes from his briefing in Rome and relaxed, taking in the view of the peaks.

326. BERCHTESGADEN BAHNHOF, JUNE 21, 1941, 2:00 A.M.

Josh was sleepy after the long train ride from Berlin, a ride made longer by a British air raid that caused a six-hour delay for bridge and track repair. He kept thinking about what Courtney had told him as he boarded the train: "No time for a plan. Just find Karl and persuade him to stand down."

The SS guards at the taxi kiosk checked papers and questioned the disembarking passengers in the queue ahead of Josh. He took out his diplomatic passport and the engraved envelope from the German Foreign Ministry that held a letter from Ribbentrop officially inviting Dr. Enzo Galifano to attend the reception that evening on the Kehlstein.

The SS Hauptmann who inspected Josh's papers was polite but brisk. "Ah, yes, Dr. Galifano. *Willkommen in Berchtesgaden.* We have a car and driver to take you to the Berchtesgadener Inn, where your embassy has reserved a room for you." Josh nodded but said nothing. As he climbed into the waiting Mercedes, he noticed a man in an Italian naval uniform waiting his turn at the taxi kiosk.

327. BERCHTESGADENER INN, JUNE 21, 2:21 A.M.

Josh stood in line at the registration desk ahead of the Italian. Josh showed his diplomatic credentials to the middle-aged woman behind desk. "I believe that a Dr. Muller from Berlin is also a guest here. He's an old friend, and I'd like to call on him."

The woman smiled. "Dr. Muller retired early and asked not be disturbed," she told him.

Not wanting to arouse suspicion, Josh didn't ask for the room number. He thought it better to meet Karl when they were both rested.

328. MINNELLI'S ROOM, 2:30 A.M.

Minnelli decided to stay out of sight. His Italian passport and naval credentials were authentic; he'd taken them directly from the dead Carlo Malzone.

One of Luciano's men had removed Malzone's photo and replaced it with Minnelli's.

He would sleep and stick close to the inn until it was time to attend the reception. He'd wait for the American to make his move. Since he was an Italian naval officer, no one would question him for wearing a sidearm.

Sitting on the bed, smoking his last cigarette of the day, Minnelli tried to envision everything that might happen. In the inevitable confusion following a thwarted attempt on Hitler's life, he would tell the Germans that he needed to return to Rome immediately to give Il Duce and Count Ciano a firsthand account of the incident, and reassure them that the Führer remained alive and in command of Germany and the war.

He would not, of course, be returning to Rome. He would leave the Italy-bound train before it reached the border and find an unsuspecting German private unlucky enough to have the right uniform measurements. Wearing the dead man's uniform, Minnelli would travel to the Swiss border where he could slip out of the Reich unobserved. Luciano's men had already provided him with a second set of forged papers for his new life in Switzerland.

329. KARL'S ROOM, 4:45 A.M.

The alarm roused Karl after nine hours of dreamless sleep. He wouldn't run or take any exercise on this morning. He'd done all the training he needed since returning from Africa. His final "street encounter" with three SS men had been only five days ago. He felt fit and rested, ready to act – and react – as events demanded.

He shaved, showered, and dressed in a summer-weight blue blazer, freshly pressed white cotton trousers, and a crisp white shirt. He folded a silver-blue striped tie in the side pocket of the blazer. Everything he needed for the day was laid out neatly on the bed. Careful to avoid any telltale bulges, he put the brass knuckles in the right-hand side pocket of his jacket. His wallet and ration book both fit snuggly, as usual, in the inside pocket of his jacket.

Karl went to the window and pulled back the blackout curtains to observe the cobblestoned town square in the early light. No one appeared to be watching the inn. He saw a light in the butcher shop. He scanned the still-empty square, focusing on the doorways and windows from which someone might be watching. A moment later, he slipped out past the sleeping man at the front desk.

6:05 A.M.

Entering the butcher shop, Karl placed his ration book on the counter.

"What's the best cut of meat available today?" Karl asked the portly butcher.

"Most of my best cuts go right up that hill," the butcher said, pointing in the direction of the Berghof and the SS barracks. He was a large, barrel-chested man well into his sixties. "Our beloved Führer may not eat meat, but the SS men in the barracks keep me very busy." He reminded Karl of Ernie, the waiter at the Ideal Coffee Shop on 86th Street. Looking out the shop window, Karl saw lights in several windows and a man lighting a cigarette near the entrance to the inn. Berchtesgaden was starting to wake up.

"I'll take the T-bone steak," Karl said. "But cut it off the bone and please cut away as much fat as you can."

He also asked the butcher to wrap the steak in some ice and place it in a plain white towel that he'd taken from the Berchtesgadener Inn. He wondered whether the butcher would suspect something and report him, but it was too late to worry about that now. "The steak's a surprise for my girlfriend," he lied. "She's a nurse at the new hospital. It's her birthday, and I'll be cooking it for her at lunchtime."

He paid and walked out of the shop with a firm grip on the paper bag that held the meat. It was just a short walk to Trudy's place.

330. TRUDY'S BERCHTESGADEN HOUSE, 6:40 A.M.

Karl scanned the vacant street but saw no one on this Saturday morning. The café across the street hadn't opened yet. The key he had taken back in August worked perfectly. Once inside the house, Karl reminded himself not to turn on any lights or answer the phone. In the kitchen, he put the steak in the icebox so it wouldn't spoil before it was time for him to eat it that afternoon. By nightfall, he would need every bit of strength the steak would give him.

6:50 A.M.

For now he was safe. If someone were looking for him, it would be quite awhile before they'd think to look at Haus Gretzler. In his mind, Karl saw the large stone building atop the Kehlstein, its large octagonal room and adjacent terrace. He saw Hitler, Bormann, and Jurgen, each moving about. Frederick and Fern were there too. So was Hitler's five-man security contingent. There was no escape from the reality that he had to control each of their movements and make things happen as planned, all in the critical moments before his encounter with Hitler. Karl went over it all again and again. He knew he had to make things happen no matter what, and no matter who intervened. The process tired him, but he was satisfied that he had done all he could.

2:00 P.M.

Karl cleaned up after eating the steak and made sure everything was just as he'd found it. Then he went upstairs to Trudy's room, set the bedside alarm for six, and dropped off to sleep.

331. THE BERCHTESGADENER INN, 2:05 P.M.

Josh had been knocking on Karl's door every half-hour or so since mid-morning. Now he asked the old man at the desk to telephone Karl's room. After three calls with no response, Josh found a young chambermaid, whose dark eyes lit up when he handed her ten Reichsmarks. She removed the "Do Not Disturb" sign from Karl's door and entered the room with caution. Josh saw that Karl had left some clothes in the room but sensed that he'd been gone for some hours and wasn't coming back.

Josh decided to take to the streets of Berchtesgaden to check the parks and cafés. He knew he had to find Karl, he just didn't know how.

332. THE BERGHOF, 4:03 P.M.

Bormann was furious. He had envisioned a small gathering, but the guest list had grown much too long. At Karl's insistence, Bormann invited Günter Jurgen on behalf of the Führer. That would almost certainly annoy Heydrich, who had let Bormann know that Jurgen was persona non grata.

If that weren't enough, the Führer now insisted on inviting a group of some twenty SS men who would be following the Wehrmacht into Russia. At least that would keep Heydrich from complaining too much about security, Bormann thought.

Frederick Wagner had been on the guest list from the start. So had his niece and her boyfriend, the Berlin detective who worked for Heydrich. And now, there were two more recent additions – an Italian naval officer and, of all things, some American doctor whose presence Ribbentrop had recommended, with Hitler's blessing.

Much to Bormann's surprise, he hadn't heard a thing from Karl Muller all day. Hadn't this reception been Karl's idea from the start? Or had it been Frederick's? Bormann shrugged. As much as he tried, he couldn't control everything.

333. HAUS GRETZLER, 6:00 P.M.

Karl had been awake for several minutes when the alarm sounded. Feeling refreshed, he got up, stretched again, and straightened the bedding. Then he took a long drink of water and started shadowboxing again. He felt fast and strong and ready. He felt butterflies in his stomach. He expected them. They were old friends.

334. ACROSS THE STREET FROM HAUS GRETZLER, 6:30 P.M.

Hans sat on the terrace of the café across the street from Haus Gretzler. He'd been tailing Karl since early that morning and had already eaten too many sweet rolls and read every story in the local newspaper. Fortunately, the café owner had a telephone. A call to Berlin informed him that the house across the street was owned by one of the architects Bormann had hired to work on the Kehlstein, who was now in Japan. The owner's daughter, a nurse, had also lived there. But she was missing and presumed dead following a recent air raid. Karl had evidently found a safe hiding place. But what was Karl hiding from? And what in hell was he up to?

335. HAUS GRETZLER, 6:45 P.M.

Karl again checked the contents of his pockets before telephoning Bormann.

"Karl, where the hell have you been?"

"Sitting in a café," he lied, "preparing for my meeting with the Führer. Could you have someone pick me up at the statue in the Berchtesgaden market square in twenty minutes. I'm ready to come up to the Kehlstein."

"I'll send someone right away," Bormann said. "Since we have so many SS men around here, we might as well put one of them to good use."

336. ACROSS THE STREET FROM HAUS GRETZLER, 6:55 P.M.

It was getting late. Hans had begun to wonder if he'd be able to pick up Fern in time for the reception on the Kehlstein. He was relieved when he saw Karl emerge from Haus Gretzler and begin walking toward the market square.

Hans telephoned Fern to say that he'd pick her up within the hour. Based on what Frau Frick had told him, Hans was all but sure Karl would be headed to the reception on the Kehlstein.

337. KEHLSTEINHAUS, ENTRANCE TO THE GREAT RECEPTION HALL, 6:59 P.M.

Martin Bormann bristled. He couldn't believe Heydrich was taking so much time scrutinizing the guest list, especially when it was full of Heydrich's own SS men, many of whom, like Günter Jurgen, would be part of the "political action" units in Russia.

"I must question the presence of three guests on your list, Martin. One, I'm embarrassed to say, is my own man, Hauptmann Günter Jurgen. The other two are the American doctor-diplomat and the Italian naval officer." Heydrich kept his suspicion of Karl Muller to himself.

"Günter Jurgen," Bormann snapped, "is here at the request of Dr. Muller."

"I wish I'd known Jurgen would be here, Martin."

"I hardly thought it necessary to inform you, Reinhard, since you always seem to know everything. If you have problem with that, take it up with Dr. Muller, not me."

"You can be sure that I will, Martin. And who is this Italian?"

"A junior officer, nobody important," Bormann said. "There could be some discussion tonight about strategy in North Africa. We wanted a representative of the Italian government on hand so we don't offend Mussolini."

338. THE BERCHTESGADENER INN, 7:34 P.M.

Worn out and worried because he couldn't find Karl, Josh collapsed into the small sofa near the registration desk. He'd spent the entire afternoon and early evening crisscrossing crooked cobblestone streets.

He went outside again to look around. Still no Karl.

Back inside, the desk clerk handed Josh an envelope bearing the SS emblem.

We have arranged for an SS driver to take you to the reception this evening. The driver will meet you at the hotel entrance at eight o'clock. Your embassy requested that we provide you with every courtesy and we are happy to do so.

Cordially yours,

Joachim von Ribbentrop

Josh hurried to his room to change and freshen up.

339. KEHLSTEINHAUS, 8:05 P.M.

The sun was still above the mountaintops. On the terrace of the Kehlsteinhaus, Karl took a moment to view the Watzmann and the Hochkalter, both capped with snow even on this first evening of summer.

Karl flexed the fingers of his right hand. His attacks on the SS men in Berlin had re-honed his skills. His Jackhammer now had far more power and accuracy than it had in Scotland. So did his other punches. And though his reflexes might not be quite as good as they'd been at his peak in New York, he was still a fast puncher – fast enough to have knocked out more than thirty SS officers in the past year, sometimes two or three at a time. Now he only had to strike one more time.

He examined the setting, comparing it to his memory of the place from when Bormann first brought him here eighteen months before. The terrace extended some sixty feet along the side of the building. The walls were thick enough to muffle the noise of any scuffle, and all the windows looking out of the house onto the terrace were some eight feet overhead, well above eye level for even for the tallest of men. There were entrances at both ends. The western doorway opened from a small dim corridor adjacent to the main hall where some of the first guests had begun to gather.

It would soon be dusk. Karl went back inside. He knew it was time to put the most important piece in place.

He saw that Hitler was standing near a corner table, deep in conversation with Bormann and Frederick Wagner. Hitler looked up as Karl approached. "Karl, rest assured I will see you at nine."

"I'll take whatever time you can give me, *mein Führer*. What I have to tell you about Rommel should take less than ten minutes."

"Rommel, yes," Hitler said, lowering his voice, his attention fixed on Karl. "I'm curious as to his loyalty and how it might relate to that anonymous memo on an alternative to Barbarossa." Hitler nodded, peering over Karl's shoulder at the other guests.

"One more thing, *mein Führer*," Karl said in a voice just above a whisper.

"As I believe Bormann has mentioned, only one security person will be present – Günter Jurgen, a highly capable SS Hauptmann with whom I served in Poland and Norway. He commands a special SS detachment that's headed east. He's also light-heavyweight boxing champion of the SS. Hauptmann Jurgen can accompany us onto the terrace, but will remain far enough away not to overhear what we say. I hope this arrangement satisfies you."

Hitler stuck his hands into the pockets of his white blazer but said nothing. "*Ja*, I've heard of this Hauptmann Jurgen," Hitler shrugged. "I'm safe enough here anyway. So the three of us will meet on the terrace at nine. Bormann has told me all this."

After he walked away, Karl turned to see Bormann still chatting with Hitler, who pointed with a subtle index finger toward his black-shirted SS guards. Bormann nodded and walked over to them. Seeing the SS men's affirmative nods, Karl felt his blood rush. He knew he had to risk telling Hitler about security – and it had worked.

To Karl's relief, the five SS men in the Führer's personal security detail were talking among themselves and at ease, at least for the moment. Still, uniformed SS men were everywhere.

Karl strolled back over to where Frederick and Bormann were talking. "Strong military presence, don't you think?" Karl asked.

"Actually, the Führer insisted on it," Bormann said. "It gives him an opportunity to address the SS officers bound for Russia. He'll be doing so in the Scharitz Room, which is right up those steps and through the doorway," Bormann said, pointing with his chin while checking his watch.

340. THE KEHLSTEIN, 8:20 P.M.

"Dr. Galifano, welcome to the Kehlstein," Heydrich said as Josh emerged from the elevator. "I've been looking forward to meeting you. We in the SS make it a practice of introducing ourselves to everyone who is about to meet the Führer. I understand that you've just spent some time in Moscow."

Josh didn't respond at first. Hoping for a glimpse of Hitler or Karl, his eyes searched beyond Heydrich. He could see past the arched doorway into the reception hall, but he hadn't expected such a crowded room. Heydrich kept talking. "I hope we might find a few minutes this evening to discuss your thoughts on the Soviets."

Now why in hell would I want to do that, Josh thought to himself. He shrugged to indicate his lack of commitment. Heydrich recognized the cold shoulder. "Please understand that I'm interested only in improving relations between our two countries."

"Well, Sir, the best way to accomplish that is to let me enjoy your Führer's hospitality," Josh responded.

"But, of course," Heydrich responded with a thin smile. No one intent on making trouble, he thought, would dare be so impertinent.

Heydrich saw the Italian naval officer emerge from the elevator. He tried to engage the man in conversation, but their brief exchange demonstrated how poorly the man spoke German. Heydrich wasn't surprised that the Italians would send someone so unqualified. He'd tell Krebs to keep an eye on the Italian nonetheless. Of course, Krebs would already be occupied watching Karl and Günter Jurgen. Even Krebs would be hard put to watch three men at once. No matter. Krebs was good. He would give him the order as soon as he arrived.

341. GREAT RECEPTION HALL ENTRANCE, 8:33 P.M.

Arriving with Fern at the entrance to the reception hall, Hans knew he had work to do. "Let's split up and mingle," he whispered in Fern's ear. "Good idea," she replied. "I'll find Frederick." Heydrich spotted Hans and led him to an uncrowded corner of the room, ordering Hans to keep watch on the Italian, as well Karl and Günter Jurgen.

8:40 P.M.

Karl chatted with Frederick, not wanting anyone to interrupt and make it difficult for him to break away just before his meeting with Hitler. Then he felt a gentle hand on his right elbow. He turned and saw Fern's bright green eyes staring right through him.

342. THE KREMLIN, 10:40 P.M. (MOSCOW TIME)

Stalin had already left the Kremlin for his dacha outside Moscow, firm in his stance that the invasion would not happen on this night. But the lights were still on in the Kremlin, as Politburo members, top military personnel, and adjutants scurried from meeting to meeting, evaluating evidence, and weighing the likelihood of an imminent Nazi invasion.

Events of the past two hours only reinforced the wisdom of not arguing with Stalin about the probability of an invasion. A German defector had crossed the frontier earlier that evening with news of Hitler's plan. Stalin declared the defector a "disinformer" and had him shot.

Cloistered in his office, Molotov took a bottle of vodka from his desk drawer and poured generous portions for himself and Beria, who sat opposite him. "What do you hear from our people in Berlin?" Molotov asked.

"Nothing for the last twenty-four hours," Beria said. "I've instructed our agents to keep their heads down. We've built a dependable intelligence network there. They're deeply embedded, and it would make no sense to risk exposing them now."

"Your young American doctor was among those who gave us intelligence on the invasion weeks ago," Molotov said. "So what does he say now?"

"I don't know. He's in Germany on U.S. State Department business."

"Why not have your top Berlin operative arrange a meeting with him, dinner perhaps, and send us an evaluation? We'll need American friends before long."

"I've already given him a phone number," Beria said, leaning toward Molotov. "I know how to do my job, Comrade."

"Relax Lavrentiy," Molotov said. "We both have more important things to do this evening than argue about some amateurish American."

343. WEHRMACHT FORWARD POSITION, NEAR THE WESTERN BORDER OF THE SOVIET UNION, JUNE 21, 10:45 P.M. LOCAL TIME (8:45 P.M.BERCHTESGADEN TIME)

Haber sipped black ersatz from a tin field cup. Despite his misgivings about Barbarossa, Haber felt the warrior in him stir as an army of more than three million men stood ready to execute the battle plan he had helped to develop. He looked up from the large map to read a typed report handed to him by a youthful officer.

"So, Hauptmann, everything has gone according to plan. Our Panzers are ready to pounce," Haber said. "And the Luftwaffe will take off at first light and fly into Soviet airspace. Never before have so many seasoned troops and so much mechanized power been poised to strike."

"I understand that the general contributed a great deal to the planning of this invasion," the Hauptmann said tentatively.

"Yes, Hauptmann, I spent many long nights working on what we're about to do. Make sure that we maintain communication with Berlin and with the Kehlsteinhaus. There may be some last-minute order from the Führer – another distraction in the Balkans or some unforeseen event in the African desert. One never knows."

344. MEN'S ROOM, KEHLSTEINHAUS, 8:39 P.M.

Alone in a toilet stall, Minnelli checked his Beretta and silencer before relieving himself. Again he reviewed his simple plan. He owed his life to the fact that he was a patient man – and patience would be essential now. He reminded himself that he would have to wait until the very last instant before Karl struck Hitler. Leaving the stall, Minnelli checked his reflection in the mirror. He liked the look of himself in the crisp white uniform.

345. KEHLSTEINHAUS, RECEPTION HALL, 8:40 P.M.

Standing next to Frederick, Fern locked her gaze on Karl. After a split second of silence, Karl reverted to the practiced liar he had become.

"Ah, this must be the celebrated Dr. Fern Wagner about whom I've heard so much," he said, offering his hand. Her fingers were icicles. If her anger had abated, she gave no hint of it. Still, Karl held her soft hand for an extra second.

"I've admired your work for a long time, Dr. Wagner. Some years ago, when I still was practicing in Africa, I read several of your articles in the *New England Journal of Medicine*. I was especially impressed by one on treating victims of tenement fires."

"Surely," Frederick said, turning to his niece, "you've heard of Dr. Muller?"

"Well," Fern responded, "for a moment I had him confused with someone else. He bears a striking resemblance to someone I knew long ago. Quite silly of me, I guess." Over Fern's shoulder, Karl could see Günter Jurgen approaching.

"You're right on time, Günter," Karl said. "I want you to meet some friends of mine."

8:46 P.M.

Now or never, Josh realized. He saw that Karl was talking with Fern, Frederick, and a German Hauptmann he didn't recognize. He realized how hard it would be to get Karl alone. He'd been hanging back, lingering near the entrance to the great reception hall, feeling out of place. The only other person who wasn't mingling was the Italian naval officer, who was standing alone by a window gazing alternately at the mountains and at Karl. There was something about the Italian Josh didn't like.

Josh marched straight toward the friend he had not seen for seven years. As he drew up next to the group, he heard Karl telling Frederick and an indifferent Fern about his recent service in Africa.

Karl tried to hide his surprise as he saw Josh approaching.

"Sorry to barge in," Josh began. "Dr. Muller, isn't it? I'm Dr. Enzo Galifano. Could I have a word with you in private?" Karl gave no indication of recognizing his old friend.

"Some other time perhaps," Karl whispered, drawing Josh aside.

"No, Karl. For God's sake – it's me, Josh."

Putting her right hand on Josh's forearm and giving it a hard squeeze, Fern led him to a wine bar in the corner. Under his breath, Josh tried to explain his sudden appearance. "I can't talk now, but I'm working for the U.S. government. I've got to stop Karl from doing something."

"Josh, do you know where you are?" Fern asked, trying to maintain a neutral expression. "Shut up before you get us all killed."

"It's almost time for our meeting with the Führer, Günter," Karl said, placing a hand on Jurgen's right shoulder. "I see that Bormann is escorting him toward the terrace. We must join them now."

8:58:30 P.M.

Bormann stopped at the terrace entrance, leaving Hitler in Karl's hands. Without any introductions, Hitler and Jurgen allowed Karl to guide them onto the terrace.

8:58:35 P.M.

On the other side of the room, Hans had been keeping to himself, chatting with guests, but doing his best to watch Karl, Jurgen, and the Italian. Now, he saw Karl leading Hitler and Jurgen up the steps to the entrance of the terrace.

Seconds later, Hans spotted the handsome young naval officer in the white uniform moving across the room toward the same stairway. Hans followed him.

346. THE TERRACE, 8:58:47 P.M.

Karl waited until they had walked half the length of the terrace before introducing Hitler to Jurgen.

"*Mein Führer*," he said, looking Hitler in the eye, "I have the great honor of presenting Hauptmann Günter Jurgen. Hauptmann Jurgen commands a special SS unit that will soon be active on the new Eastern Front. I had the honor to serve with him in Poland and Norway. He has long hoped to meet you in person."

"It's an honor to make your acquaintance, Hauptmann," Hitler said in a low voice. "I know of your achievements in Poland and Norway, and as a boxer." At ease, Hitler followed as Karl led them toward the far end of the terrace.

Hans pretended to adjust his suit jacket as he unlocked the safety catch on the Walther P38 in his shoulder holster.

"Your work in the conquered territories has been exemplary," Hitler said to Jurgen as the two men walked side by side. "Himmler reported to me that you were personally responsible for rounding up nearly a hundred potential troublemakers and Jewish leaders in Poland. We will need men like you in Russia."

"It will be my honor to serve there, *mein Führer*."

"*Mein Führer*," Karl interrupted, "before we discuss what I learned in Africa, may I suggest we enjoy this remarkable view. Once Germany has won the war, you must paint a scene like this, perhaps from this very spot."

"Yes," Hitler mused, "Perhaps when I return here in autumn after our victory over the Bolsheviks."

Karl watched Hitler lose himself in contemplation of another triumph. As a rim of sunlight faded over the mountaintops, Karl stepped behind both Hitler and Jurgen. "Those will be great days," Karl said, raising his right hand, his open palm flat and hard.

347. TERRACE ENTRANCEWAY, 9:00:08 P.M.

Hans stopped short at the entrance to the terrace, waiting for his eyes to adjust to the gathering darkness. He could just make out the silhouettes of

Hitler, Jurgen, and Karl looking at the mountains. Karl, he noticed, was standing behind the other two men.

He froze when he saw the Italian naval officer – not twenty feet from where he stood – down on one knee, aiming what looked like a Beretta at one of the three men. There was no way for Hans to know which one. Hans saw that Karl stood erect and motionless, except for his right hand, which was inching imperceptibly upward.

As he drew his Walther, Hans could hear Hitler rambling on about how he would paint the Watzmann and the Hochkalter.

Not aware of Hans, Minnelli strained to hold his fire. He had not expected an SS man to be on the terrace. Still, he kept a bead on Karl. He noticed that Karl was raising his right hand.

In the next instant, Karl's flat right hand hammered into the nape of Adolf Hitler's neck. Hitler crumbled onto the concrete floor, face down. It was then Hans understood why Karl had come to Germany.

Minnelli fired. His silenced shot grazed Karl's right earlobe. Karl spun and landed a lightning-fast left on Günter Jurgen's mouth. The Sicilian cursed to himself. He tried to get a second bead on Karl, but Karl's sudden lunge toward Jurgen had surprised him.

9:00:43 P.M.

"You fuck," Jurgen shouted, spitting blood. He threw a quick right that caught Karl's right eye. Then he slammed a left and a right into Karl's rib cage. Karl absorbed both punches and countered with a left jab that sent Günter Jurgen's head crashing against the sharp edge of the knee-high terrace wall.

Grabbing the brass knuckles from his jacket pocket, Karl seized the unconscious Hitler by the hair, climbed onto his chest, and slammed his right fist into Hitler's jaw.

One more blow like that would likely send the German Führer straight to Hell. But a dazed Günter Jurgen landed on Karl's back before he could strike again. The two men rolled away from the still unconscious Hitler.

Minnelli saw that the SS man had Karl pinned to the terrace floor. The Sicilian took his bead again, this time aiming for Karl's head, which Jurgen's grip held motionless. Minnelli's finger tightened on the trigger when a bullet from Hans's Walther blew through his brain.

9:00:49 P.M.

Hans's shot echoed across mountains and resounded inside the reception hall. Knowing he had only seconds to act, Hans slipped on a tight-fitting right-hand glove he always carried with him. Distracted by the gunshot, Jurgen turned toward Hans. Jurgen reached for his Luger just as Hans snatched the Berretta from Minnelli's dead fingers and fired, sending a single bullet through Günter Jurgens's heart. Jurgen fell dead less than a meter from his unconscious Führer.

Hans put the Beretta back in Minnelli's lifeless hand, wrapping the dead man's index finger around the trigger. He then jumped up, grabbed Jurgen by the neck, and threw him on top of Hitler.

Still down and dazed from the sting of Jurgen's blows, Karl tried to turn his head and see if Hitler was still alive, but felt a shoe pressing hard against his right ear.

"Karl, it's Hans. Now for Christ's sake, just do as I say and keep your mouth shut. Give me those brass knuckles. And stay the hell down."

"What brass knuckles?"

"Don't be cute, Karl. Give them to me now." When Karl didn't respond, Hans wrenched the brass knuckles out of Karl's right hand and grabbed the other set from Karl's side pocket. Without warning, he landed a sharp right jab on Karl's cheek.

As Karl lurched upward, Hans grabbed him by the shoulders. "Sorry, Karl, but you've got to listen. We need to show that you're hurt and can't answer questions." Hans used a handkerchief to wipe the unused brass knuckles clean and placed them on Jurgen's left hand. He slipped the other set in his own pocket. "Trust me, Karl. I'm the only one who can help you now."

Struggling to his feet, Karl saw that Günter Jurgen was indeed dead, even though his eyes were wide open, staring into the night sky. Only a few feet away, at the terrace entrance, Minnelli was sprawled flat on his chest, his white naval uniform spattered with blood. Between the two dead men, Hitler lay unconscious but breathing.

"How the . . . ?" Karl managed to ask.

"Forget everything, Karl. I'll do the talking."

They heard voices. Heydrich and two SS guards with Lugers drawn were striding across the terrace. Seven more black-uniformed SS men were close behind.

Hitler let out a sigh from deep in his chest.

"What's this?" Heydrich said with measured alarm.

"One moment, Sir," Hans said, raising his right palm. "Get Dr. Wagner," Hans yelled. "The Führer needs immediate medical attention, and Dr. Muller here is in no condition to help. Keep all guests off the terrace. No one should see the Führer this way."

"You heard him! Get Dr. Wagner," Heydrich barked to the SS man on his left. "And keep everyone off the terrace except the SS and medical people."

"Tell us what happened, Dr. Muller," Heydrich said.

"With your permission," Hans interrupted, "I can provide a better explanation since I'm the only one who saw everything. Let me tell you that Dr. Muller is a hero – he probably saved the Führer's life. He prevented this fellow here," Hans said, gesturing toward Jurgen, "from pummeling the Führer to death."

"Go on," Heydrich said, putting his Luger back in the holster and folding his arms.

"As you instructed," Hans said, "I was watching all three of these individuals – Karl Muller, Günter Jurgen, and, thanks to your latest instruction, this fellow in the Italian naval uniform. I followed the Italian to the terrace entrance, and saw him crouch down in a shooter's stance not twenty feet in front of me, his pistol aimed toward the men on the terrace. I had no choice but to assume he was about to assassinate the Führer. He got off two quick shots, one of which killed our SS friend here. To protect the Führer, I shot and killed him on the spot."

"But," Hans said, lowering his voice and drawing Heydrich away from the SS contingent, "I'd prefer not to give a report here. It's better if I go type up a full report while the events are still fresh in my mind."

"Then get to it Krebs," Heydrich said.

Fern arrived on the terrace and went directly to Hitler's side, clasping his limp wrist to take his pulse. She tore open his blood-stained jacket and shirt, took the stethoscope from her shoulder bag, and listened to his heartbeat. Then she lifted his eyelids, felt his forehead, and examined the area around his neck and shoulders.

"We need a stretcher and an ambulance," Fern said. "We have to get the Führer to the hospital in Berchtesgaden right now. There may be swelling near his brain." Her voice was calm but deliberate.

"How bad is it?" Heydrich asked, whispering so that only Fern could hear.

"He's breathing, but his vital signs could be stronger," Fern said. "He's probably in shock."

"The military situation demands that the Führer make a public announcement very soon," Heydrich said. "If not tomorrow, then in a few days. That means you have very little time to fix him up, Dr. Wagner."

"That's if he lives" Fern said. "We'll need an orthopedic surgeon to examine him and see what to do about those blows to his neck and head. Quite by chance, there's a highly skilled American orthopedist here tonight. His name is Galifano, Dr. Enzo Galifano. You may have met him earlier."

Then, turning toward Karl, she said, "If Dr. Muller recovers his wits he can assist us too. We'll need all the help we can get. Dr. Galifano and Dr. Muller can accompany me with the Führer in the rear of the ambulance. But we have to act now."

348. KEHLSTEINHAUS RADIO ROOM, 9:07 P.M.

Hans went straight to the basement radio room, which was always manned when Hitler was on the Kehlstein. He sent an urgent message to the Prinz-Albrecht-Strasse.

Immediate Priority.

Perform thorough search of Hauptmann Günter Jurgen's apartment at number 12 Geller Strasse, Berlin. Report findings to me here at once by teletype. Krebs.

Then he found a typewriter and began his report to Heydrich.

349. THE KEHLSTEIN TUNNEL, 9:20 P.M.

With two uniformed SS men at his side, Josh waited for Fern and Karl to emerge from the elevator. When the elevator doors opened, two stretcher bearers whisked the wounded Führer into a waiting Wehrmacht ambulance, Karl and Fern right behind them. The box-like ambulance resembled a delivery truck and could carry as many as six patients.

"I know these vehicles," Fern said. "We used them in France." Once Hitler's stretcher was secured, Fern addressed the driver: "My two colleagues and I will ride in the back with the Führer." She saw a Hauptmann who appeared to be in charge of the tunnel and went up to him. "If you believe we need a guard with us, he can sit in the cab with the driver. I want only professional medical people with the Führer now." The Hauptman nodded, not wanting to challenge her.

Karl started to recover. An SS medic had bandaged his cheek, and the earlobe had stopped bleeding.

Fern approached Karl. "Remember, when you greet Josh," she said "for God's sake, don't hug him or call him Josh. As far as anyone knows, you two met for the first time at the reception up on the mountain. Be sure to call him Dr. Galifano." Karl's heart jumped at the first civilized words Fern had spoken to him in seven years.

350. IN THE AMBULANCE, 9:22 P.M.

In the back of the ambulance, next to Josh and across from Karl, Fern used a sterilized cloth to swab the swollen and bloodied face of Adolf Hitler. The driver and an armed SS corporal sat in the closed-off cab. Looking out the rear window, the three doctors could see six SS men on motorcycles roar into the car park at the mouth of tunnel. Seconds later, the motorcycles began leading the ambulance down the mountain.

Fern checked to make sure the intercom was off. "It's okay to talk," she said, looking at Hitler. "He should be out for a while." Leaning forward over

Hitler's inert body, Karl realized he could complete his mission easily with one final blow.

"I know what you're thinking," Josh said. "Forget it."

"Forget what?"

"Forget what you're about to do," Josh said. "You've thrown enough punches for one night."

"Says who?"

"It's complicated," Josh said, leaning toward Karl as the ambulance sped down the corkscrew mountain road. "I was sent here to stop you, to tell you that Churchill and Roosevelt scrubbed your mission. Now they want Hitler alive."

"Why the hell do they want that?"

"So he can invade Russia. As soon as he does, the Brits gain an ally, one with a three million-man army. And the Germans are left with the impossible job of conquering the goddamn Soviet Union. For the Brits, it's heaven-sent."

Karl sat in silence for a long moment. "Okay," he said. "But why you, Josh? Why did they send you to tell me?"

"They thought I was the only one you'd believe. The Brits had hired somebody to kill you if I couldn't get to you first. I hear there are two dead guys back on the Kehlstein. It's a good bet that one of them is the hired killer."

"No time for a seminar now," Fern interrupted. "Our job is saving Hitler's life, like it or not."

351. KEHLSTEINHAUS RADIO ROOM, 9:31 P.M.

Hans stayed in the radio room to write his report while Heydrich's men interrogated guests and staff members upstairs in the main dining hall. Mindful of Hitler's distaste for tobacco smoke, he hadn't smoked any cigarettes during the reception, though he was making up for that now.

Chain lighting his third cigarette, Hans took a deep drag and resumed typing at a deliberate pace, careful to say what he needed to say and to avoid typos. Heydrich would likely interpret any crossed-out words as evidence of too much thinking, or contrivance. Some bastard might ask what he had started to say, why he had changed his mind. Hans was renowned for producing error-free typewritten reports quickly and on the spot. On this night he would do everything he could to maintain that reputation.

9:48 P.M.

Hans pulled the completed report from the typewriter and read his meticulous blend of fact and fiction.

352. MAIN OPERATING ROOM, BERCHTESGADEN HOSPITAL, 10:09 P.M.

With its bright white tiles and state-of-the-art equipment, the operating room was a facility designed to handle just the sort of emergency the three doctors now faced.

Josh held the X-rays up to the light. Hitler's neck, though swollen, would likely suffer no permanent damage as a result of Karl's blows to his neck and chin. Though Hitler's jaw wasn't broken, it had been pushed back, putting pressure on his brain.

Josh's time in Moscow had taught him to speak in a habitual whisper. "The years have taken their toll, my friend," he said to Karl. "Five years ago you would have killed him with one punch. But it's still a serious injury, and I'll have to be careful. Being a vegetarian has cost him some bone density. His jawbone isn't as strong as it should be. And it's pressing against the meninges. Even the slightest pressure in the wrong direction would kill him."

"Compared to some of the injuries you treated in Spain," Fern said, "this should be relatively straightforward. Once you fix his jaw, I'll take care of those ugly lacerations. Karl can assist us. They will be wheeling Hitler in any minute now."

10:12 P.M.

The twin steel doors swung open and two SS guards wheeled the still-unconscious Hitler into the operating room. Two nurses followed, each pushing a tray of instruments. There were no introductions, only nods. The taller nurse turned on the bright lamp over the operating table. Both nurses appeared shaken by Hitler's appearance. A short, round middle-aged man in a knee-length white coat entered the room and introduced himself as Joachim Kessler, the anesthesiologist.

"We'll need to keep the patient still as a stone," Josh explained to the nurses in German. "Until I relieve the pressure on his brain, even the slightest movement could prove fatal."

Fern recognized both nurses from her time in France. "I know you're both professionals. Let me assure you that Dr. Galifano here is an experienced, highly skilled surgeon who's performed similar procedures many times. He's worked in Madrid and has operated on prizefighters whose injuries were similar to those sustained tonight by the Führer. I have complete faith in his ability. Dr. Muller is also a highly skilled physician."

Fern waited for questions, but there were none. "Let's scrub up and get to work," she said. "Keep in mind that Dr. Galifano is the senior physician – he'll be in charge of the procedure."

11:03 P.M.

"Okay, he's going to live and should heal soon enough," Josh said, looking up from the operating table. "I've relieved the pressure."

"What about the swelling around the cheek bone?" Karl asked.

"That'll probably subside in a couple of days," Fern said, "as long as he remains quiet. The two stitches under his chin will prevent all but minimal scarring. Now he needs rest and seclusion. Goebbels can attribute his failure to appear in public to an emergency dental procedure."

Josh gestured for the nurses to wheel Hitler into a recovery area.

"Let's get some fresh air," Fern sighed.

As they walked into the hospital courtyard, Heydrich was waiting for them, sitting on the hood of a black Mercedes, arms folded.

353. ON THE SOVIET-POLISH BORDER, JUNE 22, 1941, 12:58 A.M. LOCAL TIME

In the dim light of the railway carriage, General Haber listened on the radio operator's headphones. There had been no word from Berlin or the Obersalzberg for more than two hours.

"Nothing new, Herr General?" the radioman asked.

"Nothing," Haber answered, shaking his head. In the distance, they could hear the approach of aircraft engines. Haber shook his head again.

354. ROMMEL'S HEADQUARTERS CAMP, NEAR EL ALAMEIN, JUNE 21, 11:09 P.M.

Pushing back the mosquito netting, Erwin Rommel put on his field jacket to protect himself from the cold desert night and walked the fifty paces to the radio tent.

"Any messages for me?' he asked the radio operator. "I thought we might receive something from Berlin or Berchtesgaden."

"Yes, there's one from Berlin reporting that the Wehrmacht has crossed the Russian frontier and is advancing on a broad front."

Rommel returned to his cot but didn't sleep.

355. COURTYARD, BERCHTESGADEN HOSPITAL, JUNE 21, 11:10 P.M.

Easing himself off the hood of the Mercedes, Heydrich strode toward Karl, Josh, and Fern. Karl braced himself. More than twenty SS men were standing guard at the hospital entrance. Heydrich raised his palm to fend off any questions.

"Now allow me to report on the security measures," he began. "We've posted guard units around the SS barracks and the Berghof. We're also watching all the roads and train stations. Since we have no way of knowing whether this incident is part of some larger plot, we must be thorough in the extreme.

"As for the Führer's ongoing medical care, his personal physician, Dr. Theodore Morell, along with a team of doctors from Berlin, will arrive in Berchtesgaden early tomorrow and remain as long as necessary. I would stay as well, but I must leave for the Russian front first thing in the morning. I'll be directing special operations there over the next several weeks before returning to Berlin. Tell me, Dr. Wagner, have you anything to report regarding the Führer's condition?"

"All the procedures were successful," Fern said. "But the Führer will require constant medical supervision for at least three days, probably more. I propose that Dr. Galifano remain with the Führer until his personal physician arrives."

"I'd be happy to watch him until tomorrow morning," Josh said. "Dr. Muller has a room at the Berchtesgadener, so I can reach him there if I need help."

"Excellent," Heydrich responded. "I've ordered an ambulance to take the Führer to the Berghof – he'll be able to rest more comfortably at his residence, and security is already in place there. Two nurses and two orderlies are on their way and will remain in the Führer's service until further notice. We'll furnish Dr. Galifano with a cot in an adjoining room. You'll have an eight-man SS security contingent with you at the Berghof, Dr. Galifano."

"Fine," said Josh. "I'll take all the protection I can get."

A Mercedes ambulance rolled into the hospital courtyard and pulled up to the entrance. Four attendants slid a stretcher carrying Hitler into the rear of the vehicle and Josh climbed aboard.

11:21

A second Mercedes staff car rolled into the courtyard and stopped next to Heydrich. An SS Leutnant jumped from the back seat to hand Heydrich an envelope, which he ripped open and read to himself in the glow of his cigarette lighter.

CONFIDENTIAL REPORT NOT FOR DISTRIBUTION

DATE: JUNE 21, 1941

TO: REINHARD HEYDRICH, DEPUTY CHIEF SS, SD

FROM: HANS KREBS, SPECIAL DEPUTY SD

INTRODUCTION

This report describes an incident involving a possible attempt on the life of Adolf Hitler that took place at the Kehlsteinhaus this evening. The incident started at 9:00 p.m. and unfolded over the course of several minutes. At least two men were killed. Although the Führer survived, he suffered injuries of unknown severity and his survival remains uncertain at this time.

SEQUENCE OF EVENTS

At 9:00 p.m., I noticed the Führer, Dr. Karl Muller, and SS Hauptmann Günter Jurgen walking together from the reception hall to the entrance of the sun terrace. I followed them pursuant to your earlier instruction. As I approached the open doorway to the terrace, I could see all three men standing about halfway down the terrace. They appeared to be chatting and enjoying the view.

Seconds later I noticed a fourth man down on one knee near the entrance to the terrace. In the gathering darkness, I had failed to see him at first. This man, dressed in a white naval uniform, was the Italian commander you had also ordered me to watch. He was aiming a Beretta in the direction of the three men. It was unclear to me at that moment — and remains unclear — whether he intended to shoot one, two, or all three.

There was a burst of activity just before 9:01 p.m. Hauptmann Jurgen started punching the Führer's head, striking him with a quick succession of lefts and rights. In the same instant, I heard the click of a silencer, as the man in the white uniform fired. His shot appeared to miss because no one fell or reacted to the shot. (It was later discovered that this shot grazed Dr. Muller's right earlobe.)

Dr. Muller jumped on Hauptmann Jurgen's back to stop him from striking the Führer. Hauptmann Jurgen threw Dr. Muller off and began punching him, just as the Italian's second shot hit Hauptmann Jurgen in the chest and killed him.

Did the man in the naval uniform fire to save the Führer? Or was the Führer his intended target — or his next target? I could not risk waiting to find out. I shot the man in the back of the head with my Walther. The papers on his body identify him as Commander Carlo Malzone, a special envoy, representing Mussolini and his Foreign Minister Count Ciano. We have asked Rome to verify his identity.

After shooting the Italian, I ran to the Führer, who was unconscious but breathing. His face appeared badly bruised. The dead Hauptmann, Günter Jurgen, had brass knuckles on his left hand. Dr. Muller was semi-conscious and bleeding from the right ear and left cheek.

FURTHER INVESTIGATION
Following the aforementioned events, I telephoned Berlin and ordered an immediate search of Hauptmann Jurgen's flat. I also ordered the Reich Foreign Ministry to contact its counterpart in Rome to verify the identity of the dead Italian. I am authorizing a comprehensive ballistics examination to document which bullets from which gun killed Hauptmann Jurgen and the Italian. Retrieval of shells from the victims' bodies will confirm that the shell form the Beretta killed Hauptmann Jurgen and that a bullet from my Walther killed the man in the Italian naval uniform.

Searching Hauptmann Jurgen's apartment this evening, our men found brass knuckles, face masks, and Stars of David.

I will keep you informed of further developments.

Hans Krebs
Special Assistant the Deputy Chief SD

Heydrich returned the report to its envelope. He would keep most of its contents to himself, at least for now.

"We have verified that one of the dead men is Hauptmann Günter Jurgen," Heydrich said. "But it'll take more time to verify the identity of the other dead man, the one in the Italian naval uniform. We need to confirm that the man Krebs shot at the Kehlsteinhaus is the same man the Italian government sent to Germany. We're running a fingerprint check and have transported his remains to the mortuary here for a complete autopsy."

Turning to Karl, Heydrich said, "Dr. Muller, I must ask that you take a look at the dead Italian and tell us whether you've ever seen him before."

11:41 P.M.

Another Mercedes staff car arrived in the courtyard and a distressed-looking Bormann emerged from the rear and walked to Fern.

"How soon can we get the Führer back to full strength?" he asked. "He was scheduled to leave for a forward headquarters near the Russian front tomorrow. The foreign press will expect a statement."

"It'll be at least a few days before he's up and around," Fern said.

"Martin," Karl said, "it appears that Jurgen was able to fool me. I'll accept full blame."

"Karl, it doesn't matter how much blame you accept. Hitler will hold me responsible – I agreed to your idea and exposed him to Günter Jurgen."

A second later, a startled Bormann saw that Heydrich was standing but a few feet behind Karl, close enough to have overheard them.

"What you both have to say may be true," Heydrich said, "but let me offer my own *mea culpa.* It was I who paved an upward path for Jurgen in the SS, praising his work and yes, his excesses in Poland and Norway, and exploiting his celebrity as a boxer. Yes, Jurgen was my protégé as much as he was Dr. Muller's friend. Yes, even though I eventually made him persona non grata, it remains my shame that he proved to be a madman. As it turns out, gentlemen, Hauptman Günter Jurgen has made a fool of each of us."

"Still," Bormann sighed, "I'm the one who will have to explain things to Hitler."

"So you'll get yelled at," Heydrich said. "Your skin is thick, Martin. You will survive his foul temper. I have. So has Himmler. We've lived through it several times and so will you. Remember, he needs us to do his dirty work."

Heydrich eyed Karl. "As for you, Dr. Muller, it appears from what Krebs reports that you just helped save the Führer's life on the Kehlstein, and you helped again in the operating room. And what we all need to understand is that once our Führer recovers, he'll be absorbed in the details of our advance into Soviet territory."

Bormann nodded, curious that Heydrich was being reasonable.

Karl listened but said nothing.

356. THE BERCHTESGADEN HOSPITAL MORTUARY, 11:50 P.M.

Karl shivered. He'd forgotten how cold mortuaries were. Pausing over Minnelli's naked corpse, he saw the dead man's big right hand, which lay over his left as if in prayer. "I've never seen this man before tonight," Karl muttered before the heavyset SS sergeant slammed the drawer shut. Fern's view of the dead Minnelli was just as uneventful.

357. THE HOSPITAL COURTYARD, JUNE 22, 12:02 A.M.

"Karl, what's wrong?" Fern asked, once he'd returned to the courtyard. "You look stunned."

Before Karl could respond, Frederick arrived in his Duesenberg. He told them it had taken forever to get away from the Kehlsteinhaus because Heydrich's men were questioning everyone. Frederick's driver, Max, a black chauffer's cap perched on the back of his head, remained seated behind the wheel.

Fern took Frederick's arm and turned to make sure they were out of earshot of the SS men guarding the hospital entrance. She nodded for Karl to stay with them. "Let's talk back at your place, Uncle. We could all use some of that wonderful beer and schnapps you keep there."

"No, I don't think so. After all that's happened tonight, it's too late for Max to drive those mountain roads back to the chalet," Frederick said. "I've already booked us each a room at the Berchtesgadener."

"But I suspect the two of you might find a few things to talk about. Why don't you take the Duesenberg and drive to my chalet? Just drop Max and me at the inn. There's no moon," he said, looking at the sky. "But it's a clear, starry night. Just be careful of the winding roads."

"Well we're bound to encounter a roadblock," Fern said. " Can you handle that, Karl?"

"I suppose we'll have to take our chances. This bandaged ear ought to give me some credibility."

358. ON THE ROAD TO FREDERICK'S CHALET, 12:15 A.M.

With Fern at the wheel and the top down, the Duesenberg rolled through the empty town square and away from the Berchtesgadener Inn after dropping off Frederick and Max. They had gone only a mile from the sleeping village when Karl broke the strained silence.

"Fern, I need to tell you something."

"Not now, Karl. Let's just be quiet."

Karl actually welcomed the silence. Fern was right – they both needed quiet time. They had to stay focused on survival. But there were so many questions. Did Heydrich really believe that story Hans had blurted out as Hitler lay unconscious on the Kehlsteinhaus terrace? How did Hans manage to insert himself so effectively into such a chaotic sequence of events? And why?

The petrol gauge showed close to a full tank, enough to get them to the Swiss border. But there was little chance of making it through any SS roadblocks if they appeared to be fleeing the country. And even if they could escape to Switzerland, Heydrich would wreak vengeance on Haber, Hildy, Frederick, and Hans, a man who, Karl now realized, had just saved his life.

Not long into the drive, they saw the flashing lights of an armored car that was blocking the road. The car had a roof-mounted machine gun. Six heavily armed SS men were standing around the car, pointing their machine guns at Fern as she brought the Duesenberg to a quiet stop.

An SS Leutnant stepped forward, the light at his back, and demanded to see their papers, which he examined in the bright glow of the armored car's headlamps. Saying nothing, he turned his back on them and returned to the armored car to use the field radio. The other SS guards flanked the Duesenberg. Karl heard the crickets and watched Fern's slender fingers resting on the steering wheel. If this was the end, he thought, at least he was with Fern and he'd seen Josh. He fought an impulse to take her hand.

They heard the Leutnant slam the door of the armored car, but all they could see was his silhouette against the blinding headlights. The Leutnant was smiling as he approached the car. *Another SS sadist, Karl thought. They were all Günter Jurgens. He's going to have a laugh and gun us down right here.* At last the Leutnant spoke.

"Dr. Wagner, Dr. Muller. I've just spoken to SS-Gruppenführer Heydrich. He wishes you a good night's rest. He said you've both had a trying evening and are free to proceed." He handed them back their papers. From his demeanor, Karl and Fern both grasped that the Leutnant knew little or nothing of what had happened on the Kehlstein.

As they drove away, Karl thought about how it had been seven years since they'd been alone together, except for that awful confrontation in Fern's Munich apartment. After ten minutes, Fern slowed the Duesenberg down and Karl noticed that the road become steep and winding.

"We're not lost, are we?" he asked.

"No, at least not in any geographic sense."

Fern turned and drove up a steep mountain road until the headlights illuminated a hand-carved wooden sign: *Landhaus Wagner.* Then she turned left and drove another hundred yards. The asphalt ended, and she brought the car to a stop on a clean white gravel driveway.

In the clear mountain starlight, Karl caught sight of the two-story structure with a wrap-around second-floor balcony and an expansive front deck.
Fern saw Karl looking up at the chalet. "Come, Karl. It's even nicer inside."

359. FREDERICK'S CHALET, 12:54 A.M.

Fern turned on a lamp and led Karl through the living room and into the
kitchen. "There's some excellent beer in the refrigerator," she said. "It's a G.E.
Frederick had it shipped here all the way from America just before the war."

They each took a frosted mug of beer into the living room, where Fern
sank into the leather sofa and closed her eyes. Karl went upstairs and found
a wool blanket in a walk-in cedar closet. When he returned, Fern was sitting
up and wide awake.

"What do you think that creep Heydrich knows?" she asked as they sat
back down in the living room.

"You're talking like a cop," he said, taking a seat close to her.

"I know a lot about cops. My friend Hans is a cop."

"I know he is. Are you in love with him?"

"No, I'm not," she said, taking a long swallow of beer as she moved closer
to Karl. "I'm in love with that guy back in New York. Never got over him,"
she whispered, resting her head on his chest. "Let's skip right to the good part
of the dream before Heydrich's thugs barge in and crash our party. You can
tell me your story in the morning."

"Even now, I can't tell you everything," Karl murmured, stroking her head.
"If Heydrich's goons do come crashing in here, the less you know the better."

She sat back up. "Oh yes, you damn well *can* tell me everything," she
laughed. "And you will tell me, every bit of it, all seven years. You owe me
that, Karl Ludwig. You owe me that for seven years of grief. Yes, you've been
through a lot, but at least you knew that I was alive. That gave you hope, but
I had none. Death is final, Karl, and I had to accept that finality. You know
I'm right, don't you?"

He nodded, saying nothing. He knew she was right.

"Tell me your story after we get a good night's rest," she whispered.

It had been a long time since he'd heard her whisper. She stood up and went to the front door to make sure it was locked, then took his hand and led him up the stairway.

8:00 A.M.

They woke at the same instant. Their lovemaking that night had been frantic, each knowing that it could end with a clatter of boots on the stairs and SS men barging through the door. Now, refreshed by sleep, they made love again in the morning quiet.

Karl got up and went straight to the window. He saw only the Duesenberg parked in the driveway. No sign of trouble for the moment.

In the kitchen, they listened to the news of the German onslaught into Russia on the wireless. The report emphasized that Soviet provocations had forced the Führer to take action against the Red menace in the East. Goebbels read a statement from the Führer, who was said to be personally directing the invasion, although his whereabouts were not disclosed.

After scrambled eggs and coffee, Fern put her hand on Karl's forearm. "Now it's time to tell me your story, Karl. You can't really have me back without telling me the truth, every ugly bit of it."

She stood, switched off the radio, and took a chair across the table from him. She listened as Karl told his story, from the day they parted at Sing Sing. He spilled it all. He described the unprovoked beatings in the prison recreation yard, his time in solitary, and his introduction to Channing Brown. He told her how he'd decided to accept the mission Brown offered, with all its ramifications, and about his training in London and at Thornbil Castle. He described his arrival in Germany and his life as a family doctor and Nazi Party fundraiser. He told her about his time in Spain, the contrived rescue of General Haber, and the horrors he'd witnessed in Poland and Norway. He even went into some detail about his attacks on SS men, his plan to frame Günter Jurgen, and his recent meeting with Frederick at his back-country cottage. Finally, he confided what had transpired the night before on the terrace of the Kehlsteinhaus – the blows that he, not Jurgen, had landed on

Hitler, the subsequent brawl with Jurgen, the shots that killed Jurgen and the Italian, and Hans's sudden appearance out of nowhere.

"Hans is resourceful," she said, "but never mind that now. I feel better knowing that you've been working against the Nazis, and that Frederick has been working against them too. He had me fooled. But I still don't get how the Englishman Brown identified you, why they chose you out of all the thugs and killers in America."

"They identified me long before I went to prison. I didn't grasp it all until last night at the mortuary. They framed me, Fern."

"Framed? How?"

"Go back to the fight at the Bavarian Inn. That fight was the first step in the set up. I had questions right from the start, though I didn't want it to look like I was making excuses for myself. Sure, I knew I shouldn't have slugged that guy. But I took the bait. The punches I threw set me up for the arrest, then the plea bargain, Sing Sing, and the unprovoked beatings in the prison yard – all of it to set me up for Channing Brown's visit in the prison infirmary.

"Remember, by the time Brown appeared, I'd already endured three terrible beatings. I was ready to sign anything to get out of Sing Sing. But it was only last night that I finally understood."

"But why last night?" Fern asked as they heard a car pulling into the gravel driveway. From the window, they watched as Frederick emerged from a black Mercedes.

Over a fresh pot of American coffee, Frederick explained that he'd borrowed a car from the motor pool at the SS barracks.

"I've told Fern a lot this morning," Karl said. "But I haven't yet told her what I learned last night when I saw that dead guy in the morgue."

"So tell us," Fern said.

"The guy had crossed pistols tattooed on the back of his right hand and a one-inch scar over his left eyebrow. It's funny," Karl said with a frown, "because I remembered someone with exactly the same tattoo and scar – the guy who damn near killed Josh that night at the Bavarian Inn. It all jibes with what Josh told me in the ambulance. I realized that the people who recruited me for this mission sent the same guy to kill me."

"Is something wrong, Uncle?" Fern asked, noticing Frederick's creased brow.

"Yes, because there's something neither of you know. Since we might have unwelcome visitors at any moment, I had better get this off my chest now. I pray that someday you'll understand that what I did seemed, at the time, like the right thing to do.

"It started after the Armistice in 1918. After my release as a prisoner of war, a wealthy English landowner on whose farm I worked won permission for me to stay in Britain. Look at the trajectory of my business career – I invested wisely, yes, but my early clients and customers were mostly British. Soon Brown recruited me, and I moved my headquarters home to Berlin and bought several German companies. On direction from London, I was one of the Nazi Party's earliest financial supporters. That's how I gained access to Hitler and his gang – and how I eventually won all those lucrative contracts. Over time, you see, I became something of an idea man for Channing Brown."

Frederick kept his eyes on Karl. "If you haven't figured it out by now, I must tell you. I'm the one who came up with the idea that took you away from your life with Fern and your career. Some of my friends in London wanted to stop Hitler in his tracks long ago. They knew of several failed attempts on Hitler's life and wanted a new idea, something with imagination."

Karl locked his gaze on Frederick. "*You* identified me to the Brits?"

"I'm afraid so."

"So tell me, Frederick, how and when did you come up with the idea?" Karl asked.

"The people I was working with in London were smart enough to know that conventional ideas – you know, like a pistol-armed assassin in the crowd or explosives hidden under a manhole – were unlikely to work. Security around Hitler was quite formidable, even back then.

"Then one day, just before leaving New York to return to Germany on the Bremen, I met Fern for afternoon coffee at the Plaza Hotel. She told me that you planned to stop boxing and how thankful she was that you hadn't killed anyone with your fists. I had seen you box, so I knew she had a point.

"As we chatted, listening to 'The Skater's Waltz' and eating apricot tarts, it came to me."

"So, Uncle, you're the one who planned that fight at the Bavarian Inn, the attacks on Karl at Sing Sing, and his ultimate escape?" Fern asked.

"Let's say I did a lot of work behind the scenes, though I hardly orchestrated every detail. Much of the plan was worked out in London, then in New York. We got help, including financial assistance, from Sir Crawford Ware, and muscle from the Bellacostas, who were part of the Luciano organization. The New York City Police, the Governor of New York, and the White House all had a role to play, too. Neither Brown nor I anticipated how rough things would get at the Bavarian Inn or Sing Sing. In hindsight we were a bit naive."

Fern couldn't take her eyes off Frederick.

"You both have every right to be angry," Frederick said.

"Yes, damn angry," Fern said, walking to the picture window. "But right now none of us can afford the luxury of anger or self-pity – or regret. If we do survive, I'll have this out with you one day, Uncle."

Karl laid both hands flat on the table. "We need a plan for answering Heydrich's questions. He let us through the roadblock last night, but he may just be laying a more elaborate trap."

They stiffened at the sound of another car on the gravel. Fern was relieved to see that it was Hans and that he was alone.

Hans's sweat-stained shirt was open at the neck, his tie undone, his face unshaven. He accepted a quick kiss on the forehead from Fern and took the measure of Karl. He sensed in an instant that Karl and Fern had reconciled. He had long ago begun preparing himself for that eventuality. Indeed, he felt a certain relief. His inner struggle with the demons of false hope – that Fern would one day be his – was over. Case closed.

"Pour this man a coffee," Karl said. "He's the real hero. Come join us at the table, Hans."

Hans glanced back at Fern, catching her eye for a second before turning to Karl. "By now, Karl Ludwig, I presume you've told Fern everything?"

Karl blinked. "I have," Karl answered, "and Frederick has added some deep background. But we haven't gotten to what happened on the terrace last night. That's where you come in, Hans. You can start by telling us how you know my real name."

Hans commanded their attention as he told them how he'd discovered the photograph of Fern and Karl in Frederick's New York townhouse just before the war began.

"You knew?" Fern said. "So the three most important men in my life have all lied to me? You were one of them, and you said nothing."

Hans did not respond directly. "I contemplated some dark options but rejected them."

"You mean you could have turned me in to the Gestapo or the SD," Karl said. "And no one, including Fern, would be the wiser."

"I considered it, yes. But I couldn't live with myself. Besides, if I had turned Karl in, the SD would have soon discovered that Karl Ludwig and Fern had been involved back in New York. And I knew what that would mean for you, Fern, not to mention what would happen to your mother, Frederick, and General Haber."

"So you kept it to yourself all these months?" Frederick asked.

"Yes. Needless to say, I still had a lot of questions – and no one to discuss them with. Why the faked death in New York, for example? Why the new identity? What was Karl doing in Germany? It was obvious to me that some-one had gone to great trouble to have people believe Karl Ludwig was dead. And I knew there had to be some reason."

Brushing his straight blonde hair off his forehead, Hans turned to Karl. "I poked around, visited Sing Sing, and spent time in newspaper morgues. I even inspected the scene of the accident near West Point and went to the State Police barracks in Newburgh. All the records of the accident were gone. After I returned to Germany, I realized that your presence here – hobnobbing with the likes of Hess, Haber, and Günter Jurgen – was all part of some plan. But I had no idea what that plan was."

Hans met Fern's eyes before going on and then glanced over at Karl. "I began following you at night whenever I could. I didn't learn much at first. Then one night I tailed you to a safe apartment building owned by Ziggy – and you came out with a shopping bag. I stayed on the street and, what do you know, out came Big Julius. I've been working with Ziggy and Big Julius for years. We trade information and do favors for each other."

"So you went to them?" Karl asked.

"Yes. They didn't know who you were, Karl, but they told me what you bought from them. They took you for a high-class second-story man, maybe a jewel thief, even though the brass knuckles and cocaine didn't fit with that. About a week later, I followed you again, this time to number 12 Geller Strasse. Afterward, I checked to see who lived there – and I was only a little surprised to learn it was SS Hauptmann Günter Jurgen.

"Later, when Jurgen was on occupation duty in France, I searched his flat myself and found the brass knuckles, the cocaine, and the other stuff, all of it concealed quite skillfully in the wardrobe and behind a desk drawer. If I were to guess, I'd say it had all been planted there by a well-trained professional, most likely for the purpose of blackmail or a frame-up. Still, though, I couldn't be sure. Maybe that stuff really did belong to Jurgen."

"So you kept following me?" Karl asked.

"Not every night, of course. I was getting other assignments from Heydrich, and a man's got to sleep sometimes. But when the beatings of the SS men started – and word of those beatings got around very quickly despite efforts to keep them quiet – I suspected you right away. I was even more convinced when I learned that the attacker was using brass knuckles. One evening, well after midnight, I followed you and watched as you pummeled three men at once. Three nights later, I saw you sneak up on an SS Hauptmann and fell him with an open-handed blow, just as you did to Hitler last night."

"I guess I kept you pretty busy," Karl said.

Hans then told them how Heydrich had become curious about Karl's sudden rise in Nazi circles and had ordered him to keep an eye on Karl.

"Still," Hans offered, "I had no idea what your real mission was until last night on the terrace of the Kehlsteinhaus. The instant you began swinging, I understood why Jurgen was there – that you had come to kill both Hitler and Jurgen and let the dead Jurgen take the blame. All that evidence tucked away in his flat would make it an open-and-shut case. But just then I saw the man in the naval uniform, crouching and aiming his Beretta . . . I wasn't sure if he was there to kill you or Hitler."

"So Heydrich?" Fern asked. "What will he do now?"

"Depends," Hans said. "Heydrich and Himmler both have their own hides to protect. Remember, the SS is responsible for Hitler's safety, so they'll have to face Hitler's wrath. So does Bormann. And so will you, Karl. But that could well be the end of it. The entire incident could be forgotten on purpose."

"I'm not sure I understand," Karl said.

"For one thing," Hans said, "no one in the Nazi leadership will want it known that the Führer was attacked – and nearly killed – especially now that Germany has just invaded Russia. Nor, for God's sake, would they want it known that an SS officer was the would-be assassin or that Hitler was saved on the operating table by a visiting American doctor. Believe me, this isn't a story that makes anyone look good."

"How much of this do you think Heydrich has figured out?" Fern asked.

"Perhaps more than we realize. It's possible that he had other agents following Karl – and that he knows for certain that Karl was the one beating up SS officers. Heydrich might also have had someone tailing me, or Karl, to Günter Jurgen's flat and found the same stuff I did."

"So you're saying that Heydrich may already know – or suspect – the truth about Karl?" Fern asked.

"Absolutely. He keeps files on countless people, and he never lets good information go to waste. He keeps what he knows to himself, unless it suits his purpose to do otherwise."

Fern recounted how it had been easy for them to pass through the roadblock.

"That would support my point," Hans said. "Even if he suspects something, he's likely to keep it to himself. If he wanted to arrest Karl, or anyone else, and make a show of things, last night would have been a most opportune time to do it – a swift response, order restored, that kind of thing. Instead he did nothing. In fact, he was almost pleasant."

"So should we just continue going about our business as if we were all good Nazis?" Karl asked.

"Something like that," Hans said. "It's one way to stay alive. My guess is that Heydrich will make a move only if and when it suits his own purposes. He isn't working for Hitler or even for Himmler. He's working for himself. Right now, that could play to our advantage."

"I hate to interrupt all these revelations," Frederick said, rising from the table, "but it's high time we visit the Führer. Not showing up at the Berghof would only draw attention to our absence, and that would be, let's say, awkward for Fern and Karl, who attended to him last night."

360. HITLER'S BEDROOM, THE BERGHOF, JUNE 22, NOON

Hitler was conscious but heavily bandaged, still unable to speak. He nodded as Karl, Fern, and Frederick entered the room. For the past hour, he had been listening to reports from the new Russian front. If he recalled, or even understood, what had taken place on the terrace the night before, he gave no indication of it.

They had spent a respectable ten minutes at Hitler's bedside when Josh entered the room, unshaven and disheveled after a fitful night's sleep in a cot under the stern watch of two square-jawed SS sergeants. For the past hour, Josh had been briefing Dr. Morell and Hitler's other physicians, all recently arrived from Berlin, on the Führer's condition, which he described as "stable but tenuous." Dr. Morell prepared to give Hitler a series of injections to "speed his recovery." Josh had been briefed back in Berlin not to challenge Morell, should their paths cross.

Once they left the room, Josh drew Karl aside and spoke in a low, barely audible whisper.

"I'll say goodbye to Fern here, then we'll walk outside together," he said. "Hitler's aides have arranged for a military plane to take me back to Berlin. They're kissing my ass. They don't want any trouble from the Americans."

After a brief handshake with Fern, Josh walked with Karl into the brilliant mountain sunlight. He started to put a hand on Karl's shoulder, but checked himself.

"Josh, they hired that guy to kill me. I got a good look at him in the mortuary last night. It was the same guy who beat you up at the Bavarian Inn. This all goes way back."

"They weren't *all* in favor of killing you. Your man in London, Channing Brown, the one who recruited you, he wanted to get word to you. But that was next to impossible, since you insisted that you wouldn't respond to any last-minute communications. That's why I was sent to Berchtesgaden – they thought you might listen to me."

"To hell with the mission, Josh. It's over. Tell me, what do you do with yourself when you're not saving the lives of guys like Hitler?"

Josh gave a two-minute history of how Jack Courtney recruited him. They walked to the Mercedes that would take Josh to his plane. "You'd better get moving," Karl said. "We shouldn't be having a heart-to-heart conversation before so many curious eyes. When can we meet again?"

"Perhaps sooner than you think, Karl. There's one more thing I need to tell you now. Just act as if we're making small talk, because I'm sure we're being watched from the second floor. That guy Channing Brown has developed an escape plan for you."

"I don't think I'm interested."

"Well, just listen," Josh said. "Once you get back to Berlin, go through all the motions of everyday life – tidy up your medical practice and your office as if you're being assigned to a unit on the Russian front."

Karl nodded for Josh to keep talking.

"On Thursday, take an early-morning run in the Tiergarten. Run fast enough so no one can follow you. Start early, while it's still dark, and go to the comfort station just north of the Brandenburg Gate. There you'll find a black suitcase against the outside back wall. Someone will have placed it there in the dead of night. Inside you'll find a business suit, a freshly laundered shirt, a tie, some new shoes, and a briefcase. Get dressed in the comfort station as fast as you can. Pack your running gear in the suitcase and take it with you. Then slip out of the Tiergarten and onto the street, which should still have little pedestrian traffic at that hour. Just don't leave the Tiergarten through the Brandenburg Gate – the Gestapo always keeps a close eye on that entrance. Once you're out of the Tiertgarten, walk at a normal pace to the old U.S. Embassy building on the Pariser Platz. You'll get a new identity, a U.S. diplomatic passport, and a ticket on the ten o'clock Swiss Air flight to Zurich, where you can say hello to what they tell me is a sizeable bank account. You'll be back in New York in two days."

"What about Fern?"

Josh motioned for them to keep walking as he made some feigned surgical gestures, as if he were cutting someone open. "She's invited. Her travel documents would include a new name and a U.S. passport, a gray wig, and a frumpy dress to make her look middle-aged and dowdy."

"That sounds like a complicated path that could land us in the basement of the Prinz-Albrecht-Strasse – and spell trouble for Hildy, Frederick, and General Haber. Plus, I don't see Fern going along with it."

"The other alternative would be more involved," Josh said. "We could fake her death in an air raid. We could do it for both of you. It's worked for the Brits."

"No, that takes too much time and effort. There are too many *ifs*. No thanks either way, Josh. Remember, I already died once."

"Well think it over. The suitcase will be there."

"It's been good to see you and that shit-eating grin of yours," Karl whispered as Josh climbed into the Mercedes. Karl fought the lump in his throat as he turned back toward the Berghof.

361. THE BERCHTESGADENER INN DINING ROOM, JUNE 22, 7:45 P.M.

Seated in the otherwise empty dining room Karl, Fern, and Frederick picked at their dinners of overcooked cabbage and potatoes. Frederick spoke little and ate less. Only after the coffee did his eyes meet Fern's.

"I must tell you that the British have offered me a way out," he said, wary of eavesdroppers. "On my next business trip to Stockholm, I can just march into the British embassy, piece of cake."

"But you won't do it, will you, Uncle?" Fern whispered.

"No, too easy. And what could I accomplish after that? I owe it to myself and you two to keep on fighting them, to make sure my factories don't produce as much as they really can, and to be Brown's eyes and ears in the Chancellery."

"But the risk?" Fern said.

"My penance." Frederick said.

Not enough, Fern thought. Perhaps in time.

Frederick excused himself after the ersatz. There were no hugs. He had booked sleeping compartments for Max and himself on the night train to Berlin. Karl and Fern rose to say their goodbyes at the table and then lingered over their ersatz.

"It's Russia for me," Fern said. "I'll be setting up field hospitals." As she leaned toward Karl, he fought the impulse to stroke her cheek. Looking across the room over her shoulder, he could see two stocky men in gray business suits seated at the bar, sipping beer.

"Let's walk," he said. In the deserted square, they sat together on a small stone ledge that bordered the fountain. "We can escape all this together, Fern. All you need to do is go to the American Embassy in Berlin, and I'll meet you there. The disguises are all prepared. Their plan's in place."

"No, Karl, I can't leave mother here. Lord knows what they'd do to her if I defected – they'd probably interrogate her to death in the Prinz-Albrecht-Strasse basement or send her to Ravensbrück. She's strong in her way, but I don't think she'd survive a concentration camp. Then there's Frederick, General Haber, and Hans."

She paused. Across the street they saw the same two men they'd seen earlier at the inn.

"The noise of the fountain will keep them from hearing us," Karl said. "All they can do is watch."

"Don't let my situation stop you, Karl. You've earned your ticket out of here. And you deserve the money stashed away in Switzerland."

"The money can wait. We can't. I've been away from you too long, Fern. If we pull a few strings, we might be able to join the same Luftwaffe group in Russia. Frederick might be able to help with that. Once we're there, we'll just have to be cool about it and pretend there's nothing between us – at least for a while."

"Sure," she grinned. "After seven years I think we can handle that."

"Now, *Liebchen*," he whispered, "let me tell you something else. I've seen enough of these Nazis and what they do to know I need to keep working against them."

"But let's face it," she said, "we've both been basking in a weirdly exciting Nazi celebrity. I'm ashamed to admit it, but I've enjoyed staying at the Adlon and the Ritz and hobnobbing with the elite."

"Maybe being in Russia together, but not actually with each other for a while, will be *our* penance."

"I want to work against them, too, Karl. Maybe we can work together. It won't make up for what I've done to help them – not at first – but it's a beginning. I can learn lots in a field hospital that would be useful to the Russians and Brits."

"Yes. I'll have to get word to my contact when I return to Berlin. London should welcome the opportunity of having both of us on the Russian front. Just keeping them apprised of German casualties will be invaluable."

"What about Heydrich?" Fern asked.

"We already know we're being followed. For now we'll have to rely on what Hans told us – whatever Heydrich knows, he'll keep to himself until it suits his purpose to do otherwise."

Her eyes had moistened, but she knew she couldn't wipe them. That would only give the two goons across the street something to report.

"It's time to go," she said, "before I get ideas about freshening up in your room." Karl could see that the two men were pretending to talk to each other.

"Okay then. Remember, this time it's not goodbye, but *au revoir*," he whispered, as they walked toward the Duesenberg.

"It was easier when you were dead, Karl," she said with a crooked grin. "If we fled and left Frederick and General Haber behind, they could handle it. They're big boys, important men in the Reich, at least for now. And somehow I see mother as a survivor, stronger in many ways."

"But you won't leave?"

"I won't and neither will you. That medical practice in San Francisco can wait. She climbed into the car and drove off. Karl forced himself to turn away and walk slowly back to the inn, listening until he could no longer hear the Duesenberg's engine.

362. THE ADLON, BERLIN, JUNE 24, 1941, 9:00 P.M.

Josh had met Jack Courtney earlier that evening in his small office off the rain-soaked Pariser Platz, where he provided Courtney with his account of the events on the Kehlstein and in Berchtesgaden. As Josh knew, Courtney was under strict orders to do everything possible to please the Soviets now that they were in the war on Britain's side. One thing the Soviets wanted, Courtney told him, was for Josh to have dinner with their top Berlin operative, the same agent who had provided such precise details on the Wehrmacht's three-pronged assault into Russia.

Josh entered the spacious, nearly vacant Adlon dining room and introduced himself to the headwaiter as Dr. Enzo Galifano. As instructed, he asked to see a Frau Graf, who would be expecting him.

"But, of course, Doctor. Please follow me."

Josh followed the headwaiter to a large corner booth, where an attractive woman with silver hair rose to greet him with a warm handshake. Her confident bearing rather surprised Josh.

"It's so good to meet you at last, Dr. Galifano. Please sit. I've taken the liberty of ordering us a light Rhine wine. I understand your wife is a nurse in Paris. I love Paris."

Josh felt an immediate connection to Frau Graf. She had him talking about his life in no time at all. The wine and the food, excellent by wartime standards, helped to propel their conversation. They talked of the war, of Nancy, of life in Paris, and of the tragedy that had befallen the Communist cause in Spain. For her part, Frau Graf found the young doctor to be a bit naïve, although quite genuine.

Over a cup of real coffee, she listened eagerly as he responded to her question about the fateful evening on the Kehlstein. He told her what he knew of the rumors about the botched assault on Hitler by some half-crazed SS man. He responded truthfully that he had, in fact, been at the Kehlsteinhaus on the night in question, but had not witnessed the attack. He omitted mention of the surgery he had performed at the Berchtesgaden Hospital.

With her last sip of coffee, Frau Graf advised Josh to leave first. She would take care of the bill. As he left, Josh found himself thinking that there was something about her – perhaps her voice? He knew he would have no trouble working with her if that was what Courtney wanted.

8:25 P.M.

After Josh left, Frau Graf signaled for the headwaiter. She'd been working with this waiter, a veteran Soviet agent, since before the Nazis took power. "You know what to do," she said. "Charge it to my special account."

"*Danke,*" he said with a bow. "May I have someone call you a taxi?"

"*Nein, danke.*" I'll be meeting my daughter in a few minutes. She's staying here at the Adlon. In fact, I believe she's waiting for me now over at the bar. A moment later, Fern greeted her mother with a warm hug.

363. NUMBER 10 DOWNING STREET, LONDON, DECEMBER 15, 1941, 9:00 P.M.

Channing Brown took his seat across the conference table from the Prime Minister.

"Well Channy, what can you tell me about Hitler's eastern adventure, especially with freezing temperatures in Moscow and a blanket of fresh snow covering Murmansk?"

"I won't disappoint you," Brown said. "I've just met with Frederick. He's managed to speak with both Karl and Dr. Wagner, who are at work in the same forward area of the front, not far from Moscow. Karl had informed Frederick that the Luftwaffe airmen and Wehrmacht soldiers were still wearing their summer uniforms. Karl also reported that among the German enlisted men, the incidence of severe colds and influenza is quite high. Dr. Wagner reports that the supply of essential pharmaceuticals is falling far short of the need. Frederick himself reports that, thanks to his own manipulations, the lubricant used to keep the Panzers running has begun to congeal and make the German tanks all but useless in the northern areas."

"Splendid, Channy, bloody splendid," Churchill said, relishing every word. "We're about to see a tectonic shift in our fortunes. Karl may not have killed Hitler, but he'll have a ringside seat as the Russian winter strikes a crippling blow."

THE END

Made in the USA
Middletown, DE
09 May 2015